THE PANDAHEM CYCLE II

The Dray Prescot Series

The Delian Cycle:
1. Transit to Scorpio
2. The Suns of Scorpio
3. Warrior of Scorpio
4. Swordships of Scorpio
5. Prince of Scorpio

The Havilfar Cycle:
6. Manhounds of Antares
7. Arena of Antares
8. Fliers of Antares
9. Bladesman of Antares
10. Avenger of Antares
11. Armada of Antares

The Krozair Cycle:
12. The Tides of Kregen
13. Renegade of Kregen
14. Krozair of Kregen

The Vallian Cycle:
15. Secret Scorpio
16. Savage Scorpio
17. Captive Scorpio
18. Golden Scorpio

The Jikaida Cycle:
19. A Life for Kregen
20. A Sword for Kregen
21. A Fortune for Kregen
22. A Victory for Kregen

The Spikatur Cycle:
23. Beasts of Antares
24. Rebel of Antares
25. Legions of Antares
26. Allies of Antares

The Pandahem Cycle:
27. Mazes of Scorpio
28. Delia of Vallia
29. Fires of Scorpio
30. Talons of Scorpio
31. Masks of Scorpio
32. Seg the Bowman

The Witch War Cycle:
33. Werewolves of Kregen
34. Witches of Kregen
35. Storm over Vallia
36. Omens of Kregen
37. Warlord of Antares

The Lohvian Cycle:
38. Scorpio Reborn
39. Scorpio Assassin
40. Scorpio Invasion
41. Scorpio Ablaze
42. Scorpio Drums
43. Scorpio Triumph

The Balintol Cycle:
44. Intrigue of Antares
45. Gangs of Antares
46. Demons of Antares
47. Scourge of Antares
48. Challenge of Antares
49. Wrath of Antares
50. Shadows over Kregen

The Phantom Cycle:
51. Murder on Kregen
52. Turmoil on Kregen

THE PANDAHEM CYCLE II

Kenneth Bulmer

writing as

Alan Burt Akers

Published by
Bladud Books

First published in 2011 by Bladud Books

Originally published separately as:
"Green Shadows" (1983 in *Imagine*)
Talons of Scorpio (1983 by Daw Books, Inc.)
Masks of Scorpio (1984 by Daw Books, Inc.)
Seg the Bowman (1984 by Daw Books, Inc.)

This first omnibus paperback edition published in 2011 by
Bladud Books, an imprint of Mushroom Publishing,
Bath, BA1 4EB, United Kingdom

www.bladudbooks.com

ISBN 978-1-84319-871-0

Contents

"Green Shadows"

In their engaging way the Star Lords hurled me headlong into rip-roaring, blood-pulsing adventure stark naked and unarmed—and, as well as adventure, into diabolical situations where I could get myself killed with spine-shattering ease. Like now.

The situation into which I tumbled was clear, simple and deadly. The Everoinye sent their phantom Blue Scorpion, all gigantic and glowing, to snatch me up from home in Esser Rarioch. They dumped me down here where squamous monsters with fangs and exceedingly sharp claws sought to rip me up for a light snack. In a gravel-floored cavern lit by pale phosphorescent fires I, Dray Prescot, of Earth and Kregen, had to be about my business with sharp promptitude.

"Be quick! Or we're all dead!" The woman crouching against the cave wall shrieked it out. The two men with her just screamed.

On the gravel a few paces off lay a harness of plate armor. From its breaths and sights flowed a green ichor. The cavern stank with the throat-clogging odor of rotting flesh. In the visor an Acid-Head Gimlet stuck fast. The gauzy wings of the dragonfly killer shimmering with pseudo-life reflected for a ghostly moment in the blade of the sword as it tumbled from a lax gauntlet onto the gravel.

Time only to feel a heartbeat of sorrow for the poor devil who'd worn the plate—a gloating hissing and movement against the cavern's oppressive radiance snatched my attention. In the mouth of the tunnel ahead bulked the monstrous shape of a reptile-man, and from his green-taloned hand a second Acid-Head Gimlet flew.

The wings glimmered in the phosphorescent light. The gimlet head glistened with the acid that would melt me down to the soles of my naked feet. No time to do anything but dive forward in a desperate try for the sword fallen from the armor's open gauntlet... My fingers touched the hilt, knocked it a handsbreadth across the floor. No time now to curse, to do anything but scrabble forward, seize the sword and flick it up in the way the Krozair Disciplines taught.

The Acid-Head Gimlet bounced against the blade, caromed off and smashed his deadly head against the rock wall.

The reptilian monster-man charged. He was not as deadly as his pets. His sword, a huge and ponderous affair, swung up as I slipped on loose gravel. The blade sliced down like a sickle of the Reapers of Men. A roll saved me so that I could hurl myself up and snout my borrowed weapon forward. The sword was a serviceable cut and thruster, a thraxter of Havilfar, so I gripped the hilt in both hands and drove straight on. The blade slid in and in. After a few moments in which I felt the sensations of a man trapped in a whirlwind, his convulsions ceased.

An old fighting man and leem-hunter does not wait around after a single combat. There would be plenty more monsters in this labyrinth and although I bore them no ill will I fully intended to do my best to keep my head on my shoulders, oh, yes, by Krun! Instantly, all a part of the same movement, I leaped away to the side, slimed blade up ready for the next one who came howling from the tunnel. This one tried to be clever and attempted to use a technique old when men fought with flint weapons. He went down and the rest fled.

The woman said: "Hai, Jikai!"

By the disgusting and putrid eyeballs of Makki Grodno! I shook my head and looked at the tumbled—and infinitely pathetic—heap of armor.

"A small jikai, perhaps." I said, for that word denoting a truly tremendous, heroic deed, seemed out of place in this depressing cavern of blue phosphorescence and shadows and dead men. The poor devil of a Chulik had not been altogether clever wearing plate armor down here. Despite his fanatical training from birth in the arts of combat, he'd just been too slow to dodge.

She saw my glance. "He was our champion, Nas Chendo, to whom we paid much gold to protect us."

"Let us not," said the full-fleshed man whose veined face shone blotchily red and green, sweating, "speak ill of the dead." He was dressed in dark practical leathers which, to my eyes, did not suit him. He was more of your sumptuous clothes man, used to dealing in the good things of life, a Merchant Adventurer, I guessed. The broken ends of his purse chains showed that down here in the Moder his merchanting had gone as badly as his adventuring.

The second man stared fixedly at me with his slanted, round slit eyes, yellow and bold. "Where did you come from jikai?"

Now, when you deal with sorcerers and folk of that uncanny ilk, it's best to be extremely wary. These people were venturing into the mysteries and terrors of a Moder in search of loot and magics. They'd know damn well I hadn't been with them in their party when they'd started. I used a facile excuse. The effect of the horrors employed to guard the tombs and the treasures within a Moder in Moderdrin, the Humped Land, situated in the centre of Havilfar, is to shred away disbelief in the strange.

"I've been wandering about down here—Havil alone knows how long—lost all my belongings—I'm very pleased to see you. Where is the rest of your party?"

For a moment I thought the sorcerer might not accept this explanation. His cat-face, with the arrogant whiskers and slanted feline eyes, regarded me fixedly. He was, I saw, a Sorcerer of the Cult of Almuensis, clad in splendid vestments of silk, richly decorated with gold thread. He was of the lordly ones of the shadow realms, who commanded, who wielded enormous but subtle powers. From his belt dangled gold chains. His beringed fingers touched his lips and those slit eyes stared on me, saw my naked body, the slimed sword—and this powerful man licked his lips and stumbled over what he would say.

"We have been separated—we are lost—and Nas Chendo—"

"But now we have a new champion!" The woman's voice rippled lightly in the cavern. I detected an incongruous note of amusement in her tones.

The man in dark leathers who had some respect for the dead spoke in a voice that would, in other circumstances, have been fruity. "Llahal and Lahal, jikai. This is the Lady Shamsi and this is San Ferald. I am Nath Jadrelgen ti Riptanporth."

"Llahal and Lahal. I am called Jak ti Tamlin."

That was enough for now. Jak is a name I use often. Tamlin is a charming little village on the island of Veliadrin. Dray Prescot's name is not unknown upon Kregen, what with all the stories and plays and puppet shows, and these people would scarcely be surprised to run across him all naked and unexpectedly. And so, I looked more closely upon this Lady Shamsi.

Her appearance was surprising on a number of counts, one of which was not so much the color of her hair, a deep and lustrous green, as why she had chosen to dye it that color at all. Her features were regular and decided. Her face was white. One hears of white faces; hers might have come freshly from the flour bag. Inevitably, her eyes were green and the heavy eyeshadow a subtle variation of the same color. Her mouth was red, and a white tooth showed a tip just indenting her lower lip. Some folk find that no blemish but an added attraction in a pretty woman's face. She wore a white thigh-length tunic with a shimmery green undersurface, and black tall-boots with tops of lizard skin, gold buckled. Her waist and arms were cinctured by gold bands.

From time to time she spoke softly to the clinging creature perched on her left shoulder, a hairy, bright-faced little monkey with great intelligence in his round puzzled eyes... Around his neck an emerald green, brass-studded collar, such as the chavniks of Hyrklana wear, was missing three of the flower-stamped, pseudo-golden studs. The chain attached to the collar chingled with the soft, luxurious sound of solid gold. Mili-milus, the Kregans call these friendly monkey-like creatures, and savants argue heatedly over whether their chittery sounds constitute a language, and if, in consideration of their well-proven emotional attachments, they might be considered as human beings.

This russet-haired mili-milu made no sound, squatting on the white and green shoulder of the Lady Shamsi. She reached up her hand covered by a glove very similar to the thickly-padded glove a falconer wears and stroked the hairy fellow.

Around her neck and loosely fastened by a turquoise-headed stick pin she wore a red scarf. This she now unwound, replacing the stick pin in her tunic, and handed to me.

I gave her thanks and wound the scarf around me and hauled the end up between my legs. The scarf was not, unfortunately, scarlet. The poor dead Chulik's armor yielded a broad belt with broken lockets— the scabbard was missing—and this I fastened around me. With the thraxter in my fist I went forward and took my place before the others as we left that cavern reeking of death.

One of these three people was the reason the Star Lords had pitched me headlong down here. One of them had to be protected. Which one? I did not know. Perhaps all three? That made no difference. I needed to protect them all from the eerie perils lurking in the unplumbed depths of the Moder.

Clad only in a scarlet breechclout and wielding a Great Krozair Longsword, I, Dray Prescot, Vovedeer, Lord of Strombor and Krozair of Zy, have fronted many dire perils on Kregen. Oh, yes, that wonderful and terrible, beautiful and savage planet four hundred light years from the world of my birth has afforded me great hardship and dangers aplenty, and, also, the most marvelous of joys.

Now, with only a thraxter to match the red scarf, I would have to do what I could. Yes, by Zim-Zair!

With the return of color to his cheeks, Nath Jadrelgen took on some of the self-importance natural to him. He glared at the Fristle Sorcerer of the Cult of Almuensis. "Why did you not cast a spell, San Feralf? Havil knows, the situation was desperate enough."

The wizard was still gripped by fear. With a despairing gesture he lifted the broken ends of the chains on his belt. "When we fell through that misbegotten trap I lost my Book—"

"As I lost my purse," said Jadrelgen with great malignity.

Then what the sorcerer was saying struck home. "You mean you cannot cast any magics, here in this dreadful place?"

"I tried to memorize some of the various arts—but the Book—it never leaves me—it is my life—it is more than my life—"

I said: "We must push on if we are to rejoin your party. San Ferald, as we go perhaps you might try to recall a useful spell or two you have in your head."

The Lady Shamsi laughed. The tiny mili-milu jumped.

Ahead, the rock corridor stretched unbroken to double doors at the end. We proceeded cautiously, probing and looking.

San Ferald, with some hesitancy, said: "I think—Yes! I can recall exactly Sheomanar the Mad's favorite casting. The Sleety Tomb!"

In a shrill and near-breaking scream, the Lady Shamsi cried: "Then you must use it now!"

Her voice broke into a babble of prayer and her hand pointed starkly down the corridor. I stared and, for an instant, could see nothing to warrant alarm. Then a vicious horde of winged creatures broke from the walls, buzzing, and stormed towards us.

"Fliktitors!" shrieked Jadelgren, collapsing backwards. Squamous, buzzing on glistening wings, with fangs and claws that would strip us to the bone, the Fliktitors swooped. Not one was larger than a terrestrial domestic cat.

San Ferald took a sliver of crystal from his pouch and grasped it pointing at the multitude of little horrors. He started to declaim. Like a scything blizzard sweeping across the Ice Floes, the Fliktitors swarmed upon us, screeching. Perforce, I set myself with the single sword to do what I could against them.

We would have been totally overwhelmed, there was no doubt of that, by the ponderous thighs and mountainous hips of the Divine Madam of Belschutz! From the Sorcerer's outstretched shard of crystal, a sleeting storm of ice spread in a glistening cone. Each barbed and fanged horror was encased. Each one fell to the floor numbed and prisoned in a miniature example of Sheomanar the Mad's favorite casting—The Sleety Tomb.

We spent some time waiting to recover from that ordeal and I learned some of the familiar reasons why these people had ventured down here. The Humped Land, the wide area of Monsters and Moders, attracted many diverse folk; all sought something special to them. Jadelgren's merchanting had sunk into a decline, so that financially he was at rock bottom. San Ferald had heard strongly substantiated rumors that a highly powerful Book, a Hyr-Lif of enormous thaumaturgical knowledge, had in the long ago been secreted in this particular Moder. Both men hoped to gain what they most desired.

The Lady Shamsi merely laughed so that the mili-milu jumped. "I seek my pleasure down here, and if fortune comes my way among the gallant adventuring, why, then I am doubly rewarded."

My own story was simple; I was a paktun hired as a guard.

When we'd recovered sufficiently to push open the double doors we stepped through into a vast and ebon chamber. Robed in black the walls, black the throne, black the candles and black the obscene statue of a forgotten god. The massed candles threw an oddly mellow light, out of place and unsettling, upon that somber scene and upon the two balass doors beyond the throne. The eyes of the statue glittered and seemed to watch our movements.

"Why was I persuaded to venture into this awful place?" Jadelgren's voice quivered. "By Havil! I regret it now!"

"You came, as did we all, to gain magic and treasure and plunder the tombs," said the Lady Shamsi. "As we all admitted." She smiled graciously upon the Fristle sorcerer. "You did well to remember your spell, San Ferald. No doubt you will recall more for us?"

"I do not think so, my lady. All that is in my head is a childish exercise—"

"No matter." She interrupted brusquely. Her gloved hand stroked the mili-milu who crouched down, his chain chiming. "We must go on. Which door, do you think?"

It was all one to me. Yet I could clearly see the excitement seething in this sharp and haughty lady. She'd come down here primarily for the thrill of it and one felt a certain admiration for her poise amongst all these terrors. As for Jadelgren, his face now shone as green as before, with the veins pulsing blue. He said very uneasily to me: "I don't like the look of that statue's eyes."

"If we do not touch anything and go carefully," I told him, "we should regain the safety of your main party."

"That Havil-forsaken trap! It snatched away my crossbow as well as my purse. Look!" He showed me the ring on the little finger of his right hand. A cut sapphire, it was engraved with the representation of an archer. "This ring gives me the accuracy to hit nine times out of ten."

"Very useful—if you had a bow."

Now, from my previous experiences down a Moder I had gained an inkling of the way the Moder Lord liked to toy with those bold fellows and ladies who had the effrontery to go delving down among the treasures. Every now and then as the delvers proceeded they would come across a chamber handsomely furnished with broad tables and comfortable chairs. Those fine tables would be covered with dishes containing—food! There would be silver goblets with fine wines. Needless to say, by this time my inward parts were groaning with the stark necessity of finding and devouring vittels. I surely needed a wet, by Vox!

Of course, the Moder Lord, guardian of the treasures, only sets out these tables of gourmand food and fine wines so that he may continue to keep the delvers going in order that he may torture them further.

"Aye, jikai," he said on a gusty sigh. "Well, Lady Shamsi, I do not know which door." He hunched up his shoulders in the incongruous black leathers. "Nor, by Hanitcha the Harrower, do I care to choose!"

The contrast between the demeanor of the two men and the woman struck me forcibly. They'd all fallen through the same trap, they'd encountered the same dangers, yet the men had gone to pieces. Truly, if this Lady Shamsi was not a Jikai Vuvushi, a Battle Maiden, then she would be welcomed with open arms into any regiment of Warrior Women.

She continued to babble her prayers in a low and barely audible voice, yet this did not detract from the impression of fortitude; rather, it perhaps revealed the inner source of her strength. She stroked the mili-milu. Most folk like to stroke these friendly creatures, to rub their noses in the sweet-smelling hair, to caress them. She had her face turned away, staring at the statue.

"If," quoth Ferald the Sorcerer in a quavery tone, "that thing comes to life, I can do nothing."

"But you told me you remembered another spell!" She swung about, alarmed and angry. Her green eyes slanted upon the Fristle.

"Yes, my lady, a trifle of foolishness learned when very young—a baby spell—"

The ebon statue, ten foot tall, seized a double-bitted axe and jumped for us. His eyes blazed. All the horror of this unholy place concentrated in those glaring eyes.

I leaped forward. "Leave him to me!"

Do not think I was vainglorious or wishing to prove my right to be called jikai before these people. Oh, no, by Zair! I was in deathly terror lest the Star Lords banished me back to Earth. And, also, I suppose in those days, I was stupid.

We fought. Axe against sword we battled around and around that ebon chamber with the tall unflickering candle flames and drapes black as the hour of dim on a night of Notor Zan.

Far above us the Suns of Scorpio, Zim and Genodras, sent down their streaming mingled radiance, shining ruby and jade, and down here we faced the horrors from the tomb. In the end I cut the statue to pieces and sundered him in black fragments upon the marble floor. Green smoke puffed from the splintered detritus, a stifling odor of rot stank in our nostrils. The Lady Shamsi clapped her hands together, white flesh and solid glove, calling again: "Jikai!"

The other two delvers jabbered in frenzied relief, the little mili-milu remained silent, crouched upon the lady's shoulder. I just felt a testy embarrassment that the great word jikai was being bandied about like a clipped copper ob piece.

Around the Lady Shamsi's neck a triple-gold chain hung down, its ends vanishing under her tunic between her breasts. She pulled up the chain and I caught a single glimpse of a round white object which she instantly clasped in her bare hand. She no longer stroked the mili-milu.

The merchant adventurer in his ridiculous black leathers glared at the two doors past the throne. "The wiles of Spag the Junc foil us at every turn. At his evil pleasure we are lost." He swung up a shaking finger. "If we are to choose, then let us take the left hand door."

"The right, surely?" said the sorcerer.

Once again the Lady Shamsi began her low-voiced muttering, apparently intoning private prayers for our safe deliverance. I was just thinking that her display of spirit shamed us when a stunning crash smashed into the chamber and destroyed any problems of which door we should choose.

The entire throne crashed to the floor. From the black and cavernous opening so dramatically revealed a shrieking horde of skeletons burst upon us.

There are many forms of Kaotim, the Undead, upon Kregen and these were not apim skeletons, the bones of Homo sapiens. I recognized them by the lean viciousness and the snarling reptilian jaws, the vindictive speed of their onslaught, their very blasphemous possession of vigorous life in forms that should be dead and buried. They were Schrepims, incredibly fast and deadly, inordinately difficult to kill. And I must slay them all a second time!

My sword blurred into action. Commonplace words, perhaps, but only with the aid of Zair and Opaz and the utmost exertion were we to come out whole from this fraught encounter. So—my sword swept into action, slashing and hacking, for to thrust was useless. Swords and axes swirled about me. I fought. Oh, yes, Dray Prescot, rogue and emperor, can at least fight.

In a situation as desperate as this, could there be any shame in fighting?

Now, I have been called an onker, stupid, a get onker, an onker of onkers, more times than I have mentioned. And I own to trying to see the best in people until I am proved wrong. I began to see the pattern, and to add up what I should have added up long since.

This was why the Everoinye had dispatched me here. The trap through which these delvers had fallen had sundered all their chains—purse, Book, sword—but what of the Lady Shamsi's chains? And who stroked a friendly little mili-milu wearing a heavy gauntlet? She'd not even bothered to talk to him properly, to call his name. And lizard-skin around the tops of boots—were they then lined in reptile scales? I'd not seen the Fliktitors until after she called in alarm. Perhaps the most damning piece of evidence was the relief with which she'd given me the red scarf... Her decisiveness and sharpness had earlier given me the idea that had she not been a lady she might well have acquired a sobriquet. She'd be called Shamsi the Otlora. Otlora means no nonsense. In this stark adventure down the Moder, she'd earned that name, by Krun!

As I fought and ducked and slashed, I yelled: "San Ferald! Use your spell! Now and quickly. Before it is too late."

"But it is only a silly—"

"Cast it!"

The reptilian skeletons pressed on and I chopped them. I took a nick or two, which displeased me mightily. San Ferald took a bright red ring from his pocket and began to chant.

The Lady Shamsi laughed, a shrill, triumphant scream. Her white face now quite clearly showed green traces where the artificial whiteness of cosmetics was wearing away. And I battled. By the Blade of Kurin, I fought!

Pallid with fear, Jadelgren stood close to the sorcerer as Ferald chanted. The Fristle held the red ring aloft. He pointed it at the skeletons of the Schrepims. I shrieked.

"No! No! At the woman! At Shamsi!"

He was well into his chant now. I simply roared at Jadelgren, putting all the old devilish cutting command into my bellow.

"Jadelgren! Swing him around. Pivot him at the lady!"

As a farmer swings a scarecrow, so Jadelgren swung the sorcerer. The pointing ruby ring aimed at Shamsi—the spell climaxed in babbled confusion—and all the skeleton reptile-men disappeared.

My sword slashed at thin air.

"It will last only a moment!" screamed Ferald. "It is weak and she is strong, strong!"

The Lady Shamsi stood with her left thumb in her mouth. She made sounds like: "Coo. Glug."

"It is for soothing babies to sleep."

Before any of us could move, a hairy motion on her left shoulder drew our rapt attention. The little mili-milu simply took the turquoise-headed stick-pin from her tunic and drove it deeply into her eye.

Long before she fell to the floor, her clothes, her flesh, her scales, sloughed away. A skeleton reptile-woman, she sprawled, a mere scattering of yellowed bones.

"She was sent by the Moder Master to betray us," said Jadelgren afterwards as we fought our way back. "You shout mighty loud, Jak ti Tamlin."

We struggled higher into the next zone—which is another story—and then, thankfully, we could hear the voices of the main party and lights bloomed a welcoming rose and gold along the rocky walls.

"Sink me!" I said. I stroked the little mili-milu. His collar and chains had been taken off and thrown down upon the pathetic green-dyed wig and pile of yellowed bones. His thralldom to the reptile sorceress had ended. Perched on my shoulder he chittered happily away, a warm hairy bundle of lovableness.

"I wouldn't have had to shout so loudly if I'd had my wits about me from the first. By the Black Chunkrah! All the clues were there."

But, I think, and to my shame I confess, it was the sight of my face as I fought and commanded, that old demonic Dray Prescot Devil Look, that so galvanized Nath Jadelgren into instant action.

Of one thing I was very sure. I'd have to be excruciatingly careful how I explained my foolishness, and how the little mili-milu had joined us, when I got home to Esser Rarioch and told it all to my own bewitching Delia.

TALONS OF SCORPIO

Under the Suns of Scorpio...

To those unfamiliar with the Saga of Dray Prescot all that is necessary to know is that he has been summoned to Kregen, an exotic world orbiting the double star Antares, to carry out the mysterious purposes of the Star Lords. To survive the perils that confront him on that beautiful and terrible world he must be resourceful and courageous, strong and devious. There is no denying he presents an attractive yet enigmatic figure. There are more profound depths to his character than are called for by mere savage survival.

Called to be the Emperor of Vallia, Prescot, with the Empress Delia and their blade comrades, is slowly guiding the island empire from its Time of Troubles. They must all look to the future, which is dark with the threat of the Shanks, the Fishheads, raiding from over the curve of the world. The terror of the Shanks lies over all the bright lands of Paz; but at the moment more immediate perils beset Prescot. He has often been at cross-purposes with the Everoinye—the Star Lords—during his tumultuous career on Kregen; now he is wholeheartedly with them in their desire to stamp out the unholy cult of Lem the Silver Leem.

Down in the island of Pandahem, Prescot and his comrades, having burned a temple or two, must now press on and open a fresh campaign against the Silver Wonder. Of course, life is not as simple as that, particularly on the horrific and fascinating world of Kregen where, under the mingled streaming radiance of the Suns of Scorpio, the unexpected is always to be expected.

Alan Burt Akers

One

Pompino's name affronts him

"It's very simple, Jak," Pompino said as he leaped nimbly ashore. "All we have to do is recruit a few more rascally fellows and go across and bash this Lord Murgon Marsilus. Then we burn all the damned temples of Lem the Silver Leem, sort out who marries whom—and go home."

"Simple," I said, and jumped up onto the jetty after my comrade. Always difficult that—for me to remember not to shoulder forward and be first out of the boat. The twin suns glittered off the water, gulls circled and screeched above, the air tasted like best Jholaix, and we were off to burn another temple.

Pompino started along the jetty, striding out, arms pumping, chest and head up, red whiskers flaring. I looked after him, and then down to the boat where the rest of the rapscallions who had wangled shore leave were tying up and jumping out onto the wet stones. Our ship, *Tuscurs Maiden*, lay in the roads, canvas furled, and those poor wights detained aboard hanging over the gunwales with faces like grandfather clocks.

To either side of this little seaport town of Peminswopt the red cliffs stretched, serrated, flecked with shadings and tonings of rust, orange and ruby under the light of the suns. We had made landfall within the enormous curve of the Bay of Panderk and here we were in the Kovnate of Memis. Our destination, the Kovnate of Bormark, lay to the west. I started off after Pompino. He was the Owner, the man who owned a fleet of ships, and his men knew him and would follow to keep him out of trouble.

With Pompino the Iarvin on the rampage, trouble was a natural and inevitable occurrence.

He headed toward a line of broad-leaved sough-wood trees shading a walkway beyond which rose the walls of the outer town. Much activity went on here as the sailors and fisherfolk went about their business. The smells of tar and pitch mingled with the sea air. A long string of curses rose from a ramshackle shed where tarred nets hung. Someone was in difficulty in repairing their nets. Pompino took no notice. He strode on for the land gate situated alongside the water gate with its portcullis of black iron.

Lofting over the town the fortress of Peminswopt reminded anyone careless enough to let it slip his mind that reivers and pirates might at any time roar in to do all the unpleasant things that folk of that ilk are prone to. This fortress reared up, strong and well-positioned. From those battlements accurate volleys of rocks, darts and flaming carcasses could shatter an unwary attack. Trouble was—the pirates operating here in North Pandahem were just as crafty as renders operating anywhere else. I followed Pompino, aware of the men at my back, and—I admit—comforted by their presence.

If Pompino insisted on burning the temple to Lem the Silver Leem here—a sound and righteous thing to do, seeing that the adherents of the Silver Wonder indulged in murder and torture and baby-sacrifices—the ensuing fracas would need the ready weapons of our comrades.

His reddish whiskers abristle and his foxy Khibil face shrewd, Pompino halted in the shadows of the arched gateway. A string of calsanys passed, each one loaded down with straw-packed boxes, their tails tied to the neck-rope of the one astern.

"Before we start, Jak, my throat is—"

"Aye. And mine."

As we stopped—and only for a couple of heartbeats—a Sinewy brown hand reached out between two of the calsanys and groped for the wallet hanging on my belt. I looked down with interest, always fascinated by the ways in which differing people go about earning their living. This one was smart and quick. The steel knives fastened to the inside of his fingers would have snipped through the thongs in a trice.

Pompino said: "The rast!" and snatched at the lean wrist. He gripped it, tugged, and a bundle of gray rags flew out between the animals. The restraining rope caught around the wretch's neck and hauled him up. He gargled.

"Look out for the calsanys," I said quickly. "You know what—"

"I know what they will do if they are upset."

Pompino hauled the thief upright, disengaged the rope and, taking an ear betwixt finger and thumb, ran the snatch-purse a few paces along the wharf. The fellow twisted in Pompino's grip; he did not produce a weapon.

"By Diproo the Nimble-Fingered!" burst out the cutpurse. "You're mighty quick, dom!"

"To your sorrow, you forsaken of Pandrite!"

"Leave off! I need that ear."

"As you needed my friend's wallet?"

"I've three wives and ten children to support—"

"More fool you. Where's the Watch?"

Now the thief looked alarmed.

"You wouldn't hand me over to the Watch? I'm a poor man. Renko the Iarvin I'm called and—"

I thought Pompino would burst a blood vessel.

"You're Renko the *what*!"

But the fellow babbled on. "Kov Memdo is mighty fierce in these latter days after the wars. You wouldn't—"

"Renko the *what*!"

My comrade's apoplexy was a wonder to behold. Pompino the Iarvin held onto Renko the Iarvin's ear, and bellowed purple of face into that imprisoned organ.

"The Iarvin—" Renko babbled. He squirmed and twisted like a caught fish.

I stood aside, very serious, very thoughtful as the last of the calsanys trotted past. I wouldn't laugh. No, by Vox, even though my insides pained as if about to explode.

"How dare you bear that name!"

"Why—wha—? Leave off my ear, dom!"

Now these Kregish nicknames are a jungle of meanings in themselves. They contain more than one allusion to the quality and attributes of their bearers. To translate them faithfully into a language of Earth one would need to use a considerable quantity of definitions. Iarvin, for instance, means—inter alia—a smart fellow, someone who is sharp, bright, clever, nobody's fool, impeccable—and there are more shadings. Pompino lived up to his sobriquet. Few girls bear the Iarvin as a nickname, for the meanings run differently for them, and the nearest, I suppose, would be the Iueshvin. So, now, the two Iarvins glared, one at the other, and slowly the thief of that name understood what the Khibil of the same name was after.

"You wouldn't hand me over to the Watch, dom? No—of course you wouldn't—"

Cap'n Murkizon, enormous as a barrel, black as a thundercloud, stormed up. I told him what had happened, for he and the others with him could see plainly enough what was going on.

"Aye, Jak. Clever, these folk. Tied himself alongside a calsany and waited until he could reach a likely victim." Here Cap'n Murkizon's eyes squeezed shut and tears started. "But, by the black armpit and flea-infested hair of the Divine Lady of Belschutz! Horter Pompino is no likely victim for a trick like that!"

"He's the Iarvin."

Brick red of face, brilliant blue of eye, sprouting hair every which way, Cap'n Murkizon glared about. He cocked his massive head up on that barrel body. He stared at the sough-wood trees.

"Watch?" he bellowed. "Watch? When there's a tree with a suitable branch handy! Now, thief, you may thank whatever ancient ship's captain it was who brought the first sough-wood tree all the way from distant Havilfar. How could he know that one day, when the trees had grown so fine and tall, they would serve to save a wretch from the Watch?"

Renko the Iarvin grasped instantly what this dynamic bundle of a man meant.

"You wouldn't—for a wallet? By Diproo the Nimble-Fingered! Are you then all stark mad?"

"Aye," said Quendur the Ripper, standing easily at Murkizon's side. The smile on Quendur's face would have filled a shark with horror.

The Kregan way is often an odd way. The spirit of Yurncra the Mischievous must have caught at us. The minor pantheons of Kregen are filled with spirits and demons who move men and women to willful, wanton and reckless ways.

"Where is the rope?" demanded Cap'n Murkizon.

"A seaport always has rope aplenty," observed Larghos the Flatch. He stood close to Murkizon. These two had formed a close friendship since the time Larghos had dived into the sea to save Murkizon. Now Larghos looked about with his Bowman's eye.

"No, no, horters!" yelled Renko the Iarvin. "You would not!"

Just how long Pompino would allow this charade to play I could only guess. The game was growing cold to me. This poor devil Renko, seeing the faces of the seamen around him, devoutly believed they would hang him high from a branch of the sough-wood tree. I stepped forward.

Like the others, I wore simple sailorman's clothes, blue trousers cut to the knee, a blue shirt and a red kerchief around my head. A rapier and main gauche swung at my sides from the broad lesten-hide belt. Only Pompino was dressed with great magnificence, as befitted the Owner, and Captain Murkizon wore a shiny black coat much decorated with gold, his axe swinging from a thong at his belt.

"Renko," I said, "how true is it that you have three wives and ten children?"

He jabbered, and spittle ran. Pompino eased up on his ear.

"I lied, horter, I confess, I lied! I have but the two wives, and but seven children, as Pandrite may smile on me!"

"He's more likely to laugh at you, you great buffoon!" Pompino, for all his talk of going home, had little back in South Pandahem to draw him apart from his pair of twins.

One of the crew swung up with a length of rope; but Pompino had wearied of the farce. He let Renko up. He stuck that fierce Khibil face close into Renko's.

"Now listen to me, you great heap of useless garbage. When you chose to steal from us, you chose the wrong victims. By Horato the Potent, you imbecile! You might have had your hand cut off!"

"No, no, horter! Had I known, I would not—"

"That's what Pantri the Squish said when the needleman explained to her," said Murkizon in his coarse way.

The others guffawed at the reference to the old story of unexpected consequences. This Renko the Iarvin squinted up at them, and, in truth, they wore the appearance of a cutthroat band of ruffians well enough. They'd elected to follow the Owner, they and the others of the crew of *Tuscurs Maiden*. Pompino had explained sufficient to them to justify completely this mission of burning the temples of Lem the Silver Leem, although—for obvious reasons—he could not explain all.

Now Pompino pushed Renko a little way off and glared at him in a most baleful fashion. Renko was all skin and bone, scrawny, with lank hair and the frightened face of a denizen of the stews. His clothes, mere rags, hung on him.

I said: "Do you worship any particular gods hereabouts, Renko?"

At once he was on the defensive, as any sensible person is when questioned too closely by strangers over matters of religion.

"I swear by the potent majesty of Havil the Green," he said, a little truculently. The answer was safe. Havil the Green, one of those all-purpose major godhoods, is worshipped all over the continent of Havilfar and the island of Pandahem. That folk tend to hunger for the more personal worship of a closer god gives rise to the untold numbers of minor religions and cults abounding on Kregen. This is human nature when the chief god cannot sustain all a person's spiritual longing.

Pompino caught my eye. In the partnership we had forged through a number of interesting adventures I was still perfectly happy to allow my comrade the lead. He nodded with his mind made up. He advanced on Renko with what the thief took to be a renewed attempt at hostilities.

"Renko, the crawling nit upon a ponsho fleece! What d'you know of the Brown and Silvers?"

Renko jumped as though branded.

"Nothing, horter! Nothing—"

"Speak, ninny, or—"

"They took my little Tiffti, my little girl. She went with them for sweets and candies and she never came back. And I was beaten, one night, by men—"

"All right, Renko," I said. "You needn't go on."

This was the pattern. The vile adherents of the Silver Wonder, clad in their robes of brown and silver, sacrificed little girls in the most horrific rites. They believed that what they did reflected glory upon them and stored up wealth in the paradise to come. We happened to believe differently. So far we had been able to do precious little to make the other side see our point of view, and, as I said to Pompino, burning a few temples would make little difference. But, it was a start.

"Can I go, horters? My family are starving—"

That might be true, it might not be. I fingered out a golden deldy with the face of a King Copologu on one side and a proclamation on the other suggesting that Copologu the Great was responsible for wealth, health and happiness. Where his kingdom might be I wasn't sure, somewhere down in the Dawn Lands, probably. I tossed the golden coin to Renko.

The gold did not wink a glitter of splendor in the air. A shadow fell about us and a chill gust of wind rattled between the pillars of the archway. Clouds piled in, shadowing the glory of the Suns of Scorpio.

Captain Murkizon said: "B'rrr!" And then: "Are you letting this miserable specimen go free, Horter Pompino?"

"His punishment is being what he is," observed my comrade, twirling his whiskers and obviously enjoying making a profound statement of eternal truth.

Renko the Iarvin snapped up the golden deldy and it disappeared into his rags. He shivered. He was, in truth, a sorry specimen, and I felt for him. Not everyone, on Earth four hundred light-years from Kregen, as on that marvelous and difficult world itself, can be a hero forever swashbuckling about with a sword.

"Be off with you!" bellowed Pompino.

No doubt Renko imagined these rogues would repent of their leniency and produce the rope instanter. He ran. He scurried off along the quay and vanished into the throng of folk all preparing for the coming rain.

"He'll empty a few pockets before he goes home," quoth Pompino. "But that is no affair of ours. Hai, fanshos! Are you for this wet we promised ourselves?"

So, laughing and ahurrying against the rain, we took ourselves off. Through the gate the streets presented a cobbled, close-set, pointy-roofed-houses impression of huddlement. We found a swinging amphora and a sign that read The New Frontier, and in we went.

Someone wanted to know what the sign might mean, and Cap'n Murkizon rumbled out, with a reference to his Divine Lady's anatomy, that this brave new frontier was off across the ocean in the continent of Turismond, where many nations had established ports and trading stations. The ale passed and we quenched our thirsts and watched the rain sparkling on the cobbles.

The landlord, a cat-faced, bright-furred Fristle, came over with a fresh jug. He wore a spotless blue and yellow striped apron.

"The new frontier did very well for the kov," he told us, pouring carefully. "His father, Kov Pando na Memis, made a fortune over there in Turismond. The dowager kovneva, the Lady Leona, brought the young kov back home and now he lives in great style." He wiped the lip of the jug with a clean yellow linen cloth. "Of course, Kov Pando being in the army had to go and get himself killed fighting those Pandrite-forsaken rasts of Hamalese. The wars, they spoiled everything."

"They're over now—"

"Aye, thank all the gods. But we hear tales of those Shtarkins who raid and burn. No coasts are safe, it seems, these days."

He had his worries, we had ours. That is how the worlds roll on. We drank and waited for the rain to stop and took little notice of the company in Fandarlu the Franch's The New Frontier.

Cap'n Murkizon, anxious to put right what he considered a slur upon his honor, wanted to know more about the plans to burn the accursed temple here in Peminswopt.

Pompino explained enough, and little at that.

"This hateful cult of Lem the Silver Leem—" and he kept his voice low—very low "—appears in different guises from country to country. The king here, this flat slug of a King Nemo the Second, supports the religion. It is spoken of a little more openly, and more people know of the Brown and Silvers. But they like to keep their secrets. They use passwords and secret signs. And they torture and sacrifice little children."

Murkizon drank ale, and his fists clenched on the jar. He said nothing.

Quendur the Ripper, raffish and reckless and almost a reformed character, said: "When I was a render adventuring for my own profit and leading a band of bloodthirsty pirates, we never did that. It would not occur to any civilized man."

"Draw your own conclusions."

Larghos the Flatch poured more ale and pushed the jar across to Murkizon. "Civilized people might think to raise a Great Jikai against this evil cult."

"Many do not believe what they cannot grasp. The secret powers of the Leem Lovers are great; men and women disappear in the night, others are assassinated. The followers of the Silver Wonder have friends in the highest places. The Jikai against them is difficult—"

Murkizon looked at the jar Larghos pushed across, down at the one in his fists and saw that it was empty. He exchanged the jars, drank, wiped his lips, and said: "Anything worth doing is difficult. This is not anything like the fight against the Shanks." He clamped his heavy lips shut. No one said any more about that fight, in which Murkizon had been absolutely in the right to suggest we should not fight, and when we had fought he had taken his part right royally.

Outside in the rain a file of soldiers wended past, hunched in their capes. Their flag hung wet and shining. This was the flag of Tomboram, a solid blue with the symbol of a quombora, a fabled beast all fangs and spits of fire. Tomboram utilizes the system of having a simple national flag which is differenced by each sub-use, so that the Kov of Memis charged the blue with a silver full-hulled argenter, and Pando over in Bormark where we were bound had a golden zhantil emblazoned in the center of his blue flag. This is an interesting tradition of a number of nations on Kregen. I looked at what trotted along after the soldiers.

Sleek and shining in the rain, the lethal forms of werstings appeared to undulate like a river in spate, so close their backs were packed. Black and white striped hunting dogs, werstings, vicious and trained to hunt and kill. Yet they have only four legs, and not over-large jaws or fangs. The pack humped along, chained together, and led by their Hikdar, who carried his switch tucked under one arm.

"Werstings," said Quendur. "Now those I do not like."

"Out in the rain?" said Pompino. "Some poor devil is for the chop, then, that is sure."

The landlord, Fandarlu the Franch, came back to our table. He looked after the last of the werstings, loping along with tucked-in tails, and made a face. When he offered to refill our jars, we refused, for the rain was easing and the first hints of ruby and jade across the street gave evidence that the twin suns of Kregen, Zim and Genodras, once more deigned to smile upon the world.

"Thank you, landlord," said Pompino, standing up. "Here is the reckoning." He put a handful of coins on the table. The others nodded and smiled, pleased that the Owner had treated them. We went outside where the air held that freshly scrubbed after-rain tang. Water ran in the gutters. People began appearing on the street. A few birds climbed away from the eaves where they had sheltered, heading out for the fish quays. They were gulls and small birds, not saddle flyers.

"A nice place, The New Frontier," commented Pompino as we walked along. "Clean and respectable."

I felt like stirring Pompino a little. Now the landlord's nickname of Franch means a fellow who thinks a lot of himself, and is able to prove it. It is not in the same category as Iarvin. So I said: "His nickname suited him, no doubt. Perhaps they are all cut from the same cloth hereabouts."

He stopped and glared at me. He took my meaning. Then he laughed. Pompino Scauro ti Tuscursmot, called the Iarvin, can laugh as only a Khibil can. For Khibils are a mighty supercilious folk, highly hoity-toity in their ways and when they laugh they relax from that high posture and let it all roll out.

"And there," he said when he stopped laughing, "is the fellow we need." He nodded his head.

Indeed, there was the man. He strutted along the street pompously, swinging a golden-headed balass cane. His clothes ballooned splendidly, laced with gold and silver, wired with gems. His hat glistened, the arbora feathers flaring. A few paces to his rear trotted along a Brukaj, patient, docile, carrying a satchel which no doubt contained all the fussy necessaries this puffed-up personage required from time to time.

The object which unmistakably told us that this was, indeed, the man we required, was pinned to his lapel. A small silver brooch, fashioned in the form of a leaping leem, and with a tuft of brown feathers setting it off.

"They are more open, up here," I said.

"They are safe, the cramphs. If you do not know what the silver leem and the brown feathers mean, then you do not matter. And if you do know, then you had best walk small and keep a still tongue in your head, otherwise you're likely to find yourself in the gutter with a slit throat."

"Aye. You have the right of it."

Murkizon said in his thunder-growl voice: "Shall I twist his arm a little?"

"When we are safe from observation. And the poor Brukaj slave will have to be attended to."

"I," said Quendur the Ripper, who had once been a pirate, "will treat him with great courtesy."

We followed this glittering popinjay in an unobtrusive way among the growing crowds. His slave carried the furled-up rain-shedder, a kind of umbrella, over his shoulder, and looked miserable. The popinjay himself carried a multi-colored kerchief in his hand, with which he made much gallant play to passing ladies and acquaintances. He also carried strapped to his waist a rapier and main gauche. For all his dandified looks, he'd be able to use the weapons. On Kregen weapons are carried for a purpose, and those that carry them are expert in their use. Those that are not are dead.

As the suns shone down and we dogged our quarry, I qualified that thought. Not everyone on Kregen is a roistering rapscallion of an adventurer, and, in addition, there are those who carry weapons and who have only a modicum of skill in their use. Usage and custom dictate where the twain shall meet, if they do, and how they shall conduct themselves.

"He is making for the zorcadrome, I believe," said Pompino. "The thought of a fine dainty zorca saddled to support that bulk offends me."

"You are right, and you are wrong."

"What, Jak? What in the name of—?"

"You are right to say he is no zorcaman, despite they are sturdy and strong and always willing. You are wrong to say he is going to the zorcadrome. Look. That is his destination."

The fellow we followed in our unobtrusive way lumbered up the steps of a building that gave no indication of its use. It was simply a three-storeyed structure, one of a row in this street, with a fantastical array of pointed roofs and toppling spires and chimneys. The slave Brukaj followed and the door closed after him.

"How long is the ninny going to stay in there, wherever he is?" demanded Murkizon.

Before Pompino had time to speak, I said: "Well, I for one do not intend to hang about to find out."

They looked at me. To give my comrade his due he grasped my meaning before the others. Larghos the Flatch started to say: "What, Horter Jak! Giving up so soon!"

Pompino broke in. "And I am with you!"

"Good," I said, and wasted no more words. Across the street, dodging a smart carriage drawn by freymuls, up the steps and a thunderous tattoo on the door, I gave Pompino no chance to dart in front. He was at my side as the door opened.

A small Och woman—and Ochs are small in any case—turned her head up to regard us. She wore a decent black dress and a yellow apron and her hair was covered in a white lace coif. Pompino spent two heartbeats staring vacantly down the brown-varnished hall with its side tables and vases of flowers before he looked down at the little Och lady.

"Yes?" Her voice held the timbre of a saucepan struck by a carving knife.

"Ah..." said Pompino.

He stared at me with the same vacant look.

I said in as cheerful a voice as I could manage: "Pray pardon, madam. Is Horter Naghan Panderk at home?"

The name just jumped into my head—Naghan as one of the more common Kregish first names, Panderk for the bay of that name.

She looked me up and she looked me down. Her nose wrinkled just a trifle.

"There is no one here of that name."

I looked suitably flabbergasted. Pompino picked it up at once.

"Surely there must be, madam? This is where he lives."

She shook her head and made shooing motions.

Maybe Pompino had picked up more than he ought to have done. Maybe this place was not a house where people lived at all. As though confirming that notion a hulking great Chulik of a fellow hove into view along the passageway. His yellow-skinned face and the upthrusting tusks at each corner of his mouth bore down on us, together with his beetling brows and his thin lips and his iron armor and his sword.

Perfectly normal to have a watchman, a sensible precaution in a chancy world, of course—but this fellow bore down with so evident an intention of picking us up by the scruff of our necks, of smiting at us with his sword, of doing us a mischief, that the normality of the custom vanished instantly.

He wore brown and silver favors, and that condemned him in our eyes.

"Out!" he roared. "Schtump!"

"Now this," said Pompino, and he spoke almost gratefully. "Is more like it!"

At that instant the terrified scream of a child rocketed up through the house, bounced along the corridor in a shriek of agony.

"Devil's work!" yelled Pompino.

Together, shoulder to shoulder, we charged past the little Och woman and slap bang into the raging Chulik beyond.

Two

The Devil's Academy

If the famous Watch of Peminswopt of whom Renko the Thief was so scared had chanced by just then and seen a wild bunch of ruffians breaking into what seemed a private house, they would have taken us for reivers, criminals, bandits. That piercing scream proved otherwise.

The little Och woman toppled sideways, unharmed as we crashed past. Pompino dealt with the Chulik in a summary fashion. The man was unready for such a swift and headlong assault, and he went down soundlessly.

We roared on along the passage.

"Down there!" yelled Pompino and we clattered down the blackwood stairs leading off at a right angle at the turn of the corridor. The others whooped after us. A vague orange glow from the edges of a door at the foot of the stairs abruptly bloated into brilliance. The door smashed open as Pompino put his foot to it. We all rushed through. The room beyond held four more Chuliks in iron armor and wearing brown and silver. Their weapons glistened in that orange light.

They did not hesitate. They launched themselves at us in a feral onslaught designed to smash us instantly, with no questions asked. Pompino yelled, Cap'n Murkizon's axe whistled about, Larghos switched his sword forward. Quendur simply slid down and along the polished floor on his seat and skewered upwards. A nasty trick—dangerous, of course; but then that was Quendur the Ripper, reckless and swashbuckling. I joined them and in a trice the Chulik guards were overpowered.

"They were not guarding that entrance for nothing," quoth Pompino. His sword indicated the curtained doorway at the far end.

The shrill and agonized scream broke out again, ending in a ghastly bubbling wheeze.

"Hurry! Before we are too late!"

The curtains whisked aside.

Pompino used his sword to open the drapes; what we saw beyond convinced us that swords would have to be used for a grimmer purpose before we were done with this place.

"The Devil's Academy!" Pompino's words summed up that scene. The man we had followed was in the act of dressing himself in clothes suitable for what went forward here. His assistants, meek, frightened, pallid men and women, fussed over him, oblivious of our entry. The room's lamps shed that orange light upon the cages and the basalt slabs, the racks of knives and saws. For a foolish moment I thought we might have stumbled upon a surgeon's operating room; but I saw no signs of tar barrels, and Kregans do not operate in quite that way. The man in the blood-stained smock over his brown and silver looked up. His fingers ran with blood. The girl child upon the slab would not live, not now. The saw in the man's fingers was a single bar of crimson.

He shouted: "Who are you?" And then, quickly: "Guards! *Guards!*" For he saw our swords and understood what they meant.

The man we had followed struggled to get either into or out of the smock his attendants fussed with, and he, too, screamed for guards. It was quite clear what was going on. As Pompino said, this was the place where the priests of Lem learned their butcher's trade.

We were too late to save the child who had screamed and so brought us here; we could try to save the four other children, three girls and a boy, penned in the iron cages against the walls. Their hands and feet were bound, and they wore blindfolds and were gagged. We did not think it was from concern over their feelings that they were thus blindfolded.

The half-dozen or so younger men in the ubiquitous brown and silver standing goggling to one side must be the acolytes, the trainees. Here they were taught the finer arts of sacrifice.

With a shout of pure horrified anger, Pompino threw himself forward. The others followed, yelling. This, I thought, was what the Star Lords wanted us to do, eradicate Lem the Silver Leem, root and branch. I gather that here on this Earth there have been discovered recently something over two hundred sub-atomic particles, including leptons, and things called glues which hold, or appear to hold, quarks together within protons. I'm pretty confident that the Star Lords know of many more sub-atomic particles if there are many more to know. These sacrifices were being divided and sub-divided, like atoms, into sub-atomic, sub-human, particles. If this was Lem's idea of scientific research, then the Star Lords had our whole allegiance in putting a halt to it. So, nauseated, I dived into the fray, and my prime object was not revenge but to get the four children safely out of it.

The flash of sword flickered in a most particular and sinister fashion in that pervasive orange light. My comrades rushed upon the adherents of the Silver Wonder. I turned toward the cages.

As the clangor of the fight broke out at my back I looked at the cages. The iron bars bulked each with a heavy full roundness that told of strength sufficient to hold not only children. Leems would be kept penned there when required. The bolts were shot home, the locks clumsy and intricate. To one side two angerims gaped upon the scene.

Sharp-toothed are angerims, all hair and ears, and as a race of diffs who are not Homo sapiens they are an untidy, messy lot. Staring at me they backed off, holding their mop and broom up as though they were weapons.

"Just give me the keys," I said. For the key ring at the taller of the two's waist spoke eloquently.

"Keep off!" screeched one angerim, his hair sprouting everywhere, half-concealing his brown breechclout.

"Run!" yelped the other.

They threw down the mop and the broom and started to run toward a small door set abaft and to the side of the cages. Opaz alone knew what maze they'd disappear into if they escaped through that exit. I sprinted after them.

In their mad flight they kicked over a metal bucket containing bits and pieces. The floor stained red and slippery. I jumped. They almost reached the door when I realized this was no way to get the keys.

Instantly, I yanked out my old sailor knife, poised, and threw.

The broad blade pierced the thigh of the taller angerim and he toppled over, screeching. His companion did not wait about but simply wrenched open the door and leaped through with a long wailing cry. In a heartbeat I reached the fallen diff, saw that he would live if he reached a needleman in time, and took two things from him—one the key ring and the other my sailor knife.

The noise spurted up as Pompino and his crew sorted out the problem of the Leem Lovers. The third key fitted the lock and the first cage swung open.

The best plan would be to open all the cages first and then to release the bonds and the blindfolds. To do it the other way around would see the first child running screaming every which way, probably to fling himself in the way of a sword.

Each cage opened with its own individual key. A neat touch. Remaining on the clumsy iron ring three keys promised other doors in this place it might be worth the opening. I glanced over my shoulder. The acolytes had either run or been cut down. The two chief butchers, the instructors, must have attempted resistance, for the body of one still clutched in one half-severed hand a broken sword. The other vomited out his life over the corpse of the child.

26

From the distant end of this unpleasant chamber the guards at last appeared. A group of half a dozen or so Rapas rushed into sight. Predatory, beaked and feathered, their vulturine features convulsed with killing fury, the Rapas hurled themselves at Pompino and his men. No doubt they intended to avenge their paymasters.

Cap'n Murkizon let his booming roar lift over the noise.

"Hit 'em, knock 'em down and tromple all over 'em!"

This he proceeded to do with great gusto.

Confident that all was well, I returned my attention to the cages and the children.

If you wonder why I, Dray Prescot, whom my companions knew only as Jak, did not roar into a knock-down drag-out fight, but, instead, opened cages, then you profoundly misunderstand my nature. A fight is a fight; there have always, it seems, been fights and, no doubt in the nature of man and woman's inclinations, there always will be fights. That does not mean a fellow has to hurl himself headlong into every one that comes along if there are more important tasks at hand.

Like now.

Freeing the children was easy; calming them down was an enormous task.

Only two were apim, Homo sapiens, like me. One girl was a Fristle Fifi, sleek and charming and graceful in her feline way, her fur a glorious honey-colored softness. The lad was a Brokelsh already with his coarse black body hair abristling everywhere, quite unlike the swagging growths fringing an angerim.

I'd half a mind to keep their ankles hobbled up; but after I'd spoken to them in a manner more brusque than I really cared for, they quieted. Their eyes, round and glistening, regarded me as though I was a fabled devil from Gundarlo or Cottmer's Caverns. I tried to smile for them.

"You will all go home to your parents—" And, of course, that was the wrong thing to say. At that, they began to cry. The picture was obvious and ugly enough. So, to repair the damage, I told them that as soon as the nasty men had been dealt with we would find a new home with many sweets—in fact, I said, embroidering, "We will find you a home right next door to a Banje shop!"

A Rapa blundered past with half his beak missing and his feathers bedabbled a brighter color than their usual green-gray. I merely watched him as he struggled to reach one of the other doors in this place, for the Devil's Academy was well-provided with exits. Larghos the Flatch, sweeping his sword in a slashing cut very suitable for a Bowman to use, helped the Rapa on his way. I held the little Fristle Fifi's hand, and the other children clustered around. Their eyes remained large and round and glistening.

The noise quieted. The stink of spilled blood rasped in the close atmosphere. Pompino came over, looking as though he was halfway through a chore.

"Fire, Jak," he said. "Now we burn the accursed place."

"And hope the temple is handy."

"Too right, very handy, to be consumed also."

Larghos said: "That Rapa—he must be dying; but he dodged off. He could raise the alarm."

"Then settle him, lad, settle him!" boomed Cap'n Murkizon. "By the nit-infested armpits of the Divine Lady of Belschutz! Don't waste your sympathy on these cramphs!"

Larghos ran off, swirling his sword. Murkizon trundled along after. They were forming a right partnership, that pair.

Quendur the Ripper said: "I am glad Lisa the Empoin is not here to witness this." He shook his head, raffish, reckless yet trying to reform.

"If she had been here," Pompino told the ex-pirate, "she would have been more merciless than we mere men."

"Oh, aye. That is sooth."

I cocked an eye at Pompino. The Khibil brushed up his reddish whiskers. No doubt he was thinking of his wife, who nourished ideas above her station, and with whom Pompino no longer got on. A startling confirmation—a re-affirmation—in the coincidence of the actions of Pompino's wife after a fight and what next occurred, a confirmation only that human nature is human nature, gave me a feeling of helplessness in the face of that very same human nature. Cap'n Murkizon returned to the chamber yelling with merriment. He fairly golloped out his glee.

Following him walked Larghos the Flatch, his head bent a little to the side and over the sleek dark head of a naked girl who walked close to him. We all stared.

"A cloak!" bellowed Murkizon. "To cover the Lady Nalfi!"

Quendur leaped to one of the less distorted bodies and whipped off the brown tunic. The silver hem was only lightly bespattered. He took the garment across, saying: "Until we can find something better for the Lady Nalfi."

Larghos the Flatch took the tunic from Quendur. I noticed the officious way in which he acted, taking the tunic, fussing, handing it to the girl. She was in the first flush of womanhood, firm and rosy, with bright eyes in which a pain easily understood clouded the blueness. She lifted her arms and slipped the tunic on, shivering.

"Thank you, Jikai," she said in a small voice, speaking to Larghos. He was acting as though he'd received a thirty-two pound roundshot betwixt wind and water, so we all knew his business was done for.

"The Rapa?" said Pompino, brushing aside what went forward, anxious to get on with the purpose.

"He led me to the Lady Nalfi," said Larghos. He spoke through lips stiff with some emotion we again envisaged as being all too easy to understand. "I cut him down. And a rast of a Chulik tried to bargain with us over the Lady Nalfi—"

"Standing holding her!" roared Murkizon. "But she didn't stay held long."

"She just took his dagger from his belt and slit his throat." Larghos gazed fondly at Nalfi. "A brave act for a naked girl in so perilous a position."

She lowered her eyelids and leaned against Larghos.

"I—I had to."

"Do not think of it, my lady, if it pains you—"

"No, no. It is not that. Just—"

Pompino burst over all this. "Find combustibles. Pile them up. Let us burn the place down and leave, for, by Horato the Potent, the stench is getting down my gullet!"

As we busied ourselves over this task, I reflected that the adherents of Lem the Silver Leem hired mercenaries of a reasonably high quality. Also, while it is said that Chuliks and Rapas are hereditary enemies, this is not strictly and invariably true. Of course, some Chuliks and some Rapas are always at one another's throats, just as there are misguided apims who are hereditary enemies—here on this Earth just as much as Kregen, more's the pity. But an employer will hire on mercenaries from many different races, and they will serve alongside one another for pay, and not quarrel overmuch. This system, as I have indicated, works to the employer's advantage in that there is less likelihood of plots against him or her from the ranks of the paktuns taking pay.

The combustibles were set, the children and the Lady Nalfi drew away to a safe distance, and Pompino personally set the first flame.

We had seen no sign of the Brukaj slave who waited on the man we had followed here, and I, for one, could entertain a hope that he had escaped. Slaves are controlled, and do not always believe what their masters or mistresses believe.

Flames ran and crackled and laughed gleefully to themselves. Smoke began to waft in flat gray streamers, filling the place with a soft veil, hiding the horrors.

Retracing our steps up the blackwood stairs we encountered the little Och woman at the top, wringing her hands, crying.

Some of us were for cutting her down where she stood, there and then. Others of us, though, counseled mercy as we could not know the full story and there was certainly no time to wait to find out. Pompino shouted alarmingly, and the Och woman ran off, throwing her apron over her head. The rest of us, the children and the Lady Nalfi, came up and we headed for the front door.

Now even on Kregen in a civilized city a cutthroat gang of rascals with blood-spattered clothing and blood-reeking swords will claim attention if they attempt to march down the High Street. We halted on the steps, staring about.

The Lady Nalfi in her soft husky voice said: "I know a way. The back alleys. Come, quickly."

Agreeing, we trooped down the steps and cut into the side alley between this house and the next. Murkizon trod on a gyp which howled and scampered off with his tail between his legs. Nothing else untoward occurred as we hurried along the alleys, past the backs of stores and houses, and so came out to a place where three alleys met. Here stood—or rather leaned—a pot house of the most deplorable kind. Only four drunks lay in the gutter outside. No riding animals were tethered to the rail. The Suns shone, the air smelled as clean as Kregan air ever can smell clean.

Pompino looked at Nalfi.

Larghos held her close and it was clear he would not relinquish her.

"If we clean off the blood—"

Pompino nodded. So we all went at the pump outside the pot house, sluicing and sloshing. Larghos eyed the four drunks calculatingly; but Murkizon told him that their clothes were far too ragged—and alive—for the Lady Nalfi.

Speaking in a solemn, careful way, in almost a drugged fashion, Larghos the Flatch said: "I shall see to it that the Lady Nalfi is dressed as befits her, in the most perfect clothes it is possible to find. Such beauty must be dressed in beauty."

Nalfi did not reply; but her blue gaze appraised Larghos. He swelled with the importance of the task he had set himself. Pompino caught my eye, and smiled; I did not respond. Not all marriages are made in Heaven, and not all end in Hell.

When we were cleaned up we set off still keeping to quiet and less-frequented ways down to the docks.

Confidentially, Pompino said to Cap'n Murkizon: "Captain. It would be best if you asked Larghos, quietly, what he knows of this Lady Nalfi."

Murkizon leered; but agreed.

The sea sprung no untoward surprises, sparkling pale blue with that tinge of deeper shadows past the rocks, which, in their furry redness sometimes looked perfectly in place and at others oddly out of keeping. Gulls flew up squawking as we walked along the jetty.

"Thank the good Pandrite!" exclaimed Pompino when we saw our boat was still moored up. Looking back over the spires and pinnacles of the close-pitched roofs we could see no sign of smoke. Murkizon expressed himself forcibly on the subject of fires, and when, icily, Pompino requested that he make himself plain, the bluff captain shut up.

But we knew what he was on about. Pompino had set the fires. We had all seen them burning, beginning to ease their way aloft. Why, then, had the godforsaken building not burned down?

Not until we had pulled almost up to *Tuscurs Maiden* and the watch, hailing us, prepared to receive us aboard, could the first wafts of smoke be seen over the city.

Pompino merely gave the smoke a single significant glance, and leaped up onto the deck. That glance spoke more eloquently than any "I told you so!"

Standing on the deck I said to Pompino: "I know a man, a fellow by the name of Norhan the Flame. His hobby is throwing pots of blazing combustibles about."

"Aye, Jak. A handy fellow to have along now."

"Down in Hyrklana, though—I think, for he was moving around the last I heard."

"Don't we all?"

The breeze indicated a fair passage, the vessel was in good heart, if a trifle stormbeaten, and she'd been careened and scraped at Pomdermam. Over on the shore the smoke lifted and people moved about on the jetty. Two other argenters like *Tuscurs Maiden* lay moored up. Well, being North Pandahem craft they were not quite exactly the same as our vessel which hailed from South Pandahem.

"It is reasonably doubtful, Pompino. But there is a chance we were observed. Therefore we may be followed."

"We may, indeed."

Climbing onto the quarterdeck Pompino radiated energy.

"Captain Linson," he said to the master. "While I do not profess to understand the tides and the winds as sailors do, and while it is true that I merely own the ship, I would like you to take us to sea and toward the west at this very moment."

Pompino, it seemed, had been learning that owners could not order their ships to perform evolutions like soldiers on a parade ground. His heavy-handed way with Linson, who was sharp, cutting, and with every instinct set on making a fortune from the sea, simply made the master even more indifferent. Linson was a fine sailor, knew his own mind, took enormous delight from tormenting Captain Murkizon, and was prepared to obey orders if they did not conflict too much with his own desires.

"We are able to sail at once, Horter Pompino. I made certain arrangements when I—ah—observed the smoke."

"Did you now, by Pandrite!"

As Cap'n Murkizon and I sailed as supernumeraries, we had no direct part to play in getting the ship to sea, apart from hauling on and slacking off and running. This sailor activity pleased me for reasons Murkizon, who had been born on Kregen as had everyone else as far as I knew, could never understand. As for Murkizon, that barrel of blow-hard toughness ached to eradicate the imagined slight upon his honor.

The Lady Nalfi and the children, escorted below, were safely out of it. I caught Pompino's eye as the canvas bellied and was sheeted home, and the ship began to come alive.

"Linson could see the smoke before we could, as he was higher."

"Aye. Devilish smart is our master, Captain Linson."

"Aye."

Tuscurs Maiden heeled, took the breeze, and in a comfortable depth of water headed out past the Pharos. A few small craft bobbed here and there. The lookout sang out.

We rushed to the aftercastle.

"May Armipand the Misshapen take them!" burst out Pompino.

With shining oars rising and falling like the fabled wings of a bird of prey, wedge-prowed, hard, a swordship pulled after us, her bronze ram bursting the sea into foam.

Three

We sail for Bormark

We stared aft as that cruel bronze rostrum smashed through spray after us. The oars rose and fell, rose and fell, beautiful in their way, derisive of the agony entailed in their hauling. Pompino stamped a booted foot upon the scrubbed deck.

"Now I am growing heartily sick of this seafaring life, Jak! I thought buying a few ships and trading would turn an honest ob or two, in between serving the Star Lords. Yet it seems an honest sailorman's life is bedeviled every which way he turns."

Somewhat drily, I said: "They are probably not pirates, Pompino. No doubt they are some of the Seaborne Watch of Peminswopt. They would like to ask us some questions."

Pompino eyed the pursuing craft meanly. She foamed along, yet I fancied that once we left the shelter of the cliffs she'd feel the bite of the sea and the thrust of the wind. Once out into the offing we should outrun her, if the breeze held.

"This Kov of Memis runs a tidy province, I'll say that for him."

"Do I detect a hint that our own young Kov Pando na Bormark does not?"

"Ask his mother—"

Involuntarily, I glanced down as though, foolishly, I could see through the solid planking of the deck into the aft staterooms. Sprawled on a seabed down there, Tilda—Tilda of the Many Veils, Tilda the Beautiful—would no doubt be drinking with a steady regularity from any of the splendid array of bottles provided. Never fully drunk, always a trifle lush, the Dowager Kovneva Tilda presented us with a sorry problem. We knew that the Star Lords, superhuman, almost immortal, unknowable, as I thought then, wished us to cleanse the province of Bormark of the Leem Lovers. We had burned a temple in the capital of Tomboram, Pomdermam, and now we had burned the Devil's Academy in Peminswopt, in Memis. Next along the coast in the enormous curve of the Bay of Panderk lay the stromnate of Polontia. I had not yet made up my mind if we should stop there or make directly for Bormark, at the western frontier of the kingdom of Tomboram.

The pursuing swordship foamed along. Long and lean like all her class, she presented only that wedge-shaped bow and the wings in their shining splendor, rising and falling, rising and falling. Faintly, borne across the breeze, the sound of the drum reached us.

"They mean to catch us."

I made up my mind. As Pompino the Iarvin considered he led our partnership I had to put the decision to him tactfully; this was accomplished easily enough by spelling out our alternatives. Pompino nodded decisively.

"Captain Linson!" he called. "We steer straight for Bormark!"

Linson nodded, dark and smooth and as sharp as a professional assassin's dagger. *Tuscurs Maiden* responded to a delicate helm, a trifle of canvas management. She headed directly for the open sea, bearing boldly out across the Bay. Soon the swordship was going up and down like a dinosaur in a swamp.

"Hah!" shouted Pompino, filled with childlike glee. "They do not like that, by Horato the Potent, they do not!"

"I," I said with firmness, "am hungry."

"And I. Is there time to eat before—?"

"He won't catch us now. And his oarsmen will have shot their bolt soon enough. Poor devils."

By this time in our relationship, Pompino knew this was no idle remark. He agreed, commenting on his previous remarks about the plight of oarslaves. He had been made well aware that my face was firmly set against slavery.

Sharp set, we went below.

"Of course," said Pompino as we entered his stateroom, "there remains the problem of the Kovneva Tilda."

"She expressed the firm desire to return home to Bormark. Our way lies in that self-same direction." The table was spread with excellent promise, and I addressed myself as much to the viands as to Pompino. "And Pando will not be a long away from his estates, not with the trouble he has brewing there."

Biting into a succulent vosk pie, well stoked with momolams and greens and with a gravy poured from the tables of the gods themselves, I realized how fatuous that remark was. On Kregen, wonderful, horrible, fascinating, trouble is always brewing—if it is not already here and hitting you in the back of the neck.

"Did you follow all that rigmarole of the love lives of these folk?" Pompino spoke around a leg of chicken that dribbled gravy into his whiskers. This he wiped away at once with a clean yellow cloth. Khibils are fastidious folk.

"Most. It is not an unfamiliar pattern—"

"Oh, agreed. I meant how can we turn it to our own benefit?"

Sharp, too, are Khibils, especially those dubbed the Iarvin.

I speared a momolam and lifted it. *Tuscurs Maiden*, in Limki the Lame, boasted a cook to be prized. In this, Linson merely emphasized his own approach to the important things of life. I squinted at the momolam, the small yellow tuber glistening and delicious and aching to be tasted.

"Whoever supports us in opposition to Lem receives our support in their amorous designs? Is that it?"

"Aye. Probably."

"Too simple, my friend."

"Nothing is simple where you're concerned, Jak."

I placed the momolam into my mouth and shut my eyes and chewed. Pompino was right, confound it!

I wondered what would chance if the Star Lords dispatched Pompino to Vallia to sort out a problem for them and we met up. I'd have a deal of explaining to do then, by Vox!

He waggled his knife at me.

"Your young friend Pando, the Kov of Bormark, is a rascal and yet a very very highly placed noble. He means to have his own way with this girl and to Cottmer's Caverns with his cousin Murgon."

Refusing to be drawn into a wrangle about Pando's character I said: "The Everoinye have commanded us to go and burn Lem's temples. So this we do. We are going to burn as many temples as we can find in the kovnate of Bormark. Young Pando is the kov. A great deal of his property is going to be burned up when the temples are destroyed. What, Pompino, do you think the young rascal of a kov will say to that?"

Pompino laughed and threw his gnawed chicken bone into a silver waste dish.

"Why, Jak! He will roar and rage. But the temples will be burned!"

"Humph," I said, taking refuge in that silly sailorman's noise when he has nothing to add that makes sense.

So, after an interesting space in which Pompino fussed over selecting a wine that pleased him—a light Tardalvoh, of all things—I had to say: "Yes. Pando is determined to take the girl, this Vadni Dafni Harlstam, to wife. This will not only increase his estates, for her vadvarate marches with his kovnate to the south, it will infuriate his cousin Murgon—"

"It may destroy him!"

"You think so? He struck me as dark and dangerous—"

"Oh, aye, he is. But I read him as a man to be broken rather than bend."

"With all the delays that have bedeviled us it's a racing chance Murgon will reach Bormark before we do. As for races, I wouldn't care to wager on which cousin will get there first."

Thinking of Pando and his mother, Tilda, I was of a mind that Murgon could bend or break so long as he failed in his dark designs. In this I was woefully adrift, as you shall hear.

I could not tell Pompino that over the years I'd had agents in Pandahem to keep an eye on Pando and Tilda, and that they had failed me. The reason for their failure, at the time, was easy to understand, what with the turmoil of the Wars and the struggles against poor mad Empress Thyllis of Hamal and the devil wizard, Phu-si-Yantong, known as the Hyr Notor. In those dread days men's and women's lives were cheap. We were clawing back to the light of the Suns, now, and life was resuming something of order and civilization; we still had a long way to go.

So—this meant I was not in possession of the full facts. Ahead all was murk and uncertainty.

Patting my lips with a yellow cloth, I stood up.

"I'm for a spell on the quarterdeck. I need the breeze in my face for a time. You'll join me?"

"Later. If we are to avoid the Stromnate of Polontia and head straight for Bormark there are arrangements in the bills of lading and the accounts I must make." He cocked a bright eye up, mocking and yet serious. "We great shipping magnates have our work, as well as these tarry sailors."

"Hah!" I said, not particularly convincingly, and went up on deck.

A great deal had to be thought about, and much of what I had to contend with was, of course, completely unknown to my kregoinye comrade Pompino. We headed straight across the Bay of Panderk in the days following, shipboard routine continued, the breeze blew, the Suns of Scorpio shed their mingled lights across the waves, and if a fellow had had no other thoughts in his head he might well have enjoyed an idyllic period.

We sighted no other sail until a morning of crimson and jade and hurling wind, with *Tuscurs Maiden* bowling along under all plain sail, hard braced, heeling on the starboard tack, racing along—well, racing along for a stumpy argenter.

"You'll get no damned renders in this weather," exclaimed Cap'n Murkizon, bristling, grasping a ratline. He stared off across the tumbled sea. "Up by the Hoboling Islands you'll find 'em creeping about, pirating honest sailormen."

"You've experience of the Hobolings, Cap'n?"

"By reputation. I heard that once they sent a fleet to fill the oceans down to Tomboram. That was a time ago, now. They've not repeated that kind of raid, to the glory of Pandrite the credit."

That was a most serious statement from our Murkizon.

Carefully, I said: "I heard a chief pirate was Viridia the Render. Does the name mean aught to you?"

"Only as a render leader. She fought better than a man, I am told." Before he or I could continue this hazy conversation, the lookout bellowed. For want of anything better to do and the desire to know, I scampered up to the cross-trees and wedged myself and stared at the distant speck bobbing on the horizon rim.

The breeze blustered past and the ship gyrated as any ship will on almost any board and the old sailorman's trick of holding the glass steady enabled me to center the sighting.

She was no pirate. She was a Galleon of Vallia.

Satisfying myself that she was on an interception course, I shinned down the backstay and found Pompino on the quarterdeck with Captain Linson. Both looked grave.

"A Vallian?" Linson rubbed his chin. "We cannot outsail her, then."

Pompino huffed up; but he had to accept that when it came to sailing ships, the Galleons of Vallia were the finest sailing these seas—apart always from the damned Leem-Loving Shanks from over the curve of the world, blast their eyes.

"The days of enmity between Pandahem and Vallia are over," I said. "By Chusto! Those days are dead and gone!"

Both men swiveled to regard me. I realized I had spoken with some warmth. The subject was close to my heart, as you know, and I was wrapped up in schemes for the future when Pandahem, Vallia and the other land masses of Paz must cooperate against the Shanks.

"I picked up rumors in the Captains' Saloons, here and there," remarked Linson. "Not all Vallians share the friendship for Pandahem proclaimed by their new emperor."

I said: "There has for many seasons been friendship between Vallia and Tomboram."

We spoke lightly of Pandahem, which is an island cut up into kingdoms and kovnates, when each nation was an entity unto itself. Just how much truth there was in my last observation I still was not sure; maybe that was just a pious hope.

"Well, Vallian galleons have pirated ships of Tomboram, along with all the other nations of Pandahem. I think," said Linson in his hard way. "I shall prepare for any eventuality."

"Of course."

No captain was going to risk his ship through lack of preparation.

"You think, Jak," said Pompino, "we should run up the flag of Tomboram? Of Bormark? This will safeguard us from the Vallian?"

"It should."

I could hear that infuriating quaver of doubt in my voice as I spoke. By Vox! Hadn't these idiots grasped essentials yet? My idiots of Vallia? Pirating each other, which is what it came down to, how did that help us against the greater foe?

As though further to emphasize the difference between a Vallian galleon and an argenter of any other seafaring nation, the breeze slackened, backing, and *Tuscurs Maiden* although sailing well lost a deal of her speed. Not so the Vallian. He came on at a great rate, and it was now transparently plain that he was, indeed, steering an intercept course.

Linson eyed the other craft meanly.

"If he means to fight, then we can accommodate him."

This idea dismayed me. Of course, from the first moments I'd realized that as a member, supernumerary, of the ship's crew, I would expect to fight her enemies. Those enemies were seamen of my own nation. Before I believed that, I had to cling to the belief that seamen of Vallia no longer preyed on the seamen of Pandahem. But—some still did. I knew that. It was no good blinking at facts. If that galleon over there, foaming along with the bone in her teeth spuming white, all her canvas drawing, was in truth a pirate—why then I, Dray Prescot, Emperor of Vallia, had better keep that fact very quiet. Very quiet indeed. A gang of cutthroat renders would as lief string up the emperor as spit at him—they'd more than likely spit on his corpse. My Delia had experienced something of this dilemma in her brush with the Sisters of the Whip, when to be acknowledged Empress of Vallia would have brought not instant obedience and protection but chains, the whip and a death in torment.

The crew took up the positions they occupied at action stations without the usual rush and scurry. The drums did not beat, the trumpet remained mute. Quietly, fingering their weapons, the men and women of *Tuscurs Maiden* stood to. Up on the forward platform our varterists waited around their ballistae. The forward boarding party, the prijikers, kept close, waiting for orders. Weapons were held down, inconspicuously out of sight of the Vallian. Captain Linson nodded as Pompino finished speaking to him, and issued orders.

Very shortly thereafter, the blue flag charged with the golden zhantil rose above our decks. We sailed under the flag of Bormark of Tomboram. How would the Vallian react to that?

Itching with impatience to know the outcome of the puzzle I took a glass up to the crosstrees again. The galleon neared. She was a splendid craft, one of the new construction we had put in hand after the Times of Troubles. She would be able to range *Tuscurs Maiden*, outsail her, riddle her. As to her crew, well, the Vallian sailorman is a fearsome foe upon the sea, as I knew and joyed in. If it came to a fight, the Pandaheem were on a losing wicket.

The circle of the spyglass roved across the approaching vessel. She was splendid! Soon I could discern the features of the men upon her quarterdeck. I did not recognize any—but at this range I could easily be mistaken.

I thought one man looked remarkably like Ortyg Fondal, and another like Nath Cwophorlin, both capable ship-officers of the old emperor's navy; but I could not be sure.

The glass carried my gaze forrard and picked out the superior grosvarters of Vallia arranged on the forecastle. I stared. One man leaped into focus. His lean body was bare to the waist and his buff breeches were cut off at the knee. He wore a close-fitting leather cap, and there were not one but three red feathers sporting there. I could visualize the thin streak of black chin beard under his jaws, the lean eager look of him, the broken nose. Well, Wersting Rogahan had served me well and fought for Vallia; but he would just as easily fight to line his own pocket with pickings from a Pandaheem as not. I had to hope. Wersting Rogahan would listen to me if I spoke, that was certain.

I switched the glass back to the quarterdeck.

A man climbed up out of the aft cabin, and stretched, and looked across at us.

I felt a suffusing tide of relief. Upright, strongly built, lithe, the figure of the captain of the Vallian moved purposefully to the bulwark. He stared at us, and an outstretched hand was instantly filled by a telescope. He raised the glass to his eye. I felt like waving, and did not. I kept still and small, for Insur ti Fotor, with whom I had fought the Shanks, would recognize me wearing my old Dray Prescot face. He wore a trim naval officer's uniform, with a little gold lace, just to let folk know he was the captain. For since my Delia had had him promoted to ord-Hikdar, he had climbed past the ninth and tenth grades of Hikdar, and was now a ley-Jiktar, into the fourth grade of Jiktar. He ran a taut ship; a single glance showed, unmistakably, all the marks of a vessel and crew on the top line, thrumming with energy and spirit. I counted Insur ti Fotor as a friend, and so I breathed again. *Tuscurs Maiden* would not be attacked and sunk by Vallian renders.

Trade was reopening between the two islands, and Insur must be here with his fine ship as protection for Vallians against pirates of any nation. That was why he sailed down on us, to reassure himself that we were honest merchants.

That could be left to Pompino and Linson. I could make myself scarce. The relief was intense. The thought of having to fight Vallians had been unpleasant for a variety of reasons. I decided to stay in my perch aloft as the formalities were observed.

At Captain Insur ti Fotor's side a fellow lifted a speaking trumpet to his lips. He was a Womox, and his own horns were nearly as large as the horn used to fashion the trumpet. He bellowed, his words rolling out flat and booming, magnified across the water.

"You are a prisoner of war! Heave to!"

Wersting Rogahan's forrard varter let fly and a rock hummed fearsomely across our forecastle.

"Heave to or I'll sink you!"

Four

The instructive history of a zan-talen

A second rock hurtled dangerously low over our deck. Wersting Rogahan was a remarkable shot with a varter, and could split the Chunkrah's Eye at tremendous distances. A horrific thought occurred to me in the chaos of the moment—how would a shoot-out between Wersting and our two varterists, Wilma the Shot and Alwim the Eye, turn out? Impossible! I could not let that happen!

Captain Linson bellowed furiously.

"Prisoner of war? Prisoner of war! The Vallian is mad!"

People scurried about the decks, confusion held them all, and the sudden powerful smell of the sea reached up to me in the cross-trees, blowing all the aromas of the ship away.

"You said we could not outsail him!" screeched Pompino. The breeze blew words about like gulls over a cliff. Wilma and Alwim looked aft, ready for the signal to loose.

The Womox bellowed again.

"Heave to! Strike your colors!"

"Never!" raged Pompino. He had drawn his sword and he waved it—somewhat foolishly—about his head.

Over on the Vallian's forecastle, low enough in the sleek galleon build, Wersting's crew was hard at it rewinding the gros-varter. The next rock would not skim harmlessly above our heads. The next shot would crunch sickeningly in, to gout a fountain of splinters into bodies, to smash and rend, perhaps to bring down a mast.

It seemed to me in the midst of this madness there remained but the one thing left to do.

In that old foretop-hailing voice that had cut through more than one gale in Biscay I yelled down to Pompino.

"Heave to, Pompino! Buy some time!"

"You wouldn't surrender, Jak!"

"No. But we must find the explanation—"

"We can pulp that damned varterist on their forecastle!" shrilled Wilma the Shot.

"Belay that, Wilma!" If Linson refused to obey the order to heave to, if Pompino's proud Khibil blood got the better of him, we'd all be pulped. "Just heave to!"

Fiery whiskers flaring, Pompino glared up. He stuck his hands on his hips. His chin jutted.

"You're up to some deviltry, Jak!" he howled.

"Aye. Fighting won't save our necks now."

The two vessels eased close alongside running sweetly, and the galleon shortened sail to reduce her way and so pace the argenter. She creamed along, handled superbly, and the snouts of her varters and the arms of her catapults bore upon us. Her flags were of Vallia—the new Vallian Union of the yellow cross and saltire upon the red field—and the crimson and pale blue of Ovvend. The symbol of the kovnate of Ovvend down on the south-west coast of Vallia is a galleon. That is fitting.

For what seemed to me a damned long time the ships sailed together and the canvas all about me drew strongly. With a rat-tat of the drum and a shrill of calls accompanied by the slap of bare feet upon planking, thankfully, *Tuscurs Maiden* responded and lost way, her canvas fluttering as she first backed her main tops'l and then gathered her canvas in. No doubt Linson had performed the evolution in this manner as a sign to the hostile ship's captain that he did so under pressure.

Whatever the reason, the argenter lost way and soon we rolled sluggishly as the galleon, matching us, paced alongside.

Men clustered at the falls of a longboat over on the galleon's spar deck. A boarding party would come fully armed and ready for trouble. Now, it was all down to me...

The water looked a long way down.

That was the quickest route.

Once, I had dived into the Eye of the World, the inner sea of Turismond. That had been a longer dive, far longer; I took a breath, readied, and dived. The water came up like a brick wall.

Deeply under, with the water thick about me, turning palms upward and so planing around and rising, rising... The blueness turning from indigo through the lightening colors until the silver sky above my head broke into a bursting dazzlement. My head popped up. I felt fine, strangely enough. Instantly, suspecting the worst, I drew a breath and dived again, twisting as I went down.

I'd been right.

A vicious scaled form flicked for me, tail thrashing. Jaws opened and rows of needle-teeth gaped.

The old sailor knife, well-greased, slid from the sheath over my right hip.

If this Opaz-forsaken Styrorynth thought he was going to gulp me for his lunch he would have to be persuaded of the error of his belief. He was infernally quick and lethal in his own element. Accounted a superb swimmer and diver though I may be, I'd only have the one chance against him.

He swooshed in, mouth wide, needle-teeth ready to clench upon this tasty tidbit. Sliding down and under him, foaming in his pressure wave, I managed to avoid that rat-trap mouth. The knife scored along his underside and the water fouled. Without waiting to hang around I kicked hard—not for the surface but in a direct line for the dark shimmering hardness ahead that was the galleon's keel.

The Styrorynth rolled away aft and no doubt those little fishes upon whom he preyed would swarm up to feast. Swimming strongly, feet churning, I went clean under the galleon's keel. Before I surfaced I checked—as far as was possible—to see no other predators of the deep waited to seize me in their jaws.

For the distance I could see underwater with that shimmering silver sky dancing above my head there appeared to be no further danger. No danger, at least, from that direction. When I broke the surface and looked up not a single face peered over the bulwarks upon me. The galleon rolled gently. Well, they had no doubt seen a man fall from the argenter and vanish into the sea. They knew what manner of beasties lurked below the surface. They might cast a cursory look down; they would hardly expect to see the self-same man surface on the other side of their ship.

I hollered.

Three times I sucked a deep breath and dived, knife in fist, warily watching, and three times, seeing nothing, I surfaced and shouted.

On the last time a shock of hair showed over the bulwark above me and a thick voice said: "Whey-ey! Where'd you come from, dom?"

"Throw down a rope and I'll tell you."

"Oh, a rope—oh, aye."

Moments later a coil hit the water by my head and I seized the end and was hauled up over the side, streaming water. I had the sense to stuff the old sailor knife away. It was clean enough from the sea water.

On deck a shake of the head and a few blinks, snorts and shakes set me up to face the perils ahead.

The owner of the shock of hair was Brokelsh, and his nose was a mere flat sponge. He goggled at me.

Over on the other side men clustered, staring at *Tuscurs Maiden*, who rolled listlessly beyond. I said: "Thank you for the rope, dom. I'll do the same for you one day," and headed straight for the quarterdeck ladder.

The Brokelsh shouted after me: "I'll remember that, dom. Make sure you do, too. My name is Bango Barragon, from Ovvend, so remember it when the time comes."

I did not laugh although, by Krun, his shock of hair and his squashed nose and his manner were enough to make a fellow split his sides. I put a hand on the rail of the ladder and a boarding pike came down thwack! I jumped. I looked up and my face must have shone a very nasty glow.

"You nearly had my hand off then, dom!"

"Aye," quoth the fellow at the head of the ladder, clad in leathers, brass-studded, and with the crimson and light-blue banded sleeves of Ovvend. "And if you try to come up here without an invite I'll have your head off, by Vox!'"

A few sailors and a couple of Pachak marines came over to stare at me, dripping water on their deck. They held weapons; they were in no wise scared of me, of course; just curious and cautious.

"Tell Captain Insur ti Fotor I wish to speak—"

"*Tell* the Capt'n, is it, now! A civil tongue in your head might keep that object upon your shoulders."

A young lad with a flushed face looked over the quarterdeck rail. I did not know him. He wore a helmet of silvered iron flaunting the feathers of Ovvend. He would be a noble youngster training up in the galleons so that one day he, too, might command one of the sleek sea greyhounds. He could be a fop, a ninny, an autocrat of sadistic humor; he could be a stout-hearted lad ready to learn his trade. I stared back at him, and then yelled: "Captain Insur ti Fotor! If you value your hide, lad, jump! Fetch him!" And, then, I used the word to make 'em leap about. "Bratch!"

He flushed even further, tightened up, opened his mouth—saw my face—and bratched.

The guard at the head of the ladder tried to hit me over the head with his pike. You couldn't blame him, really. I dodged, took the pike away, so that he fell down the ladder on his nose. A Pachak lifted his upper left arm; his comrade stuck out his lower left arm. In another moment they'd all leap on me, and I had no wish at all to fight them, all at once or one at a time.

"Insur!" I bellowed at the top of my voice.

Now Insur ti Fotor's family name—it was Varathon—had been scarcely used by us. He'd always been known as Insur ti Fotor, for Fotor was a tidy little township of Ovvend and Insur Varathon came from one of the chief families there. So, all I could do was bellow out: "Insur!"

Give him his due. He did not hang about. His face appeared over the rail, beside and higher than that of the middy's. He saw. At once he shouted: "Send that man up here. Handle him gently."

The guard sat up rubbing his nose, which did not bleed much.

"Your pardon, dom," I said. "It was your nose or my head."

He sneezed red.

"We'll see, dom, we'll see."

Up the ladder with the two Pachaks at my back I went. Insur turned away, glaring at the middy.

"Please return to your duties, Hikdar Varathon!"

"Quidang!"

The lad scuttled.

Insur simply shouldered on to his aft cabin, shouting to his first lieutenant: "Do nothing until I tell you!"

"Quidang!"

At the carved companionway entrance, Insur half-turned, still not looking at me. "You may return to your duties, Pachaks. My thanks. I will take charge of this man."

"Quidang!"

The Pachaks trotted off and I followed Insur down into his cabin. He waited with the handle in his fist, and he slammed the door after us. Then, at once, he bowed, and said:

"Majister."

I took his hand.

"My thanks, Insur. That was splendidly done."

"If I say I am amazed—flabbergasted—to find you here..."

"You would match the pleasure I feel in meeting you again."

He motioned to a chair, and so I had to sit down, otherwise he'd remain standing, half-bent, forever. "Well, Insur, tell me all about it."

He sat down and instinctively poured parclear. The sherbet drink fizzed and sparkled in the glass. "I will tell you everything, majister. But—what? I am bereft of words."

"First of all—you did right to keep my identity safe. Second: What is all this nonsense about taking the argenter from Tomboram a prisoner of war?"

He straightened.

"It is hardly nonsense, majister." He wouldn't mince words. "The Opaz-forsaken devils bear heavily upon us. We strive to thwart their designs, but—"

"Press? Designs? What are you talking about? Is not Vallia at peace with Pandahem? All the nations of Pandahem—well, perhaps with the exception of the Bloody Menaham."

"No, majister. Not so."

I gaped. Then I said, harshly, "Tell me."

So he told me.

Down in the southwest of Vallia, the land I had made my home on Kregen and which empire had fetched me to be their emperor, down there in the southwest in the kovnate of Kaldi a pretty little revolution had broken out. I knew about that. My son Drak had taken his army down there to sort them out, for Kov Vodun Alloran had proclaimed himself as king. During my most recent adventurings I had been somewhat out of touch with the latest developments.

Insur said: "Alloran sought help from Pandahem. He got it. Armies were landed and Prince Drak has fought many hard battles—"

He saw my face and stopped speaking abruptly. Drak! Suppose he was killed in one of these petty little battles, for hard battles mean casualties. Insur saw at once.

"The Prince Majister is safe, and leads the army brilliantly."

"Thank Opaz!"

"Aye."

"And so you cruise the sea lanes to prevent the ferrying of more troops to feed this mad King Vodun Alloran?"

"Yes, majister."

"But—Tomboram! They have been friends for many seasons. I would have thought it of Menaham—"

"They were defeated in a great battle, and Alloran desperately sought fresh allies, and found them in Tomboram."

"Well, I suppose it all adds up," I said in a grudging fashion. "Although it stinks worse than the Fish Souk in Helamlad where there is no ice for fifty dwaburs around."

"Where Helamlad might be, majister, I do not know. What I would dearly like to know is where you came from—oh! Unless—"

"From *Tuscurs Maiden's* ship's company, Insur, that's where. And she's not of Tomboram, being of Tuscursmot in South Pandahem. We flew the colors of Bormark just because we imagined Vallia and Tomboram, Bormark, allies."

He shook his head; but he was no man's fool.

"Your designs are none of my business, majister. You know I will do all in my power to aid you."

"I know, Insur, and I thank you. So that means you can't take the argenter prisoner."

"Quite."

"I spotted Wersting Rogahan at the forrard varters."

"He will know you, for sure. And Ortyg Fondal and Nath Cwophorlin have made your acquaintance in the past. Once made—"

"I know, I know," I grumped. "They say I've a face like a leem at times."

A tiny smile licked around his lips, and his face, all bronzed and sea-beaten, creaked alarmingly. He was no salt-laden old sea-dog but a fiery and consummately professional naval officer. Men had given their lives to save his. I looked hard at him. "And," I said, "that young Hikdar Varathon...?"

"My son, majister."

"Congratulations. He looks likely."

"A sight too likely at times. But—the argenter!"

"Aye, well. I am on passage for Port Marsilus. I can tell you that I and my comrades over in *Tuscurs Maiden* have a mission to burn temples of an evil cult. Pray that cult never sets foot in Vallia. It has tried and we have rooted it out. This affects all the peoples of Paz."

He spread his hands. "I and all my people here in *Ovvend Opandar* are at your disposal, majister."

I nodded. "It is a temptation. You have a first-class command, and if the lads are anything like Wersting Rogahan, they are a fearsome bunch. But—I think not, Insur. Your duties lie elsewhere."

He looked disappointed, for he, like many a man and woman of Kregen, well knew that if they followed me they'd get into scrapes and adventures enough to last two lifetimes. I managed a farcical kind of smile.

"The Shanks, Insur, the everlasting damned Shanks. There will be fighting enough and to spare when they arrive."

His eyebrows went up.

"Oh, yes, my friend. They are on the way to invade our lands. We have some tidying up to do first before they get here."

"Do you know where and when they expect to make landfall?"

"I wish I did. I know only that a vast fleet is on the way."

A knock rapped discreetly on the paneled door. Insur did not look annoyed, as a lesser man might well have done.

"Yes?"

"A Khibil from the Pandahem argenter demands to see you, captain. Demands, no less."

The voice beyond the door betrayed amusement.

I sighed.

"Time I was gone, Insur. That'll be a vastly intemperate Khibil whose acquaintance I have the honor to claim. Perhaps if you just tell him that

Vallia and Tomboram are allies, ask him to convey your respects to Kov Pando Marsilus na Bormark, and then get rid of him, the quicker we can all get on with our jobs."

"If he's been long in your company, majister, he is likely to demand damages, recompense, an apology."

"I'm sure you can accommodate him."

Insur did not smile; but his nod was of the thoughtful variety, betokening a careful estimation of what he could get away with in dealing with an intemperate Khibil who was the friend of the emperor.

Insur opened the door. There was much we had not spoken of; but Pompino had effectively put an end to deliberations. I bid Insur remberee, and slipped quickly up on deck.

The two vessels rode close, their yards almost interlocking. I cocked my head up. Like a monkey up the ratlines I went and so out along a yard and leaped for *Tuscurs Maiden's* main yard and so down to her deck.

Cap'n Murkizon regarded me as one might regard a ghost.

"Jak! We thought you done for, for sure! You are not broken from the ib?"

"No, Cap'n Murkizon. I am no ghost."

"By the hairy black warts of the Divine Lady of Belschutz! Right heartily glad to see you!" He seized my hand and pumped away as though extinguishing a conflagration. Others came up. Pompino was not among them.

Larghos the Flatch said: "We saw the finny back of a disgusting Styrorynth. Then we saw blood. And yet—you live!"

"The Vallians hauled me out."

Captain Linson, master of *Tuscurs Maiden* and mindful of responsibilities, congratulated me on a miraculous escape, and then added: "Here comes Horter Pompino. He looks pleased."

Pompino leaped onto the deck, hitching his sword out of the way. He brushed up his whiskers in a gesture that told us—or, at least me—that he was feeling very pleased with himself.

"It was all a mistake," he said, strutting up. "The moment I spoke to their captain he understood. We are to proceed at once."

"What, Pompino," I could not forbear from prodding. "And did he offer an apology?"

"I did not ask for one, Jak. Besides, he had his damned varters swung in my direction. Ugly, those artillery pieces of Vallia. Damned ugly."

I did not laugh.

Then he extended his hand, palm uppermost. A single golden coin glittered. It was a zan-talen, worth ten Vallian talen pieces.

"The captain, an unhanged rascal called Insur ti Fotor, requested me to treat the crew to a wet. Of course, he knew better than to attempt to pacify me in that way."

"Naturally."

Inwardly I was laughing—chuckling, really—over Insur's audacity. The likeness on the coin was of a remarkably ugly fellow, all chin and beard and beaked nose. No one, seeing that indifferent portrait, was going to recognize its subject as me, plain Jak. This had been in my mind when old Larghos Valdwin had carved the original, and I'd told him to make me look as ferocious and unlike myself as possible. He'd made the expected sly remark on that. The other side of the coin, which I regarded as the more important, showed the glory of Delia, beautifully fashioned and, yet, again, a portrait from which it would be difficult to recognize her.

Self-advertisement for your ordinary everyday emperor and empress is no doubt a worthwhile objective. For folk like Delia and myself, adventuring off around Kregen as we did, a trifle of anonymity paid handsome dividends.

Linson gave his orders and Chandarlie the Gut, the Ship-Deldar, bellowed them into action.

Pompino sniffed.

"You were given up for lost, Jak."

I did not reply. The breeze had backed a few more points and now we could sheet home our full spread of canvas. *Tuscurs Maiden* bowled along merrily. An altogether different air now pervaded the ship's company. It was as though we had come through a dire experience far worse than that through which we had really gone. Such is human nature. Men sang about their tasks. The coast lay ahead, and Port Marsilus, and taverns and dopa dens, no doubt, and a golden zan-talen nestled securely in the Owner's strongbox, to find its way down the thirsty throats of the crew.

"I am glad you were not chomped by that Styrorynth. Ugly customers, with jaws like the black gullet of Armipand himself, Pandrite rot him. No doubt he snapped up some other victim, for there was blood."

"No doubt."

"And, Jak, just think. If you'd been killed, would the Everoinye have held me accountable? The thought has often plagued me."

At once I felt contrition.

"Look, Pompino, as I have told you, I do not think the Star Lords hold me in very high esteem. I curse at them and attempt to evade what they order when it conflicts with what I desire. But I serve them more willingly now than I once did. All the same—if you were killed, I think that perhaps they would frown most unkindly upon me."

"Well," he said, brisking up and giving a twirl to his moustaches. "As we are not about to allow ourselves to be sent off to the Ice Floes of Sicce, let us push these doleful thoughts aside. I'm for a wet."

"I am with you. Port Marsilus is not far off, now. There we can start our deviltry. If the Leem Lovers were other than they are, it might be in my mind to feel sorry for them."

"You may begin being maudlin after they are all safely howling in Cottmer's Caverns!"

Five

Aye

"Look!" said Pompino as we sailed in for Port Marsilus. He did not point as one might expect a man to point as he indicated the object of his interest. "D'you see him?"

"Aye. I see him."

As *Tuscurs Maiden* ran on with the bluffly blown spume from her round bows breaking and her canvas drawing as full-bellied as a noble after a feast, and the coast of Tomboram neared with the pinnacles of Port Marsilus already in sight, I stared up.

Up there circled a giant raptor, a golden-and-scarlet-feathered bird with sharp black talons extended. He was the Gdoinye, the spy and messenger of the Star Lords.

"They keep watch upon us, Jak." Pompino spoke in a low tone, for we leaned on the quarterdeck bulwarks and Captain Linson and his officers and men on watch stood close.

"You can see the Gdoinye, and I can see him. But, of late, I remark that no one else sees him—"

"Of course not! Why, only a kregoinye, one who has been selected by the Everoinye, can ever see—"

"Yes. But I have known a few people in the past who have seen him."

"I find that hard to believe."

The spoken Kregish tongue is modulated by many tonal variations, so that Pompino's simple words, by being given different inflections, could mean that he was calling me a liar, to an amazed agreement with my statement. This latter meaning he now intended.

"True, Pompino. I believe a certain innocence of mind has an influence, for a lad I know saw the bird, and a caravan master from Xuntal, a true child of the Great Plains. Also, this Kov Pando Marsilus, when he was a youngster, saw the Gdoinye."

"So that is behind your remark. But he is no longer a coy, young and fresh and green and innocent."

"Ha," I said in a kind of grunt. "If ever he was, poor lad."

Pompino let that by.

I did not say that the lad I knew who had seen the scarlet and gold raptor was my eldest son Drak. Pompino was under the impression that I was fancy free and unencumbered by a family. Just why I'd allowed that impression to remain might seem petty and obscure; it saved a quantity of explanations.

The bird circled, a menacing silhouette as he passed beneath the Suns of Scorpio, a glittery glory as the streaming radiance touched his feathers.

"He can only report that we are on our way to carry out our duties," said Pompino.

"Aye," I said in an ugly voice. "And we are on our own time in this."

"True. But I think the Everoinye are now completely involved with us, and we can—"

"We can expect no help from them!"

Pompino let his lips compress. That was true, at least for me, and despite Pompino's attachment to the Star Lords, I suspected for him, also.

There was no sign of the white dove sent by the Savanti. Even Pompino couldn't have seen that bird.

It occurred to me to wonder if he'd ever seen or heard of Zena Iztar, who as a superhuman woman exercised mysterious powers. She had assisted me in the past, and although I might suspect she stood over in opposition to both Star Lords and Savanti, I was not certain of that. She it was who had helped us when the Brotherhood of the Kroveres of Iztar fought their early sacrificial battles. Now the Kroveres with Seg Segutorio as their Grand Archbold were dedicated to righting wrongs, uprooting slavery and injustice, and of countering the Shanks. Naive ends for an Order, you may think—all except the last—but of such naiveté are new and fairer worlds formed.

Continuing his train of thought, Pompino went on: "Here in Bormark we will have to go about the business in a rather different fashion from Memis and Pomdermam."

"Oh?"

"Aye! Look you—I burned a temple to Lem here. No doubt others have sprung up to take its place. But now we have the Lady Tilda with us."

He used the general word for lady—shiume—which has so many gradations of rankings Kregans more often than not omit all these subtle shadings, and say simply "The Shiume" and then the lady's name. This applies from Kovneva to Kotera. I know my Delia has trenchant opinions upon this subject of lick-spittling fawning. Pompino and I, when we did not call Tilda the Beautiful, Tilda of the Many Veils, Kovneva, we addressed her as Shiume, my lady.

I agreed. Then, with a note of caution, I said: "We are duty bound to see her safely to her palace. This may lay us open to observation. It is certain sure that Murgon Marsilus will have spies, no less than the Leem Lovers."

"Then we proceed under cover."

Any Kregan knows the nightly tally of Moons. Tonight we were due the Twins, the two second moons eternally orbiting each other, and the largest moon, the Maiden with the Many Smiles. The fourth moon, She of the Veils, would appear wanly toward dawn. As for the three smaller moons, they hurtle past in their headlong courses, casting little enough light, in so much of a hurry Kregans have a whole repertoire of jokes about them and their resemblance to the energetic hyperthyroid types of people to be found everywhere.

We agreed the best time would be a couple of glasses before the hour of dim, just before the Maiden with the Many Smiles put in her appearance.

All details of entering the harbor and of finding a berth could be left to the captain. We roused out the four hefty fellows selected to carry Tilda's sedan chair, the luxurious palankeen in which, besides cushions and pillows and fans and toiletries and other essential requirements she would have a considerable quantity of interesting bottles stashed away. Everyone knew that the Lady Tilda drank, and was usually a fraction on the other side of lustiness and yet was never ever drunk—or, at least, never intoxicated to make it noticeable or herself a nuisance. The chair swung up onto the deck and settled on its clawed feet. The curtains were drawn.

"It might," observed Rondas the Bold, his red feathers whiffling in the breeze, "have been easier to have hauled the gherimcal up with the lady seated inside."

One or two of the hands laughed.

As a serious suggestion it was perfectly sensible. To have dropped the gherimcal back down and put Tilda inside and then have hauled the pair up would smack of the undignified now the damned chair was actually on deck. Tilda, despite the drink and her grossness, was, after all, a kovneva and a lady.

Pompino said, "I, for one, am having nothing to do with getting the lady on deck."

Chandarlie the Gut stepped forward. "Leave it to me, horters." His stomach swelled in its magnificent bow shape; he and Tilda would make a likely pair.

"And handsomely, mind," I said.

It is worth mentioning that of the four men selected to act as calsters and carry the chair, two were apims, Homo sapiens like me, one was a Brokelsh and the other a Brukaj. It has often been said that apims make the best sailors on Kregen, and Fristles among the worst. Brokelsh are found in surprising numbers following the nautical profession. A captain usually has a crew consisting of a mixed bunch of races under command and it is up to him to knock them all into shape.

Tuscurs Maiden negotiated the buoyed channel and we tied up alongside a stone quay with long black-painted sheds across the cobbles. The port officials descended like warvols and these were left strictly to the master and to the Relt stylor, Rasnoli. They knew how to handle these fellows.

The declining suns threw long radiances of jade and ruby across the houses and water, casting umber shadows against the terraces and towers, limning in light the opposite cornices. Gulls winged looking for last minute morsels for supper. The air held an evening tang.

The argenter's new first lieutenant, a shambly man with a pebbly skin, one Boris Pordon, went about his tasks with a worried expression. I could fully sympathize with the tribulations of the Ship Hikdar, by Vox. And, as we went down for a final meal, I suddenly realized that I might be leaving the sea for some time. What we faced with such casual ease was likely to be exceedingly fraught and filled with the clangor of swords. This was very much a case of frying pan and fire.

Pompino must have shared much of this foreboding. As we sat to Limki the Lame's latest creation he chewed thoughtfully.

"We had best take a goodly supply of weapons with us."

"Aye."

"And Captain Linson will spare us enough men."

"Aye."

Pompino eyed me. He took a forkful of Limki's roast quindil and paused, opened his mouth to speak, and then stuffed the quindil in instead. I am not overfond of poultry, and the quindil, a kind of turkey, however beautifully roasted and stuffed, scarcely merited comparison with the vosk chops Limki had prepared for me.

When he had swallowed, Pompino said: "Superb! Limki lost no time in buying fresh foodstuffs—yet you stick with those giant chops—and we will need to take provisions with us, also, I think."

"Aye."

He slammed his knife down hard.

"You are infuriating, Jak! Is that all you can say—aye!"

"Anything else would appear superfluous."

"We are likely to have Murgon Marsilus, King Nemo, the Pandrite-forsaken imps of Lem, and who knows who else, all buzzing about our ears and trying to part us from our heads—yet all you can do is chomp down Vosk chops and say Aye."

"I forbore to point out the facts you have just related with such fervor out of respect for the delicacy of your stomach during a meal." He might have blown up then; but I went on in what I hoped was an imperturbable tone: "However, if you wish me to add from all we have unearthed and what we can surmise, my own observations, why, then, I will willingly do so."

Then he had me. He said: "Aye."

I almost laughed around a mouthful of vosk chop.

"Well, then: Firstly—and there may not be a secondly—the Kovneva Tilda wishes to return to her palace here in Port Marsilus for a number of reasons. She wishes to consult with this mysterious Mindi the Mad, whoever she may be. She wishes to see the twins Pynsi and Poldo Mytham. Also she feels safer in her own palace." I took up a glass of wine, a full-bodied red—a Jeu O'fremont, I recall—and watched Pompino. He sat munching his bird and watching me. I went on: "The Leem Lovers have committed themselves too deeply in the attempt to kill her and must continue—"

"Ha!" said Pompino. "We've blattered 'em once—let 'em try again, Pandrite rot 'em!"

"Quite. As I was saying. She must have friends in her own capital city, and in her palace... Surely?"

"One would judge so, yes."

"Once we can place her safely in their hands we can breathe more freely. And we can get on with burning temples."

"Aye."

"It also strikes me that young Pando got in over his head. He joined up with the Leem Lovers in order to strike at his cousin Murgon. I think that association with Lem the Silver Leem was too strong for his blood. People get to know about these things—people who count, in responsible positions, who run things. The old values wither. The whole of this kingdom of Tomboram is in a mess, and the kovnate of Bormark is in the worst mess. And Pando is at his wits' end."

"With that reading of the matter I concur."

So, inevitably, I said: "Aye."

We drank a little in silence for a space.

Then Pompino said: "This young lady, the Vadni Dafni Harlstam, whose lands adjoin those of Pando. Murgon designs to marry her to aggrandize himself. So does Pando. One is allowed to wonder, I think, if she, too, is an adherent of Lem."

"Ah," I said, wisely.

"What is sure is that she is not the cause of the quarrel between them. That has festered since their respective births. She is the catalyst that has precipitated the latest outburst. And she is likely to be the last."

"That is a bleak enough prophecy. But, if you look on the bright side, it might be a good one."

He reached for more wine, his whiskers very red under the lamps.

"You mean, Jak, that after we have finished with them all, all their problems will be settled? Aye!"

You had to hand it to Pompino the Iarvin. Confidence was his middle name in these matters. Once he stepped ashore he became a different man.

Nath the Apron came in with the dessert. Limki had prepared looshas pudding, a soldiers' favorite, and both Pompino and I tucked in. There was a cream and fruit trifle to follow that, and Nath the Apron, a quiet and unobtrusive cabin steward, brought in the bowls of fruit and the palines. The wine passed, and we sat, thinking of what lay ahead.

Thankfully, on Kregen, no one was foolish enough to light up and smoke. Although, and sometimes I admit this with a quiver of guilt, a fine after-dinner cigar would not have gone amiss...

Presently, Pompino stretched and thumped his glass down.

"Time?"

I stood up. Preparations had all been made. So there was but the one rejoinder to make. I said it.

"Aye."

Six

The Lady Nalfi hides in the Chunkrah's Eye

"Where in the name of Suzi the Bowgirl have you been, Nalfi?" Larghos the Flatch sounded both distraught and relieved.

The Lady Nalfi laughed lightly.

"Why, you silly man, I went ashore to buy certain things a girl must have, with the money you gave me. And I became lost—"

"Think what could have happened to you! Why didn't you ask me—?"

"You were all so busy. Anyway, it is of no moment."

We were crowding down onto the jetty, the four calsters were manipulating Tilda's chair down, we were trying to keep quiet and stop our weapons from clinking. Murkizon was breathing like a whale.

"Once Larghos rescued you, my lady, you placed yourself under his protection. I have done so, and joy in it."

"As you stand by me, Cap'n," burst out Larghos. He looked wild. He'd had a fright.

The Twins shed light enough, too much for nefarious purposes I fancied, with an uncomfortable hitch to my shoulders. Somehow or other, and even allowing for my act with Pompino, the whole business of this night looked awry to me, not quite handled in a logical and successful fashion. But Pompino was trying to shout in a whisper, and his Chulik, Nath Kemchug, dropped a spear, which clattered, and Rondas the Bold, still not abandoning his mail, let it clash slightly as he negotiated the gangplank. Pompino looked to the Moons and stars above, and clutched at my arm.

"A pack of famblys, the lot of them, by Horato the Potent, famblys all."

I did not reply but looked about into the moon-shot darkness of the jetty. The black sheds glistened with runnels of moonshine. The cobbles swam in glisten. I could see no shadows moving out there.

Tilda's chair had been draped with canvas to make it appear less grand, and the fake chair done up out of packing crate wood and painted canvas had been sent off earlier with most of the escort. That should have drawn off any unwelcome attentions; now we simply ran straight for the palace.

That, as I say, was the plan...

We were to follow in a slightly different path from the decoy party. The walls and towers of the palace provided a clear target, and I was perfectly prepared to wake Tilda up and shake information out of her if we could not find an easy road through.

As the Owner, Pompino had selected the composition of the parties, and he had undeniably put more weight into the genuine escort. The Ship Hikdar, Boris Pordon, commanded the fake escort with more men in numbers but not, Pompino judged, in fighting ability.

Also, the fake escort with its wood and canvas dummy chair carried torches to light the way. We, with Tilda in the real gherimcal in our midst, hurried along with only the light of the Twins to guide us. And, as I have indicated, that light was of a sufficiency enough.

Past shuttered houses we sped, the gherimcal swaying as the bearers moved in rhythmic steps. Nath Kemchug had his spear firmly grasped, and Rondas the Bold's mail—as befitted a proud Rapa paktun—no longer chittered, link against link. As was his right and duty, Pompino led. Because of that old itchy feeling betwixt my shoulder blades—usually an infallible sign, not always, of approaching danger and action—I prowled along at the tail end. My head kept on trying to twist itself off my shoulders as I turned this way and that watching our backtrack. Every window could conceal a marksman, every shadow a shrieking swordsman, every archway a charging axeman...

The Brown and Silvers hit us from up front.

They were waiting for us.

They simply rushed out into the mouth of an avenue leading to the palace, fronting a square, and charged.

At the first yell, the first clatter of iron-shod sandals on stone, I was raging up, quivering—and remaining in the rear. Pompino and the others would have to handle the frontal attack. I still suspected a treacherous stab in the back.

"Hit 'em, knock 'em down, tromple all over 'em!" bellowed a fruity voice.

The wicked tinker-hammer of steel against steel racketed up, echoing against the walls.

Anybody who tried to break a way through that powerful human hedge of steel was in for trouble. In the time I'd known them, the comrades I'd made in *Tuscurs Maiden* had proved themselves. Now, once again, they were fighting and earning their hire. I closed up to the chair, setting my back against the curtains, and staring forward and aft. Mainly, I looked to the rear. This ambush was just right for the attack from the rear that would smash into the unprotected backs of the fighters defending in front. Grasping my thraxter, I watched.

The two apims, Nath the Clis and Indur the Rope, and the Brokelsh, Ridzi the Rangora, and the Brukaj, Bendil Fribtix, remained grasping the handles of the chair. They were ready to run like stink to smash a way through surrounded by the fighting men. They had a tough task, and one not to my liking, I can tell you, by Krun!

Something kicked my ankle.

I looked down, the thraxter snouting.

A shapely foot and ankle with a silver bangle kicked and then withdrew. I bent and lifted a flap of canvas, and the sword in my fist nuzzled forward.

"Oh!" gasped Nalfi, twisting around, her pallid face staring up in shock.

"It's all right, my lady. But I do not think you are particularly wise. It is not safe under there if—"

The dagger in her fist glimmered as she crawled out.

"Larghos told me to seek shelter and this seemed the best place. I am frightened—"

We had fixed up boards and bronze in the gherimcal against arrows. Nalfi knew this. All the same, the chair was the target and she had chosen to shelter in the chunkrah's eye, as it were.

The fight up ahead swayed back and forth as we spoke in snatched whispers. Dark shadows moved in convulsive gyrations, and men screamed and died. The noise would bring other men and women, soon, that was sure.

Nath the Clis holding the front near side handle looked back and called: "Larghos was right, Jak. But the lady is still in danger here."

Even if Nalfi could have somehow squeezed into the chair with Tilda and all her belongings, the additional weight, together with the bronze and wood, would slow us too much.

"Crouch down small, Nalfi. Here." I handed her across the shield I'd taken from Nath Kemchug's armory aboard ship. "Hold this over you. We'll see off this rabble up ahead. It won't be long."

"I do hope so!"

Larghos the Flatch ran back to the gherimcal, his bow over his shoulder and his thraxter stained dark.

"You are safe, Nalfi?"

"Yes, yes—"

"They're giving way up there. We can move on now—"

And at that moment the back stab I had anticipated and thought to be a mere overwrought fever of my brain erupted in a yelling mob of Brown and Silvers, hurtling down upon us.

Instantly we were embroiled in a vicious fight to stay alive and to protect Tilda. The four bearers had to thwunk the gherimcal down, draw their weapons and hurl themselves into the fray. We struggled in a mass of contorting bodies across the cobbles, smashing back at the attack, striking and defending, roaring in a mind-wrenching phantasmagoria of action under the light of the Moons.

Having given the shield to Nalfi, I was in no mood to foin with this mob of would-be assassins. The left-hand dagger whipped free of its scabbard. With the stout cut and thrust thraxter in my right fist and the main gauche in my left I felt that the combination would prove an interesting variation. The things one dwells on in the fractions of a heartbeat!

The swirl of action revolved away to my left as, with Larghos at my side, we swathed a way through on the right. The Brown and Silvers wore their colored favors openly. Their faces were not masked as assassins' faces are commonly concealed. We hit them hard, and they hit us hard.

Ridzi the Rangora catapulted backwards. A thick spear transfixed his belly. Larghos, with a cunning sideways belt of his sword, dispatched the fellow, all eyes and teeth, who had thrust his spear through Ridzi.

The Brokelsh sank down. For a tiny moment his voice reached me through the hubbub.

"By Bridzilkelsh the Resplendent! I am done for!"

Blackness gushed from his mouth.

"Hold up, dom," I said. "We'll carry you—"

But the Brokelsh, Ridzi the Rangora, keeled over onto his side, the spear haft drawing up his knees in a rictus of agony. In the next heartbeat he was dead.

In a heavy rush of bodies more of our fellows joined in from the fight up front. Quendur the Ripper cut down his man, swirled at another, called across in a high, bright voice: "They run in front, Jak! Now we have them here!"

I did not reply, catching a heavy blow in a slanting glide on the dagger and thrusting with the thraxter. Recovering, I ducked and belted a blow sideways to take the knees from a Rapa who gobbled and, before he could fall over, had his beak removed by Murkizon's enormous axe.

"Tromple all over 'em!"

"Hai!" roared Pompino, catching a Brown and Silver trying to get at the gherimcal. The man sank down in a puddle. My comrade glared about. Quendur was in the act of swiping at a Fristle who now clearly wished to backpedal. The fight was all but over. The remaining Brown and Silvers drew off.

"Hurry!" I said in that penetrating whisper that cuts like splintered glass. "They'll be shafting us now."

Quendur saw where Ridzi lay, doubled up over the spear, the black stain on the cobbles. He stepped forward, took up the handle of the gherimcal, the other three calsters took their handles. Tilda gave no sign of life. The chair lifted. In a bunch, weapons naked and stained, we ran for the palace.

Unwilling to leave a comrade, I hoisted up Ridzi, breaking the disgusting spear off. I hurled the broken haft into the radiance of the Moons, cursing stupid waste. With the hairy bloody body of the Brokelsh over my shoulder I ran after the others.

The avenue leading from that kyro where we had been ambushed led on for a couple of hundred paces and then opened out into the plaza fronting the palace. The building of itself appeared to be no great size under the moons. Some of its towers lofted to a goodly height, and one dome gleamed silky-sheened in the radiance.

There was no moat or drawbridge. Instead a double gate flanked by watchtowers protected the entrance. I did not give that fortification a long life against an expert siege-master.

Two apim guards in little sentry boxes, their spears slanted, watched us running up.

As we approached in a rushing wheeze of panting breaths and staccato cracks of studded sandals, the gates creaked open. They creaked. Through the noise of our progress the wood and iron creaked loudly and distinctly.

We did not stop but rushed straight through into a walled courtyard where torches flared.

The gates creaked and closed at our backs.

"Safe," said Pompino. He looked wrought up. "We've done it!"

"Aye," I said, as they put the gherimcal down. "And here is some of the cost." Over my shoulder, Ridzi lolled.

There was no decent answer Pompino could find to that.

Tuscurs Maiden's Ship Hikdar, Boris Pordon, appeared. He looked worried sick.

"Thank Pandrite you are safe, horter!" He spoke to Pompino directly. "We were about to run out to your assistance—"

Pompino brushed that aside. "The whole affair was over before you could have reached us. It was a hindrance only."

The decoy party and the fake chair had made a simple, safe journey here, unmolested. The canvas and wood construction stood to one side and I looked at it critically. Well... Seen like this it might have fooled the Leem Lovers. It had not done so, and that luck played against us.

The torches streamed a ruddy light upon the folk clustered in the court-yard. Their faces wore apprehensive looks, they fidgeted and fingered their weapons. They hardly looked the people to defend a palace against deter-mined onslaughts.

In the light an Ift stepped forward, approaching the carrying chair.

"I bid you welcome, horters, horteras," he said. "Is the Kovneva safe?" He bent to the curtains.

Pompino bristled up.

"Just who are you, horter?"

The Ift straightened. He was under man height, although some Ifts can grow to overtop a full-grown apim, so it is said. He was clad in clothes of varying shades and tones of green, and here in a palace he was out of his usual habitat, for Ifts are folk of the forest. They are accounted fine bow-shots. Wayward folk, Ifts, with tall pointed ears reaching almost to the crown of their head, and with slanted, devious eyes. Now this Ift stared challengingly at Pompino.

"Were it not for Hikdar Pordon, I would demand of you the same ques-tion, Horter Pompino. But he mentioned that we were to expect a Khibil."

Here Pordon gave a little jump, so I guessed he'd told this Ift a little more about Pompino than he'd care to have the Owner hear.

"I am waiting," said Pompino in his menacing voice.

The Ift reached a thin brown hand to his sword hilt. Then he nodded. "I am Twayne Gullik, the castellan here. My word rules while the kov and the dowager kovneva are absent."

My foxy Khibil comrade wouldn't be foxed by that.

"As the kovneva is now within her palace, you no longer rule. Make sure the lady Tilda is cared for. Summon her handmaidens. She has had a try-ing journey. She will, no doubt, in her own time, acquaint you with your future duties concerning me and my people."

Twayne Gullik opened his mouth. Even in the radiance of the Twins, slanting into the courtyard, the color in his face darkened ominously. I was not going to step forward. This, now, had become a matter of will-power and of honor between these two. Of course, if they started the nonsense of a ritual fight in the ages-old dueling system of the Hyr Jikordur, I'd have to try to prevent that.

Then Cap'n Murkizon's genial bull-bellow broke into the strained silence.

"By the infested armpit of the Divine Lady of Belschutz! My throat is as dry as Golingar Desert dust! A wet, for the sweet sake of Pandrite!"

That broke the tension. Larghos bustled forward, servants took the poor limp form of Ridzi the Rangora from me, Quendur the Ripper and the others yelped for wine, and so we were able to hustle along. The chair was carried off after Pompino took a look inside. The moment he withdrew,

Twayne Gullik looked, also. As they both appeared satisfied, although saying nothing, I surmised Tilda was safe and asleep.

We all trooped into a side corridor and thence to a hall where we sat at tables and the servants poured wine. We were thirsty, at that; but wine would never solve any serious problem.

"That superior Ift," said Pompino.

"They are a haughty and fractious people," said Quendur.

"Twayne Gullik," I said. "By Chusto! Whoever gave him that name marked him from birth."

"Let him go back to his forests," quoth Murkizon, lifting his goblet. "And take out his spite on the tumps, who, being shorter than he is, if broader, and just as mean, stand no nonsense from the Ifts." A few smiles broke out, for the notorious antipathy between Ifts and tumps has been the basis of many a play and many a buffoonery-filled farce in Kregen's playhouses over the seasons. The tumps are, indeed, a race of diffs short of stature; but they are immensely broad and stoutly built, and the men folk grow beards down past their protuberant waists. They are a mining people, delving deep underground, and there is little they value above red gold. "The point is, my friends," went on Murkizon, we have brought the lady Tilda safely home. So—now what lies in store?"

"A few fires?" I suggested.

Pompino clicked his compression tube. "Always ready..."

They laughed.

It would not be as easy as that.

Mind you, nothing in this life is easy, by Zair, unless it be going astray—or shuffling out of life altogether. The itch between my shoulder blades I'd wanted to scratch when we'd hurried through the nighted streets of Port Marsilus persisted. It did not go away. They called this place the Zhantil Palace, for the kov's predilection for the zhantil. I knew why Pando favored that marvelous wild animal of the untamed ways, the golden mane and the superb air of dignified lethality. Something more within this palace caused that itch between my shoulder blades.

And that was not caused by a mere irritating little Ift called Twayne Gullik.

Seven

Twayne Gullik

Despite being quartered in a corner of the garrison's barracks within the Zhantil Palace, Pompino and I set watches for the night.

The barracks was practically empty, the long rooms echoing to our voices and footfalls. The rows of bunks, each piled with bedding, lay dustily under the dusty beams. Of men at arms to serve the palace there were but twenty-four. Two dozen fighting men to guard the kovneva, and of these some were not fit to be called paktuns.

The cadade, the captain of the guard, turned out to be a Fristle with patches of fur missing from both cheeks. At least, he saw to a proper burial for Ridzi the Rangora.

For this I thanked him, and gave him a donation in thanks.

"Kov Pando took most of the guards with him when he went to Pomdermam," said Framco the Tranzer, pulling his whiskers, a little unsure at this arrival of a bunch of harum-scarum sea dogs. He took his duties as cadade seriously. "He could not know how things were going to turn out."

"And," said Pompino, "how have things turned out?"

We spoke on the steps outside the mess hall, with the archway to the next courtyard and the more splendid buildings of the palace beyond. The night had passed uneventfully and I for one was anxious to speak to Tilda. We had to make a start somewhere within the city, and she ought to know the most likely places.

"Things have not turned out well," said Framco the Tranzer.

Pompino just brushed up his whiskers with a gesture which said, more or less that, oh, yes, he was used to things not turning out well and that, by Horato the Potent, when he was around he soon had the things sorted out, or they'd know what's what.

"The kov's cousin, the Strom Murgon, bears the kov a grudge. He has stirred up the city against him. It is very black." Framco the Tranzer pulled his whiskers unhappily, frowning. "I have a few good men; but the rest are—"

"Little better than masichieri," stuck in Pompino, unarguably.

"Yes."

"But," I said, feeling alarmed. "Surely the citizens would not make an open attack on their kovneva within her own palace in her own capital city? Surely that is not to be believed?"

"You were attacked last night, Horter Jak."

"Yes, but—" And then I stopped. We who knew of Lem the Silver Leem knew the way his followers organized their secrecy and their ways of wielding power. Would the cadade know this? I doubted it, but it was possible.

So, I went on: "They seemed to us a bunch of brigands, drikingers who kill and rob wayfarers and who mistook our mettle."

"That they did, thanks be to Numi-Hyrjiv the Golden Splendor. But I am mindful of my duty to the kovneva. I am from the kov's estates, and no hired mercenary."

"Do you or do you not think the people of Port Marsilus will attempt to storm the palace and harm the kovneva?"

He jumped.

"I cannot tell, horter. There is a cult abroad of which I know little, merely rumors and fearful whispers. I fear that the kov is mired in this evil, and I pray Odifor he is not. But it is certain sure that the Strom Murgon Marsilus will take every opportunity to strike against the kov through his mother the kovneva."

It seemed to me, and I am sure to Pompino, that the cadade, Framco the Tranzer, probably knew a great deal more that he was not telling us. And fear of reprisals from an unknown hand held him. The sound of footsteps took our attention to the castellan, the green-clad Twayne Gullik, marching up with a group of his Iftkin about him. Gullik looked savage, and yet contained, as though biding his time.

Now I have mentioned that the color green is splendid for certain purposes, and I would add to that list regimental colors and facings. At this moment on the steps of the mess hall in Tilda's palace I tried to remember that the green connotations here were of Robin Hood and Sherwood and not of the Grodnims of the Eye of the World. With Twayne Gullik's attitude thrust, as it were, under our noses, the effort required was considerable.

He did not beat about the bush.

"I thank you for your efforts on behalf of the kovneva." He stood straight, one hand on his hip. This morning he wore a bow over his shoulder, a short compound-reflex weapon, and a quiver of arrows across his back. Each arrow was fletched green, glistening in the growing power of the Suns. "Now that you have delivered the kovneva safely home, your task is done. You may leave at once. I shall provide an escort for you to the jetty."

Pompino started to let rip, and I said—sharply!—"Escort, Gullik? In daylight? Why do we need an escort in broad daylight in peaceful Port Marsilus?"

He didn't like the way I'd called him Gullik. But he liked the question even less.

"A mere precaution. You will recall you were attacked last night."

Pompino burst out: "How did they know which way we were coming? And why did they not attack the Ship Hikdar and the chair he was protecting? Someone told them, Gullik. Perhaps you told them, hey?"

Twayne Gullik's sword was out. His pallid face, sharp with those slanted eyebrows and those pointed ears, darkened with passion. A man of temper, this.

"If you were not under my protection, Horter Pompino, you would answer for that. Any fool could see that contraption was not the kovneva's chair."

Truth to tell, the thing did look ridiculous in the suns light. But it had been hurried along through moons lighted streets. The puzzle would remain.

"There is no need to quarrel over this," said the Fristle guard captain, hissing more than usual. His cat face reflected his own puzzlement and uncertainty. "We have enemies enough outside without making more within."

Whatever relationship existed between the castellan and the cadade, these words did have the effect of making Twayne Gullik rein up a trifle, and of Pompino's immediate half-apology.

"I meant no harm, Gullik. We are all on edge."

I notched up one for Pompino. Not like a haughty Khibil to acknowledge anything to an Ift, just down from the trees, all green and dewy. Pompino felt the same unease over this situation as did I. We had a gross half-drunken woman to care for, and her enemies could strike as and when they liked. The responsibility sawed at our nerves.

"Your apology is accepted," said Gullik, and I stepped a little sideways and trod on Pompino's foot.

He glared in hurt surprise.

"The question is," I said, in a voice louder than necessary, "why it is needful for us to leave so soon. I must speak with the kovneva—"

Gullik broke in.

"That is out of the question. The kovneva is—indisposed—and is being cared for by her handmaidens. And as for your leaving, we cannot feed you all comfortably. As it is—"

"As it is," bellowed Pompino, "a mere matter of gold, then we will pay for the kovneva's hospitality!" He lifted up his foot and rubbed it, half-bending down, kneading the soft leather boot. "Pandrite help the poor traveler in this land!"

I said: "It is just after breakfast and I am thirsty, having drunk a mere six cups of tea. I'm for more. Are you with me, Pompino? You have, I recall, a golden zan-talen to spend."

Before Pompino could answer, Twayne Gullik said with a snap: "You may swill your tea, and then you will all immediately leave the palace and return to your ship."

Pompino just said: "Or?"

"Or I shall have to ask the cadade to assist you."

Framco the Tranzer looked decidedly unhappy at this, rolling his eyes at us and fair pulling his whiskers clean out of his furry cat face, it would seem. He, it was clear, wanted no part of any attempt to eject us.

Pompino laughed. "Listen, Twayne Gullik. We are not leaving here until we choose to, until we are ready. Do you understand that?"

"I understand," said the green-clad Ift, "that if that is what you choose you will sorely repent your choice."

With his Iftkin about him he stomped off. Pompino watched him go, laughed, and twirled up his reddish moustaches.

Eight

Concerning the traitoress Ros the Claw

The Zhantil Palace proved to be an odd sort of residence. Stately halls, winding staircases, cubbyholes, corridors lined with door after door leading to a maze of apartments beyond, lavishly ornamented windows, arrow slits, dovecots—oh, yes, Pando's palace boasted them all. And yet, the place seemed odd. There was a quantity of good porphyry from Molynux, carpets of Walfarg weave, ceramics—naturally—of Pandahem ware. And yet, it was scarcely a place in which to live comfortably or happily.

If there had been no doubts about Tilda's safety, I'd have been overjoyed to get out of Pando's Zhantil Palace.

"That pipsqueak Ift," growled Pompino as we went along the north corridor toward the barracks. "If he thinks he can throw me out just like that he is vastly mistaken."

"It did occur to me to wonder why they had not given us rooms in the main part of the palace. There are guest rooms there which, if mean and unwholesome looking, would perhaps be preferable to the barracks."

"Perhaps, and perhaps not."

"Aye, Pompino. You are probably right."

He twitched that new rapier of his up and down in the scabbard.

"We have yet to meet this person Mindi the Mad. And we must speak with the kovneva. Then we burn temples."

"As I pointed out earlier, I devoutly hope we do not burn down too much of Pando's property. Or that of honest folk."

"From what little we've seen, I doubt there are any in the whole of Port Marsilus, by Horato the Potent!"

From which it was perfectly clear my comrade itched to get his fingers around a tinderbox or compression tube, with a sizable pile of kindling to hand.

Despite the estrangement between him and his wife, the Lady Pompina, I judged he was deeply worried over the threat to her from the Leem Lovers. And if his pair of twins, four beautiful children, were harmed, he might lose his reason. Such an event, for a proud Khibil of passionate convictions, would not be impossible. He had hired swords to protect his loved ones while he went about to root out the evil at its source.

I gave Twayne Gullik few odds if he tried to stand in the way of Scauro Pompino the Iarvin. The Ifts might scorn and play tricks where tumps were concerned, the two races of diffs detesting each other to the point of obsession; a Khibil's feelings of superiority stood in quite another league.

A couple of Fristles marched past, trailing their spears, their armor reasonably bright and cared for. They were hurrying, leaving the barracks, and we guessed they were late for guard duty. They gave us a quick nod of recognition as we passed.

"Humph," said Pompino, staring after them. "A right couple. Like 'em all here, slack, damned slack."

"You going to blame Gullik for that? Or for the state of the people in the city?"

"If I've a mind to, I will. I expect the citizens of Port Marsilus are a spineless lot, undermined by the war and the absence of a strong authority. Oh, yes, I know." He went on speaking quickly. "I know this Kov Pando is a friend from your past. And so is the Lady Tilda. But, all the same—"

"All the same, Pompino, I think you are right."

"As I said. And this Twayne Gullik is no better than a damned masichier, a confounded bandit masquerading as a mercenary. I own I have itchy fingers when he's about."

"Don't forget, my friend, that he will have itchy fingers, too."

"Ha!"

The north corridor contained a long row of tall windows, not quite slit windows affording cover for archers; but windows that were not particularly good at admitting light. They overlooked the north courtyard and the battlemented gate which, as the palace faced west, opened onto a side road. The noise of hooves and the clash of iron-rimmed wheels on cobbles attracted our attention, and we hauled ourselves up on the narrow windowsills to peer over and down. Green slate roofs spread beneath us and, far below, the hint of the north courtyard.

The polished roof of a carriage, partially concealed by a brass-bound traveling trunk, was just disappearing under the archway, the rear of the vehicle and its wheels concealed by a mounted escort whose lances slanted in ungainly fashion. From this angle we could make out few details. The escort, a dozen totrix men in mail, clattered out and the courtyard lay empty.

Pompino said: "The jutmen carried no colors on their lances."

"By their flags shall ye know them," I quoted. "And, so, we do not know them."

"When," said a mocking voice at our backs and below us, "you are quite finished, the kovneva will see you."

We let go the windowsills and dropped to the floor. The fellow who spoke held a golden-bound balass stick, ivory-topped. He wore long blue robes with a plentiful supply of silver, and his hat—flat, wide, puffed—supported a bunch of cut feathers of so inordinate a height one felt he would take off in a breeze.

"Who the devil are you?" demanded Pompino.

The fellow's puffy face, all pouched eyes and purple nose and sagging jowls, quivered in outrage.

"I am the kovneva's grand chamberlain, Constanchoin the Rod. She has graciously condescended to see you now, and you had best not keep her waiting."

"And," Pompino said, in a brittle voice, "not a horter in all this farrago."

I'd been thinking that a chamberlain, grand or not, would use the simple polite term of horter to a couple of gentlemen, here in his mistress's palace. Mind you, by Krun, most of the time it is difficult to take me for a gentleman, and I do not pretend to be a member of that ilk. I am content to be a plain sailorman, a fighting man or, when it comes to it, an emperor.

All the same, folk called Pompino and me horter out of simple politeness.

The grand chamberlain banged his black staff on the stone floor.

"There is no time to waste. Follow me."

I put a hand on Pompino's arm.

"It would be a sensible idea if we are to see Tilda to take Lisa the Empoin or the Lady Nalfi—"

Pompino's forearm bunched under my fingers, quivered, and then relaxed.

"Agreed." He spoke with some stiffness. "But, if they go, it is certain sure Quendur and Larghos will wish to accompany them, and if Larghos goes, Cap'n Murkizon will—"

"Quite. And, why not? After all," I said to this Constanchoin the Rod, "the kovneva will be glad to see all of them, seeing they risked their lives to bring her to safety."

Three flunkeys in a sillier version of the grand chamberlain's attire stood at his back. Constanchoin flicked the pomander on the end of a stick he carried in his left hand. If the gesture was a mere command, or signified what he thought of us, I neither knew nor cared.

"Planath," he said to one of the flunkeys. "Go to the barracks and summon these people. Tell them to hurry in our footsteps."

The flunkey mumbled a reply—not the military quidang—and trotted off, banging his balass staff—bound with silver—against the shins of a slave who almost fell over getting out of the way. A number of slaves passed and repassed, most of them carrying water, for that is a never-ending task in Kregan palaces. Other people had stopped to allow the grand chamberlain to go about his official duties and, also, to watch and enjoy whoever might be discomfited.

Followed by Pompino and me, Constanchoin the Rod started off back the way we had come. Four slaves with a carved lenken box strapped with bronze pressed against the wall to allow us to pass. Just beyond them a girl with a fluted vase of flowers—where she might be going was anybody's guess—waited. She wore a decent gray slave breechclout, and her hair was bound with a grass fillet. Apart from that she wore nothing else, and her feet, besides being dusty, showed a trace of blood. I had to walk on. But, by Zair, the maggots festered, believe you me.

Then I stopped dead.

The fellow who stood like an ale barrel against the wall wore a pale blue tunic, and dark blue trousers, with black boots. He did not wear a hat and his brown hair was cut short. He stood short, stout and robust, on thick legs that waddled when he walked. He wore a pallixter, the Pandahem form of thraxter, belted to his waist—and the word waist was merely a euphemism for his girth. His nose was a mere chunk of gristle, and the redness of his cheeks vied with the sunset of Zim, the red sun of Scorpio.

Pompino swung to look at me in surprise.

I walked on a few paces, as though in thought, and then said: "Do you go on, Pompino. I'll catch you up in a moment."

"But—"

"Hurry!" called the grand chamberlain. His flunkeys pressed close.

"Go on, Pompino. Tilda is, after all, a kovneva."

"What's going on? By Horato the Potent, Jak—you—"

"Something I must do—I'll be along with the others in no time."

Now Pompino is no man's fool. His frown did not lift; but he nodded and swung back to follow Constanchoin and the flunkeys. I breathed out.

There was no danger, I estimated, that the barrel-shaped fellow by the wall would throw himself into the full incline and start majistering me. He was too sly for that.

He started to walk off and turned into the first cross-corridor. I followed. Not too fast, not too slow, walking as though needing to go on an errand of purpose, I followed Naghan Raerdu along the cross-corridor and so into a small room stuffed with dusty barrels and boxes. He closed the door after me and stood back, looking at me.

Then he said: "Jak, is it, majister?"

"Aye, Naghan. And well met. I am glad to see you."

"As I am surprised to see you here: The Prince Majister's latest intelligence is only that you left Ruathytu in the devil of a hurry. But, of course, I have had little news myself in the past few sennights."

I answered in order. "I am not surprised to see you, Naghan, but I am pleased that my son chose you to spy for us here in Pandahem. I've been some way since leaving Ruathytu, and am now engaged in rooting out temples of Lem the Silver Leem. And, although any secret agent must be kept informed, it is his job to gather intelligence."

"Assuredly, Jak, assuredly."

Here Naghan Raerdu shut his eyes and the tears squeezed out from under the lids. He quivered. His red face became even more startlingly colored. Naghan Raerdu laughed in his own special rib-crushing way, spraying tears. When he laughed no one took much notice of what else he was doing.

This, of course, made him a very dangerous man and a first-class wormer out of secrets.

Presently he told me that his cover was a simple ale tradesman—and this fitted, for Naghan Raerdu seldom passed a bur or two without a glass tilted to his lips. Drak wanted to find out all there was to know of the people organizing the opposition to the warmongering factions here in Bormark. Armies were being sent across to the southwest of Vallia to support Kov Vodun Alloran—as I had learned aboard Insur ti Fotor's galleon—and my lad Drak felt we should assist those here in Bormark who stood against this plan.

"And there are such people, people who do not wish to fight against Vallia? You have contacted them?"

"Tsleetha-tsleethi," quoth Raerdu. "Softly-softly. There was a group I had just contacted when half of their number turned up in the River Liximus with slit throats and the other half vanished."

I looked sternly at him.

"If you turn up in the river with your throat slit, Naghan, I shall be extraordinarily annoyed. Not as much as you, perhaps. But remember! If you take stupid risks and such a fate should befall you, the ale would never reach your stomach."

He glared back.

"Few men call me stupid, majister."

"Sink me! If you were stupid you'd be dead twenty times by now."

I was not prepared to go into a long, involved and probably incoherent explanation of my feelings over sending men and women into danger and the risks of nasty deaths. They fought for Vallia, as did I. I'd had my share of risks, and, by Vox, a hell of a lot more lay ahead, as you shall hear. But, as always, I fretted at the unwholesome necessity of sending men and women into dangers I could not share.

"I'm still alive, Jak. That must prove something."

Although in the end we're all going shuffling off to the Ice Floes of Sicce and, if we are fortunate and of stout hearts and hew to the right path, make our way to the sunny uplands beyond, we all feel we wish to push that time off for as long as possible. I've been around Kregen under many assumed names, as you know; I believe I have only once been called Davy Prescott. Amusing as an indication of scholarship though this is, for me it is merely another prod in the direction of staying away from any Alamo, unless something stupid like honor gets in the way. It was in my mind that Naghan Raerdu would never let the stupidity of honor betray him, for all that he was loyal and courageous. He gave me further news—which does not concern my narrative at this time—and he reassured me that those people for whom I had a particular care were still in one piece.

Then he said: "The Princess Dayra was down in the southwest. I was not assigned there, until later, and so cannot vouch for the rumors—"

I congratulated myself on my iron control.

I did not leap forward and seize Naghan Raerdu around his neck and choke him, screaming: "Rumors? Princess Dayra? What rumors? Spit 'em out or you are a dead man!"

No. My self-control was admirable.

Naghan Raerdu jumped, staring at me in that dusty room. His color patched into white and pink.

"Majister..." he stammered, and licked his lips, and said quickly—very quickly—"A colleague said that the Princess Dayra was actively assisting Vodun Alloran..."

I put a hand on a barrel. The dust lay thick.

"And?"

He swallowed.

"As I said, majister, I cannot vouch—"

"Tell me what the rumors are concerning my daughter Dayra."

He straightened, for he saw the crisis had passed. A large number of people knew how much of a trial Dayra was to her family. She was known as Ros the Claw, having been through Lancival where she had been taught the secret Disciplines of the Whip and the Claw. The Sisters of the Rose had taught her, and her mother had loved and counseled her; but during the time of her growing up there had been no father in her life. That great rogue had been banished to Earth, distant four hundred light-years, by the Star Lords. For that I had, I thought, forgiven them, for they and I had reached a tatty kind of agreement in these later years. But, as now, the hideous results of that parting from my family came home to me with deadly remorse.

The truth was, of course, that even had I been around like any normal father, Dayra would still have gone off the rails, although perhaps not to quite the extent she had. She had been lured off course by bad companions. Some of them were due a hempen necktie—when they were caught.

Dayra's mother, the incomparable Delia of Delphond, had herself been constrained by duty to the Sisters of the Rose. It was perfectly reasonable to suggest that the SOR themselves, as much as any other factor, had contributed heavily to Dayra's wildness.

Naghan's rubicund composure returned. Sweat glimmered on his red forehead.

"The usual things, Jak. Smashing up wine shops, wrecking restaurants. But she was seen riding with Alloran when he led an armored host to war—"

"But he was fighting the Prince Majister! Do you think I am to believe that my daughter Dayra would go out to fight her brother?"

"There were no reports of her presence on the battlefield."

"Thank Opaz for that. Is there more?"

"This fellow Zankov was also seen in her company."

"Him," I said, and drew a breath. "I tell you this, Naghan, for your information. Zankov is a young devil, spurned by his family and out to make himself master of whatever he can lay his hands on. He is the man who slew the emperor, the Princess Dayra's grandfather. I do not think she can know this."

Naghan's brown Vallian eyes widened. "I did not know this. By Vox! What a coil!"

"Oh, the coil is tighter than that. For the Princess Dayra hates and detests her father, Dray Prescot, Emperor of Vallia."

All Naghan said was: "That I knew."

An emotion, and I hardly care to call it pride, for it was more a kind of affronted despair, a desperate call for a fraction of self-esteem, made me say: "Although when she thought she could slay me, dubious though the chance was, she did not strike, and held back the blow. It is in my mind that, perhaps, her hatred and detestation are not the powerful forces in her life she thinks they are."

Naghan Raerdu said: "I pray Opaz you are right."

I shook myself. The dust was getting up my nose.

"We have spoken long enough for now. We shall meet again. Now I'm on my way to see the Kovneva Tilda, for there are temples to be burned."

"The kovneva?" Naghan looked puzzled. "She left the Zhantil Palace very early this morning, Jak. She took a large escort, and no one knew where she had gone."

Nine

How a blood-stained switch changed hands

The problems of my family and particularly of Dayra had to be pushed aside—yet again. The Star Lords overlooked my actions here in Bormark, even if they had not directly commissioned Pompino and me. Because I had defied them in the past they had banished me to Earth for twenty-one years. In those years Dayra and her twin brother Jaidur had grown to maturity. Useless to harp on what might have been...

I found Constanchoin the Rod in a small, black-hung chamber, superintending the chastisement of a slave girl. The under-flunkey I dragged along by an ear had let me know that I was sealing my doom by my actions. But he led me where I wanted to go, even if he dragged along after, his ear stretching.

The slave girl, naked, hung suspended by her ankles from a cross beam. She was past the shrieking stage, and blood ran down to drip from her forehead into her hair and so onto the iron floor. The Rapa who, stripped to the waist, wielded the switch, halted his blow as I bundled in.

Two Rapa guards immediately rushed across, their spears ready to degut me. I threw the junior flunkey at them and took time to take the switch away from the Rapa and hit him a belt across the head. His beak bent. I kicked him as he went down, thus proving the grand chamberlain at least half-right when he'd omitted to address me as horter.

The two guards disentangled themselves from the flunkey and heaved up. The grand chamberlain was shrieking out something about kill him, you fools, kill him. They charged with their spears low. They'd have killed me, too, I believe, even before anything had been sorted out. As it was I whipped the thraxter out, swished left, cut right, ducked away, got inside the second spear and thrust.

Two Rapa guards lay on the iron floor, bleeding messily.

Three naked and chained girls at the side did not scream. But their eyes were as wide as the Sunset Sea.

No doubt they were next in line for punishment. There had been enough time since the grand chamberlain had summoned us to the kovneva for just the one girl to be chastised.

The tendril-like antennae growing from her forehead and shrouded by her soft dark hair looked limp and woeful. Her small pinched face with the bruised eyes and the full yet small mouth made me kick the Rapa switch-wielder again, hard, and say to him: "Be thankful you are still alive, dom."

The only other person in the chamber, a little six-armed Och in a brown tunic, crouched beside the chained slave girls. Mutely, he handed me the keyring. I did not take it.

"Unchain them," I growled, and then dived for the grand chamberlain who was attempting to scuttle out.

"C'mere, grand chamberlain," I said, and lifted him up by his fancy silver-worked blue robe so that he squeaked. I stuck my ugly old beakhead of a face into his and said: "Where's the kovneva?"

"I don't know!" He chittered it out, swinging with his toes scraping the floor. I shook him.

"You summoned me to see the Kovneva Tilda. She has left the Zhantil Palace. She had left long before you spoke to me. So, dom, where is she?"

His eyes were popping. There was foam on his lips.

"I don't know!"

I did not hit him, for that would have solved nothing. I looked at him sorrowfully. I cocked my head at the beam and dragged him across. Holding him with my left fist I used the thraxter in my right to slash the girl's bonds. She fell into the arms of her three companions who, unchained, were ready to help in this impossible and undreamed of situation. They were girls of spirit, then, and not broken slave grakvushis.

The girls were all trembling, as was natural, yet with that quick summation of their characters I surmised they had not been slave long. One was a Sybli, one a Sylvie and the other apim. They were all pretty, and I sighed.

Constanchoin went upside down with some ease and I looked at the girls.

"Two of you tie his ankles to the beam."

The Sybli with her childish face just smiled and went on bathing the girl who had been beaten. The Sylvie and the apim girl leaped up, eagerly sorted out fresh bonds, and fastened Constanchoin upside down. I half bent to stare into his engorged face.

"You know what is going to happen, grand chamberlain. But, of course, you won't let it happen. You'll tell me where the kovneva is."

He was hysterical now, shattered by shock and fright.

But he still chittered out: "I do not know! A great crowd of Twayne Gullik's Iftkin came and took the kovneva away. I was not told—"

I frowned.

This had the ring of truth. That Twayne Gullik... Maybe Pompino was right and the Ift was an out and out rogue.

The Sylvie picked up the bloodstained switch.

With the feeling a man gets when he realizes the bottom of his ship has been ripped out on a coral reef I saw that the situation had now overtaken me. What I had begun in so febrile a manner would be continued and probably finished by others with their own interests to slake. I bent again to Constanchoin the Rod.

"If you know, tell me. These girls will not be easy on you."

"I do not know!"

"Well, where would Gullik most likely take her?"

"His kin have a castle at Igbolo, deep in the forest—"

The Sylvie whistled the switch around with a hiss and the grand chamberlain yelped although not touched. His blue robes hung around his head, but I felt sure the girls would remove the rest of his clothes before they started.

"Igbolo," I said. "That is not much help." Igbolo was like saying Greentree. "You'll have to do better than that."

"I can take you there—I think." He spoke with a rush, seeing a way out of his predicament. I wasn't at all sure I could stop these poor girls once they'd started.

"What do you mean, you think?"

"The way is guarded by traps. It is lost in the forest. I have never been there—" He regretted saying that instantly. He tried to cover. "But I have been told."

By this time I felt reasonably confident that he didn't know where the kovneva was. She might be at Gullik's Iftkin's castle of Igbolo. But she might not be. Gullik would know for sure that the search would be prosecuted there.

"Anywhere else?"

"No! I don't know—save me, save me, Horter Jak!"

I did not smile.

"If you insist on tying up girls and having them beaten painfully with a switch, you surely cannot complain if girls tie you up and reciprocate? Is there not justice in that?"

"As you love Pandrite, save me!"

"Horter," said the Sylvie. "I do not know who you are; but I am growing tired of waiting."

"We take turns," said the apim girl.

"Of course, Natalini, we take turns. Only I go first."

"You always do get first go at the men, Sharmin."

"And this time it will be different, by Shiusas the Insatiable, vastly different."

As all Kregans know, if anyone is cognizant of insatiability, it has to be the Sylvies, of whom most men are strangely ignorant—or, perhaps not strangely, seeing that they wish to remain on speaking terms with their own womenfolk. Or, so it is said.

Constanchoin fell into an incoherent mumble, interlarded with prayers and pleadings. The broken-beaked Rapa slumbered. The two guards lay in their own blood. The Och had vanished. There seemed to me nothing left here for me, except a difficult decision. Why did I have to become embroiled? I'd told this damned grand chamberlain that, hoisted with his own petard as he was, he could expect no other punishment than that which he had meted out. But was this a civilized action? It was not, certainly in many areas of Kregen. Just as I had decided—and, I might add, with some reluctance—to halt the girls in their revengeful beating after each had had a whack or two, the whole problem was terminated in an unsurprising and typical way.

The black-hung chamber echoed to the clash of iron-soled sandals on the iron floor and a mob of guards burst in.

Since I stood in front of the upside-down grand chamberlain hanging from the beam, all the newcomers would see of him would be his ankles bound up. They took as little interest in those as they did in the wounded and unconscious Rapas. Most of the guards were Fristles. They looked at the Sylvie.

I said in a hard voice: "Have you seen the kovneva, Framco the Tranzer?"

The cadade hauled up and looked at me. He recognized me.

"The kovneva? No, of course not. We had report of a disturbance, of a wild man—what's going on, Horter Jak?"

"Why, only that that rogue of a Twayne Gullik has kidnapped the kovneva. As for the business here, your grand chamberlain was about to taste his own switch. But I think that may not be necessary now."

The Fristle cadade peered around. He saw what had been going on. I readied myself for a bout of handstrokes; but what I'd said worried him far more than the plight of the grand chamberlain. It was not difficult to guess that Constanchoin had given Framco a hard time in the past.

"Gullik's kidnapped the kovneva! You are sure? It is a most serious allegation." Framco did not pull his whiskers. He looked competent, on a sudden, in his mail. "Forgon—cut down the grand chamberlain. Catch him before he falls." To the Och, who ran in grimacing and ducking his head: "You, Nathamcar, see these girls back to their quarters." To an ob-Deldar whose whiskers were dyed blue: "Anfer, take two men and guard them. I'll question them, if ever I get around to it... Now, Horter Jak, perhaps you'd best tell me all about it from the beginning."

"Gladly, if I knew what the hell was going on."

Constanchoin, cut down, was carried past, moaning.

Framco said: "You'll have to answer as to what has happened to the grand chamberlain. Although if he's in the plot I'll be the first to string him up again."

At the time I found nothing unusual in the cadade's immediate acceptance of my story. That there was strong animosity between him and Twayne Gullik was obvious, and that antipathy extended to the grand chamberlain. Also, Framco the Tranzer was no hired paktun. He came from Pando's estates, and would be expected in the normal way to be loyal, given fair dealings. That he had been chosen to be the captain of the guard indicated something of his mettle.

The girls walked past, the antennae of the fanpi drooping as she was carried by two men.

The Sylvie, bold, stopped by me and looked up.

"You deprived me of my revenge, horter."

I said: "You will be thankful, one day, that you did not take your revenge. When I see the kovneva I will buy you and your friends—"

She showed her teeth.

"I would not willingly be slave to you—"

"I do not keep slaves. I will manumit you all. That is a promise."

Her face changed color.

"What is the name of the fanpi who was beaten?"

"Tinli, horter."

"I shall remember the four of you, and see you are freed, for you can face nothing but pain here now. Tinli, Suli, Natalini—and Sharmin. I shall remember."

"If you do, horter, then Shiusas the Insatiable will surely reward you."

Framco said: "We have to find the kovneva first."

"Aye. But where has Gullik taken her? And," I said, for I was still unsure, "It could be he has merely taken her to another place of refuge..."

"That is a possibility, of course. But I know that rogue Gullik."

"Suppose he mistrusted us?"

"Had you wished to kill the kovneva, I am sure you would have done so long ago, and run no further risks in bringing her into the Zhantil Palace. By Odifor! I may be wrong in this, but my whiskers tell me I am right!"

The smiling Sybli girl with her childish face turned as she passed. They are simple folk, the Syblians, but not as simple as they look.

"The mistress wanted to take me to the estate at Plaxing, if that helps, horter. She told me so last night."

I looked at her, said thank you and she smiled, her babyish face rosy and now free from worry, for she, like any truly sensible person, might look into the future but refused to worry over it, unlike most of us.

"Tilda spoke to her last night, when she was supposed to be unwell." I could hear the edge in my voice. "There has been a plot at work here."

"Yes," said Framco, agreeing. "But I do not think Gullik would take the kovneva to her estate at Plaxing."

"You agree there is a plot. Tell me what you think has been going on." For my money the cadade knew nothing, and Twayne Gullik had, following his name, gulled him. "You'd better send some of your men to make inquiries. A party of Iftkin with a chair or a coach may have attracted attention."

The carriage Pompino and I had seen leaving might belong to the plot. When I mentioned it, Framco sent to make inquiries. Then we went off to find Pompino.

On the way through the corridors with scared slaves keeping out of the way, Framco told me that if there was a plot, as he now believed, he knew nothing of it. He'd always mistrusted the Ift from the day Pando took him on as castellan. No doubt Pando had his motives in the appointment; I could not guess what they were. Some of Pando's estates consisted of entire stretches of forest. Maybe that was the answer.

We found Pompino and the rest of the people from *Tuscurs Maiden* fuming.

"Kept me waiting like some cur dog!" Pompino started off. "No formality, no courtesy—"

He quieted down when I cut in to explain what had happened. Then he broke out afresh.

"We'll scour every street, every tavern, every hole and corner! Someone, somewhere, will know where the kovneva has been taken."

"That," I said, "will take time."

"If only Mindi the Mad were here," said Framco. I noticed that he'd started pulling his whiskers again. "She has the power. I am confident she would be able to spy out the kovneva's whereabouts."

"A witch?" demanded Pompino.

"A good witch, a female wizard, a sorceress, a seer, yes."

"You trust her?"

"Oh," said Framco the Tranzer, "no."

Towards the hour of mid when we thought of taking a little light refreshment, one of Framco's men reported back that a party of Ifts with three wagons had been observed leaving the Inward Gate, which led out into the hinterland.

"After them!" he cried. "Mount up, all. We'll overtake them and demand a reckoning, by Odifor!"

A bunch of hersanys were brought from the stables and saddled up. Big ugly brutes, hersanys, with coats of thick chalk-white hair, and their six legs are as ungainly as any totrix's. But they have stamina, and do well in the bruising jolt of a cavalry charge. Framco's guards mounted up, and Pompino called down to me from his saddle.

"Mount up, Jak! This is nip and tuck."

"Listen, Pompino." I walked across and put my hand on his bridle. "Do you go on after the Ifts. You may find the Lady Tilda with them—"

He looked alarmed.

"You think not?"

"I don't know, by Pandrite! But I do not think it wise to expend all our energy in one direction."

He nodded. "Then I'll follow this clue. If you root out anything, send a messenger—these locals will know the direction we've taken."

"I'll do that."

"Maybe I should stay with you and let Framco go—"

"That is your decision. But I want to poke about myself. I want to use my nose."

"A damned great beakhead it is, to be sure. Very well. I'll give this chase a day, then I'll be back."

"Agreed."

They clattered off, like a hunt after leems, and I went back into the palace, free to go about my own nefarious activities.

Ten

Of the power of the Lemmites

Looked at dispassionately, the perfectly logical deduction from what had happened was that Twayne Gullik, a conscientious castellan, concerned for the safety of his mistress and much distrusting us rough new arrivals, had taken her off to a place of greater sanctuary. This was perfectly possible. His attempt to get us out of the palace had failed. But—we knew that the kovneva had left the palace before Gullik spoke to us. Copper-bottoming his bet? Maybe.

One way or the other, we had covered the options. If Tilda was safe with Gullik, no harm would have been done. If she was being abducted—and one could hardly say against her will because she was probably in a state of happy befuddlement—Pompino and the crew from *Tuscurs Maiden* and Framco and his guards would take the necessary measures to secure her from the rascally Ift. If he was a rascal.

Framco had left a handful of men under an ord-Deldar to hold the palace. They'd be occupied if anything untoward happened. My judgment was that some of the peril we had anticipated, directed as it was against persons and not property, might have been exaggerated. It might not have been. If a howling mob broke in to loot the palace the guards would see them off; if assassins sneaked in they'd find no quarry, their kitchews all flown, and if any of the other folk who wanted Tilda dead attacked they'd have dust and ashes to show for their pains.

So, feeling discontented but aware that in that direction nothing further remained to be done, I set about the next task.

If I burned a temple before Pompino got back to join in he'd feel cheated of his amusement. But, I could see about finding the locations of the temples. As I did this I'd make inquiries after the Ifts and the kovneva.

A change of costume being desirable I went along to see the grand chamberlain.

He was still in a distressed state, lying shivering in his bed in his apartments. A couple of flunkeys wanted to cut up; but I looked at them, and went across the carpets to look down on Constanchoin.

He glared up, feverishly, black rings under his eyes.

"I refuse to feel sorry for you," I told him. "If you order girls to be beaten then you must expect to be beaten yourself. As it was, you came off lightly."

He moaned. This was all shock, indignity, fright; he hadn't been physically harmed.

"I need a change of clothes. I came to see if you were all right and to tell you that I am plundering the kov's wardrobe. He will be pleased to let me have whatever clothes I wish to take, believe me. As for you; when you are recovered you will take great care of the people, both men and women, in your charge. Otherwise—well, in the Blue Distance of Pandrite, anything may happen. *Dernun?*"

That rather fierce way of demanding understanding jolted him. He managed a feeble nod. A slave girl wiped spittle from his lips. I looked at her, a Fristle girl with silvery fur and a tail adorned with a blue and green bow.

"If he hits you, fifi, tell me. He will not hit you again."

With that foolish statement echoing in my ears I went off. As you will observe, I was a trifle warm about the domestic arrangements young Pando kept up in his palace.

In the lavishly furnished apartments given over to the kov's personal use I found he did himself proud in the wardrobe department. His tunics wouldn't stretch to fit my shoulders, of course; but I needed a Pandahem hat, and a loose cape-like upper garment known in Pandahem as a puttah. I chose one with a blue ground and not too much black and silver embroidery, for they are foppish in these things. With this slung over my shoulders, the wide hat pulled down, and a fresh pair of gray trousers, I was perfectly decently dressed.

The Fristle ord-Deldar, who reported himself in as Naghan the Pellendur, offered me a hersany. I told him I'd prefer to walk, thanked him, and sauntered out of the gate. I felt a tickle of amusement as the two guards in their little sentry boxes slapped up their spears in salute. I touched the brim of the hat to them, shoved the puttah over my left shoulder in the style of a pelisse, and took myself off to explore Pando's Port Marsilus.

His hat, I should mention, was of a fine pearl-gray color, most elegant, with a black velvet band. In that band a jaunty tuft of green feathers gave, I now admit, life to the combination. With a gesture I admit, I admit! was entirely petty, I ripped the green feathers out and scattered them on the roadway. Of such things are a fellow's life made. Meaningless gestures, irrational loyalties, a childish approach to the serious things of life...

The way to handle children... Well, I knew that, didn't I? Of course I did—or thought I did like any fond parent. But children do not grow up in the same mold as their parents. I couldn't honestly say that a single one of my children took after me—except in a twisted sense that Dayra would like to take after me with her Whip and her Claw. Although she hadn't struck that final blow...

So, thinking dark and unpleasant thoughts, all occasioned by a bunch of green feathers, I tried to brisk up my steps. The first port of call would be a tavern, by Krun!

At the sign of the Hersany and Queng I downed a tankard of ale and devoured two cheese sandwiches with a great deal of pickle, and all the time I sized up the clientele—middling tradesmen, a fellow who was clearly an artist from the paint on his fingers and the well-worn portfolio leaning against his chair leg, a farmer into the big city over important affairs and dressed up in a hideous mélange of color and style, a mercenary—a little out of his milieu—who was tazll and being unemployed had a lean and hungry look. To this last customer I insinuated myself with the usual tricks of introduction, and bought him a tankard, and so sat down easily at his side.

The suns light struck across the settle so that he stood out in fine detail, whereas I leaned back in the shadows.

"And they say they're taking anybody. Masichieri, most likely, so a paktun like me can expect a good position."

"Hikdar?" I said, lazily.

He blinked.

"Well—perhaps not at first. But shebov-Deldar, at the least."

Shebov-Deldar—seven steps up the ladder of promotions within the Deldar ranking—would be handsome, I judged. He was apim, like me, well-built, and with a crop of dark hair tied into a knot with a blue ribbon at the back of his head. He wore a leather brass-studded jerkin, and carried a pallixter. He had no helmet I could see.

He said his name was Apgarl Apring, called the Strigicaw; but I did not believe him.

His business on that score was his own; what he could tell me of the recruiting going on was going to be mine also.

"You looked a fine handy fellow when I saw you come in," he said, quaffing the ale I'd bought him. "Why don't you come along o' me, and we'll sign up together?"

"Why not?"

He looked pleased. If he'd run off from some scrape he'd welcome a friend. He wore neither golden zhantil-head nor silver mortil-head at his throat; but in these latter days on Kregen he called himself a paktun, which is really a name reserved for mercenaries who have acquired renown.

He knew nothing of any party of Ifts, and allowing my voice to rise when the question was posed, I received no response for my pains from anyone else.

This Apgarl Apring possessed no saddle-animal, no helmet, no spear, no shield. The obvious conclusion was that association with him would bring accumulated suspicion down on my head. This might work both ways, of course...

We went along to the Street of the Jiktars where, at an imposing structure stuccoed white, we went in to see about signing up. The courtyard was busy with comings and goings of military men and women, and the place hummed with activity.

In many of the countries in this part of the world in the days following the great war against Hamal, employment for mercenaries had thinned. Men and women to be hired for guard duty and to protect caravans or ships were always in demand; now the markets were overflowing. In the normal course, then, one would expect Apgarl to find some difficulty in securing employment.

No such thing. Oh, no! The moment we sized up the layout, saw the different regimental tables with their recruiting Deldars, the heaps of gold coins, the busy bustle, saw the speed with which any new arrival was snapped up, we saw there would be no difficulty. Apgarl looked at the different tables.

He smiled and then he frowned.

"I shall, of course, choose a first-class regiment."

"Of course."

I'd seen enough—already. If they wanted men so desperately as to take on Apgarl Apring—who was in all probability a decent enough fellow except for his unfortunate circumstances—then an expedition of some size was planned. Given the information I was already possessed of, it seemed to me that the destination of the expedition had to be southwestern Vallia.

"Where are you off to, then, Nath?" Apgarl looked surprised. I'd told him I was Nath the Bludgeon.

"A previous appointment, Apgarl. Don't wait for me."

"I won't, by Acker of the Brass Tail! But if you're in the Hersany and Queng I'll treat you out of my first pay."

"Done, Apgarl. Remberee."

He trotted off to sign up and I wandered in the other direction where a bulbous-nosed fellow wearing a gorgeous uniform that had been stitched together to close the rents, and chalked over the white and painted over the colors, stood at a table and bellowed fruitlessly. A standard of blue and white with yellow slashes hung at his back. Its edges were shredded. His own uniform of similar colors looked as though he'd been ridden over by the same charge of armored cavalry.

"Come along, dom," he called to me. "You look a fine upstanding fellow." His spiel followed the usual line of desperate recruiting Deldars. Things were hot, then!

"Tell me, Deldar," I said in an easy voice. "Just where are you expecting to fight? For, I can tell you, I have a weak stomach. If there're ships involved—"

"Weak stomach!" He managed a laugh, although his cheeks, bearded and pitted with tiny blackheads, for he was apim, changed not at all and his eyes remained dull. "Why, we can soon cure that for you! We'll see to it that you get a first-class berth, with all the trimmings. Come along, lad, sign up and take the silver in your hand." He tossed a silver dhem up and down on his palm.

This time of day the recruiting Deldars might wait at their tables here in Headquarters in the Street of the Jiktars; their serious work took place later in the various taverns about the city. They expected eager volunteers now.

"So it is over the sea," I said, looking downcast.

"It don't matter to a fighting man where he fights! When you take up the profession of arms, you look no further than the next meal and the purse o' gold, the next jovial company and the next battle."

"Who, Deldar, are you fighting?"

Still his expression remained in that pathetic joviality overlaying deadness.

"That's for the orffizers to say, dom. Here, take the silver and we'll make two men of you—"

"You look, Deldar, as though you've just staggered off a battlefield. You're not a good advertisement for your regiment."

He goggled at me now, taken aback. Then he banged the ornate brass badge set in the front of his leather helmet. Half the blue and white feathers were missing from the socket.

"See that, lad! That's the badge o' the Corrundum Rig'ment, known as the Korfs. Proud, we are, and don't you—"

"Archers, then... You don't know I can pull a bow."

He laughed now, and there was some amusement there. "I seen your shoulders, dom. I know a bowman when I see one."

A Deldar at the adjoining table shouted across.

80

"Corrundum Krasnys! Step over here, dom, and join a *real* rig'ment!"

He wore a splendid uniform of blue and yellow with much gold ornament and a veritable peacock's tail in his helmet. Giving him a casual glance, I was held by the small silver brooch at his left shoulder, fastening the flamboyant sash. A small tuft of brown feathers surmounted the silver image of a leem.

About to saunter across, ignoring the pleas of the Deldar of the Corrundum Korfs, I had to step aside as a great wash of men surged in, shouting and laughing, stamping their boots and swishing their capes.

"They'll pick and choose," said the Corrundum Deldar. He clearly regarded me as a lost cause. "Proud we are, right enough; but we've had hard times lately."

If a pang touched me I had to thrust it aside.

"Been in it, lately?"

"Aye, dom. Down in Hamal, I was. Paktun." He was a true paktun, for he wore the silver mortilhead at his throat. "Fought them Pandrite-forsaken Shtarkins, the Shanks. Beat 'em, too—"

Jolted, I said, "You were at the Battle of the Incendiary Vosks?"

His eyes opened. "Aye, I was. You, too?"

"Aye."

He looked alive, suddenly. I could not afford to get involved in old-soldier campaigning talk, much as I might have enjoyed it over a wet. He was a mercenary, last season fighting with me against a common foe, this season fighting for my enemies against my own country. All the time, if he were your true paktun of Kregen, he would remain loyal to the employer to whom he had sworn his allegiance. I edged a little away, not because of any ill-feeling against paktuns, but out of the pressing necessity of getting on with the task in hand. I looked at the sumptuously-clad Deldar in the blue and yellow with the badge of the Silver Leem.

A fellow, a moltingur, all proboscis and carapace, was speaking to the Deldar. He wore brass-studded leathers and carried a formidable armory. He leaned over and I heard him say: "Yes, indeed, Deldar, I am choosy; but, as you can see from this I am not your ordinary paktun." And he touched his own silver and brown badge pinned to his shoulder.

The Deldar simply asked a question, couched in the ritual—and rigmarole—of the secret passwords of the Leem Lovers. I was privy to these secrets, having been inducted into the vile cult to save my life down in Ruathytu. The moltingur had no idea what was being said, and gave a noncommittal answer that branded him as one who knew nothing of Lem the Silver Leem.

Fascinated, I listened and watched.

The Deldar of the Corrundum Korfs sniffed at my back and said in a growly bass: "That lot get promoted, right enough."

I faced him.

"You know about that badge—the leem and the brown feathers?"

"I know nothing and I want to know nothing. But you see it more and more every day. That moltingur will get made up to ord-Deldar on the strength of it, you mark my words."

I thought not; I did not say so.

Loath though I was to give any credit to anyone belonging to the Leem Lovers, in what next occurred I saw that, perhaps, some men and women—and particularly the military—might sign up with the cult out of other reasons than religious fervor, misguided ambition and love of orgies. I fancied that this Deldar might be absent when it came to torturing and sacrificing children.

He spoke swiftly to the Moltingur, in a low voice, and then called across to the Deldar of the Corrundum Korfs.

"Hai, Deldar Poll! Here is a fellow for you—"

The Moltingur's proboscis shoved forward and he grabbed the rich uniform before him, starting to protest. That, as anyone could see, was a great mistake.

The Deldar did not hit him, made no move to withdraw. He simply called: "Glemshos! Autmoil!* *Bratch!*"

The next few moments witnessed a boil of fellows in bright uniforms descending on the unfortunate moltingur and beating anywhere they could reach with stout and heavy cudgels. They knocked him down and kicked him, and then they dragged him up by his ears and threw him into the center of the courtyard.

One of them, a pinch-faced fellow whose brown and silver badge was of an ornateness surpassing the others, spat down: "If you attempt to deceive or impersonate us again, you will try to swim with a slit throat, by Flem!"

The moltingur lay on the flagstones, shattered.

The pinch-faced fellow swaggered back. "That's the way to deal with that trash, Deldar Loparn. We are not people to be fooled or trifled with."

The word used by this Deldar Loparn—Glemshos—intrigued me. Clearly the shos part came from the common word fanshos, being a band of companions, a gang of likely lads, all pals together. The Glem was merely one of the ways the Leem Lovers disguised their adherence. But the use of the word in just this way meant that here in Bormark the cult of Lem the Silver Leem operated much more in the open. The words spoken and the acts performed testified eloquently to this. I'd seen Lem the Silver Leem worshipped openly in Canopdrin, seasons ago, and we'd settled up that question. Now the Canops lived on the island of Canopjik and kept watch and ward for the Shanks who raided up into Havilfar. Deldar Poll at my back coughed and said: "Bad cess to 'em."

---

* Autmoil: stranger

"You don't fear them?"

"Of course I do, dom!"

He wiped a sleeve across his mouth.

I said: "There's little enough doing here. Come along for a wet."

He hesitated; but agreed when I took one of Pompino's golden deldys out and twinkled it between my fingers. He called a shiv-Deldar out to take over, not that there would be much doing, for this fellow's uniform was in almost as sorry a state as Poll's. We went off toward the wing of the Headquarters turned into an alehouse for the recruiting period.

Our conversation followed along traditional lines. As Nath the Bludgeon I contrived to put on a half-vacant look, not quite imbecilic, although my friends claim that this is a natural expression. He said he was Tom Poll called the Nose. That organ was not as colorful or as plentiful as many nourished in the taverns of Kregen, but it was of a certain quivering splendor.

A vague idea that I could join up with a Brown and Silver regiment and thus worm my way into the heart of things had been dashed. Tom the Nose said his commander, Jiktar Naghan Lappartom, was a fair man, but short of the readies, both of cash and equipment.

"We've been in Vallia, and we had a tough time." He was into the confidence stage now, past trying to recruit me.

"This new army they're putting together will probably beat the Vallians; but you never can tell. They fight hard."

"So I believe."

"You must have heard of them at the Incendiary Vosks. By Pandrite—they and those devilish Djangs! I was with a regiment contracted to old King Hot and Cold. I can tell you, I'm glad we did not have to thwack it out with the Vallians."

I hoisted my stein and gave him a quizzical look.

"You sound as though the Vallians you saw then and the ones you fought over in Vallia recently are not the same."

"Too right, dom! The best Vallian regiments are still in Hamal, or are up in the north of Vallia. It won't be easy; but this time we can do it. Their King Alloran will sweep most of his section of the country clean. There'll be rich pickings. I wasn't at the sack of Rahartdrin—"

"Sack of Rahartdrin?"

He slopped ale.

"What's wrong?"

"Nothing. I knew someone from there. That's all."

He leered, his nose wobbling. "A girl, hey?"

"Yes."

"Don't we all."

"By the way," I said, trying to sound casual and making a pretty poor fist of it, "d'you hear anything of what happened to the kovneva there: Katrin Rashumin, I think her name was. My girl slaved for her."

He cocked an eye at me.

"She ran off, was all I heard. And the Vallians don't keep slaves anymore—"

"Figure of speech, dom, figure of speech."

I drank ale, to hide the fury in my face. Being caught up in my own wishes and orders! Ironical—and infuriating with it. The fact that Vallians had done away with slavery in almost all their provinces was now a well-known item of news even though it remained a marvel.

"So this King Vodun Alloran has conquered Rahartdrin." That kovnate consisted of a large island off the southwest coast. Katrin Rashumin was a loyal friend to Delia. And this maniacal king was on the move, clearly taking other islands and also making his way up to the northeast. Soon he might reach Delphond—what the hell was Drak doing?

This Tom Poll the Nose, with whom I sat companionably drinking ale, was a zan-Deldar. He wore the silver mortilhead. Now he quaffed ale, and said: "Oh, yes, right enough. As soon as we get there we'll be off, you mark my words. We'll be off into Vallia and bring their capital city, Vondium, down about their ears. King Vodun Alloran has vowed to cut off the emperor's head." He drank again, a paktun discussing his trade. "It's certain sure. This Dray Prescot emperor is for the chop this time." He eyed me. "What's stopping you from coming along and helping us fight this Dray Prescot?"

Eleven

How the Great Lie spread

"What's stopping me from going and fighting Dray Prescot, Emperor of Vallia?" I said. "Why, Tom, I told you. I'd get seasick."

He looked over the rim of his stein at me, quite clearly nonplussed.

"You were down in Hamal—"

"Certainly. Never again."

The large hall in this wing of the grandiose building given over as a tavern for the military resounded with the clink of bottles, the surf-foaming-roar of voices, the occasional quick snap of argument. Most of the men were recruiters, conscious of their dignity; the arguments did not degenerate into fights. They'd come later, out at the taverns, when the competition grew fiercer.

I leaned closer.

"Did you see this Emperor of Vallia at the Incendiary Vosks?"

"No. He kept out of it. That's his style."

"Oh?"

"Surely. Why, dom, it's no secret. He was built up as the Prince Majister of Vallia, before the old emperor died, given false credentials, a fake glamour, made out to be a fighting man, when in truth he's nothing more than a ninny."

"I'd heard that. But I thought those old stories had been disbelieved by now."

"Some folk were gulled. But we've been told the truth. We know what kind of a devil Dray Prescot is. Cunning, cowardly, scheming, as soon murder a friend and run from an enemy as stand and take decent hand-strokes like a warrior."

"You've been told?"

He let a satisfied smile twist his lips. I'd summed him up as a decent sort of fellow, one who followed his profession with devotion, probably pushed into it when he'd been so young and wet behind the ears he knew no better. But, at that, a real paktun on Kregen, a man of honor, has no need in those terms to feel shame. I'd known mercenaries one would put down as a blight upon civilization; others helped to ensure that that civilization endured.

"Oh, yes, dom, we've been told. We know the truth. Prescot is no good. Even if he was as brave as two zhantils, which he isn't, he'd still be evil and crooked and ripe only for the chop."

Patiently, I said: "It is difficult to believe—"

"Would you believe it if it came from his own family?"

So, then, of course, I knew.

To delay, now, the moment, I said: "He has a son Drak, the Prince Majister. He is fighting you now. He has a daughter, the Princess Majestrix—"

"And who knows where she is? No, dom, this Prescot's daughter, Princess Dayra. She knows her father only too well. She's had trouble with him before. She's the one who knows the truth."

My fist closed on the jug, and clenched, and I could not speak.

Tom the Nose drank ale, flushed with this imparting of high affairs. I felt sick. I managed to get the jug to my lips, and drank, and wiped the back of my hand across my mouth and did not say: "By Mother Zinzu the Blessed, I needed that!" although it was true, by Zair!

"She must hate her father."

"Hate? No. She told us, just before the Battle of Corvamsmot. Contempt, that's what she feels."

"Did she—did she ride out to the battle? Did she fight?"

"A princess? Not likely!"

Little he knew of the princesses I knew, then...

I had to go on, although Tom the Nose would start to wonder pretty soon at my insistence on matters so far removed from our station. "But you mean she urged you to go and fight her brother?"

He put his stein down. It was empty, and I signaled the Fristle fifi nearest with a replacement. As the ale was poured Tom the Nose picked his teeth, reflecting. He looked just a little puzzled.

"Well—she was there, on the high platform when we formed ranks. Most of the talking was done by King Vodun Alloran and his Kapt-Crebent, a great noble who had been cheated of his estates and inheritance by this Prescot."

Patiently, now, stalking the meanings like a leem, I said: "Oh? Who was that, then?"

"A great noble called Zankov."

So it all began to fit into place...

"Zankov? Just that? Nobles usually have a long string of names—"

"Of course! But he called himself that until he'd won back his rightful titles from this Dray Prescot."

No true paktun was going to get fuddled on three or four steins of ale in the mid afternoon. Tom the Nose was prepared to talk on while I bought the drinks. There was little more he had to say on these scores that burned so painfully in my brain. I decided that I'd better go and see Naghan Raerdu, Drak's spy, and sort something out of this mess.

As I say, Tom Poll the Nose had little more to say until, as I was rising to leave, he looked up.

"You ought to change your mind. There will be good pickings in Vallia, although we of the Corrundum Korfs always respect the proprieties in these matters. We do not go in for wholesale rapine and slaughter against the ordinary folk. It's these nobles and emperors who cause the trouble—"

"You are indisputably right there, dom."

"Well, come with us. Anyway, whether what the great Zankov says is right or wrong, and whether or not the Princess Dayra told him or not is all beside the point." He suddenly looked fierce, his bountiful nose quivering with a new menace, quite without mirth. "I lost my mother and father when I was a youngster, and I never knew my grandparents. But I wish I had. Any person ought to respect their parents and grandparents."

"Agreed—"

"This Dray Prescot, Emperor of Vallia—d'you know how he got to be emperor? Why, dom, I'll tell you. He murdered the old emperor. He killed the Princess Dayra's grandfather. D'you wonder she wants to be revenged?"

I tottered out.

This was so new, so shattering, so—

I came to my senses wandering along the Street of a Thousand Clepsy-dras. People looked at me and then walked on swiftly. I'd been very fortunate not to have been taken up.

The Suns of Scorpio were very low, streaming their mingled radiance along the street and turning everything into a golden-tinged glory of amber, jade and ruby.

The taste in my mouth was of ashes, and dung heaps.

By the time I reached the Zhantil Palace the Suns were gone. I did not feel hungry, just empty.

Then I said to myself: By Zair! So I am Dray Prescot, Emperor of Vallia, for my sins. I was fetched to be the confounded emperor and I've tried to do a decent job and have the place in a reasonable state for Drak. All right! It's this bastard Zankov—the man who really murdered the old emperor—who's poisoned Dayra's mind against me. Quite apart from my absence on Earth which she blames on me—rightly enough, given her under-standing. That, I thought, was settled when she refused to strike when she might have done. I marched up toward the gate with the little sentry boxes, and the two guards stiffened up into columns of iron. What my face must have been like, Zair alone knows. Right, I said to myself as I marched on through. Right. That does it. I'll settle Zankov's hash and tell Dayra the truth—when I can find the girl—and she'll believe me. Oh, yes, she'll believe me.

With that high-sounding and exceedingly hollow promise to myself, I went in to seek Naghan Raerdu.

"Sink me!" I said to myself as I marched along the palace corridors. "When Pompino gets back what am I to say to him when he asks me what I've been doing all day?"

I had the nastiest of suspicions that Pompino and Framco would return without Tilda. This was just a hunch, of course, and depended on no cere-bral deductive efforts on my part. They might catch up with Twayne Gullik; they might not. Tilda might be with the Ift; she might not. All I could do was repair my fences by questioning Naghan Raerdu.

I found him superintending the broaching of barrels for the evening. He was fussy, for where ale was concerned Naghan was a connoisseur. The ripe smells in the cellars, the tang of dust, the gonging notes as the slaves worked, the lively feeling of the slaves all served to rouse me. Naghan Raerdu was of Vallia, a good man, and he had abjured slavery. Forced to conform to the customs of another country, he did what I hoped any mod-ern Vallian would do. The slaves were well treated and they knew that this job, broaching ale barrels and bringing supplies up to the mess halls and dining rooms of the palace, would hold plenty of perks. They'd get a skin-ful tonight, or they weren't smart know-it-all slaves!

"Jak."

"Naghan."

"You look—if you will pardon my saying so—mind that spigot, Olan the Fumble-Fingered!—as though you have had bad news. I trust I am mistaken—hammer it in soundly, you great fambly, Nodgen Nog-Ears!—for your new comrades and the cadade have not returned nor sent a message."

"It does not concern them, Naghan. I must talk to you—"

"Assuredly, assuredly, Jak—tilt the bucket, you enormous heap of famblys!—catch the ale, the wonderful ale!"

Froth spilled across the stone floor. Naghan did not go down on his knees and lap up the spilled beer; he might well have done and no one feel surprise. He had proved loyal and wise during the affair at the Headless Zorcaman. I felt he could be trusted; that was not the reason I wished to talk to him.

Presently, the barrel chuckling itself empty into the procession of carrying buckets, Naghan could devote all his attention to me.

I gave it to him straight.

"Says you murdered the old emperor, does she? H'mm..." Here Naghan pulled a face. "One can well see why she hates you."

"I intend to take this Zankov by the neck and choke the truth out of him, so that the Princess Dayra makes no further mistake."

"A highly desirable ambition, Jak, if uncomfortable for Zankov."

"You never saw him?"

"No."

"A pity. Still, you'll recognize him—"

Naghan Raerdu had kept half an eye on his slaves as they carried the ale away. Now he turned to face me.

"He's here, in Port Marsilus?"

"Probably. That is what I want you to find out."

"That, of course, I can do."

I told him what I'd been doing and he nodded, and the tears squeezed out from under his closed lids. "They'll take their fine fancy new army across and the Prince Majister will whip 'em, like he did last time."

"This fellow, Tom the Nose, and he seemed your decent paktun, was mighty confident."

"Name me a recruiting Deldar who isn't."

"You were Relianchun of the Phalanx, Naghan. We don't employ mercenaries in Vallia. I am confident that Drak will whip 'em; but it's up to us to do what we can to help him before this damned army even steps ashore in Vallia. It would be a beautiful thing if they never did so."

"Your son, Prince Drak, saw them off at the Battle of Corvamsmot. He will do so again, if we can't prevent the army sailing." He looked around; we were not overheard, all the same, he leaned closer. "Majister! Brace up, brassud! You give me a queasy in the inward parts."

Naghan Raerdu and I were old campaigners; I took no offense. Rather, I felt a quick spurt of gratitude to this short chunky barrel of a fellow with his red face and his blob of gristle for a nose. By Zair! I was not acting like your high and mighty emperor—which I was not, anyway—and I had to get the future into perspective. My own personal problems had, as always, to be pushed aside to serve greater ends.

"You're right, Naghan, by Vox. You find Zankov for me and I'll try to put things right with the Princess Dayra. Also, there is the kovneva Tilda to worry me—"

"Us."

"Yes, Naghan. If we Vallians can't stick together, then the whole wide world of Kregen will tumble down."

"My people," said Naghan, and I did not inquire what he meant. Any good spy will set up an apparat as soon as he can, and it was clear that Naghan had recruited people to go about spying for him. In all probability many of them just didn't realize what they were doing for this happy laughing merry fellow who was so lavish with ale and gold. "They report the city has seen more Ifts than usual recently. I do not wish to sound negative or pessimistic; but I fear the party of Ifts and the three wagons your friends chased after do not carry the kovneva Tilda with them."

"You do not surprise me. I felt that in my bones."

"I am having inquiries prosecuted."

You had to laugh when Naghan Raerdu said that. He was so unlike the chief spymaster of Vallia, Naghan Vanki. I'd set up my own inner circle of espionage, independently of Naghan Vanki, not because I mistrusted the spy chief but because I wished to have my own sources of information. The thought made me say: "What are Naghan Vanki's people up to here?"

His laugh was a wonderful phenomenon of nature; his cheeks glistened, red as Zim, his closed lids sprayed tears. He spluttered. At last he said: "They poke and pry. One of 'em—Nath the Long—signed up with the army and they put him to peeling momolams—the great fambly. Another of 'em, Ortyg the Sko-handed, broke into the Headquarters building at night and only got away with half his trousers missing. I tell you, Jak, Naghan Vanki, for all he is a clever spymaster, needs better folk to serve him. At least, by Vox, here!"

From this it was perfectly apparent that Naghan Raerdu had a source of information within the Official Vallian spy network in Bormark. This seemed to me eminently satisfactory. I just hoped Naghan Vanki never got to find out. Loyal to Vallia, he was a dry master at his craft with whom I'd had a few run-ins before now...

An under-chamberlain clad in his fussy flunkey robes came in looking all hot and bothered.

"Naghan Raerdu!" he called. "You are to be blamed! You must keep a tighter control on the slaves, who are fit only to be beaten."

"Now what?"

"Two of them are rolling down the half-stairs, drunk as kovs. And they spilled the buckets—"

"Pandrite rot all!" yelped Naghan. "There's no harm in a few slaves getting a bellyful of ale like any honest fellow. But when it comes to spilling the precious fluid—" He scuttled off on his waddling legs, scarlet and snorting, and I took myself off, mightily cheered despite all.

Naghan did not work for the palace; he supplied ale and superintended its initial distribution. The under-chamberlain would no doubt get the rough edge of Constanchoin's tongue when the grand chamberlain recovered. Who would have to pay for the spilled ale would most certainly prove an enjoyable exercise in argument and legal debate.

Suddenly discovering I had an appetite, I headed for the mess hall. The place would be practically empty; that would not worry me.

At the end of a cross corridor a woman stood looking down as I approached.

My way lay off to the right. At the time, just why I looked at her with such sudden interest did not register. I just looked. She stood completely still and composed. She wore a long pale blue gown that reached to a circle around her feet. Her hair shone a glimmering auburn. Her hands were folded before her, half-hidden in the full sleeves of the pale blue robe. Her head was bent down, shielding her face, so that I had only a suggestion of a small nose and high cheekbones. I walked on and a hurrying slave passed, getting out of the way, in the natural reflex of his daily life, and when I looked back the woman in blue had vanished.

Thinking no more, my thoughts on a choice vosk pie, or perhaps a prime cut of ordel steak, I hurried on toward the mess hall.

Just before I entered I saw the woman in the blue robe again. She stood in exactly the same posture, fixed and unmoving, her auburn hair a bronze shimmer in the lantern light. As I looked she shimmered, wavered, vanished. I blinked.

One of Framco's guards, hurrying to get to his evening meal, almost collided with me as I hauled up.

He started to swear, saw who I was, and apologized.

I said, "Did you see that woman? In the blue robe?"

"Yes," he said. "She went into the mess hall. I wouldn't mind making her acquaintance."

He went on and I followed. The woman had vanished, it seemed to me, far too quickly to admit of a normal method of going into the hall. Maybe I'd missed something, maybe I'd blinked at the wrong time. All the same, as I went in to find a seat I reflected that the woman in the pale blue robe had taken herself off mightily fast. Mighty fast!

Also—she was nowhere in the mess hall I could see...

The meal turned out to be Leavings Pie, and none too savory leavings at that. Raerdu's ale was on the table, fine and frothing, and after a single jugful I pushed the plate of Leavings Pie away and stood up. It would be a tavern and a lash-up meal for me, this night.

The clothes I'd worn all day could do with a change, and once more I plundered Pando's wardrobe. This time my outfit was of the refined yet adventurous sort a young blood might wear when he went on the town. If they had anywhere here in Port Marsilus to compare with Ruathytu's Sacred Quarter, then I was dressed for the part.

The color combinations of gray and green and blue were entirely conventional. The puttah over my left shoulder in a base of apple green reeked of gold wire and embroidery. Gold and silver embellishments smothered the rest of the outfit. The low boots were soft-leather engraved and encrusted with gold, almost as fine as the leatherwork of Magdag. My hat, very dark gray, sported a dark blue feather in its jeweled clasp. Knowing Pando's fortunes I wondered if the jewels were superior fakes; they looked genuine but I did not test them. I felt this would demean Pando and me—foolish fellow!

With this fandango of clothing draping me I ambled off to the city. If you wonder that I thus fabulated myself in phantasmagorical clothes—well, I'd done it before and was to do it again. I looked your true fop, me, who was far more used to swinging along in a scarlet breechclout wielding a two-handed Krozair longsword!

Finding a slap-up meal—that cost the better part of a golden deldy—in the Paline and Brunestaff, I washed it down with a miserly allowance of ale. When I shifted onto wine I needed to remain crystal clear. The Paline and Brunestaff was a superior establishment. Most of the patrons were senior officers of the military services. That was why I had chosen it. I tended to stick out like a coy in the arena's kaidur pairs.

Striking up conversations was easy enough, particularly when the wine went around; discovering anything of moment was quite another venture. I found out nothing. No veiled hints, no cautious questions, elicited what I wanted to know. They started singing when the Twins rose in the night sky to shed gold and rosy light upon the cobbled street outside. The lanterns inside the tavern swamped that moonshine outside. They began singing with a Pandahem ditty: "The Song of Patoc Punji the Neemu."

I didn't mind that. It starts: "When I was a lad in jolly old Panj, my life it was a bore-o. Then I went for a paktun to be, and made my name in the war-o." This is, as you will readily perceive, a poor translation; but it conveys something of the original. Patoc Punji went on his expeditions, performing incredible feats, rising from the rank of Patoc to that of Deldar, and thence to Hikdar, and—in some versions—to Jiktar before—horror!— he got himself into trouble with the lord's lady, and found himself busted back down to Patoc again.

So, as I say, I sang along with the rest, trying to think I was accomplishing something, anything, of help to my quest. Then they started up on "The Swingeon of Drak the Devil."

The tune was a famous old tune of Vallia. The words were, apart from being obscene, grossly contemptuous of Vallia. So I went out, fuming, helpless, and ready to go back to bed.

You could in all honesty say that the Emperor of Vallia had been bested by a song. The way I felt...

The troubling factor was that Pandahem ought to have been in alliance with Vallia, since Vallia had been instrumental in flinging out the hated Hamalese conquerors. I'd had some of this stupid nationalistic intolerance in Hamal. By Vox, I said to myself, I'll have a few sharp questions for Pando when he gets here.

So, feeling I'd accomplished nothing and found out unwelcome facts, a day not so much wasted as unwanted, I crawled back to the Zhantil Palace.

Twelve

Of the Pied Piper of Port Marsilus

The next morning I awoke and rolled over and groaned. One of the fancy tooled leather boots lay in a corner of the barracks and the other halfway along the side wall where I'd hurled them the night before. I went along to Pando's apartments and routed out a somber kit of grays and blues, and then trundled into the mess hall where the morning porridge was not laced with red honey, and the bread was stale, the palines wilting and the tea weak. Disgruntled, I ambled along to see Naghan Raerdu.

Here was I wasting my time on bad commons, doing nothing, only finding out unwelcome facts, when my comrades were out no doubt having exciting adventures chasing rogues through the forests.

As I walked along the corridor toward Naghan's cellar entrance a slave girl undulated up to me. She wore a gray slave breechclout and her feet were bare; but she had a flower in her hair, which was combed, and a string of beads around her neck. She pouted up most artfully, and—I swear it!—fluttered her eyelashes.

"Horter Jak—"

"Well?"

"My master requests you see him at once."

"He does, does he," I said, most weakly. "And who may your master be?"

"Why, the Alemaster, of course, master."

"Lead on, for that is where I am going."

She led me past the cellar door and through a curtained archway into a narrow room where on shelves along one wall row after row of crystal bottles caught the morning sunlight through a high window. Apple green and palely pink, that morning light of the twin suns, Zim and Genodras. They were called that quite often in North Pandahem, for the culture of the island is split between north and south. Down in South Pandahem Zim and Genodras were often called Far and Havil. One pair of the most common Pandahem names for the Suns is Panronium and Panigium; one heard them sometimes from the older folk.

Naghan Raerdu was carefully siphoning a deep orange liquid from one crystal flask into a retort. He looked up, nodded a cheerful good morning, and finished off his task.

Then he said: "Thank you, Saffi. Now run along and find me a nice loaf of bread and a piece of Loguetter. I am famished."

The slave girl, Saffi, nodded and ran off instantly. She was an impish thing, with smoothly rounded shoulders, and a swing to her hips. I fancied Naghan would manumit her in Pandahem terms the moment this assignment was through.

He looked out of the door, closed it almost shut and stood so that he could see through the slit if anyone should come by. Over his shoulder, he said: "I have certain news that Strom Murgon Marsilus will reach the city today."

I felt disappointment.

Then I said: "I was hoping Kov Pando would be here first."

"My source was imprecise. She seemed to think the young kov was on his way. She said that the king was much displeased with him."

"Now that is a disappointment. I had cherished a thought the king was dead, burned up in his palace."

"That is why he bears so heavily on Kov Pando. He blames him for the fire."

"As I said, Naghan, my comrades set that fire in the temple of Lem the Silver Leem that was underneath the king's palace. When I find the temples here, we will burn those also."

"Praise be to Opaz. There is no word on the Ifts."

"If Pando is in trouble with the king," I said, fretfully, I admit, "that will heap more problems on his shoulders. I just hope his mother Tilda is found before he arrives."

"That ninny Trandor the Broad, who claims to have been an archer before his fingers were chopped off, is headed this way. He will gossip, mark me. Can you meet me in the Awkward Swod at the hour of mid? It is in the Kyro of the Sword. I have ale to deliver there."

"Yes. Any reason?"

"I hope to have intelligence of Zankov by then— Hai, Trandor, you old soak! Come to cadge a few mouthfuls, have you?"

Trandor the Broad smiled and grimaced, a lowly servitor in the palace and not a slave. He possessed only the thumb and little finger of his right hand. A barbarous practice, that, reminiscent of the Hundred Years War on this Earth. Some nations fear bowmen above all else.

I walked off with a polite word to Trandor and a mock thank you to Naghan for wares I had not sampled, and so trundled off to find a decent breakfast. This accomplished at a little stall in one of the side streets off the main Avenue of Triumph, I thought that I had a few burs to go before meeting Naghan. In that time I might redeem myself in my own eyes.

Depressingly enough, there were plenty and to spare of folk walking about sporting the brown and silver favors.

With so many Leem Lovers openly flaunting their allegiance, even if only the cognoscenti—in their estimation—would recognize and understand, there shouldn't be too much difficulty in finding one of their Opaz-forsaken temples. I followed a few Brown and Silvers, and the more I went about Pando's Port Marsilus the more I was dismayed. The place seemed alive with the evil cult. At last I selected a place that had once been a theater of some kind and was now in ruins. The door looked solid enough and the loungers outside lounged with a purpose. All were armed. There were at least a dozen. I wondered if news that their temples were being burned had reached the cultists here.

Down a side street and around the back I went, and found three fellows talking on the corner. The back of the theater had been propped up at some time; but the walls looked perilous. These were just the sort of premises the cult might choose. I sauntered up to the three. All wore the little silver leem and the tuft of brown feathers.

They didn't waste time.

"Shove off, dom. Move along!"

"But," I said, in a high falsetto. "I only wanted—"

"You'll get a smashed skull. *Schtump!*"

So I, instead of schtumping, leaped for them.

I drew two-handed and used the hilts on them. They went to sleep peaceably enough, one, two, three, ob, dwa, so.

Their limp forms had to be dragged into the rubble out of sight. This I did. I confess I was drawn on. I'd intended merely to scout this place; but one thing led to another, and, well, I penetrated past the outer ruined wall and so came across a fine new wall, built of baked brick, with a new door of lenk, bronze bound. This opened to a touch. All beyond lay swathed in darkness but for a distant ruby wink of light. So, in I went. There was no excuse. I chafed for something to do after the days of relative inaction. What Pompino would say I didn't care to dwell on.

The ruby light from a lantern illuminated a turn in the corridor. At the far end another door tempted me. I tried to tell myself to turn around. Quite clearly, this *was* a temple to the Silver Leem. Ergo, return, fetch up Pompino and a gang of our lads, and deal with the foul place. But, on I went, like any onker.

The door led into a maze of alleyways and storerooms, mostly disused, at the back of the building. As I cautiously worked my way forward I was sorting out the combustibles in my mind, seeing what would burn easily and what might need a little encouragement.

The sound of crying drew me to a small door with a single opening, iron-barred. Very quietly, I looked in.

The room was jam-packed with little girls. Children, not above six years old, I'd guess, most of them naked but a few with dingy scraps of cloth around their waists, they lay supine or huddled in fetal positions, they ran about screaming, they fought each other, they added to the filth of the room. They were all gargoyles of mud and dirt, as though just dragged in from the gutters. You could carve a slice of the smell and serve it out on a plate.

Down at the far end of the room an opening door made me duck down until only my eyes showed above the iron-barred grille. A woman wearing a yellow smock and gloves walked in. She just hoicked up the nearest child, swung her over her hip in a most professional fashion, and walked out.

The door was solid, iron-studded, and I wasn't going to break it down in a month of the Maiden with the Many Smiles. That child had been taken off—for sacrifice, for torture, perhaps just for experiments, training in how to chop up a baby girl. There had to be a way around to the back through the maze of corridors. I started off, hurrying...

For the sake of the person concerned, it was fortunate that I bumped into no one on that crazy rushing progress through the dusty ill-smelling rooms and corridors.

Evidently, the front of the abandoned theater had been turned into the temple, and all these backstage areas used only occasionally or never. Keeping my bearings and twisting through the twisting corridors I hurried on and so came into a small foyer-like place with double-doors to my right. These were bolted on the inside. Faintly—very faintly—from outside came the sound of animals' hooves and the grinding rattle of wheels. Ahead a door with a glass panel gave ingress to a chamber I felt reasonably confident must lie at the opposite end of the room of children. Only a fellow in a yellow apron tried to stop me and I put him to sleep, with some care, and looked around.

An opening to the side glowed with orange light. From there came the sound of cries, and splashings, and the tinkle of running water. I stuck my head around the edge of bricks framing the opening.

The woman I'd seen take the child out was bending over a bathtub. The child in the tub, yelling blue murder, was being given a thorough, a rough, a very hard bath. There was soap in the girl's eyes; that was for sure.

Rows of white dresses hung from a line of pegs. On a side table stood an open box bulging with candies.

I knew this set-up of old.

There was even a cabinet full of pretty satin ribbons.

I took the woman by her yellow clad shoulder and turned her around. She did not hesitate. She tried to hit me with the soaped scrubbing brush.

That powerful instrument went flying. I looked at her.

"You are a dead woman if you make a commotion."

She stared back, flushed, her brown hair in rat-tails over her sweaty forehead, her forearms hot-water pink. She had that hard, institutional look about her, perennially harassed, suspicious, always on the lookout for number one and ways to beat the system.

The child was rubbing her eyes and bawling.

Soap flew. I shook the woman. "You have stolen these children from their mothers. Is that any work for a woman?"

She spat back at me. "They are not stolen! Each one has been paid for—"

"Aye," I said. "Aye, paid for by a silken dress and gold coin."

"The bargain was just. The guards will cut you into very small pieces—"

"As small as you would cut these girls into?"

"You do not understand." She wasn't afraid. She was just impatient that some boorish buffoon had happened along to interfere with her work. No doubt she had to get a certain number of the children ready in time.

Now I faced a quandary of some magnitude. Just how many girl children there were I could only guess; certainly no less than twenty-five and probably as many as forty. By Krun! What a mess!

"What do you want?" The lines around her mouth showed a pinched look. "I must bathe ten girls—"

"You will not be bathing anymore, I think, for what you intend. They will be bathed, in love and care; but not by you or any of your-harridan crew."

She sneered, and—despite all—you had to acknowledge her courage. "What can you do? Let them all go into the street? Don't you think the guards will be here soon?"

So, feeling the idiocy of the bravado, I had to say: "Let them come. They can all die if they choose."

Tired of this fruitless wrangling I hoisted her upside down and shook, and among a cascade of oddments out fell the keys. I upended her and dumped her down, hoicked the child out of the bath, not without a soapy chubby finger whistling perilously close to my eye, and heaved the woman in.

Her knees stuck up past her nose.

"Stay there. If you cry out, or try to run off, you are most certainly a dead woman."

"There is no need to call or run for the guards."

With those ominous words floating behind me I ran to the door, opened it and then surveyed the appalling sight within. If you imagine an ant's nest, disturbed... Well...

Not having a pipe handy I'd not be able to play the Pied Piper. But some device had to be discovered to organize the girls, just for the time it would take to get them out—of course! I scuttled back, ripped out the box of candies and nipped back to the door. I held up a sweet and threw it to the nearest girl. The one I'd taken from the bath hung onto my legs, and bellowed: "Banje! Banje!"

"Here," I said, and gave her a sweet.

The others caught on quickly. I backed off. By Zair! What an unnerving sight! A host of unwashed naked girl children, all screaming and howling and rushing down on me demanding candies! I just fled.

I did not drop a single sweet until we were at the bolted double doors leading outside. Here I gulped a breath, said a prayer to Zair, and unbolted.

In those few seconds the girls reached me and were all over me, clawing at the candy box. I put my foot against the door, closing it. I seized up the girl from the bath, who was chewing her sweet with dedication and demanding more.

"What is your name?"

At last, she mumbled out something that sounded like: "Lobbi."

"Look, Lobbi—over there. Wouldn't you like a nice new dress? And a pretty ribbon?"

She was off like a woflo after cheese.

The other girls saw, and between grabbing candies from the spilled box and plundering the dresses, they resembled the ladies—and gents—on opening day of the January sales.

By the time each girl, grubby as she was, had struggled into a dress— and, by Krun, half of them didn't fit—I felt it was past time for the guards to appear.

The double-doors opened easily enough. The Suns said it was almost to the hour of mid. Naghan Raerdu would have to wait. We trooped outside, and I went last, and then, late but deadly with their swords and spears, the guards rushed after us.

The woman bath attendant led them, the soap suds still glistening on her yellow smock.

"There he is!" she screeched. "The vile Lem defiler! Kill him!"

Thirteen

The Little Sisters of Impurity

There were only six guards, and I felt I could handle them, allowing always for my caveat that one day, apart from Mefto the Kazzur, I'll meet a better swordsman. There was no time for fancy work. The children were out on the street, gawping, some still crying and huddling, but enough of them wandering off. Those loungers on the corner, who lounged with purpose, should not be allowed to see their sacrifices wandering off...

So it was a case of skip and jump, of duck and bash.

"Take that, you tapo!" screeched the first, a fine big Rapa with bright yellow feathers around his beak. I took the flung spear from the air and almost in the instant he cast it it returned embedded in his chest. The woman screamed and urged them on, getting in the way. The next two, Rapas both, seeing what had happened to the first bore in with their spears at the port and a few quick and meaty thwunks had to be dealt to see them off. One fell awkwardly, breaking his spear which jammed in alongside his body, point up.

The next three, the final three, came on together. They wielded swords. Two foined—a waste of time in a bashing match of this description—and went down and the last faced me, his thraxter held in a professional fighting man's grip.

The woman pushed him on, shrieking: "Get on, Nodgen, get on and spit him!"

He gave her an impatient thrust of his free hand, clearing her out of his way.

"Stand back, Mitli, stand back—"

She tripped on a body and fell helplessly. The point of the upright spear pierced her through. Even as this fellow Nodgen, who was a bit of a swordsman, yelled and charged again, I saw the bright blood leap from the woman Mitli's mouth.

"Stand and fight, you tapo! By the Blade of Kurin, you are for the chop now!"

He was very good for a mercenary, not a paktun, hired out as your ordinary kreutzin, a light infantryman. He wanted to fight as he had always fought, sword against sword, and to him the victory.

There was no time for that.

I took him with a nasty little trick that left his thraxter twirled up with my main gauche while my rapier went stick-plink through his throat above the brass rim of his leathers. He choked and dropped.

Instantly, the bloodstained blades naked in my fists, I had to hare off to round up the wandering children.

Controlling their direction, I found, could best be accomplished by shouting: "Naje! Candies!" to them, and shooing them along. Only when we'd crossed that street and were well down the next could I afford to relax a little. A couple of folk hurried past, avoiding us. They were gauffrers, with flat hats pulled well down over their rodent-like faces, minding their own business. City folk, gauffrers, suspicious of trees and grasslands, making their varied livings out of city customs.

The half-imbecilic face I'd put on to assuage any fears my ugly old beakhead might inspire in the children did little to reassure the gauffrers. The bloodstained weapons in my hands... Well, on Kregen that sight is not as infrequent as it ought to be. Carefully wiping the blades on an inside flap of the little cape I wore, I thrust them back into their scabbards. A matched pair I'd received as a gift from Captain Nath Periklain aboard *Schydan Imperial*, they ought not to be maltreated. Then we set off on the next stage of this Hamelin-like progress.

This crocodile of girl children could be taken down to the docks to join the other children we had rescued aboard *Tuscurs Maiden*. What Captain Linson would say almost made me decide to do just that. They could be taken back to the palace. Wherever they went, they and I would attract attention and the spies from the Leem Lovers would smell us out. Wherever we went we'd bring grief with us...

That meant *Tuscurs Maiden* was out of the reckoning. The girls would have to go along to the Zhantil Palace. It was high time that young rip Pando took the running of his kovnate seriously. If he faced grief from the adherents of Lem the Silver Leem, that might make him shake himself up. If he still pretended to be a member, maybe he could get away with that. Either way, I wanted to unload this pathetic collection of human and juvenile detritus—for that is what the girls would be in the eyes of most folk in Port Marsilus—and get on with the job. For a start—Pompino would gape at me when I told him of this damned adventure, and say: "By Horato the Potent, Jak! And you didn't burn the temple down!"

Huh, I said to myself, he should've been there!

The chances remain problematical whether or not I might have shepherded the girls all the way safely to the palace. We passed along the street before the low-doorwayed entrance of a building of slate roofs and many small windows. Few people walked the streets this close to the hour of mid. Over the doorway which crouched bowered in Moonblooms a sign showed up in weathered gold leaf. The gold leaf was a reminder of past glories.

The sign said, simply: "If you are of impure heart you are welcome, stranger, for purity exists only with the Dahemin."

Without pulling the bell cord I pushed the low door open and we all trooped through into a flower-bowered courtyard. The Dahemin, the twins, the god Dahemo and the goddess Dahema, had fallen out of favor when the green religion of Havil was new. The pious women here, the Sisters of Impurity, kept up the old mysteries and beliefs. I felt I could appeal to them for help. If I could not, there was nowhere else as far as I knew in all the city.

The Sisters oohed and aahed over the children and, fluffing clear yellow kerchiefs around their noses, led the girls off to be bathed. This bathing would be of an entirely different order from that in the Silver Leem's temple. The Mother Superior—to give a bowdlerized form of her title—made me sit down to a glass of parclear and a plate of miscils. As the tiny cakes melted on my tongue she asked me and I told her. I told her that the adherents of Lem the Silver Leem would seek out the whereabouts of the girls to take them back for sacrifice. I did not expect her to keep them here in her house of seclusion. I did not tell her where I intended to take them.

She said her name was Mistress Mire. She was not old, clad in a severe gray gown with a rope girdle and bare feet, a flap of gray cloth over her hair, which shone most beautifully. The Little Sisters of Impurity ministered to any who sought their services, and the small charges they made sustained them in their frugal way of life. I refused to pass any judgments.

Pompino's gold spilled out of the purse onto the table between us. I'd take up a loan from Pando next, if necessary. Sister Mire smiled her sweet smile.

"We can offer you a refreshing personal service—"

"I am in need of keeping an appointment, sister. I hope I do not offend by this refusal?"

"When you feel the imperfections of the spirit and the flesh, you will call on us. We are here to minister to your needs in the supernal name of the Dahemin, man and woman both."

"Quite. I give you thanks. I will make arrangements to collect the children later when the Suns have gone."

There was clear disappointment on her face. No doubt she was hoping I'd just leave the girls and clear off. They'd make a capital addition to her house of seclusion when they were a few seasons older.

When I left I started to make the rote farewell along with the remberees—"May Pandrite have you in his keeping." I halted myself. These women followed a religion old before the religion of Havil, which here in Pandahem had been materially supplanted by that of Pandrite. She might have considered that I blasphemed her. In impurity are all hearts as one.

As they say in the inner sea, the Eye of the World: "Only Zair knows the cleanliness of a human heart."

Bidding Mistress Mire remberee I hurried off to the Awkward Swod, keeping a sharp lookout. Naghan was still waiting. He'd secured a side table under a wide black beam, and ale stood upon that table, and a meal which, covered, was still edible.

"Trouble, Jak?"

Eating, I told him. "I'll have to arrange tonight to—"

He lifted a hand. "Leave all that to me."

"My thanks."

"It is now certain that Kov Pando follows Strom Murgon as fast as he can. It is said that when they meet one will die."

Naghan would have messages carried by relays of merfluts, or possibly some other form of Kregan homing pigeon. Merfluts are exceptionally fast and reliable.

"And Pompino is not back yet, I'll warrant."

"He is not."

"And no message from him?"

"None I'm privy to."

I didn't say that if Naghan Raerdu knew of no message it was certain sure no message existed. But that was so near the truth as to convince me Pompino had sent no message. Or, rather, no message had been received at the Zhantil Palace.

He drank and then said: "I must tell you that this morning someone unknown burned down the Vallian embassy here."

Quelling my annoyance was not difficult; after all, with the temper of this place it was a wonder they hadn't burned our embassy before this. I said: "Was anyone hurt?"

"No, thankfully enough. The ambassador sought refuge in the palace. It adds another complication."

"Too right it does, by Chusto! I don't want him catching sight of me up there."

"Strazab Larghos ti Therminsax knows you well enough, I'd think, seeing he received the title of Strazab at your hands."

One of the Vallian diplomatic corps, Larghos ti Therminsax was an earnest, serious man who, loyal in the Times of Troubles, had made a career in the diplomatic. As a strazab, an imperial creation on a level with a strom in the regular nobility, he was of the right rank to be ambassador to Bormark. In fact, ambassadorial status was high for a mere kovnate within a kingdom, and that was because of my personal feelings regarding Pando. I frowned. I'd been using the Zhantil palace as a base; I didn't really fancy poking around to find a new.

With a squeezing shut of his eyes and a copious flow of merry tears,

Naghan said: "It may be that Strazab Larghos will happily return to Vallia. If it is suggested."

In rather too sour a voice, I said: "Well, you can't suggest it to him, and neither can I."

Naghan Raerdu was not discomfited.

"I will go down to see Captain Linson and have a messenger return with word from Vallia. It can be arranged. Strazab Larghos can be recalled."

"H'm. It might work. Although Linson's a stickler, and you'll have to cross his palm with gold, not silver. And that reminds me. I paid all the gold I had to the Little Sisters of Impurity—"

Naghan Raerdu laughed so much he almost choked.

"—so, my friend, I shall crop your ears for a loan."

"Done, Jak, done!"

If Strazab Larghos believed a Pandahem argenter brought the signal for his recall from Vallia, it would be a wonder. But honest and loyal though he was, he'd be in the frame of mind for a recall. Then I expounded my scheme to Naghan, and he listened, growing grave, although every now and then whetting the throstle with a glug or two.

At one point he said: "I refrained from setting anyone onto keeping an observation on you. I surmised you would object."

"I'd have been glad of some help when those poor girl children were running about all over the street, I can tell you!"

"Just so. The riding animal is easily obtained—a totrix, or hersany—?"

"No. A freymul, I think, the poor man's zorca. That will suit the style."

"You'll see to providing the robes and badge yourself?"

"Oh, aye," I said. "I'll see to that."

"Until you spoke so freely to me I had taken little interest in this Lem thing. There has been little time. But I fancy, with some help from Opaz, that I can insinuate a fellow into—"

I looked sternly at this unlikely-looking secret agent.

"I caution you most strongly, Naghan. The Leem Lovers have their rigmaroles of secret signs and passwords. If you try to put any poor fellow in without sure knowledge, he's done for."

He rubbed a finger around his blobby gristle nose.

"I believe I have paid good red gold to just such a one. A little questioning more, a little suggestion—and the fellow has a girl, too. She might be the more useful."

"Just don't get good people killed on my behalf."

We were sitting comfortably in a tavern, the Awkward Swod, and drinking and eating and taking our ease, and we plotted dark doings and nefarious expeditions. What we decided could cause many deaths, could cause riots and conflagrations, and not always to the evil ones of the world. We had to step with great caution.

Naghan said: "Just in case, then. Tipp the Kaktu. Monsi the Bosom."

"I'll remember."

As I may have remarked before, a number of times, if you want to stay alive and in one piece on Kregen you have to remember names.

"My information contains nothing on Zankov, Jak."

"Confound it! By Chusto! I was hoping—still, no matter. He'll turn up like a hole in your sandal."

"Strom Murgon will be coming in through the west gate. The Inward Gate is not grand enough for him, it seems."

"As they say in a place I know—when the chavnik's away the woflo will play."

"I'll meet you there in three burs."

"Capital."

Naghan rose on his stumpy legs, puffing, finishing the last of his ale. He plunked the jug down, lifted his purse and unlatched it and thunked it down on the table. I picked it up. It weighed.

"My thanks, Naghan."

His laugh was a marvel of compression and of explosion. The one of his eyelids, the other his tears.

"You paid it to me, Jak, you paid it to me."

"Aye. And you'll have it all returned, with interest. I'll see you at the west gate in three burs."

On that, with the remberees, we parted.

Going out of the Awkward Swod into the streaming mingled radiance of the Suns of Scorpio, two thoughts made me reflect that, one, it was a grand comfort to a fellow to have loyal helpmates, and, two, it was just as well that Pompino the Iarvin was still not with me. By Krun! I'd have had one hell of a job keeping his itchy fingers off a tinderbox!

Fourteen

Strom Murgon puts on a show

Pando's chief city of Port Marsilus was set into a cup-shaped indentation of the coastline on the western edge of the Bay of Panderk. Consequently, the north and eastern sides were washed by the sea, and the southern flank, being walled off by a ridge of ground the locals called the Spine of Lhorcas, the road wound in and around this ridge and so fetched up with the main gate of the city, the west gate.

There were other gates; but I fancied, along with the judgment of Naghan Raerdu, that Strom Murgon would choose to ride in through the chief gate of the city.

Murgon Marsilus, Strom of Ribenor, cousin to the Kov of Bormark, stood no nonsense from anyone. A powerful man, dark of temper, an adherent of Lem the Silver Leem, he was not content to lord it over his little stromnate within the kovnate; he lusted after greater power.

If Pando was in trouble with King Nemo—and why hadn't he burned up with his damned palace?—Murgon would step forth more openly in his ambitious designs.

They both craved this Dafni girl to increase their domains and power. When two men want the same girl, and the girl has a mind of her own, empires may totter and fall. I did not know how much credence to put in Tilda's words when she'd told me that Dafni Harlstam had settled on Murgon and then Pando had happened along to upset the arrangements. If he had, it could mean that Dafni Harlstam herself had wanted that. Otherwise Pando's suit would have fallen.

But, then, he was a kov. Dafni was a vadni, and her vadvarate of Tenpanam marched border for border with Pando's lands. It was a coil. Maybe I'd have to wring the answers from each of them in turn. As to why it concerned me, that was obvious. One, Pando was a friend. Two, I was the Emperor of Vallia. And, if you cared to admit it, Three, we hadn't much liked Murgon Marsilus, even though he had put himself in jeopardy to rescue us from a scrape.

He'd done that because he thought Pompino and I were adherents of Lem the Silver Leem.

Three burs exactly saw Naghan Raerdu trot gently up in the shadows of the west wall. He rode a freymul and he led another on a headrope. Both animals were fine examples of their breed. He saw me and halted and dismounted. His face, in the shadows, short still in mid afternoon, looked a mere splodge. I guessed he was laughing. He tied the second freymul to a hitching ring stapled into the wall. Plenty of people were about, going about their business, with the gray slink of slaves gliding unnoticed through the throngs. Then Naghan mounted up and trotted off. I ambled over.

The freymul had a scrap of paper tucked into his harness. One word—FRUPP.

"Hai, Frupp," I said, knuckling in behind his ears.

He bowed his head and twisted it around. Freymuls do not have the single spiral horn of the zorca, and they are, although willing in their fashion, limited in performance. This Frupp had curly amber streaks below and a chocolate-colored coat. His eyes were bright. I liked him instantly.

Along the wall beside the gate sat a line of beggars, cripples, folk in buckets, folk on crutches, folk hideously disfigured, women exposing themselves to show deformities and scars and the tied ends of amputations. By this time in my life upon Kregen, that wonderful if horrific world four hundred light years from Earth, I had become, if not inured to sights like these, at least understanding of them. This was one unpleasant facet of life. Some of these people were in the begging profession. As small children they would have been mutilated by their parents, all in the name of earning a living. As usual, I distributed a few coins; but too great generosity, harsh as this may sound, was a mistake.

Among those pitiable morsels of near-humanity, I wouldn't mind taking a wager, squatted one of Naghan's people.

The noise burst all about me, chaffering people, the beggars whining, saddle animals jingling, the discordant music from the juggling troupe. Outside the gate lay the main Wayfarer's Drinnik, the wide space where caravans formed up or disbanded. Although this scene was wildly familiar in many aspects, and even although the Star Lords—as I thought—had for their own purposes imposed some uniformity upon peoples and customs, there was no doubt I was in a foreign land. This scene before me was not one that would be enacted in Vallia, or even in Havilfar. The elements might appear to be the same; the underlying structures might appear to share the same rules; but the effects were totally different. Kregen is a world of violent contrasts, and of uniformity, and of a never-ending wonder.

An armored man astride a hersany clip-clopped in through the gate, followed by a string of calsanys, all laden with straw baskets, two each side, lolling along held by the guide ropes. Guards prowled. This was a caravan destined for some specific destination and pleased to be within the walls before sundown. The juggling troupe carried on, and now they were rivaled by a group performing some kind of primitive play, full of bladders and false tails. A musician with all his instruments lashed about him jigged up and down and, I found with pleased surprise, producing a not unattractive melody—punctuated, of course, by many bangings of the drums and the cymbals between his knees.

I mounted up on Frupp and gently guided him out through the gate when space permitted. I wished to attract no attention. Outside, and past Wayfarer's Drinnik, the land opened out. Here all the trees had long since been cut down. Any lord with any sense does not allow cover for hostile archers within bowshot of his walls. The track stretched away, rounding the curve of the Spine of Lhorcas. I ambled along astride Frupp. Presently the forests began, closing up to the road. This made me fret over Pompino and that rascally Ift, Twayne Gullik, and the fate of the Kovneva Tilda. What I was doing riding out like this had seemed to me to be a sensible idea. I'd catch sight of Strom Murgon early on.

That wouldn't help. Not really. I was riding to still the quiver in my nerves. So, incontinently, I turned Frupp's head and rode back. He did not complain.

I needed to find my turkey; that would be more fruitful.

Riding easily about the streets might not prove to be the best plan. But it was no use leaving it too late.

I needed somebody not too unlike me. The obvious problem would be that the fellow would be well-known. How to legislate against that concerned me; apart from asking him, there was no way I'd find out. Eventually, I found a likely recruit to my nefarious plans just leaving a tavern, the Boiwink and Clooke, reeling just enough to betray him to my grasping fists...

This happened down the side alley into which he'd reeled to relieve himself. He made not a sound. I didn't particularly want his clothes, which were not greatly different from my own—or, rather, Pando's—or his money or weapons. I took his waist-length cloak, which, gray on the outside, was brown on the inside, edged with silver lace. His badge—that I had. The silver leem was finely chased, the tuft of brown feathers rampant. I trusted this fellow was not too high up. His pouch yielded what was perhaps the most important necessity of all—his silver leem mask. I'd worn these things before. It fitted up on leather straps, a snarling vicious countenance all whiskers and fangs. Once a Leem Lover wore his or her silver leem mask, all restraints vanished.

The mask went back into the velvet-lined pouch and was hooked onto my belt. His purse was one of those vainglorious items you could buy in the flash zouks, a thing of stringed netting so that the gold within could glint through and proclaim your wealth. It fastened with a jeweled clasp. Vainglorious, yes, and foolish, too...

As I straightened up from the fellow's unconscious body the first shafting ray of ruby radiance of Zim shone down the alley as the great red sun of Antares dropped beyond the corner building. A party of tumps trudged past the end of the side alley. No doubt they'd come into the city to spend their gold for new tools to dig more, and for ale and provisions. They lived in their mines and caves in the countryside, and quarreled with the Ifts and anyone else. They saw the bright wink of gold, they saw me crouched over the body on the ground. Instantly, on their stumpy legs, their heavy-headed hammers raised and their beards flying, they charged.

Without any self-consciousness I jumped up and ran.

Bashing a posse of pint-sized tumps over the head was not on the agenda this evening...

Also, and this I freely concede, short and stout though they are, and massively bearded, if a tump hits you over the head with his hammer you're likely never to hear the famous old Bells of Beng Kishi. Those hammers are reputed to stove in vosk skulls, although this I doubt.

Mounting up on Frupp I nudged him and obediently he trotted off and out onto the main street. I turned toward the west gate. There could not be much time left now...

You had to say this for Strom Murgon Marsilus. He knew how to put on a show.

First of all trotted a posse of trumpeters mounted on gray zorcas. They tootled away, the golden notes blasting into the warm evening air and proclaiming the imminent arrival of a great lord. A strom is not ordinarily a great lord, just a lord of the upper middle rankings. But Murgon had great plans.

There followed a troupe of dancing girls, scantily clad, who scattered flower petals. Unquestionably they had been brought along in wagons from Pomdermam, and would have alighted and begun their flower-strewing dance just before they entered the west gate. Onlookers crowded up, forming a lane along which the procession wended its colorful way.

A half-pastang of hersany lancers rode next, and then the first of the infantry, kreutzin in light equipment and little decoration. A yell broke from the crowd at the next sight to lumber through the gate. Murgon had brought a pair of thumping great dermiflons, lurching, idiot-headed, ten-legged, their blue skin glistening like olive oil under the Suns. They were often a favorite with the ordinary folk; some nations could not abide them. There was no doubt the people of Port Marsilus considered them a rare treat.

More cavalry and infantry followed, the sword and shield men, the churgurs, and—which interested me more than a trifle—a whole regiment of swarthmen. These cavalrymen rode their two-legged reptilian mounts with almost, almost, the confidence of well-trained jutmen. I fancied the swarths were new to their riders. Certain sure it was, the riders were new to swarths.

Music of a tin-banging, rattling kind was provided by splendidly attired bands which marched along at ear-splitting distance. Murgon would have positioned his baggage wagons at the tail of the procession, with a rough-rider band to look after them. Folk might still hang about admiring the number of wagons in a rich lord's entourage. If Murgon was as rich as this show attested, he would have a sizable train. If he was as rich as Pando had implied, he could never in a thousand seasons afford all this.

The strom himself rode a black zorca, whose spiral horn, adorned with silver, nodded up and down in a fretful way, for Murgon held him on too tight a rein. The animal was superb. Murgon, too, clad sumptuously, looked superb.

His black beard, cut short, his sharp and haughty features, the level arrogant unseeing stare in his dark eyes, all stamped him as a notor of Tomboram. I did think that there was about him more than a hint, a definable impression, of defiance. Pinned to the front of his tunic, partially concealed by the massed gilt-lacing to the edge of his cape, he wore a device. From this distance what it might be was problematical to all save those who would know.

He wore the imago of the silver leem, with its brown and silver ribbons. Openly, the strom wore the badge of Lem the Silver Leem. Many a man and many a woman in the crowd wore their own silver leem badge, with the tuft of brown feathers or the brown and silver ribbons. They would know, and, knowing approve...

The cheers that greeted Strom Murgon bellowed to the evening sky. They depressed me, by Vox, they depressed me.

I remembered how, in the cabin of *Tuscurs Maiden*, I'd discussed with Pompino the chances of Murgon or of Pando reaching Bormark first. It seemed that Murgon had won. He clearly had the people with him. He did not harm his chances or his popularity by the lavish handfuls of silver men dressed in fantastic costumes scattered from wicker baskets. Murgon was displaying his wealth, his largesse, and thereby his power. Again, I pondered—where was all this hard cash coming from?

Pando, in the nature of a kov, would be rich. The king was displeased with him, his cousin was buying his people—Pando was getting the cold shoulder, the Big E.

This, I believed, must tie in with the enterprise against southwest Vallia. I'd be hitting two birds with one shaft this night, I fancied.

Discreetly, after the great man had passed, I guided Frupp through the throngs, following on. Jollity broke out, Murgon's silver being immediately put to useful purposes.

Now I knew just how many Stromnates and eltenates and other of the lesser nobilities existed in Pando's Bormark, for I had made it my business to know. I knew, also, who did and who did not keep up villas in the kovnate's capital city. Murgon maintained a modest villa along the Avenue of Miscils... The procession did not make for the villa of Ribenor. Oh, no, they headed for a certain tumbledown old theater.

Gradually, the bands ceased playing, the soldiers parceled themselves off to seek billets, the dancing girls disappeared, the men had emptied their baskets of silver.

With only a small escort and retinue, Murgon reined up before the old theater. People still followed him, and I was not at all conspicuous.

The twin Suns were almost gone. In the flaring light of torches his face showed, dark and brooding. I caught the fierce impression that he dearly loved to order his men: "Clear me this rabble away!" Instead, he called a courteous remberee and then headed into the side street. One of his aides, a Gon whose bald head shone butter-bright in the torchlight, shouted: "The strom bids you all a restful night and he wishes you well and your wonderful families and now he wishes to be alone and will quarter in the Speckled Gyp and remberee one and all." All on a breath.

The high-class tavern and hotel called The Speckled Gyp did lie in the next avenue across. I did not think Murgon would reach there. He'd be in that side door like a leem after a ponsho, going through the dusty corridors, making his way to the chambers reserved for him. He'd be attending the rites of Lem after he'd eaten and freshened up.

Now that I knew his location I could see about my own inward hollowness. As Kregans are fond of telling you, there is nothing like six or eight square meals a day.

Trotting gently back to The Awkward Swod, I attempted to put the pieces of this puzzle together.

On the face of it, a kovnate like Bormark, or even a kingdom like Tomboram, would stand little chance of invading a still-powerful empire like Vallia. Oh, yes, Vallia was still rent by factions. The empire remained partitioned. There was a king in Evir in the far north, there was a king of Womox Island to the west, and now there was this King Vodun Alloran in what he called Thothclef Vallia. Also, there were dissidents still resisting unification in the northwest of the island of Vallia. But with our capital at Vondium, and our armies and air cavalry and vollers, we were no pushover.

If Alloran made an alliance of convenience with this King of Womox, for instance... He'd taken Katrin's kovnate of Rahartdrin. He was attempting to march to the northeast, which would bring him into immediate conflict with loyal provinces. My lad Drak resisted; but that blob-nosed Deldar, Tom the Nose, had merely confirmed what I suspected, that Drak did not have the best regiments with him. We'd all have to rally around: Delia could get regiments from Valka, Seg could send men up from Hamal—although, confound it! Seg was off somewhere lost in the jungles of Pandahem south of the central mountains. I'd call on Inch in the Black Mountains, and Korf Aighos and Filbarrka, and anyone else. We could not afford to allow a fresh collapse of our hard-won hegemony.

But none of the thoughts in my old vosk-skull of a head as I dismounted and hitched up Frupp revealed to me who might be financing this latest enterprise against Vallia.

Once the first bites were taken in the southwest, once the swarms of tazll mercenaries learned what was afoot, we'd be swamped with the rogues, reivers, flutsmen, aragorn, all the vile batteners on human misery that had before tried to ruin our land and whom we had thrown out. We'd be right back to the Times of Troubles again...

So, troubled myself, I went into the tavern and ordered up whatever first struck my appetite, and ate almost without tasting. I went sparingly with the wine.

Vallia had been invaded before. No doubt Vallia would be invaded again in the future. However much a part of life that might be on a turbulent maelstrom of a planet, it remained damned unsettling, by Vox, highly unwanted.

However important my mission here was to destroy the evil cult of the Silver Wonder and not destroy but attempt to convert back to decency its adherents, maybe my responsibility to Vallia should come first. Once the island empire was whole and healed again, once the old empire had been reestablished and the people lived together in harmony, these constant invasions would no longer take place. The reivers and flutsmen and aragorn of the world would think more than twice before they set out on an enterprise against Vallia.

Into the equation I must add the promise I'd made that I'd hand over everything to Drak, let him be the poor bewildered emperor, as soon as the empire was whole. Well, Deb-Lu-Quienyin, a famous and mystically powerful Wizard of Loh and a good comrade, had advised me to let Drak handle affairs down in the southwest. Drak was the intense, serious, level-headed one of my sons. He'd make a splendid emperor. But maybe, just maybe, I ought to have gone back home and sorted things out myself, first...

I quaffed the last of the wine—I've no idea what it might have been—and tossed down two silver dhems, and then added a third to pay the reckoning. A Fristle fifi with a yellow apron and a green bow to her tail had been attentive and had put up with my absent-mindedness. She deserved recompense for my ill humor and reward for her smiling service. I stood up and she handed me my cloak and I found some sort of skull-faced smile for her.

The hostler had seen to Frupp, and I tipped him a few coins, and so mounted up and turned the willing and well-fed freymul in the direction of that infamous theater.

Under the archway at the end of the deserted yard, the hostler having taken himself off with his hand clenched on the coins, a lamp burned in a crooked holder. The iron bars shed bars of shadow across the yard. The scent of moonblooms hung heavily in the air. Under that crumbling archway a woman appeared.

She stood with her head bowed; but not bowed enough that I did not realize she studied me. Her auburn hair caught some of the lamplight; it did not shine in quite the way it should have; the angles and the shadows threw projections in the wrong places. Her long pale blue gown draped in a circle about her feet, and her hands were folded into the sleeves of the gown.

She stood, silent, unmoving, her head just that tiny bit bowed, her nose and her high cheekbones washed with a light I swore did not come from the lamp above her head.

Abruptly, she moved.

Her figure wavered, as objects swim beyond heated air.

I started forward on Frupp, anxious to question her.

She looked up, and then she looked around. I saw a face that, piquant and dainty as it was, yet held a darker and more profound power than any elfin face might hold. She looked at me, and her eyes took in my senses, and she lifted a hand as though to ward off a blow.

Then she vanished.

She vanished.

I was not discomposed—well, not overly so.

Apparitions and ghosts, these are not unknown upon Kregen.

Only a moment ago I'd been thinking of Deb-Lu-Quienyin. I would not have been surprised, I'd have been overjoyed, if he had appeared under the archway. Wherever he was, in Vallia or Valka, or down in Hamal, he could put himself into the trance state of lupu and using his kharrna send out a ghostly image of himself to survey what might be of interest in distant places. Good old Deb-Lu! But he did not appear, and the lamp under the archway shone on stone and cobble.

Frupp's ears pricked up. He reacted uneasily to these weird comings and goings. I patted his neck, bending forward, soothing him.

Now if, I said to myself as we trotted out under that haunted archway onto the street beyond, now if I knew whose side you supported, mysterious witch-lady in the pale blue gown, that might be more than useful.

One fact was absolutely certain and without doubt.

On Kregen it is a far far better state of affairs to have a witch or a wizard on your side than opposing you.

By Vox, yes!

Fifteen

Dafni

When I contemplated what might lie ahead I had half a mind to go along and torch the temple of Lem the Silver Leem. The temptation was very great. Mind you, as I may have remarked on previous occasions, many of my blade comrades would agree with vast enthusiasm that, yes indeed, I did have only half a mind.

If I wanted to find out the truth behind the enterprise against Vallia, it behooved me to proceed with far more caution than I would have done if it had been a mere case of burn, hack and run, or if Pompino were here with free advice.

The excitement engendered by the strom's arrival lingered on in the streets and squares of Port Marsilus. Folk would be up late this night, roistering. Everyone bore an eager look, as though they all knew exactly what was going on, had a hand in it, and couldn't wait for the off. That this was a totally misleading impression was beside the point. They were merely caught up in the atmosphere. But, with the problems I had, that impression was galling, I can tell you, damned galling.

Going along gently on a slack rein I neared the abandoned theater that was now a hidden temple. The sound of hoofbeats astern and a chorus of shouts warned me, and I nudged Frupp into the side, out of the roadway. I reined in and sat, hunched, my face down under the hat, watching.

A party of zorca riders rattled past. They conveyed the impression of flaring cloaks, feathered hats, the dark glimmer of weapons, a bunched group of riders on an errand of importance.

They clustered about the figure of a girl, for as she passed me the light of a torch fell across her face under the hat. A girl, then, surrounded by armed men. Escorts are of two kinds—those that protect you and those that imprison you.

The impression I'd taken, fleeting and as swiftly gone as a snowflake falling into flames, was of a fine pallid face with wide dark eyes. The look, and I could easily have been mistaken, on that face was of absorption, a kind of rapt inner awareness that denied exterior objects. I shook Frupp's reins and walked him on toward the temple.

The party of zorca riders turned into the side alley.

By the time I'd reached the mouth of the alley they had vanished.

People who had moved aside to let the cavalcade pass now resumed their apparently casual evening strolls. About half of them were mounted, so I attracted no attention as I allowed Frupp to go easily with the drift. We circled the building, and on the farther side the people moved into the shadows under an overhang where an arch, much weathered, supported a flying wing of the place. I went along.

A row of stalls to the side accommodated the riding animals, and hostlers in brown tunics took charge as the people alighted and entered the building. Without a word I dismounted, handed the reins to a villainous-looking fellow and followed on. Casually, I turned the waist-length cloak inside out so that the brown side showed, the silver bullion thick along the edges. Around me the flowering of brown and silver glinted menacingly under the light of torches.

In the random and erratic shafts of light we all went through into the foyer where debris and splintered beams told anyone looking in that this was a deserted and abandoned place. As we went along, the silver masks came out of the pouches. The light flicked from silver eye-holes, silver whiskers, snarling silver masks of primeval savagery.

I put the silver leem mask on, thankfully, over my face. At least, I would not have to suffer the bee-sting agony of holding a different face for too long a time.

Beyond the portal in the far wall where guards stood ready to deal with any unwanted intruders, the congregation turned left and right to enter the auditorium. Lights spattered the curtains concealing the stage. The floor was swept. People stood in clumps, talking in low tones, waiting. I eased along to the side, taking as my aiming point any one of the small exits under the side balconies. What struck me most forcibly was the casual lack of real secrecy. Despite the guards, despite the obvious attempts to make the old theater appear as merely an abandoned building, the Leem Lovers were arrogant in their use of the place. They congregated here, and if any outsider observed them then he knew what he could do—keep silent or suffer the consequences.

Voices suddenly lifted in what was a coarse way over by the other side of the auditorium. People moved in an agitated way. I stopped under a balcony and looked back.

Presently the cause of the disturbance reached the group of men and women nearest and they turned to one another, gesticulating, obviously annoyed, and yet, even so, subdued.

"It is so disappointing," a woman protested.

"Tomorrow, my dear. We shall come back tomorrow."

People were now leaving the hall.

Walking quietly up to the group I had no need to ask what had happened, for the woman's husband turned to me and said: "The strom has canceled the ceremony for this evening. He gives no reason; but quite clearly he is tired and we hear important developments have taken place."

"Quite," I said, and went back into the shadows under the balcony as though mightily disappointed. Well, by Krun, I was and I wasn't. The auditorium cleared of people; before the last of them went I slid through the side exit and found myself in a long dusty corridor. Down this I went, padding light-footed.

The first door, half-open, showed a room full of dancing girls. They were taking off their jeweled bangles and beads, unpinning their feathers, and putting their clothes on. Among the apim girls and Sylvies and Fristles were three lieshas and a couple of numims. I was surprised to see the lion-girls, for numims are generally above that sort of occupation.

Two doors along I found a room full of guards, also standing down from duty, coughing and spitting and stacking their spears and looking forward to a night off drinking. I scuttled past there rapidly and went on.

More rooms lay empty, dusty and cobwebbed. Here I was on the other side of the building from where I'd found the girl sacrifices and their bathing establishment. I prowled on.

The fellow who'd turned and told me the ceremony was canceled for this evening had referred to Murgon as the strom. This, alone, was intriguing. Normally the Leem Lovers concealed their identities under a farrago of nonsense names, all high-flown and pompous. This, surely, must be just another example of the power and eminence the cult had reached here in Bormark.

Toward the corner of the building I came across a stairway leading up. Just a simple wooden affair, it led through an opening onto a higher corridor. At the foot stood a man in half-armor, carrying a sword, who stared at me in my leem mask and said: "They have all gone, no one—"

He said no more as he sank down, mightily surprised, I feel sure, that the world had gone black. I dragged him into a doorway and left him breathing heavily, out to the wide, and padded quietly up the wooden stairs.

These old buildings are often warrens of tiny rooms. The sound of voices led me to a narrow window at the side of a closed door. There were two voices, and one of them was Murgon's. Without a doubt. I remembered that harsh, overpowering and yet resigned voice. The other voice was that of a woman.

I put my eyeball around the edge of the narrow window, looked in, and listened.

"You will marry and that's an end of it!" Murgon's voice pulsed with menace.

The woman was the one I'd seen ride up here closely surrounded by her escort. Her pallid face, still half hidden by the flap of her hat, looked distraught.

"I cannot, Murgon! It is against nature to ask me!"

"You will!" He reached out both hands and shook her by the shoulders. He put his face close to hers, shouting. "You will!"

"No—please—"

He had his two cronies with him, the giant malevolent Chulik, Chekumte the Fist, and the sly and slinky Dopitka the Deft. They stood to one side, watching, ready instantly to do whatever Strom Murgon commanded them.

The woman crumpled. She slid to her knees, her arms trailing down Murgon's body. She stared up under that silly hat.

"Dafni," said Murgon in that grating voice. "There is no sense arguing. This you must do—this you will do!"

As though unable to argue longer, her head lowered, and she lay, trembling, grasping his knees. It was not an edifying scene.

Murgon gestured to his henchmen.

"Take the vadni away." Then he added, almost as an afterthought: "Treat her gently."

The two plug uglies started forward.

Now, as I may have mentioned before, on Kregen it seems to me rescuing ladies from villains is a perfectly normal occupation. You usually have to be quick. There is no sense in hanging about. Unlike other normal occupations on Earth, it's a job at which you can get yourself very messily killed.

Still wearing the snarling silver leem mask I kicked the door in and leaped.

Chekumte the Fist simply hauled out his sword and rushed at me. His tusks, gilded and polished, caught the light from the samphron-oil lamp. His dangling pigtail flew out like a bolt of blue rope. I did to him what Pompino had already done once and he flew up and over and fell, to lie snorting. Then I did to Dopitka the Deft what Quendur the Ripper had done to him and he fell to lie beside his fellow.

Murgon's rapier was out.

As he flew at me he tangled up with the lady Dafni. I eluded that first attack, gripped his wrist, ready to pull, twist or break, and Dafni, shrieking, fell all over us. Murgon caught me a nasty whack alongside the head. For a moment dizzied, I stumbled back. The rast nearly had me and I just managed to evade his savage thrust. Dafni fell all asprawl against him, I jumped up, head ringing, to hit him and he toppled back over the girl. His head hit the floor. He sprawled, rapier tinkling away. I shook myself.

The blow had struck shrewder than I'd realized. Maybe there was not the full campanological chorus of Beng Kishi's famous Bells, but my head clanged like an old bucket kicked over down an alley on a moonless night.

A hand to my head I staggered up. The four of them slumbered. What a mess! Vadni Dafni came up in my fists and I slung her over my shoulder. She flopped like a sack of meal.

"By Krun!" I said to myself. "The things a fellow does!"

Out the doorway and with a swift look up and down—no one in sight— and a careful pad down the stairs—still no one about—and a cautious quiet prowl along the dusty corridor—and still no one to challenge me. I could taste the dust on my tongue. The smells were laced by the after-scents of the dancing girls' perfumes.

There seemed to me to be few chances of getting away scot free. Someone was going to be about still, that is the nature of the beast. Instead of re-entering the temple area I turned in the other direction and wended on, looking for the first doorway out. That the door I found was bolted had little to do with it. I put the lady Dafni down, propped against the wall—where she immediately flopped over like a baby—and gave the door a thumping kick. The bolt snapped.

The night breeze blew in, scented with the fragrance of moonblooms. Moons shine glistered on cobblestones. A corner of the building jutted here in an angle where the roof dropped low, and a couple of the loungers who did not lounge were just strolling back. Watching them, I waited until they turned in their apparently casual amble. Then I leaped.

The luck that was with me in that they had been at the far end of their patrol when I'd kicked the door open persisted. Both men went down without a sound. I straightened. For all I could see in the Moons shine, no one had seen me.

I ran around to the front of the building. A couple of the hostlers in their brown tunics hung about, and the stalls contained perhaps a dozen or so riding animals. My freymul was brought out and I mounted up. Over this matter of tipping, a little dash, I could betray myself if they didn't go in for it between the members of the cult here in Port Marsilus; and although it went against the grain to hand out money to the people in brown tunics, I handed down a couple of silver coins.

"Our thanks," said the fellow with the most silver spattered over the brown. He took the money all right.

I trotted off, letting Frupp flick his head up and down as though pleased to see me again.

By the time I'd ridden around to where the door I'd broken open flapped more than I liked, I was reassured that the hostlers suspected nothing. Also the pain in my head, still throbbing, was beginning to lose some of the scarlet claws that dug into my brain.

The lady Dafni lay half on her side, half on her front, sprawled, and she made snoring sounds that, I felt convinced, would have offended her had she known she was making them. I hefted her up, went outside and arranged her across Frupp. Freymuls, like zorcas, are close-coupled animals with room enough for two people if they squeeze up tighter than peas in a pod. I decided to walk alongside. The silver leem mask would have to come off now. It had served well, the damned thing, and I stowed it away in the velvet pouch.

Frupp and I with our limp burden walked sedately through the nighted streets of Port Marsilus.

There was going to be a pursuit, as surely as Zim and Genodras would rise in the morning sky.

No sense in rushing along in a galloping lather, attracting the attention of everybody on the streets this late. Just a nice careful walk along in the shadows, with the girl over the saddle held gently, and Frupp acting as though well aware that he carried a burden somewhat different from that to which he was accustomed.

In the kyro where we had first been ambushed I wended around on the shadowed side. The memory of that first attack made me screw my head around, watching every opening and doorway. A couple of passersby gave me a look; but I'd put on a nondescript face, one of the sort that Deb-Lu-Quienyin called a gyp-face, quite unremarkable. Deb-Lu's powers as a Wizard of Loh had enabled him to overcome ferocious sorceries, and give me sage advice, and they had taught me through his own charisma how to alter my own harsh physiognomy.

She of the Veils rode the night sky, flirting with skirts of cloud, gilding the night with beauty, casting roseate shadows through which I walked with Frupp at my side. The lady Dafni was showing signs of returning consciousness, and I wanted to be along the avenue and into the palace before she awoke.

The guards in their little sentry boxes were a couple of Fristles I recognized, men serving under ord-Deldar Naghan the Pellendur who, I trusted, was keeping the palace functioning and intact. I say I recognized these two cat-men; they did not recognize me.

They stepped out and the two spears slapped across forming a saltire to bar onward progress. I halted and Frupp let a little ripple of breath escape his nostrils. I patted his neck, and said: "All right, all right, old lad. The stables and a bale of hay are coming right up." Then, to the Fristles: "Lahal, doms. Naghan the Pellendur, ord-Deldar. He'll want to see me at once, or before that if it were humanly possible. I'll wait inside, if I may, while you summon him or a patoc—patoc Lurgan Crooknose might be on duty now, might he not?"

Lurgan Crooknose happened to be a Fristle whose name I recalled from hearing Naghan the Pellendur bellowing at him.

The cat-men took no offense at my easy way; they carried out their duties punctiliously, bidding me stand fast, not letting me through the gate— whereat although not faulting them I waxed a trifle warm, and looked back over my shoulder—waiting until patoc Froindarf the Clis arrived.

I said: "Patoc. Kov Pando sends me with this lady to his palace. You—"

He interrupted. "You seem to know a deal about us. You ask for Naghan the Pellendur, so you must know he commands here while the cadade is away. Yet—how could you know this if you did not spy on us?"

Mind you, I ought to have got rid of that confounded gyp-face before this; but I'd been dwelling on other items in the night's doings. I went on with great patience, realizing the farcical waste of time this was; but trapped by my own stupid cleverness.

"You are right to say I spy—but I spy for Kov Pando." He moved across to the freymul and lifted a hand. One of the guards hauled a torch from its becket and swung it over Frupp.

"This lady," said patoc Froindarf the Clis. "This is the Vadni Dafni! You'd better bring her in." He ran back to the gate and helped to open it wider, and yelled: "Send for handmaidens! Hurry! The vadni needs assistance!"

Frupp ambled through. Just as the gate was pushed shut, and I put my shoulder to it, I can assure you, I saw through the closing gap a string of torches debouching from the avenue, and the dark exaggerated forms of zorca riders, and the wink of steel. The gate slammed solidly. I let out a breath. And—I nearly lost that gyp-face. It did not sting overmuch, and I could hold it for some time.

The courtyard buzzed with activity. Naghan the Pellendur arrived, sorted out the confusion, and came over to Frupp. Dafni was assisted down. She opened her eyes as she stood up, supported by a couple of scantily dressed handmaidens hastily dug out, and she looked about in a bewildered way.

"It is all right, my lady," I said. "There is nothing to fear."

"Where—oh, this is Pando's palace—I recognize—what? How did I...? Murgon!"

"Hush, my lady. Murgon need no longer concern you. You have been rescued from his clutches—"

For a moment I thought she would collapse again. The handmaidens held her, trying to fuss, patting her clothes straight. Then she drew a deep breath and opened her eyes and looked at us surrounding her. She could see the concern on our faces.

"By the agate-winged jutmen of Hodan-Set," she whispered. "It is scarcely to be believed."

"Kov Pando will be here soon. You must rest and recover from your ordeal."

"Ordeal? Yes, you are right. You were the man who burst in wearing the silver mask? Yes, I remember—"

"Then forget that, my lady. Murgon can no longer harm you here. You are now under Kov Pando's protection. All his people will care for you."

"Pando... So I am here, then. It is da'eslam. What I am fated to do I will do. Da'eslam."

The lady Dafni Harlstam, Vadni of Tenpanam, put out a trembling hand to clutch at the handmaid, and she burst into a torrent of tears.

Sixteen

Mindi the Mad

The lady Dafni, so Tilda had told us, was a vivacious girl.
Tilda was right.
Too right.
There are a couple of apocryphal squibs, not, I hasten to point out,

attributed to San Blarnoi, which go something like: "Why is language called the mother tongue, because father doesn't often get to use it; and when a woman tells a doctor she is exhausted he asks to see her tongue."

Yes, Dafni chattered.

She recovered from what she kept on referring to as her "Ordeal." When, the following morning, I turned up in different clothes and wearing my ordinary face, I was able to ooh and aah along with the rest as she told her story again and again. Vivacious. Yes, she was that, all right. That and a lot, a whole lot, more.

Pompino and Framco the Tranzer arrived back during the day. They brought all the people with whom they had set out, not having lost a soul. They did not return with Tilda or Twayne Gullik.

Pompino was disgusted.

"Not a sight of 'em. Then we got a trail, turned out to be a bunch of idiot Ifts taking supplies back to their forests. Waste of time, complete and utter."

"You did not send a message."

"Not send a message? Of course we sent a—oh!"

I waited.

We were sitting in the mess hall, drinking sazz and parclear, for it was too early for wine. Framco said: "That messenger, then, either betrayed us or was waylaid."

"But you returned with everyone—"

"A numim who said he was going to the Zhantil Palace—he was not a great lord; but he had a retinue of stout fighting men—took the message."

"And you trusted him?"

"He was clearly a man of honor—"

"All numims look like that, for the sake of Pranxco the Gullible!"

"Well—" began Pompino truculently.

"Did he give you a name?"

"Of course. We made the pappattu. He was Mazdo the Splandu."

I said nothing more on that, and changed the subject of conversation immediately, by trying to tell Pompino that my priorities had changed, and not tell him why.

"Leaving me to burn the temples?" he said, outraged. "Here I've been traipsing up and down those diabolical forests and you've been idling your time away here! By Horato the Potent, Jak! What are you up to?"

I couldn't tell him that these confounded people were hiring on an army to invade my home country. Rather, I *could* tell him, and after all the marvelings and wonderings, he'd just say something like: "Well, you know, Jak. You have to serve the Star Lords first!"

To hell with that. I had to stop these villains from invading Vallia. That was the priority number one.

"There wasn't time to burn the temple in the old theater because I was rescuing the lady Dafni at the time."

"Yes, yes, a fine handy piece of work. But the temple is still *there!*"

"I," I said with a great show of magnanimity, "left it all for you!"

"In all this," put in Framco the Tranzer. "What of the Kovneva Tilda?"

There was no sensible answer we could give to that heartfelt question.

I did not want to lose my freymul, Frupp, for I had grown attached to him. So I hummed and hawed, and then said: "There was a fellow in a silver leem mask who helped me with the lady Dafni. He brought her back on my freymul. Nath the Bludgeon, he said his name was. Useful. He—"

"Ah!" said Pompino, brushing up his whiskers. "Now we are getting the truth! This fellow Nath the Bludgeon did all the rescuing while you were admiring the scenery—I see!"

"We-ell," I said, choking up a trifle, and determined not to let Pompino catch on.

"So now perhaps we'll find the real reason you didn't burn the confounded temple!"

I was saved on that one by the arrival of Constanchoin, just about recovered although still inclined to shiver a trifle when he saw me—which was a pity, really. He thumped his black balass wood staff down. He looked put out.

"All these children!" he said, crossly. "Do you know anything about them? They're running everywhere like a flood of tinklehoils who've just lost their tails."

"Ah, now," I said, and leaned back in my chair, and picked up a paline from the pottery dish. "Well, now—"

"Yes, Horter Jak?" Constanchoin had learned one lesson, apparently.

"They are the guests of Kov Pando. He will welcome them when he arrives. Just give them lots of sweets—bring in a Banje shop's stock, if you can."

"But they're getting everywhere! I just managed to stop them swinging on the bellropes—"

Framco the Tranzer started up, aghast.

"By Odifor! If they ring the bells...!"

"Quite," said Constanchoin in a kind of moan. "What are we to do?"

"Keep them occupied." I was glad the girl sacrifices were safe; they were the past at the moment, and only in the future would they become part of the present. That damned army recruiting to sail against Vallia... That was the conundrum.

Murgon and the army, they were the present and immediate future. But I could not abandon Pompino. So I said: "They postponed their diabolical ceremony until tonight. No doubt they'll buy some more sacrifices." I rattled through what had happened with the smells and the bathing glossed over. Constanchoin, clearly, wanted to hear nothing of this and took himself off. Framco listened, pulling his whiskers and every now and again saying: "I don't know what we are to do."

Pompino crowed. "So you've been to the place twice, and it still stands! And all these girls—"

Warm, I snapped out: "We'll burn the dump tonight, if you wish. But we'll have to get any more sacrifices out first. You burned a temple here. I do not see it has lessened the worshippers' zeal in the slightest."

"By Horato the Potent! You speak hard!"

"As I told you; we have to find a more successful method of uprooting the cult than merely burning temples. We have to change the minds and hearts of the worshippers—"

"Part their heads from their shoulders. That'll change their minds, ha!"

The arguing and wrangling went on and then, with an amusement in which I delighted, I remembered the catty remarks about Dafni and her incessant chattering. By Vox! These men had been nattering away fit to rival Dafni in full flow.

On Kregen there are many and various delightful stories concerning Hyrzibar, a shishi who exclusively serves the minor godlings of various mythologies. Her chatter fills many a fat tome and many a guffaw-worthy anecdote. The lady Dafni and Hyrzibar were, in the opinion of those able to make the comparison, well-matched.

From the vantage point of the battlements of the Zhantil Palace the Sea of Opaz glittered under the lights of the Suns. That sea represented a highway between Pandahem and Vallia. In my mind's eye I could see it filled with the sails of argosies, fleets of ships all bearing on toward Vallia, carrying hordes of armed and armored fighting men to invade and, once again, lay waste to the island empire I called home.

The thought of all I and my comrades had striven for once more being destroyed, put to the torch and the sword, hacked down, was not to be borne.

Out I went along the ramparts, ignoring my friends here, letting the breeze cool my fevers. Was I not Dray Prescot, Lord of Strombor and Krozair of Zy? Was I not the Emperor of Vallia? Well, then, I had to prevent that enterprise from sailing against Vallia, or clip its wings—at least, I felt the thankfulness, here in Pandahem they would have to use sailing ships. They did not possess the airboats of other nations, or the flying sailing vessels. They had no vollers to pelt through thin air and descend upon my land of Vallia.

A racket of footsteps on the ramparts at my back did not halt me. I strode on, feeling the breeze, staring at the dancing sea.

"Jak! What the hell...?"

I took no notice.

Ahead along the stone ramparts by an embrasure stood a woman. Her head was downbent, and her pale blue robe descended in straight folds into a circle around her feet.

She lifted her head and the auburn hair blazed in a light that never came from the twin suns overhead.

Her mouth, small, almost black in that odd lighting, circled. She was speaking. I heard nothing, only the screeching of gulls as they chased tails over the battlements. The breeze blew, the Suns shone and a few high clouds parceled off toward the east.

She spoke to me. There was strain on that face. And I could make out nothing.

"By Horato the Potent! A ghost!" Pompino shoved up beside me, and I could hear his breathing, ragged and hoarse. "A witch, broken from the ib!"

"She is trying to say something—but what?"

The phantasmal form beckoned. A slim white hand lifted from an enveloping sleeve. And the lips writhed in pantomime over words—a word—that I could not grasp.

A high, excited voice at our backs shouted.

"*Mindi!*"

She spoke now, a torrent of soundless words.

Then, as a feather is consumed in the Furnace Fires of Inshurfraz, she vanished.

I swiveled.

"Framco—if that was Mindi the Mad, what was she trying to tell us?"

The Fristle cadade pulled his whiskers; but he looked fierce, determined.

"I think, horters, I am sure—she was saying Plaxing—"

"That is where the Sybli, Suli, said Tilda wanted to take her, on the evening we arrived."

"This," said Pompino, "could be some sorcerous trick."

"You said, Framco, that you did not trust Mindi the Mad."

"I do not. But she has been of great use to Kov Pando and his mother the kovneva in the past. I am not sure..."

"It is certain sure we must send to Plaxing. That is the least we can do." Pompino sounded vexed. "I would offer to go. But time has been wasted, and there is a temple to burn. Framco, you will go?"

"It is my duty."

"Good. Then that is settled."

"There is one concern," I pointed out. "If we all go haring off we leave the palace open to Murgon's attack. He may guess this is where the lady Dafni is held for her safety..."

Pompino spoke up with the obvious answer; although it was one I disliked muchly.

"The lady Dafni will have to go with one of the parties. And she cannot go with us, therefore..."

Framco nodded heavily. "I agree. For her own safety she will have to ride with me."

I didn't like it. But it made sense.

So it was arranged. Orders were given. I was interested to see the way in which Framco the Fristle, Nath Kemchug the Chulik, and the Rapa, Rondas the Bold, acted, one with the other. I have previously remarked about the Rapas and Chuliks, and even more that this so-called hereditary enmity between Fristles and Chuliks is a matter of particular subdivisions of the races. At the least, these three specimens of their peoples rubbed along.

Rondas the Bold and Nath Kemchug would stay in the Zhantil Palace with the guards Framco would leave. They would deal with any attacks. They promised this in a species of sullen resentment that they were not included in our force to go and blatter the Leem Lovers.

Pompino was all fire and eagerness to start. He just wanted to work for the Everoinye and burn temples to Lem. I wanted to get hold of Murgon and obtain a few answers from him.

As though pointing up that Rapas and Chuliks and Fristles and most of the other splendid array of diffs on Kregen share with apims a divided heritage, Nath Kemchug came in swearing that: "He'd rather spend a sennight in the Cheerless Barracks in Vorcheng." And that, believe you me, by Chozputz, is a legendary location to set the shivers up anyone's spine.

Rondas the Bold said: "By Rhapaporgolam the Reiver of Souls! If any wight tries to break into the palace tonight, his beak will be bent to inspect his backside!" which is, as you will perceive, a mighty oath for a Rapa.

We took what comfort we could from this manifested fighting spirit of those left on guard.

Nath Kemchug had a clever trick some Chuliks are capable of employing. Always fascinated, I watched as he used the sharp blade of his spear, flat on, to polish up his tusks. He had such control of his weapons that the steel blade kissed up and down the tusk, sweetly. So, this time, I said: "If you'd stuck a few diamonds in your tusk, Nath, or banded them with gold, you'd find that trick more difficult."

"By Likshu the Treacherous, folk who do that are plain mad! I don't hold with the custom, although it is common enough. For one thing, if you don't clean your tusks with extra care you'll get tusk rot for sure."

"I can believe it."

So, we divided our forces into three, and settled down to wait out the hours of daylight, we who were to raid the temple and we who would remain on guard. Framco led his party off to ride for Plaxing. We ate and rested and tried to contain ourselves in patience for the derring-do that lay ahead.

At the least, although we had kept away from most of it, we were now spared the incessant chatter of the lady Dafni.

Pando possessed a fine library and I sought solace there for a bur or so; but was driven out by half a dozen remarkably clean-looking girl children who rolled in with the utmost determination to get themselves as dirty as they could in the shortest possible time. As I scuttled off, one of the under-chamberlains panted in, puffing and sweating, trying to get the girls to come along and behave. It seemed to me that Constanchoin and his underlings were being most severely punished by this juvenile invasion, and I found that of a come-uppance most sweet. Opaz alone knew what we were going to do with the quondam sacrifices; I fancied a good life lay in store for them—if they survived the consequences of their own conduct. On that uncharitable thought I went off to get dressed up for the night's entertainment.

As we gathered in the courtyard I was instructed to learn that the Divine Lady Of Belschutz had, no doubt in some wayward and long-forgotten escapade, contracted a most painful condition affecting certain of her more tender parts. Captain Murkizon was on form, in fine fettle, and his swishing axe was going to be a danger to all his comrades until we got into action.

Larghos the Flatch kept asking people if they'd seen the lady Nalfi. No one had lately. In the general hubbub more jocose remarks were thrown at him than real concern; she had proved a girl of her own mind and spirit and Larghos was not having an easy time with her. Eventually he discovered her, so he told everyone, leading her back and fussing over her, bravely doing up her own armor, trying to buckle the straps over her back. He strutted as he paced beside her, and one could not help feeling both sorry and envious—and a little of some emotion no sane man would give a name to—as one looked at him and the lady Nalfi together.

In the end it was decided that Lisa the Empoin and the lady Nalfi would not go with us.

They protested; they were overruled.

All day there had been no sign of Drak's spy, Naghan Raerdu. Carefully casual inquiries about ale in the pantry brought forth the information that Raerdu was expected tomorrow with a fresh consignment of Amber Spirit, a fine ale of which he could supply the finest quality. This was inconvenient; but I took comfort from the thought that had there been any startling intelligence Naghan would have found a way to convey it to me.

We set off in small groups, walking inconspicuously, riding separately. I'd taken pains to discover what there was to know of the ruined theater, and found that it had been badly damaged in a raid by the Bloody Menahem, repaired and then ruined all over again, only worse, during the time the Hyr Notor ruled in Pandahem. Its name was The Playhouse of the

Singing Lotus. Fine and fanciful, I thought. A new playhouse had recently been completed two blocks away, called the Golden Zhantil. Pando had contributed heavily to its construction. Grimly, I wondered how long it would be before the adherents of Lem the Silver Leem took it over.

The Bloody Menaham, as the Tomboramin called their neighbors to the west, readied themselves for further raids against Bormark. Pando's province usually took the first brunt of the attacks from Menaham. Defeated they may have been in Vallia; the Bloody Menaham who had been the most vociferous supporters of the infamous wizard called the Hyr Notor would not long delay in having a fresh onslaught started against their neighbors.

As we went along through the dimness with only two of Kregen's smaller moons hurtling low above us in the sky, I reflected that it was a great pity that the Pachaks Pompino had signed on in Tuscursmot were no longer with us. Brave and loyal, devoted to their employers under their honor code of nikobi, they had been among the first to die during the affrays and combats we had endured reaching here. I thought of them and the fights we'd seen, and consigned their ibs to a successful passage beyond the Ice Floes of Sicce to the sunny uplands beyond. As you know, I have tremendous admiration and affection for Pachaks among the splendid diffs of Kregen.

The Twins, eternally orbiting each other and shedding light enough to reveal desperadoes to the eyes of honest men, even if the honest folk were thus illuminated for the drikingers, sailed into the sky. Some of the nearer stars paled; but the sparks of light above scintillated brilliantly. The air tanged with night scents. Ah, a night on Kregen! There can be no other planet in all this wide galaxy, it seems to me, to compare with Kregen— beautiful, terrible Kregen under the Suns of Scorpio.

So through the splendid Moons' glitter we went, and I recalled how I'd begun this adventure with the simple object of burning a temple or two. Then I had been deflected by what seemed to me to be more important objectives. What a single man was going to do against an army I was not as yet perfectly sure. That I must contrive something was the only thought in my head on that score. But, this being Kregen, I began this night's jaunt with one priority ousting another, only to come full tilt against what was in my estimation another and altogether overriding priority...

Pompino's plan was simple, as he had indicated to me earlier on. As to the sorting out of who married whom, that had been materially furthered, I fancied, by the rescuing of the Vadni Dafni from the clutches of Murgon Marsilus. Ha!

"We all take different doors, bash 'em in, and throw in the firepots. That'll smoke 'em out, the rasts!"

So, that was the plan.

I'd demurred on one point.

Pompino's reply, brisk, no nonsense, summed it all up.

"Very well, Jak. We'll arrange a party to go in and get the sacrifices out. We'd better take—"

"No. I'll do it alone. I have the silver leem mask."

"You believe it can be done alone?"

"Yes."

"Then may the brightness of Pandrite shine upon you."

So, here we were, at the temple to Lem the Silver Leem, and the firepots were being brought to a fine state of combustion, cloaks were thrown back from sword arms, and we were spreading out to cover every bolthole. I put on the silver mask and marched boldly into the entrance from which I'd brought the freed girl sacrifices. From here I could strike any way. Pompino would not burn here until the last.

In the event, striding out, I met no one who offered to stop me. This, I judged, had something to do with the amount of silver lace on the brown cape, and the embroideries which, as far as I could fathom out, put the owner of this rig around halfway up their devilish hierarchy. He must have been discovered by now. Entering at the back instead of the front, I hoped, would avoid any checks. The corridor matched the one on the other side, and I entered the auditorium under a balcony matching the one I'd sheltered in the previous time I was here. This time the place was full, agog with anticipation and expectant excitement. And the girl sacrifice was there, in her iron cage, to one side of the stage, with all the blasphemous impedimenta of the Lem cult spread out.

The place reeked of unwholesomeness. Incense stank. Candelabra burned, and I eyed these with a view to incendiary activity. No one took any notice of me as I joined the congregation.

The girl in her white dress in the iron cage sucked on her sweets and played with a scrap of satin ribbon. Next to her the slab waited, flanked by ranked instruments. The statue of Lem in a silver glitter hovered above.

Three turns of his pocket glass, Pompino had agreed, would give me time to infiltrate and position myself ready. My own sense of timing told me the three glasses must be almost spent. I eased a little forward. The stage remained empty of all save the girl sacrifice, and I was minded to feel disappointed on this score for I'd marked any of the vile crew who tried to stop me for instant destruction.

The high priests and their acolytes and sycophants did not appear just yet, and the congregation waited, talking, excited, keyed-up.

The crash of splintering wood and shattering tiles jerked everyone's astonished gaze upward.

From the balconies to either hand men leaped down, their weapons flashing in the lights.

These startling newcomers wore armor, and helmets tufted with yellow feathers. But their faces! Each warrior's face was covered by a mask—but not by any ordinary assassin's mask—oh no. As the fighting men leaped down and ripped into the shrieking congregation, their faces snarled with the savage and frightening golden semblances of untamed zhantils.

Seventeen

A Rose between two thorns

Without hesitation I roared up onto the stage, leaping a screaming woman and kicking her companion in the face—quite accidentally—as I whipped up onto the boards. The girl in the cage held the scrap of blue satin ribbon before her face, her eyes wide, staring, not quite ready to start crying at all the hubbub.

Just about then the first firepots sailed in.

This place would burn like dry shavings.

The cage of the sacrifice, which, as I knew, sometimes held leems, was bolted. The bolt clicked back with a snick audible in the hullabaloo. I reached in.

"I have some more sweets for you," I said in what I tried to make a modulated and reasonable voice. "We're going to a special Banje shop—"

"You won't take me back?"

She drew away, the ribbon held like a shield.

I knew what she meant. These Leem Lovers knew where to go to buy their sacrifices.

"No. I promise you. To a Banje shop, that's where."

"There's a fire."

She spoke in her light treble, interested in what was going on, allured by the thought of candies, ready to cry or laugh as the occasion warranted. I flung a quick look back.

Pompino's lads were hard at it. Fire raced up the drapes and smoke roiled from two of the side openings flanking the main doorway. In the auditorium the zhantil-masked warriors were cutting down men and women indifferently and some, who appeared to be in authority, superintended the rounding up of those worshippers who threw down their arms and surrendered. It was frighteningly obvious that whoever the men in zhantil masks were, they were not over-bothered if the Leem Lovers fought or surrendered.

I snatched up the girl and leaped for the drapes at the rear of the stage.

If I cut to the side through any convenient doorway I ought to get back to the clear way out. Thank Zair there were no more girl children imprisoned there.

Others besides me had the same idea. They knew the layout and a bunch of them followed me along the dusty corridor. There was no point in fighting them at this stage, for however much the itch might have trembled my sword arm, fires burst up at our backs, and if we didn't get out we'd all be roasted—the girl sacrifice and me along with the rest.

People who attempted to escape through other exits would be met by walls of fire. Up ahead the corridor stretched empty both of flame and smoke. Pompino's folk would wait until I was out—and they wouldn't wait overlong, by Krun—and then this place would fire up, too. If, that was, the temple hadn't burned down already.

Empty of smoke and flame this exit might have been—it was not empty of golden-masked zhantil men.

As we broke out of the last doorway and made for the double doors leading outside, a line of fighting men in the zhantil masks fronted us, weapons glittering.

Now anyone who resisted Lem the Silver Leem was an ally of mine. Also, I had an idea I knew who had sent these men here, who employed them, who would use the zhantil mask as an emblem in defiance of the leem mask.

It was no part of my plan to fight allies.

To the side lay the other corridor, and there might be a way past there, so that I could circle... Clutching the girl child, who was now, most understandably, crying at all the din and confusion and the roar of the flames, the stink of the smoke, I turned sharply to break a way through. The zhantil-masked fighters crowded up to the rear. The Leem Lovers, yelling, pressed back. Smoke choked down, obscuring much of what was going on, and the evil crackle of the flames beat against the din of combat.

A hand clutched my elbow.

A leem mask glinted as a slender fellow in a short brown cape with little silver adorning its folds tugged at me.

"This way, Jak! Hurry!"

At his side a woman, more bulky than he, urged me on.

At once I realized these two must be Tipp the Kaktu and Monsi the Bosom, Naghan Raerdu's spies.

They guided me through the smoke away from the main mass of struggling people; three or four of the Lem worshippers spotted our movement and followed. Seven or eight of us crowded along, stumbling, coughing as the smoke retched into our mouths. Tipp the Kaktu threw up a trapdoor in the floor, Monsi the Bosom held out her arms to take the girl sacrifice.

"Quick, Jak—we must be quick!"

There was nothing else for it.

Monsi took the girl and bundled through the opening in the floor, I followed, dropping onto a straw-scattered floor with only the dim glow of the fire angling down to provide illumination. A body dropped after me and Tipp's reedy voice husked: "Go on! Go on!"

He smashed into me, and he cursed as more bodies dropped down after. The quick-witted among the Leem-Lovers desperate to escape the zhantil-masked killers had not missed this chance. In a bunch we ran along the murky corridor.

Naghan must have given strict instructions to his two agents. They would have had me under observation all the time, discreetly shadowing my movements. Just how far into the cult were they? They knew their way about what had been the Playhouse of the Singing Lotus. The cellars wound about confusingly and we had to backtrack at one point where the roof had fallen in, a mass of blazing timber. In the lurid orange light I saw the Leem-Lovers with us. Two men and a girl, quick and active figures, swinging around at once and retreating and then waiting for Tipp and Monsi to take up the lead. These were survivors, that was clear.

Gobbets of flaming wood tumbled about our ears as the floor above burned through.

One of the Leem-Lovers gave Monsi a savage thrust, shrieking: "Get on, you cramph, if you know the way out! Hurry!"

This behavior was normal for the Lemmites. Monsi stumbled and the girl cried out in terror. I caught Monsi about her waist—surprisingly slender for so large a woman—and took the Leem-Lover by the arm. I bent a trifle to him.

"Ill-treat this woman again and you go headfirst into the flames."

His silver mask ran with ruddy highlights. He tried to hit me and I threw him away, one-handed, and then hustled on with Monsi. "Shall I carry the girl?"

"I can manage, I thank you."

We did not use names.

As I say, the sequence confused. One moment we were hurrying along the cellar passageway, the next the whole roof collapsed. Monsi sprawled forward and the girl, her legs flailing, rolled over and over. Tipp screamed and jumped.

The woman Leem-Lover fell on top of me. The others were mere contorted shadows, writhing in the smoke and turmoil. I struggled to rise, pushing a burning bulk of timber away. I hauled the female Lemmite up and she sprang to her feet, lithe and lissom, swinging instantly to the help of her male companion. The way ahead was blocked. The three of us were cut off, walled in by flames.

"Which way?" shrieked the man.

"Any way so long as it is up," said the girl.

Again the sequence confuses. We tried more than one of the cellar passageways and boltholes, and we passed gagging through the space where, behind bars of solid iron, the leems were caged. No one thought of releasing them, poor dumb brutes though they were, in the common parlance, for the whole section of roof and wall collapsed into the thunder of an inferno as we shielded ourselves and ran on.

The girl had to drag the man past a tongue of flame that scorched across a narrow alleyway. I jumped through when it was my turn, and the Furnace Fires of Inshurfraz were no doubt hotter, but not by much, by Krun!

Beyond that point the girl sniffed out a way where fresh air was drawn in. We bundled along, colliding with the old worn projections of walls, barely seeing where we were going, finding steps with their treads hollowed into half moons, panting up, pushing desperately at the wooden trapdoor above.

The two halves of the trap flapped back. There was an impression of the night sky speckled with stars, a cool night breeze. Blocky silhouettes moved against the stars. A hoarse voice shouted: "Here are more!"

And the answer, begun: "Hit them gently for—" and a blurred shadow in the corner of my eye and the black cloak of Notor Zan swooped down and engulfed me.

As I must repeat, the sequence blurs.

Looking back at that frightful period I think I must have made an attempt to fight, so they hit me again, perhaps they hit me many times. My memory, which in the normal course of events, because of the immersion in the sacred Pool of Baptism, is well-nigh perfect, fails me in this. When exactly the dark cloak of Notor Zan enfolded me is open to conjecture. I recall nothing with clarity after that brief glimpse of the stars of Kregen, for I remember nothing of any internal stars in my old vosk-skull of a head. A pain in my wrists kept pricking at me, and I couldn't move my feet, and I felt awful, and my head hung down.

They'd hung us up in a row on hooks against the wall.

A hoarse voice croaked out: "By Lem! They'll pay for this."

The girl's voice, next to me and from the same direction, on my right: "Who will make them pay?"

Ungluing my eyes may not have been as painful as the uproar clanging away in my head; it was agony enough. I could see my feet, bound together, and the rough stone of the floor below, with an air gap between. I could see my legs, and the scarlet breechclout which I had, when I'd dressed myself up for the evening's entertainment, donned without a thought that this might be the outcome. Scarlet. Well, I'd chosen the brave old color out of sentiment, and because we struck a blow which might aid Vallia. So they'd stripped us of clothes. Yet they'd left the silver leem masks on, and the reason for this was made at once clear by another voice, harshly dominating, that broke across the girl's pointed question.

"Aye, you rast. The girl is right. It is you who will pay when our master arrives. Your masks are the badges of your shame and I spit on them and you!"

I swiveled my eyeballs and squinted at the fellow who spoke. That I shared his sentiments would not be believed. He wore bulky armor, and the yellow tuft of feathers in his helmet, and his zhantil mask glittered golden in the light of the becketed torches.

Just so we were kept alive until this fellow's master arrived... I was so sure that master had to be Pando I had already fathomed out his whole scheme, and approved, and wished I'd thought of it, and determined to put it to the best use of which I was capable as soon as I could.

There were four or five of the zhantil-masked guards and they began an argument among themselves whether or not the leem masks should stay on or come off the captives. I managed to get my eyeballs to swivel to my right and saw the girl hanging as I was hanging, her arms spread out and hooked to the wall by leather thongs. Her body, stripped to a breechclout, as was mine, arched in an instinctive and futile struggle to free herself. She, like me, wore a red breechclout and this—I confess—amused me. It seemed odd. As for the fellow beyond, the glimpse I could catch of him showed a wiry body and a green breechclout. In other circumstances if it came to a fight, my natural ally would be the red and my natural foe would be the green; here they were both Leem Lovers, Lemmites, as the word was, and they could both go hang.

As, by Vox, would I!

Eventually the zhantilman who wanted to keep the leem masks on was overruled. One of his companions, a potbellied individual, said: "I'll jump up and down on 'em!"

Another one—and, in the nature of these things he was thin and quick—said swiftly: "Aye, dom, you do that. And when you're finished I'll melt 'em down. They'll fetch a fair price down the Boulevard of Silversmiths."

Thick fingers reached out to unlatch the leem masks, the thin quick fellow merely slashed my latchings away so that the mask fell into his clawed hand. He laughed, a hollow rattle behind his own mask.

I blinked.

With the skills taught me by Deb-Lu I managed to fashion a gyp-face; but it stung like the devil, and I guessed the repeated knocks on the head had done me no good at all. I'd recover fully, thanks to the Sacred Pool of Baptism in far Aphrasöe, but right now I was still muzzy, not quite in command of myself, and feeling as though I'd been in a fight with a leem...

My head hanging, I watched dully as the guards, chuckling over their booty, left the cell. The door clanged.

There seemed little chance that this dungeon cell was in the Zhantil Palace. Probably Pando had set up his headquarters for his zhantil masks in a safe house in Port Marsilus. The quicker he got here the better, for I surmised his delay had been caused by the arrangements for this sort of exercise. The problem from his point of view was that the Vadni Dafni, whom he had been trying to rescue, was already rescued.

The fellow in the green breechclout started a long complaining monologue, filled with imprecations and obscene curses and threats. He would have his powerful friends carve up the zhantil faces. His sorcerous friend would blast them into black cinders. He would scatter their ashes across the Sea of Opaz, and glee as each cinder fell. He did not sound at all pleasant, and with the Bells of Beng Kishi ringing and clanging away in my head I found him tiresome. Also, muzzy as I was, I thought I knew that voice.

The girl said: "Do leave off! Think of a way to get out of here, by Vox!"

Jolted, I said: "If you're a Vallian they'll kill you twice over here." My head hung down, and I was too shattered to open my eyes against the sparking glitter of the torches.

The man said in his shrill hiss: "Vallia is doomed! The great enterprise will most certainly destroy all that proud and haughty land!"

And the girl, in her hard yet modulated voice, said: "The battle is not yet won, Zankov, and if we're dead before it begins, where is the profit in that?"

Zankov!

The bastard was hanging up helplessly—and so was I.

And this girl...

I opened my eyes against the sting and squinted.

I could remember her only as a grown woman. All the time she had been growing up, as a little child in her white dress with her toys—her dolls and beads and daggers—I'd been on Earth. I'd seen her as Ros the Claw, fighting splendidly for what she believed in. She had tried to slash my eyes out. I'd carpeted her, and carried her out of a pit of evil. She had, when she understood that—at last and so late, like any cretin—I knew who she was, she had withheld her blow. She had not slashed her lethal Claw and taken off half my face.

Confident that Pando would soon be here, light-headed with the blows I'd taken, muzzy, I cast all thoughts of caution aside.

So few words I'd spoken to her, so few, and now the important ones had to be of death...

"Dayra," I said. "That fellow Zankov, hanging next to you, killed your grandfather. He slew your mother's father, not me."

In the silence, the torches spat and crackled.

She turned to look at me. The gyp-face was gone, smoke blown with the wind.

Yes—she was my daughter Dayra. That face, passionate, willful, stubborn, beautiful in a way that her mother Delia was beautiful and yet with an added darkness that—to my despair—I knew must come from me, that face that had haunted me now regarded me with a look I could not comprehend.

Then she said, in a whisper: "So you continue to lie and cheat and betray! How typical of you—the man I most loathe in all the world!"

My old head was going up and down like a swifter in a rashoon. I swallowed down the sick. I couldn't shake my head for fear of the consequences.

I said: "You are willful, and also a fool. Zankov betrayed you, more than once, and plotted to take the crown and throne and to kill me—which might not be altogether a bad thing—and to kill all the family. He tricked you at the Sakkora Stones—your mother was chained up, and he would have slain her. Barty Vessler—"

Zankov's thin bitter voice cut in, hatefully.

"Do not believe this kleesh! He lies! It is clear he lies!"

"I do not lie. You have betrayed Dayra too many times—"

"Perjurer!"

"There is no need for me to lie. What I say can be tested by witnesses—"

"Foul cramphs like yourself!"

The whole dungeon spun about me and the heavy blows inside my head beat and reverberated. For a space I could not say any more, only dwell agonizingly upon the bitter memories, while these two hung up beside me spoke in fierce, staccato whispers I barely heard, let alone comprehended.

Odd words spurted out, as they do from vaguely heard conversations. "Great enterprise." "Argenters." "Galleons." "Delphond." "Gold." The word gold spat out, more than once, something about the treasure and its safekeeping in trust.

Why didn't Dayra ask this bastard Zankov? Why was I so useless? Zankov had killed the emperor, slain him before witnesses including the Lord Farris and others, chief among whom was Delia. Delia! Hanging there in my agony I thought of her, and—as always, as always, thanks be to Zair and to Opaz and Djan—her presence in my life, whether beside me or on the other side of the world, uplifted me and strengthened me, gave a spark of courage to go on.

"Ask him!" I bellowed out and my words husked like a dry broom sweeping a gutter in the stews. "Ask him why your mother was hung up as we are hung up now, and he with a dagger in his fist. Ask him how Barty Vessler was slain! Ask him to his face, and let him deny that he killed the emperor your grandfather!"

"Hold your tongue, you stupid old fool!" came that bitter venomous voice. "Dayra knows who her friends are."

Desperately, reaching out with all the willpower I could muster, I said: "Dayra—you know your mother. I plead for myself in a despicable way, now, I admit. But—but, Dayra, do you think she would remain with me if I had killed her father?"

Her face turned to me and I saw that she was far more troubled and disturbed than I had thought, imagining her hard and brittle, and hating me so. "I—have wondered. Mother would not tolerate... No... I have not seen her since—"

"Since that cur-dog there tried to kill her!"

"Do not listen to him, Dayra!"

"Your mother and I miss you sorely—I own to my misdeeds. If you spoke to her, you would learn the truth—"

Zankov spluttered out in his staccato way: "Your mother believes this rogue, of course! She is easily duped. No doubt she lusts after him as a—"

"Zankov!"

But he rattled on, letting all the bile spill out, conscious of his own illegitimate ancestry and the deviltry to which he had resorted to place the crown of Vallia upon his own head. He'd had the help of the arch-Wizard of Loh, Phu-si-Yantong, the Hyr Notor, who was now—thank Opaz—dead and gone. He had the aid of many enemies of mine.

If it does not sound too bombastically pompous, too egomaniacal, they were the enemies of Vallia, also...

If I reiterate that the blows on my head interfered with my thoughts, turned my brains into a sludgy puddle, I do so, I believe, as much to explain the fogginess of my perceptions as the lacunae in my memories. Head hanging, a thread of blood running down from scalp to ear and so dripping drop by drop upon the stone floor, I persisted in this petulant obsession—why did not Dayra question this bastard? The grayness swirled about my eyes; yet my ears picked up drifts and snatches of their words—and, yes, Dayra did question him, I hoped, and his answers, at first convincing, gradually became more incoherent, more shrill, so that he ended by simple blasphemies and kept harping on the enterprise against Vallia and his ambitions and the great treasure. He was greatly concerned about the treasure.

"...damned treasure," said Dayra. I strained to hear in a lucid moment, only to have the sounds in the cell swirl away as though caught in a silent storm. When I could hear again, Dayra was saying: "...you and everyone said my father was a ninny, a puffed-up propaganda hero of a prince. Yet I found out differently, when he fought under the voller and escaped you all."

"Tricks, Roz, tricks only!"

"Because of you and our friends I tried to kill my own father! By Opaz—" and here her voice shook with more than the pulse of blood in my own ears. "You've never properly explained why mother was treated so cruelly at the Sakkora Stones—"

"We had to convince her! You know that!"

"So you told me and so I believed. But chained up—"

Then the grayness returned and when I could take stock of what was going on again they spoke more harshly, one to the other, with more bitterness.

"I wish Hyr Brun was with me," and Dayra spoke passionately of the yellow-haired giant who was her faithful bodyguard.

I croaked out: "I hope Hyr Brun is not dead, Dayra, for he is a good man, and the child, Vaxnik, also, a brave proud spirit—"

"They live. They are not here. Had they been—"

"Thanks to Opaz they are alive—and I hope the girl sacrifice I sought to rescue is safe, also..."

"Who cares for a slave girl bought for the glory of Lem!" Zankov spoke as any worshipper of Lem the Silver Leem.

Stung, I said, "Dayra—I am disappointed, I find it hard to believe—how could you descend to this evil nonsense of Lem the Silver Leem—?"

"And you! You wore the silver mask! You are a Leem Lover! That damns you, that causes me to distrust and hate you—" She did not go on. Banal words, but spoken with a fire that scorched.

So—I took heart!

"Listen, daughter, and mark me well. I and my friends oppose Lem. We set fire to the temple tonight. Aye! My comrades burn the stinking temples to Lem. I wore the silver mask only so that I would have the chance to rescue the girl sacrifice..."

"How can I believe!"

"He lies, Ros, he lies!"

Then Zankov stopped his shouting, abruptly. Dayra spoke slowly. "If he lies, then... And if speaks the truth, then..."

Zankov was caught both ways. He blustered and raged, swearing most vilely. I kept silent, head hanging, feeling awful. How I had contemplated this meeting with my daughter, the Princess Dayra, known as Ros the Claw... How often I had imagined its circumstances. How could I have foreseen that it would be like this—with Dayra hanging like a Rose between two thorns!

Their voices blended, one shrill and bitter and loaded with invective, the other hard and growing harder, suspicious, horrified. I'd started this adventure with a simple objective, as Pompino had said, but that had been deflected by a greater urgency, and I was now in a peril so great as to cause me to tremble, me, Dray Prescot, father of this girl who was troubled out of her wits... Bad advice, no advice, bad example and no example... Her life, despite the connotations and her connection with the Sisters of the

Rose, had been no bed of roses... She deserved more from me than I could repay.

I do not think any words of mine—the stupid, stumbling, feeble words—tipped the balance. Dayra had been misled, deceived; but she was not a stupid girl—how could she be, how could any daughter of Delia's be stupid? She must have harbored doubts. That she had rationalized the sight of her mother hanging in chains must have caused her intense agony; doubts persisted, engendered despite all the wily and malevolent advice heaped upon her by her friends.

Zankov confirmed my suspicions.

Among the threats, the taunting, the obscenities, he reproached Dayra. "You have proved stubborn in the past, and have grown worse lately." The thin bitter words crackled as the torches spat sparks. "I have lost a great deal of the hope and trust I once had in you. You are an ingrate—and this miserable kleesh, your father—"

"I have tried!" She sounded distraught and yet, and yet, through all her desperate despair, that hard note of reawakening reality heartened me. "I believed you and our friends. The Kataki twins—I believed what they said. All of you—because my father was not there. And the calumnies you put about regarding my mother—are they lies, also?"

My blade-comrade Seg Segutorio had been forced to kill a few folk for these false and vile rumors about Delia. I'd experienced horror when he'd told me—death for a few words! Now, seeing the havoc they had wrought, these few words, I could wish Seg had dispatched all the dispensers of lies and calumnies regarding Delia... Dayra had suffered, and I had not known how she had been affected.

I croaked out—and Dayra turned her head to listen to me even as Zankov spluttered and blasphemed on her other side!—"Dayra—your mother is above reproach from anyone, she cannot be touched by the stinks of offal like that."

The effort of speaking nigh exhausted me. I could feel the blood dripping down my face. I'd been sore wounded before, far worse than these clumsy blows on the head, and I'd recover well enough. But I needed to be alive and vigorous right now. Right at this moment I needed all the strength and willpower I could muster. This schemer Zankov had to be unmasked, and now. Dayra could not be expected to change her mind about the conduct of her life in an instant. The painful process would take time. She had to be convinced and then when she had thought it all through for herself and seen the truth, why, then she would make the decision.

All I could do was hope Pando got here in time.

And—I could go on through the dizziness and put in what arguments I could, explain, keep calm—keep calm!—and try to make Dayra's agonizing reappraisal an experience that would not destroy her. That, I shuddered to think, was a real danger... But, was it? Would a daughter of Delia's be shattered? I took heart. No—not while the Ice Floes of Sicce exuded their chill breath!

Intermittently I heard Dayra trying to question Zankov, and he slid away from the quizzing and harped on the great enterprise and his powerful friends and the treasure they had entrusted to him to pay for the ships that would carry the army to Vallia. I struggled to listen and learn of this, although I cursed the fellow and willed Dayra to press her inquiries.

"The Lord Farris?" shouted Zankov, answering one of her questions at last. "Yes, he was there. When I see him he will tell you the truth, him and Lykon Crimahan both!"

Spluttering, I coughed out: "Lykon Crimahan! I did not speak of him, Zankov, so how—?"

"It is common knowledge—"

"It is not common knowledge. Lykon Crimahan, the Kov of Forli, returned to his kovnate and fought the aragorn and the slavemasters. He was no friend to me. But now he is loyal, and he saw you slay the emperor..."

"He saw you, you cramph!"

"I think," I said to Dayra, "that unless Crimahan is very careful, if this fellow here is let free, these words have signed Crimahan's death warrant."

"He and Farris, all of you!" shrieked Zankov.

Dayra turned those gorgeous brown Vallian eyes on me. I could see her mother there. "And you truly joined the Lemmites and wore the silver mask to rescue the sacrifice and burn the temple?"

"You saw me carrying the child to safety. The temple burned."

"Yes..."

"Did you, Dayra, become a Leem-Lover—?"

"I never was! D'you think I could—?"

"No, my daughter, no, I do not think you could."

"We'll see!" shouted Zankov. "You have betrayed me, Ros. I am finished with you! When my friends get here—"

"Or when the Zhantil masks return," I put in, hard.

We hung there, the three of us, breathing hoarsely. This Zankov, for all his villainy, had courage. And I saw what the plan was against Vallia, the thoughts ringing in my head. They would land the enterprise in Delphond—my Delia's Delphond!—and march to cut off my lad Drak. They'd catch him between two armies, crush him, and then turn like leems on the capital of Vondium. It all fitted together. And Zankov had the money to pay for it all. A deal of that gold had gone to Strom Murgon, that was clear. They were all in it. Pompino's actions and mine against the Leem Lovers had been, also, against the foes of Vallia.

It all fit.

And I was strung up like a bird in the kitchen to be plucked, stuffed and roasted...

The time dripped away. Zankov kept on railing against Dayra, and she protested that she must have time to think and he made it perfectly plain that if she was not wholeheartedly for him then she was against him. He became more malevolent. He was confident. He knew the strength of the forces arrayed on his side.

The sound of iron-shod sandals, the crash of the bolts on the cell door brought a cry of triumph to his lips.

Eagerly, I looked, aching to see the golden masks appear, and Pando, and to have this ghastly ordeal over.

"Now you will see!" he crowed. "The silver leem-masks will destroy you forever, Dray Prescot!"

And I said in all my stupid arrogance: "And the golden zhantil-masks will rid the world of you, Zankov!"

We three stared in awful fascination as the door opened.

The wood creaked back. Torchlight flared brilliantly.

In that eye-watering radiance as the door opened—we stared—warriors broke in—in that brilliance the wink and glitter of silver overpowered in the stinking stone cell.

Eighteen

Of the spitting of Ros Delphor

"Cut me down! Cut me down!"

Zankov's voice cracked with triumph.

The silver-masks rushed in and then halted at the sight before them. One jumped as though stung when Zankov shouted, and leaped forward, dagger lifted. He slashed the bonds and as the thongs fell free so Zankov collapsed forward onto his knees. He breathed in huge gasps. Wiry, vigorous, alive, he wore the green breechclout drawn up tightly.

Green is a perfectly ordinary color for a Vallian, and Zankov was Vallian, if nothing else. Dark blue is the color Vallians shun, to my sorrow. Pale blue is acceptable in seacoast provinces, and the old Vallian Air Service used to wear dark blue and orange in a fashion that did not last upwards of ten seasons. So, the importance of colors was not lost on me as Zankov shoved up, turning lithely, fighting the cramps, to gloat upon us, and I recognized that, yes, indeed, green in all the evil connotations of that otherwise admirable color was fit garb for him.

An Ift wearing the leem mask reached up his dagger to cut Dayra free.

Zankov knocked him aside.

"Give me the dagger, and stand away, rast!"

The Ift obeyed instantly.

Zankov took the dagger and fronted Dayra. He laughed; his eyes were very merry.

"Hurry, notor, there is not much time," said a fellow whose dark beard sprouted around the edges of his leem mask.

"There is time for this, Handroi." Zankov spoke in his thin and bitter voice and yet he was filled with elation. "You are a fool," he told Dayra. "You have failed me. I have suspected you for some time past, and now I know your allegiance to Lem the Silver Leem was mere make-believe. Well, shishi, think on this, before I kill you. You have a sister, you have two sisters, and a niece. When you are dead and gone wandering the Ice Floes imagine me, wed to Lela, or to Velia. Either will do. Or, if they fail me, I shall wed your niece, Didi. All are in the line of succession. And, all the others, all, will be dead and gone and moldering!"

With that, triumphantly, he lifted the dagger to strike out the life of my daughter Dayra.

She spat in his face.

Now, if I repeat that I am Dray Prescot, Lord of Strombor and Krozair of Zy, too often, you may well think of me as a braggart. But this repetition arises from humility that life has afforded me so much. I do not boast. I state facts that mean a great deal. The bonds cut into my wrists. My head still felt as though it had been battered around a camp of my Clansmen in Segesthes. But, just because, I had to try.

The bonds broke—at last. Of course, as I fell in a heap to the stone, I expected to die at once. That mattered little—save for one or two items of unfinished business—but Zankov would not dagger the life from my daughter while I lived and could prevent it. And, if I thought of my daughter Velia, the first Velia, as I staggered up and bundled all any old how into Zankov, that, too, I think you will understand...

I butted him a thwack in the ribs and he bowled over like a ponsho brought down by a leem. The dagger remained fast clenched in his fist, and I couldn't reach it. It was vitally necessary to roll over and over, away from the expected slash of blade or shaft of arrow.

"Father!" screamed Dayra.

Zankov, screeching, staggered up, the dagger glittering. Beyond him a fellow in a leem mask lifted his short bow. The arrow head centered on me and I dived aside, pivoted, put a foot into Zankov's green breechclout. His face joined that color scheme.

He fell away and a bulky Brokelsh rushed, sword uplifted. I twisted him over my shoulder so that his head and the leem-mask hit the floor with an almighty thwack. Blood spurted, but the damned sword skittered across the stone flags, and I reared up to dodge the next arrow or front the next attacker.

The chances were not entirely hopeless... Frantic action, constant movement, swift, savage and sudden...

Two more leem-masks dropped, broken, and my fingers reached for the hilt of a thraxter. In the corner of my eye a blurred rush—Dayra's passionate yell: "Your back!"—a twist, a vicious thrust of the sword—blood gushing over my wrist—a blow sending me staggering sideways—a recovery and sight of a silver-masked Rapa lifting his bow. Off balance, I tried to twist to avoid the shaft. The Rapa did not loose. He swiveled sideways. An arrow stood in the center of his back. He fell forward onto his beak, bent within the mask.

The heavy tramp of footfalls and a voice, a booming bull voice just finishing saying... "Tromple all over 'em!"

Yet, despite that Pompino and Cap'n Murkizon and Quendur the Ripper and Larghos the Flatch bustled in, roaring, laying about them with the deadly flicker of steel, the first into the cell was Tipp the Kaktu.

Instantly, belting an inopportune Fristle over the furry head to make his whiskers wilt, I leaped for Dayra. The thraxter sliced bloodily through the bonds. She fell against my chest, and I held her, held her, as she trembled.

"Listen, daughter. Call me Jak. I am just Jak. Remember—"

"Jak the Drang?"

"No. Just Jak—sometimes Jak the Shot."

She recovered with the swift catlike ability that must have kept her alive in many a perilous situation when there was no mother or father to keep an eye on her.

"And me—Jak?"

"A friend. We have both been accustomed to using aliases. Are you still Ros?"

"Yes. But not the Claw—"

"Very well." The uproar bellowing away, as Pompino's fellows from *Tuscurs Maiden* and Tipp the Kaktu who had watched me and brought the crew here, fighting mad, sorted out the Lemmites, formed a chorus to Dayra and my quick words. "Yes—then you must be Ros the Radiant—"

"No. Delphor. Ros Delphor."

"As you wish—" A body with its head hanging and the silver mask slashed across tumbled past. "I'll have to help the lads now—"

"You said I am to be a friend. It won't be as easy or as quick as that."

"No. But it will—Ros Delphor!"

And I went roaring harum-scarum into the fight and, lo! it was all over.

Pompino brushed up his whiskers and stared around.

"By the tangled and nit-infested locks of the Divine Lady of Belschutz! What a mangy crew!"

Cap'n Murkizon's axe glimmered darkly with blood. Pompino said to me: "You are unharmed, Jak?" Then he laughed. "I seem to be saying that with distressing frequency, by Horato the Potent!" He stared at Dayra.

She stalked arrogantly across the floor, kicking bodies out of the way, ripped off a few capes and cloaks and things until she found a decent gray cape to swing about her shoulders. With a gray tunic—with only a few spots of blood—to go under the cloak, and a thraxter in her right fist and a dagger in her left, she paced back. She moved with the lethal grace of a hunting leem, and—as I thought in my admiration for this woman who was my daughter—with the nobility of a zhantil.

I made the Pappattu quickly.

"Scauro Pompino the Iarvin. Ros Delphor." And the others, swiftly, for we had to get clear of this place, and there were certain acts I had to perform this night before I could think that this adventure was over.

Together, we hurried from the cell. Needless to say I'd clothed and armed myself. We climbed stairs, and as we went I made it my business to say to Tipp the Kaktu: "My deepest thanks, Tipp the Kaktu."

Without the leem mask his face showed quick, intelligent appreciation of events. His nose was on the thin side; but his mouth was finely formed. "Naghan Raerdu is a generous paymaster. Also, he is very sudden. And, again, I do not care for people who chop up children."

With those sentiments, I fancied, we had the beating of the Lemmites.

We saw no more masks, either silver or golden, as we went through the house, apart from masks upon corpses. Stopping, I bent and freed the leather latchings of a golden zhantil mask from a dead man. He looked peaceful enough lying in his own blood. I stowed it away with a fine silver mask in the pouch taken from a fellow whose swag belly held more than the pouch. We pushed open the last door and so walked out onto the streets of Port Marsilus under the radiance of the Moons.

Among all the twisted corpses—and, believe me, I'd looked with attentive care—not one revealed the thin and bitter features of Zankov.

When I asked, Larghos the Flatch said, crossly: "That one, I shot, but a hulking Brokelsh got in the way and took the shaft in an eye. When I looked again this fellow—Zankov?—was gone."

"We'll blatter him yet!" boomed Murkizon, cheerfully. He mentioned the Divine Lady of Belschutz, and added: "That sort run hardly upon their noose."

Ros the Claw, Ros Delphor, said nothing.

I said to Tipp the Kaktu, and I own I felt concern: "Monsi the Bosom? She is safe—you both got out of the fires in the cellars?" He saw my concern. "And the child?"

"Yes, Jak. And the child."

"Thank the good Pandrite."

Dayra favored me with a swift liquid upward glance; again, she said nothing. Pandrite, a chief god of Pandahem, sat oddly on the lips of a Vallian. In a bunch, desperadoes, all of us, we moved along the street, our cloaks and capes flaring in the night breeze.

The glow in the sky suffused drifting clouds with orange; of flames, nothing, and of smoke, none in the night. The temple, that had been the Playhouse of the Singing Lotus, had not taken long to burn to the ground. But, by Krun, she must have made a splendid spectacle when she roared in fury!

Moderating our progress now we were away, we still kept a sharp lookout. Pompino fell in on my other side. He glanced across at Dayra, at ease and most gallant in his haughty Khibil way.

"My lady. Where may we have the honor of escorting you?" And then, before she could answer: "You appear to be friendly with our Jak, which he does not deserve. Perhaps you would care to favor us with an account of your acquaintance, although, of course, one would not press..."

Jesting though he was, he struck shrewdly.

Dayra did not flinch.

"I give you thanks for your timely rescue, kot— horter Pompino. Jak claims friendship with me; I am not sure I give mine so freely."

"Aha!" exclaimed Pompino, bubbling now with the aftereffects of the fight in his blood. "I knew it! I always said he kept secrets too well. You see, my lady—"

I broke in. "Some secrets—like secret wine drinkers, and some not so secret, like Herry Tarkness, of the great spirit and dedications, steeling themselves to face the edge—some secrets remain so, and, therefore, by definition, cannot be known."

He eyed me and licked his lips and did not brush up his moustaches. "The point is, Jak, we are collecting a great harem of womenfolk, and what are we to do with them all?"

"The children could always join your two pair of twins and Ashti of the Jungle."

Abruptly, he slapped his thigh, laughing. "Capital. And my dear lady wife would welcome them, too, for her ideas encompass far greater imaginative leaps than that."

"As for the ladies—Nalfi and Ros for the moment—they will do what they will to do."

"I will to see about Zankov," said Dayra. She spoke with a rasp. "Jak— you heard him talk of the treasure?"

I was there, already, ten leaps ahead. I nodded. But it would be boorish to tell Dayra her own plans.

"Treasure?" said Pompino, bristling up.

I had to say, gently: "My lady Ros—if treasure is in the wind I must warn you these lads have sticky fingers."

"They may take it all, for me, provided they take it from those who possess it now, and those who covet it for gain."

"Well, that last category covers the crew, for a start."

But, for all the banter, we were deadly serious. And Dayra was shrewd enough to see she did not have to spell it out.

"How many do we have to knock over?" Pompino transparently gained in good humor. "For I realize the generality of this army they're hiring would not be privy to the secret whereabouts of the pay chests."

"No one trusts anyone. Zankov admitted—back there—he had lost his trust in me." She sounded hard, determined, not bitter or resigned; but changed. Oh, yes, Dayra had changed in those traumatic hours. I was not fool enough to imagine that the change would encompass my good graces—not just yet, anyway. She went on: "Like any undertaking of this sort, they set up a complicated series of transactions. They used agents and tools of accomplice. Kov Colun Mogper of Mursham, which is in Menaham and therefore suspicious to these Pandaheem, had a hand in it. He worked with Strom Murgon."

"But the treasure?" persisted Pompino.

"I do not know where Zankov got it from. He fell out with his master, the Hyr Notor, and when he died, Zankov seemed relieved of a great burden. But it is certain sure Zankov could never lay his hands on so much gold. There is someone—or some group of people—anxious to harm Vallia—"

"Anxious to open the gate to plunder and slavery," I put in, quickly. Dayra might be an accomplished agent in Vallia; here in Pandahem she would have to be more careful. Already, she'd said "kot" for koter, the Vallian word for horter, and now she was showing a lively concern over the island empire that, to most Pandaheem, could sink into the sea to general joy and thanksgiving.

As though echoing these unpleasant thoughts of mine, Pompino said: "That might be a capital adventure."

Casually, being careful, I said: "Better to lay our hands on the treasure now. That is real and within our grasp."

"Aye. You are right, Jak. By Horato the Potent! What it would be to return home with gold enough to make my lady wife blink—maybe then the gold might match her ambitions." He considered. Then: "No. No, I do not think gold enough exists for *that*."

"I," quoth Dayra with great firmness, "am starving hungry."

"And I!"

While on Kregen some taverns stay open all night, not in general being irked by licensing regulations, we deemed it prudent not to patronize a public eating place. To the best of our knowledge no one spied on us as we hurried into the Zhantil Palace. Our friends were relieved to see we were still alive. The temple had blazed awesomely. Some of Pando's property had burned along with it, and Pompino and I exchanged glances. That problem was for the future. Just when young Pando would get into Port Marsilus remained unknown. Framco had not returned, and this was perfectly understandable; there was no message from him.

Tipp the Kaktu had disappeared en route here—gone home, clearly. He and Monsi would not know who I was, if Naghan Raerdu exercised his usual caution. Only my daughter Dayra was aware of my true situation; and, as you may imagine, there were very many things we had to talk about—very many, by Zair!

Also, you may imagine my relief when no one had heard or seen the Vallian ambassador, Strazab Larghos ti Therminsax. Naghan Raerdu must have shuffled him off successfully in some other way than involving Captain Linson and the ship. *Tuscurs Maiden*, I gathered, had pushed off from the jetty and moored up a few hundred paces offshore. A sensible precaution, that...

We ate hugely, plundering Constanchoin's best, and drank moderately, refreshing ourselves, and then we slept ready for the morrow's exertions. Like the day that had gone, tomorrow would be a big day...

We stood to as the mists of dawn curled silvery vapors above the battlements and the twin suns began their daily shafting of emerald and ruby light across the world. There was time only for the Fristle ord-Deldar, Naghan the Pellendur, to shriek out a single warning.

The main gate simply erupted as the iron-headed ram burst through. Smashing the splintered wreckage aside, leaping ferally into the palace, armored men shocked into instant combat with the guards. The clang of steel and the hideous uproar of battle told us we were abruptly faced with mortal danger. Men swarmed into the palace, the Brown and Silvers brandishing weapons and seeking to destroy all within and take back the Vadni Dafni—for, striking magnificently in the warriors' van, Strom Murgon led that devastating onslaught.

Nineteen

Sheathed Talons...?

In a twinkling, Deldar Naghan the Pellendur's men were tumbled back from the gate and the first courtyard. Rushing up I was in time to join the defense as we sought to hold the inner wall. The uproar flowered to the rising suns.

Arrows shafted in; but the overhang prevented them from striking down upon us. That first abrupt onslaught was held—somehow—and we gained a breathing space. When the next attack came an odd thing happened.

Now, as you know, I am not one of your fighting men who believe they must have one special weapon in battle. Any paktun who depends on a particular sword is likely, if he goes adventuring, to be parted from it smartly. If, then, he feels incapable of fighting well with another weapon— oh, no! Oh, no. Your true paktun will fight with whatever comes to hand, a master of any weapon.

I own that I have gone to some lengths to retain a particular Krozair longsword, or a matched set of rapier and main gauche. But not to extreme lengths, by Zair...

So, as we fought, I used a thraxter. The stout weapon, shorter and fuller than a rapier, served well in the crude bash of the melee. A warrior, brave undoubtedly, tried to get at me over the wall, and I cut him down. His companion, a moltingur, tried to stick me from the side. I blocked the blow and, even as I struck back, recognized the weapons the man wielded. They were the rapier and main gauche I'd had from Captain Nath Periklain in *Schydan Imperial*, the very matching set I'd lost when the zhantil-masks knocked me over. Without hesitation I trampled the moltingur down—in turn, in turn!—and snatched the weapons. The fellow wore my belts, also. In the next few moments, as we drove back that assault, I was able to drag him in by the proboscis and strip the leather from him.

Pompino said: "You're getting fussy, Jak." Then he saw the weapons, recognized them, and said: "You know what you told me—"

"Aye. But, right now we are like rats in a trap."

"True. But you must admit we are trapped with as bonny a bunch of fighting men as you could wish."

"I'm past being choosy in whose company I die."

"Ha! By Horato the Potent, you speak sooth. And, my friend, I'd like to know how this Murgon knew and why he chose to attack now."

"Spies, Pompino, spies. They get everywhere."

"We can hold them in that chamber with the zhantils painted along the walls—for a time..."

"I'll tell you one thing that is no longer a puzzle. This rapier and dagger were taken from me by the zhantil-masked people. Now they turn up here with Strom Murgon. That means that moltingur was a leem-mask who slew the zhantil-faces."

"And they roar out into the open—and here they come again!"

So, once more we went at it, tinker fashion, hammering them back. Just how many men Murgon would commit we had no way of knowing. We

145

did know that he'd have more men than we did. Also, through his lavish dispersal of the funds provided by Zankov, he'd have no trouble from the ordinary folk of the city. No doubt they fancied they'd be better off under Murgon than serving Pando. I did not share that opinion...

As we battled and then drew back, using all the tricks of which we were masters to delay the foe, everyone became aware that we were never going to halt Murgon until he had destroyed us all. The odd little thought occurred to me that one was entitled to wonder what Zankov would think of this use of his money...

The booming roar of Cap'n Murkizon as he exhorted us to: "Hit 'em, knock 'em down, tromple all over 'em!" heartened us. The two varter-ist sisters, Wilma the Shot and Alwim the Eye, highly displeased there were no ballistae they could shoot, got stuck in with bows and then cold steel. Rondas the Bold, in his element, fought magnificently. Nath Kem-chug, dour, fought as only Chuliks can fight. Quendur the Ripper, like quicksilver, slashed now here, now there, battling back. Larghos the Flatch shot superbly—I even fancied Seg might have nodded a quiet approval. Chandarlie the Gut had a gigantic boarding pike and this dripped red. As for Lisa the Empoin, despite Quendur's entreaties, she stood shoulder to shoulder with us in this fight to the death. The Lady Nalfi was not with us and for the sake of Larghos the Flatch we welcomed her absence.

In a quick breathing space as the enemy pulled back and the remnants of the Fristle guard joined us, with Naghan the Pellendur shaking the drops from his scimitar, Pompino spoke in a fretful way, as though affronted. That this, in the midst of battle, was highly amusing was almost—almost but not quite—lost on my comrade.

"We're trapped here, Jak—and for what? We do not have to hold the pal-ace, for Pandrite's sake!"

"True. Murgon can bring so many men he'll push us back until there is nowhere left."

"It will be dead men and women who reach there, that place at the end," said Rondas the Bold. He whiffled a finger through his facial feathers. "But I shall not reach that end. I shall charge into them, going forward—"

"Yes, Rondas," I cut in, "admirable. But wait a few murs first. Strike with us, together; that is our strength."

"Normally, yes—but this is not your usual battle."

They had all missed my meaning.

Pompino, I knew, although he talked of retreating until we were all slaughtered in some hole or corner, would instantly seize the other course. He would, even though it meant us all rushing out to what appeared cer-tain death. Each one of us would believe that he or she would scrape through somehow.

So I spoke the obvious words, and they all agreed.

"Although," said Lisa the Empoin, "and remember I stick with Quendur—although this Kov Pando ought to be here soon. I stayed in the palace, and they talked of nothing else."

"My heart," said Quendur, gently—and with the blood splashed gorily upon him, "Do not put too much store by a miraculous rescue—"

"You know me, Quendur, by now! I merely pointed out what I had heard—onker!"

So, we were all in good heart.

In good heart to rush out upon our sudden deaths.

Constanchoin was told to take all his people and the slaves and those who could not fight and find some secure place where they might bargain for their lives. At that, a number of sturdy slaves volunteered to join us, and we provided them with weapons, to the horror of the good Constanchoin. He would, we felt, strike a bargain with Strom Murgon.

The best place to make the break lay toward a side entrance. Naghan knew the palace. In furtherance of these preparations we had pulled back swiftly, abandoning a whole block of the building within the courtyard, and barricading doors and windows behind us. We collected in the ground floor hall of what we were told was the Nathium Cupola. That lofted many stories above our heads. We prepared to rush out.

Someone called in excited shock. Heads turned.

Through the distant clangor as Murgon's men broke down our improvised barricades, through the buzz of the people, through the nervously clinked sounds of steel against iron, that voice lifted high.

"*Mindi the Mad!*"

She was there, standing as before, head lowered and her pale blue gown depending in its straight folds into that neat circle about her feet. She stood against a small and insignificant door leading to a slave's cleaning room. She lifted her head. Her hand rose, a forefinger beckoned.

Naghan yelled: "Mindi!" Then he rounded on us. "She is a witch and she knows many strange things—"

As Mindi beckoned again, I said: "And she knows a secret way out of the palace, that is clear."

"Aye!"

They roared out, now, most of them, yelling: "Show us, Mindi, show us!" And: "Lead us to safety, Mindi!"

Rondas looked thoroughly put out. Murkizon whistled his axe about.

"Now then, you two!" and Pompino spoke with barbs in his tongue. "No fighting without cause—remember where we are going and what to do, and then think again!"

"Aye, you are right, Horter Pompino, although I was set upon the last great fight—"

"Not today. Let us follow this Mindi the Mad."

So, that is what we did. We trooped along through the slave's cleaning room and down stairways and along flang-infested corridors and so, after a goodly distance, came to a blank end to a side corridor. The pale insubstantial specter beckoned us.

We looked at the blank masonry, dripping and green with lichen, and our torches struck sparks from nitre specks.

"Is this it!" demanded some.

The dead-end corridor contained a broken chest to the side, holding rusted iron, and the place stank of rotting vegetation, a dank, stagnant stink.

Pompino brushed up his reddish whiskers and stepped forward. No haughty and smart Khibil, his manner proclaimed, could be beaten by a small mystery like this—no, by Horato the Potent!

Cap'n Murkizon let rip a bellow. "The lever to open the secret block is here, in this rusty iron." He stalked over to the broken chest. "It is obvious!" With that, he bent to grasp a projecting rod of orange-rusted iron.

With a liquid flash of blue the spectral form of Mindi the Mad reared before Murkizon. He staggered back. One arm flung up to protect himself and the other groping futilely for his axe.

Mindi pointed up. She stabbed up twice, and then brought her palm down, flat and squashing. Her face reflected the greatest alarm.

It was clear—as Pompino acidly pointed out.

"Had you pulled that lever, Cap'n—a great block of stone would have dropped on you—and us! Squash!"

Cap'n Murkizon stood back. He did not mention the Divine Lady of Belschutz.

Mindi the Mad pointed to a certain junction of masonry where a finger hole showed, black and oozing water. Into this Pompino stuck a finger. He did so with great aplomb. He might have had it bitten off, and he knew it. He twisted. With a groaning like a miser paying out gold, a doorway-sized block of stone revolved before us. The stink gushed out, gagging us.

Quietly, Dayra said to me: "I think I like your Khibil friend very much—for a Khibil and a friend of yours."

People pushed through the opening. Dayra and I stood aside as the crocodile of children went along. We'd brought them with us when a chance of escape favored by Mindi had presented itself. Caring for them were Natalini, Sharmin, Tinli and Suli.

One little girl's slipper fell off and she was too scared and too pushed along by the others to stop for it. I bent and picked it up.

"If we leave any signs Murgon will know where we've gone."

And—I swear it!—even as I said this we heard the first sounds from the maze of corridors at our backs. The tread of iron-studded sandals, the clink of spear or sword against stone, told us we had to hurry. A small group remained to the last, ready to bash anyone who tried to stop us. Rondas was still in half a mind to rush out to the last great fight; we did not quite drag him into the opening; but he was highly reluctant. As for me, I had greater schemes afoot than enjoying a bout of sword-fighting in the cellars, by Krun!

All the same, I managed to persuade Pompino to go on and sort out what lay ahead while I brought up the rear. So, it chanced that I was the last to go through into that dark opening and Dayra the penultimate.

A wooden horizontal bar across the inside of the slab afforded purchase to close it. I put a hand to this, Dayra stood at my side and helped. The slab began to revolve to close us off in secret and, far off down that main tunnel the sounds hastened on and a gleam of light struck into the nitre flecking the walls, reflected like an accusing host of eyes.

I stopped shutting the slab.

"What's up now?" demanded Dayra, still pushing on.

"Wait a moment, Ros." With that I turned sideways and slid through the narrow crack. I reached down to the certain junction of masonry where a finger hole showed. From it I drew out a palm's length of ribbon. Water stained the ribbon darkly, but the stripe of zig-zag silver down the center had reflected that accusing flicker of torchlight. Dayra's whistle of surprise was stifled instantly. I stuffed the ribbon into my flap-pouch, squeezed back into the opening and together we closed the slab.

The stink really got up my nostrils, and Dayra said: "By Vox! What a pestilential place!"

I said: "Use Pandrite, or Chusto or Chozputz—"

We crept along a narrow and slimy ledge with the sounds of the others before us and the erratic light of their torches to prevent us from stepping into the sewer at our side.

"Chusto?" said Dayra. "Chozputz? I've never heard—"

"Nor has anyone else. I made them up."

"Oh!"

"And we have someone in our midst who leaves ribbons to mark where we went."

"You have no suspicions?"

"None. It is probably one of the slaves we armed and brought along. Or, possibly, one of Naghan's guards. They seek to earn a disreputable coin or two from a grateful Murgon."

"They will earn something a little different from me, by Vo—Chusto!—when they are unmasked."

"When."

The small sewer led into a medium-sized sewer which led to a large sewer. The striking fact was the stinks did not improve or lessen; the folk of Port Marsilus were median in their ablutional functions. Scurrying claws fled from us; we met no fearsome monsters and I was mightily thankful for that. I thought of the girl children and the way their new dresses were being ruined. At last we reached a manhole where Pompino's fiercely whiskered face peered down, and he said: "Come on, Jak! We're waiting for you! Oh—my lady Ros—here, take my hand."

With great gallantry he assisted her up. We were in a shadowed shed racked with implements like shovels and brooms and water-carrying equipment. So we could wash some of the muck off before we started out into the daytime streets of the city.

"To skulk off from a fight does not please me," Pompino said. "But the greater good demands this dishonor."

"Gold demands it," I pointed out—with little pleasure.

"Lead us to the gold," quoth Cap'n Murkizon. "I fancy we know what to do with it after those pestilential sewers."

"Beng Dikkane will wax fat," said Larghos, his arm protectingly around the lady Nalfi. She looked disheveled and unhappy.

We decided not to split up to slink through the city but to go in a bold body down to the docks. Dayra guided us. We met no one who offered to stop us; we guessed word of our presence would quickly reach Murgon. We just had to beat him for speed.

At the jetty the children were ferried out to *Tuscurs Maiden* with the lady Nalfi and some of the slaves who had escaped with us and were not fighters. Then we went along to where Zankov's ship, the swordship *Igukwa Valjid*, lay moored.

The watch saw us coming, of course, and attempted to resist. But with gold in the nostrils of our fellows we were not to be denied. The watch either went overboard or fled. Dayra knew exactly where the chests were stored; the iron bars presented no problem to gold-hungry rascals like us, and we began to pass the strong iron-bound lenken chests aloft.

About the time we had a sizable pile at the jetty and the first boatload had gone across to *Tuscurs Maiden*, the sentries shouted the alarm.

Mounted men galloped down onto the stones of the jetty, shrieking, shirling swords and slanting lances. We formed to meet them and that first impetuous charge was shot to pieces.

"There will be more of the rasts," panted Pompino, shaking his bow. He shouted back over his shoulder. "Hurry up, there! Get the chests aboard!"

"Quidang!"

The next attack combined a few kreutzin with the cavalry so that we shot and then came to handstrokes. Still we had the beating of these disorganized attacks. When Murgon and Zankov brought the full weight of their new army to bear it would be a different story. By this time the holes we had punctured in the bottom of *Igukwa Valjid* had admitted water enough to bring her deck level with the waves. A pity we could not have seized her and pulled her out; that was not on in our circumstances. We braced for the next onslaught and saw that off, and then there remained but the one pile of boxes, a ship's boatload.

All this time Dayra had placed the balass box she'd brought from Zankov's vessel by her feet on the dock. She did not move from that spot overmuch as she shot with the precision taught by Seg Segutorio. The bows from *Tuscurs Maiden* were the short compound reflex bows of Pandahem, with a few crossbows; with them we wrought great execution. But our time was running out.

I said to Dayra in a pause in the fighting: "Do you go with this last load of chests, Ros."

"I think—Jak—I will remain for a while yet."

As she spoke she looked at her balass box and then searchingly at the files of soldiers trotting out at the far end of the jetty. Her face lit up. I whirled.

He was there, leading on a group of men, Zankov, arrogant, brittle thin, nervous, yet filled with courage. I marked him and shot, and missed, and Dayra laughed.

"I do not think that one is yours, Jak."

"I'm glad Seg didn't see that."

Zankov rushed on at the head of his men. Larghos the Flatch reeled back with an arrow in his shoulder, whereat he cursed wrathfully. Rondas the Bold's mail was slashed and dangling. Nath Kemchug's Chulik pigtail gleamed with blood from a head wound. Cap'n Murkizon whistled his axe ferociously.

I said: "Mayhap we had best leave this last pile of boxes."

"I'm not leaving the gold for this mangy pack!" roared Murkizon.

Working like demons the men hefted the chests into the boat. The second boat pulled frantically for the shore to take us off. We might still do it. The Suns glittered on the water, gulls screeched and winged overhead, the air scented sweet with the sweetness of Kregen—it was good to be alive and futile to die for a handful of gold. But gold is gold and people are people; there is no gainsaying that on two worlds...

The front rank of soldiers hit us and we battled back. We halted them and sent them reeling and someone screeched: "The gold is loaded! The boat is here!"

"Time to go!" roared Pompino. "No arguments, anyone!"

We knew what he meant right enough.

"They come in again!" yelled Rondas. "Hai, Jikai!"

Ros bent to her bronze-bound balass box. From its velvet-lined interior she took her Claw, the shining razor-sharp Talons, and strapped them up on her left arm. Now she was a Taloned Demoness, a Sister of the Rose, one who could slash the face from an opponent and stick another with her rapier.

We jumped into a last mad affray, a jumbled affair of leaping and ducking, of slashing and hacking. We were pressed back, and a slave, brave with his new-won freedom and his spear, died under our feet. I felt the rage at the waste and pressed in ruthlessly. Ros the Claw, slashing, slicing, merciless, cut the face from a fellow and instantly swirled to take the side of a face from another. How her wicked Talons raked in! How they smashed in and twisted and left merely a red wrecked pudding!

With horrified disbelief I saw she was down. In a twinkling she slipped on spilled blood and took a vicious glancing blow from a thraxter. Instantly I dashed the brains from the fellow before me and hurdled his body and reached and scooped up my daughter. Ghastly visions of Velia floated before my eyes—I would not lose two daughters, not while I lived!

Zankov rushed me. His sword blurred. He would have gutted me then and there, but I managed to twist and kick him in the shins. He did not howl but staggered back. His thin and bitter face shone with effort, his eyes were wide and drugged and hating. He gathered himself for the final spring when he anticipated he would finish us once and for all.

A broken axe haft whirred past his head. He ducked in reflex action. A broad, barrel-like form hurtled past. Arms spread wide, red face a Zim-set of fury, that compact thunderbolt of muscle crashed into Zankov.

"...of Belschutz!" Massive arms wrapped about the thin and brittle form.

"Back to the boat!" screamed Pompino. "Bratch!"

I did not hesitate. Oh, no, not me, not puissant Dray Prescot with a wounded daughter in his arms! I simply scuttled for the boat and the waiting arms of the crew. I saw Dayra safely into the boat and then turned back, sword out, ready once more to hurl into the fray.

I saw Zankov was bent across Cap'n Murkizon's knee. The barrel body strained as a woodcutter casually strains to break a branch for the fire. I do not believe Cap'n Murkizon needed great strength or pressure. He jerked his arms downwards. Zankov stiffened and went limp. He drooped. Murkizon threw Zankov away and ducked back, haring for the boat. Arrows fleeted past, feathering the first of those who tried to follow.

We all bundled into the boat. Covered by arrows we pulled for *Tuscurs Maiden*. We were all flushed, wrought-up. I bent to Dayra. Her eyes opened.

"It is nothing," she said, most acidly. "A worse knock is suffered in training—"

"Lie still, Ros Delphor, lie still."

As we neared the vessel her canvas rose. Captain Linson was all prepared to go—no doubt he'd have gone if we hadn't reached him in time. The boat hooked on and we were hoisted bodily from the water. *Tuscurs Maiden* heeled and headed out to sea.

Wearing an untidy yellow bandage around her head, Dayra insisted on staying on deck. I joyed in having her at my side, and trembled, yes, trembled in terror at what lay ahead for us in our prickly relationship. I could not expect to be received back as a dear and doting father in the blink of an eyelid. Also, by Zair, the young miss needed to be thoroughly conversant with the magnitude of her follies.

Pompino said: "Without pay, the captains of what ships Murgon has will never chase us. By Horato the Potent! We've hamstrung him finely!"

Certainly, no movement could be observed among the small scatter of shipping. *Tuscurs Maiden* sailed splendidly, carrying us well out to sea.

Mantig the Screw, one of the few apims in Framco the Tranzer's guard detail, reported in. He'd been sent with the message, and reaching the Zhantil Palace to find it besieged, had very sensibly gone on to *Tuscurs Maiden* to find us. A sharp-set young man, with a pointy look to his face—his nose was not exactly screw-shaped, but the general suggestion could not be denied—he delivered the message briskly.

"The cadade informs you that the Kovneva Tilda is safe at Plaxing. Kov Pando is with her. He is aware of the situation—"

"Is he, by thunder!"

"The kov has with him the Mytham twins and Mindi the Mad, who keeps his intelligence."

"That explains that, then," said Pompino.

I was amused. Pompino, who like me was a kregoinye, working for the superhuman and supernatural Star Lords, took their incredible powers perfectly matter-of-factly. But when it came to a witch performing a little lesser magic the short hairs bristled!

Naghan the Pellendur, dourly, said: "And I'll wager, by Numi-Hyrjiv the Golden Splendor, that unhanged rascal Twayne Gullik played both ends against the middle. He's loyal again because Kov Pando is with him."

"A fellow to be watched," observed Pompino.

The breeze tautened our canvas and the bluff bows smashed through the billows. The stout lenken chests were stowed below, and Cap'n Murkizon and Nath Kemchug, with Rondas the Bold and others of our friends, oversaw the stowage with exactness.

Cap'n Murkizon gave his opinion that the few swordships in port might follow for the gold. This would not worry us once we were well out into the offing. When Murkizon joined us, Dayra looked at him searchingly. He huffed and harrumphed, and then said: "I think his backbone was broken clear through, my lady; but he was not dead."

Dayra said to me: "I think I will go below, now—Jak."

At the head of the companionway she halted and looked back. "Call me if there is a fight." She went below. We had a great deal to clear up; but, first, another important matter had to be dealt with.

"Gold," said Pompino, "equals dead men and women."

If in the ordinary way a mercenary received a silver piece a day, less if he was an Och, more if he was a Pachak or a Chulik—or a Khibil!—and if Murgon had recruited something like thirty or forty thousand men, with ships to transport them and ration allowances, plus the mounts for the cavalry, then we might expect to find a treasure of considerable size. How long the enemies of Vallia expected the campaign to last with their own gold before they could subsist from the Vallian countryside, must remain conjectural. Pompino was confident we had laid our hands on the equivalent of two hundred thousand gold pieces, for much of the treasure would have to be in silver coins. This treasure would be shared out among us according to the usual customs. We would have to set reliable watches and sleep with our swords naked at our sides.

Just where all this gold was coming from I could not know for sure. I had a terrible belief that I did know. Well, if I was right, then the future, dark though it might be, held also the promise of vivid action and headlong adventure, together with intrigue and peril enough to frizzle the scales from a dinosaur.

All that had to wait. Now I could luxuriate in the thoughts I had been keeping at bay and now was unable any longer to resist.

When I saw Delia! By Zair! What a story to tell her—Dayra, the fierce and ferocious taloned miss, the merciless Ros the Claw, our little Dayra—at last true to Vallia and to herself. Yet this was not a facile example of the return of the Prodigal Daughter, oh, no. Very much it was the return and redemption of a Prodigal Parent—for Delia had always retained Dayra's love, of that I was very sure, despite what I had seen to the contrary in times past.

If I could win my own daughter's affection, if I could sheathe those Deadly Talons—wouldn't *that* be a thing to tell Delia?

MASKS OF SCORPIO

Masks of Scorpio

Masks of Scorpio, chronicling the headlong adventures of Dray Prescot on that marvelous world of Kregen four hundred light years from Earth, is, like all the volumes of the saga, arranged to be read as a book in its own right. Dray Prescot is a man above middle height, with brown hair and eyes, brooding and dominating, an enigmatic man with enormously broad shoulders and superbly powerful physique who moves with the deadly grace of a savage hunting cat.

The Star Lords, mortal but superhuman beings, have a grand design for Kregen and employ Prescot and his Khibil comrade Pompino to perform the derring-do sections of the plan. Often at cross-purposes with the Star Lords, Prescot is now wholeheartedly with them in their desire to stamp out the unholy cult of Lem the Silver Leem.

Down in the island of Pandahem, Prescot, using the alias of Jak, has burned a temple or two, has rescued his wayward daughter, the Princess Dayra, Ros the Claw. They have seized the treasure of an army outfitting to invade Vallia.

Always looking forward, Prescot must face this new relationship with Dayra. With the crew and mercenary marines of Pompino's ship *Tuscurs Maiden*, they are sailing into fresh adventures under the streaming mingled radiance of the Suns of Scorpio.

Alan Burt Akers

One

Gold

How do you get on to civilized speaking terms with a daughter you haven't met until she was a grown woman, a tiger-lady with Whip and Claw who once sought to rip your face off? It's not all that easy. No, by Vox, not at all easy!

We sat together in the mizzen top, looking aft. Far astern two shining triangles showed where the pursuit gained remorselessly upon us in the quartering breeze. Soon they would overtake us and attempt to board and we would fall to handstrokes in the red roaring madness of battle—but far, far more important than that were these first stumbling steps in building a relationship between father and daughter.

My daughter, the Princess Dayra of Vallia, known as Ros the Claw, could not be expected to become suddenly all Sweetness and Light. After all, she'd hated and loathed me all her adult life. To find out that she had been betrayed and deceived, lied to, misled, and that I wasn't quite the rogue she thought—not quite, but nearly, by Krun!—must have hit her with a shock that might topple less resilient minds.

As our ship, the stout bluff-beamed argenter *Tuscurs Maiden*, sailed on across the Sea of Opaz, bursting the water to a dazzlement of foam, she said to me: "What am I going to say to mother? I feel such a—such a—"

"I'm prepared to take most of the blame there is floating around," I told her. "Most, but, by the Black Chunkrah! not all! You've got to face up to it, too. And your mother shares no part of the blame. Frankly, I don't know how she has managed over the seasons, what with me going off and the children turning into a bunch of rapscallions—well, except for Drak—"

"Drak!" She laughed, high and perhaps a little too tensely. Her face—that gorgeous passionate face so much like Delia's face darkened by the undercurrents of character she must inherit from me—regarded me in a wild, self-hurting way. "Drak is a sober-sides! He's so high and mighty and filled with his own sense of integrity he'll—he'll..."

"He's a good brother to you, Dayra."

"Perhaps he tried to be. He did try to speak to me a few times... But I was surrounded by brilliant and clever people who told me—"

"Who told you a pack of lies!"

She did not answer but held out her hand for the spyglass.

"They're catching us," she said, the glass centered and swaying with our movement. "But they're slow about it."

With that characteristic half-tilt of the head and a swift squint up she established the positions of the Suns. The great red sun, Zim, and the smaller green sun, Genodras, the twin Suns of Antares shed their streaming mingled radiance upon the face of Kregen and Dayra wrinkled up her nose and said: "I doubt they'll overhaul us before nightfall."

"The Maiden with the Many Smiles is due early," I pointed out. As the largest of Kregen's seven Moons, the Maiden with the Many Smiles would afford light enough for boarding.

"True. But there will be cloud."

"You're sure?"

"No. But it is likely. Zankov was always complaining about the clouds."

I made no reference to Zankov, the chief instigator of my daughter's ills. My comrade, Cap'n Murkizon, in breaking Zankov's back, had not quite killed him. I couldn't honestly say I wished greatly for the rogue's recovery.

As though the thoughts in our heads followed a similar train, Dayra said—and with a tartness that was not all mischievous twinkle: "Suppose I told this bloodthirsty crew you've gathered around you just who you are? If I told them you were the Emperor of Vallia—what d'you think they'd do?"

"That's easy. They wouldn't believe you. I'm just Jak, or Jak the Shot, or Jak the Whatever Has Recently Happened. They'd laugh in your face. But, still, if you care to, try it. Tell them."

"And your foxy Khibil partner, Pompino?"

"Well, I'll allow he might believe it. He has heard the name of Dray Prescot mentioned before."

She steadied the glass upon the two pursuing ships.

"Oh?"

"The lord of Bormark—whose coast is just visible to the southward—Kov Pando, and his mother, the Kovneva Tilda, knew me when I told them I was called Dray Prescot. They remain firmly convinced that I used the name as an impostor. They believe I am Jak, for they met the real Emperor of Vallia on an unhappy occasion for them. That, they tell me, was not me. So I think Pompino will take the same tack. It is not easy to persuade ordinary folk that emperors and princesses go wandering around among them—as you should know, Ros the Claw."

"You call me Ros Delphor!"

"Agreed. I merely made a point."

Mind you, young Dayra for all her artistry with the Whip and the Claw, the rapier and the dagger, for all her cunning and resourcefulness, was still not yet your fully accomplished spy. She unthinkingly used Vallian expressions. She swore by Vallian gods and spirits. Down here in Pandahem, whose various nations had over the seasons fought many costly campaigns against reivers from Vallia, Vallians were not welcomed with open arms. She'd chosen to adopt the new name of Ros Delphor. Now, I happened to know where Delphor was, although it boasted but one claim to fame, and that within the boundaries of Vallia.

Delphor was a tiny, insignificant, placid village situated in a pleasant and verdant spot in Delia's Imperial province of Delphond. Its one claim to fame was that, some five hundred years or so ago, the puissant and much-respected Sister of the Rose, Vasni Caterion ti Delphor, had been born in a tiny thatch-roofed tumbledown. As I say, this information would mean nothing outside the island empire and, one has to admit, precious little inside, except to those who cared. I just happened to know through the insights vouchsafed me into the Sisters of the Rose and allied sororities by the Everoinye, the Star Lords. The point was, Delphor was a Vallian name. It had the ring of Vallia. Dayra ought to have chosen a name either more neutral or positively Pandahemic in its associations.

So said I, watching those two bloodhounds forereaching on us, and gauging the descent of the Suns, and worrying over Dayra, and, in general, not overmuch enjoying myself.

"You all right up there, Jak?" bellowed up Pompino from the quarterdeck.

I leaned over. His reddish whiskers bristled, his arrogant fox-like face shone ruddily. I bellowed back.

"All all right. They gain on us steadily."

"May the black flux of Armipand suck them down!"

Dayra said to me: "Do I detect a querulous note in our proud Khibil?"

"Oh," I said. "Pompino's top class on land, and in a fight on the sea. But since he bought his fleet of ships he's turned into a worry-guts over them, coddling them like a hen over chicks, always worrying that something will bring disaster—"

"Something usually does!"

Those sort of laws operate on Kregen as on Earth...

Dayra had only recently won free of her evil friends, and we had had little time together in which to pack all the talking necessary. Mingled with the wondering reflections on our previous conduct when we had met were all the painful readjustments we had both to make. There was no sense in trying to rush all this.

Pompino yelled again, and the lookout perched in the crosstrees screeched down the enlightening information that our pursuers gained on us, slowly but relentlessly.

"I'm for a wet," I said.

"I'll race you down." With that Dayra hoicked a long and shapely leg over the side and started down the ratlines, going like a grundal of the rocks. To do what any self-respecting middy would do, and slide down the backstay, would see me on deck well in the lead. I did not. I clambered down after her and we touched the planks at the same time, flushed and with something of that mad helter-skelter enthusiasm that comes of rapid descents. Eiffeltoweritis, you could call it.

"Ha!" Pompino greeted us with a flourish, twirling up his mustache. "You two have something to cheer you up, then."

"Unlike you, Pompino, who has the cares of a fleet of ships on his shoulders."

"Aye! Well may you mock! Every time I put to sea I am beset with pirates, with storms, with everything to upset a fellow!"

"That's the way of it when you're a sailorman."

No one aboard knew that Dayra was my daughter. She was known as Ros Delphor, a good companion, and handy with a rapier. If those two ships tracking us managed to board, Dayra would be in there, hacking and slashing with her Claw and thrusting with her rapier. She was worth two in a fight like that.

That I felt absolute horror at the prospect, that I heartily wished my daughter was not involved, is only half the truth. Certainly I wished that Dayra was not into all this fighting. But, as this was Kregen and she was a princess, a Sister of the Rose, and engaged on hazardous missions, then what must follow would follow and there was precious little I could do about it.

Captain Linson, master of *Tuscurs Maiden*, spoke in his brisk efficient manner. A valuable man, this, one who while seeking his own fortune enhanced the fortunes of the Owner. That Pompino would see this arrangement the other way around was, besides being amusing, a part and parcel of the relationship these two had.

"We're in for a blow," said Linson.

I stopped myself from the instinctive snuff at the air. For what may appear simple reasons, I had pretended to have no knowledge of the sea. This was a foible which amused me at the time I'd first begun it; now it dragged a trifle. All the same, I would persevere...

"You think so!" exclaimed Pompino. He bristled. He took it as a personal affront when the gods of the waves heaved in wrath and upset his insides.

"Green Nasplashurl of the Seaweed Mane will ride tonight, I think," went on Linson with dry relish.

Pompino cast a hunted, a furtive look around.

"Is there no cove where we may shelter, captain?"

"With those two beauties on our tail, horter?"

"Oh, we'll blatter them, good and proper, when the time comes. I'm thinking of my supper."

"You mean, dear Pompino," said Dayra, "that it is likely not to remain your property for long?"

A booming laugh brought Cap'n Murkizon, barrel-bodied, startlingly red of face, fiery-eyed, alongside. "I'll warrant you'll keep your supper down, horter Pompino, if we get to handstrokes with those fellows! By the decaying gums and putrescent eyeballs of the Divine Lady of Belschutz! There's nothing like a little blattering to tighten up a fellow's insides!"

I felt for my comrade. He and I both worked for the Star Lords and carried out perilous missions for them. We'd come to this strange, unspoken, understanding that each was responsible for the other in the eyes of the Everoinye. They might not see it that way, for they were superhuman, mysterious powers who spoke to us through the agency of a giant scarlet and golden bird. But we felt it. For sure.

"The pity of it," I said, "is that this ship is from South Pandahem. Up here in the north—well, what do you know of the shoals, the navigation points, the hazards? Cap'n Murkizon? Captain Linson?"

Both shook their heads.

"We sail without charts here—and that is a fool's pastime." Linson had not suffered to let his view on this folly be known.

"Unless we take charts from some wight or other..." Cap'n Murkizon let his words trail off, uncharacteristically.

"From them?" I said, and jerked my thumb sternwards.

The rascally leanings of these rapscallions were proving a joy to me, used as they were in the service of the Star Lords and Vallia. In the fertile loam of their scheming brains the idea rooted itself instantaneously, grew, flowered, and their reactions exploded in a thunderous chorus of: "Aye!"

I was, as the saying goes, showered in petals.

Since the time when he'd counseled us to refrain from fighting the hideous Shanks and then we went ahead to fight them, Cap'n Murkizon fancied his honor impugned and considered he continued on in life with a slur attached to his name. This was not so. What it did mean was that, the Cap'n Murkizon with us at the moment would not, most certainly would not, be the one to mention the odds. He would not point out that we would have to fight two ships. A few moments ago all we had been thinking of was running away from them and taking the treasure we had—liberated was the right word here, by Krun!—to where we could share out the spoils; now we turned our scheming minds to the question of how best to ensure the destruction of our pursuers.

Well, that is not only the way of Earth as of Kregen, it is a way to gain your ends, or gain your end.

Wilma the Shot stepped forward. She and her sister, Alwim the Eye, had proved themselves fine varterists who could shoot their ballistae with great accuracy. Also they had fought with us with cold steel, and we valued them with their free ways and their ready comradeship in hard times as well as good.

"We cripple one of them," said Wilma, with firm confidence in her and her sister's expertise in loosing the rock or the dart from their ballistae. "Then we draw off and—"

"Take the other like a plucked fruit," finished Alwim the Eye.

"Sound," said Pompino. "Very sound. Your thoughts, Captain Linson?"

"I sail the ship, horter. I can handle her to run rings around those two." He pointed a casual hand aft. The glint of sail was visible from the quarterdeck now.

No one was fool enough to comment that these two had the heels of *Tuscurs Maiden*. Argenters are built for carrying capacity and for comfort, not for speed.

The two varterist sisters, well-pleased, went off to check their weapons which needed no checking. Between them they could knock over just about anything those two sea wolves on our tail might put up against them.

The rest of our company would be as ready to fight as they ever were. An interesting little problem cropped up as clouds began to build and some of the refulgent glory of the twin suns dimmed. Our two pursuers would surely catch us before nightfall; if the brewing gale broomed in with any power before that the whole picture would change. If the storm held all night as it might well do, we might never see these two sea wolves again. And that, it was very clear, would suit us admirably. With the treasure we had won aboard and crying out to be divided up according to the customs, a fight would at best be merely a distraction from the important work, and at worst might mean we could lose the gold.

"Pantor Shorthush of the Waves holds a personal grudge against me. I am sure of it," said Pompino. He spoke fretfully. Up here in Pandahem they called Shorthush of the Waves Pantor, instead of Notor, his lordly title down in Havilfar. He was one of the armada of Kregen lords who out of spite or mere idleness, mere mischief, send the gales to sink honest men's ships.

"I think Pantor Shorthush may be smiling, if wickedly, upon us, Pompino, for if the outskirts of the gale strike us early we can use them to escape those two fellows back there."

"Escape? I thought we were going to blatter them for charts—?"

"Oh, we will if we have to. But we have more important ends than that." I stared up at the massing banks of cloud. "Anyway," I added with deliberate carelessness, "we can always buy, beg or steal charts at a more convenient time."

"I suppose that is sooth..."

I wasn't about to tell my comrade that I wished devoutly to avoid a fight because Dayra was aboard.

And that reason, of course, was highly ludicrous. Ros the Claw was a formidable fighting phenomenon, well able to take care of herself. All the same, in the brutal slog of a boarding action even the finest swordsman of any number of worlds—and I am not that one—can get a knock on the head and drop into the sea with a splash that ends all...

And, I admit to a fascination in finding out just how good Dayra was. That she was very good indeed was obvious from her training with the Sisters of the Rose, from her exploits, and from the simple fact that she was still alive.

Tuscurs Maiden ran on in her lumpy wallowing fashion and Captain Linson kept casting black looks aloft to match the gathering sky. He was reluctant to take in any canvas. If he did so the pursuers would race up to us; if he did not and the breeze increased with sudden ferocity he could lose a sail or two, perhaps a spar. The situation was tricky.

Down in the Shrouded Sea in the great continent of Havilfar, south of the equator, sailors have to deal with volcanic disturbances almost as often as gales. Down there they call on Father Shoshash the Stormbrow, imploring him through Mother Shoshash of the Seaweed Hair not to destroy them. Up in Vallia the seamen of the superb Vallian galleons call less on the gods and spirits of the sea in terms of supplication, demanding a live and let live policy. Vallian sailors trust to their ships and their nautical skills. They apostrophize Corg from time to time; but he and they rub along.

Had we been in a galleon of Vallia now, I would not have been so concerned. As it was, I owned to a lively feeling of imminent disaster. And this, as you will perceive, was because I sailed with my daughter as shipmate.

So it was that when the blue-glimmering apparition appeared on the forecastle of the ship I was among the first to leap eagerly for the help promised.

"Mindi the Mad!" yelled those who knew her. She had helped us before and now she was going to help us again...

We crowded up. She stood on the castle which, in an argenter was a real castle-like construction containing varters and not the low lean fo'c'sle of a galleon.

"Mindi! Mindi the Mad!"

She stood there in her usual pose, head downbent and her auburn hair shining from a light that never came from the suns above us. Her pale blue gown reached in its straight folds to a circle about her feet. Her arms were folded in the gown.

Yet her figure wavered. She shimmered. We all knew the witch was not really standing on our forecastle; but her apparition presented far less of the solid reality it had shown before. A dark blur of the bowsprit showed through her, until her blueness coalesced and she was fully fleshed before us; then the image flickered and wavered erratically.

Naghan the Pellendur who ran our guards with admirable correctness in the absence of the cadade, said: "She is having great difficulty. And there is no wonder at that!" He spoke with a crisp disdain which embraced the sea and all things to do with the ocean.

The blue-gowned apparition lifted an arm. A pale hand pointed landward.

We all craned over the bulwarks to look.

A shadow raced across the sea. Clouds massed above and the radiance of jade and crimson lay low across the water beyond the shadow. Rimming the horizon the coast of Bormark lifted jagged peaks.

Captain Linson said: "If we sail inshore I will not answer for the shoals—"

"Yet she clearly intends us to do just that." Pompino tugged at his whiskers.

"She must know a way of safety." Naghan the Pellendur looked decidedly unhappy. He was a Fristle, and it is notorious that that race of catlike diffs are not enamored of the sea. They make atrocious sailors, and are generally not employed aboard ship. Naghan, for one, would dearly love to set foot safely on dry land once more.

Cap'n Murkizon let rip a bellow.

"Put good men in the chains, Captain Linson! Go craftily. If this witch leads us, we can find a safe passage. By the unwholesome armpit of the Divine Lady of Belschutz! For an expert captain such as yourself the risk is not so great!"

The mockery with which Linson habitually treated Murkizon was now being turned back on his own head. It was amusing. The situation itself, also, held amusing overtones. I simply stood back and didn't even bother to take a mental wager on the outcome.

An abrupt blast of wind that stretched our canvas and heeled *Tuscurs Maiden* settled the issue.

We were convinced that Mindi the Mad knew the coast and that she would not send us hurtling down onto rocks driven helplessly by the wind. There was a secure cove there sheltered from the gale. That had to be so...

In the refreshing way of your rapscallion Kregan they would have fallen into a sprightly argument, well-spattered with flowery oaths, before deciding to do what was obvious.

For some unfathomable reason—no doubt connected with my thoughts of Dayra—I was jolted into a memory of the time I'd spent as a kaidur in the Jikhorkdun of Huringa in Hyrklana. The arena's silver sands had wallowed in spilled blood and I'd fought as a sworder against horrific beasts and wilder men. In those days I'd dreamed of my baby twins, Drak and Lela, for the rest of the children had not yet visited Kregen. I'd thought, even then, that babies grow up and face their own problems. Well, by Zair! My children had grown up and they did, indeed, face their own horrific problems. The amusing kicker here was that Dayra's twin brother, Jaidur, had grown up to become the king of Hyrklana. I could never have expected that when I'd fought in the arena in Huringa's Jikhorkdun!

So, impelled by these old thoughts, and perhaps with more of that old, lowering, black, devil's mask that was the real Dray Prescot, I stepped forward.

"Let us follow Mindi's direction and seek a safe cove and to Sicce's Gates with these rasts who follow us! Then we can divide up the treasure and see each one of us obtains his just share and reward."

Pompino glanced at me with a perplexed look. Then, at once, he shouted: "Captain Linson! Kindly steer the ship where the witch directs. As soon as we find a safe anchorage we can—" here he brushed up his whiskers in a way which said that, by Horato the Potent, he might not know much about ships; but he was the Owner, and he knew a bit of sea-going jargon or two "—where we can drop the hook."

Some of the old sea salts down in the waist laughed at this; but the situation eased dramatically.

As for me—I felt the relief that Dayra was going to be kept out of another fight. She was a trained fighting girl, a mistress of the Whip and Claw. She had sheathed her Talons for a space. Those wicked razor-sharp talons affixed to her Claw that could rip a fellow's face off as soon as look at him, they would remain sheathed if I had my way.

And that, as any onker could tell you, was as unlikely a happenstance on Kregen as anything else. The future would not hold that Sweetness and Light I craved, and yet the darkness would be illuminated by flashes of that lightning that comes only from good companionship and stout hearts and a brave striding on against fortune.

Running before the wind we sped rapidly toward the coastline. Any skipper in his right mind would have nothing whatsoever to do with this madness—running freely down onto a lee shore! Insanity! But we trusted the pale-blue glimmering apparition of the witch-woman, Mindi the Mad.

The moment an upflung headland of gaunt striated rock passed away to starboard the wind moderated spectacularly. Our canvas flapped. We moved on sluggishly in the wayward eddying currents of air spilling over into this wide expanse of sheltered water.

We had way enough to continue and to enter the mouth of a funnel-shaped bay. The land swept away and upward into mountain crests, and all clothed with strongly green vegetation. A river no doubt spilled down between those hills. The thought occurred to me, idly, that in all probability the water we now sailed was perfectly drinkable.

Islands scattered reflections of themselves, many islands, and flocks of birds, driven to seek shelter by the oncoming gale, wheeled and squawked in the preliminaries of settling down. The shafting light of the Suns lay low and bewilderingly, glittering up refulgently from the water.

Selecting one of the islands we rounded to in a good depth of water off a yellow beach. Here we did as Pompino in his newly won nautical expertise had prescribed and dropped the hook.

"A goodly shelter, this, far from prying eyes," said Captain Linson. He was well pleased. He, it was clear, saw no sense in risking his ship in a combat against twice his number. And also, he like us could foresee the time when we'd come by charts of these waters, honestly or otherwise.

When a ruffianly crew of us went ashore for fresh water and firewood, Pompino roundly declared that, by Horato the Potent, he would spend the night on honest solid ground. A tent-like shelter was rigged, the fires were started, and the ship's cook, the superb culinary artist Limki the Lame, with his assistants, prepared our evening meal. An anchor watch was left aboard *Tuscurs Maiden*, and we had to promise them their partners would oversee their share in the gold.

Sharing out the treasure!

Ah! That was now the single most important fact in all the universe to this bunch of rapscallions.

The apparition of Mindi the Mad vanished to our shouted remberees. We could not hear her speak when she was in this trance state that allowed her spirit to visit us, and we doubted if she could hear us, but being good Kregans we shouted the remberees in good heart. The two pursuing ships might snuffle about these scattered islands all night; we had no doubt that they'd never spot our fires, and if their captains had any sense, they, too, would anchor up for the rise of the Suns.

The general opinion, heartily shared by Pompino and the Fristles, was that we ought to make camp here and spend some time reorganizing ourselves. Fresh water tinkled in the brook, game abounded, we were well-provisioned. This little paradise would mightily suit us for a spell.

The chests were dragged across the sand and ranged in neat rows. The men clustered in the firelight. Their faces—well on the faces of the apims, members of Homo sapiens like me, the avaricious gloating could be plainly read. On the faces of those folk who were diffs, races of those splendid people of Kregen who are not fashioned like people of Earth, the expressions might differ. There was no doubt that everyone here looked forward with the keenest anticipation to dipping their hands into the gold and silver...

Treasure!

Well, I in my dour sour cynical old way anticipated trouble. I was right; but not as I'd anticipated...

"We will do this thing according to immemorial custom."

"Aye!"

The proportions to be taken by each and every person were regulated by rank, position and prowess. We had upward of two hundred thousand gold deldys to distribute, made up of various gold and silver coins. There was no rush. This could take all night and still the rascals would be on their feet with a flagon in their fists, gloating. Pompino stood on a chest with the list prepared by Rasnoli, his gentle Relt stylor, and read out the distributions.

Each name was met with a cheer or a groan, a chorus of good-natured banter. The firelight glistened on flushed faces and whiskered cheeks, glittered in eyesockets, caught the rows of jagged teeth. Dayra and I stood together, a little in the background. She had brought the treasure to us, taken from the enemy led by Zankov; she would come into a handsome share.

"Gold," she said. "Ha—the Little Sisters should be pleased."

I did not inquire which particular set of Little Sisters she referred to.

I did say: "In your own time, Dayra, you would do well to return to the Sisters of the Rose. They would welcome you—"

"What do you know of them! You cannot tell me that!"

"I do not seek to uncover the sorority's secrets, my girl. But you could do worse than seek their blessing once more."

"I will think on it."

Now the treasure was being divided. It had all been counted, every last silver piece. The men formed up, and the women took their places. Each one held out a sack, or a cap, a stout wooden box, and the coins were counted out by Rasnoli as Pompino, Captain Linson, Cap'n Murkizon and other of the more trustworthy members of the crew stood by. The process took time. No one minded that.

Gambling began at once, of course.

The slaves we had freed and who had fought with us were entitled to their share. Also we had agreed that the multitude of girl sacrifices we had rescued should also receive each one her share. There was a certain amount of self-serving in this, for as soon as we reached civilization we could unload the girls with a small fortune each. That was the general consensus of opinion. Dayra, I had told, and she had agreed, that I wanted to look out for these waifs more particularly. If they were simply cast adrift with a pocketful of gold they'd be dead or slave again in a twinkling.

The share-out went on. The principals, in which number Dayra and I were included, would receive their portions later. The amounts were known. This was not a scheme to defraud our shipmates, merely an example of the protocol in which Kregen abounds.

This amused me. Limki the Lame stomped past, his nose in a flour bag. The bag bulged with the shape of coins.

"By Llunyush the Juice!" he said, coming up for air, his face whitened in splotches. "As fine a sight as any honest man can hope to see!" We agreed. Cooks are important folk.

A vast amount of jollity broke out around the campfires. Wine passed freely. Every man felt himself a king and every woman a queen. There were quarrels. Inevitably so. One or two knives flashed; but it was noticeable that these were mainly gripped in the fists of the newcomers to our band, and the old stagers moved in swiftly to break up the disturbances.

Pockets bulging with gold coins, men and women strutted from the pay-out table to join in the celebrations. If trouble was to come, I was thinking, a few of us retained clear heads—I was thinking that when the lambent blue glow spread across the level sands by the water's edge.

For two heartbeats, and two heartbeats only, I thought the Star Lords were sending their enormous blue Scorpion to snatch me away from this island beach and hurl me down all naked and defenseless on some other part of Kregen where I would sort out a problem for them. For two heartbeats only...

Other folk yelled. Some screamed. A panic movement away from the beach began and Rondas the Bold fell all sprawling on those yellow sands that were stained with the indigo fires spurting from the apparition.

This was not Mindi the Mad.

A face stared out at us from the center of the deep blue fire. A walnut-crevassed face surrounded by whiteness, a face sharp and piercing, a face of illuminated sorcery. Dayra took my arm. We stood, scarcely breathing, watching. And the hooded eyes in that grotesquerie of a face looked out in a gleam like summer lightning. Those eyes saw the beach and the campfires, the carousing people, the heaps of gold and silver, the broken open chests.

"D'you recognize her?"

"No," Dayra answered, on a breath.

The spectral image of the witch remained hard and fiery edged, studying us. The outline of blue flames expanded. The woman's body rose into view. She wore a white form-fitting gown after the fashion of the Ancient Egyptian women of our Earth, banded under her breasts, which were small and hard and cone-like. The gown emphasized the shape of her figure, the swell of her hips, the slight protuberance of her stomach. Around her neck a massive circlet of interlocked gold lozenges, studded with gems, stood out vividly against the mahogany-colored skin. Her hair was remarkable. Frizzed and fluffed in the Afro fashion, it surrounded her head in a sheen of chalk-whiteness—startling and yet in no way incongruous. A tiara of blinding light crowned her forehead against that chalk-white mass of hair. The sound of a multitude of tiny tinkling bells shivered in the night air.

In the fashion of many ladies of Kregen she wore a glittery linked chain from a bracelet on her left wrist. But the other end of the chain did not attach to a necklet on some friendly furry little creature, a doted-on pet, a warm cuddly bundle—oh, no. That necklet fastened up a winged, fanged, scaled reptile of hideous appearance, who yawned widely, revealing a scarlet mouth and serrated teeth and a forked tongue that licked wickedly this way and that.

The witch gazed upon us on the beach and we stood, petrified after the first frantic moments of panic. Not a sound disturbed the night except the tinny tintinnabulations of the silver bells.

As though an artist wiped a chalk mark clean with a single swipe of a wet cloth—the sorceress vanished.

No one had the strength to speak.

We trembled in the night air as the sounds of the crackling fires, night insects, the gentle susurration of the sea, returned to the normal world. An after-scent of musk hung in the air. I felt Dayra's fingers gripping my arm.

I'd made no move to put my hand on hers, to give her that physical comfort, for I felt sure she would not welcome that, regarding it rather as a patronizing gesture. But I did look at her, and as I turned my head a man yelled down by the beach, and then another shrieked in agony, and a chorus of agonized howls burst out.

Dayra jumped.

"The devil! Vomer the Vile take it!"

She clawed frantically at her tunic, tearing at her pocket. I smelled burning. She had to rip the tunic off and hurl it down and jump on it to extinguish the blaze.

All over the beach men and women were leaping about, yelling blue bloody murder, ripping off burning clothes. I saw Limki the Lame's flour bag burst into flames and a lava stream of blazing gold run swiftly across the sand, molten, to hiss in eruptions of steam into the sea.

So, of course, we understood what had happened.

All the treasure had turned molten.

Gold and silver alike, it melted into puddles and then wisped and shrank and vanished. We were left, dazed, smelling the stinks of scorched flesh and burned clothing, left with not a single coin of all that marvelous treasure.

Dayra said it.

"By Chusto!" she said, her eyes bright. "That gold soon burnt a hole in our pockets!"

Two

Pompino simplifies the future

"She may have been a Gonell, for they have white hair they do not cut off."

"She suffered from chivrel—"

"Powdered with flour—"

"The witch! I'd like to powder her with hot coals!"

"With red honey and let the ants—"

Oh, yes, as you can see, the company of *Tuscurs Maiden* was not at all enamored of the witch who had so summarily reduced our worldly wealth, whoever or whatever she might be.

We sat moodily around the decaying fires as the Suns rose. Someone would have to stand guard and the rest would try to sleep. No one felt like doing anything. We were in all truth a most depressed bunch of desperadoes...

"Well," declared Dayra. "I never expected to be rich in this life."

"But that is always an objective, a dream, something one can yearn for," protested Pompino. "Although, mind you, I own my disappointment is in not seeing my dear lady wife's face when I emptied the gold chest before her."

It was in my mind that I ought to do something about the Lady Scaura Pompina, just to give my comrade the sight for which he yearned. But then, being a haughty Khibil, he'd resent at once the implication that he was accepting charity.

That reminded me of something I had to tell Dayra. I drew her a little off and we sat down as Pompino selected off the unfortunates to take the watch.

"Well," she said. "I am disappointed. But, at least, the enemies of Vallia do not have the gold. They cannot pay their soldiers or for their ships to invade us at home."

"True. There is something that may make you smile, although I am always heartsick when I recall—"

"What?" She cut into my maundering. I braced up.

"Barty Vessler—"

"Oh. *Him!*"

I felt the rage mounting, and quelled it. Barty Vessler was one of your true koters of Vallia, a gentleman in every sense, filled with notions of honor and duty and with a sense of proportion in everything except risking his own neck. Delia and I had both liked him immensely, for he was upright and honest and if foolhardy of his own person in pursuit of his ideas of honor was always considerate of those with whom he came into contact.

"Barty was a fine—" I began.

"Oh, yes. He told me he loved me and I believed him, I think. But he was so—so—and, anyway, he wouldn't come out with the companions and—"

"Smash up a few taverns? Terrorize a few innkeepers?"

"And so?" she flared. "Life was so *boring!*"

I wasn't going to get into the strict parent bit at this stage. I held on doggedly to what I wanted to say.

"I shall speak of your antics later, my girl. Now I must tell you what Barty has done for you—"

"Done for me? He's dead, isn't he?"

I felt the pang.

"Aye. Barty's dead. When your mother was hung up in chains by that rast Zankov, Barty roared in to the rescue. Kov Colun Mogper of Mursham killed Barty, treacherously stabbed him in the back. It was..." I held my breath for a moment and Dayra had the sense to say nothing. Then I went on heavily. "Jilian Sweet-tooth has a personal score to settle with Mogper. I believe she has come here to Pandahem—"

"Jilian in Pandahem!"

"We are hardly likely to meet up with her. The island is as large as Vallia."

"I have had words with Jilian. You know her well?"

"We have fought shoulder to shoulder—but she is her own woman and your mother's good friend. Now, Barty said in his Will that you were to have his stromnate of Calimbrev—"

"He did!" She stared at me in genuine surprise. "Barty Vessler left me his stromnate! But—but there must be relations to claim the title and the lands, surely?"

"No."

"But I was not there. You know that tenure must be established. Inheritance has to be fought for."

"I know. I sent good men there to hold Calimbrev for you."

"Oh, yes, I can see that." She tossed her head. "The great high and mighty Emperor of Vallia would send an army to gain land for his family."

"Yes," I said.

She looked away.

"So—you are the Stromni of Calimbrev, Dayra."

"You won't be calling me Stromni here—and do you forget I am Ros Delphor?"

"No—"

"I suppose you are so accustomed to being the emperor now that grandfather is dead. No doubt you are majister this and majister that—it makes one sick—"

This, clearly, was a part of what had gnawed away at Dayra when she was younger. I said: "My friends at the palace usually just call me majis. And there's an interesting development in the services, where they're using jis to address superiors." I couldn't say that this use of jis was similar to our Earthly use of sir in that context. Some time would have to elapse before Dayra learned her father had never been born on Kregen, but on a funny little world four hundred light years off with only one yellow sun and one silver moon and not a diff in sight.

We spoke on for a space and the hurt in Dayra hurt me, also. I hewed to my purpose. Tsleetha-tsleethi, softly-softly, as the saying goes.

Pompino came across looking put out, as he had every right to be.

"This is a fine mess! By Horato the Potent, Jak! I believe the gods have aligned themselves against us."

"Not the gods, Pompino. Just a witch."

"Just a witch!"

"I'd like to know her interest in all this."

"I," said Pompino the Iarvin, "am not often wrong in anything. But I own that when I said this would be simple, I erred."

I didn't laugh; but you had to hand it to my comrade.

"You said, if I recall, that we would recruit a fine gang of rascally fellows, go across and bash Strom Murgon, burn all the temples to Lem the Silver Leem, sort out who married who, and then go home." I counted off the points on my fingers. "We have a few fine fellows; we could do with more. Strom Murgon more bashed us than the contrary. We have burned one temple here, and there are more hungry for the flames. And as for who marries who—"

"Tell me," said Dayra, "about that."

"Oh," said Pompino. "Kov Pando and Strom Murgon both lust after the same girl, the Vadni Dafni Harlstam. Both want her estates. There are the Mytham twins, Poldo who himself yearns for Dafni, and Pynsi who wants Pando to marry her." He gave his whiskers a fierce upward brushing movement. "It is all very simple, as I said."

Dayra put a finger to her lips and regarded Pompino calculatingly. "Simple?"

"Of course."

"And the rest of it. You really do go around burning temples of the Silver Wonder?"

"The quicker they are all burned the sooner the air will smell sweeter."

I made a small sound, a hesitant beginning to an expression of my personal doubts that burning the temples of the evil cult would change the minds of the worshipers.

Pompino glared. "Oh, yes, Jak, I know your views! But if there are no temples—"

"They will build more," said Dayra.

"Then we'll burn them and perhaps deal more harshly with the cramphs who chant the praises of torturing and cutting up small girls into smaller pieces, may Armipand take 'em all into his black jaws!"

As he spoke so my comrade looked at Dayra. His foxy face showed a shrewd scrutiny. No fool, Pompino the Iarvin, as his name testified; I thought he would not penetrate very far into her secrets. He waited a moment, and as neither of us spoke, he nodded. He was about to go on when I interrupted his train of thought.

"We may burn temples as much as we desire. We must win over the credulous fools who believe the nonsense they are told. And that means—"

"That means," said Dayra, interrupting in her turn, "finding who gives the instructions."

By the way she used the word we understood she meant instructions to imply far more than simple orders.

"The priests, the chief priests," said Pompino. "Aye, we'll find them. And I, for one, know what to do with 'em!"

He spotted Captain Linson approaching, and finished: "Well, we'd better see about sailing again. Now we've lost the treasure these sea-leems will be a fine cutthroat crew, I think. Anyone who crosses them will rue the day." He went off to speak with Linson about resuming our interrupted voyage.

Dayra said: "Jak—when mother was chained up, there at the Sakkora Stones. And Barty died—"

"Was treacherously stabbed in the back with a poisoned dagger, girl!"

"So you say—"

"So it was!"

"I had to go off—if you were there—"

"Oh, yes, I was there, with a damned great arrow through my neck. You were concluding the legal wrangle about marrying Zankov—"

"I do not think I ever really wanted that, for all my words at the time. At any rate, I never did."

She looked splendid with her heightened color and the spirit in her; I remembered how she had warned Zankov not to harm Delia. As they say in the Eye of the World, only Zair can tell the cleanliness of a human heart. She spoke in a rush, emptying herself of this particular emotion.

"And Barty? I know it sounds stupid, banal; but tell me, for I must know. Did Barty suffer at the end?"

"The poison worked swiftly. He might well have died from the blow alone; he did not suffer, thanks be to Opaz."

She made a sideways, empty gesture. Down by the water's edge they were hauling a boat out, and splashing, and calling to one another. The camp site was being broken up, and we were due for the off again.

"We had to fly from the Sakkora Stones. I found out at once that mother still lived. I did not hear about Barty until much later. I didn't know."

"And you had no feeling for him?"

"Oh, yes, I liked him, as one would a puppy."

As though it had no bearing on what we were saying, I said: "I was slowly curing him of his ideals of honor. They killed him before I could—" I couldn't go on. I turned away and stomped off and got my shoulder to a boat and so shoved her savagely out into the water.

"Come on, you lubbers!" I roared. "We've lost one treasure! Let us go and find another!"

Three

A hairy fighting bunch

Precious little chance we had of finding any more treasure for that day; we sailed between the islands, each one floating on its twin reflection, and entered the mouth of the river, and we saw not a living soul, on the sea, on the land or in the air.

We might have only rudimentary charts of the north coast of Panda-hem, and nothing at all detailed of the navigational hazards here; but we knew where we were well enough. Quite a number of the folk aboard had knowledge of the kingdom of Tomboram outside as well as inside Pando's kovnate of Bormark.

The gale, moderating overnight, had not disturbed us once we'd passed into the shelter of that massive uplift of rock, the Sentinel of Bormark. The river was known by two names. This was just another example of the infuriating way in which even simple agreements failed to be reached by two folk, both living not only on the same island but in the same kingdom. Pando's Bormark to the west called the river She of the Mellifluous Breath. Apgarl Superno's kovnate of Malpettar to the east called the river He of the Bright Face.

Fishing villages had to be carefully sited because of the infestations of pirates. Here there had—inevitably!—been two, one each side of the river. Both lay in blackened ruins. We sailed past silently, not caring for the ugly memories those heaps of overgrown refuse brought to mind.

A few birds hopped about mournfully. No doubt the woods were still filled with game. No doubt the insects still sang. We sailed past that desolate scene and if only a few of us reflected on the waste of man's intemperateness to man, most of us were affected by the sight.

Captain Linson said to Pompino: "I cannot take you past Pettarsmot, horter." He'd had that information from one of the slaves we'd freed. The town stood at the end of navigation.

"Well," said Pompino with cheeriness that didn't sit ill on him, "by Horato the Potent! We'll march the rest of the way!"

The traitorous thought occurred to me that we'd hired on these mercenaries in Pompino's home port of Tuscursmot. Most of them were from South Pandahem. We'd picked up a few more folk along the way. But everyone served one end only; each and every single one of them. Oh, yes, we burned evil temples and we rallied around the Owner; but—but! The crew had thought the fortune made each one dreamed of. We'd lost the gold, sorcerously melted into slag that burned our pockets and skins. The salve had gone around, believe you me. So, now, why should any of them follow Pompino into the heart of Bormark? Why should they go to Plaxing to find Kov Pando and all the troubles we expected there? For pay—oh, yes, for their silver sinver a day. But when all is said and done, money has its limitations.

I said to Dayra, whom I carefully addressed as Ros: "Care to take a wager on those who will go and those who will stay?"

She sniffed.

"Typical! You know them far better than do I—"

"Ah, yes, but you have the eye to search out their hearts."

"I'll tell you one thing. That barrel of a fellow, Cap'n Murkizon, will go. And if he goes Larghos the Flatch will go. You won't keep Quendur the Ripper away, and that means Lisa the Empoin will go. Nath Kemchug, Pompino's Chulik, will go, and so will Rondas the Bold."

"You pick a hairy fighting bunch, Ros."

"The two girls, the varterists, they have not yet accepted me. That is understandable. But they'll go and I think it worthwhile to try to gain their confidence."

I refused to be surprised at her words.

"The ship's company will be split, then. For the crew will mostly stay, I think. Linson will insist, and rightly so."

"I've noticed you do not have many Hobolings—"

"Oh, Hobolings are extremely fine topmen; but *Tuscurs Maiden* is from South Pandahem—"

"True. But Hobolings travel the world like anybody else."

"So that leaves Naghan the Pellendur and his guards."

"They're paid by this Pando fellow, aren't they? Surely they'll earn their hire?"

"Some, I fancy, will not."

"You make me wonder if I should bother to accompany you—"

"I noticed you did not include the lady Nalfi when you mentioned Larghos the Flatch among those who would go. Why was that?"

Dayra put a hand to her hair—that hair so like Delia's, brown and free and gorgeous—and said airily: "Oh, she has no affection for Larghos the Flatch!"

I was startled.

"But they are inseparable! Larghos dotes on her!"

"A man may dote on a woman; that does not mean she is duty bound to have anything to do with him—"

And then, as our thoughts flew to Barty Vessler, Dayra stopped herself. We stood for a while looking over the bulwark as the green banks drifted past.

You had to admit that a girl as sharp as Dayra would spot anything amiss in that sort of relationship. Zair knows, it made me wonder. The lady Nalfi was now a part of our band, generally respected. She kept herself aloof, true; but that was perfectly natural on two counts—one, for the love we supposed she bore Larghos, and, two, for the rascally band we were.

The breeze turned fluky and the river's confined waters meant we had to turn out and put our backs into it. The longboat lowered, and lusty fellows settled at the oars to pull. For a relatively clumsy sailing vessel like an argenter the river, wide though it was, represented confined waters. The fluky winds ruffled the surface and rippled the tops of the trees. Higher up low-flung clouds went racing past, driven by a breeze that scourged inland.

The small cock boat had just brought me back to the argenter from a stint at the oars, hauling upriver, when Pompino let out a yelp. Other people, all staring up with astonished expressions, joined in the exclamations of wonder.

I looked up.

Among the driving masses of cloud a sailing ship of the sky plunged on, driven helplessly. She had once possessed three masts; their wreckage dangled overside in a tangled confusion that merely assisted the wind to propel her onward. She was considerably larger than our vessel *Tuscurs Maiden*, with four decks and high-lifting fore and after castles, with fighting towers above and fighting galleries below. The snouts of varters showed in serried ranks. A single flagstaff reared at her stern, which was squared off and blunt, like the end of a house rather than the stern of a ship. Being of the air she had no need of the robust construction necessary to withstand the shock of the sea.

I recognized her.

She was *Vol Defender*, registered in Vondium, the capital of the island empire of Vallia.

On that single flagstaff floated two flags, and each tresh whipped and snapped in the breeze. One was the yellow cross and saltire upon a red field that is the Union flag of Vallia. The other was a solid blue, with a quombora at its center, the flag of Tomboram. The blue flag floated above the red and yellow.

I stood on the quarterdeck and looked up and I held my face in a stasis of emotion, as though sheathed in ice. A Vallian flying sailing ship, captured by the Tomboramin! Dayra started to say something, and I said, harshly: "Can you see anyone up there?"

"There are a few heads peering down," said Pompino. "If they drop firepots on us—"

The breeze blustered the shattered aerial vessel over our heads. Very few of the folk aboard had seen one of these flying sailers before. They were not vollers. Vollers contained power derived from their two silver boxes that could drive them through thin air, up and down, forward and backward, soaring immune to gravity and the bluster of the wind. The flying sailing craft, which we in Vallia called vorlcas, did not possess in their silver boxes all the necessary magical mix of minerals. They could lift up against gravity and by exerting power on what the wise men called the lines off ethereal magnetic force, could tack and make boards against the wind. The vessels of this kind were known as famblehoys in Havilfar.

We in Vallia had made great use of them in our wars against the Hamalese.

"Bad cess to her," said Naghan the Pellendur. "She is Vallian and up to no good here."

"Look!" called Quendur the Ripper, pointing. "There is an airboat!"

Lying alongside *Vol Defender* and in her shadow, revealed as the vessels flew past, a voller snugged tightly. She was not an airboat built in Hamal or in Hyrklana. From her lines I fancied she'd been built in one of the countries down in the Dawn Lands; I could not be sure.

Dayra said, "But the Pandaheem do not have vollers!"

I looked at her and spoke up quickly: "Pandrite the All-Glorious has seen fit to provide us with one at least, Ros."

She did not put her hand to her mouth or stutter out some fatuous remark; but she got the message all right.

The sight of solid objects floating in air fascinated these folk of Pandahem. Hamal and Hyrklana refused to sell their vollers to Pandahem or to any of the countries of the continent of Loh. They had sold to us in Vallia, for we were a thorn in the flesh of Pandahem. Only—in the old days the vollers we bought from Hamal continually broke down. That was policy on the part of Hamal, and one of the contingent reasons for the wars—apart from the insane ambitions of the Empress Thyllis, who was now dead and wandering about the Ice Floes of Sicce. No one would take a wager on how long it would take her to reach the sunny uplands beyond.

The two vessels, the enormous vorlca and the smaller voller, blew away before the wind. We watched until they vanished out of sight among the clouds. Then, as though a spell had broken, we could return to our normal tasks.

Yet the aerial vessels remained the subject of talk for some time. Pandaheem were unused to flying ships. As to the business that had brought a Vallian here—that was easy to guess.

One interesting item was that the Pandaheem had little idea of the difference between a voller and a vorlca. To them both were simply magical. They were vessels that flew. I managed to have a quiet word to Dayra—to her, for she flared up at once.

"I know, I know! But I am learning and soon I'll be as good a Pandaheem as you! The thing is—she was one of ours and she's been captured! *That's* the important thing!"

"She looked in a sorry mess. That'll be the gale. Jiktar Nath Fremerhavn was in command the last I heard. He's a good sailor. Something else happened, that's certain sure."

"Yes, but what?"

"One thing, Ros. We'll have to act as though we, too, are overjoyed that a Vallian has been captured. We're always in danger. It's no good forgetting—"

"I know."

Her color was up, her head high and her eyes bright. Useless to push anymore, as I well knew. She was my daughter all right, by Vox!

We took turns hauling at the oars, shift by shift, and our vessel slowly forged upriver. The banks proliferated with vegetation of wild and exotic varieties; the birds flocked in prodigious numbers, fish leaped in the water, and the suns shone. Here, between two provinces who were not on friendly terms, the land, quarreled over, went its own way. The king in far off Pomdermam might rule his kingdom; out here what the local lords said went—double. This river, running between the two kovnates, was neglected. Once it was brought under a single control it could bloom and produce amazing riches. Trouble was—who was to rule, Kov Apgarl na Malpettar or Kov Pando na Bormark?

"From what I've seen," said Pompino, giving a twirl to his whiskers, "I wouldn't back either of 'em with a single copper ob. If you want my opinion, the man to put the money on is our villainous Strom Murgon—"

"What!" exclaimed Dayra. "You're backing our enemy?"

She was trying to fit into her new part, then. Until recently Strom Murgon had believed Dayra, with Zankov, to be his staunch allies against everyone including their homeland of Vallia.

"Not with any pleasure, Ros. But I've seen little of this Pando our Jak here knew as a young man. Murgon—well, he'll get more money—"

Dayra, Ros Delphor, half-lifted her hand. Her face looked stricken.

"What is it!"

"Why," said Dayra, "why—the treasure the witch melted, that disappeared—it will—"

Pompino jumped up and down. His whiskers bristled. He looked incensed past all bearing.

"Of course! By Horato the Potent! The devils!"

I must admit that with all the experience we had of sorcery we'd been slow in arriving at the obvious conclusion. That striking white-haired witch in the body-hugging gown, whoever she was, would not just melt down the gold and let it run into the sea, wisp away, vanish. Oh, no. No, she'd collected it up through her thaumaturgical powers. That mass of gold and silver coins once more rested in the coffers of Strom Murgon.

"May the obnoxious and pestiferous odors of the Divine Lady of Belschutz overwhelm them!" roared Cap'n Murkizon. "Then it is all to do again!"

"We will, Cap'n," said Pompino, with a snap. "We will."

"It is not quite the same this time, though," I said.

"True. Maybe I spoke a little too harshly about your friend Pando." Pompino was not going to apologize for a trifling matter like this. "If the chance affords itself of sinking a blade into Murgon, that we'll do right merrily."

Naghan the Pellendur walked up, perhaps a trifle more relieved that the ship sailed quiet waters with green land on either beam. He still tugged at his whiskers with the same nervous violence. "Pettarsmot, horters," he said. "My advice would be that if we sail in we will not be received in any friendly spirit. Quite the contrary."

Pompino said: "My thought, exactly."

"We're from South Pandahem," objected Murkizon. "They won't know we have the welfare of Kov Pando at heart."

His words should not have surprised me. When a fellow signs up to do a job one may sort the leems from the ponshos. Murkizon was a ship captain, temporarily without a command, employed by Pompino. He was not quite the same as any of the other mercenaries. Yet they shared this common feeling. I truly believe that what they had witnessed of Lem the Silver Leem had wrought marvelously upon them. They shared our dedication. Dayra had seen that, too.

"So we land on the Malpettar bank and march in, a normal group of travelers. If we tried to enter the town from the Bormark side we would face more awkward questions."

"That is the best."

So, that is what we agreed. Captain Linson was most heartily pleased and relieved. He would keep most of his crew and they'd return downriver. As to what he did then...

Cap'n Murkizon was not prepared to push his opinion after the disastrous—to him—decisions he had made before we fought the Shanks.

Anyway, it seemed best to us all to try to handle the forthcoming day or two with cunning and quietness rather than violence. That, we all felt, would come later, and in plenty. Well, as you shall hear, we were right, well and truly right...

Naghan the Pellendur told us that Mindi the Mad, who was with Pando at Plaxing, would probably be able to contact Captain Linson. We breathed easier after that, and many of the fellows were vastly engaged by this use of sorcery on their behalf.

A simple pull on the whipstaff and a hail to the boat's crew were all that was needed to let us glide gently in to the bank. Preparations were rapidly made. We took a great quantity of weaponry, and provisions, and there was a certain amount of scuffling and laughing, for these lads were your real paktuns, dour and doughty fighting men who could let themselves go when the mood was on them. We watched as the sailors who were not going with us pulled *Tuscurs Maiden* out to midstream and then set off hauling downriver.

We shouted the remberees, and watched, and presently were left on the bank, a party of fighting men and women dedicated to two main objectives—if you did not count the paramount objective of staying alive. One was to deal with the vile adherents of Lem the Silver Leem. The other to win a fortune that did not magically disappear before it could be spent.

We marched along the riverbank to Pettarsmot, and saw few folk working the fields close to the town. The place was solid enough, with a fortress from which the flags flew.

They left the gate open for us. As we'd trudged along so the folk in the fields had followed on, their day's work done. The evening light lay mellow and rubicund upon the bricks and the masonry. The shadows looked purple under the archway. We walked in, ready to shout the Lahals and to slake our thirsts at the nearest tavern.

A guard consisting of two ranks of spearmen waited, at ease, and their officer sauntered across. He wore metal armor. His sword was scabbarded.

"Llahal!" called Pompino. "We are weary travelers going inland. We do not wish—"

The officer—he was a so-Hikdar—said in a cold voice: "What you want or do not want is not important. Just look up there."

We looked up to the walls. Rows of armored men drew bows, and every arrow head pointed at us.

"Now just throw down your weapons, all quiet and peaceable."

Useless to rage. Some of us no doubt could have escaped; most of us would be shafted. We threw down our weapons.

They marched us off to the lock-up and tumbled us onto foul-smelling straw with water-running stone walls about us. The sound of iron bars clanging shut rattled through the cell and through our stupid skulls, by Krun. We'd been taken up like brainless milbys in a snare. Fine warrior paktuns of Kregen we were!

Four

I learn about Ros the Claw

"Well," I said in what I hoped was a reasonable voice, "you can't really blame them. We'll see a local dignitary in the morning and explain. Then we can set off for the interior."

"You're a fambly, Jak!" foamed Pompino. He strode up and down the stone cell and folk drew their legs out of his way. "Onker! We should have come in here with drawn swords!"

"Then," said Dayra in her level voice, "we'd all be dead."

In circumstances like these, people display their own peculiar characteristics. Murkizon was all for hitting the first guard over the head and breaking out. They'd taken our weapons away, of course; we were in no doubt that we'd pick them up, or others, in the nearest guardroom.

Rondas the Bold, his vulturine features beaked and grim, seconded Murkizon. Nath Kemchug was perfectly prepared to bash a few skulls to win free.

Surprisingly, Quendur the Ripper and Lisa the Empoin sided with me and counseled caution. They, too, felt that in a civilized country the mistake would soon be cleared up.

"Mistake?" said Larghos the Flatch. He held the lady Nalfi close. "Mistake? The only mistake we made is in not doing as horter Pompino and Cap'n Murkizon suggested."

If we fell to a quarrel among ourselves, well, that would be perfectly natural. It wouldn't help at all.

Dayra had expressed her surprise that the lady Nalfi had elected to accompany us. But, Nalfi had, and here she was, penned up with us between dank stone walls behind iron bars.

The others of our group expressed their opinions. Naghan and his guards were all for a bashing spree. I went across to a far corner where Dayra sat, and plumped down, and decided I wouldn't waste energy arguing over hypothetical actions. Come the morning, and we'd know for sure.

"Then," said Dayra, whom I had to call Ros Delphor, "Then we go out and blatter them." She spoke with feeling. They had taken away the canvas and leather bag in which she carried her Claw. She was clearly concerned over its welfare.

"Aye," I said. "If they will not see reason."

She laughed. There in that fetid den, my daughter Dayra laughed.

"Since when have you ever bothered about seeing reason when you want to do what you want to do?"

"You'd be surprised."

"I doubt it."

We were a little separated from the wrangle, which in the sprightly Kregan way promised to last a long time and be of consuming interest to all involved. A torch cast a spluttery kind of mildewy light upon the scene.

After a time, Dayra said: "You were always gone, so mother said, always off somewhere or other."

"That is true."

She cocked her head and glanced sideways at me.

"I own I was surprised to see you here in Pandahem. Vastly surprised. I thought you in Vallia, seeing about the empire."

"Your brother Drak is doing that."

"So you say. I suppose—" and here she shuffled herself more comfortably against the wall. "I suppose why you were so often away from home was because you were off doing things like we're doing now?"

"Yes."

"I've heard the stories about a devil in a red breechclout leaping about with a great sword—"

"Just stories."

"Folk tend to look over their shoulder when they tell these 'just stories.'"

"And," I said, "the breechclout is scarlet."

"Ah!"

We relapsed into silence, each occupied with thoughts the other might, perhaps, only guess at. Water dripped in that noisome place, and little beasties scuttled across the floor. Of food and drink we had none. Our stomachs rumbled and our throats were dry, believe me. But the time passed and we slept fitfully, on and off.

At one point or another, speaking quietly in the glimmer of the dying torch, I said to Dayra: "I well remember when your mother and Lela were off searching for you. You were smashing up taverns, and whatever other deviltries you were up to—I didn't know then, for your mother wouldn't tell me, and I forbore to ask." She turned to face me and the vague light lay orange curves down her cheek. "Wait, Ros—all that's gone now, smoke blown with the wind. When your mother and Lela searched for you—it was during that time we had to combat the Black Feathers of the Great Chyyan—I was frantic with worry. Often and often we've been parted. I don't want those old evil days to return."

She whispered, "I heard about the Black Feathers of the Great Chyyan. A false creed. I do not think it to be much like this Lem religion."

"No."

She settled back. "Now I've tried to find you, I do not wish to be—" She stopped speaking and yawned, and said, "By Chusto, Jak! Try to get some sleep."

In that guttering light I glanced swiftly about the cell. The people were mere misshapen lumps upon the stone. Some snored. I did not think anyone could have overheard us. And, truth to tell—I was beginning to grow tired of this Ros this and Ros that. Well, not so much the Ros, for that is a fine name, as the pretense that Dayra was a mere friend and not a precious daughter. If Pompino knew, he was horter enough to know when to stop his questions.

Then Dayra shifted over again. I could just make out her face in the last of the torch glow.

"The Black Feathers of the Great Chyyan. If we are to enjoy an honest relationship..."

"Yes?"

"Zankov thought he could bargain with Makfaril, the leader. A golden numim hoodwinked him, a lion-man called—"

"Rafik Avandil."

Her eyes opened in a surprise she concealed at once.

"I might have guessed... They ill-treated Zankov and imprisoned him in a horrible underground temple abandoned for centuries—"

"The ruined temple of Hjemur-Gebir. A monstrous toad-thing of stone, a malignant idol, at the center of the underground—"

"Yes. I imagine afterward many people went to gawp."

"I believe they did." I stared at her, my face in shadow. "And you were there. It was Zankov with a broken arm—"

"How...!"

"I saw it. I saw—you!—rescue him. You were there, there, so close, and I wished you well and went on..." I recalled all that old and horrible adventure. "I did not know who you were—except that you were a tiger-girl, powerful and gorgeous, very quick and lethal, and you went away with that rast Zankov..."

"You—saw—all that..."

"Aye." Someone moved restlessly among that heap of sleeping bodies, and I finished quickly: "Sleep now. We can talk over old times tomorrow."

But, before she lay back to sleep, she whispered, "I heard the uproar. I was carrying Zankov along—and we could not find a way out. And then Rafik Avandil was there in his golden armor, raging, cursing, insane with despair and rage, and—"

"It was your mother's dagger. The gems in the form of a rose..."

"Aye. It went through his neck sweetly..."

So I lay back. What one learns about one's children as they grow old enough to confide!*

My penultimate thought as I drifted off to sleep at last was that there would be many more horrific stories to learn of my wayward daughter's headlong career upon Kregen; but I took heart from this, for I felt the trueness of the bridge we were building between us.

My last thought before sleep, as it is every night, was the same; although on this particular night it was of Makfaril's Sacrifice...

We were roused out just after dawn by apim guards who kicked us awake. We stumbled into a stone-walled courtyard, blinking in the early light, apple-green and palest rose. We were given no breakfast. We husked about, and tried to spit, and waited while the guards went through their tiresome rigmarole.

The women among us had been offered no indignity, and we were generally agreed that this was a wise action on the part of the jailers of the Pettarsmot prison. We were, for the sake of the Bright Pandrite, in Mappeltar, in Tomboram, a civilized country! When I said to Naghan, speaking in a dry, a very dry voice, that I thought the place was called Malpettar, he managed a hissing sort of laugh.

"Malpettar or Mappeltar, depending on north or south; for us in Bormark they are all tarred with the same brush."

"Well, keep your black-fanged winespout shut about Bormark," rasped Murkizon.

We were herded along to the gateway and here we were joined by another bunch of decrepit-looking folk. They were prodded up from adjoining cells. They had been worse-treated than us, that was clear. Many were wounded and their bandages were all what they had provided themselves. I felt Dayra's hand on my arm; and I did not look at her but fastened my gaze on those poor devils who were whipped and beaten along.

They wore shreds of uniforms. There were apims and diffs, men and women, in that sorry line. Those uniforms wrung a savage gasp from me. Dayra squeezed my arm.

I—I, myself and Delia, and many another comrade, had helped design those uniforms.

"They're from the vorlca *Vol Defender*."

"So I see." I managed to speak the words in the kind of grating hiss a pile of pebbles gives when it slides off a truck, in my old gravel-shifting voice.

She said, breathlessly: "We must—"

"Aye. We must. Now keep quiet and pay them no attention."

As we were prodded along she flung her head up, glaring at me. She spoke softly; but it was a struggle.

---

* For Dray Prescot's adventures with the Black Feathers of the Great Chyyan, see *Secret Scorpio*, Dray Prescot #15.

"Is that it, then? I see! You will do nothing because no one must know who you are! And there are friends over there—good friends—there's Sosie ti Vendleheim, and—"

"Ros! Shastum! Keep quiet!"

She flinched at my tone, and I blundered on: "If we start anything now we'll all be killed. If we fight now, all our friends will fight—all of them!—and we'll all die!"

"What was that, Jak!" called Pompino, shuffling along. "Something about fighting?"

"When the time comes, Pompino. When the time comes."

"By Horato the Potent! My insides are more hollow than the nine empty bladders of Pantora Hemfi of Promondor! Just let us have a bite to eat and drink before we come to handstrokes."

Murkizon guffawed at that, and a guard hit him with the butt of his spear, and Cap'n Murkizon took the blow and rolled with it—and laughed the louder.

I began to feel sorry for these guards of Pettarsmot.

The two bunches of prisoners trudged side by side only for the time it took to cross the next yard. Here we were shepherded under an archway and so into the building; the last we saw of the aerial sailors of *Vol Defender* they were being bludgeoned through the opposite archway.

Dayra would not look at me.

She walked along, her head high, nostrils flaring, her face wild. I managed to crab alongside Lisa the Empoin, for whom I had a high regard.

"Lisa—would you speak to Ros? Tell her how a prisoner and a potential slave behaves. She'll stir up—"

"At once, Jak. You're right. She's acting as though she's a princess!" And Lisa the Empoin wormed her way swiftly to the Princess Dayra's side, and said: "Ros Delphor, listen!"

Quendur the Ripper looked after Lisa. "I think," he said in a matter-of-fact tone of voice. "I really think when I make Lisa a princess, as, of course, I shall one day, she will remember Ros Delphor. If ever a girl should have been born a princess as well as my Lisa, it is Ros."

Do not think I enjoyed suffering under my daughter's haughty contumely. She was in the right, if you took into account only the high Jikai kind of headlong glory-hunter who got himself killed half a dozen times. She probably did not fully grasp that the comrades with us now were of Pandahem; they'd fight for themselves, they wouldn't get stuck into a fight with little chance just to rescue some damned rascally Vallians. Ros knew that well enough when she thought about it; at the moment she wasn't thinking but letting all her Prescot and Valhan blood surge passionately into her actions.

The guards bustled us into a chamber where a fellow halted us and formed us into ranks. We stared about owlishly. The walls were draped in deep blue. A railing fenced off a podium whereon stood four chairs, richly decorated. Guards watched us alertly. A woman hurried in from a side door, hitching up her blue robes, climbed onto the podium and sat down in a middle chair. She peered at us with great displeasure.

A small woman, with a smooth yet knowing face, dark hair and eyes, and a mouth that would take off the leg of a granite statue, she used her power without thought.

A flunkey bellowed: "The great and puissant lady Moincy, Under-pallan of Justice, in session." He banged his staff. Murkizon laughed, and Pompino hushed him.

I leaned a little toward my Khibil comrade.

"I trust you have a good, a very good, story ready?"

He swelled. He brushed his whiskers. "Trust me!"

Nobody in this hick town was going to overawe or catch out a foxy fellow like a Khibil, no, by Horato the Potent!

The woman, this lady Moincy, looked down on us.

"You are fortunate that today there are bigger fish to fry. I cannot waste time on you. What have you to say for yourself before you are fined?"

Pompino yelped: "Fined! What are we fined for?"

"You do not have to know why you are fined, only that you are fined. Is that all you have to say? Very well—Each fined two gold Deldys."

Pompino's mouth was opening and closing like—well, like a clever foxy fellow called the Iarvin who had had his breath temporarily snatched from him. Temporarily only, mind...!

"They've had a good look at our belongings," pointed out Quendur. "They know how much gold we have—"

"And she's pitched it just right! The slag heap!" said Murkizon, bristling.

Murkizon, unfortunately, was wrong. The lady Moincy had barely started. She wasn't in so much of a hurry as not to be able to spare a few more moments fining us.

Pompino at last got out: "We are honest paktuns seeking employment—"

"Thieving masichieri, more likely!"

"Never! We—"

"Silence." She motioned down and a guard hoicked out our possessions from the chest into which they had been thrown. You may imagine with what hunger we gazed upon our weapons tumbled there. The guard produced a canvas and leather bag. From this he took out and held aloft the shining, ugly, cunning Claw.

"To whom," said the lady Moincy in a voice on a sudden silk soft, "does this belong?"

Five

Of fines, songs and fliers

My left arm flew out, as it were on its own, and palm back pressed Dayra away. I held that arm rigid so that she could not step forward, and Murkizon's barrel body concealed my action. I stepped out before my comrades. I looked up.

With my back to them I could put on an imbecilic face, a vacuous grin, a semi-leering simpleton look that I can do so well—as I have all the natural advantages for it, according to my comrades. I stared up happily at the woman and said: "Why, lady, that is mine." Before she could answer I rambled on in a loud bucolic voice: "My comrade, poor Nath the Kaktu, brought it back from some outlandish place, don't ask me where, somewhere beyond the Pillars of Rhine where men have eyes in their stomachs; leastways, that's what poor Nath said, and he won it in a game of Jikalla, he said, although I wonder, for you know how these brave paktuns are, and Nath, he said—"

"Shastum! Silence!"

"Why, yes, lady," I said, and wheezed, and looked up at her grinning like a puppydog.

"And do you know what it is?"

"Why—in course, lady."

I heard the low gasp from Dayra at my back.

"Well, onker? What?"

"Why, it be a back scratcher, o' course, and right handy at bath nights, although it's a mite sharp if you're—"

"You fool!"

"Why, yes my lady."

She glared at me. "You are fined a gold Deldy for being a fool, fool!"

"Why, thank you, lady—"

"And now," she went on, hunching herself up and taking on an altogether different appearance, as though she had sprouted wings, horns and a tail. "And *this*!"

From the chest the guard lifted aloft a glittering star-sparkling silver mask, a snarling mask of a devotee of Lem the Silver Leem.

"Why, my lady," I spoke up before anyone else had a chance to speak. "Poor Nath did say as he valued that there mask above a flagon o' best Jholaix, which as I told him is plain silly for an honest paktun to talk, seeing that it is never and nowise ever was real silver, leastways, that's what poor Nath said, he said, 't'ain't silver, he said—"

"Shastum!"

"Why, yes, my lady."

As I subsided I wondered if I was verily the fool the lady dubbed me, or clever. I had the strongest feeling that the cult of Lem had either bypassed Pettarsmot or not been well-received here. To claim allegiance to Lem, as would have been easy, would not, I judged, have been our best course.

The guard hoisted up the golden zhantil mask worn by the people who slew the worshippers who wore the silver masks. We thought, although we did not know, that Pando had started the idea of having his fighting men wear the golden zhantil mask in opposition to the leem mask. I glared up with my lopsided grin, the simpleton to the life, ready to brazen it out, or to leap—very quickly!—seize a sword and so go red-roaring headlong into action...

"And, fool, this?" The woman's voice purred now just as a big cat purrs—sometimes—before he has your head in his jaws.

"Nath said that was not real gold, lady, and you can see it is not real gold by reason of the bit of brass off behind the left eyehole which I saw at once and told poor Nath and he said, he said—"

She sighed. She looked down.

"Fined three gold Deldys for being a fool of fools."

"Why, thank you, lady."

Somebody at my back was having the devil of a job, spluttering and wheezing and fairly bursting to stop themselves from laughing out loud, long and uproariously.

Grimacing away to the woman on the podium I got a quick glance back. Trust Pompino! He was in no case to step forward and take charge of the situation.

But I misjudged my Khibil comrade. He shut his eyes, squeezed, opened them, took a whooshing breath, and then stepped out beside me.

"My lady," he roared out, very brisk, very correct, your upright paktun to the life. "We seek honest employment. Do you have any openings for guards here in Pettarsmot, for, my lady, we are all experienced mercenaries, and take our full pay as prescribed—"

"The land crawls with mercenaries since the wars, fellow. Go along to that pest-hole in Bormark, Port Marsilus. They recruit an army there. They will welcome riff-raff like you."

"Thank you, my lady—"

"Fined one gold Deldy—"

"What for?" Pompino was outraged once again.

"Fined two gold Deldys for speaking importunately to a lady, and two more for speaking improperly. Guards!"

I tensed, but the guards merely ran us out of the chamber and into a narrow hall where they told us to wait.

Presently slaves appeared carrying our gear. We checked it over, grumbling, and found the gold vanished. The lady Moincy had pitched it exactly—proving Murkizon right, after all—and there was not a single gold coin left to us.

We belted up our armor and weaponry, and were all of us in a fine foul mood, I can tell you!

"This place is worse than the Diproo-Blessed Tavern on pay night," said Pompino. "The quicker we are out of here the better."

"Absolutely right," I said.

Dayra looked at me, her face rosy with repressed passion, and then she turned away. Her shoulder lifted against me.

Surrounded by guards with arrows nocked and ready, we were escorted to the town gate.

The town of Pettarsmot was just a town. The houses were neat and tidy, and no doubt the hovels were well out of the way, the folk were well-dressed and walked about with a brisk air of business. At the gate the towers were manned by guards. Flags flew. The Suns shone. Dust lifted. The hikdar in command waved us through.

"On your way! If you come by here again you will no doubt be more circumspect."

"Oh," said Cap'n Murkizon before anyone could let rip some noise, any noise, to drown him. "We'll be back."

"And what does that mean?"

"Why, horter," I said, pushing forward and grinning that silly sly grin. "We did enjoy your night's lodging—and your supper and breakfast."

His pudgy face blanked with rage, blood rushed under the skin, then Pompino shoved me aside and roared out: "One has to suffer loons these days, hikdar! Never fear. We shall bid you all remberee, and depart!"

Poor Dayra was so wrought up I saw her press her hands together. Her fingers writhed and coiled one within another. I felt for her. But her life was precious, far, far more precious than anything else.

All the same, if these idiots of Pettarsmot thought they had done with me, they were vastly mistaken.

Now it chanced that I'd been wearing a plain blue tunic with short trousers cut to the knee. I strode off along the road, with the irrigation ditch alongside, until we'd passed beyond the first stand of trees where we were out of observation of the guards on the gate towers. Here I halted.

Advancing along the road toward us came the first of the incoming produce from the country, heavy wagons drawn by shaggy old quoffas like perambulating hearth rugs, carts hauled by low-slung mytzers with their multitude of legs. Country folk walked along, children clinging to their mothers' skirts, the men in simple country clothes of smocks and tunics, some with shaggy jerkins, smaller editions of the quoffas they guided.

Pompino at the head of our people passed.

I said: "Do you go on, Pompino. I'll join you later."

"Oh?"

"Aye."

He looked at me. He'd experienced my desires to go off by myself before. He brushed up those reddish whiskers and started to say something, thought better of it, and yelled at the crew: "Step lively, there! We've a ways to travel before we reach breakfast!"

As Naghan the Pellendur reached me I said to him: "Naghan. Would you have one of your lads carry my bundle, please? I'll claim it later, and intact, I trust."

"Of course, horter Jak. But—?"

I was stripping off the blue tunic and cut-off trousers. In their place I wrapped a length of green cloth about myself, unblinking of the color. An old brown blanket went over my shoulder in a roll. I handed Naghan the rapier and main gauche. He took them, mightily puzzled. I handed him the sword, the straight cut and thruster, and he took that, too. Over my right hip was sheathed a sailor knife. That would suffice. Perhaps I'd find a stout stick from a hedge.

The Fristle guard Deldar said: "Horter Jak. Do you know what you are doing?"

"Yes, Naghan, strange as that may seem. Now go along with your people. I'll catch you in time for dinner."

He shook his catlike head, and tugged his whiskers, but he yelled at his men and off they went along the road.

In the shadow of the stand of trees I watched them, searching for the form of Dayra. I did not see her. I frowned. A quoffa-cart creaked along toward me, loaded with what looked like cabbages. The man leading the animal chewed a straw and wore his hat pulled down. I simply fell in at the tailgate of the cart, and Dayra said, "And about time, too!"

I refused to be discomposed.

"Look, Ros, this is no place for you—"

"They're Vallians—and there are others who are friends besides Sosie—"

"Yes, but—"

"It is no use arguing."

So, in a kind of armed truce, we walked back to Pettarsmot where we had been imprisoned, fined—and not fed.

She wore her own blanket in a kind of poncho, and had changed her russet tunic for a blue skirt and bodice. I saw I was going to have trouble with this smart daughter of mine if I wanted to sneak off in the future...

She'd retained her swords, also, under the poncho.

Going along quietly at the tail of the wagon we reentered Pettarsmot. The place looked no different, as indeed, why should it? We went along to the prison block and stopped outside to have a scout around. For all our casual attitude, this was not going to be easy.

"Bash somebody over the head and ask," counseled Dayra.

With a little devil prodding me, I said: "Now if we had a carpet handy..."

She stared at me. "I haven't forgotten!"

"Well, this is how we do it, then."

We found the fellow standing guard at a small side door. As we rounded the corner we both stopped. Dayra gasped.

Out in the center of the parade ground lay the imposing if wrecked shape of a flying sailing ship of the air. *Val Defender*, masts trailing over the side, a raffle of cordage cumbering her decks, squatted like a child's toy trodden underfoot by a careless adult.

I brightened up when I saw her.

"That's more like it!"

"What—?"

"Grab this fellow and let's get inside."

The guard went to sleep standing up and as I eased him to the ground Dayra slid the door open. Light from an open roof spilled down, revealing an empty corridor. We stuffed the guard into a corner, tied and gagged, and padded off looking for trouble. How odd, and yet how exhilarating, to be out adventuring with my daughter Dayra! I thought of the times I'd gone off on adventures like this with Lela, my eldest daughter, known as Jaezila, and I vowed certain vows and if I thought of my daughter, Velia, well, then, I did, and the whole world might stop and still make no difference...

By a side wall in a patio where a well covered by a sharply pitched blue slate roof lorded it, we found a flunkey who was only too pleased to put down his water bucket and take us along to where the Vallian prisoners were confined. Usually, when you are on a rescue mission of this nature, it is not as easy as this... I watched the fellow in his gray slave breechclout. Dayra paced ahead eagerly.

We heard them before we reached them.

They were singing.

It seems to me entirely unnecessary to say that I'd borrowed the sword from the guard who'd gone to sleep. Now I lifted the weapon, as it were, for all the silliness of it, for all the stupidity of it that it may reveal, I lifted the sword in involuntary salute.

The men and women of Vallia, prisoners, sang.

They were not singing one of the great songs of Vallia, a patriotic paean of glory and valor and nobility. Oh, no. They were not singing one of the rollicking Vallian songs that poke fun at the various enemies Vallia has had to contend with from time to time. Oh, no.

Oh, no. They were singing "The Song of Logan Lop-Ears and His Faithful Calsany." This, in its enumeration of the terrible problems poor Logan Lop-Ears faced taking his father's calsany to market to sell the poor beast, adumbrates stanza by stanza the vicissitudes of folk's lives and mishaps. It provokes, needless to say, considerable mirth.

And the Vallians roared out with gusto, particularly those stanzas that often have their words subtly altered to fit circumstances.

Dayra glanced back at me. Her color was up and her eyes were bright. I nodded. For that moment, I, too, could not speak.

The slave flunkey could. He said: "There will be guards with swords, masters. They will kill you, and me too. Let me go, I beg you—"

"We will not harm you, dom," I said truthfully. "Just bide quietly and see what will be."

There were guards, four of them. They were just about to bang on the door to stop the singing, and then, for the Vallians would not stop for that, more likely than not go busting in to crack a few heads. Dayra leaped. There was a steely, diamond-bright glitter before her. One of the guards fell back, trying to scream through a wrecked face. His companion staggered drunkenly sideways as Dayra's rapier licked back. The other two were barely aware of what was going on until they slumped, and Dayra took one of them, also...

The fattest held the key ring at his belt. Dayra stooped. I stepped back a pace, half-turning, listening.

"Tell them to keep singing, but softer. You go on, Ros. I will see if—yes!"

Around the corner behind us came five more guards, big beefy fellows carrying stuxes as well as swords and spears.

Dayra gave them a single comprehensive glance.

"Come to change the guard. Very well—father!"

She leaped for the door, the key in her fist.

I swung back to face these five who ran on, shouting.

Now if I say I was pleased to see them, you may wonder. I was. The reason, simple enough, was that they carried weapons. My folk of Vallia would need those weapons.

The guards ran up, hurling their javelins. These stuxes flew with varying directions and power, for two of the fellows were apim, one was Brokelsh, one a Rapa and the fifth a bleg. He'd be difficult to knock over. Now it was vitally necessary that I allowed not a single stux to pass me. If one flew over my shoulder it could strike into Dayra's slender back as she bent to the prison lock. So—I caught the first one, deflected the next and the next and the fourth, damnably, nicked me along my left forearm. I used the stux in my fist to swat away the last one—that hurled by the bleg who came from a race of diffs not noted for their hurling ability—some of them— and then I was able to roar on and get to handstrokes.

The tinker-hammer stuff could not be allowed to last. It was all charge, knee-up, dirty stuff, bash and trample on. And, as I'd guessed, the bleg with his four legs arranged rather like the legs of a chair took the most knocking over. That he was half-dead when at last he slumped had little to do with it.

As he hit the floor a raspy voice at my back said: "Hai, Jikai!" and a bulky body crashed past, diving for the fallen weapons. Others of the Vallians crowded up. The singing, which had faltered, now resumed. Dayra joined us. It was all very quick, like gears meshing smoothly. No time for lahals; we had to fight our way out.

There was only one place for us to go, of course.

With Dayra and myself in the lead we raced off. The slave flunkey lay in the angle of the corridor; he was not dead, he had fainted clean away. I commended him to his patron spirit as we dashed past.

Dayra spat out as we ran: "The Pandaheem have been cruel to them! Young Paline Vinfine has been killed. I do not think the crew of *Vol Defender* will have much mercy."

"Can they all keep up?"

"Yes. The worst wounded are being carried."

"Good. Is Jiktar Nath Fremerhavn alive and with us?"

We skidded out onto the verge of the parade ground where the forlorn lump of wreckage that was a proud flying ship of Vallia lay abandoned. We stared calculatingly out across the open we must cross to reach our goal.

"Jiktar Fremerhavn was posted into command of *Val Neemusjid*," said a firmly built woman who halted at my side and stared keenly out, not looking at me. "Jiktar Vanli Cwopanifer was posted to command *Val Defender*. He—is not with us."

"Guards," rasped the bulky fellow who'd been the first to scoop a weapon. On the rags of his uniform he wore the rank badges of the Ship-Deldar. "By Vox! I am going to enjoy blattering the rasts!"

"Hold, Edivon! Do not let your rage blind you. We hit them when they reach the shadows."

"Quidang, Hik!" rasped this Deldar Edivon.

So the woman was the Ship-Hikdar, her first lieutenant. I gave her a single searching look. Her face was taut, naturally, hard and lean, with a prominent nose and cheekbones. Her eyes and hair were good Vallian brown. There was about her a calm competence and yet an eager blaze. If I say that one could easily visualize her with a whistle on a cord about her neck, calling: "Now, come along, girls!" I indicate the admirable qualities. If anyone is foolish enough to regard the comparison as in some way derogatory, even sexist, then all I can say is, let 'em rot in their own effluvium.

The guards reached the shadows. The people of Vallia pounced. Then we were up and racing across the open toward their ship.

I felt the fierce leap within me as Dayra was first up and onto the deck.

Magnificent, she looked, wild and free, the silly skirt thing ripped away, her legs long and lithe as she clambered up. The crew followed her and they went raging over the bulwarks and the shattered watch of Pandaheem were overwhelmed. Dayra's Claw slashed and her rapier twinkled, and there were no more enemies holding a ship of Vallia.

Without even thinking about it, the Ship-Hikdar took command. Her orders cracked out. Deldar Edivon attempted to moderate his bellow. Folk dived below to assess damage, and an urchin wearing a rag around her waist came up and slapped up a cracking salute and said: "The silver boxes are unharmed, hikdar."

"Very good, Pansi. Get to your station."

"Quidang!"

That young ragamuffin, that grimy urchin, was probably a high-born-noble lady of Vallia learning her craft as an aerial sailor. This woman, this Ship-Hikdar, knew her business. I watched as everything that should be done was done. Walking slowly across the deck I looked down on the opposite side. At once I was galvanized into fresh action.

Down there, snugged in alongside the vorlca, the slender petal-shape of the voller lay quietly waiting for me to leap down and take her into the air.

"Ros!"

She ran up. "Yes?"

I nodded over the side. Dayra looked.

"Oh, yes!"

The flying sailing ship moved under me. Duty personnel were at the levers of the silver boxes, drawing them closer together so that the power inherent in the minerals in one box and the mysterious substance cayferm in the other could exert their force and lift all that solid bulk up into the air as light as thistledown. The raffle of masts and rigging clattered and groaned as it swung inward and upward as we rose. That could all be cut away later.

Without hesitating I jumped onto the bulwark and took a flying leap out into thin air.

I hit the deck of the voller and staggered and was up, sword in fist, searching for guards.

Dayra landed beside me, fleet, sure-footed, her Claw a diamond-glitter.

"No guards."

We were alone on the voller—then half-a-dozen folk dropped down. A lad looked about wildly. I said to Dayra: "We'd better—"

She was into the small steering cabin amidships before I'd framed my thought. The aerial sailors might know how to fly a sailing ship; they might not know how to pilot an airboat.

We lifted away as Dayra manipulated the control levers. Down below on the parade ground soldiers were running out, many of them. They were foreshortened figures, glinting with steel and bronze, and they could not touch us.

A girl wearing a Claw came across to me. She wore precious little else; but on the scrap of red cloth over one shoulder the embroidered representation of a rose glowed in colored silks.

"I can fly an airboat," she said. There was no blood on the talons of her Claw. "Do you know Ros the Claw?"

When folk ran below to sort out their possessions and to make sure the ship was sound, this girl had seized up her Claw from its hiding place. No doubt she was sorry the fight was over before she could use it.

"Yes. You do?"

She drew herself up.

"I am the lady Royba ti Thamindensax."

"Then Llahal and Lahal, lady. Pray, tell me the name of your Ship-Hikdar and what happened to your Jiktar."

She eyed me. That she felt puzzlement was clear. I did not know her. Of her town, yes, I had heard but never visited. By Vox! An emperor can hardly visit all his towns in one lifetime. We were lifting up now, matching speeds and courses with *Val Defender*. The breeze had veered in the night and we floated along splendidly. Then Dayra popped out of the steering cabin, and through the ports I could see a lad at the controls. I hoped he knew what he was doing! Dayra walked up to us, and she was smiling.

She began unstrapping her Claw. She nodded to the lady Royba's steel bright Talons. "I see you didn't have a drink, Royba."

"That Sosie!" Royba was obviously in a truculent frame of mind. "She beat me to a weapon—but I did kick a damned Pandaheem where he will be sore for a sennight!"

The ships sailed on, suspended between earth and sky.

Royba gave me that puzzled look again. "This great hulk tells me he knows you, Ros. Is that—?"

"Jak? Oh, yes, he knows me—or thinks he does."

I said, "I was inquiring after the name of the Ship-Hikdar and what happened to the captain—"

"That lady was Vylene Fynarmic of Fallager."

I knew of Fallager, it was a prosperous town up in Turko's kovnate of Falinur.

"As for the captain, Vanli Cwopanifer was—was—" Here Royba glanced around as though seeking the right words. "We were caught in the gale and a spar fell and crushed his head. He was—he was insistent upon maintaining command. Yet it was clear to all of us that he was makib, and this insanity led him into strange actions."

This is, as any first lieutenant, any ship's officer will tell you, a horrible predicament. Cwopanifer had kept up a string of orders, the gale had broomed upon them, the ship had lost her spars and her masts, and then the damned Pandahem voller had leaped on them. It had all been over before most of the crew were aware.

Looking up to the rearing side of the flying sailing ship, I could see the hands already hard at work. They were carefully cutting the tangled lines and hauling spars and yards inboard. If I knew my sailors of Vallia, they'd be jury-rigged in no time. I turned to Dayra.

"Ros. Can you take command here? I must go across to have a word with the lady Vylene Fynarmic."

"Of course. And tell Sosie from me she is getting fat." Dayra laughed. "No. Better not. Her Claw is ferocious!"

"This Ship-Hikdar," I began. "Is she—?"

"No." Ros shook her head. "She is a Sister of the Sword."

"And they're a right tearaway bunch!" I said, whereat Dayra looked at me as though demanding to know how I presumed to such knowledge of any secret society of women.

She went into the steering cabin to conn the voller herself as we rose above *Val Defender's* deck. I slid down a rope and dropped exactly plumb less than three feet from Vylene Fynarmic.

She looked at me calmly.

"I believe we owe our escape to you and to Ros the Claw," she said in that firm hard voice. "You have my thanks, sincerely. Although," she added matter-of-factly, "we were ourselves maturing plans for a break. Those cramphs would not have held us for long."

"That is true, lady—" I was saying.

She interrupted. "I am told you are called Jak. Can you hand, reef and steer? We can use you aboard."

"I am not exactly at liberty at the moment—"

"Nonsense! You're a Vallian. Well, then. That is settled. Report to the Ship-Deldar. He will post you to a watch."

"But—"

"That is enough, Jak! We are an emperor's ship!"

It had to happen, I suppose, sooner or later.

A strapping fellow clad only in a red breechclout was lustily hauling on a spar as it was angled inboard. The jagged end lashed and he staggered back into me. I caught him and stood him up on his feet. He turned, already shouting his thanks. He was florid, handsome, with bright eyes. He saw me. He knew me. I knew him.

"Majister!" At once, crack, up he went into that rigidity of attention the old hands can always muster.

"Majister! Lahal and Lahal!"

"Lahal, Nath the Cheeks," I said. And then, and I shouldn't have but I couldn't help it, I said: "And now I suppose everyone will know I'm the blasted emperor."

Six

"The Emperor of Vallia is aboard!"

"The emperor!" The buzz went around faster than the wine cups on pay night. "The emperor—the Emperor of Vallia is aboard!"

You had to give this lady, Vylene Fynarmic, full credit. Oh, she was a splendid person! A Sister of the Sword, first lieutenant of a proud sailing ship of the air out of Vondium. She looked me straight in the eyeball.

She said: "I give you the lahal, majister." Then, still in that same hard voice: "So you are Dray Prescot."

She stood there on her own deck, in command, and I had some inkling of what must be in her mind. She saw Nath the Cheeks standing as stiff as a lance at our side.

"You! Nath the Cheeks! Get the lead out! About your business, you fambly, and no lollygagging!"

He was about to rap out a reply when I said in a carefully neutral tone: "Oh, Nath the Cheeks and I are old campaigners. We were together in *Vela* at the Battle of Jholaix. Nath was a nipper, then."

He bellowed: "Quidang, majister!" and fairly bolted back to putting his weight into shifting the splintered spar... Vylene looked after him with a grim set to her jaws.

She turned to me. "You had best come below, majister. They are fixing my cabin last, when we are airworthy once more. But I can find you a stoup."

"When," I said as we descended the companionway, "did you last eat?"

"Just before we were captured."

"Then everyone is starving?"

"When the ship is ready to fly, then we will eat."

I had to agree. But my insides were railing at me like a pack of blood-thirsty werstings.

She found a bottle, and at least I could slake my thirst. She wore the rags of her once-proud uniform. The breeches were tattered, and the bodice was ripped. There were bruises on her shoulders. Her rank insignia had been torn off.

"What grade of Hikdar are you, lady?"

"Ley-Hikdar, majister."

She was four rungs up the ladder of promotions within the Hikdar grade; when she reached zan, ten, she might become a Jiktar. Now we had latterly amended the rank required to command the larger ships of the air. Once an ord-Hikdar could command a large flier. This had bothered me, used as I was to the idea of a person commanding a regiment of soldiers being of the same rank as a person who commanded a goodly sized ship. So, now, Jiktars commanded the great sailing fliers of Vallia.

I said: "I cannot promote you immediately to Jiktar, lady, much though I would wish to do so. The Lord Farris has final jurisdiction in the Air Service. But I can and do right gladly promote you to ord-Hikdar. At once."

She took that calmly, with a grave nod of her head. Strong-willed, resolute, she knew what she was about.

"Thank you, majister."

She told me a little more of the terrible time when the late captain had gone insane, and the Pandahem voller had bounced them. Any sailing ship, whether of the sea or the sky, has always to be particularly cautious of a powered vessel. I tried to lighten the tone of these proceedings.

"Well, you can see now that I am unable to sign on with your ship's company. I have things I must do here."

"Of course."

"I would be grateful if you would furnish me with pens and paper. Now I have the opportunity, I will write letters. I would ask you to deliver them for me."

"With pleasure."

So, down I sat at her desk, with pens and much of the superior Kregan paper, and wrote. To whom I wrote and what I wrote will, in general, be obvious. I wrote cautioning Drak that armies were being raised in Pandahem against him in southwest Vallia, which he knew, and went on telling him much of what had occurred, and that he could rejoice that his sister had... At that point I fell to chewing the end of the pen and staring vacantly about the ruined cabin. That Dayra had reformed, seen the error of her ways, rejoined the fold? That was not quite as we saw it.

In the end I wrote that Dayra worked actively for Vallia and that the great rascal Zankov had suffered a broken back, and if he was not dead then the spirits of Hodan-Set had missed their mark. Also, I told Drak that he must summon regiments of our best from Hamal. Down there we had been triumphant; now it was up to the Hamalese to work out their future. I would write, as well; but if Drak was to be Emperor of Vallia—as he was, as he was, the stubborn prideful fellow!—then he had to show Vallia and the world that he was the emperor.

After a dozen or so letters Vylene came in to see how I was getting along. She carried a pewter plate on which reposed four exceedingly hard and gritty biscuits. She put the plate down with a clatter on her desk.

"I decided we should all take a short breather and have something to eat. Some of my girls are faint with hunger."

With perfect composure, I said: "I give you thanks, lady." The way I spoke, the cut of my jib—both gave me intense pleasure. I'd remained calm, cool, perfectly polite. By Djan! That, I tell you, was a great victory!

In one corner of the cabin stood a brightly painted wooden tub with an earthenware inset, filled with good rich earth of Vallia. A pathetic-looking stump stuck up from the middle. She saw my glance.

"Those devil-spawned rasts of Malpettar took all our palines, and cut down my bush."

About to make a reply that, I felt, could not be the right one—for any ship's company sailing without palines to suck and chew on and to find the surcease those remarkable berries can bring, is a ship's company in deep trouble—I was saved by Dayra's breathless entry. I stood up.

With all the cracking relish of a ship's captain, Vylene snapped out: "You do not enter here without knocking and waiting, Ros the Claw! Now go—"

"To hell with that! We're all starving—and all we get is this!" She threw a biscuit onto the desk. "Hard tack! Weevilly biscuits and no palines!"

Vylene handled herself well.

"Go away at once, Ros the Claw, and I will forget this incident. You are subject to naval discipline aboard my ship. If you have come to appeal to the emperor—" Here she half-turned to look at me, and I fancied the gleam of a tinge of uncertainty caught at her.

At once I said: "The lady Vylene commands here, Ros."

"But my guts ache!"

"As do everyone's. We shall be leaving soon. Now—"

Dayra simply turned around and rushed from the cabin.

Not prepared to continue this scene, I sat down again. What Vylene was thinking of my choice of traveling companions made uncomfortable reflections. It was clear that the alias of Ros the Claw well-concealed the identity of the Princess Dayra. As it should do, of course...

Vylene did say, being human: "These Rosy ones, beloved of Dee Sheon. I must crave your forgiveness, majister."

I said, "If I write to the empress, can you make arrangements to deliver the letter into the right hands?" This was an appropriate moment for the subject.

She looked at me, a strong, competent, firm-faced woman in her rags of uniform.

"I am of the Sisters of the Sword. I will call Sosie ti Vendleheim for you."

I nodded and sat down to the sweetest writing task any man may have in two worlds. Sosie came in and stood quietly waiting. She was just such a Sister of the Rose as so many of them were, lithe and limber, flushed with the graciousness of youth and high spirits, wearing her tatters with panache and with the marks of hard toil upon her. When I had finished I turned and said: "Sosie."

"Majister."

"I entrust to you this letter for the Empress Delia. You, I believe, will see it delivered safely."

"As Dee Sheon is my witness."

As she spoke she made that small secret sign. I nodded, satisfied, and handed the sealed packet across.

When she had gone I stood up and stretched and said to Vylene: "I thank you for your courtesy, lady. Now I must be about my business."

"You will take the flier?"

"Aye, Vylene. Aye, I will take the flier. She will be invaluable." Then I outlined some of what was going on across in Port Marsilus, and finished: "So they continue to recruit an army there to invade southwest Vallia."

"We are on patrol against just such a threat."

"Good. But you'll be sailing for Vondium directly."

"Yes. The yards will soon refit us."

I said: "One last boon before I go." I touched the green cloth about my waist. "Have you a length of scarlet cloth in exchange for this?"

Well, that was swiftly provided.

Out on deck I saw Dayra with her head down talking to Sosie ti Vendleheim. My Val! but they looked splendid! As I walked across ready to go overside into the voller, Dayra looked up. Sosie moved away, discreetly, stuffing a packet into the remnants of her russet tunic. Dayra smiled at me.

"Well, Jak! And are you ready now?"

"Quite ready. You?"

"Oh, aye," and here she put the little finger of her left hand into her mouth and wriggled the nail around her teeth.

"Didn't your mother ever tell you—?" I began.

"Yes. But you know how roast ponsho gets between the teeth!"

"You little minx!"

She laughed and hoicked a leg up and so slid down into the voller. When folk's insides sound as cavernous as a bat hell then there are tricks aboard a ship to provide the necessaries... I was still sharp set—sharp set! I was starving. But young Dayra had gorged good roast ponsho...

The folk crowded to the bulwarks to look on us as we shot off, waving and calling the remberees. *Val Defender* was already in process of resuming some semblance of a fighting vessel of the air. Her crew were in good heart. I settled back as Dayra at the controls sent the voller slicing through the bright air of Kregen. If a man can ever be content, which by nature he cannot, I suppose that was a moment of minor contentment as Dayra turned and extended a hand.

"Here."

I took the wrapped bundle, a yellow cloth folded over, and unwrapped it, and so looked at a chunk of roast ponsho, a heel of bread and a dip of butter. The ponsho was cold; but it was superb. Eating, I looked at Dayra, and out across the cloud-castled sky, and sighed, and chewed. Life, life... A funny old business, by Zair!

She said with an abruptness that revealed her indecision: "I am glad you wrote to mother—"

"I would not have thought Sosie would tell you that."

"Why not? I sent a letter, also—"

"I see. So Sosie knows—"

"Well, of course! We went through Lancival together."

"Then I am glad you wrote to your mother. She has been through perilous times since I last saw her. The quicker we can settle this affair of Pando's up, and sort out that army in Port Marsilus, and burn a few more temples to Lem the Silver Leem, the quicker we can go home."

She regarded me with an odd expression.

"You are the emperor. What really keeps you here? You could easily fly home directly, now—why not?"

She knew nothing of the Star Lords.

Obscurely, not fully certain, I felt this was not the time to tell her of the Everoinye. That would come. Instead, I said: "It is a matter of plain common sense. If we can prevent the army sailing, or hurt it in some way, we fight for Vallia."

"That is true."

"And this flat slug King Nemo of Tomboram. Now if we can handle him aright he might be more friendly—"

She fired up. "Friendly! I'll tell you what we should do with this flat King Nemo. We should chuck him out and get someone else in—your friend Pando, perhaps?"

"The thought had occurred to me. But—"

"But what?"

"Life is not as easy as the Shadow Plays, or the Farces they knock about in the Souks of Lanterns—"

"I know that!"

Well, she did, she did, as I could testify...

I talked to her for a time as we drove on southward through thin air about the greater problems of Paz, our grouping of islands and continents. She shared the general aversion and horror everyone felt about the Shanks who raided us. We talked companionably, and I felt these recent adventures had helped to bring us at least a little closer together.

Following the road, we passed over forests and open areas and just about the time we calculated, working on the assumption of speed of Pompino's party, we spied them trudging along below. They were all looking up and pointing and already unslinging their weapons. We had taken in the flags of Tomboram, for this was a king's ship, and mightily unusual for Pandahem. We leaned over and waved.

"Hai! Pompino!" I bellowed. "Are your feet sore?"

"Jak! You're the greatest unhanged rascal that ever—" So, amid the shouts of lahal and the uproar, we landed. Soon, with everyone loaded aboard, up we soared, on course for Plaxing, Kov Pando, and what the future might bring of disaster or triumph.

Seven

We name Golden Zhantil

"Clearly," said Kov Pando, "the airboat will have to be returned to the king. I'm in trouble enough as it is. He was telling me the last time I had civil words with him of how he had negotiated the purchase of an airboat from the Dawn Lands. Mighty proud he is of it. Armipand the Malignant will not spare any horrors for the malefactors who stole it." He glared at me in a most stern fashion.

Pompino burst out most wroth: "But, kov! We cannot send it back! Anyway, we have named the airboat *Pride of Bormark*."

I said, "Anyone who takes the airboat back to King Nemo is likely to be thrown from her deck, very high in the air, or, talking of air, he may find an air gap between head and shoulder blades."

"Too right!"

We sat at Pando's high table in his great hall in his steading of Plaxing. We had eaten until we could burst. The samphron oil lamps gleamed. A party of musicians twiddled their instruments, waiting for the kov to give them leave to begin. Because a Kregan kov is like and yet not quite like an Earthly duke, some of his functions appear odd. As for young Pando himself, well, he worried me. His sharp alert face with the jutting beard, the intelligence in his eyes, as the popular conception goes, the marks of authority about him, might have reassured me; but his irritability of manner, the way his left hand kept rubbing over the pommel of his sword, the way his energies appeared almost manically directed, yes, as I say, young Pando worried me.

We had not yet seen his mother, Tilda of the Many Veils, and everyone knew this was because by this time in the evening she was lushly into her third, or fourth, bottle and would not be disturbed for an earthquake.

Pando had greeted us kindly. He was a great lord, even if he was for a moment in disgrace and in what amounted to hiding. He'd been disgraced before and had won back into the king's favor. But my comrades were aware that Pando was a kov, one of the great ones of the world. Also, we had been very swift to tell him that we held no allegiance to the Silver

Wonder, and were aware that he had joined the worshipers of Lem only so as to strike at his cousin, Murgon Marsilus.

As for Plaxing itself, it was a fine estate set in connected clearings in the forests, run by a curmudgeonly old fellow called Mankar the Horn, an Ift, and although the place was just a lord's estate, used for hunting as much as produce, it was unlike the other hunting lodges and estates I have seen in other parts of Kregen. One could scarcely expect a hunting lodge in, say the country inland of Magdag, or an estate in Hamal, to be the same as a similar place in Pandahem. Yet the similarities existed as well as the differences.

Pando said, "The airboat will have to go back to the king, and there's an end to it."

Pompino scrubbed up his whiskers. He had eaten and drunk well. "The airboat was lost from Malpettar, kov. No one knows who stole it—"

Almost, I was about to break in with: "Liberated—"

I halted myself. Dayra glanced at me, and smiled, and I warmed to her. If young Pando got ideas in Dayra's direction, I'd have to think on. Of course, she was a grown woman and mistress of her own fate, as far as anyone can be on Kregen. That would be for later.

A lively fellow with clear eyes and curly hair, dressed carefully and yet with a soberness to the cut of the clothes, leaned forward. "But, you said there were Vallians in the town. What happened to them?"

Dayra spoke easily, holding an apple in one hand, the fruit shining and ripe and ready for the crunch of white teeth.

"I believe they managed to escape. There was a great deal of confusion at the time."

"There!" exclaimed this young fellow, who had been introduced as Poldo Mytham, taking an interest in the argument. "You see! The loss of the airboat will be blamed on them!"

The buzz of agreement rippled around the high table. They were free and easy among themselves, I'd noticed, except when Pando spoke. Then the strained attentive silence was close to embarrassment.

Poldo seldom took his eyes off the lady Dafni Harlstam, who sat at Pando's right. She talked—well, she talked all the time so that in the end you tended to be able to carry on with other conversations and interests without actually hearing her—and as well as talking she did not look particularly happy. She'd been rescued from the evil clutches of Strom Murgon Marsilus and brought here. Pando was determined to marry her for her estates, Murgon wanted her for the same reason, only poor Poldo wanted her for herself.

Across from him his twin sister, Pynsi, a girl who looked withdrawn, with pale hair banded about her head, seldom took her eyes from Pando, as her brother seldom left off looking at the vadni at Pando's side. It was all a conundrum.

Pando said, "Are you questioning my orders, Poldo?"

"What—? No, no, kov, of course not!"

"Oh, Poldo!" breathed Pynsi.

"I say the airboat goes back to the king. You, Poldo, can take it back."

Pynsi looked stricken.

I pushed my wine cup away across the table. I said: "That will not be necessary. The airboat which once belonged to King Nemo no longer is his. She belongs to me—to Ros Delphor, and to me. To no one else. We say what will happen to her."

"Aye," said Dayra into the shocked hush. "And we're not giving her back to that flat slug Nemo."

Well! I can tell you! A right royal shindig began then.

I had the shrewdest of suspicions that all Pando's people, all his paktuns and Ifts, would not have stood against Pompino's crew had it come down to handstrokes. For, make no mistake, Pompino was using Pando for his own ends just as were the rest of our cutthroat band.

Over the hubbub Pando glared at me. Now, remember, he'd known me when he was a young lad, when Inch and I had taken back his kovnate for him from Murgon's rascally father who had usurped the title. He knew I'd called myself Dray Prescot, and thought I'd used the name aping the man who was to become the emperor of Vallia. He thought I was Jak. But Dray Prescot or Jak, Pando knew that I'd stand no nonsense from him in these latter days. I'd told him. Had I been firmer with him when he was a lad he might not have turned out as he had. His mother, Tilda the Beautiful, had held my hand to both their griefs.

So, he spoke up. Instant silence fell.

"Very well, Jak. I agree the airboat is your stolen property. This means I cannot accept you as a guest. If you keep the airboat you must leave—or I will arrest you and send you and that woman in chains to King Nemo."

Cap'n Murkizon said: "I am weary of walking everywhere. I prefer to sail in a ship, even if she flies in the sky." He did not mention his Divine Lady of Belschutz, and he made his position perfectly plain. Larghos the Flatch, instantly, agreed. So did the others.

The green-clad Ift, sitting along from me, who had not so far taken a great interest in the conversation, by reason of his continual baiting of a tiny tump serving girl, leaned forward.

"Better if you left at once, then, Jak," said Twayne Gullik.

I regarded him. His tall pointed ears stuck up almost past the crown of his head. His narrow slanted eyes conveyed that devious look that so marks Ifts, a wayward folk, at home in the forests, clad all in varying tones and shades of green. This Twayne Gullik was the castellan of Pando's palace in Port Marsilus. He'd taken the kovneva Tilda into hiding here, taken her away from Pompino and the crew of *Tuscurs Maiden*. We fancied he was a man who backed both ends against the middle and we trusted him as far as we could throw a dermiflon.

"Far better, Gullik," I said, knowing he did not like this bald use of his name. "The problem over that easy course of action is that Kov Pando is in some trouble and as we are his friends we must rally round."

Some folk took that well, some ill, and Cap'n Murkizon laughed, and poured more wine.

Pando slouched back in his high chair. The people around the table rattled and chattered away, and in all this talk there was precious little of any planning. And Pando grew more and more irritable and jumpy. I just was not happy with that young imp, not happy at all...

When folk are immersed in animated conversations and the room fills with the racket, there often occur on this Earth unaccountable sudden silences. These occur at twenty minutes to or twenty minutes past the hour. In one such abrupt silence two things happened.

One—Twayne Gullik craftily snitched out his sword scabbard, tangled it in the busy legs of the little tump serving girl and toppled her over. The tray with its freight of half-empty wine cups spilled. Twayne Gullik laughed, a clever Ift scoring over a stupid tump in the eternal rivalry between the two races.

Murkizon snorted, and turned away, disgusted.

And, two—I said, hard edged to Pando: "Tell me, Kov Pando, why did you choose the zhantil as your emblem?"

He knew. Of course he knew, and he damned well knew I knew, too.

Pando gripped a gem-encrusted golden goblet. He looked down the table at me. "I recall a certain day, with the caravan, out in the New Territories of Turismond. I lost the pelt, seasons ago. But I said, then, and I kept my promise. The zhantil is the noblest wild animal—" He stopped himself, and then went on: "You called yourself Dray Prescot then."

"I have used the name, I admit," I said casually. "And the zhantil-masks we spoke of? I admire your craft there. It is a great gesture, potentially a Jikai, to smash the leem-masks with zhantil-masks."

"And that is our true purpose!" cried Pompino, very bristly. "And not this unseemly wrangling among ourselves."

I hid my smile as I drank. My haughty Khibil comrade Pompino not enjoying a bout of wrangling! Come the day!

"Murgon has the king's ear," said Pando. He spoke moodily. "He is ensconced in the Zhantil Palace in Port Marsilus. He raises an army. I begin to think that perhaps he has won this bout, and maybe this is the last contest."

"Nonsense, kov!" said Pompino. "Do you not have the Vadni Dafni at your side!"

I must admit I wondered what the talkative Dafni would have to say about being lumped together as what amounted to a chattel along with the king's ear and the Zhantil Palace. Mind you, given the circumstances and the customs, that was exactly the situation, and she was enough of a noble lady to understand that. I wondered, too, what she would do about it.

What she did do was to stand up and say—inter alia with comments about the new dress she had ordered and the way she required her eggs in the morning—that now she would retire. Her handmaids went with her. Of all the ladies left only one, I judged, might not wish to join in the drinking and singing that would follow. Perhaps two, if Pynsi Mytham was feeling too frail. The lady Nalfi stood up. "I, too, will retire."

So that was a simple wager won.

Pynsi stayed on and this, I judged, was because Pando did. We sang a few songs; but they did not rollick out with the required gusto. We were not, all told, a happy band.

In the end I'd had enough. I said to Dayra: "I'm for bed."

So, Dayra, Pompino, two or three others, we made our respects and cleared off to our quarters. Larghos vanished. We slept. We awoke. We breakfasted. All that day we argued back and forth, and Pando did not put in an appearance. We renewed acquaintanceship with the cadade, the captain of the guard, Framco the Tranzer. He was pleased to see us, for he recognized the crew as seasoned warriors. Naghan the Pellendur had copied his cadade's habit of pulling his whiskers.

Everyone wanted to go and inspect the voller.

I said to Pompino, "We can't call her *Pride of Bormark*."

"True. Well, let your young friend Pando sweat. We'll call her *Golden Zhantil*."

"Capital!"

At our own request we saddled up zorcas and rode through the forests, admiring their richness. The animals were very fine, not as fine as Filbarrka's zorcas of the Blue Mountains of Vallia, but then, as he would be the first to say, there are no zorcas in all Kregen to match his.

Three days thus passed in idleness and chatter.

On the fourth day we cantered back gently through the falling shadows of indigo and bronze, looking forward to a good meal. Pando had not put in an appearance, and I was seriously considering going and trying to induce some sense into his thick vosk-skull of a head.

The longer we delayed, the greater Murgon's ambitions would rise, the greater his power extend.

We rode into the stockaded yard of the steading to find absolute chaos, stark raging madness.

When we'd shaken some sense into the nearest wight we could lay hands on he shook himself in fear. He was a Fristle guard, and he bore a great wound down his arm.

"Lords, lords! They came and took her away!"

"Who came? Took who?"

He shivered.

"I do not know who they were. They wore silver leem masks. And they took the Vadni Dafni away with them."

Eight

A roll of gold for Jespar the Scundle

The first question to ask in these circumstances is: "Which way did they go?"

Murkizon growled out the question and the Fristle shook and shivered and stuttered: "Lord, lord, I do not know."

"Where's Pando?"

The uproar in the yard we now saw was mostly from slaves scared witless, men and women who had been wounded, and not a needleman in sight, and folk who just rushed about aimlessly. The kov, we learned, had ridden out in pursuit with a large party of his retainers and most of the guard led by the cadade.

"So he knew which way to go," said Pompino.

The hubbub continued unabated. Slaves were taking full advantage of the confusion to do what slaves tend to do given half the chance. I saw one fellow staggering off to the back quarters carrying an enormous jar—ale, probably—and followed by a raggle-taggle of his cronies. Other slaves were upsetting the side trestles, and roaring, and running. The bedlam battered on. We found a tump slave calmly sitting with his back against a wall stripping palines from a branch and popping them one by one into his mouth. He was happy. Well, not all tumps are your dour, taciturn, mining people who just dig in the ground for red gold and continually bicker with the Ifts of the forest—though tumps and Ifts bicker all the time, of course.

He wiped his mouth where the whiskers sprouted, for his beard reached to his belt, and swallowed the last morsel of paline and stood up.

"Masters, that Ift castellan, Twayne Gullik, led the pursuit."

From his manner, cowed and abject in the slave fashion though it was, you could tell what he thought of Ifts.

"So the kov did know which way to go." Pompino swung away energetically. "Well, that settles it." He drew me a little apart from our comrades, who were now intent upon finding their own suppers. "Jak, we have wasted too much time here shilly-shallying. We should be about the Star Lords' business, burning temples—"

"But this was part of the plan—"

"Assuredly. But burning temples to Lem the Silver Leem is by far the most important task we have at the moment. If your friendship for the kov Pando—whom I cannot profess to care overmuch for—prevents you from carrying out your duty to the Everoinye—"

I spoke hotly.

"I've told you, aye, and the Everoinye, what I think of their duty. They have caused me much anguish in the past. I know I distress you with these sentiments, Pompino; but they are sincerely held. The Star Lords plunk me down in unhealthy places and expect me to sort out their problems for them. All right. And I agree we must smash the Lemmites. But, right now, at this moment, I am concerned for Pando."

"Nobody knows which way he's gone!"

"True. But we can take the airboat and search."

He put his fists on his hips and glared at me, whiskers bristling, face flushed, foxy and brilliant and altogether a sharp customer.

"If I order my people to follow me, then—"

"Then I'll be on my own."

"And—you would?"

"Aye, Pompino, by the Black Chunkrah, I would!"

The moment blew up into the promise of a full-grown gale—and then the tump walked across. He was around four foot high, so he was well-grown and he looked up. "Masters?"

"Aye, what?" growled Pompino.

"That haughty Ift shouted out as they galloped off—"

"What?"

He shuffled from one splayed foot to the other. He screwed up that knobbly face with the long nose, squinting up at us.

I said, "I know how you tumps love to dig in the ground, and sing about your work, and bring forth ripe rich red gold. But if I gave you a gold piece, now, for your words, well—you are slave. What could you do with gold now?"

"I was not always slave, master, and I will not always be slave. There is a scheme. The red gold—"

"Your name?"

"Here they call me Jespar the Scundle, master."

I reached into my pouch, and my fingers felt the leather and the stitching and not much else—perhaps a dead moth—and I almost laughed.

"All our gold was melted or spent or fined away, Jespar the Scundle. Now, we must hurry. The kovneva will give you gold." I started off at a trot, and I yelled the old man-driving word I seldom use: "*Bratch!*"

Jespar the Scundle bratched.

Tilda's handmaids were outraged and Naghan the Pellendur who had been left as a guard demurred. I brushed all that aside. Into Tilda's private apartments we went. I was after the loan of a gold piece; I need not have bothered.

Mindi the Mad stood beside the kovneva's bed. She wore her pale blue gown in that shadowy chamber of heavy drapes and mellow lamps and thick rugs. She lifted her head within the hood and I saw that pale, narrow, high-cheekboned face in the flesh for the first time. But, of course, I knew her well.

"You are the man they call Jak?"

I said: "A gold piece, Mindi. The tump here is entitled to his due. We must be after the kov and Dafni—"

"The kov is being misled—"

"Ha!" broke in Jespar, with a most unslavelike rasp of humor. "The haughty Ift Twayne Gullik is foresworn again!"

"Sink me!" I burst out. "If you knew Pando had gone the wrong way, why didn't you stop him?"

She did not flinch.

"I did not know then, for I have just scryed. And, anyway, they were out of the steading like a pack of wild leem."

A slushy, slurred and yet full voice from the bed said: "Is that...?"

She sat propped against pillows, half in the shadow of a curtain draped from the bedhead. Her gross form mountained the bedclothes like The Stratemsk, across which monstrous mountains I'd ventured just before my first meeting with Tilda. She held out a hand. The cup slanted at an angle.

"Natalia! My cup is empty. If my cup is empty, you know—you know what—what will..."

Her thick voice trailed off. A wisp of gossamer, the flash of a slender form, white arms tilting an amphora, and the kovneva Tilda's cup was once more full. She slopped some wine, drank some, stained the bedclothes a deeper pink, and said, "It is no use chasing after Pando. Or after Dafni. He will not—not find her. Let—let her go. No good will come of them..."

She was, for this latter-day Tilda of the Many Veils, remarkably sober and lucid.

Of course, the suns had only just gone down. It was early in the evening yet.

A superb russet-clad form moved gently beside Pompino, and Dayra said: "Mindi the Mad. You can scry. Can you not tell kov Pando? And put us on the right path? You have the power, *I know*..."

For a moment I held my breath. The Sisters of the Rose could produce girls whose command of sorcery ran deep, who were thaumaturges of a very high order. Delia had not taken her Witch's Vows. The SoR did not deign to call their girls with the magical powers sorceresses or witches, instead dubbing such a girl a vibushi. I glanced sideways at Dayra. Was she a vibushi, then, a mistress of the magical arts as well as of the Whip and Claw?

Mindi the Mad looked at Dayra.

"The kovneva has just expressed a wish that the lady Dafni be left to ride away—"

Pompino blew up then.

"That's it! By Horato the Potent! This is footling. Come on, let's leave this pestilential place and set about our proper business!"

By Krun! And wasn't that the temptation!

I said, "I believe our best ends will be served if we can prevent the union between Murgon and Dafni. As to any future marriage between Dafni and Pando, that is entirely a different matter."

"How serve our best ends?"

I couldn't tell Pando all of it. But, by Zair, I was in the frame of mind to cut through all this skullduggery. If Pompino knew the truth, he would change in his attitude to me, of course he would change. But then we might get things done quickly that now I had to beat about the bush to accomplish.

With her smooth voice modulated and level, Dayra said: "If this Murgon takes Dafni, he wins her province, that will make him even stronger with the king, and the temples you speak of will proliferate and flourish..."

"All the more to burn!" grunted Pompino. But Dayra's words had made him think afresh.

He drew his dagger. Mindi flinched back and half raised her hand. No one really believed she could turn him into a little green toad. But the thought was there, stark in our minds.

Pompino presented the point of the dagger to Jespar the Scundle's throat. His left hand seized the long beard and jerked the tump forward and up.

"I am not a silly forest Ift, tump. I am a Khibil. Now you will tell me what I want to know."

Jespar strained on tiptoe. He remained calm.

"You may kill a slave, Khibil; you will not then learn what it is you wish to know."

Oh, yes, tough these tumps; tough as the rock they dig their red gold from.

I drew my knife; that broad heavy sailor blade caught a glint from the lamps and glittered. Jespar swiveled his eyeballs in my direction. I heard Dayra take a breath.

On the footrail of Tilda's bed, exposed by the drape of the clothes, the golden inlay gleamed lushly. The point of the knife slid in, I twisted, pulled, got the strip in my fingers and hauled. I was able to roll up a good arm's length of the golden inlay into a bundle. This I held out.

"You'd better put Jespar down, Pompino. You'll have that beautiful beard out by the roots else."

The Khibil laughed. He socked the tump back onto the soles of his feet, and said: "Well, tump? Tell us!"

Jespar the Scundle shook himself straight, grabbed the roll of the golden inlay, stuffed it away somewhere into his gray slave breechclout and drew the belt tight.

"Yes, Jespar," I said straightly. "Tell us it all." For I had not missed the inner significance of the tump's words.

"That haughty Ift, Twayne Gullik," he began. Then he realized just what I had said. He slid those deep eyes of his around to goggle at me again, and said in a rapid staccato: "The Ift shouted out Benorlad; but I knew the men in the silver leem masks had not come from there."

"Benorlad," jerked out Naghan, his Fristle whiskers quivering. "That's Murgon's damned great fortress in his stromnate of Ribenor—"

"Why, Jespar?" I said.

"Why—wasn't my second cousin's wife's brother there, with the men in the silver masks, with a chain around his neck and sitting on the back of a zorca? Tumps don't ride so grandly. And we don't like straying far. No, that wight Tangle the Ears—and I can't say I care for him over much for he got disgustingly drunk when my second cousin was married—was being made to act the guide. They're off to the mines up around the headwaters of the River Oonparl, up beyond Erronskorf."

I stared at Mindi the Mad.

"You knew this?"

She, in her turn, looked at Tilda. The gross form moved spasmodically as Tilda turned over, slopping wine, having had her say determined not to hear any more. Mindi took that as permission.

"Since you have discovered where Murgon is going, through chicanery—why, yes."

"Then," I said, swinging about and grasping Jespar, "do you scry and warn kov Pando. Tell him we are headed directly for Erronskorf. If he rides hard he may come up with us to be of use."

"But—" she began.

"You would be well-advised to do it," said Pompino. He spoke gravely. He meant what he said.

Jespar squealed in my grip.

"Lord, lord! I cannot ride a jut, let alone aspire to straddling a zorca!"

"Oh," I said. "You won't have to worry about riding any animal the way we're going."

And, so, without more ado, off we trooped to gather our lads and to take after Strom Murgon and his silver leem masked rogues and the Vadni Dafni.

212

Nine

We drop in on Korfseyrie

Hurtling through the windrush under the Moons of Kregen we pelted headlong for Erronskorf.

Pompino gave orders for the crew to sleep by watches; I suppose some of us caught a few moments of sleep as we hurtled on in that streaming radiance from She of the Veils and the Maiden with the Many Smiles. One of the small moons bustled past above, swinging wildly through the star fields.

Because these Pandaheem were totally unacquainted with vollers, Dayra and I had to fly *Golden Zhantil* ourselves. Dayra proved a first-class pilot—well, by Zair! and didn't she ought to be, seeing her mother had taught her? Delia had also taught me my piloting. As for Delia, well, no doubt there were better pilots who flew vollers all day for a living, no doubt; my view remained exactly the same as the view which told me that Seg Segutorio was the best bowman of Kregen—Delia, likewise, was the best pilot in all the world. So said I.

Sitting quietly at the controls with the port-windows thrust wide I was privy to a vastly entertaining conversation between Rondas the Bold, our Rapa paktun, and the diminutive tump, Jespar the Scundle.

"Now, tump," said Rondas in his big blustery way, "you are very welcome to join our company. Why, we are fearsome and ferocious paktuns, aye, and at the moment we are serving without pay, seeing it was all fined away from us by a scoundrelly woman."

"I never thought to live to see the day mercenaries would serve without pay—"

Rondas's answering snort must have riffled his feathers splendidly. "No more did I, tump, by Rhapaporgolam the Reiver of Souls! But, and listen good, we are in the habit of going agio when we go into action—"

"Agio?" Jespar's voice was an alarmed squeak.

"Aye, dom, agio! You see, all of us put in our gold, into the kitty, all of it. Then, when the battle's over we share it out again."

"You mean, to keep it safe?"

"Fambly! No! Why, those who share it out are less than those who put it in, onker! That way a fellow can make a little on the side from a fight."

"I don't think—"

"It's all fair and above board. It's in every paktun contract, I expect—anyways, it's in ours. So, you see, tump, when we get to wherever this fight is to be, your roll of gold will be in good hands."

"But...!"

I concentrated on flying the voller. By Krun! But they were a rascally bunch, right enough.

The two girl varterists came up and when Jespar appealed to them, they gravely told him that as far as they were concerned they went in for agio and—had they any gold about them—it would have gone into the kitty along with Jespar's roll of gold inlay.

"Why don't I just keep my own gold—?"

"What! And suppose you are killed!"

"Why, as to that," said Jespar, "I don't intend to get into any fights!"

"Amazing!"

"Incredible!"

"Not believable," amplified Rondas. He must have been mournfully shaking his great beaked head, very vulturine, very menacing. "Coming with us and not getting into a fight!"

"I didn't want to come!" squeaked Jespar. "Anyway, I'm just a guide. I wouldn't have come at all if that great hulking apim fellow hadn't hauled me along—"

"Oh, you mean our Jak. Why, dom, you want to walk very small when he's about. He'd as lief fry you up and gulp you down as a tasty morsel between meals."

"I don't—" began the tump.

Alwim, very hard, said: "You'd better believe it."

"I do! I do!"

"Just as well," said Wilma, as hard as her sister.

With the light of two gorgeous Moons of Kregen in the sky we deemed it not altogether opportune for a swift and undetected onslaught. Below passed away forested hills, very ghostly silver, most eerie in that streaming light. Those we pursued would have ridden hard at the beginning, and then have husbanded their mounts. We could cover in a single bur the distance it would take them to progress in ten or twelve.

This thought occurred to Pompino, for he walked up and said, "I think we may reach this damned place before them."

"That is likely. I hope so. The advantage will lie with us, then."

"Only if this tump Jespar the Scundle speaks right."

"He speaks right, as far as he knows and guesses. If he is wrong—"

"I'll chop his ears off!"

"It seems to me our little tump Jespar is in for a very rough ride..."

"Oh, he'll survive. Very tough, they are. And I'll tell you something else. They're not as dull and stupid as the Ifts make out. Both races tend to want to occupy the same areas of forest, the Ifts for the trees and the tumps for the gold under the ground. Why they don't go and dig for gold somewhere else escapes me."

"Why should they? If the gold is in the ground, they'll dig it out, and if a few trees are in the way—"

"The Ifts are mightily upset, by Horato the Potent!"

Because we took a circuitous route so as not to fly directly over the hamlet of Erronskorf we took longer than the flight strictly required. All the same, we were very quickly there, and Dayra guided the voller down into the shadow of the trees.

"And you are sure this is the path they must take?" demanded Pompino.

"Aye, lord, this is the path." As we crowded out of the voller under the stars and gazed around on the gently swaying masses of trees, Jespar sounded confident. He was back on his own stamping grounds. That perked him up.

He pointed upward along the path between the tree-clad slopes of the mountain.

"Up there lies the mine—more than one, belonging to different branches of the family. Down there—" and the jerk of his thumb was highly dismissive, "lies the forest of the Ifts. This is the path they will follow to go up past the mines to Korfseyrie."

I just hoped Jespar was right, as much for his ears as anything. Murgon could hide Dafni away up here and no one the wiser. Then he could strike where he willed.

He as good as held the provincial capital, Port Marsilus. He was entrenched in the Zhantil Palace there. Now he sought to erode further Pando's fast waning power.

Pompino's mind must have followed a similar train of thought, for he growled out: "A pity that flat slug of a King Nemo did not burn with his damned temple and palace in Pomdermam. While he rules and supports Murgon—"

"Murgon has a free hand here. Aye."

A pair of voices that were usually lovingly gentle broke out in passionate argument in the shadows. We turned.

"Lisa! You are the most stubborn and willful of women!"

"And you are the most thick-headed and stubborn of men!"

Pompino brushed up his whiskers. "I would not care to step in to settle that," he observed, in a fine free way.

Quendur the Ripper quite clearly had not heard Pompino's heartfelt remark. His face alive and working, with passion, Quendur stormed over to us. The golden mask hanging from its straps in his fingers shook violently.

"Horter Pompino! I appeal to you! Tell Lisa the Empoin that as I love her I will not have her with me in this fight! Tell, horter, spell out the recklessness of her folly!"

Pompino flung me such a look I had to turn away.

"Well, Quendur—you see—that is—" Pompino stamped his foot. "By Horato the Potent! Am I to mollycoddle you, Quendur, you, the great roarer of a pirate?"

"But—!"

"But nothing! If I tell Lisa not to join in the attack, do you think she will listen?"

"We have kept her out of fights before."

"That was different."

Lisa walked up, quietly, contained, already fastening the leather straps of her zhantil mask over her head.

"You see, my love, I am in the fight, and shall stand by your side to keep you out of trouble."

"And may Pandrite aid me!"

"He will, he will." And Lisa the Empoin pulled the straps up tightly.

Larghos the Flatch pulled his bow from his shoulder and set about stringing it. He looked sullen. Then, looking up he said: "I could wish, Quendur, that the lady Nalfi shared the spirit of Lisa the Empoin."

At my side Dayra moved and was still. She was too much the great lady to say: "See? I told you so!"

"Rather, Larghos, you should praise your gods that the lady Nalfi does not foolishly run headlong into danger." Quendur swung his golden mask about dangerously in itself. "Where does she rest now?"

"She remained in the airboat. She said her foot pained her, and she would bathe it in hot liniment."

Quendur grunted something unintelligible, and then this part of the preparations was over. Each one of us pulled on a golden zhantil mask provided from Pando's armory. Some were of brass, some steel with a wash of gilding. They did not restrict vision, and were light enough not to discommode a person in the heat of a fight. They might stop a blow across the face, although I was not too sanguine about that.

The two Moons, the Maiden with the Many Smiles and She of the Veils, slanted beyond the tree line and the Twins would be later this night. For a space, a fragrant darkness englobed us in the perfumes of a Kregan nighted forest.

While there was little necessity to give orders to so cutthroat a band about how to lay an ambush, Pompino went along each side of the pathway, making sure the dispositions pleased him. We settled down to wait.

Well, we waited. When the Twins rose and the forest trail lit up in a fuzzy pink glory, I went over to Pompino, about to make a certain suggestion. He was holding Jespar by one ear.

"Now, Jespar, you have had us out here on a fool's errand! Confess! My blade is hungry for your ears!"

"No, lord, no! Master, my ear!"

I said, "You should know, Jespar the Scundle, that Horter Pompino can be very severe on villains' ears."

"That is sooth!" roared Pompino.

"You should be lucky your sobriquet is not Iarvin," I went on. "Had it been—" I sucked in my breath, and fell silent.

Pompino took the point. He let go of the tump's ear. "Now," he said in a more reasonable voice. "Where are they?"

"Perhaps they have been delayed, lord—lord, I am certain sure my second cousin's wife's brother would be used to guide them here. Otherwise, why did they have a chain about the neck of Tangle the Ears, and why mount him astride a zorca, where he was always in mortal peril of falling off?"

"Perhaps he fell off," I said.

"That great rast Murgon would stick him back and tie him on," quoth Pompino. And, that was true...

"I'll have a look down the path a ways," I said.

"I'm with you," said Dayra.

"That will be enough!" snapped Pompino, quelling the instant desires of the rest to take a break from lurking in ambush. So, off down the trail went Dayra and I, looking to see what there was to see.

We found enough, and easily enough at that, to tell us what had happened.

Zorca hoof prints, many of them, in a milling marking of the ground. They had ridden up, and then they had halted, and then they had struck off through the forest and skirted our pretty little ambush.

When Pompino came down to see he was beside himself with rage and mortification. I realized I had to handle this situation—and especially Pompino the Iarvin—with fastidious care.

"They must have caught wind of us," said Pompino, when he could speak coherently.

"Highly unlikely, surely, with such a band as ours?"

"Aye, you are right. So—?"

"So let us not worry too much over that now. Jespar can lead us to Korfseyrie."

Pompino pulled his whiskers.

"An onslaught is different from an ambush."

"That is true. But we can use the voller—"

"The airboat? How?"

He'd taken off his golden zhantil mask and dangled it from his fingers. He was pretty livid with anger and frustration and primed to abandon the night's doings and return to Plaxing.

Dayra, also, removed her mask, as did I. The breeze zephyred over my cheeks, and I felt pleased that shadows dropped down to conceal my face. Dayra spoke up briskly.

"Why, my dear Pompino, we all climb aboard, we sail over their heads, and we drop down on top of them."

"Ha!" Pompino swung his arms about. "That sounds a sure recipe for disaster, my lady—"

I said, "We believe from what Jespar and the others said there are between twenty and thirty of them. We either go now and drop on their heads, or we give in and go back."

"Who said anything about giving in?"

"This was the gist of your observations, surely?"

Pompino glared about truculently. He breathed hard. He scrubbed up his whiskers. As a kettle on the stove bubbles and boils before either being removed or blowing up, so the haughty Khibil bubbled and boiled.

"Very well. We drop on their heads. And if you are killed do not come whining to me with your head all a-dangling."

At his words I turned sharply and blundered back down the path. Dayra had suggested the stratagem, and she was coming with us, and if Quendur the Ripper thought he had problems with Lisa the Empoin, then he didn't know the half of it...

Delia and I had called our youngest daughter Velia, and we had done this out of love and grief and prideful memory of the older Velia, our second daughter. I did not wish to contemplate all the agonies that might follow on this night's doings.

There was enough of the night left in which, if we hurried, we could finish this affair.

Lisa said she was coming, and that was that, and the lady Nalfi expressed the perfectly natural desire not to be left alone in the forest. She looked flushed. It was decided she would stay in the cabin out of harm's way. We did not intend to make our call a long one.

Korfseyrie was well named.

During the day no doubt the korfs would wing about the high towers, darting specks of color in the suns shine as they sought their prey. Now they'd all be tucked up with heads under wings along the niches and crevices of the stone walls and towers. In the mingled lights of the Twins we slanted down.

The place was a solid fortress, buttressed against attacks from the edge of the forest, its walls lofting sheer, its towers dominating every access. Being built in Pandahem no thought had been given to attack from the air.

"How well d'you know the place?" demanded Pompino.

Jespar whiffled and evaded; but in the end he admitted that he had a passing acquaintance with the fortress.

"How passing?"

"We-ell..."

"Spit it out!"

The place spread below, coming up fast, a confusing medley of lights and shadows. Dayra flew the voller in a tight circle aiming to land us on a flat-roofed construction high in the center. The flatness glimmered pink. Each corner of the roof supported a squat tower.

Jespar looked over the sides as Pompino's groping fingers sought his ear.

"If you land there you'll get wet!"

"A damned rooftop reservoir!" said Pompino. "Catches the rain. My lady Ros, we must find another—there! That courtyard looks promising."

Dayra said nothing but flicked the flier into a tight turn, scraped past the edge of a corner tower and brought her to ground in a superb display of flying which was completely wasted on these Pandaheem to whom the vollers were simply magical and to be expected to do magical things.

The moment I'd clapped eyes on this place I'd regretted my suggestion of attacking it.

So maybe it was not planned to defeat an onslaught from the air, so maybe the sentries were single-mindedly watching for our approach up the narrow and tortuous path to the summit, so what... We were down in a yard high in the complex, Jespar could show us the way; but we were dreadfully few to accomplish a mission against a stronghold and its garrison as strong as Korfseyrie.

Pompino had secured enough directions from Jespar to take us through to Murgon's quarters. We didn't then discover just what were the passing acquaintanceships the tump had with this fortress; but Jespar was perfectly confident in his directions. Soundlessly we leaped over the bulwarks of the flier and raced into the shadows.

Ten

Jak Leemsjid

We reached the first shadowed doorway unobserved and I paused and looked back at the airboat.

If a satisfied grimace cracked my battered old features into a gargoyle smile, I was not only allowed that—and deserved it, by Vox—I joyed in it!

From the bulwarks, Dayra stared after us. She saw me stop and look back, and she shook her fist at me.

She had said, very hot, very intemperate: "Why should *you* go and *I* stay?"

"Because you can fly the voller—"

"I believe you have some small skill in flying, Jak the Onker!"

"That is beside the point—"

"Or is it that you think me not a ferocious enough fighter to go?"

"If ferocity were all, then you would outdo all of us—"

"Then it is my skill and prowess at arms that disqualifies me in your sight?"

"Not at all, your skill—"

"Well, then, what?"

Pompino and Murkizon and Quendur and the rest looked on and took their own enjoyment from the scene and my predicament. I couldn't burst out: "Because you are my daughter, Dayra, that's why! And I'm not having you uselessly killed like Velia!"

I did say in my churlish way: "By the disgusting diseased liver and lights of Makki Grodno, girl! You'll stay with the guard and fly the voller out if you're attacked, and you can hang about and fly down to pick us up when we get out!"

She opened her mouth—and I looked at her, and Dayra or no damned Ros the Claw, she shut up.

I admit to no proud feelings in this, on the contrary, to my discomfiture; but I knew what was what and Dayra was the pilot among us to stay in the voller.

Queyd-arn-tung!

There is no more to be said!

As we took breath in the shadowed doorway a second figure appeared beside that of Dayra at the bulwarks.

A fierce raspy voice said in my ear: "I give you thanks, Jak, that you made Ros Delphor see sense, for Lisa the Empoin was constrained to obey me—for a change."

I said, "They'll be up to mischief, don't fear, Quendur."

"I know. I do not wish to contemplate that—"

"In here and stop lollygagging!" rapped Pompino.

Dutifully, we all went into the first of the chambers and looked about, our weapons ready, our senses alert.

Jespar mumbled: "I should have stayed, too. You know the way—"

"Think of your ear," said Pompino, "and lead on!"

Korfseyrie was large enough to require a sizable garrison and it was highly unlikely that the twenty or thirty with Murgon would spread out. When we bumped into one, we'd find most of them, or so we reasoned. The place smelled of damp and decay and bore an abandoned feeling, for Pando seldom ever came here and the place, designed to guard the mines worked by the tumps as well as the forests below, had been bypassed in the late wars. Murgon had shown craftiness in selecting it as his temporary headquarters.

We passed a tall window from which the glass had long since fallen. The stars glittered through the opening and a zephyr stole in and rippled the tapestries on the wall opposite.

Instantly, the movement at his side registering in the corner of his eye, Rondas struck.

The tapestry split. Dust puffed out chokingly. The whole tapestry simply ripped and fell into pieces, whole soft swaths of it disintegrating and collapsing across the corridor.

Nobody passed a comment.

A mail-armored and axe-armed man could have been waiting behind the arras, ready to leap out and decapitate one of us as his comrades roared into the fray.

Those decrepit tapestries were symbolic of the whole fortress. Decrepit, dusty, disintegrating. Just how old it was we didn't care to guess; it was old...

However unwilling and complaining he might be, Jespar led us in what I considered to be a reasonably straight line through the corridors and chambers. For all Pompino's tough manner, and the paktuns' casual menace when they suggested agio, we all felt affection for the little tump and the fearful threats made were merely that, threats and not to be acted upon. At least, I trusted that was so...

Cautiously we descended from that high courtyard going down broad staircases and narrow spiral staircases, prowling along corridors darkened by shredded tapestries and drapes. No statuesque harnesses of armor, no stands of weapons arranged in decorative patterns, adorned the walls. They had all long since been taken away to be used in the red tumult of battle. Weapons and armor must serve many seasons when the wars are on.

Now the castle-builders of Kregen do not usually construct their fortresses so that any raggle-taggle-bobtail crew may calmly stroll in as though out for a Sunday promenade. They set traps. They confuse by winding stairways and corridors. They trick the unwary in a myriad of cunning, ingenious and lethal stratagems.

If you are unable to garrison the whole of your fortress, then you seal off those parts undefended and set the traps. We had the great advantage that we descended from the upper levels instead of fighting our way in over the ramparts as any sensible Pandaheem besieger would have to do. Jespar was aware of many of the places where we would have been slain for sure, and our own expertise took care of most of the rest.

Most of the rest...

"There are murdering holes in that ceiling," pointed out Rondas the Bold, "and arrow slits in the walls."

"Aye," agreed Pompino. "Where is the trigger?"

Jespar professed himself at a loss.

"This must have been set up after Kov Pando left."

"Well," I said, venturing an opinion, "if no one has been here much since, this could be Murgon's work, therefore we look for places where the dust does not lie as thickly—as there!"

The plate in the floor was suspiciously free of the dust that clung stubbornly everywhere. We could mark our route in the dust of the floors.

"You could be right."

"We shall see," said Rondas, and he took off his heavy helmet, swung it by the straps, and hurled it full onto the plate. The metal rang gonglike.

Instantly, the nearest murdering holes disgorged a fuming liquid that stank in the confines of the corridor, and the nearest arrow slits ejected barbed darts that flew to smash rendingly against the opposite walls.

Bold as ever, Rondas laughed, and stepped forward to retrieve his helmet, no doubt concerned lest the feathers were damaged.

"Wait!" screeched Pompino.

Rondas took two steps more and bent, and the whiz of the dart passed just over his head. From the murdering holes more fuming liquid poured, stifling us in the stench. Rondas let out a yell, and leaped back, half-straightening as he jumped. The second dart took him full in the back. It punched through his carelessly flung cape, and as he reeled under the blow I leaped, grabbed him, hauled him in like a fisherman reeling in his catch. Rondas fell all of a heap.

We staggered back.

Rondas said, "May all the devils of Gundarlo take it—my back, horters, my back!"

We turned him onto his front so that his great beak jutted to the side and lifted the cape away. The barb had dinted into his armor, breaking a way through. Dark blood welled.

Pompino pursed up his lips.

"It is deep; but not so deep as to be fatal, as I judge. You have been lucky, my Bold friend."

"Lucky! My back feels like it has been broken in two!"

"Well, the dart must be got out, and that is a job for a needleman, of whom we have none. So—"

"I can make it back to the flying boat," gasped Rondas. "Even if I crawl. Do you go on."

I said, "I am not prepared to see Rondas die for lack of attention—"

"What do you suggest, then, Jak? Abandon our rescue?"

"If necessary. The Vadni Dafni can always be rescued another time—this whole venture is—"

"I know! It is foolhardy, harebrained and stupid! But we are in for it now, mostly thanks to you. So I shall go on, by Horato the Potent!"

"Very well."

He glared at me, very huffy, very arrogant, brushing up those reddish whiskers into a bristling stiffness.

"If that is your desire, Jak the—Jak the—"

"Call me Jak the Onker, and it would fit. We cannot go on through that corridor, I judge—"

"That is right, master!" broke in Jespar, babbling in his eagerness. "The traps are fresh and strewn thickly."

"So you will have to find another way through, Pompino the Iarvin."

Cap'n Murkizon, who appeared somewhat at a loss because of the absence of Larghos the Flatch on guard by the voller, banged his axe about, mentioning his Divine Lady, and suggesting we stop blathering and get on with it. I believe he had missed a deal of the byplay, the words not spoken, between Pompino and me.

Now Pompino cast about and spotted a secondary corridor. He pointed that way, nose in the air, filled with a quivering fury.

"Let us go, then, by Horato the Potent!"

The way led for a time back the way we had come and if Pompino noticed this he did not comment thereon. I supported Rondas, fairly hauling him along, concerned at the state he was in. Arrow and dart wounds are the very devil if they are not treated correctly. I judged that the barb although not overly deep was deep enough to present problems. It could not be pushed all the way through, as a slender arrow might with a smart blow, mainly because it was aimed directly into the vitals of the Rapa. It would have to be cut out. This I could do, and had done aforetimes; it was not something I was overly fond of having to do. Also, to weigh the balances in our favor, Rondas was a tough bullyboy of a fellow, able to stand the shock of my rude ministrations. He would not keel over like others might have done who had previously caused Seg and me some headaches.

The Fristle guard commander, Naghan the Pellendur, told off one of his men to assist me, and between us we carried Rondas along more comfortably.

As we went along, I decided that I didn't care what Pompino might do. He was my comrade and we both worked for the Star Lords. If he wished to continue the rescue attempt then he would do so and I would not seek to prevent him. I did know that I was taking Rondas back to the voller where I'd put out my utmost exertions to see that he did not die from his wound.

The others pressed on and Naghan half-turned.

"Maybe it would be safer if a couple of us went with you, horter Jak."

"My thanks, Naghan; but with Nath the Gristle here to help, we should manage."

The Fristle guard assisting me made no comment.

The Pellendur nodded, satisfied, and swung off after the main party.

We'd reached a bend in the corridor where the Twins shafted their light, still eerily tinged with a ghostly silver glow, across the walls covered in faded paintings, from an arched opening above.

Dust motes spun in the still air. The men ahead seemed phantoms, specter figures moving in moonbeams and magic. The whole wall at our side collapsed and fell away on hidden hinges. A pit gaped beside us.

The Fristle guard, Nath the Gristle, and Rondas would have fallen, tottering off balance. I managed to give them both a fierce twisting shove, a gasped effort like the release of a spring. They toppled away from the pit.

Then, in the same instant, I was falling, spinning head over heels through thin air.

A frenzied hullabaloo started above, a chorus of shocked yells and oaths. The sounds racketed between the stone walls. I hit with an almighty thump, thwacking down flat on my back onto a heaping pile of filthy straw. Mangy bits of straw fluffed, the stink was immense, and all the stars of Kregen flashed before my eyes and the cacophony of the Bells of Beng Kishi clamored in my skull.

"You all right, Jak?"

Pompino's shout was an echo, floating around in darkness, an alarmed yell of despair.

I couldn't—for the moment—answer.

"*Jak!*"

I drew in a breath that nigh gagged me.

"You'll wake up the whole damn fortress..."

"Thank Pandrite—we'll soon have you out."

A hiss, a particular venomous malevolent hiss, drew my shocked attention. I came quiveringly alert. I knew, at once and without a doubt, what kind of creature stalked me from the shadows.

Up above on the lip of the pit, out of jumping distance, my comrades crowded to peer down. They saw. They saw the lean slinking form lope out into the shafts of moonlight.

That lethal shape halted when the first shaft of moonlight struck down. In that pallid radiance the eyes gleamed, gleamed—oh, how those eyes gleamed!

The wedge-shaped head sank down, low to the stone, and the mouth gaped wide revealing rows of yellow teeth and the purple-black gums, from which spittle-foam dribbled down. Slavering, those jaws opened wide.

Delicately, step by step, two feet at a time, one from each side, the eight clawed feet lifted and fell and the long lean body bore down on me. The tail flicked from side to side, sinuous, quivering, and the tip was truly tufted by a clot of black hair. The muscles stirred the furred pelt, long iron-hard muscles, moving with smooth precision under the ocher hide. Low to the ground, head out-thrust, two feet after two feet, tail flicking, death stalked me in that moonlight-drenched pit.

One of the Fristle guards hurled his spear and thankfully he missed the leem.

More usefully, Nath Kemchug shouted: "Hai!" and threw down his spear to me. It clattered on the stones and the butt end rested on the pile of stinking straw by my foot.

At the Chulik's shout the leem paused and his wicked head with the whiskers stiff as steel spikes tilted up. I reached out a slow, steady, cautious hand for the spear.

My fingertips touched the iron-bound wooden butt; and then froze. The leem snarled at me, ignoring the people up above who were all now shouting and screaming trying to draw the beast's attention.

Two more spears flew.

"Belay that!" I yelled, risking an immediate attack. "You might hit him!"

No more spears hurled down.

Two clawed feet at a time, eight feet lifting and putting down, the leem moved from the shadows into the light of the Twins. His two shadows lay close together, so for a bewildering moment it seemed there were three leems stalking me in the pit...

My fingers wrapped around the iron-shod butt. Nath Kemchug was proud of his spear. It was stout and sturdy, with plenty of steel weighted in the head. He could polish up his tusks a treat with it.

The saliva glimmering on the teeth of the leem dripped down from those purple-bruised gums. His tail flicked from side to side—was he one of the sort who straightened his tail into a bar in the instant he charged? Or was he of that diabolical sort who waggled his damned tail even when he leaped? I did not know. My fingers eased up the smooth wooden haft of the spear, and I was at full stretch, and knew that if I moved too much too quickly the bolt of ocher-furred lightning would strike...

Sensations fined down. I could feel the polished wood as rough as sandpaper. The stink wafted away and became as nothing, the dung-heap stench vanishing, and instead my nostrils filled with the smell of leem. I could see the way his whiskers indented, each in its own little black pit. I could see the sparkle of each drop of spittle. I could see the angry-red tongue, lolling behind those fangs. His ears lay close to his head, swiveled to catch the first sound of an enemy elsewhere than where he knew he had his prey firmly fixed. And his eyes! Partially veiled by a downdroop of brow, semicircles of hate, the eyeballs turned up so that the eye looked a blot of mirror darkness cupped in a rind of yellow-white, those eyes fastened on me with such merciless determination I knew that I'd have one heartbeat and one only to save myself.

As that thought shot through my head I realized I was glad Dayra was not up there, crowding to the lip of the pit with the others.

I do not know how long the interval was between my falling into the pit and the instant the leem charged. It could not have been very long. Leems are sudden beasts in their ferocity; to me that time passed in an agony of slowness. It seemed a long time to me, a damned long time.

Then I had the spear in my fists, had thrust the butt into the crack of stone just beyond the pile of straw and the leem was in midair above me, his paws widely extended, his mouth a single vast cavern...

One way and one way only to go—

Headlong I dived under him, between the rows of taloned paws. His belly shot past above and the steel spear point penetrated his breast and went on and on and he went on also. Had I stayed another heartbeat, he would have landed full on me. The spear passed completely through him, jutting up a reeking and gory splinter above his back.

His screeching scream shattered against the walls of the pit and echoed crazily in my head.

I was on hands and knees, was turning, seeing his tufted tail quivering before my face. He thrashed and screamed and pawed at the spear, and blood sprayed.

He wasn't dead. Not by a long long way do you kill a leem by merely passing a spear through his body. Even if you hit one of his hearts, the other will pump fresh anger and power into his muscles.

If my comrades were yelling, I could not say. If the world had blown up, I didn't know. The noise in my head, compounded of the leem and my own blood, drowned out sanity. My thraxter was in my fist. What a weapon to fight a leem! I leaped to the side, skidding, and he turned and tried to leap again and this time I was poised and ready. The thraxter went in neatly and I swear the last foot of the blow was in midair, for I was already turning and leaping away and snatching up one of the Fristles' flung spears.

Give a leem no chance—he never gives anyone or anything a single chance in all of Kregen—give him no rest... The first spear, muscled by desperation, flew to embed itself in his flank and bit, as he swiveled to leap again. He did not move as fast as he had... His blood choked upon the floor and fouled among the foulness of the straw...

Flashing the second spear before his face, shooting a jagged reflection of moons shine into his eyes, checked him for a tiny moment. He was a fine specimen—powerful, savage, a killing machine. I believe the spear in his flank must have nicked his secondary heart; for as he swiveled and prepared to leap again he was slow. I poised the spear. I drew a breath, realizing that that simple act meant I was back in control of myself and was a fighting intelligence rather than a mere primordial warrior-savage. His tufted tail lashed. His eyes fastened on me like leeches. His scarlet cavern of a mouth gaped and the yellow fangs glittered with saliva. Blood pumped from his side.

In the next instant he would leap...

So, mastering myself, remembering I was Dray Prescot, Lord of Strombor and Krozair of Zy, I bellowed out: "Hai!" and charged in full tilt.

Savage against savage, beast against beast...

The cruel steel spearhead drove deeply into the ocher beast's breast as the apim beast that was myself forced on the shaft with bursting muscles.

Almost, he had me then.

A paw swiped from nowhere and even as I ducked a claw razored down my cheek. Had he connected full that blow would have split my head as an axe splits kindling, a child squashes a rotten fruit.

Hanging onto the spear I twisted, grinding it in, shouting, redness and haziness everywhere.

Someone shouted: "Hai!"

Pompino was there, before me, a spear in his fists driving down.

I said, "Thank you, Pompino—"

He said, "It was fast, too fast—my help was not necessary."

Staggering back, feeling the wetness of my own blood on my face, I gulped air. The stench was prodigious. The leem lay on his side, eyes rolled up, a last long shaky quiver trembling his lean flank. The dark tufted tail gave a last twitch.

"Hai!" bellowed down Murkizon.

The others set up a yelling. I sat down, plump, on the blood-soaked straw.

Probably the perfectly natural reaction of a fellow after a fight overwhelmed me then. Normally I can contrive to carry on with some at least of the old functions still operative after combat. But, for some reason, on that occasion, with the dead leem and the blood and the stink—and the very real horror coiled in me at thought of what might have occurred had Dayra been with us when I fell into the pit—I babbled like a green young coy after his first brush with the foe.

"A leem!" Quendur said, leaping down and giving the dead carcass a kick. "That is a jikai—a lone man—"

So, loose-tongued, chattering, I said: "A leem? But I had a sword, and spears, so I had all the advantages. I've fought leems before. Once, I recall, I fought a leem with a kutcherer, that silly butcher knife with the spike at the back. That was a bad one. He chewed me up; but I got him in the end. Leems? No, doms, I do not like leems and have fought them many times, and each time I swear will be the last."

"You speak strangely, Jak." Pompino turned his head to stare at me instead of the leem. The furred, feline and vicious fighting cat lay there in his own blood, and he looked pathetic now, as so many dead creatures do...

"Strangely?"

"Aye. A lone man against a leem no matter what his weapons and skill is a jikai not lightly to be undertaken. Even professional leem-hunters, who are all mad anyway, do not operate alone. You were a leem-hunter?"

"Not a professional—I only fight leems when I have to..." And, as you know, that was not strictly true...

"A jikai," boomed Murkizon. "That is what I call this deed and that is what it is, a jikai. Hai, Jak Leemsjid!"

Jak Leemsjid...

They all took up the cry.

So, I had acquired a sobriquet, at last, after my simple name of Jak.

Leemsjid, leemsbane...

I said, "If that is so, we must prove myself equal to the name. The Leem Lovers—"

"Aye!"

I stood up. I retrieved the thraxter. I cut off that dark tuft at the tip of the leem's tail. This I tucked down into my harness. Then we were hauled out of the pit and so set off again, and now Rondas the Bold was assisted along by a rascally savage fellow rejoicing under the new name of Jak Leemsjid.

Eleven

We assist at Strom Murgon's feast

The way before us was blocked solidly by a mass of masonry extending from wall to wall and from floor to ceiling.

"The devil take it!" exclaimed Pompino.

He twisted up Jespar's ear.

"Well, tump!"

"I do not know, master! Maybe, maybe the noise—we were heard—maybe Murgon has triggered more traps—"

"That cross-passage fifty paces back may lead us in the direction we wish to go," suggested Naghan the Pellendur. He glanced at the slumped figure of Rondas the Bold. "We must hurry—"

"Aye," said Nath Kemchug, busy with rags and oil.

I took great heart from this small exchange. I have said many times that most of the folk of Kregen did not get on with Rapas. But one became accustomed to their smell after a time. Not all were evil. No more than any other of the races of Kregen—excepting Katakis and some others, who were damned of the devil and doomed in all men's eyes.

Now a Chulik and a Fristle were concerned for the life of a Rapa.

As I say, that heartened me.

We retraced our steps in the dust to the cross-passage and ventured along it in semi-darkness.

Pompino said to me: "I suppose that damned great gash in your face will heal up with uncanny speed, as always?"

I grunted something. Pompino was not aware that I'd bathed in the Sacred Pool of Baptism in far Aphrasöe and this gave me seemingly miraculous healing abilities. There was so much Pompino did not know of me, and I was his comrade, a fellow kregoinye. Well, the dark glass holds the future, as they say. Now, as we shuffled on through the dusty corridors, I felt the weight of Kregen pressing down on me.

The walls and ceiling floated echoes down oddly from up ahead. Pompino and Jespar were yammering away, and although they spoke in fierce staccato whispers, the sounds bounced off the stone and reached us at the tail. They might, also, reach other ears, set each side of heads filled with plots for our destruction. There was no doubt we had made a lot of noise. Now ordinary noise in a castle can fade and attenuate from one ward to another, muffled by thick walls and lost. A fight can bring the guards arunning, as all of us here knew. That damned leem... He must have been a precious part of the Leem Lover's paraphernalia, for the slinking lean forms of leems are not easily come by—alive in good condition.

So, we expected company at any moment.

Nath Kemchug's ministrations on his spear were almost finished. He carried oil flask and rags like any warrior to keep his armory clean, and again like any warrior wasn't too choosy whose wall he knocked over to get some brick dust. Of spittle we usually had a plentiful supply, except when our mouths dried in the fear and clangor of combat, and then we were not particularly thinking about cleaning blood off our weapons—quite the reverse.

But with Pompino's mercenary Chulik the cleaning of spear took precedence over all of his other weaponry. There was obsession in this. Chuliks, trained from birth to handle any weapons, continue to perplex and baffle me, and while they could handle—and clean—any weapon, Nath Kemchug remained obsessed with his spear. As we were making so much noise, I did not hesitate to call across to him over Rondas's drooping shoulder.

"I give you thanks, Nath Kemchug, for the use of your spear. The weapon served well."

He was down at the butt end, meticulously picking away at the junction of wood and iron, removing all traces of the leem's blood. He did not look up as he spoke in his apparently surly Chulik way.

"You fought well. In the name of Father Chalkush of the Iron Brand, I give you the jikai for that, Jak Leemsjid."

Rondas, sagging in my grip, let out a gurgling groan of a laugh at that.

Surly, Chuliks appear to the world; I was beginning to believe that my original estimate of them, founded as it was upon ignorance and prejudice, might be more in need of rethinking than I supposed. And, the same estimate applied to Rapas, and to Fristles. Truly, the more I spent my life on Kregen and learned of the ways of that ferocious and mysterious world, the more I understood how little I really knew!

Men are men and women are women, and that is the beginning and end of the mystery.

Pompino's voice floated up. He sounded absolutely revolted at what he had just heard. He sounded disgusted.

"What, tump! Down *there!*"

"Aye, master. It seems to be the only way through."

Another of those uncannily appearing blocks of masonry walled off the passageway ahead. If we went back we'd only run into the other block, or be forced to try the passage where Rondas took his wound. At the side of the block the dark round opening of a hole promised fearful terrors. The smell was bad enough; there was no leem stink mixed with it as far as we could sniff.

"By Horato the Potent! This expedition is not turning out as I expected!"

"Strom Murgon is a very clever man, master—"

Pompino turned to look down, and he turned and looked very slowly and with great meaning. Now by this time we'd all taken off our zhantil masks—if I'd been wearing mine when I fought the leem I wondered how little protection it would have afforded my face against those horrific claws—so that Pompino's haughty Khibil face could fully express the depth of his feelings. He stared at the little tump.

"And are you then suggesting that I am not?"

Jespar quaked.

"No, master! Of course not—"

For a reason not at all obscure I said: "Jespar is too wise in the ways of this world to make elementary mistakes, apart from being made slave and then of going with us. I think he should be listened to—"

"But, Jak, down there!"

Cap'n Murkizon boomed out: "Show us another way, horter Pompino, and we will gladly follow it."

There being no answer to that, we all dropped down the black hole into the stink, one after the other. And, of course, Pompino dropped down first.

We managed to bring Rondas down without causing him overmuch pain. His mail had saved his life. But if we did not get the barb out within a reasonable time, and patch him up, he could easily lose that precious commodity.

Jespar's squeak said: "We are approaching Murgon's quarters. I am sure of it."

Nobody could see a blind thing. We shuffled along a narrow ankle-breaking slit in which muddy water ran. If this was a drain and someone pulled the plug up aloft, well, we'd be neck high, or mouth high, in filthy water—or drowned.

I made up my mind I'd see to it that Jespar was lifted up so that he stood the same chance as folk of races not dumpy and near to the ground.

We came to a fork where our hands met emptiness each side.

"Which way, Jespar?" growled Pompino.

"To—to the right, master, lies Murgon's suite—I think."

"And to the left?"

"I am not sure. If this drain lies under the Corridor of Fountains, then the left would lead to the drain opening onto the cliff—"

"To the right, then."

A moment's thought assured me that to emerge onto the cliff, separated from Dayra and the voller by the bulk of the fortress, would not serve my purpose. We had to go back and up. If that way lay through Murgon's apartments, then that was the way we would have to go.

When we came across a ladder, Pompino halted.

"I am going up. I am heartily sick of this drain."

Perforce, up we went. When Nath the Gristle and I maneuvered Rondas up onto the paving through the manhole we found ourselves in a narrow space walled by masonry and brick. Lanternlight fell through a latticework a score of paces off to our right. That was the way Pompino led.

Now we padded along silently, feral, alert, and with weapons in our fists.

The sound of voices reached us, and at this we all took heart.

Soundlessly, we approached the latticework and peered through.

Had an observer chanced to spy us he must have jumped back, aghast. At the best of times an unruly, fearsome, hairy bunch, after our experiences with Murgon's traps, our struggles in the corridors and pits, and to top it off the trudge through the slimy stink of the drain, we must now appear a truly awful, horrendous bunch of scarecrows.

Pompino put his nose against the stone latticework. He sniffed. That sharp cunning foxy nose wrinkled, and he sniffed again.

About to make a tart comment that we were aware that we all stank, I stopped. I, too, sniffed.

"Undoubtedly," pronounced Pompino.

Cap'n Murkizon said with enormous satisfaction: "Roast vosk for a certainty."

"And momolams."

We were all sniffing away at the delectable odors drifting in through the latticework. Our own stinks were forgotten.

Everyone smelled out his favorite dish. They were all there.

"If this is not another trap..." said Pompino.

"It's got to be Murgon's kitchens."

"True. But I have the deepest suspicions of anything that man does. None of you will rush upon the viands. If you do—"

Rather tartly, I reminded them.

"I do not believe Rondas the Bold will go rushing anywhere for a time."

That was cruel of me, of course; for they were all aware of Rondas' plight; but I felt the responsibility in an odd way. As the others led off, going cautiously, and Nath the Gristle and I followed on with Rondas between us, I reflected that I'd taken enough responsibility in my life, Zair knew, and taken it damned ungraciously usually. Responsibility to others, to some shadowy creed, to your own damned stupid self, sometimes weighs a fellow down more heavily than all the iron shackles in Kregen.

When we fetched up with the others in a vaulted barn-like place with two walls roaring with fireplaces, with broad tables groaning with provender, with pots abubbling and pans afrying and spits aroasting, the glorious mouth-watering scents of any gourmet's paradise enclosed us in a world of enchantment.

The cooks and serving folk huddled against the one wall that held only shelves, and a posse of Naghan's Fristles prodded absently at them with their spears one-handed, while they gorged on whatever came to the other hand.

Nothing loath, for like them all we were sharp-set, Nath the Gristle and I plunged for the nearest food-piled table. Rondas, comfortably on his side, appeared not the least interested in food. We took him back a drink, which eased his thirst but was probably not too clever, although I was confident the dart had not penetrated into his intestines.

Pompino rolled over, swallowed down, hiccoughed, and said: "Murgon is in the middle of a feast. I imagine he will not wait too long for the next course."

"He won't tolerate slack service." I spoke solemnly, already gleeing at what was to follow.

For, of course, Pompino the Iarvin, as a smart kregoinye, saw as fast as did I—probably faster—what the next ploy would have to be.

"Although, Pompino, I also won't tolerate delay in attending to Rondas."

"There's a needlewoman at the feast. I asked."

"Then I am with you and let us try to knock some sense into these rascals of ours... They'll stuff themselves silly given half a chance."

With superb food distending their stomachs, their blood still hot from the insults they had received within this place, the lads were very much inclined to go and do nasties to Strom Murgon and his cronies. An eye for an eye, reprehensible though that may be, tended to operate at certain levels.

I said to Pompino: "Mind you, Murgon is feasting late. The night won't last forever. One wonders what was the occasion, apart from the lady Dafni, of course."

"A fellow doesn't really need an excuse for a feast, Jak Leemsjid!"

I agreed. As Pompino spoke the new name, I realized that there was a certain lack, a wanting of euphony. The name needed a lightening syllable...

In no time at all, once the idea had taken hold on their evil imaginations, the crew and the guards dressed in the flamboyant if shoddy festive robes of the servitors. They disguised themselves amid much stifled laughter. Weapons were hidden. Quendur stuffed his sword into an enormous pie, and swathed a yellow hot-serving cloth about the hilt, guffawing.

Soon, choking to keep down their merriment, their weapons hidden and ready, their festive serving garments, all swathing multi-colored cloths and feathers and baubles, disguising the grimy bodies beneath, they were marshaled into a procession. Trays bearing a bewildering assortment of foods for the next course hoisted high to conceal their faces, they marched solemnly for the doorway leading into the banqueting hall.

I, Dray Prescot, walked with them, clad as were they, my weapons hidden as were theirs.

We were going to serve up Strom Murgon with an unexpected delicacy.

Every one of us wore a golden zhantil mask.

And, with us, clinging like a vile miasma, the stink of our passage through the sewers floated about us.

So, dressed up, kitted up, with sharp weapons, stinking to high heaven, we entered Strom Murgon's banqueting hall.

Twelve

Golden zhantil-masks

"Bratch, you rasts, bratch!" called a silly foppishly dressed fellow who must be the overseer of the servers. We ignored him. We marched on in stately procession, carrying the viands high to conceal the golden zhantil-masks.

Strom Murgon sat in state in this banqueting hall of Korfseyrie. The chamber bore none of the marks of long disuse of the other parts of the fortress. Tapestries glowed upon the stone walls. The beams above were carved and gilded. The tables in the form of a horseshoe carried fine yellow napery, and silver and gold vessels, and banked vases of flowers. Incense hung in the air, which stank worse than we did from the sewers. Murgon's cronies sat about the tables, facing inward to the hollow center. Among them lolled many painted girls in transparent draperies.

In the space between the arms of the horseshoe tables a troupe of erotic contortionists performed. This explained the lack of urgency in chasing up the next course of the feast. They'd been sitting here enjoying themselves since they'd avoided us in the forest and settled down to a night of debauchery, and they were not halfway through yet.

The orchestra in a grilled enclosure to one side donged and plucked and tootled away. The performing troupe performed. There were Sylvies there—as one expected—and they always gave within the expertise of their art superlative exhibitions.

From a bulky grotesquely clothed form with a silver tray bearing a whole roasted bird stuffed with smaller birds ad infinitum a throaty rumble said: "...Belschutz!"

"Such decadence is to be expected," whispered Pompino.

"But there are still guards lining the walls."

"Oh, aye, I see them."

We advanced in procession, and the foppish personage realized that this was not according to plan. We would clash with the high spot of the Sylvies' performance.

He tried to halt us.

"Wait, you cramphs! Wait by the nine-towered serving tray of Beng Forlti."

Although adjured to stop by the patron saint of all waiters and waitresses, we marched on.

The guards, the musicians, the erotic performers, did not wear masks. Everyone else did.

The glitter from the samphron-oil lamps' reflections blinded in silver.

Masks of Lem the Silver Leem—snarling silver leem masks!—adorned every face in that blasphemous assembly.

No need to describe the color or ornamentation of the robes of those feasting so merrily here!

High against the end wall the monstrous silver statue of the leem glittered down.

There was no iron cage, no little girl sacrifice in her white dress.

There were bloodstains upon the stone floor in a cleared area to the side.

Scuff marks in the stone flags told where the sacrificial block had been dragged away after the gruesome rites had been performed.

"Stop, you misbegotten cramphs, you spawn of Hodan Set! Stop or you will be flogged jikaider."

The foppish personage fairly danced with frustration, probably well knowing that if the servitors fouled up he would be flogged in that cruel crisscross fashion also.

Now I happened to be carrying a silver tray which bore a large, sugary, creamy confection, a ziggurat of a cake the Kregans call annimay cake. While undoubtedly too rich, too sugary, too creamy and altogether too fattening, it is, even to a soured old forager like me, delicious.

About this time the bewildered and bothered chief steward, this overseer of the servers, woke up to the bizarre assortment of dishes we carried in so solemn a procession.

He fairly gobbled his alarm.

"What, what, what? You, there, with the bird... And you, a trifle... And is that vosk and taylyne soup? What in the name of Llumino of the Sauces is going on?"

Pompino—he with the taylyne and vosk soup—said, "It is about time."

"Aye."

Murgon in his silver mask and his Brown and Silver robes sat at the head of the table, and the woman at his side must be Dafni—and she, too, wore the Brown and Silver, and the silver leem mask covered her face. Murgon's two trusted thugs must be among that company, the Chulik, Chekumte the Fist, and the sly little apim, Dopitka the Deft, if they had not so far been slain. One or two of the silver masks angled in our direction and the lamp-glow glittered with inquiring menace.

"Let slip the hounds and let loose the shaft!"

Without more ado, having achieved complete surprise, we leaped into action.

The overseer of the servers had just reached the clear conclusion that all was not as it seemed with the servitors. He began to dance up and down in wrath.

"As certain as my name is Nath the Tureen, you will all be flogged—"

He went flying helter-skelter, this Nath the Tureen, as we threw the viands in all directions, tore out our weapons and leaped.

Pompino had marked Strom Murgon and for him he roared, shouting, his sword lifted. Cap'n Murkizon hurled the stuffed bird at the nearest table and followed it in a tremendous billow of outrageous clothes, smashed into the table, upending it. It crashed down on the feasters beyond.

Shrill screams sliced into the air and echoed from the ceiling. Viands crashed and splashed. The wicked silver glitter of swords rose to combat the evil glitter of silver leem masks.

The annimay cake sailed up into the air from my silver tray. It arched up and over. It descended.

Splat!

The two guards who rushed in from their position along the wall were smothered in the sugary gunk. Without masks to protect their faces the creamy cake blinded them.

Two swift chunks with the hilt disposed of them.

It seemed very necessary to me to make sure of the folk here who carried weapons. After that the more important task of sorting out the needlewoman might be attempted.

Well, we went at it with a will. Tinker-hammering uproar filled that opulent chamber.

No one felt inclined to pull their blows, to let these miserable specimens off the hook.

Men staggered away from the tables, their blood gushing over the brown robes. Men—and women, too—screamed and fought to win free, and Pompino and Cap'n Murkizon and Quendur roared into them. Nath Kemchug and Naghan the Pellendur and his guards smashed forward.

Some of the guards in their Lemmite uniforms fought well. Quendur had a right to do until Cap'n Murkizon reared up and his new axe went around in a flat and vicious arc, chunk into the side of Quendur's opponent.

Quendur didn't bother to shout a thankyou—he just swiveled and slashed the legs from the wight who attempted to brain Murkizon from the blind side.

Together, the two flailed their way on.

By this time, with a few of the guards coughing up their guts on the floor, I'd spotted the woman I took to be the doctor.

She wore the Brown and Silver and a silver leem mask covered her face. But she had not leaped up, either to escape or to fight. From the corner of my eye as I raced on I caught a fleeting glimpse of Murgon dragging Dafni along, and a couple of the guards making a valiant effort to protect their lord. Pompino was hard after them.

I fancied Pompino and the others had the situation well in hand now. Straight for the needlewoman I jumped.

She tilted her head to regard me and the mask caught the lamplight and gleamed dully.

"You would slay me, then?"

"Only if you deserve to be slain."

I backhanded a fellow off who tried to stick a short sword into my side, and he yowled and fell away, his sword arm shredded.

"You are a needlewoman?"

"That is why I sit here and do not take up a sword to strike you Unbelievers down."

I regarded her in that tumult of action and blood and death.

The fight was just about over. I do not believe I could have abandoned my comrades in the midst of action had they not been so signally successful. The sheer scale of our surprise had granted us the victory from the moment we had unsheathed swords and leaped.

Pompino was leading the lady Dafni back.

Her silver mask dangled from its straps. Her face was distraught. She sobbed in convulsive, ugly heavings, and she twisted and struggled and Pompino, gentle with her, guided her to a seat.

"Bring wine for the Lady Dafni!"

So she was being attended to.

I called across.

"Hai! What of that rast Murgon?"

"Like the flat rock-basement inhabitant that he is, he escaped through a secret door in the masonry."

"It closed up and snatched my sword away," yelled Mantig the Screw, and he went busily off to find a fresh weapon.

"So your great chief," I said to the needlewoman, "abandons you. That is his honor."

"If I repeat a proverb, you will understand."

She had spirit, this lady doctor.

"Oh, aye. He'll run to fight another day. And when he does, he may be killed, or he may run again. But you are here and—"

"And in your power!"

I looked down. She could see my golden zhantil mask. She could not see my expression, as I said: "Yes."

Her head jerked back.

"What do you want of me?"

"There is a man sore wounded. I need your skills and your arts to attend him."

The leem mask swiveled sideways. She regarded that luxurious banqueting hall where the blood stank rich and smoking upon the yellow napery, upon the floor, upon the bright tapestries. Bodies lay in grotesque positions.

"There are many who need my ministrations."

"Probably. But this man, you will attend first."

I held out my hand to assist her to rise, and she disdained that brown and clutching claw and stood up. With a flick she adjusted the brown robe.

I pointed to her silver-banded balass box.

"I will carry that for you, sana."

She laughed.

That startled me.

She laughed at my use of the honorific of sana, which gave her the honor due to a sage, a mistress, in the arts of healing.

But, natheless, I picked up the box which would contain her unguents and her acupuncture needles and the medicines in which she would be skilled. I guided her sedately over a few corpses and around the spilled blood and so brought her into the kitchens where Rondas the Bold lay.

"Your name, sana?"

"I am called Shula the Balm."

"Well, Mistress Shula, here is your patient."

"He is a Rapa!"

I bent my head to glare at her, the zhantil mask glittering.

"He is a Rapa. I would suggest you remove that vile silver leem mask before you attend him. He is likely to thrust a dagger through your guts if he sees that obscenity above him."

Her hands, very white, very nervous, fluttered; then she began to unclasp the fastenings of the mask.

Well, even on Kregen you sometimes expect the ordinary, which is a foolish fault.

The capacious brown robes with their silver embroidery concealed and disguised her bodily form. I'd expected an apim woman.

I was wrong.

She was hiosmim. Oh, yes, her face bore resemblances to an apim face; but the pixie look, the width of the high cheekbones, the curve of the chin, the spacing of the eyes, all spoke eloquently of hiosmim blood. Her skin was white with a creaminess to the coloring vastly different from any chalk-white semblance. Her hair of a pale blue was confined in a silver band. About her clung an aura of calm, of competence, of that certain sureness of inner certainty that normally arouses complete trust.

In these moments her racial characteristics aroused in me only horror.

That such a woman, devoted, sure, blessed, should have been swayed by the cult of Lem!

But I would not allow doubt to enter my mind.

Or, if I did, it was to be refuted instantly by what I knew of the habits of the Lemmites.

Wordlessly, I pointed at Rondas.

At once, she opened her medical box and set to work.

Thirteen

Shula the Balm

"So much for his share of my agio!"

Jespar the Scundle crawled out from under a table and stood up. He chewed on a chicken bone. He was not the least whit abashed that he had not charged in with us and struck a blow. I, for one, could hardly fault him for that.

Shula the Balm looked up. Difficult, of course, to translate the facial expressions of one race into a meaning to another—did that wrinkling of the brow indicate anger, fear, contempt, amusement?

She said, "Tump. Hold this."

Jespar jumped.

He had been a free tump, a mining man, and then he had been slave. His instincts had been sufficiently overlaid by discipline to make him instantly reach forward and do as he was bid.

The woman barely acknowledged him.

The "this" he was requested to hold was the hideously blood-smeared dart embedded in Rondas the Bold. Acupuncture needles festooned our comrade and, thankfully, all his pain was eased away. He closed his eyes as the needlewoman began with her sliver of knife on his wound.

As she worked with an exactitude I found pleasing, she spoke: "If I save this man I assume I have your promise of my life?"

I pondered this—oh, the answer leaped fully formed into my head at once, of course—but I had no wish to allow any thoughts of mercy to devalue her due recognition of her position. This was not the shameful attitude it might be thought to be in a company of knights errant—any persons who followed Lem the Silver Leem put themselves beyond the pale of civilization at a stroke...

Then: "Your life is of no consequence beside that of this man and of my comrades." I could hear myself mouthing the words—and I refused to regard them as despicable—and I went on in that grating tone: "But I am not in the habit of wantonly slaying little girls in white dresses or of offering up their hearts, still beating, to a filthy silver statue. You may perhaps live if you serve well."

Her fingers did not quiver. But her head bowed a trifle lower under the onslaught of my words.

She said, "It is time. Help the tump."

So with the keen knife easing the way, Jespar and I drew the cruel barb from Rondas.

His feathers were blood-spattered. The wound gaped.

"Hand me the box."

Jespar jumped to obey.

She took out unguents, bandages, began to dress the wound with a skill I admired.

"The bleeding will stop very soon. I have removed all the detritus. But the dressings must be changed frequently—"

"You will be alive, Shula the Balm, to see to that."

"I would suggest that you and your comrades bathe as soon as possible."

Suddenly she turned that pixie-like face up, and the tiny nose wrinkled. "You stink."

"Aye."

Footsteps on the flags of the kitchen heralded Pompino. As usual he was brilliant and heady, brushing up his whiskers, a fine foxy Khibil, master of the situation.

"They never knew what hit 'em!"

"Quite. I think Murgon merely evades his fate. The Lady Dafni?"

"A strange one, that. Oh, and she has stopped her eternal chatter for a space. She was confused. She resisted her rescue because of the golden zhantil masks."

"I see."

Pompino dangled his mask. The gold caught the lamplight, glimmering in that chamber of culinary splendor.

"The fanshos are tired, yet we can march back to the airboat. Can Rondas travel?"

I turned to the needlewoman.

"It would be better not to move him—" she said.

"Better, perhaps. But can we carry him safely?"

She hesitated.

I said: "I have conditionally promised this person her life, even though she is a Lemmite. She—"

"No lover of Lem should be allowed to live and breathe the same air as honest folk!"

Again, was that a shadow across her face, a minuscule flinching back? I could not fathom this doctor—yet.

"Nevertheless, she will go with us to attend Rondas. Now, Pompino—are there more wounded?"

He grunted.

"Poor Faplon the Chuckle took a spear through the guts, and as he fell a sword half-removed his head. And Nath Kemchug lost half his pigtail—"

"I hate to think of what befell the wight who did that monstrous deed!"

"Bits of him lie here and there."

"As for Faplon the Chuckle—a pity. He was always cheerful, and a good Fristle."

"Yes. Otherwise, apart from a few scratches, we were too fast for them, thanks be to Horato the Potent."

True to their calling, our mercenary comrades now busily occupied themselves in collecting up all the plunder displayed on the tables and spilled onto the floor.

In a tremendous smother of white, Quendur emptied out a flour sack. He darted back into the main hall and there he would quickly stuff the flour sack with golden cups and dishes, silver knives, ornate candlesticks.

Strom Murgon did not stint himself when it came to the good things of life—in this instance the lavish furnishing for his table.

"Those two hirelings of Murgon's were not among the dead," said Pompino. "I turned the bodies over with them particularly in mind. Chekumte the Fist and Dopitka the Deft could not have been here. I'm certain sure no one else escaped with Murgon, apart from a hairy Brokelsh with one arm hanging off."

"Aye. He carried a leather sack. Murgon almost ran him down escaping through that devilish slit in the wall."

Jespar the Scundle had, like me, received a liberal blessing of Rondas's blood when the dart pulled free. Now, as we went across to the sinks to wash, he looked nervous.

"My second cousin's wife's brother—Tangle the Ears. Masters—did you see a disgusting tump lying in his own blood among the corpses out there?"

Pompino laughed.

"No, Jespar."

"Hmf," sniffed Jespar. "It would be like him to be found dead drunk in the wine cellar."

Our two girl varterists had found a splendid tapestry which they were arguing over.

Wilma the Shot said: "It should be cut lengthwise."

"Not so, sister," said Alwim the Eye. "Cut it across."

"If you cut it across you will part the pictured peoples' heads from their bodies."

"But if you cut it down you leave almost all the gold thread in one half—"

"Maybe so. But it is more artistic—"

"Then who is to have the golden-heavy half?"

"Why," said Wilma, cheerfully: "You may have the golden section, sister. The picture is the important thing."

So, their argument settled in sisterly fashion, they chopped the priceless tapestry down the middle.

I wiped myself on a fluffy yellow towel and looked about.

"Time we were moving on, Pompino. I begin to fret over the airboat up aloft—"

"Agreed. We may have to thwack our rascals to make them move."

"They'll move."

A very few words proved sufficient to convince our comrades that it was time to go. A party carefully carried Rondas on an improvised stretcher. After a last look around that chamber of death, we started our march back to the voller.

Shula the Balm walked with a lissom swing beside Rondas's stretcher.

She had applied unguents to bruises and stuck a few needles in furry hides, here and there, to ease the pain of wounds. But, mercifully so, we had suffered miraculously few injuries.

Jespar's relative, Tangle the Ears, had not been discovered, drunk or sober. The little tump knew a straight way from the banqueting hall to the yard above. He mumbled something about generations of tumps coming here to pay their taxes to the Marsilus family, damned iniquitous taxes, he said, and we strode on feeling more and more confident.

Although we kept a sharp lookout we saw no sign of Strom Murgon.

Nothing Pompino or the crew had been able to do had opened the secret panel in the wall. No doubt dusty passageways led through the fabric of the building to a hidden doorway. By this time Murgon should be well away.

No one minded that too much.

That villain would run upon his fate soon enough.

For the time being he must be considered out of the game. We had rescued the Lady Dafni—again!—and before long she would be reunited with Pando.

So up we went and entered the last corridor that would take us to the yard upon the roof.

The various unpleasant traps Jespar pointed out, we were thankful to avoid. We would have had a much harder journey of it this way, even, than we had going the tortuous route we had followed.

Two guards, Brokelsh both, lay on the stone, their hairy bodies slack in death.

At the far end of the corridor the opening glowed with a penumbra of light. Outside, the twin suns of Scorpio were rising, casting down their mingled streaming light upon the world of Kregen.

From the shadows a voice, hard and yet gasping, said: "Hold! Stand fast, or you are dead men!"

We had seen the shafts transfixing the bodies of the Brokelsh guards.

"Hai!" called Pompino. "It's us! Hold fast your shaft, Larghos."

"Quidang! You are well met—"

We hurried forward, alarmed by the hoarseness of Larghos's voice.

He stood in the shadows of a groined arch, his bow lifted. As we approached he lowered the weapon.

"It's this stupid wound I took when we snatched the treasure upon the quay. It bothers me."

Brisk, efficient, Pompino said: "We have a needlewoman with us, Larghos. A Mistress Shula. She will treat your old wound, even if she is a misbegotten Lemmite."

Larghos did not look well. His face held a grayish cast I, for one, did not like.

"I welcome that, horter Pompino. There have been only those two Brokelsh who came by. No one else. I own I am glad to see you." He peered at the stretcher. "Rondas?"

"A bad stroke; he will survive. Let us all go along to the airboat."

Cap'n Murkizon took a firm grasp on Larghos, supporting him, and as we covered the last few paces out to the suns shine, started to tell him of our adventures.

Out in the yard, with the early light, palest lemon and shimmering apple-green, suffusing the stones with a luminescence, we stopped.

We looked about, gaping.

There was no voller there waiting for us.

Pompino quelled the outcry.

He gestured widely, fingers stabbing upwards.

"What a pack of famblys!" He laughed, expansively. "The lady Ros heard Larghos the Flatch dealing with those two stupid Brokelsh. She has taken the airboat up to be on the safe side—"

Larghos pushed himself straight from the embracing grip of Murkizon's arm.

"No, horter Pompino. No." He wet his lips. "After I dispatched them I went back to the flying boat. It was still here, and the lady Ros was talking to the lady Nalfi—"

A buzzing arose then, of unease. Quendur stepped up.

"And Lisa the Empoin?"

Larghos shook his head.

"I did not see her. The lady Ros said she had ventured down a passageway again—"

"Again!"

"Aye. She was most wroth that you had forbidden her to accompany you. The lady Ros and she went down this passage and came back. Then the lady Lisa the Empoin went again. The lady Ros went after her as I came back to my post."

"This I do not like," quoth Pompino. He brushed at his whiskers; but the gesture was far removed from his usual confident flourish.

I looked up and about the morning sky. A few clouds offered some cover; I did not think they would have concealed a voller for the time I searched the sky.

No sign of the airboat—and no sign of Dayra.

In a hard and exceedingly unpleasant voice, Quendur the Ripper said: "Which way, good Larghos, did the lady Empoin take? Which particular passage?"

Larghos gestured.

"That one."

Without another word, Quendur started off for the indicated passage leading from the yard at right angles to the one we had adventured down. Instantly, I was at Quendur's side. Together, we plunged into the dimness.

A few slotted windows at the side were mostly blotted by choking festoons of spiders' webs. A little light seeped through, mottling the dusty floor with ruby and vermilion.

Quendur's sword snouted forward. His fist looked hard and knobbly, and the patterned light painted a trick upon his face, so that he looked like a puppeteer's dangled nightmare. I paced him.

Shouts reached us as we moved along, distant at first, and as Quendur—recognizing those calls for help—broke into a frantic sprint, growing louder every second. We found Lisa the Empoin neatly entrapped. Cobwebbed spider strands engulfed her, strands cunningly interwoven with thongs and slender iron-linked chains. The whole lot had fallen upon her from the ceiling as she brushed through.

She saw Quendur and the color rose in her face.

Quendur put his hands on his hips and his sword angled up alarmingly.

"So, my lady, this is how you amuse yourself when I am away—"

"Stop jabbering, you great buffoon, and get me out! Oh, and there are spiders about as big as soup plates you would do well to avoid—or squash instantly." She glanced to the side.

She'd squashed one of the creepy horrors, fairly pulping him. A thin yellowish ichor trailed from the broken body. The thing *was* as big as a soup plate.

As Quendur, tight-lipped, started to cut Lisa free, I peered around, sword and feet ready to pierce or squash.

"The chains—" she said. And then: "My love—I am—"

"Save your breath, Lisa the Empoin."

"But, my heart–"

"You—" Quendur let rip a long groaning sigh. "You are the most obstinate of women!"

"Yes."

"And you are right. I cannot break the chains."

"There are no skeletons that I can see lying about," I pointed out, helpfully. "So they did not expect to leave a victim entrapped here. Perhaps those two Brokelsh were patrolling this way—"

"Probably."

"The chains—"

"I am going back to the yard," I said. Before they had time to register their surprise or disapproval, I went on briskly: "If Cap'n Murkizon will lend us his axe—"

"Hurry, Jak Leemsjid," Quendur said.

I hurried. Murkizon came back personally and hacked Lisa free of the chains. As she staggered forward into Quendur's arms, the gallant Captain Murkizon said: "The notches in my blade are well bought for the sake of so fine a lady, aye, by the scabrous belly and verminous hair of the Divine Lady of Belschutz!"

"I will buy or obtain the finest axe for you, Cap'n Murkizon," said Quendur. "And with it goes my thanks."

He did not look at me.

I knew the unspoken thoughts seething away in Quendur's mind, as they must soon seethe away in all my comrades' skulls when they heard this tale.

Lisa cut that knot—thankfully.

"The lady Ros tried to make me return with her—and I would not. Quendur—I own sometimes I am headstrong and foolish—but—"

"You are," quoth Quendur the Ripper, firmly.

We walked back along the passageway and Murkizon trod flat-footed upon a scuttling spider, and thought nothing of it. I swallowed and said: "Lisa—the lady Ros?"

"When I would not go back to the yard with her she said that the Lady Nalfi was probably more at risk than I was. She was perturbed, and I shall apologize to her, for I put her in a difficult position."

"If she has returned in the flier."

That meant Quendur had to explain our predicament to Lisa.

"Ros Delphor would never desert us." Lisa spoke as firmly as Quendur. "I have talked with her, as she with me. She is a lady—oh, I know how we all laugh. But it is sooth. There must be another explanation for her absence..."

She stopped herself speaking then.

By Krun! Didn't I know there could be another explanation! A dark, horrible and altogether unbearable explanation...

Fourteen

"Prepare for the Scorpion!"

Pompino, twirling his whiskers, said, "I have not burned a temple for some time and I am beginning to feel chilly."

Pando, bright, arrogant, hugely relieved, said: "I thank you again for the safety of the lady Dafni. I am at your disposal when it comes to burning the Lemmites' temples."

We'd marched down from Korfseyrie and met up with Pando's force, flushed from their forced march. We had slept off the effects of our adventure, we had eaten enormously, and Pompino was fretting to be up and about and doing.

Of course, I shared his views. But my concern of a father for Dayra fretted away at me.

Pompino scoffed at my fears.

"Ros Delphor can look after herself, Jak! Perhaps the airboat—wonderful though it truly be—developed some defect and drifted off with the wind."

"The lady Ros," said Pando, "is a formidable lady, in all Pandrite's truth."

"So—" I began.

They wouldn't hear of querulous hearts.

Larghos the Flatch was so down in the mouth we all guessed that his concern for the lady Nalfi weighed on him far more than the aftereffects of his wound. Shula the Balm treated him, so he would recover; he shared with me the agonies of not knowing what was befalling a loved one.

The camp we'd made in the woods served us well enough for the time we recouped our strength. Now Pompino, mindful of the long journey entailed in reaching the nearest likely site of a temple, itched to be off.

Rondas the Bold made a terrible scene when we told him he'd have to go along with Kov Pando's party back to Plaxing.

"I do not skulk when there is work to be done, by Rhapaporgolam the Reiver of Souls!"

He appealed with Rapa fervor to Shula the Balm, his feathers whiffling, his beak snouting, his crest wild.

"If they tie you upon a beast so you do not fall off, you might go, Rapa. I would not answer for your life."

"I do not ask you to, Lemmite! That commodity, precious though it is, is now back in my keeping."

"So be it."

Rondas the Bold, therefore, would come with us.

Nath Kemchug, a dour, hard, merciless Chulik, said, "If you fall off, Rondas, I will catch you." Then, with a thumb along a tusk, glistening it up, he added, "And I'll tie you back on so tight your eyeballs will pop."

We were all glad that Rondas had recovered so speedily. He expressed his gratitude to us. In our turn we chaffed at him—for Rapas do, indeed, possess their own weird brand of humor—and the moment that might have become mawkish passed in amiable insult.

The crafty Ift, Twayne Gullik, spent only the briefest of times at the camp, and then he went back at once to Plaxing with his people, claiming that his duties called him.

Jespar stared after the cavalcade.

"And good riddance," he said, unknowing that he was overheard.

Pompino and I, who had gone a little way off, ignored that. Tump and Ift—well, the up and the down, the dark and the light—and perhaps the twain never would meet.

Pompino started, suddenly, and he looked up with such an involuntary look of apprehension, my sword was halfway out of its scabbard before I, too, saw what had startled him.

Up there, floating in tight hunting circles, the giant golden and scarlet raptor of the Star Lords looked down upon us.

That bird was undeniably beautiful. Its golden feathers gleamed with a brilliance outshining mortal gold. The scarlet of its coat of feathers emphasized that glitter of gold around its throat and eyes. The wicked black talons outstretched, scarlet tipped, golden tipped, raked down as though to seize us up and rend us to pieces.

The Gdoinye up there circled, his head tilted, surveying us. He was the messenger and spy of the Star Lords. They watched us, those superhuman near-immortal men and women, they watched us.

Pompino, I often fancied, must have fallen to his knees when first the Gdoinye appeared to him, and spoke, and gave him orders. Now he remained standing; but he remained stiff, quiveringly alert, receptive, a perfect tool in the hands of unknowable despots.

My own relations with the Gdoinye had been of an entirely different character—altogether on a coarser plane. My reactions and antics alarmed my Kregoinye comrade.

Both of us were well aware that no one else in our company could see or hear the messenger from the Everoinye.

The bird swung lower, cutting across the face of Zim, the giant red sun, and so turned himself into a wedge of blackness against the light. He volplaned out, turned, glinting in radiance, arrowed down for us.

"Scauro Pompino, known as the Iarvin!"

The Gdoinye's hoarse croak reached us with clarity as he circled, hovering.

"Dray Prescot, Onker of onkers!"

"Aye, you rascally, injurious, supercilious bird of ill omen!" I roared back. And, in the old way, I shook my fist up at him.

He croaked a squawk that might have been a laugh.

"Jak! Jak!" Pompino fairly bristled with anxiety.

"We are on our own time now," I said. "We choose to oppose Lem the Silver Leem because it appears a seemly thing to do. We know the Everoinye also oppose the Lemmites; but we were not sent here by the Star Lords—"

"Cease your stupid babble, Onker!"

I glared up at the bird. Pompino put a hand to his whiskers; but for some reason failed to brush them up in the old arrogant way.

"Jak!" He almost writhed in his alarm and embarrassment. Then he tilted his foxy head back and called up: "We obey your commands. We burn the temples of Lem—what—?"

"Yes, Pompino the Iarvin, there is yet more!"

"Certainly!" I bellowed up. "Certainly, there is always more! And what help do we ever receive from you?"

"*Jak!*"

"You do not understand the help you are given. You are human. I am not here to bandy words. I am here to warn you of a summons. Prepare yourselves."

"Damned considerate of you!"

Well, it was, really, given the Star Lords' usual endearing habit of plunking me down naked and unarmed in a devilish tricky spot to pick their hot chestnuts out of the fire.

The Gdoinye winged up, a blurring of gold and scarlet.

"Prepare for the Scorpion!"

His blunt head pointed up, those powerful wings shredded the air, in a smother of wingbeats he lifted away, dwindled to a dot against the brightness of the sky, vanished.

"Humph!" I said. I did not spit.

"Jak—you run hard upon a leem's nest!"

"Oh, the Gdoinye and I have sharpened many a rapier together. I admit that talking to him is like saddling a zhantil—but, all the same, he has warned us."

"I believe this will make our task, as it were, official in the eyes of the Everoinye. Thanks be to Pandrite the All-Glorious."

"It was official enough for me before, by Chusto!"

The others in the camp were going about their duties without taking the slightest notice of us. The Star Lords were perfectly capable of putting the whole of Kregen under a spell if they wanted to, I did not doubt. That they did not do so, that they worked toward the fulfillment of their plans through fallible human tools like us, was all a part of their mystery. I did not think—then—that I would ever penetrate that mystery. I persuaded myself that it did not concern me. I refused to worry over it. By Vox! I had enough worries of my own, what with Dayra going off and Opaz-alone knowing where she was. All the same, there had in these latter days been a growing rapport between the Star Lords and myself I had viewed with interest—with unease, of course, and with confidence for the future.

Now, it seemed, we had a fresh task set to our hands.

"Jak—" began Pompino.

I turned to look at my comrade. I turned slowly.

I'd taken the name of Jak for perfectly obvious reasons—reasons I have explained and that are easily understood. But, sometimes, it irked me, this answering to another name. My name is plain Dray Prescot. I may be the

Lord of Strombor and a Krozair of Zy, which privileges and responsibilities I take seriously. I was also Emperor of Vallia, King of Djanduin, Strom of Valka, a whole pretty kite-tail of titles and folderols. But, all the same...

"Yes?"

"Once again the Gdoinye did not call you Jak. He would know that you are now Jak Leemsjid."

"Of course he'd know, the cunning, onkerish—"

"Jak!"

Instinctively, Pompino glanced up. No doubt he expected lightning to blast down for my impiety. Pompino dealt with the Star Lords on the basis that they were supernal gods, demanding and worthy of obedience. He was privileged to serve them. And they'd rewarded him. Their machinations had brought the gold into his fists, gold with which he'd bought his fancy fleet of ships.

As far as I knew, they'd not put a single copper ob my way.

"Jak—why does the Gdoinye call you by the name of the Emperor of Vallia, a name which you adopted as a ruse long ago, when he knows the truth?"

I did not pluck my lower lip; I did not scratch my head. I did not narrow my eyes on my comrade. Had I done all those things they would have been perfectly proper.

"Well, Pompino..." I began. Then, as Seg Segutorio would have said in his fine free way, I also said: "...My old dom. It's like this."

And then I stopped.

No. No, I wouldn't shatter our relationship. As I had surmised earlier, if I told Pompino the truth, he'd never regard me in the same comradely way again. How could he? If I was an emperor, then he'd have to start treating me like an emperor, like one of the lordly beings of Kregen, and I detested that. I valued Pompino. Perhaps, when the situation was clearer, he might know, and then we would work out a modus vivendi. For now—no. No, I couldn't tell him the truth.

"Well, Jak Leemsjid?"

Now we had talked together of our experiences beforetime with the Star Lords. I'd been circumspect with Pompino, anticipating he had not penetrated to the Star Lords' hugely vaulted chamber of scarlet, seen the world spread out below, ridden in one of their hissing chairs, understood just a trifle of their plans. So he knew somewhat of my history regarding the Everoinye.

I said: "Must be because that was the first name they knew me by. They don't have the sense to get up to date."

"They know everything!"

"So they must forget a lot, mustn't they?"

"That, I cannot believe."

It sounded lame, even to me.

I tried again.

"The Everoinye were once people as we are. I am sure they still possess a sense of humor. It may be vestigial. I think they amuse themselves by thus dubbing a poor wight like me with the name of the emperor of Vallia—"

"A most puissant and terrible man!"

"Oh, aye."

"He was dreadfully severe on the slavers in Vallia. His name is not one lightly to be conjured with. If ever you venture up into Vallia, Jak, you had best beware."

I said, and I blurted it out before my stupid babbling tongue could be halted: "One day, Pompino, I look forward to the time when you and I go in friendship to Vallia."

His bushy, foxy eyebrows rose.

"Oh?"

I blustered it out.

"Surely. There must be fine pickings there."

And I laughed, forcing myself, as a free-roving reiver and paktun would laugh at the thought of loot.

Pompino, severely, said, "If you try any tricks in Vallia these days, the emperor will put you down, cut off your head, dangle you over the walls of his stupendous deren in Vondium—Jak, Jak! Think on!"

"Well, there's a damned army forming in Port Marsilus, paid by gold from somewhere—gold that was once in our possession. When that army sails for Vallia, the story might be different."

"You would join that army against Vallia?"

"Join it?" I pretended to ponder. Then: "Aye, Pompino! I'd join it. Then I would sabotage it and destroy it and scatter it to the winds. Why, then, man, I'd go up to this high and mighty Dray Prescot, Emperor of Vallia, and stare him in the face, and demand a fitting recompense for saving his empire for him!"

And Pompino guffawed at the conceit.

He sobered. "If we are to be snatched up by the Scorpion of the Everoinye then I must warn Cap'n Murkizon and the others. They will have to make their way back to the ship."

"Aye."

Pompino nodded and walked off, moving briskly, going among the trees toward the camp.

I stood for a moment, all my thoughts of Dayra making me feel the miserable stupid fool I really was, that fool, that onker, that I was dubbed by the Gdoinye.

As I stood there, the blue radiance grew about me.

The coldness of an arctic wind cut through every fiber of my body, the silence of a rushing wind drowned thought. The world fell away. I saw above me, towering and enormous, the gigantic blue outlines of the Scorpion, immense, awful, and then I toppled away into the blue radiance of the Star Lords' commands.

Fifteen

Gold Mask vs. Silver Masks

Sometimes the Star Lords procrastinated unbearably in their casual dumping of me down into action. Often and often I'd find myself in some desperate situation, quite without a clue, unable instantly to decide exactly what the Everoinye were demanding of me. They acted like this, I was more than half convinced, not out of malice but out of sheer indifference.

This time there was no misunderstanding.

Normally the Star Lords catapulted me into danger naked, unarmed, and half-bedazzled from the effects of the blue radiance, the baleful form of the gigantic Scorpion and the stomach-unsettling topsy-turvy fall through nothingness.

This time I felt limber, alert, ready for what might befall.

I needed to be.

By Zair, I needed to be!

I was, as usual, naked and unarmed.

Still the Everoinye must have sensed the lessening of regard for them that would have been engendered had they provided me with a spear, a helmet, a shield. They summoned, I went and did.

But—this time—there was something new.

In the rough canvas bag dangling on its cord over my shoulder snugged a hard, metallic object.

Without thinking twice—in all the uproar that surrounded me—I drew out the golden zhantil mask and snapped the straps about my head. I glared out through the eyeholes.

The scene was cut straight from nightmare.

The cavern lofted into purple shadows, bruised and swollen. Torchlights fluttered against that encompassing presence. The leering silver image of the Leem lowered over all, high against the far wall, silver glints striking and sparking from its body.

The iron cage stood empty. The door opened onto a stone ledge. On this ledge two acolytes of Lem the Silver Leem drew on the eager form of a little girl clad in a white dress.

Candy juice smeared her chin.

She was laughing.

Below, to the side, the altar crouched. Dark, misshapen, stained, it humped a blot of blackness against the torchlights.

The worshipers, all wearing their silver masks, swayed and gyrated, caught up in the expectations of the moment. The butcher-priests stood beside the altar. Their assistants held the implements of their trade upon cushions. The air stifled.

And the stink was diabolical.

I was one man, alone, naked and unarmed.

The worshipers mustered upward of a hundred. The priests and their assistants and acolytes another thirty or so.

Even as I started forward I was saying to myself but so that the damned Star Lords—wherever they were!—might hear: "Right, Star Lords. You've dropped me into a real beauty this time! By Vox! What a mess!"

A knee in the back of a fellow who was clutching at the woman next to him, ready for the bloodletting to follow, sent him toppling. Before he fell the thraxter in the scabbard at his waist was gripped in my fist.

I hit the next fellow a nasty slash along the neck and swiveled immediately to hack down his companion.

Run—run! Straight for the altar and the cage and the girl sacrifice! Run as I'd never run before—get into them, as Cap'n Murkizon would roar: "Hit 'em, knock 'em down, tromple all over 'em!"

The pandemonium began as I legged it, spreading from my hurtling body as the ripples spread from the thrusting prow of a swifter of the Eye of the World.

People tried to stop me.

They were cut down as the reaper cuts corn.

They saw the blazing gold of the zhantil mask.

Shocked cries burst out.

"The Golden Zhantil masks! Kill him! Kill!"

At least the Star Lords had had the sense to dump me down at the back of this unholy crew. They'd not seen me arrive, or don the mask. Now they saw a fleeting naked figure roaring along, cutting left and right, lopping heads, disemboweling, amputating limbs, the glinting glory of the zhantil mask ferocious upon them.

They crushed in to prevent my onward movement and to slay me.

Swords whipped up. Men and women screamed and gesticulated and tried to get at me.

I did not hang about.

The thraxter snapped off clean.

I hit a corpulent bastard over the head with the hilt and took his sword and degutted his crony at his side. The next two went down, the next reeled away with his face reflecting the effects of a foot in the guts, and I roared on.

It was all a blur, of course, a blur of action and movement, of the silver twinkle of swords and the quick spurt of dark red blood. Even then I don't believe I thought that I would never surface from this dank spot. There was no time for coherent thought. As each fresh opponent or pairs or threes or fours of opponents presented themselves they had to be taken on their merits. What the floor looked like in the wake of that intemperate bloody bashing onslaught I hesitate to contemplate.

I do recall that one thought hit me with scarlet intensity.

Where the hell was Pompino in all this frantic bedlam?

Had the Star Lords fouled up again?

Nobody of this ripe bunch possessed a bow, or, at least, no one shot at me.

One fellow hurled a stux and the javelin flew straight.

I took it out of the air with my left hand. I did not return it whence it came, a favorite trick of the Krozairs. Instead I lobbed it at the Chief Priest in his brown and silver robes and his ornate mask, the butcher knife in his hands. It sheared through his neck, half-severing it. I was disappointed his head did not fall off.

The Brown and Silver at his side jumped away, flinging up his hands in horror. But he didn't drop his own cunning little instrument of torture.

In the next half-dozen heartbeats I was past the chained-off area separating the main hall from the preserve of the priests. Here the incense stank away, stiflingly.

There was time—just—to throw two of the torches at the brown draperies, and then I leaped for the man who was now turned away from the fallen body of his chief. The other acolytes ran. I hit the second in command over the head—not too hard—hurdled him and scooped up the girl.

Two hard and unmerciful blows disposed of her guards.

The second-in-command staggered. I put the girl down—of course she was crying now—and said: "It is all right. Stand still."

I put an inch and a half of the thraxter into the second-in-command's guts and said: "Where is the way out?"

The repulsive idiot must have imagined I was setting up a bargain with him, making a compact.

"Behind the drapes there," he babbled. The sword must have been tickling him up. He wriggled like an insect on a pin. He pointed painfully. "There."

I finished him—and he still clutched the shiny instrument he would have used to put this girl child to so much pain—snatched up the sacrifice, and hared for the drapes.

Another stux hit the wall beyond as I wrenched the panel open.

We bundled through into dimness relieved by mineral-oil lamps at intervals. The air smelled stale and musty and yet clean by comparison with the stinks in that chamber of abominations. The door snapped shut. There seemed no way of bolting or barring it, so I just ran full tilt up the corridor.

The girl sacrifice, following the usual habits of girl sacrifices rescued against their wills, was yelling her head off and banging her heels against me.

The corridor opened into a square stone-cut chamber.

The congregation would be after me like a pack of leems.

The Chulik in the chamber, clad in leather armor with brown and silver flourishes, seeing me, immediately drew his sword and dropped into the on guard. He was ready for a pleasant foining match before he dispatched me.

The point of my flung thraxter took him in the throat. The blade punched on, ripping tendons and throat and all to smash in a welter of blood.

I ran on without stopping, scooped his sword up, went racing on along the far corridor.

Howls from back down the passage echoed from the stone walls. The helter-skelter rush and hammer of feet roared after me. I fled on, carrying my cargo in her white dress as carefully as I could. Blood spattered the dress from the splashes and stains covering me. She was blubbering away now, a fist stuffed into her mouth and her nose all running and I felt for her, I felt for her. But that mob of hyenas baying after us—if hyenas bay—had to be outdistanced before we could stop. Outdistanced—for I was not sanguine of slaying them all, much though that would have cleansed the world of Kregen.

Steps hewn from the rock led up.

A few lanterns glowed to point out the broken treads and the darkly greasy patches where water seeped. The smell of the earth, dank and rich and sweet, began to oust the charnel-house stench of the chamber of worship and sacrifice with its unholy freight of incense and blood.

Through her sobs the child gasped out: "Put me down, put me down! Let me go!"

Now the treads were fashioned of wood, cutting through the dark earth, and my feet hit them with the hard smack of callused skin.

In these frantic moments of flight there was just no way of explaining, and my concern for the child had to be adjusted with what might appear to be the same callousness that affected my feet. She had been promised sweets and candies, a pretty white dress, and these goodies she had received. To be snatched from them by a naked hairy sweating devil in a glinting gold zhantil mask! No, oh, no, explanations at this moment could never explain.

The wooden door at the head of the stairs was not guarded from the inside, whereat my heart sank, for I judged it would be bolted and guarded from the outside.

The only way to find out was to put a shoulder to it and heave.

The door resisted.

I felt—I felt that demeaning rush of blood to the head, the scarlet curtain, the furious obsessive rage that trembles all along the muscles and bursts out in blinding ferocity.

I smashed at the door.

It flew open and the mingled emerald and ruby radiance of Kregen flooded in.

The splintered ends of the shattered bar thumped to the ground. Clutching the girl sacrifice, my sword snouting, I leaped through the opening.

The two Chuliks who had been lounging on the wooden bench beside the door that let into the grassy bank scrambled to their feet. They wore the brown and silver and leather harness and they'd been playing at the Game of Moons. The pieces went flying. The Chuliks ripped out their swords and jumped for me silently.

Like all Chuliks I'd known, they were quick, professional fighting men. There was no chance of repeating my trick with a flung thraxter here. They were on me in a twinkling.

They did not attack one after the other like actors in a play who must never harm the hero; they leaped in together.

Tackling two Chuliks is difficult enough, Vox knows, without the encumbrance of a squealing, wriggling, kicking girl-child in your free arm. I dumped her down, yelled: "Stand still!" and ripped into the Yellow Tuskers.

They were good—well, that is a stupid remark! Any Chulik who goes overseas and takes employment as a paktun is good. No thought of fancy work entered my head. This had to be quick—damned quick, by Krun.

The grass afforded firm footing, so that we three could leap and pirouette and strike and withdraw with ease. They whipped in side by side and I avoided the first blows and curled my blade in and the left-handed one contemptuously foined me off. I had to skip and jump to miss his comrade's slash. The next onset went much the same way, although as in a mirror, for the right-hand one parried and the left-hand one struck. That round, like the first, ended with us fronting across the grass, warily seeking an opening, circling.

Of course, they tried to circle me from each side.

This was more like it.

They had to split up so that one could go clockwise and the other widdershins. They'd crush me between them as an ear of grain is crushed in the mill.

So they thought.

Without hesitation I rushed upon the left-hand fellow, making a bit of a pantomime of it, not actually screeching a war cry, but making enough of a menacing growling challenge to set the Chulik quivering.

As I thus rushed on him, his companion, invisible at my back, let out a yell.

"Hold him, Changa!"

This fellow before me whirled up his thraxter, and a wild light came into his yellow face. His tusks were banded with silver. He set himself to meet my attack and, so I guessed, deal with me before his comrade arrived, and thus gain the kudos, what some Kregan warriors call the *absteilung*.

Without the shadow of a doubt, the other Chulik was haring across the grass toward my back, hungering for his share in what *absteilung* there was to be gained from one naked apim warrior.

I halted. I whirled.

The onrushing Chulik, all froth and foam, eyes glaring, tusks flecking spittle from his gaping mouth, gasping with the effort, reared up, sword high.

The one called Changa screeched.

"Beware, Tincho, beware..."

I slid the blade into Tincho, twisted, withdrew, and instantly, without thought, flung sideways and snatched the thraxter aloft. Changa's blow clanged down. Then it was a twist, a thrust, another ugly twist, and a withdrawal.

Slowly, they collapsed. Each mirroring the other's actions, they fell to their knees. The swords dropped from lax fingers. Together, they pitched forward onto the grass, sprawled, limp and done for.

One—the one called Changa—managed to gasp out: "By Likshu the Treacherous... the apim fooled us..."

I looked down at them.

"By the Black Chunkrah," I said, and the sadness tinged my voice. "I salute you both, Chuliks."

The blood dripped from the thraxter.

It was the work of a moment to strip a length of brown cloth free and wind it about me. I looked about, and if I say my breathing was even and steady, do not be deceived.

The bank rose at my side with the smashed open door leading to the horrors within. Within a few moments horrors on two legs would come roaring out of that cavern seeking my blood.

Below me down the hill spread a tree-dotted expanse leading to the sea. The light of the suns sparkled on that sea. Just what sea it might be in all of Kregen I could not then know.

A seaport nestled in a bay with a spit of land to give protection. The roads were clustered with shipping. Away to the right on a flat grassy area of considerable extent the long ordered rows of tents of an army glistened in the light.

The scents of grass and trees came pleasantly to my nostrils. And a scampering white dot on twinkling bare legs skipped heedlessly down the grassy slope toward the town.

Picking up my sword, I followed.

Sixteen

A price for Carrie

"Twelve gold pieces, my friend, and I'll throw in an extra five dhems."

Carrying the girl sacrifice—her name she had whispered was Carrie—I tried to brush past in the crowded souk. The fellow with his black chin beard and gold chains and oily hair was persistent.

"Come now, my friend! I know why you are here! You cannot do better than deal with me, Honest Nath Ob-eye the Trancular. Fifteen gold pieces, then—"

He wore a patch over his left eye. His clothes were ornate if greasy, and he carried as well as a sword a whip coiled up over his left shoulder. If I sold Carrie to him he'd have no compunction in using that evil instrument on her. He'd do it in such a way as not to mark the merchandise. Slavers know how to strike in the pain ways.

Carrie and I had hidden in a brake of greenery as the pursuit from that devil's pit roared past. We'd cleaned ourselves up in a brook that led into the river that reached the sea where this seaport stood. Its name was Memguin and it boasted a powerful fortress. I'd never been here before. But I knew where we were.

By Krun! I knew!

The Everoinye had dumped me down in Menaham.

Menaham, whose inhabitants were known to their neighbors as the Bloody Menahem, stood immediately to the west of Pando's Bormark in Tomboram. Hereditary enemies, the two countries, and this bloody place had joined up willingly with Phu-si-Yantong when, as the Hyr Notor, he had taken over in his crazy schemes to conquer the world.

Well, he was dead, the black devil.

But his evil legacy lived on.

"Look, dom," wheedled this Nath Ob-eye the Trancular. "There is no need to fear. I can see your situation at a glance. You are a poor man, and you have too many children. It is common, men and women being what they are and the good Pandrite blessing them with fecundity. Your girl will be placed in a good home where she will learn to sew and stitch and perhaps, if she has the aptitude, be trained in the arts. A harpist, a dancer, perhaps if she has the gifts of the gods an actress—the lords hereabouts are partial to—"

"Go," I said, "away."

"But, dom—"

The souk bustled with activity. The spicy scents rose, and with them the tantalizing odors of food reminded me that my insides were as hollow as a blown egg.

This unpleasant slaver tried a new tack as I pushed on through the throngs.

"Twenty gold pieces will set you up for life! Why—"

His offer was as nonsensical as to price as the situation was to my purposes.

I ignored him and settled Carrie more comfortably on my shoulder. She took considerable interest in the busy scene, with its sights and colors and scents and ceaseless activity, crying out in wonder from time to time. We'd got along in the time it had taken to reach Memguin. By Zair! And hadn't I had considerable experience lately in the psychological handling of bewildered little girl sacrifices?

"Look, my friend, let me put this to you. You have a sword. Perhaps you think of joining the army being raised by Kov Colun Mogper of Mursham?"

My intense interest was at once aroused. So that was the way of it! The treacherous Mogper was once more reaching a tentacle into my affairs. As to the sword, I had, perforce, to carry it naked in my free hand.

"Perhaps, my friend, you are not the girl's father at all. Perhaps you have stolen her away, kidnapped her for gain. If I call the watch..."

A tall and emaciated thin Weul'til joined the proceedings from the side, using his furry mouth to fashion a grimace that passed for a smile. Not as tall as your average Ng'grogan, your average Weul'til, but skinnier, decidedly skinnier.

He adjusted his black clothes, shiny in their fashion, wriggled his antennae, and said: "Hai, Nath Ob-eye the Trancular! My friend—" Then to me: "I will match this thieving trader's best offer, aye, and increase it by five gold pieces—"

"You are too late, Lintin the Ancho! I was about to call the watch to apprehend this kidnapper."

I own I almost smiled.

This pair of villains waxing righteous about a kidnapping! For the Weul'til, at once serious, exclaimed: "A kidnap! Then let us call the watch at once."

No doubt they were working a variant of the badger game; but I had had enough. I restrained myself.

I looked at the pair of them, and if that old devilish Dray Prescot look flamed across my face and turned me into the semblance of a demon from the deepest pits of hell, I do not think I can be overly faulted.

"If you do not at once run away, you will not ever run again! Get going! *Grak!*"

Well, if I used that ugly word then, it fitted.

They flinched back, hovered—and then they grakked.

I'd not said "Bratch!" nor even the more correct "Schtump!" which means clear off or get out. No, I'd said grak, and this pair of villains had used that word enough times goading on their slaves to appreciate its meaning when applied to them by a wild, sword-armed fellow with a devil's face.

I walked on. The air smelled sweeter.

The little Och from whom I'd inquired directions had directed me through this souk—the Souk of Sweetmeats—as my quickest route. A few moments later I emerged from the arched roof onto the Street of Desires and so turned right onto the Boulevard of Pandrite All-Glorious.

This was a prestigious thoroughfare, and more than one passing person gave me a curious glance. Carriages passed with a flicker of wheels, people paraded in fine clothes, and among them the quick flitter of the slaves in their slave-gray breechclouts passed unnoticed. I carried a sword, and so was clearly not slave, for most if not all Kregans when trusting slaves with weapons dress them up in ornate and pompous finery so as to mark them. I pressed on until I reached the lime-washed wall with its wrought-iron gate, closed, set between stone pillars.

Each pillar was surmounted by a satyr carrying off a virgin, sculpted in bronze, most lifelike if twice life-size. I did not know whose embassy building this had been before the Times of Troubles. I pulled the bell ring.

Now—I was doing something I usually eschewed.

More often than not, of course, the Star Lords hurled me into action where what I was up to now was either not possible or against my best interests. I waited as the pleasant chiming of the bell dwindled to silence.

An almost naked wild-looking fellow, carrying a bare sword, with a girl child perched on his shoulder, might be an apparition not well-received at someone's front door.

That thought had scarcely crossed my mind, incensed by those two slavers in the souk and by concern for Carrie and that ill-starred army mustering under the command of one of the vilest rogues yet unhanged.

I just rang the bell and waited for the porter. I'd convince him easily enough.

There was no need.

The door in the gatehouse opened smartly and a fellow with one arm trotted out across the gravel. He wore buff breeches and buff shirt with red and yellow banded sleeves. His face was red and purple, beetle-browed and cheerfully pugnacious. The empty red and yellow sleeve was pinned up defiantly across his chest like a sash.

"And what does a fellow like you want...?" he began as he came up with Carrie and me.

He stopped.

He opened his mouth and closed it. His beetle-brows rose as though on stilts. He opened his mouth again and this time he got out: "Now may Opaz the Saver of Souls be praised!"

He fairly scuttled to the bar and lifted it with his one right hand with a smooth and powerful swing.

Then he slapped that right arm across his chest with rib-crushing force.

"Lahal, majister! Lahal and Lahal!"

Seventeen

In the embassy

You cannot expect an emperor to know the name of every soldier in his army, an empress the name of every voswod in her aerial forces. Some of them are canny enough, like Napoleon, to have themselves briefed before a parade so that they can talk to a soldier and use his name in a familiar way. This builds the legend.

Well, by Vox, I knew a large, a very large number of people on Kregen, and once I'd met them I'd normally remember names and faces.

This one-armed ex-soldier, beaming away, his purple face an enormous smile, I did not know.

I would not prevaricate. So—I ruined one legend.

I said, "Lahal and Lahal. Your name?"

He looked not one whit disappointed, and, to be truthful, he'd have been a fool had he been.

"Llando the Ob-handed, majister, that was Llando the Pilinur, Bratchlin in the Sixth Kerchuri when we won the day at Kochwold!"

"Aye, Llando. When the Second Phalanx trembled, the Sixth Kerchuri saved the day. I do not deny it. The Third Phalanx... You lost your arm there?"

"A hairy Clansman astride a vove would have chopped young Larghos the Fair, my sister's boy, had I not been quick..."

He wore three bobs on his chest, medals of campaign and valor. I nodded, gravely, saluting a brave man.*

He smiled easily. "I have my job here, gatekeeper, the pay is good, the company fine, and although we may be in a nasty sort of land with uncommon nasty people in it, why, majister, one must do what one can, surely?"

"You are a philosopher, Llando. And you are right."

He beamed and swelled up as though to burst.

It did not occur to me then to ask why he was not more surprised at seeing me than he was at my appearance. Later I realized that the tales and stories of Dray Prescot—of how the emperor sallied forth in headlong reckless adventure clad in a red breechclout, wielding a deadly Krozair longsword—were part of the tapestry of life in Vallia.

That Dray Prescot, Emperor of Vallia, might turn up anywhere to join a fight, to rescue honest folk, to put down slavers, was an article of faith to Vallians. But they'd expect him to come leaping in with the scarlet breechclout flaming and that deadly silver brand a glitter of destruction before him. And here I was, in a miserable scrap of brown cloth and with a wide-eyed little girl perched on my shoulder!

Well, Llando the Ob-handed made no more of that, and soon I was escorted through into the embassy.

The ambassador, Strom Ortygna Felheim-Foivan, met me with immense kindness. He did not fuss; but he saw that the right things were done. A short, stout, abrupt man, he held two small estates down by the Great River in Vomansoir and was therefore one of Lord Farris's men. Farris and I were good comrades, and Felheim-Foivan an old acquaintance.

"The Little Sisters of Benediction have a chapel here, majister; they will care for this girl child admirably."

"Excellent, Ortyg."

We sat in his private withdrawing room, the remains of the repast still on the table, the silver dish of palines to hand, the wine standing ready. The suns declined and Carrie had been half-asleep when the sisters carried her off.

"I admit, majister, to grave doubts when I was offered this post. Vallia and all of Pandahem have been hereditary enemies since times immemorial. But you have changed all that. The Bloody Menaham are an unpleasant lot; but I am growing to understand them better, and with understanding comes—"

"Liking?"

---

* For the Battle of Kochwold see *A Life for Kregen* (Dray Prescot #19). A.B.A.

He chewed a paline, thinking. "Hardly that. But tolerance. I know I speak perhaps out of turn. But the habits of a lifetime, to turn a phrase, are not easily changed."

"That is true."

We talked for a time on the problems of Vallia, how the island empire must fulfill its obligations to all the peoples not only of its own fair lands but also of the new allies we had made overseas. There were many men now in Vallia like this Strom Ortyg who had come to the fore in recent days when a great deal of the old corruption had thankfully been banished. He served Vallia to the best of his ability, and within the framework of his labors and understanding shared the visions of the future dominating the best minds. He had outfitted me in proper evening style, a comfortable robe of dark material, and also I took the opportunity of writing some of the letters that were once more overdue.

My anxiety—and that was too mild a word—over Dayra had to be put into perspective.

She was a big girl now.

The imperatives, as I saw them, were to regain contact with Pompino and our comrades, to continue the struggle against the Lemmites, to sort out Pando's problems with Strom Murgon, and to scupper the damned army they recruited against Vallia.

"Against Vallia, majister?"

Strom Ortyg paused with a paline halfway to his mouth. He stared at me. Then, heavily, he said: "This Kov Colun Mogper of Mursham is—is not a pleasant person. But I am assured he raises this army to march against Tomboram, their hereditary foes."

Picking up the point that interested me more out of curiosity, I asked Ortyg: "You have met this Mogper?"

"Aye—well, briefly, only. He is an elusive personage."

"Most."

The word came out dry and harsh.

As I waited, Strom Ortyg realized what was required and went on: "He is a brilliant man; merciless, resolute, dominated by a sense of his own importance and the bending to his will of all with whom he comes in contact."

"Yes. And?"

"His appearance, majister? Tall, strong, with features regular yet marked by his character. Fair of hair, I believe, and yet most unfair in all other things. He affects armor gilded so that he presents the semblance of a golden statue, an idol to be worshiped."

That was as good a description as I could expect of the man I had once seen riding amid his armed cronies.

I said: "If ever a lady called Jilian Sweet Tooth should seek your aid,

Strom Ortyg, in the matter of this Kov Colun Mogper, you would earn my gratitude if you would afford her every assistance of which you are capable."

He looked at me a trifle oddly. Then he nodded.

"If ever the lady seeks my assistance, I will do all in my power to aid her. And with pleasure."

"Good. And now—" A knock at the door heralded a young lad, Tyr Stofin Vingham, with news that a Courier airboat had just arrived from Vallia. Moments afterward the Courier himself, Hikdar Naghan Veerling, walked in smartly. Clad in flying leathers, wearing the neat pin on his tunic fashioned into the likeness of a silver zorca that was the badge of the Vallian Courier Service, he bore a thick wallet of messages. Not quite in the same class as the merkers, these couriers, but close. He saluted, saw me, smiled, and said: "Lahal, majister, lahal, Strom Ortyg."

So, the next three hours or so were spent in dealing with the information brought by Naghan Veerling.

Vallia prospered, I kept up with the news, and I could send back my own letters and messages by a rapid route.

Of course, I did not fail to recognize this odd phenomenon I had encountered plenty of times before this. My people of Vallia did not seem the slightest bit surprised to see their emperor popping up in the most unlikely places. Wherever they went, well, if the emperor happened to be there too, wasn't that perfectly natural?

After all, by this time they knew that Jak the Drang, Dray Prescot, was not like your ordinary emperor.

So it was that, knowing young Hikdar Naghan Veerling was one of your high-powered tearaways, I said to him as we took a breather: "Naghan. Before you fly back to Vallia, are you game for a little excitement?"

"Of course, majister."

I grumped inwardly at that, this calm acceptance of whatever deviltry I might have in store for him. Still, that was your Vallian, oh so respectable to all when it pleased, and your right villain when pushed.

"Strom Ortyg," I went on. "If I might borrow a few of your lusty lads of the guard detail. And anyone else in the embassy who would like to join...?"

"Naturally, majister."

I stood up and looked down on them, at the desks with the papers and pens and inks, at the packets ready to be sealed. "Well. And aren't you interested in what you'll be doing?"

"We'll be off on an adventure with you, majister."

By Zair!

Naghan the Courier added: "Anyone fortunate enough to go on an adventure with Dray Prescot, Emperor of Vallia, is more than fortunate."

"Aye. He might get his fool self killed."

Naghan laughed.

"When I flew the old vollers, that was an occupational hazard."

As a Courier, a fellow spending his time flying airboats, he called them by their Havilfarese name, as was proper.

He rubbed his chin. "Nowadays, with these fine new vollers you have secured for us, majister, life is more than a little tame."

"Give me a few burs sleep. Then gather the lads together, armed and ready, and we'll set off."

"Quidang!"

I looked at them.

"And still you do not ask where?"

"When the time is right you will tell us."

"I'll tell you now. We're off to burn a stinking temple to Lem the Silver Leem. That's where!"

So it was that, before the last of the seven Moons of Kregen was paled into a luminous echo in the sky by the glory of the twin suns, Zim and Genodras, we went up to that place of evil in the hill, entered through the door that had been hastily repaired, leaving four Chuliks set to guard the stable when the horse had bolted, stretched upon the grass, and so burned the vile place.

We found no worshipers, no interior guards, no acolytes or priests. We found no unnatural women preparing children for torture and sacrifice. We found no little girl children penned and waiting.

What we did find we burned.

Then, as the Suns of Scorpio flooded down in shimmering veils of color, we marched down the hill and so by devious ways regained the Vallian Embassy.

No one saw us.

Which was as well for them.

The men who had done the work had previously been informed by me of the nature of the beast they burned.

As a consequence they decided to celebrate, to hold a small thanksgiving service dedicated to Opaz the Just, and then in continuation that evening to hold a right roaring shindig. At this they drank and sang and told stories and the ladies present danced turn and turn and joined in the celebrations and, in short, everyone had a rousing good time. Which is the Kregan way.

There was no doubt in my mind that Strom Ortyg Olavhan of Felheim-Foivan ran an efficient, brisk and as far as the circumstances of being stationed in an unfriendly country allowed, a happy embassy.

Despite having only one arm, Llando the Ob-handed still had two legs and a voice. He joined in the dancing and singing with gusto. So did young

Tyr Stofin Vingham, who was by way of being an apprentice in the Foreign Office trade, so to speak. And the Vallian Courier, Hikdar Naghan Veerling, proved to possess a truly fine voice.

He gave us the Canticles of the Rose City, and we sang the old songs of Kregen, and especially of Vallia, and Llando regaled us with "The Brumbyte's Love Potion." Then a calculated and diabolical plot was hatched and I heard the good folk gathered there audibly wondering just what song the emperor would choose to delight them with.

Well, now!

I can rumble out a hoarse chorus on the march, and I'll willingly join in when the swods sing—but to perform a solo under the admiring gazes of these people? I'd done it before, of course, and no doubt would again, but, all the same...

In the end I chomped and chewed and spat my way through a fine rousing swordsman's song: "Kurin and the Risslaca of Fire-Cavern."

After that we sang for some long time and after that again a few of us were gathered in a comfortable nook and I showed them the golden zhantil mask I kept still in the sack in which it had been catapulted along with me by the Scorpion. We'd not had time to make golden zhantil masks for ourselves when we'd gone up and burned the temple. I felt confident that these men, knowing of the evil, might themselves fashion golden zhantil masks.

Then Strom Ortyg said: "I have no doubt from intelligence gathered by my agents that the army recruiting here is bound for Tomboram. I have sent notice of that to Strazab Larghos ti Therminsax, our ambassador in Tomboram. Such information could prove useful to him."

"The people of Port Marsilus burned our embassy there, and Strazab Larghos had to escape to safety, which I am assured he did—"

"Majister!"

"Aye, Ortyg, an unpleasant business. The truth is, both armies forming here in North Pandahem are aimed at Vallia—"

The people in that group reacted in their various ways, from surprise and indignation, to fury and determination to hit back.

"—and they would interfere with communications. There's a Strom Murgon along there in Tomboram who is in league with this Kov Colun Mogper. They are receiving their pay from some agency that, as yet, we have failed to uncover. We will. We will. This Murgon aims to kill his cousin, the Kov Pando, and, I guess, seize the throne from under the flat slug of a King Nemo. Then he and Kov Colun will be left ruling the roost. And Vallia will once again be in flames."

"No! No!" They bristled now, alarmed and ugly with resentment that after all we had done the stupid damned Pandaheem insisted on fighting us.

Ortyg, as I judged, was too tough a character to look shaken. He might be shattered within the turmoil of his thoughts; but a diplomat he was, and with a diplomat's habitual smile and bland words. He did allow himself to voice the thought that would now torment him every day.

"When will they get around to burning *my* embassy?"

I said, and not with much courtesy: "Find some agents you can trust and who can worm out a little more than the fellows you have so far managed. Call them spies. It often gees them up."

Here in this building on its grounds we were sitting in a tiny enclave that was Vallia surrounded by land that was not. It is not a particularly enviable position to be in when that surrounding land and its people turn nasty.

I had had personally to argue long and emphatically with the Presidio of Vallia to persuade them to sanction an embassy to Menaham in Pandahem. The Bloody Menahem were anathema to honest Vallians. But, after the death of Phu-si-Yantong and the break-up of Empress Thyllis's crazy schemes, I'd imagined a new and brighter era was beginning. Convinced though I was that such an era was beginning, I had to face the fact that there were a few hiccoughs at the outset.

Like all this imbroglio.

Well, as you will readily perceive, what we had to do was obvious. Bloody obvious.

The trick would be in finding out how to do it.

Eighteen

Naghan Veerling's adventure...

"Some people, you know, majister, really want to be slaves—well, not exactly slaves, I don't mean grak-fodder—I mean—"

Hikdar Naghan Veerling stumbled to a halt occasioned not by my questioning look as by his suddenly apprehended inability to sort out his thoughts. He had been a staunch supporter when we'd cleared out the aragorn and the slavers from Vallia. He knew my views. So he was being honest and trying to put across a point of view sincerely held.

"I know what you mean, Naghan, even if you have it twisted up." I didn't laugh as we flew swiftly through thin air toward Port Marsilus. Naghan had easily been persuaded to drop me off outside the city before resuming his flight to Vallia. "Some people do seem to be born to be slaves, and cruel men and women just enslave them. But that is not the truth of their birth or inclinations. It's simply that some folk are less able to come to terms with life and need help and support. To enslave them has been the universal answer for seasons and seasons. The correct response to their plight is sympathy and then a program of education with an ibmaster."

"But, majister, surely you would agree that Opaz has fashioned some folk to lead and others to be led?"

"You can lead many people without making them slaves."

He glanced up quickly from the controls.

"Do not misunderstand me. I abhor slavery for what it does not only to the slave but to the slave masters. But I fell into the habit of debate during my time at the University of Bryvondrin. And, as I say, Opaz in his wisdom has seen fit to make some people—as you aptly put it—unable to comprehend what life can mean. They are the weak flock."

"Quite so. The abolition of slavery in Vallia will not miraculously give these bewildered people the capacity to handle the problems of living. We're working on that."

The Kregan scientific and religious mind functions in ways somewhat at a tangent if you take Earth as a norm. To their philosophies, Kregan thinkers bring the concept of mind and body as twins. All that is not corporeal is of the ib. This subsumes mind, soul, spirit. Yet the divisions are more subtle than a simple division; it is realized that, for instance, when a fellow is bashed over the head and his brains gush out they are the physical home of his ib, along with residual pathways in his body. But you can be "broken from the ib" and wander as a ghost. And, again, in various parts of Kregen, entirely different philosophies struggle to understand and explain truths that—well, perhaps—mere mortal man was never meant to grasp. Perhaps...

"Look," Naghan broke in. "Up ahead. Voller."

Any airboat flying over Pandahem was news.

We scanned the airy reaches ahead, the clouds low to the ground spinning away beneath and reflecting back a tumultuous glory of radiance from the suns.

I caught a quick glimpse of the voller before she flickered past an upflung pinnacle of cloud.

"D'you make her out?"

"She was gone too fast."

I frowned. "It might be—" I began.

"I always said so," quoth Naghan Veerling, and he laughed out loud. "If one travels with Dray Prescot, Emperor of Vallia, one is in for adventure—without a doubt!"

"Maybe an adventure not to our liking," I grumped.

"What Opaz wills Opaz wills."

"That's truth, by Vox! And any new vollers in Pandahem have to mean mischief."

We had flown out over the sea to avoid observation on the trip from Memguin in Menaham to Port Marsilus in Bormark of Tomboram. Maybe the fellow up front had the same idea. Moments later the voller popped out of the cloud. I stared narrowly. Then: "By Zair! She's *Golden Zhantil*!"

At once a sickening host of tormenting emotions hit me, swarmed all over me, drained me, left me shaken and haggard—

"Majister!"

"You will have to fly as you've never flown before, Hikdar Naghan Veerling."

At my tone he braced up with a snap, immediately aware that the time for this adventure he craved had arrived.

"I hope, I am confident—hell, I pray!—that that voller is piloted by a lady, the Lady Ros Delphor. She is very dear to me. I would give my life for hers. If she is in danger, trouble, under duress in that flier—"

"Majister! We will rescue her—who can stand against Dray—"

"Plenty, Naghan, plenty. Now let's go down and see what the position is."

As we went whistling down I had time to reflect that my habitual regard for aliases and secrets, and the desire to protect Dayra's identity, must have an odd repercussion here. Naghan might well be wondering why a puissant emperor would be willing to give his life for some unknown lady. Well, if he found out, he found out. I stared ahead as the gap narrowed with the windrush blustering past. *Golden Zhantil* leaped up to meet us.

Among the embassy guards had been three Valkan longbowmen and they'd been blazingly anxious that I should choose their best bow. Strom Ortyg had outfitted me, of course, and provided me with an armory. Any Kregan will have a plethora of weapons if he can. Each Valkan longbowman was confident that his choice weapon was the best. I did not wish to burden myself with three bows, and so I'd chosen the finest and then attempted to cheer up the other two crestfallen Valkans. Being of Valka, they naturally called me Strom and regarded me as pertaining especially to them.

Which was proper.

Now I lifted the bow and nocked a shaft. I had the usual fleeting thought of regret that Seg was not here...

"There is a slave woman at the controls, majister. That is damned odd, by Vox!"

I had to control the furious burst of anger that threatened to deluge me in scarlet hatred. I had to concentrate on the loose.

Golden Zhantil turned below us. Her decks appeared deserted, although anyone could be below. At the controls the slim figure of a woman in slave gray was partially surrounded by four hulking great Chuliks looking up at us. Their weapons were drawn.

"Bring us in sweetly, Naghan. I'll shaft two and then it's handstrokes."

"Aye!"

We plunged down.

Naghan Veerling handled his little Courier craft superbly. As we came in I leaned over the coaming and loosed twice. Each shot struck. Then I was over the side, my sword in my fist, slamming into the two remaining Chuliks.

I was quick, nasty and the result was very messy.

She said: "I am well aware of all your bad habits. This is one of your better habits. I approve."

Then—and, by all the Names—this should have happened before, I took her in my arms and she hugged me and so for a space neither could speak.

A footfall on the deck heralded Naghan Veerling. He'd parked the Courier flier on the deck of *Golden Zhantil*. Now he stumped up as we turned to watch him. His face was furious.

"By Vox!" he burst out. "This is terrible! What will I say? It is too much, majister! Damned unfair!"

"What...?" said Dayra.

"Why," went on Naghan passionately, completely ignoring any conventions of meeting and of lahals, "I dare not tell a soul I went on an adventure with the emperor! They'll ask me: 'Wonderful, Naghan! And how did you fare?' And I'll damned-well *not* say that I did nothing! That it was all over before it had hardly begun! And me gawping from the back like a loon—"

The bubbling relief that Dayra was safe burst up inside me. I laughed. I, Dray Prescot, roared with merriment.

I spluttered and managed to get out: "You did well, Naghan—"

"Who is this young man who is disappointed he didn't give a Chulik the chance to degut him, father?"

I turned and Naghan said: "Father?"

So I made the pappattu between them, and Naghan was suitably quieted down and impressed. Dayra was a princess when she wanted to be, by Krun!

Her story was soon told. After leaving Lisa the Empoin she'd returned to the flier. Nalfi was missing. Then, as Dayra said in a resentful tone: "I made a mess of it. That bastard Strom Murgon caught me prettily, a point at my throat and nowhere to turn. He made me fly him away. Since then he's used the voller nonstop. It is amazing how much work there is for a lone flier in this country."

"I give thanks to Opaz you are safe, Dayra."

"Oh, they didn't harm me. I could fly the voller. They couldn't. I'm on my way back from dropping a party of spies in Vallia—"

That explained why the voller was empty apart from the Chuliks set to guard her. I said: "Give Naghan all the information you can. When he reaches Vallia a party will have to pick up these spies as soon as possible."

So that was arranged.

When Naghan was ready to leave, Dayra said: "I knew a Nath Veerling once. We were in Bryvondrin at the time—"

"My twin. He is regarded by the family rather as the zorca with the splintered horn.* But we got along. I have not heard from him in many seasons."

Dayra smiled, the color in her cheeks, her eyes bright. By Zair! She'd taken her rescue mighty coolly; but I guessed what she was feeling now. She masked all that by saying: "Yes, we had some rollicking times."

That, of course, was in Dayra's madcap days when she and her gang of cronies went around wrecking restaurants for fun. Out of that had grown the darker evils of Zankov.

Hikdar Naghan Veerling, a Courier for Vallia, lifted away.

"Remberee, Naghan!"

"Remberee, princess, majister."

We were left on the deck, Dayra and I, and I could feel a warming of my blood, a treacherous feeling of contentment. There was so much to do, by Krun, and yet the clouds about us seemed to me to take on a roseate tinge.

Now with Dayra safe, surely we would win through!

Nineteen

Duurn the Doomsayer

He brushed up his reddish whiskers under that smart foxy nose and his bright eyes appeared almost crossed, so shrewd were they.

"If we steal away the treasure again—which we could do, by Horato the Potent, which we could do!—that misbegotten, white-haired she-witch will melt it all back."

"Let us take the treasure, anyway; then, by the oozing sores and desiccating limbs of the Divine Lady of Belschutz, if the witch does, she does."

Other voices lifted in passionate argument, each demanding to go down and seize Strom Murgon's treasure and let that damned frizzle-haired witch try to do her worst.

---

* Equates with "The black sheep of the family." *A.B.A.*

We were all sitting or lounging in the main saloon of the voller *Golden Zhantil*. After that beautiful reunion with Dayra, I had, instead of going on to Port Marsilus, flown to seek out Pompino and our comrades, finding them marching not particularly happily down the trails to reach civilization. They were overjoyed to see Dayra and me—and, I truly think, far more in *Golden Zhantil*. These Pandaheem were very rapidly acquiring the taste for flying.

As I saw it, this particular situation was both comical and alarming.

I had to prevent that army sailing to Vallia. We had already taken the army's treasury, and that damned witch had retaken it. If we just swingled in again to repeat the process, would the lady-necromancer not do the same?

When we had chance for a private conversation, Pompino, with natural quick eagerness, wanted to know what the hell had happened to me when the Everoinye snatched me away.

"They left me behind, Jak. Ignored me. They chose you—"

"Only because I was there and you had gone back to the campfires. If I had gone, you would have been chosen."

"You think so?"

"I'm certain sure."

"Hmph," he sniffed. "Well, and what happened?"

A considerable degree of caution had to be employed in my recital. He'd be vastly energized to discover just how I'd inveigled a party of soldiers from the Vallian Embassy to assist me. So, I confess, it seemed like boasting when I ran it all together and rescued Carrie and burned the Lemmite temple all in one coup de main. One day, I supposed unhappily, Pompino would have to know I was this puissant and frustrated Emperor of Vallia. Then he'd change. Then I might lose a comrade.

Pompino possessed this exaggerated respect for the Star Lords that would, inevitably, spill over into his dealings with emperors and kings. Even so, even so, he was well up to liberating an emperor's property if the chance came...

"We will have to find another way of stopping the army," I said to Dayra when we, in our turn, had the chance for further private conversation. "Pompino and the lads would go for the treasure again; but that, I am convinced, would be merely a waste of time. And they would think twice—even those hairy rascals—of taking on the entire army to strike at supporters of Lem the Silver Leem. It's not so much a puzzle of what must quite clearly be done—"

"That's obvious, father."

"Quite so. But the doing of it will upset a number of people." I looked at my daughter. "It will not please me, Ros Delphor, and can you understand that?"

"You are just an old romantic."

"True."

"Although I wonder which will displease you most; the cause or the effect?"

"The cause will be objects, the effects people."

"And in this wicked world that does not answer the question!"

And, by Zair, she was right.

"We will have to contrive some excuse to get the lads off the voller. All of them, without exception, have no reason to prevent an attack on Vallia." I sounded sad and tired even in my own ears. "On the contrary. Despite all we in Vallia have done to create friendships with them here in Pandahem, they'll approve of an attack on us."

"Even Pompino?"

"Of course. He's a good Pandaheem, from the South, maybe, like most of them. But I'll wager young Pando would rejoice to go and swing a sword in our land. Despite all."

"Then," she said, and her lovely mouth tightened into a resolute bar. "They must be taught differently."

I did not reply to that. Dayra was still very much of an enigma to me, to my sorrow. Any sensible father takes an intense interest in all the doings of his daughters; but he does not pry. He worries his guts out over them; but they go their own way. I was not fool enough to make a stupid blunt inquiry as to Dayra's feelings for Pando. I had the strongest hunch that that young man would not measure up to what Dayra fancied she wanted, and I also felt even more strongly that Dayra would remain free from emotional entanglements for some considerable time. She wouldn't even think of marrying yet; she might never marry.

But she'd have a damned good time, all the same.

As a part of those thoughts, I spoke as though musing aloud.

"I hope Hyr Brun is well and safe. And the child, also, Vaxnik—"

"He is a child no longer! He is a fair limber young man—"

"I believe it, and with joy. He and Hyr Brun—they served you well."

And still I would not pry. The central aching question could not be asked.

Dayra said: "I do not think you realize how much we missed you when we were young, Jaidur and I. We knew only that we had a father who was nowhere. We didn't miss *you*—we lacked a father. Jaidur said he would call himself Vax and seek adventure. You know that my idea of adventure was—somewhat different—"

"Aye." I wanted to listen, silent and fascinated by these revelations. But I said, "Jaidur went out to the Eye of the World, became a Krozair, called himself Vax Neemusjid. And you smashed up honest folk's restaurants—"

She made a small dismissing motion. "One of my closest friends was

Patti na—" She stopped herself. Then: "Never mind her real name. I thought she and Jaidur would—but they did not. Patti married the one we called Vondo. They were both slain in an affray. And so I became responsible for their son, Vondonik, and called him Vaxnik."

Did I feel a deliquescence of hope? Was I pleased or disappointed? I did not know. I waited in silence.

She half-turned, not laughing; but bright, bright, the old memories stirring her. "You will have to wait to hear of Hyr Brun for here comes Pando. And he concerns us here and now much more than—"

"Hai!" called Pando as he advanced across the deck of *Golden Zhantil.* "Here you are! I have made up my mind. I have waited too long. I am going to teach my cousin Strom Murgon a lesson he will not forget. The final lesson."

Pando became very much the fire-eating young noble, a gallant kov determined to strike for what was rightfully his. No more hesitation, he said, and issued orders left, right and center.

The nub of the scheme was to destroy, banish or capture Strom Murgon.

Pando was not fussy which one it happened to be, although in private bets we tended to favor the first solution as the one most pleasing to young Kov Pando.

Although, after we touched down in a forest camp set up some miles inland of Port Marsilus, Pompino confided in me: "Your young friend Pando doesn't appear to have any really sound plan of operations."

"Don't underestimate him, Pompino. You know how these young bloods are when they have had a taste of power and it has been dashed from them. Anyway, the nub of his plan is the Ifts. Twayne Gullik has at last declared openly for Kov Pando his master and has, at last, brought in the Forest Ifts actively to assist."

"Oh, yes, I know all that. Gullik was his usual supercilious smirking self when he rode in. And they intend to use the secret way into the Zhantil Palace."

That was the tortuous secret passageway system we had used under Mindi the Mad's direction to escape. A crowd of warriors pressing in through there could well take the palace, particularly if... "And we drop in from above in *Golden Zhantil?*"

"Aye."

"It is after that. Pando will hold the palace, and this time the army with Murgon will be actively hostile. He cannot resist for long. Then what?"

"I tend to the opinion," I said, a trifle cautiously, "that Pando hopes to have finished with Murgon by then."

"He'll need to be slippy. That one is a sly customer, and cunningly tough with it."

"It is my view, and I regret the necessity although joying in the venture, that I will have to lie to Pando." I added quickly, "Oh, not actively lie. I'll lie, as it were, in absentia. It won't be a personal falsehood."

"Do what?"

"You'll see."

He grumped off then to see about the next meal, and I sought out Dayra, who must be a party to the scheme.

She fired up at once, and made all the preparations.

So it was that toward the rise of She of the Veils, ever, I believe, my favorite Moon of Kregen, a grotesque figure shambled into the camp among the trees.

Cap'n Murkizon and Nath Kemchug led him forward into the firelight. Then they moved away, out of smelling range.

Grotesque, that figure, aye, and weird. His heavy beard was checkered into red and blue, and likewise his whiskers. His hair stuck up in spikes, colored yellow and orange and blue. His face was streaked with indigo and vermilion. His eyes glared frightfully. He was clad in a mangy animal hide of uncertain parentage, cinctured by a belt of monkey's paws, fastened by a bronze clasp in the form of an apim skull.

At his side swung a pallixter, a heavy knife snugged in a sheath over his hip, and he leaned on a mighty staff of twisted wood, the convoluted root of balass, black and grained, festooned with small evil-smelling bags, and tintinnabulating with a myriad tiny bells.

Men and women shrank away from that uncouth figure. He breathed an aura of mystery and repellent blasphemy.

"Llahal and Lahal!" he called in a strident, nerve-sawing voice. He moved with a heaviness and a hint of unsteadiness. He advanced toward the fire, and halted, and spread his arms wide, and then thumped the great staff down so that all the bells danced and clamored.

"I am Duurn the Doomsayer!"

Pando and Pompino stepped up, shoulder to shoulder, not one whit discomfited, although Twayne Gullik hung back well to the rear, and the guard Fristles congregated on the far side of the fire. Cap'n Murkizon gripped his axe and stood four square. Larghos the Flatch, who was not himself since the loss of the lady Nalfi, stood at Murkizon's side, lowering and hating. Rondas the Bold, just about recovered from his wound, stood with them, ready and alert.

"Lahal, Duurn the Doomsayer," quoth Pando. "And what is it you want with us? Whose doom do you say?"

"The doom of all in Bormark, all in Tomboram!"

A gasp went up at this. No one seemed to know if they should scoff at this weird, or freeze with fear.

"A mighty army marches on Bormark. They come like the sands of the seashore, marching from Memguin, out of Menaham. They march with a golden glittering lord at their head. They come to destroy all who oppose them and seize your steadings, your wealth, your women—"

Pando believed this at once.

Pompino said: "And how, mighty warlock, do you know this?"

I was highly amused at the look this Duurn the Doomsayer bestowed on my comrade.

"Unbeliever! Blasphemer! What know you of the Arts! Tremble lest your impiety bring you low!"

And, then: "I saw the host, marching."

At that, Pando shot out: "How many? What forces? Their captains? Their rate of march? Their order? Tell me all you can, Duurn the Doomsayer, and you may name your price."

"There is no price in all Bormark that could rise to my just desserts! For I have the Eye! I have the Ear! I can scry past the mundane veils of the known! Beware lest idle curiosity burn you up as the moth is consumed by the candle."

Dayra moved with all the grace of a hunting cat leaping after her prey. She slid in from the side, quick and deadly, while Duurn the Doomsayer began to thunder more rhetorical outpourings extolling his sorcerous powers; Dayra, passing by, halted momentarily, then went on past the firelight.

In that slight pause, as she passed, she whispered: "You're overdoing it, father!"

So, incontinently, vanquished by common sense, Duurn the Doomsayer thundered his last dire doom saying, and turned away and stumped off, out of the firelight, back into the forest.

Twenty

How lord and lady cried their Remberees

So the great plan of Pando's went into operation.

Twayne Gullik together with a host of his Ifts and a sizeable force of men still loyal to the Kov of Bormark, entered the secret passageway and penetrated into the Zhantil Palace through the hidden corridors. We, for our part, flew down in *Golden Zhantil* bristling with weaponry.

The attacks were timed to coincide a full four glasses after the rising of the Maiden with the Many Smiles. We hoped to have the palace cleared by dawn.

In the fuzzy pink moonshine we soared down and leaped from the voller, teeth bared, weapons sharp, raging to get into action.

I'd been spoiled for choice in the matter of weapons. The only real lack was a Krozair longsword. Still, the drexer gladly given me by Strom Ortyg served supremely well. I had the Valkan longbow. And I had repossessed the rapier and main gauche kept by Pompino when I'd been hoicked up by the Everoinye. We went howling in like a pack of wild beasts.

With the twin onslaught the defenders of the palace crumbled and broke. That furious assault smashed them, drove them like chaff, swept them up as a slave girl sweeps up the dust of the lord's Great Hall.

Panting, flushed, triumphant, we broke the last of Murgon's mercenaries as they attempted a stand, according to their lights, swirling in headlong combat down the grand staircase and along the luxurious halls and corridors. They could not stand before us.

Like good quality Kregan paktuns who earn their hire in blood, they fought well. There was no quailing, no shrieking panic flight; these men and women had taken their pay and now they earned their hire. In honor, when the situation cleared unmistakably and the steel-bokkertu could be offered and made—why then, and only then, would these paktuns change their allegiances.

As usual I was most anxious to get all this nasty fighting business over and done with as soon as possible. Pando, exalted, a single trembling entity on the point of explosion, took some time before he set the steel-bokkertu in motion. By then, more men and women had died earning their hire.

Fragments of poetry echoed along in my skull; and I am sure, Kregen being Kregen, many a savage fighting warrior—female or male—kept up a ragged rhythm of swing and strike as the stanzas seethed in their brains. Poetry and death—ever the two are twinned...

"Do not, my heart, get your fool self killed at the last moment—"

"I shall not hang back in dishonor, you great dear buffoon—"

Quendur and Lisa, striking blow for blow, were at their accustomed arguments.

Poor Larghos the Flatch watched them in hopeless envy.

The Divine Lady of Belschutz entered the conversation from time to time, fruitily.

Rondas the Bold wished to take out some repayment for his wound. Nath Kemchug, like any Chulik, sowed death in his wake. As usual when divorced from their beloved varters, Wilma the Shot and Alwim the Eye shot in their bows with deft precision. Naghan the Pellendur, recently appointed shal-cadade,[*] led his Fristle guards with our onslaught. The

---

[*] Shal-cadade—Under (or vice-) captain of the guard. From the root word "umshal" meaning shadow. The shal-cadade stands in the shadow of the cadade, a neat conceit. A.B.A.

cadade, Framco the Tranzer, had been assigned the secret entrance and this, I felt, was as much because Pando wished to keep an eye on Twayne Gullik. Mantig the Screw distinguished himself during that fight. Jespar the Scundle was not with us—he had thankfully returned to his own people.

"I," said Dayra to me as we cleared one of the ornate chambers leading onto the hallway below the grand staircase, "abhor killing people unnecessarily. Why doesn't this young onker Pando negotiate? We have clearly won. Is there no one with enough authority over him to make him see sense and initiate the steel-bokkertu with the surviving paktuns?"

Dayra halted stubbornly at the entrance to the chamber and stared malevolently out onto the hall where the foot of the grand staircase swept out into a recurve. Statues decorated every other tread of the staircase, and the high balcony above was just visible from where we stood. She shook her head. "The get onker!"

"We keep referring to Pando as young Pando," I said, and I, too, stopped beside the entrance and looked out onto the last dying flickers of the combat. "But he is not so young these days. Like any hot-blooded lord he is difficult to control. And, it is perfectly clear, he will not desist from this fight until Murgon—"

"Ah! Malignant, then—"

"Not really." I'd given Dayra most of my past history in connection with Pando and his mother, Tilda the Fair, Tilda of the Many Veils. She did understand, of course; but like me the sight of wanton slaughter filled her with revulsion.

The stink of spilled blood, the feel of sweat in the air, the harshness of all this, gave us pause, there in the doorway of the hall with the grand staircase lofting above.

Dayra had not worn her Claw in this fight.

A Sister of the Rose normally keeps her Claw in its bronze or silver-bound balass box, secret. But that box would be an awkward encumbrance to a girl in a fight before she dons the Claw, and so usually the talons are secreted in a leather and canvas bag which can be slung on her back out of the way. These bags normally are quite plain, perhaps with a row of fancy red stitching to distinguish them one from another. The Claw itself will have each separate tooth masked by a sheath of ivory or bone, or perhaps of wood. Now, through the insights afforded me by the Everoinye, I happened to know that these sacks are called jikvarpams.

In the fight Dayra had used thraxter and shield.

She had also been armored.

I own I'd raised my voice a trifle when we'd been equipping ourselves before the off. I'd been insistent. She'd said, with a toss of her head, words more or less to the effect that if I wanted to make a scene then she'd damned well wear armor, and carry a shield. I'd replied that I'd make more than a scene if she got herself killed. We were, you will perceive, improving in our relationship.

Now she reached around and fretfully began to pluck at the jikvarpam on her back, the blood from her thraxter staining the canvas.

"Where is Pando, or Murgon? By Vox! I need a wet!"

"By who?"

She glared at me.

"By Chusto, then, you—you—"

Dayra, like all my children, knew how to use a sword and shield with superb skill, having been trained by Balass the Hawk. She slid the shield off her left arm, and dumped it against the doorjamb. She looked pretty ferocious, I can tell you.

A step at our backs brought me around sharpish. I relaxed. The Lady Dafni walked up. She wore a middle-length white gown, belted in gold, and there were flowers in her hair. Her face was composed, yet I detected an overbrightness there, a quivering sense of panic suppressed by sheer self-preservation. Odd.

Pando walked with her, dignified and warlike in armor, carrying a naked sword. With them among the retainers came the Mytham twins, Pynsi and Poldo. Both were outfitted for battle, both carried bows.

Pando did not look pleased.

"We have gained the day," he said, surly and vengeful. "But where is the rast Murgon? He hides away like a skulking pest of the sewers. Jikarna, I brand him, jikarna!"*

"Not so!" The lady Dafni pointed aloft. "Look!"

Up there on the head of the grand staircase a brisk little fight finished with a couple of Rapas falling, and Strom Murgon, blood-bespattered, flushed, waving his sword in contempt at us clustered below.

Pando rushed out to get a better view, yelling that the cramph would escape. We followed.

Murgon brandished his blood-befouled sword at us. He looked magnificent, filled with elan and fighting spirit, defying us to the death.

Poldo Mytham did not hesitate.

He lifted his bow and on his face the shattering hatred filling him rendered him demonic. He loosed.

The shaft struck Murgon in the neck, above the corselet rim.

He stood for a moment, surprised.

He dropped his sword. He swayed. Then he pitched over the railing and fell headlong to the polished marble below.

Poldo lowered his bow. He loved Dafni with a hopeless longing. Perhaps he thought... Well, who knows what he thought?

With a horrified shriek, Dafni rushed forward. In a smother of white

---

* Jikarna—coward.

dress she collapsed onto her knees beside Murgon. His head was a ghastly red pudding. She took that hideous object in her arms and rested it in her lap and bent over him, her face stained with his blood as she kissed that crushed and ghastly face. She crooned hysterical words...

"Murgon! My only true love—my heart—*Murgon!*"

"So," said Dayra softly, at my side, "so that was the way of it. It explains much."

"Aye."

From somewhere in the shadows—and to this day neither I nor anyone else knows who loosed—a crossbow bolt lanced the air, thudding into Dafni, smashing her forward. She collapsed over the shattered body of her lover. Together, blood mingling with blood, they lay in death.

No one spoke.

The part Dafni had played in this business now appeared plain. She and Murgon had loved each other—and in furtherance of his plans he had used her to bedazzle Pando. The interview I had witnessed was now explained, and when we'd rescued Dafni—she had not wanted to be rescued. Pando had been the victim all along. Tilda of the Many Veils had seen much; but her intoxication as a way of life had precluded any clear statements to aid us. And the Mytham twins?

Poldo was distraught. And Pynsi—would she now be able to marry Pando? Only the future could answer that.

The immediate task was to ensure the loyalty of Pando's people, and the army waiting outside Port Marsilus. Into that hush the sound of a man yelling in pain penetrated and Pompino appeared, brisk and bright and most foxy, dragging along a wight by one ear.

"Says he has a message for Strom Murgon which, I think, with a little persuasion, he might tell us!"

Pompino halted as he saw the two bodies, blood-befouled, sprawled together. He whistled.

"That takes care of *that*, then!"

The order of events had to be kept in a correct sequence. The cadade and his Fristle guards went off to secure the palace. Palace slaves and servants set about clearing away the detritus of battle—which is a way of saying that they collected up the corpses. Pando shouted passionately that they should treat Dafni with care and that she should be laid out in state in a bedroom. As for Murgon; he turned away and it was clear to us all that he didn't give a damn if they bunged Murgon's corpse on the dung heap.

Dayra went off to make sure that that didn't happen. At least she knew how to treat a beaten adversary.

In all this bustle, Pompino's capture stood sullenly waiting to be questioned. He was a Brokelsh, hairy and uncouth, and one eye was black and his face was cut.

I looked at Pando curious to know how he would react to the knowledge that Dafni had been beguiling him all the time, under orders from Murgon to secure Murgon's desires to control the kovnate. For all her ceaseless chatter, Dafni proved herself to have been a lady of spirit.

Pando just pushed all that aside. His choleric noble attitude just brushed away the implications. He rounded on Pompino. "Well, Khibil! Don't just stand there! What is the message this rast has for Murgon?"

Pompino twisted a red whisker, and most mildly said: "Speak up, Bargal the Ley. Strom Murgon is dead and Kov Pando is your liege lord."

"Yes, well—" began this Bargal the Ley, mumbling.

Pando roared: "Speak up or your hide will decorate the battlements!"

"Message from Kov Colun Mogper of Mursham, pantor!"

Dayra appeared at my side, silently, like a jungle predator. She touched me lightly on the arm.

"Oh? Yes?" bellowed Pando, incensed. "And?"

"He is ready for the great expedition against Vallia, pantor! He awaits word from you to finalize the date! Send me back with this information and the two fleets can sail."

"There is treachery here." Pando fairly snarled in his bewilderment. "Mogper advances to attack Bormark!"

"Your pardon, pantor!" No one contradicts a great lord when he is incensed without peril. "Not so! The kov is in alliance with Bormark. The venture is against Vallia."

His brows fairly writhing in indecision, Pando half-turned to look at us, all standing in a half-circle and watching in fascination. "That is certainly what I believed. That bastard Murgon at least had that right. But the grotesque, Duurn the Doomsayer—could he have been mistaken?"

Taking this as a direct question, everyone started off on a passionate braying of their own beliefs. Dayra and I remained quiet. I glanced at her.

The rustic hermit she'd found in the woods and from whom she'd borrowed the trappings of Duurn the Doomsayer had been rewarded with a handful of gold and seen safely on his way. As a powerful inducement to belief, the guise of the grotesque had seemed to me to be excellent. Not many other visitors could, I thought, have impressed Pando so strongly. But—was all that skill and artifice to go for nothing?

Then Pompino—my good comrade, my kregoinye companion, Scauro Pompino the Iarvin, stepped out and spoke.

"I believe what this messenger, Bargal the Ley, says. The army here and in Menaham is paid for in gold that can only be used for that purpose for which it was intended. Pay the army from Murgon's treasury. Set them forward in the venture against Vallia. For, kov, if you leave them idle around here they will prove a permanent and costly threat."

"Aye," rumbled Pando. "That is sooth."

At my side, Dayra whispered: "Nice friends you have."

"Pompino is a Pandaheem. He is right. If the army out there contains very many officers loyal to Murgon they can walk in here and we'll never stop 'em. Pando's best bet is to pay 'em and ship 'em out—"

"Out—against Vallia!"

"Aye."

"So much for your wonderful Duurn the Doomsayer!"

The movement among the throng indicated that Pando had made up his mind. Murgon's treasure would be distributed to the army and the ship-masters. The armada would sail for Vallia. Win or lose for that army, Pando would come out ahead.

I looked out over that bright and busy bustle as folk ran to do Kov Pando's bidding. Oh, yes, he'd come out all right, sweet and smelling of violets. But what of the country that was my home, what of Vallia?

"Very well," I said, and although Dayra listened, I was really speaking to myself. "Sink me! If it's got to be done it's got to be done. And let Opaz take care of my conscience."

Twenty-one

Of one broken leg

Having made up his mind, Pando was all blaze and eagerness to get the thing done and over with.

Murgon's treasure—that same hoard of wealth we in *Tuscurs Maiden* had seen melt and run fuming into the sea—being distributed to the army and the ship masters delighted all of them. There was no talk anywhere of pulling down Kov Pando in the name of the dead Strom Murgon. Kovs, after all, are kovs.

Pompino and the crew went about looking over their shoulders in momentary expectation of the ghastly apparition of the white-haired witch. Had she turned up and blasted us all no one would have been vastly surprised.

From a dusty and hidden portion of the palace a figure that was surprising emerged, blinking in the suns' radiance. Cap'n Murkizon, axe aslant, sent immediately for Larghos the Flatch.

Stumbling, her clothes in ruins, her face streaked with dirt and tears, the Lady Nalfi was caught up and clasped close to Larghos. He could hardly believe his good fortune.

We left them to their reunions, and later Larghos and Nalfi joined us where she was able to tell her story.

Dayra watched, a comically quizzical little frown denting in between her eyebrows.

We gathered in a little outdoor arbor furnished with cane chairs and striped awnings and wobbly-legged tables. In a siege the place could be converted to take a catapult. Nalfi professed to bewilderment, loss of memory, misery, fear. Yes, she remembered the flying boat and watching Lisa and Ros Delphor leaving her alone. She had been terrified.

Here Dayra pursed up her lips.

Nalfi had hidden somewhere within the voller and only hunger had been enough to conquer her terror. She had crept out to find herself back in the Zhantil Palace, and had somehow slunk out of the airboat and found a succession of hiding places. That part was easy enough to believe, on Kregen where most of the palaces are stuffed to bursting with slaves and retainers and very few people know all the souls under the same roof.

Pompino expressed our general pleasure at seeing the Lady Nalfi alive and well. He congratulated her on her courage in adversity.

Dayra said to me, sotto voce, "Huh!"

"It is true, though. Nalfi possesses great courage, and resourcefulness."

Dayra glanced at me as though I had straw sticking out of my hair.

Looking out over the sea the eye was caught instantly by the assemblage of shipping. Seabirds wheeled and cawed amid the forest of masts. Nalfi expressed herself as most pleased that Menaham and Tomboram were cooperating. For two countries of Pandahem to act in this way was a fine augury for the future. I'd have been more inclined to agree with these pious sentiments had the target of the cooperation not been my home of Vallia.

The departure of the fleet could not now be long delayed. To no one's surprise, Pompino and the crew decided to sign on for the expedition. As Pompino said, twirling up his right whisker and gripping his sword hilt with his left fist: "Those rasts of Vallians are bound to worship Lem and their evil land be teeming with temples to burn."

Dayra said, a trifle too sharply, "The cult of Lem was once brought to Vallia. I hear the emperor was most severe with them—"

"I wonder," sniffed Pompino. Then: "This is sooth?"

"So I heard."

Making some excuse, I managed to drag Dayra off. We spoke alone out on the battlements.

"All right, father—I know!"

"Forget that. We have to try something interesting before... Duurn the Doomsayer failed. I think we have a more sure tool to our hands."

She was a true daughter to Delia, Empress of Vallia. Quick, by Zair! Sharp and devious and intelligent and altogether lovely. "Yes. You have seen how Larghos the Flatch goes about these days since Nalfi returned? Like a puppy that has lost his favorite chewing slipper."

"You were quite right when you said she had no affection for him. I think that was the key that unlocked the rest of it for me."

We had regaled Dayra with the tale of how Nalfi had joined our company back in Peminswopt along the coast. We'd cleared out the Devil's Academy where they trained up the priests to torture and butcher children to the greater glory of Lem, and Nalfi, all naked and alone and held captive by a Chulik, had calmly taken his dagger from his belt and slit his throat. He had been standing in front of her, ready to fight Larghos and Cap'n Murkizon as they broke in. Dayra saw.

"So she slew the Chulik who was trying to protect her."

"What better recommendation?"

"So she's a Brown and Silver, then."

"A most courageous and resourceful Lemmite, as I said. She saw she'd be for the chop; she joined us and ever since has been a spy in our midst. When we rescued Dafni—Murgon knew. Nalfi was missing, and joined us with some excuse—and more than once."

"And the scrap of brown and silver ribbon that would have betrayed our escape, down in the sewers—"

"As I said. Courageous and resourceful."

"Maybe I should have a word with her with my Claw."

"Perhaps over the matter of Larghos, at some later time. Right now, Dayra my tiger-girl, we must go in for some theater."

I admit it with great pleasure—we arranged this little piece of live theater exquisitely.

Fortune favored us to the extent that Larghos and Nalfi indulged in a real row in a small room, almost a broom cupboard, off the snug withdrawing chamber where Dayra and I sat. They exchanged wearily familiar accusations and disclaimers. The truth is, like marital infidelities, one side seems to wander around as though struck blind. Larghos stormed off in the opposite direction without seeing us, and before Nalfi could follow, Dayra spoke up in her clear voice.

"I feel for poor Larghos; but he will cheer up wonderfully when we reach Menaham. When he takes his part in the sack of Memguin—and that's just for starters!—he'll have so much gold—"

"Ros Delphor! Careful! You speak of secrets, and you do not know who may be listening."

"No one. They've gone." She laughed in a conspiratorial way, almost giggling. "Because you knew Kov Pando when he was a young boy means he trusts you above many others. I think his scheme to gull Kov Colun Mogper with messages that we sail to Vallia, and then to march straight to Memguin and seize the place when Mogper is away—"

"Oh, yes, Pando is mighty clever. Colun Mogper will suspect nothing. His army will be cut up in that heathen Vallia, and probably never return, and we'll be busily burning temples to Lem the Silver Leem. Any Lemmites left are likely to find themselves in small pieces. Very small."

"Like the pieces of their sacrifices."

A tiny, birdlike sound from the smaller room...

Dayra said, "I am for a wet, Jak Leemsjid."

"And I am with you, Ros Delphor."

Later on Twayne Gullik, the castellan of the Zhantil Palace, reported in great annoyance that some cramph or cramphs had stolen two zorcas. Fine animals, they were worth much gold. If food had been stolen, as it would have been, by Vox! then it would not be missed among the mounds of forage produced at all hours in the kitchens.

Dayra told me with great satisfaction: "She's well on her way to Memguin to report the terrible news to Mogper."

"May he have joy of it, by Zair!"

"Being what he is, he'll start at once his riposte."

"We have to move before they start loading the ships here. I've organized Naghan Raerdu, our local Vallian agent—"

"Naghan the Barrel, the Nose, the Ale! I know him!"

I sighed. "He is a most remarkable and trustworthy man. He made it possible for me to penetrate the Lemmite temple, where we met—"

"Hanging in bonds on the wall and that rast Zankov—"

"That is past. We look to the future."

"Aye, by Chusto!"

Naghan Raerdu, a most adroit spy within the emperor's private apparat, spluttered and wheezed and laughed his way into providing all we required. He employed tools who, I am sure, had no idea they worked for Vallia.

"Why, majister," he choked, laughing, his face as scarlet as the radiance of Zim, his eyes shut and streaming happy tears. "These poor folk of Pandahem cannot tell one airboat from another. The work will be finished before the Suns set, aye, and the paint dry!"

He was right. If you do not understand aircraft you're not likely to spot the difference between a Bf109 and a Mustang when there is only the flick of a wing to see. If you don't understand ships you will not spot the subtle differences between the t'gallants of a Johnny Crapaud Seventy-four from a British Seventy-four, pitching off there just above the horizon rim.

Naghan Raerdu had the work completed in a clearing in the forest at a distance removed from Port Marsilus. He ensured there were no nosey Ifts about. His people splashed on the blue and green paint, rigged awnings, fabricated the many flags. These treshes were all the same; blue and green diagonal stripes separated by narrow strips of white. This was the flag of Menaham.

When Naghan Raerdu said what I expected him to say, I replied: "No, Naghan. Absolutely no."

"But majister! Princess—I appeal to you—"

"Look, my friend. As a purveyor of best ale, as the emperor's most valued secret agent, you are far too valuable where you are, doing what you do. If you risk your neck with us—"

"Majister! If I thought there was a risk, well, I am not sure I could agree to you both going. Also, I would not be very keen to go myself..."

Dayra laughed delightedly. Even I smiled.

Naghan Raerdu, as a Vallian spy in a hostile land, ran his neck into plenty of risks every day.

He fussily superintended the stowage of the earthenware pots, making sure they were well packed down in straw. His cover as an ale merchant well qualified him for this task.

Despite all the jollity and the coarse remarks, I was decidedly unhappy about what we set out to do. Of course, it was obvious. Painfully obvious. All the same, much of the pain was experienced by me, for, do not forget, I am a plain sailorman. I do not profess to be an honest sailorman, by Zair; but this destruction saddened me.

Well, they say men sow corn for Zair to sickle.

We stood, Dayra and I, to watch Naghan Raerdu and his people ride off aboard their lumbering wagons, pulled by patient Quoffas like perambulating hearthrugs. For a treacherous moment we waited as the last wagon vanished into the surrounding forest. We were very late. From the opposite direction a scurry of zorca-mounted warriors broke from the screen of trees. They hared for us as we stood like a pair of loons on the grass, the mass of the voller at our backs.

We heard their war cries as they charged.

"Rasts of Lemmites!" And: "Charge, for the Golden Zhantil!"

Each warrior wore a golden zhantil mask.

"By the disgusting suppurating eyeballs and putrescent fingernails of Makki Grodno!" I yelled. "Up with you, my girl!"

Dayra sprang for the voller and began to clamber aloft to reach the controls. I stepped onto the fighting gallery and turned, watching the rush. One man led out, whirling his sword, low over his zorca's neck. The airboat did not move. The zorca fleeted nearer.

The leader outdistanced the rest of his cutthroat gang. He roared in, the zorca a splendid sight, all flashing hooves and wild eyes and tossing horn.

The voller moved. She shifted from the grass and lifted a hand's-breadth. I let out a sigh, knowing that in the next instant Dayra would slam over the controls to full lift and we'd skyrocket aloft.

In that instant, this ferocious warrior in the glittering golden mask leaped from his zorca. He hurled straight at the fighting gallery below the airboat. His clutching fingers scrabbled, caught a purchase and as we went whisking aloft so he flopped over and dangled by one hand, suspended over thin air.

I had no quarrel with him. I could not let him fall to his death. His companions were left far below, dwindling dots in the clearing, brandishing their swords. I looked down.

The voice within the golden mask puffed out, muffled.

"Jak! Jak Leemsjid, you great fambly! What are you playing at? Haul me aboard, for the sweet sake of Horato the Potent!"

I jumped forward, grabbed Pompino by the wrist and hauled him inboard, all tumbled in his war harness along the fighting gallery. His head clanked into a straw-stuffed box filled with pots. He sat up, ripped the mask off, and glared at me, filled with fury, reddish whiskers bristling.

"What the hell are you playing at, Jak!"

"And what the hell d'you think you're doing?"

He sat up and rubbed his head. "Mindi the Mad scryed out and managed to tell us a mysterious airboat skulked in a clearing in the forest. But you—what's going on?"

"Damned half-Ift witches!" I said, most grumpily.

"Well—and what is it, Jak. Tell me!"

This, as you will readily perceive, was not part of the careful plans at all. Not at all...

The voller lifted and turned and steered for Port Marsilus.

I eyed Pompino. He looked bewildered and wild. At least he'd lost his thraxter; but a rapier and left-hand dagger swung at his belts. I took a breath.

"You always were a mysterious fellow, Jak." He began to gather himself. He shook his head, and rubbed it again. "Boxes of pots—and I know little of airboats; but this looks remarkably like *Golden Zhantil*. Have you—?"

I said, "Look down there, Pompino the Iarvin."

"Do what?"

I pointed down, over the side. He turned around and leaned out to look down and I put my thumb under his ear and he went to sleep. I caught him as he fell and eased him to the deck of the fighting gallery. What a mess!

When he was thoroughly tied up and unable to move, I went up to see Dayra and told her. She looked cross.

"He would have to come poking his clever Khibil nose—"

"Yes. Well, he will not stop us."

"Of course not!"

The blue and green voller bore on, flaunting the flags of Menaham. She roared on over the forest and out over Port Marsilus as the suns declined in the bright sky. Down below, crowding the roads, tied up to every wharf, the ships of the invasion fleet lay. First thing in the morning they'd begin loading. Some of the troops would go aboard before dawn.

That armada could not be allowed to land in Vallia.

Dayra spoke and I saw she spoke diffidently. "Father—do you want to fly the voller? Would you like me to go below and—"

"Thank you, Dayra. No. I abhor this, but I'll do it."

"Very well. I'll cover every last one."

"I won't miss."

So, down below I went, back to the fighting gallery below the keel of *Golden Zhantil*. Pompino had been tied up so that he couldn't move, as I thought. He was a crafty, great-hearted, fighting Khibil. He'd wriggled himself into a position from which he could look down through a grating.

I said nothing, ignoring him. I took a torch from its becket and set it afire with flint and steel. He looked on and his Khibil face drew down.

"Jak! What—?"

I had to say out of compassion—for myself, mark it, for myself!—and not very prettily: "This had to be done."

I set the first firepot ablaze and poised with it in my hand. Pompino looked from that horrendous incendiary device down to the glinting sea. He writhed and stared back at me.

"*Tuscurs Maiden* is down there, Jak! *My* ship! A vessel you have sailed in and loved, as anyone could see. Jak! You would not burn *Tuscurs Maiden*!"

"And perhaps you should not have told Captain Linson to offer your ship to Kov Pando for his fleet."

I hurled the firepot down.

As we passed above and the next firepot hurtled down *Tuscurs Maiden* was well ablaze.

Well, I, Dray Prescot, sailorman, cannot coldly chronicle the burning of that magnificent fleet. The ships burned. The ships burned...

I'd burned ships before; the *Eye of the World* had witnessed a burning. Many enemies had perished in flames of my setting. But this—no, I cannot draw that horrendous picture for you. I threw the firepots and there was a red blaze before my face and a scarlet haze in my eyes. The smoke, black and evil, drifted off before the wind.

I did not miss a single ship.

That once-proud armada sank in rinds of grimy ashes.

Long and long afterwards I learned to my great joy that not a single sailor was lost, and some poor fellow called Slow Mando broke a leg. That was the only injury—to men.

The injury to the ships was great. It was no greater than the injury to my feelings. Sentimental nonsense to feel this way about mere creations of wood and canvas? Of course. Even though they would have carried an army to ravage my home; still, I could not remain unaffected. So, I spoke half aloud.

"As I said, let Opaz take care of my conscience."

Pompino glared up. "Opaz?"

The voller steadied on course and I knew Dayra had put on the ropes to control the levers and in a moment or two she appeared in the fighting gallery. She was smiling.

"I did not see you missed one!"

"I do not think there are any left."

"By Vox! What a day!"

Pompino swiveled to look at her. "Ros Delphor? Vox?"

I said: "Poor Pompino lost his famous *Tuscurs Maiden* down there."

Dayra, it was evident, shared my sentimental nonsense about ships only so far. "So Pompino lost a ship. You can always find him another—"

I nodded. "That is true." I looked at Pompino. "How would you like a real Galleon of Vallia, Pompino the Iarvin?"

Now Scauro Pompino was a Khibil. He was smart, shrewd, quick. His foxy face congealed. His shoulders twitched where the ropes bound him, and I knew he wanted to brush up his whiskers. I unsheathed my sailor knife and stepped forward.

"You have always considered yourself the leader in our partnership, Pompino, and that has seemed to me to be just and useful. But when I cut you free, if you attempt to fight me, I think both you and I know you will come off worst."

The ropes fell away.

He stretched and shivered. He put a hand to his whiskers, and then stopped himself. He spoke with an effort.

"I think—" He swallowed and started over. "The Everoinye—they would not be deceived. Perhaps I have known for a long time and would not admit what seemed impossible."

"Now look, Pompino. You and I are good comrades. We've been in plenty of tight scrapes. We've each fought for the other. You like to get away from your lady wife because of reasons. And, I can tell you this, you don't get much fun being a stay-at-home emperor. Believe me."

"Oh, yes, Jak Leemsjid—Dray Prescot—I believe you!"

I eyed him warily. Would he start the full-inclining and bowing and scraping? Had I lost a good comrade?

He was a smart and foxy devil. He said, "When do I get the Vallian Galleon?"

Dayra let rip an almighty guffaw.

"I'm going to repaint this airboat and destroy the Menaham flags. Then I'm going down to Pando and make sure he sets his army in motion against Kov Colun Mogper. After that I'll probably have time to nip across to Vallia. If you can wait until then, why, then, I'll find you the best galleon the yards of Vallia can build."

"If I can't wait?"

"I think you will. But there will be time for Ros Delphor to fly you across to Vallia. You'll have to make up your mind—"

"Oh, I've made up my mind already. I know when I'm on to a good thing. If we continue as we have, burning temples to Lem the Silver Leem, following the dictates of the Everoinye, then I see no reason for a drastic change."

Well, as they say, don't expect a river to change course just because you throw in a boulder. Even a boulder of the size I had just thrown.

I nodded. "Good. And remember, Pompino, it is Jak Leemsjid, as ever."

"As ever."

Moving away ready to go aloft and resume control, Dayra passed me, and whispered, "He hasn't really taken it in yet. When he does—"

"He isn't called the Iarvin for nothing."

Dayra swung away going nimbly up the ladder and I sighed and thought of Delia... Delia...

Well, as soon as we'd sorted out Pando, which should not take long now, and done more about the Lemmites, I could go back to Vallia and find Delia and tell her what had happened.

There would be a fine spanking galleon to prepare for Pompino, too...

Just how would he take this revelation that his comrade was Dray Prescot, Emperor of Vallia?

Then I smiled. Far more important was what would Delia make of Pompino the Iarvin!

SEG THE BOWMAN

Seg the Bowman

Seg the Bowman is the story, complete in itself, of the finest archer of two worlds, a man courageous and resolute in the face of adversity, a wild, fey, reckless fellow, blade comrade to Dray Prescot, a man of parts. Of Seg Segutorio it has been said that perhaps he is too kind-hearted for the harsher aspects of the world of Kregen.

Kregen, a planet orbiting Antares four hundred light years from Earth, is indeed a harsh world; but it is also beautiful and mysterious, exotic and immensely rewarding, where many a dream may be realized, many a nightmare become reality.

The story begins where Seg and Dray Prescot and a party of adventurers have successfully quitted a maze of monsters and sorcery. Prescot is called away by the Star Lords, as related in *Fires of Scorpio*. Now Seg steps forward into fresh adventures wherein he discovers the passionate problems of agreeing to act as the lady Milsi's knightly protector.

The warmth and pride suffusing Dray Prescot's words as he tells the story of Seg Segutorio confirm the powerful friendship between the two and illuminates their mutual loyalty. For they are blade comrades upon the haunting world of Kregen beneath the streaming mingled radiance of the Suns of Scorpio.

Alan Bun Akers

One

Phantom of the Jungle

The woman in the blue tunic halted just inside the edge of the jungle and, shading her eyes against the twin suns, stared out toward the lake. The two men walking toward her might be deep in conversation; she knew well enough even in the short time she had made their acquaintance that if she moved another step they would see her at once.

A vague blue haze pulsed unexpectedly about the men, making her blink her eyes. She did not move. The twin suns threw down their mingled streaming lights and in the early morning radiance shadows still stretched short into emerald and ruby blobs. The strange blueness appeared to swish into her eyes like the bewildering swirl of a dancer's cape.

When she looked out again there was only one man on the little path by the lake.

Alarmed, she called out.

"Seg the Horkandur!"

At the sound of his name the man looked up instantly. He was in the act of picking up from the path a length of scarlet cloth and a longsword. From these two items he drew his attention not so much reluctantly as regretfully. He faced the woman.

"Yes, my lady?"

"Is all—is all well? Where is the Bogandur?"

"He has been—called away."

She laughed uncertainly. "Called away? Here in the midst of this terrible jungle?"

"Do not fret over him, my lady. He will turn up in his own good time."

"Yes, I believe that. For I thought him dead back there in that horrendous mountain."

"As did I. He was not an apparition, I assure you. Stand very still, my lady. When I shout run, run!"

The scarlet breechclout and the longsword went thump onto the path. The longbow snapped into Seg's left hand, the shaft was nocked and the string drawn in a blur of speed. The first arrow sped.

That shaft passed a scant hand's breadth past the woman's ear. Seg bellowed as he loosed.

"Run, my Lady Milsi, run!"

Milsi ran.

A gargantuan screech burst out from the jungle just to her rear. A bellow and a thrashing of densely packed foliage drove her on, panting with effort. A second arrow flew, and a third followed on while the second was still in the air.

Milsi panted down out of the jungle edge, pursued by what horrors she did not know. But she had complete confidence in Seg the Horkandur. She had known him for so short a time, yet he had proved to be the perfect jikai, the honorable warrior, devoted to her person.

With the same blurring speed Seg thrust the bow stave up over his left shoulder and whipped out his sword.

Yelling in a deliberate attempt to engage the monster's attention, he drove forward venomously.

The sword flamed in his fist.

He roared past Milsi without a glance, a word. Every instinct of his body concentrated on the slavering thing lashing about by the jungle edge. The three shafts had done their work. For Seg, a Bowman of Loh, anything else would have smacked of the impossible in any world, ordered or not. He brought the sword down and around and hacked a gouting chunk from the beast's neck. One eye remained, a glaring orb of hatred. That eye blacked into a gush of ichor as the sword punched in.

Seg leaped back.

The thing, scaled and vicious, lashed about in its death throes. As long as a man, it reared up on six legs to waist height. Its head, sharp with jaws and teeth, twisted from side to side. Twice it reached up on its four hind legs, the front claws slicing at empty air.

A voice bellowed from farther into the forest.

"Hai!"

The scaled beast attempted to turn itself around, and weakened by loss of blood, fell. It toppled into the scrubby undergrowth by the side of the trail. It thrashed about. And then it died.

Seg gave it a last calculating look, and turned and ran back to Milsi.

"You are unharmed, Seg?"

"Aye. By the Veiled Froyvil! I am glad you came to no harm."

"Thanks only to you. I give you the jikai."

"Aye," bellowed the voice as its owner pounded out into the clearing. "Hai, Jikai!"

Seg ignored all that. It was not a jikai in his estimation. He'd shafted the poor thing thrice, and then chopped it a trifle. A mere nothing before breakfast for a warrior upon the world of Kregen.

"What is it, anyway?"

"That is a toilca—"

"Well, Hop, it is dead now."

"Maybe." Hop the Intemperate spoke through the mass of hair about his mouth, his gross body as hairy through his harness as a quoffa. "But they do not hunt singly. They wander in packs."

Seg looked at the toilca, seeing the way the scales were patterned in brown and green to give superb camouflage. The shape was adapted to slinking through the jungle, and when the toilcas surrounded their victim, they would rear up on their hind legs and tear the poor devil to pieces with their front claws.

"In that case, friend Hop, we had best get back to the others sharpish."

"I'm with you, Horkandur. Master Exandu sent me to follow the Lady Milsi. He complained that she wandered off into the jungle like a—" Here Hop the Intemperate belied his name, for he stopped talking at that point.

Quite clearly Exandu had passed uncomplimentary comments about a woman wandering off into the jungle like a loon.

The Lady Milsi fired up.

"I could not sleep. I was worried about where Seg the Horkandur had gone, so I followed—"

"Let us go back to the others," interrupted Seg. "But, first..."

He ran back down the path and snatched up the scarlet breechclout and the longsword. When he got back to Milsi and Hop, the latter said: "They belong to the Bogandur! I thought the demon ate him."

"So did I. But he has had to go off—"

"A mighty strange fellow, that. More strange even than you, Horkandur!"

Seg made no reply to this, for he agreed. Maintaining a close watch upon the forest, they walked back along the rudimentary trail to the clearing where the party were rousing out after the night's uneasy sleep. The smell of the first breakfast filled the air with mouth-watering aromas.

Looking at the Lady Milsi as she swung along, Seg reflected that she was, in Erthyr's very truth, a wonderful person. Her body, firm and voluptuous, filled the blue tunic. Her face glowed with the remembered horrors through which they had passed to arrive here, and of which that poor toilca had been but merely the latest. She had managed to wash her hair in the last of the chambers in the mountain where the party had rested and eaten before at last quitting the abode of horrors. Her hair was of a bright and sheening brown, and the dinginess and stringiness were gone. She held herself proudly. Well, and so she should, seeing that she was a lady in waiting to a queen—well, poor Queen Mab was dead now. He and his comrade had taken the Lady Milsi from the next cell.

And that made Seg wonder where the devil his old dom might be now. Anywhere on Kregen, perhaps been spirited back to that funny little world he'd spoken of, called Earth, a long long way away, where they only had one little yellow sun and one little silver moon, and only had apims like him, instead of the multifarious and wonderful assemblage of diffs inhabiting Kregen.

"You look—severe, Seg."

"It is nothing, my lady. I but thought of the Bogandur. I wish him well. But now we must look to ourselves and get out of this pestiferous jungle."

"Yes. But where to?"

He looked surprised.

"Why—surely you will wish to return home? Of course, I shall escort you. That is, if you wish it."

"You know I wish it..."

"So that is settled."

"I hope so. It may not be so—so easy as all that."

Seg sniffed and put on an air of long-suffering. He was not the kind of fellow to allow himself to be down in the dumps for too long.

For her part, Milsi looked at Seg and saw a man endowed with superlative attributes. He possessed the archer's build, broad of shoulder, trim of waist, with the muscles like live snakes upon his bronzed body. He wore a scarlet breechclout, cinctured by a broad lesten hide belt. He carried his Lohvian longbow, and the quiver of arrows, each fletched with rose-red feathers. His sword was of a pattern with which she was not familiar. His moccasins, like hers, were supple of uppers and stout of sole. The party had worn through a good many pairs of those arriving here, and were like to wear through a lot more before they escaped this place.

These surface attributes were apparent to other people as well as to Seg and Milsi when they looked one upon the other. But each saw more than the surface. Each saw in the other a spark of life, a steady sureness of purpose, loyalty, cheerfulness, a sense that each yearned for targets that more mundane folk might consider eternally out of reach.

Seg had sworn to be Milsi's jikai, and to care for her and escort her. For her part, she had promised him nothing. They had met in the maze of the mountain when the party sought bandit treasure, and Milsi had been rescued. Her party, led by the queen in search of the king, were all dead. Now, Seg realized, she would have to return and report that fact.

For some people the fact would not be sad. For some of the schemers the news would brighten up their day...

Although Milsi had said nothing to make him think he stood more highly in her affections than anyone else, he felt confident she regarded him with approval as her escort.

That was a start.

He sniffed the breakfast scents approvingly.

Milsi glanced up at him as Hop hurried forward toward the bulky and complaining figure of Master Exandu.

"It is odd, Seg. You say you are from Loh. Of course, I know nothing of that continent; but I have heard that all Lohvians have red hair—"

He laughed, his fey blue eyes very merry.

"Come and have something to eat! No, no. I come from Erthyrdrin, which is in the very north of Loh. Up there we mostly have black hair and blue eyes. There are red-headed folk among us—and I can tell you, we make jokes about that!"

"I'm sure."

"What!" yelped Exandu. He spluttered, tottering. "This is terrible! We must move on at once, get away from this fearful place—oh, my insides. Shanli! Shanli! My insides burn—it is that infernal vosk rasher I have just eaten... Shanli, for the sweet sake of Beng Sbodine, the Mender of Men!"

Clearly, Hop the Intemperate had just told Exandu that a crazed pack of toilcas was on the loose and threatening to rush headlong upon the camp and devour everyone about the fires.

Shanli hurried up in her graceful fashion of not seeming to fuss or hurry at all but of always being on hand to fetch Exandu a sip of wine, a potion, liniment, and most importantly of all soothing words.

"A potion of Mother Babli's Stomach Balm, master. And I have mixed it with just a sip of Honeyed Jholaix."

"Oh, Shanli, my treasure... Honeyed Jholaix!"

Seg noticed the way Milsi reacted to this pathetic tomfoolery. Her eyebrows rose. Yet, she was well aware of the parlous state of Exandu's insides, and of his interminable lamentations about his liver, and bones, and aching head.

She saw Seg looking at her.

"Honeyed Jholaix, indeed! That is pure decadence."

Jholaix, being the name of the country and of its wines, the finest, so folk swore, in this part of Kregen, was well known as a wine and not often sampled. A poor man could not afford to buy a prime bottle of Jholaix with a year's wages.

"Yes, but, lady Milsi," said Shanli with her deep and resigned manner giving her a transcendental appearance of purity. "Master Exandu deserves all and more anyone can offer—"

"I'm sure."

"Toilcas!" burst out Exandu, taking a heartbeat to chatter around the cup Shanli held to his shaking lips.

"They shall not harm you, master, not with Hop the Intemperate and Seg the Horkandur and all the other fine guards with us."

Seg caught the eye of the Pachak, Kalu Na-Fre. Kalu walked over carrying a morning cup of tea in his tail hand, his upper left hand holding an enormous slice of bread, his lower left hand a pot of preserves. His single right hand dipped a knife into the pot and smeared the golden-yellow preserve upon the bread. He wore his full harness and carried an assortment of weapons. Even taking breakfast upon Kregen, especially in a Kregan jungle, a fellow did not wander about defenseless.

"Toilcas?" He sounded pleased.

"Aye. And, Kalu, you and I know that Exandu here will swing his sword lustily enough if the time comes."

"Do you not think, masters," put in Shanli, still spooning the potion into Exandu, "that we should pack up and depart at once?"

"The question is one upon which a fine argument might be built," observed Kalu the Pachak. His straw-yellow hair swirled as he turned to regard Shanli. Short, Pachaks stood in general, but fierce and ferocious warriors with one of the strongest honor codes in all the world.

"Argument, argument?" cried Master Exandu. He was a man who enjoyed the good things of life. Normally his face was rubicund and merry, with fat scarlet cheeks and eyes almost hidden in cheerful folds of flesh. And his nose! Ripe, protuberant, of a size awesome and a color glowing like the finest plumtree fruit. "There is no argument. We must leave before the monsters are upon us and devour us limb from limb."

"Oh," said Kalu, casually. "I believe they're more inclined to swallow you whole, and make you last a whole sennight. Although," and in his Pachak way he looked meaningfully at Exandu. "Although, Master Exandu, they might make you last a pair of weeks; they'd not take you down whole."

Mistress Shanli decided that her poor dear master could stand no more of this, and she urged him off between the campfires to a resting place more seemly. She was not slave, for the comb in her long dark hair glittered, and although, like the others in the party, she had been at pain to strip away her old clothes and contrive fresh, she still wore her bronze-link belt.

There were six principals in this party adventuring after treasure in the mountain of the Coup Blag. Each principal took along his retainers, all except Seg, who had now lost his comrade.

The sixth member of the party, Skort the Clawsang, had been lost within the depths of the maze in the mountain. Now Fregeff, the Fristle Sorcerer, walked calmly across to Kalu, Seg and the Lady Milsi.

"Toilcas are merely corporeal," said the catman in his hissing way. He brushed his whiskers with the bronzen links of his flail. Fregeff was an Adept of the Doxology of San Destinakon. The lozenges of brown and black patterning his gown bewildered the ordinary eye with their subtle shifts of alignment, suggesting awful superstitious fears to believers. The bronze chain about his waist led up to the necklet of the small winged reptile that perched upon the peak of his left shoulder. Now Fregeff put up a hand and stroked the volschrin.

"And, also, my Rik Razortooth would tear out their eyes—as you know."

Hop, about to follow Exandu, said in his bluff way: "We do know, San Fregeff. But the monsters hunt in packs. There will be many of them."

"And if I shake my bronzen flail at them?"

Hop shivered.

"That is not for mere mortal man to say, master."

The hissing sound from the catman might have been a laugh of satisfaction, if anyone there believed the sorcerer could take satisfaction from so small a point.

"All the same..." said Seg, and looked around. A man of parts, this strange wild archer from Erthyrdrin, and a gallant man in important matters. "Mayhap we had best move on smartly. If not for poor old Exandu's sake then for the sake of the ladies and the slaves."

The Lady Milsi's beautiful eyebrows convoluted themselves again at this. "Ladies, Seg—commingled with slaves?"

Seg remained quite unabashed.

"Certainly. I lump them together because they are unable to defend themselves—"

"Seg the Horkandur!" Now Milsi really looked annoyed. "A woman is perfectly capable of taking on and beating a craggy idiot of a man any day—"

"Some women, some men, and some days," said Seg. He spoke gently.

"Your point admits of further extension to its basic parameters," said Kalu, twitching up his tail hand but pausing to speak before he drank. "All the same, I am of the same opinion as Seg."

"Good, Kalu. I wonder if we will receive the usual tiresome contrariness from Strom Ornol?"

"Here," said Fregeff, with an indicatory jerk of his flail that did not stir the bronzen links, "he comes now."

A strom, although a little below the middle of the table of precedence, was still a rank of the higher nobility. Stroms were folk of consequence. This Strom Ornol never forgot that fact, and made sure that those around him were not forgetful, either.

The catman moved a few paces away, a small and apparently meaningless movement; but Seg was well aware that the sorcerer by that gesture was indicating that he wished to take no part in the inevitable quarrel Strom Ornol would bring with him. Fregeff, as an Adept of San Destinakon, was quite capable of taking care of himself in unpleasant circumstances, and it seemed that here and now the onrush of a pack of maddened toilcas was not an occurrence to make him worry overmuch. Let, he seemed to be saying, let you lesser mortals decide for the best for yourselves.

Strom Ornol, pale-faced as always, high of temper, a blot in the eyes of others beside Seg, came striding up in his usual furious temper.

"What is all this blathering? Toilcas? Who says so?"

Seg had really just about had enough of this insufferable young dandy. He knew that Ornol, as a younger son, had been kicked out by his noble father. He'd been into mischief from the day he could toddle, more than likely. Because he was a lord, Ornol had assumed that he was in command of the expedition. Seg had acquiesced in that. It went down well or ill with the other members; but only now and again had they shown open revolt. After all, they were equal members in the treasure hunting party.

"Well? Am I to receive no answer?"

Ornol fidgeted with the hilt of his rapier. The matching left-hand dagger swung over his right hip. This fashion of using rapier and main gauche was still new in the island of Pandahem, although well established in other parts of Kregen. Now Ornol glared about, his face with its pallid sheen of sweat working as though he had constipation.

"I saw one," said the Lady Milsi.

Seg said, very quickly: "Yes, pantor, that is correct."

He glanced at Milsi. She returned his look, and then glanced away. She sometimes forgot that one addressed lords properly, and here in Pandahem called them pantor, lord.

Kalu spoke up. "Well, strom. We have taken some treasure out of the mountain and are still here and alive. Unless you intend to return we may begin our return journey in all honor."

"Return? Into that hellhole?"

"That's settled, then," said Seg. He made it brisk. "Let us pack up and move out."

"I shall give the orders," started Strom Ornol.

Fregeff called in his hissing catman way: "Evil approaches."

Everybody jumped.

The Fristle sorcerer had powers, that was undeniable. If he said evil was on the way—evil was on the way.

They all looked about, and hands gripped onto sword hilts, and Seg slid his great bow off his shoulder.

"There!" yelped a Gon guard, and in the same instant they all saw the apparition floating in over the tops of the trees.

A throne-like chair hung unsupported in thin air. Its outlines were not clearly defined; it shimmered with power drawn from a source far beyond the confines of the normal. Seg blinked. He could make out the throne and the trailing silks that did not blow in the wind of the chair's passage, he could see the chavonth pelts and ling furs scattered luxuriously upon the seat and the arms, see the mantling canopy rearing out above the throne. That canopy was fashioned into the likeness of a dinosaur's wedge-shaped head, jaws agape, fangs glittering silver. The eyes were hooded ruby lights. Anyone approaching the throne must perforce stand in awe and terror of that demoniacal head above.

And—all these awesome appurtenances were as nothing beside the woman who sat on the throne.

Clad in black and green, picked out in gold, with much ornamentation and embroidery, she sat stiffly erect. Her pallor of countenance made Strom Ornol look as flushed as Master Exandu. Her eyes were green, sliding luminous slits of jade. Her hair, dark, swept in long black tresses about her shoulders and descended into a widow's peak over her forehead. She wore a jeweled band about that sleek black hair, and a smaller representation of the horrific dinosaur wedge-shaped head jutted from the center.

A guard lifted his bow. He was a Brokelsh, a member of that race of diffs who are coarse of body hair and coarse of manner. He loosed. Everyone saw. The arrow struck cleanly into the woman's breast. It passed on, transfixing that glowing phantasm, shot on and curved out and down to plunge into the jungle.

Somebody screamed.

As though nothing had happened the woman peered down from her throne. Her mouth was painted into a ripe bud shape of invitation. There was not a single line or crease upon that pallid countenance. Gold leaf decorated her eyelids. She looked down upon the mortals below.

Each one felt the force of her gaze pass over, a psychic probe, questing and passing on.

Fregeff the sorcerer stood supremely still. His bronzen flail did not quiver.

With a gesture that even in so simple a movement was all seduction, the woman lifted her left hand. Diamonds glittered. She made a sign, her forefinger pointed down at the camp in the clearing.

Among them all, Seg devoutly believed that lightning, fire and destruction would pour from that condemning finger.

Instead, the apparition wavered, the outlines flowed like gold within the smelting pot. The throne lifted away, turned, vanished beyond the tops of the trees.

In the next instant a horde of flying creatures swept out over the trees, the men astride them brandishing weapons. In an avalanche of fury, the flying warriors swept down upon the camp, lusting for the kill.

Two

Seg the Horkandur collects arrows

Seg's instincts clashed.

His first instinct was to loose as many shafts as he could, skewer a clump of these damned flyers, and then rip out his sword and go plunging into the fight.

But, also, his first instinct was to grasp the Lady Milsi about the waist and, honoring his sworn promise to protect her, hurry her into the problematical safety of the jungle.

He could follow either course.

Where lay the course of honor?

His old dom, whom these people called the Bogandur, used to say that honor didn't bring in the bread and butter. Despite that, he was the most honorable of men that Seg knew, his concept of honor not being of the rigid kind. Rather, it adhered to seeking the best solution to any problem that arose.

Without turning, Seg rapped out: "Milsi! Run to the edge of the jungle! Hide! Do not go too far in—"

As he spoke he lifted the bow, drew, released and had another shaft across the stave, nocked, and the bow lifting for the second shot, all in a twinkling.

Milsi said: "If you think I'm going to run off and leave you—"

"I do not want you to be killed." He loosed again, and again with that incredible speed slapped up another shaft and loosed. "Run, Milsi—*please!*"

"No."

"Then I must take you."

"You would not dare!"

His three arrows had knocked over three of the flyers. They were not all apims like him, some were diffs, for he saw Rapas, Brokelsh, a Gon, a couple of malkos.

The saddle birds they flew were brunnelleys, large and powerful, wide-winged, gaudy of coloration in blues and mauves and browns, yellow beaks and clawed scarlet feet. Plates of wafer-thin beaten gold adorned the birds. They swept in over the clearing, and their bandit riders did not bother to shoot down but landed their birds in great wing-ruffling swirls. The men leaped off, screeching, swirling their swords about their heads.

Seg sniffed and shot a fellow through the breastplate, instantly nocked and drew again and shafted his comrade.

Milsi said, "I am not frightened while I am with you, Seg. If—"

"Yes, yes. I can stand here and shoot the rasts. I suppose—"

"That is best."

"Until they come to handstrokes!"

The fighting broke into clumps as the bandits rushed in. Each member of the expedition fought as custom dictated. Strom Ornol, being at least in this wiser than one might have expected, disdained his rapier and used a hefty cut and thrust sword, swishing the thraxter about with powerful contemptuous blows. Kalu and his Pachaks simply tore into the bandits, ripping them apart whenever they made contact.

Master Exandu, as Seg had rightly observed, hauled out his single-edged sword and hit anybody who came near him. All the time he complained in his loud hectoring whine, but he kept Shanli safely tucked in behind him. Hop became most intemperate, and raged into a whirlwind, knocking bandits over and tromping them in his eagerness to get to the next.

But these were professional bandits—drikingers—and they were used to overcoming opposition. They lived by terrorizing the neighborhood, and stealing what they wanted. The expedition had in their turn taken the treasures away from the mountain hideout. Located by that gruesome apparition of a beautiful evil woman on her throne, the expedition was now about to pay a price for their audacity.

Master Exandu sliced a fellow's arm nearly off, and stumbled back, shrieking: "San Fregeff! For the sweet sake of Beng Sbodine the Mender of Men! Cast a spell! Reduce these cramphs to jelly!"

Fregeff replied in a somber voice, clearly heard through the tumult as a bell tolls through the lowing of cattle.

"The Witch of Loh has negated all spells here save my own self-preservation."

Exandu let out a yell of utter despair, and sloshed a Rapa over the head so that the Rapa's vulturine beak hung all askew and a gouting puff of brown and gray feathers spurted into the air.

The aerial onslaught of the drikingers pressed on. Seg found more and more difficulty in selecting a target who was not involved in handstrokes.

"I can't just stand here, Milsi. You constrain me."

"Look, Seg," her voice remained firm, the quaver bravely concealed. "Here come three of them to kill us."

"Three," grumped Seg, and shot, flick, flick, flick. "Now, Milsi, please. Either go into the jungle or—"

"I think," and there was a comfortableness in her tone. "I think the jungle is much more dangerous. You will not be there."

"Women," said Seg, and sought a target.

He reached up to his quiver, and groped, and brought out a rose-fletched arrow. After nocking it, he reached up and felt, carefully. There was but the one shaft left, and he knew that was a blue-fletched one of the supply with which he'd begun.

He saw Exandu, swishing and swashing, and complaining away. With a quick snap-shot, Seg disposed of the bandit about to jump on Shanli, dropping him a mere foot short of his target. The blood in Seg demanded a more direct participation... He did not nock the blue-fletched arrow. He slid the bow up his left shoulder. He half-turned.

"Milsi! I must go to Exandu's aid. The time for shooting is past. Now, you must—"

"I must go with you, Seg!"

There was no time for anything further. The sounds of combat boiled menacingly in the jungle clearing. The raw harsh stink of spilled blood broke through the jungle scents and the aromas of cooking. Shrieks and yells, the tinker-hammer of steel upon steel, the puddling of blood in the trampled mud beneath... Seg ripped out his sword and flung himself forward. Milsi followed hard in his footsteps.

He was barely in time.

Exandu, for all his moaning and groaning, could handle his heavy single-edged blade. But he was not in the same class as the guards, or the bandits.

Seg reached him in time to chop a man down, jump over him and skewer another as he was in the act of bringing an axe down on Exandu's undefended head.

For a brief instant, the fight ebbed away as the two dropped. Seg looked about, glaring, worked up. Exandu emitted a groaning laugh, a weak splutter.

"I think they run."

And it was so.

Milsi did not seem to see the corpses strewn everywhere about the clearing. She possessed a serenity in moments of crisis that warmed Seg. He knew practically nothing of her, of her life, her history, and it was most positively certain that she knew nothing of his. Yet, as Kregans say, they had been shafted by the same bolt of lightning at the moment of their meeting. If fate was to be held responsible, then fate would rejoice in their meeting. In the great circle of vaol-paol, the infinite circle of existence, they had met and the circle was complete.

The remaining bandits scrambled into their saddles. The brunnelleys fluttered and scooped wingfuls of air, soared flapping aloft. The birds whose riders had been slain joined in the departure.

"By Vox!" said Seg. He leaped for the nearest bird.

His clutching fingers almost reached the dangling clerketer, the harness which held the rider securely upon the saddle. The bird twitched a beady eye on him, reared away, flapped his wings madly. With a gouting of broken stems and leaves and detritus, the bird was airborne. He lifted away and as he went he let rip a squawk that, to Seg at least, came as a mocking screech of triumph.

"Bad cess to it!" shouted Seg. He stood, hands on hips, head upflung, staring as the birds bore away through the radiance of the twin suns.

Walking across to him, Milsi also looked up.

"You know about these wonderful birds, Seg?"

"Something."

"They are very strange to us here in Pandahem. Yet I have heard of them, of birds and animals that carry people through the sky. And now I have seen them. I wonder where they could have come from?"

"From Cottmer's Caverns, that's where, the damned unnatural things." Hop the Intemperate looked up, and in his face the look was one of bafflement. "What could you have done with one, Pantor Seg, had you caught it?"

"Why," said Seg, surprised. "Flown the thing, of course. What else?"

"You can fly a bird?"

Seg sobered. He made himself hum and haw.

"We-ell—I could have tried!"

"You'd have fallen off. A copper ob to a golden crox, you'd have toppled head over heels."

"Aye," agreed Seg, routine caution at last returning to him. "Aye, Hop. Probably."

The fact that the jungle clearing lay encumbered with corpses had different effects upon each of the people there. Most were inured by terrors to a dour acceptance of what might befall. They gave thanks to their various gods that they were not numbered among the slain.

As for clearing up—

"Leave them all," ordered Strom Ornol, striding about, still wrought up, brilliant and commanding. "Pack everything we need at once. We are leaving now."

"Strom Ornol!" Exandu waddled up. Shanli was busily cleaning his single-edged sword. "We cannot leave our poor fellows unburied, unhallowed."

"We can. The jungle will bury them for us. You know that."

"I know that. But it is not right—"

"Then you may remain here and perform your religious observances, while we march through the Snarly Hills and out of here."

"As to that—"

Seg took no part in this altercation. Like any professional warrior, any Bowman of Loh, he went about the clearing seeking his targets. He drew his knife. Cutting the arrows out had to be done carefully. He might hack a chunk of flesh away, all bloody and dripping; he had to harden himself against that. The most important item was not to damage the arrow.

Milsi did not join him during this proceeding.

During this recovery process, Seg took automatic reckoning of his shots, their effect, the accuracy of his aim.

He realized as he worked that he missed the wagers he and his old dom would have as they shot in the midst of combat. That was not a cruel or insensitive habit. They understood perhaps a little more of what possessed a man in a battle than most. There was absolutely no doubt in Seg's mind, no doubt whatsoever, that he sorely missed his blade comrade, the man these people called the Bogandur.

Kalu and his Pachaks did what any sensible mercenary would do, and helped themselves to the best of their fallen enemy's weaponry.

"Although, Seg, these drikingers use parlous poor weapons. All Krasny work. Look at this spear! The point wouldn't puncture a maiden—"

"Aye, Kalu. And their bows, which to our untold advantage they did not use, are crossbows."

Kalu laughed his Pachak laugh.

"You are not a crossbowman, Seg."

"Oh," sniffed Seg. "I have been known to use a crossbow."

The expedition had lost a number of guards in this fight. The slaves had run screaming, and now some of them returned. Some appeared to have run too far into the jungle, for they did not return. Ornol expressed his great distaste. "If they are a monster's breakfast, that is what serves them right. But it leaves us short of porters."

Seg could not stop himself.

"We're only carrying treasure, after all."

Ornol's pallid face turned on him like the head of a dinosaur above the swampy vegetation, seeking prey.

"You are above taking treasure, are you? You can joke about so important a matter? Perhaps you can afford to be disdainful of gold and gems, Seg the Horkandur!"

Milsi put a hand neatly on Seg's arm.

"Oh, no, pantor. It is not that. Seg but thinks of the provisions we must carry to take us safely through the perils of the Snarly Hills."

"As for me," quoth Exandu, scarlet, puffing, "I can barely drag my poor old bones along. Oh, how my joints ache! They are on fire—Shanli—"

"I am here, master, with a potion of Mistress Cliomin's Marrow Virtue— you will be eased in no time."

"Oh, Shanli—you are my treasure!"

"And that," said Seg, sotto voce to Milsi, "is Erthyr's sweet truth!"

The slaves set to to pack up the camp.

"Erthyr?" said Milsi. "That is—"

"He is the Supreme Being," Seg told her. "Well, of Erthyrdrin, that is. You believe in Pandrite, of course, being of Pandahem?"

"Of course. I do not call myself an overly religious woman. But I know of the power religion can afford. Pandrite is the most powerful god in Pandahem, as Armipand is the most powerful devil. But there are many other gods and many other pantheons. I have heard you speak of Vox, and of Opaz—"

"Aye."

She half-lifted one eyebrow at him; he did not elaborate.

They walked a little apart from the others, for Seg carried everything he possessed with him. Like him, Milsi had no retainers. What they could not carry they could not have.

In the end the adventurers sorted out their bundles.

Slaves carried more than slaves cared to carry. The guards, with a deal of haggling over increased rates of pay, agreed to carry bundles. The threat of the pack of toilcas remained with everyone. If that eerie witch woman in her throne could detect them and direct the bandits to them, surely she might do the same for the toilcas?

"She looked at each one of us," said Fregeff. Rik Razortooth upon his shoulder stirred a membranous wing and crept forth from the sorcerer's voluminous hood. "She searched for someone, that is clear."

"Well, we're all here," pointed out Kalu. He and his men were loaded with loot. That was their profession, venturing into tombs for treasure. They were good at their chosen task in life.

"Perhaps she looked for someone she knew, a friend, or something," said Exandu, a trifle querulously. "And when she saw us she didn't like us hanging about here."

"And we are not hanging about for long!" Ornol had unearthed a whip from his baggage, and now he cracked this with a fearsome bang.

"March! We put a long distance between us and this devilish Coup Blag before nightfall. March!"

Idly, Seg wondered what might happen if the strom accidentally flicked one of the principals with that whip. Or, come to that, if in his arrogant way he mistook a guard under a bundle for a porter and tickled him up...

That should prove amusing, at the least, by Orestorio with the Broken String!

During the fight the Lady Ilsa, Strom Ornol's traveling companion, had hidden beneath a heaped-up pile of baggage. Her corn-colored hair had never recovered from her experiences, along with the others of the expedition, in the Coup Blag, and was now a fluffy yellow mass badly in need of the attentions of a first-class hairdresser. The neatness of Milsi's hair, the severe smartness of Shanli's, were in marked contrast.

Shanli carried her accustomed burdens. Milsi had taken a part of Exandu's baggage, after a sidelong look at Seg, who humped along with a massive chest on his shoulder, out of the way of his bowstave. That chest was Exandu's. They owed the merchant nothing, of course; they carried these things out of comradeship.

The Lady Ilsa walked along freely, the new clothes she had discovered in the bandits' hideout flowing about her, her head up, unencumbered.

Well, Seg reflected not a little sourly, the silly girl fancied she was a great lady, and the very first time he'd met her she'd treated him like a slave, like dirt.

The memory cheered him up and he smiled. Milsi observed this. She did not sigh. She did realize that this craggy man with the smooth suppleness of a superb athlete had a past, just as she had. She felt for him sensations new and strange to her. She might not be frightened—too much—by a ferocious onslaught of drikingers out to slay the men and capture the women; she was deeply disturbed by her own fascination with Seg and by the turmoil of her feelings. She consciously used the word turmoil, for that word was often quoted by the poets, and used in the many plays she loved, to denote a woman's perplexities.

A turmoil of emotions had never meant much to her before, rather, she had experienced anger and resentment, for her life had not been easy. Now she was beginning to grasp a little at what the poets meant.

For a woman in her position to fall in love—actually to commit that gross folly!—would be disastrous.

And to fall in love with a wild, reckless, headstrong warrior of fortune would be the stupidest act of all.

So the expedition set off and left the horrors of the Coup Blag and struck boldly down into the Snarly Hills.

Three

Milsi expresses a considered opinion

The bold expedition had set off, full of high hopes, from the tavern called The Dragon's Roost in Selsmot. That was a small place, a stockaded area of thatched huts and houses, open and free to the air, rather grand, all things considered, to aspire to the title of town. The smot in the name might cause offense or ridicule in other folk more used to the smots of civilized places out of the jungle.

"I do not particularly wish to go to Selsmot," said Milsi quietly to Seg as they traipsed along a vague trail through the jungle.

"Oh? Well, everyone else started from The Dragon's Roost, and naturally they wish to return there. From Selsmot I suppose they'll all go off home."

"Or to more adventuring. The Pachaks, for whom I have a high regard, are indeed a most interesting party. Fancy! They make their living going around and robbing tombs—"

Seg cleared his throat.

"I'm not sure they'd appreciate your dubbing their profession a robbery. They don't just dig up graves and take away the grave-goods. Far from it. They venture into dungeons and caverns and perils where the owners set traps, both physical and sorcerous, to slay them. I'd say they earn their living. And, anyway, the whole business is a kind of game."

The trail wended past immense trees, each one isolated by its own capacity to discourage rival growths, and the way was relatively easy. Milsi looked up at Seg, and shook her head, and tut-tutted.

"When someone is out to kill me, I hardly call that a game!"

"It's not an unreasonable way of looking at it, though. At least, it helps to take the edge off the horror."

"All the same. They are stealing treasure which is not theirs."

"As I just said, my lady, if they merely robbed graves then I would agree with you. But the owners of the dungeons and tombs the Pachaks visit agree to a kind of compact with the intruders. It goes something like this: 'If you venture in here after treasure, then I will try to trap you. If you win through, you are welcome to what you have found.' In my reckoning, a great many parties of adventurers never do get out alive."

She lifted her shoulder at this.

"I suppose you are right."

"I have heard of a place called Moderdrin, where the land is studded with mounds covering immense dungeons. There the wagers go on all the time. It is well known that parties fly in from all over Paz."

"Paz?"

Seg looked at her in astonishment.

"What, my lady?"

"Paz. What is Paz?"

Seg almost groaned aloud. If his old dom were to be here and listen to this!

He explained.

"The grouping of continents and islands on this side of Kregen is called Paz. It includes this island of Pandahem, and the island of Vallia—"

She fired up at once.

"Don't talk to me of Vallia! A vile lot! They're worse pirates than those drikingers from whom we've just won free. Vallia, indeed!"

"Well, my lady, that is as may be. Paz contains the three continents of Havilfar, Segesthes and Turismond, and also the continent of Loh, which is barely regarded these days after the collapse of the ancient Empire of Loh."

"You surprise me, Seg. How do you come to know all this, or are you merely amusing yourself at my expense?"

He didn't even bother to deny the charge.

"I know, my lady, because the union of all the countries and peoples of Paz is essential if we are to face the dangers of those who raid us all."

"You speak of the Schturgins?"

"If you mean the fish-headed reivers who sail up from the other side of the world and slay and burn all our peoples and places, yes. They are variously called Shants, Shtarkins, Shanks. Usually, they are killed whenever the opportunity offers. But they are very hard to slay."

"I have heard of them only. As I said, I do not wish to go to Selsmot or this Dragon's Roost, which sounds a most deplorable tavern. I am from farther inland, upriver, where the jungle no longer chokes everything, and the plains are free..."

She stopped abruptly.

Seg could guess she was homesick for the superior climate farther north, nearer to the massive mountain chain that bisected Pandahem in an east-west direction.

He said, bending to her as they walked along: "I have nothing to detain me in Selsmot. Do you know the way to wherever it is you wish to go?"

"No questions, Seg?"

"Are questions necessary?"

"No. I find myself hardly believing in you."

He wrinkled up his eyebrows at this. He was not fool enough, after what had passed between them in the unspoken way of growing confidence, to think she meant she did not believe what he said. But he shied away from the idea of thinking that her disbelief stemmed from what she obviously meant, that he was her perfect jikai.

Seg had seen the folly of boasting. He had seen the idiocy of bloated self-esteem. This idiot Strom Ornol, for all his high-handed ways, was a mere beginner in the league of self-lovers and worshippers of their own importance.

Like a painted and caricatured devil, popping up through a trapdoor in one of the knockabout farces they loved in Vondium, the capital of Vallia, Strom Ornol came storming back down the line of marching men and women. He let his whip lick about, stinging a buttock here, striping a back there. He saw Seg.

By this time they were all aware of Ornol's penchant for quarreling. He thrived on it. No one reacted to his goading these latter days of the expedition, and this infuriated him the more. But the Lady Milsi was a newcomer, brought out of capture within the mountain.

"The drikingers did not fight particularly well, did they, Pantor Seg?"

Seg became cautious on the instant. "Perhaps they were out of practice, Strom Ornol. Mayhap they had not met real fighting men for some time."

Ornol had him in his verbal trap now. Seg's caution came from the way Ornol addressed him as pantor. Both he and the Bogandur had been recognized as lords out for adventure; their particular titles and claims to lands were left vague. Now Seg realized he had opened the way for Ornol to release the venom troubling him.

"Real fighting men? Oh, yes, of course. I, personally, slew four of them. I saw the Pachaks fighting well, as Pachaks always do. Even Master Exandu managed to knock two of the bandits over. But I was not aware of your presence, Pantor Seg, until the very end. I believe you managed two, did you not, when it was all over?"

Seg did not laugh in the popinjay's face.

He was thinking that a quiet, easy reply would be best. In the old days, he'd have just given the idiot a slap around the face and dared him to carry the matter further. These days, his recklessness had been much tempered by hard-won experience.

So that he was completely unprepared for Milsi's outburst.

"Four, you slew, did you, Ornol? Four of them! A great total! Why, Pantor Seg the Horkandur here slew four of them before anybody turned around. And then he shafted four more. Aye! And slew the last two you spoke of and the only two you happened to see."

Ornol's pallid face froze.

Seg did not bother to sigh. He didn't think with any regrets of the loss of companionship on the march back to civilization. He just dumped down Exandu's burden, took Milsi's bundle from her and threw that down.

As he was doing this, Milsi went on in a voice that cut like best Valkan steel.

"Why, you great bloated buffoon! Don't you understand anything? You're just a barrel of lard rendered down fine and dribbling over the pantry floor! Onker! Idiot! You owe your lives to Pantor Seg!"

Seg grabbed her around the waist, using his left hand. Ornol was ripping out his rapier in such an access of anger he fouled the draw, and struggled and cursed with his baldric. What he would have done had he drawn the rapier Seg did not dare to contemplate by reason of his own reply.

He just stuck his knobby fist into Ornol's jaw.

The dandy lord fell down, his mouth half-open and gargling. Seg didn't bother to hit him again. Guards were running up, yelling. No doubt he'd manage to kill a lot of them before they did for him; that was merely a foolish path. With Milsi to protect, he had to be clever and cunning, rather than brainless and muscle-bound.

Without a word he bundled Milsi up, carrying her bodily with his left arm around her waist.

He wanted to take a wager with himself that he'd reach the jungle edge before they shafted him.

He ran. He nipped between the tree trunks, using their gigantic boles to give him cover against the cruel iron birds. Suns light glowed above and the undergrowth of the rain forest opened up. Thankfully, Seg plunged into the choking green thickness, forcing his way past bushes and scrub, fending off thorned vines, smelling new stinks, feeling his feet squelching into mud, battling on.

Milsi hit him over the head.

"Put me down, you great lummox! We can get on more swiftly if I run too."

He plunked her down onto her feet so that her moccasins slurped deep into the mud.

"All right. Keep moving on, and don't talk."

"Yes, certainly—"

"Shastum!"

At that harsh command to keep silence she bit her lip. Then she started off to follow him.

Seg was not at all surprised to feel her hand grip round inside his belt as she hung on as he forged ahead.

The nature of the forest changed. Gone were the tall solemn trees with each giant isolated and denying life to lesser growths. Now the deciduous trees clustered, tangled and thickly growing, admitting light here and there and each fighting a long-drawn struggle for existence. Epiphytes twined about everywhere, sucking sustenance from the trees, and vines depended, looping, sensile, as ravenous to eat as any predator.

Over the centuries the trees shed their leaves into a deep congestion upon the floor of the forest. The leaves took time to rot down. The smell rose high, thick, cloying, a stench that gagged. Seg and Milsi moved on more through than over a giant compost heap.

The way grew hard and more hard.

Presently Seg halted.

He found a niche where a many-rooted tree left a space beneath the out-branching roots. Dampness cloyed. They were both sweating. Their clothes clung unpleasantly to them. Seg was not at all sure that the space beneath the roots was safe. A vine looped down inquisitively and he lopped the end with a slash from his sword. Milsi jerked back.

"Keep still, do not speak, and keep your eyes open."

Dumbly, she nodded.

She had known this warrior to be sudden and quick; now she was seeing a new side to his character.

Seg peered about. He felt confident that any pursuit would have given up by now, especially when the pursuers hit the choking, dense, almost impenetrable forested area. The heat was stifling. Insects buzzed and pirouetted everywhere. Pin-heads clustered and started to suck blood. Seg and Milsi, cautiously, kept on slapping them away.

As for Milsi, she could barely comprehend how she had contrived to find herself in such a terrible predicament.

What would her people say if they could see her now!

She had to persevere. She could tell this warrior Seg the Horkandur much; she knew she could not bring herself to tell him all. Not yet, at least...

A monster, all teeth and scales and spikes, blundered past, forcing his way through the tangle by bulk and power. Even he had to pick a path that avoided the worst of the natural obstructions. Seg and Milsi were quite content to let him pass without comment.

"We will wait here until I am sure no one is following us. Then we will think about a drink and some food."

"Very well, Seg."

So meek, her answer! She surprised herself!

The sounds of the forest rose and fell with the ceaseless activities of life and death. The heat sweltered. The great red sun, Zim, and the smaller green sun, Genodras, cast down a muted, entangled radiance among the fronds and branches. The pin-heads stung and were slapped away with increasing irritation.

Presently, Milsi said, "You mentioned something about eating and drinking, Seg."

"Aye."

"Well?"

Her question was not so much tart as resignedly amused, as though she was waiting expectantly for a miracle.

Patiently, keeping a continuing observation along the backtrail and all about the tangled root mass, Seg told her: "Food is no problem. As for drink, we must boil every drop of water we touch."

"I see."

She waited, sharing his patience.

Then: "Do we eat and drink now?"

"Wait."

"But—"

Still he did not look at her. He sat comfortably, relaxed and yet, as she could clearly see, immensely alert. He was so still as to appear graven from stone, the only movement the occasional impatient flick of a finger to ward off the pestering pinheads.

"Listen, Lady Milsi. In the jungle—or anywhere else, come to that— patience equals life. Impatience equals death."

"I do understand—"

"I think not."

She bit her lip in vexation. What a crude barbarian warrior he was! And yet, well, this was a part of his life she had not shared, could not have shared. The idea that this way of living might be hers from now on gave her a shudder that was not entirely delicious with romantic terror; but was not too far removed from that silly notion.

If she told him the truth about herself, he might react in a wild and unpredictable way that would spoil everything. No. Far better to get back home to safety and then sort things out.

She had no doubts whatsoever that with Seg the Horkandur to protect her she would see her home. She would arrive in the end safely; the trouble was the journey at this rate was going to take an unconscionable amount of time.

At last—at long last—Seg said, "They did not follow us this far. Now we find our meal."

A single shaft brought down a small creature of large ears and thin tail and orange and green furriness. Thankfully, as far as Milsi was concerned, it was a mammal and not a reptile. Brusquely, as Seg set about preparing the poor creature, he instructed Milsi to collect wood and break open the crumbly interior from the outer bark.

He produced his tinderbox from the soft leather pouch attached to his belt and the janul worked splendidly. In a secure cover of a mass of roots affording spying eyes no flicker of flame, Seg got the fire going. The small prepared animal, a forest colo, went on a spit over the fire.

Milsi watched fascinated as Seg's powerful hands molded and worked a chunk of the mud. He fashioned a pot and made it watertight. Water was at the moment no problem for the rains left puddles here and there— which Seg ignored. He climbed a tree alert for any unpleasant denizens with prior rights of habitation, and fetched down a cup-shaped leaf filled with liquid.

This he emptied into his pot and boiled up. It was a messy process, and twice the pot split so that he had to start afresh. But, eventually, Milsi drank water of a brackish and vegetation-tasting quality. It tasted fine.

The little colo went down well.

"Now we march."

"The way is dreadfully hard."

"We follow where these blundering great monsters open a way for us. We go quietly. We listen, and we smell. We will see them before they see us."

"I hope to Pandrite you are not mistaken."

"You can only die once."

"Oh, I agree. But that is one time too many for me."

He smiled, did not answer, and set off.

Although, of course, with the fiendish cunning of some wizards to command unholy skills it might be perfectly possible to die and be resurrected and so die all over again... This prospect was one which displeased Seg enormously. His upbringing, wild and free though it had been, had inculcated in him a respect for the processes of nature.

His respect was genuine and extended universally—save in one thing.

Seg had no respect for anything that interfered with his procurement of the finest bowstaves he could cut.

A vine studded with short hard spikes lashed in from nowhere. A shiny brown spine caught in Milsi's tunic just to the side of her navel and whipped back, tearing the blue cloth around to the small of her back. She yelped, and Seg's single slash dropped the vine onto the forest floor, wriggling and squirming.

"Did it—?"

"No, thank the good Pandrite."

The skin had not been punctured, no blood had been drawn. Very seriously, his face expressionless, Seg shifted the ripped blue cloth aside and inspected Milsi's stomach, side and back. He could see no lacerations in that tanned pink skin. He breathed out a relieved sigh.

"That is one problem of walking down a trail made by the monsters."

"It is still far preferable to struggling through that awful jungle."

As they went on it occurred to Seg to wonder how Milsi's skin under her tunic was so smoothly tanned. Since he had known her she had always had clothes, of some sort or another, rags mostly until the last chamber of the Coup Blag, to cover her. The suns would give you a wonderful tan if you stayed out for a responsible length of time.

Well, when the time was opportune he'd mention it to her. Her answer would probably involve carefree days of sunbathing at home. Her home, he gathered, was situated not in the capital of this land of Croxdrin but, as she had indicated, farther north out in the open plains in Mewsansmot.

There was no chance of conversation as they walked along the monster-opened trail so that much as he would have liked to find out more about her and her history, as any wandering fellow lusted after details of people and places and things, Seg was constrained to follow his own dictum of patience.

He had the map of the area fairly well embedded in his skull. The river, known as the River of Bloody Jaws, looped in an enormous arc around the Snarly Hills. Traffic went by river. The teeth and jaws ferociously at work in the Kazzchun River were not as fearful as the terrors of the forest.

From where they now were any direction other than a heading with west in it would bring them to the river.

North with a touch of easting, he decided, would be best. If the distance to the river was the same no matter in which direction they went, then by going north the distance to cover on the river would be shortened. When they stopped for one of the periodic rests he insisted on, mindful of the husbanding of marching men's—and women's!—strengths, Milsi began prying in order to open up a little more of the story of this fearsome warrior bowman.

"For a start, Seg, how did you come by your cognomen?"

At that Seg laughed out loud.

"Horkandur?" He was clearly delighted by his own thoughts. Milsi smiled in response. She enjoyed being with Seg, and for this space of time at least forgot her own problems in their shared perils.

"I know it means you have gained renown as a great archer—"

"In that, the sobriquet does not lie overmuch, although I detest braggarts. No, my old dom, he whom you know as the Bogandur, gave it to me, when I gave him his nickname. This was when we met up with the expedition at The Dragon's Roost—"

She showed her astonishment.

"But that defies honor! You give each other resounding titles, just like that? Really, Seg, you amaze me."

"We did not wish to give our true names."

"On the run?"

Again he laughed.

"In a fashion; but not from any just pursuit. We felt it more prudent. My name is Seg Segutorio."

Very gravely she inclined her head, and said: "Lahal, Seg Segutorio."

"Lahal, my Lady Milsi. And the rest of your name?"

Her smile faltered.

A flutter seized her, so that she looked up, and exclaimed at the sight of two bright red eyes staring down at them from a branch of a nearby tree. Seg looked and saw the little furry body, the tail wrapped about a thinner twig, and said: "Another little colo. Perhaps we will have to eat his cousin tonight. For now, he is safe."

The pathetic interlude gave her time to decide what to say.

"My father's name was Javed Erithor the Good. My mother's name was Natema Parlaix. I may use either name, as I wish."

"I know of the custom. In Erthyrdrin we have a different system of naming of names. I was able to assume the honor of the torio when my father died. He, too, was a good man, if a trifle reckless—"

"Like his son?"

"Oh, aye. But I learn. When I die my son, my eldest son, Drayseg, will become Seg Segutorio."

She felt a distinct stab at her heart.

"You have children? You are married?"

Seg's face abruptly took on the look of a sky at nightfall, before a thunderstorm. She did not flinch back; had she done so no one watching would have been surprised.

"I am blessed with a family of three, and, yes, I was married."

"Oh—I am sorry."

"I will tell you. But we have rested enough. We must push on."

"Of course."

Only when they were once more marching along the blundering monster's trail did she think to wonder just where his family might be now, what place in all of Kregen they called home. Seg—who was Seg Segutorio—had taken on a new dimension. He remained a wild and reckless wandering warrior; but he had roots.

As for Seg he was trying to puzzle out the inner meaning of the names of Milsi's family. They did not sound like Pandahemic names.

Four

Diomb and Bamba

A clattering commotion broke out ahead along the trail. A trilling noise as of a cage full of parakeets all shrilling away and fluttering their wings against the bars of the cage mingled with sharper shrieks of rage and pain.

Seg put out a hand to halt Milsi and she walked on for a moment so that her stomach pressed against Seg's sinewy palm. She was highly conscious of the contact; Seg did not notice.

He stared evilly along the trail, tensed ready for action and yet perfectly relaxed. When he had sized up the situation out there his brain would tell his muscles what to do. They would respond instantly. That was the secret, albeit a simple one, of readiness for action.

Presently, as the uproar continued unabated, without gaining or losing volume, he padded cautiously forward. He kept to the side of the trail, and he whispered so that no one more than two or three paces away could overhear.

"Watch for those dratted killer vines, Milsi."

"Oh—yes!"

The trail bent here as the monster who had made it failed to break through a tree all of five hundred seasons old. With his side against the tree, Seg peered cautiously around, and along the farther extent of the trail.

What he saw filled him with astonishment. Milsi joined him, and sucked in her breath, and said: "They are dinkus. Savage. They used poisoned darts."

"So I see."

The dinkus appeared to be caught up in a situation at once horrific and comic. They were pygmies. Each dinko stood about one meter tall, built like an apim, with the exception that from the cunningly fashioned shoulder blades swung four arms instead of two. Each man was stark naked apart from a bark apron.

They did use poisoned darts, which they shot from blowpipes.

They were engaged in a fight between two different tribes, as was evident from the colors of the feathers they wore in their clay-matted hair, and their private fight had been interrupted by a toilca. Therein lay the comic aspect of the horror. To a dinko a toilca was a monstrous beast.

"I really do think this is no concern of ours, Milsi."

"You are right. Yet they are so—and they cannot shoot their darts at the toilca's scales and hope to penetrate."

Looking out, Seg saw that the toilca had already ripped up or squashed half a dozen of the dinkus. The two opposing parties had, perforce, joined forces to fight the monster. Seg made up his mind.

He stepped out into the center of the trail.

"Hai!"

So wrapped up in the combat were most of the pygmies that they did not hear him. Some did. They swiveled to stare down the trail, and the long blowpipes switched up most evilly.

"Hai!"

And Seg loosed twice, swift accurate shots that punched clean through the eyes of the toilca under the horny protecting scales. The monster lashed about, writhing, and the pygmies leaped for their lives.

With bow ready, arrow nocked and the shaft half drawn, held by his left hand, Seg walked forward. He lifted his right hand.

"Llahal! I trust I have helped you, friends."

They chattered out, parakeets flinging their wings at a cage. Their voices chittered.

Then one with the most feathers in his matted hair stepped forward. Instantly another stepped up alongside the first. He wore just about as many feathers, but they were red as the first's were blue.

"Hai! Llahal. Are you friend?"

The blue-feathered pygmy was not to be left in the shade.

"Hai! Answer me quickly, or you die!"

"Now hold on," shouted Seg. "Just hold on a minute. I've shot the poor dratted toilca for you. I do not expect much in the way of thanks, but I do expect a little friendship—"

"No boltim is a friend to any dinko."

"Boltim?"

"That means big man," whispered Milsi.

"I know that—oh, I see. Yes." Seg retained that cunning archer's left-handed grip on bow and shaft.

"I may be a boltim. I bear you no ill will. By the Veiled Froyvil! I could have passed by and you'd all be dead, chomped up by that monster!"

The fellow with the red feathers said: "That is true, by Clomb of the Ompion Never-Miss."

"Whoever he and it may be," said Seg—to himself.

Blue feathers wasn't so sure.

"You speak with a false tongue," he started.

"And if I had not spoke you'd be quietly digesting in that toilca's insides. Why, man, he could eat all of you and look around for more!"

"Seg!"

Assuredly, that had not been a politic thing to say.

Seg blustered on.

"We are just taking a little stroll along here, doing no harm to anyone, least of all you, noble dinkus. We have helped you. Now we will go on our way and give you the remberees."

A chattering gobble of argument among the pygmies followed. They spoke the universal Kregish that had been imposed on the world, heavily adulterated by accent and local dialect words. They began to form up into two separate bands. Beside the long blowpipes and the quivers of darts slung over their shoulders by straps they carried cudgels. These were, by ordinary standards, puny. If one was laid alongside the head of one dinko, powered by the angry muscles of another, the results could be fatal.

Seg did not speak again.

He slowly withdrew to the tree, and stood, silently, watching. Before very long, tribal hatreds flared up. The red feathers and the blue feathers started off, bashing at one another. And Seg noticed a curious fact. They did not puff out their cheeks into twin balloons and blow darts tipped with poison at one another. They slung the blowpipes down or over their backs and started in a-slugging one another with the cudgels. He understood what he was seeing. This was survival of the species, survival of the dinkus, against the perils of their home in the jungle.

Presently the fight was of such an intensity that he and Milsi could edge along on the fringe of the trail and pass by without any one of the battling pygmies bothering his head about them.

They reached the far side of the conflict and turned to rejoin the trail out of sight of the dinkus.

Seg fell over a couple of naked bodies entwined beside a bush. He staggered and regained his balance with the litheness of a cat. The blowpipe quivered three inches from his chest, the lad's cheeks distended like twin red apples.

Without hesitation Seg's left hand holding bow and arrow swished around, deflecting the blowpipe. The lad expelled his breath in a mighty gasp and the dart shot off into the jungle. At once a shrill squawk sounded.

Seg said, "I hear you hit your target then, my lad. For, of course, you were not shooting at me, were you?"

His gaze beat down on the pygmy lad. He was a young dinko, and he was cuddling up to a younger dinka, who still lay by the bush, rigid with terror.

"No," said the lad. He swallowed. He looked up and up to this monstrous boltim who towered like an ancient tree of the forest. "No."

"That is wise."

"Oh, the poor things!" exclaimed Milsi. She came forward in a rush and gathered the girl up and cradled her as she might a child. The girl was crying.

"So that's the way of it, then," observed Seg.

He sighed. Sex and passion and tribal taboos had played tricks with Kregen's past, and no doubt would continue to do so into the future.

The lad wore red feathers.

The girl wore blue feathers.

"They will surely part us if they find us," said the boy. He spoke up bravely. "If they do not kill us."

"I do not think they would kill you. Life has to be precious to anyone living in the forest and fighting its perils."

"You don't know them—they are rigid as a petrified tree. Blood lines, inheritance, taboos—and I love Bamba."

The girl Bamba, cradled in Milsi's arms, sniffled out: "And I love Diomb."

Seg released the arrow grip and stowed the shaft. He was not about to allow himself to become embroiled in the half-comical, half-tragical affairs of these little people of the forest.

"Well," he said with some brutality. "I don't know what you two were doing. But if you can't go home to your tribes you'll have to run away. I wish you well."

"We were running away and they caught us. Then the toilca came along, and—"

"The toilca is dead and your respective tribes are trying to bash each other's brains out. You'd better cut along sharpish."

"Oh," wailed the girl. "Would that Clomba of the Fruit Tree Eternal would aid us now!"

The pygmy lad, naked save for a bark apron, clutching his blowpipe, stared up at Seg. His face was formed pleasingly, with regular features, and his dark eyes showed a bright intelligence. Just as Seg was telling himself that any eyeball can shine up nicely, that does not mean its owner has any brains at all, Diomb rapped out as though a bottle-cork burst from the neck: "We were running away. We were going to cross the river and seek our fortune. We can come with you. That is excellent."

"Do what?"

"Why, boltim, Bamba and me will walk with you. Together we can see the wide world."

"Oh, aye!"

Milsi spoke up and shattered Seg afresh.

"Oh, yes, Seg! Do let them come." Then, forgetting for the moment where she was, she added: "I shall take Diomb and Bamba with me. They are very welcome."

Seg looked at the Lohvian longbow in his left fist. He shook his head. Then he shoved the bow up onto the peak of his shoulder, snapped it fast, turned about and said, "Very well! Let them come. And you take care of them, my Lady Milsi."

She flared up at this, angry, and yet despairing of ever making any man see sense.

"I shall! Do not fret over that, Seg Segutorio!"

Five

Out of the Snarly Hills

In the time it took them to march through the forest to the River of Bloody Jaws, Seg was forced to admit to himself that the dinkus, Diomb and Bamba, proved themselves to be a fine addition to the little party. They knew this place, for it was their home. Diomb had only recently gone through the mysteries and ordeals of manhood and emerged as a dinko hunter. Bamba and he were quite clearly intoxicated with each other.

That was very nice for them—now.

Seg scowled a bit, and looked loweringly on Milsi, who, for her part, disdained to notice.

When they heard up ahead the clink and clatter of bottles and glasses, the apparent murmur of happy human voices, Diomb brightened up.

He was a mischievous fellow. He glanced up sideways at Seg, half-laughing.

"Ah, Seg, do you hear that? Friends are waiting for us."

Seg had enough human tolerance to wait awhile before believing the dinko meant what he said. The sounds reached them from beyond a screen of vegetation, for the forest appeared more open here and they knew by this that they must be nearing the river. The trackways criss-crossed, and not by man but by the increasing number of animals living here.

"Friends?" said Seg. He decided to play along with Diomb for a time. "They sound as though they are having a good time. And I could do with a wet."

"A wet?"

Seg smiled in his turn. There were so many things these pygmies did not know. Their life was primitive. They had a lot to learn.

"Yes. A drink of something other than water. It *sounds* as though up there they have plenty of bottles."

Diomb caught the inflexion in Seg's voice.

"Yes, Seg. Bottles. I know of them but have never seen one. They must have some over there."

"Well, then, I suggest you toddle along and ask."

Seg stopped beside the bush and looked down on Diomb. He quite expected the pygmy to stop, also. Then there would be a crestfallen explanation. For, of course, there were no happy drinkers up ahead celebrating. The clinking sounds, the murmurous voices, were produced by a killer plant known to civilized men as the Cabaret Plant. What the dinkus called it Seg didn't know, and was not just at the moment particularly interested to find out.

Instead, boldly, Diomb marched out past the bush and into the clearing.

Seg watched.

Out there in its cleared area the Cabaret Plant carried on its audio-pantomime. The sounds were remarkably realistic. To a forest-dwelling dinko who hadn't even seen a bottle or glass, the sounds must come as mysterious and evocative. The plant itself was a fine full-grown specimen.

The gourd-shaped main body was capacious enough to hold three or four people. The sounds of voices trilling and laughing and the clink of bottle against glass increased in intensity. From the top of the gourd rose a tall stem crowned with an orange flower. Seg's lips drew tightly together.

He drew his sword.

Diomb carried a large leaf plucked from a greenish-blue low-growing bush and as he stepped out he bent his legs, his knees like springs, and he moved gently from side to side.

The orange flower lashed.

It swept viciously down toward the pygmy. As it struck it opened wide to reveal its flower-petalled head encrusted with spines.

The deadly orange flower slashed at Diomb. He waited, then sprang swiftly to the side, trailing the leaf which was smashed full out of his hand. He darted back, and his face blazed with pride and prowess.

"Hai!" cried Bamba, glowing with reciprocal pride.

"Huh," grunted Seg, sourly. "Some of the tribal fun and games, is it? Proving you're a man among men?"

"More than that, Seg." Diomb waited, judged his moment exactly, and darted in, snatched up the leaf and withdrew. The orange flower lashed about in baffled frenzy.

"I have never done that before," remarked Diomb. "I have practiced, of course, with my friends slashing at me and pretending to be the Naree-Giver."

"It was well-done, Diomb," declared Milsi, with a glance at Seg that put him in his place.

"All right, Diomb," said Seg, almost growling. "I knew what was what the moment we heard the Cabaret Plant. What you call a Naree-Giver." He looked at the leaf which Diomb was now most carefully inspecting. "Narees, is it? This is how you come by the poisoned darts for your blowpipes?"

"This is one way, yes."

The leaf was struck through by the poisoned spines from the plant. There must have been thirty of them. Now Diomb began a painstaking removal of each spine, putting them into a bark pouch in his apron.

"We splice the spine to the main shaft of the naree. These will make very good weapons, you will see."

"I daresay."

Seg decided not to feel chastened. He'd had a nasty experience with a Cabaret Plant before, and he'd been classing them as among the more hideous of the horrors of the jungle. And here this little pygmy lad trotted along and baited the ferocious plant and took from it its spines to use as his blow-pipe darts—and had the effrontery to give the thing a name that indicated the esteem in which he held it! Enough to make a bluff tough fighting man spit.

The last Cabaret Plant Seg had encountered had cost him ten gold pieces...

Milsi broke into his thoughts with a pert suggestion that it was high time they stopped for something to eat.

Diomb's skills as a forest hunter provided ample food. Water continued to be boiled. They selected a good campsite and settled down. By the signs within the forest they hoped to reach the river on the morrow, or the next day.

Seg inquired if Diomb shot his dinner with his poisoned naree and then ate it, poison and all.

"We usually snare our food, as I have done since we met. But if we have to shoot with a poisoned naree there are ways of boiling or baking the poison out. I can bring a small quarry down with an unpoisoned dart, of course."

"Oh, of course."

Milsi gave him a look.

When they had eaten, Seg felt that a small rest would be in order. He wanted to know more of Milsi's life story; yet he was reluctant to press too hard. He did not wish to reveal very much about his own life, for that would take a clever man to explain and a trusting woman to believe, by Vox!

"Seg," she said as they lay side by side, some way apart from the two dinkus who were out of sight together. "Why are you so hard on Diomb?"

"Hard? Me, hard on the little fellow?"

"Perhaps you are jealous of him?"

The torrent of images, desires, passions that flared into Seg's brain made him almost gasp aloud. He rolled over and stared off into the forest, away from Milsi. He was vividly aware of her presence at his side. Jealous? He was conscious of all that he was missing, that until his meeting with Milsi he had banished from his life. Well, now was the time to tell her a few home truths that might explain a little more...

"I told you I was once married."

"Yes."

"My wife was called Thelda. She was a—a funny woman. She always meant well. I could see how she tried. Yet—"

Milsi could not see his face. She said: "You need not explain, Seg, if it is painful. I think I understand. One meets these people in life who mean so well, and yet whose every effort turns to disaster."

He rolled over to look at her.

"Well—it wasn't disaster all the time! No. I won't have that. I loved Thelda. I truly did. We had a good life together, and there were the children, and our friends, and life to be lived."

"And she died. I am sorry, truly sorry."

"I thought she had died."

"Oh?"

"There was a difficult period. We called it the Time of Troubles. We were separated. I was sore wounded. I searched for Thelda, searched for her where I knew she would be, and then in our home. I could not find her. I was made slave—"

"Oh, Seg!"

"It was not pleasant. My old dom hoicked me out of that and I had to spend time recovering from my wound and, well, everyone said Thelda was dead. So I believed it, too."

"And she wasn't?"

"I got over Thelda. I said I could not continue to love a ghost, a person broken from the ib. I put her out of my mind. But I did not look at another woman. I was a husk, you see, until..." He stopped, and plucked a thin twig from the bush by which they lay and stuck it between his teeth. He chewed reflectively.

Milsi said nothing.

"Only recently my old dom told me that Thelda was alive. She believed me to be dead, as I believed her. She had found a man, a man I knew slightly, an honest, upright man. They loved and were married and there was a child. This was done in all honor."

"Oh, Seg!"

"Yes, well, that is all ancient history now."

She felt perplexed.

"You did not say how old your son—Drayseg—was."

While the people of Kregen could live to well beyond two hundred years—if they did not get themselves killed off before then—they did not alter a great deal in appearance from the time they reached maturity to a few years before they died. Despite this there were small signs by which one person could estimate the age of another with fair accuracy. Without this subtle judgment unfortunate liaisons might occur; a passionate romance between a young person of twenty-five with another who looked just the same but was a hundred and twenty-five, might be acceptable to them, might be warmingly wonderful an example of human faith and love; it was also a cruel trick to play on frail humanity by fate.

Milsi wrinkled up her eyebrows at Seg. He was clearly a mature man, strong and craggy, and a man she found undeniably handsome and attractive. He was a few years older than she was. But he talked as though these events had taken place seasons and seasons ago.

"How old Dray is means nothing," he said at last. "The twins are a bit younger. They're all off in the great wide world adventuring and having fun, I hope, and all my prayers to Erthyr go to protect them from the perils of life."

This was the difficulty, Seg knew, that his old dom had had to face many times. They'd both bathed in the Sacred Pool of Baptism in far Aphrasöe, in the River Zelph, along with their families and good friends. This assured them of a thousand years of life, together with the capacity to recover from wounds with an amazing rapidity. Seg judged Milsi to be a few years younger than she appeared to be, the age he'd been when he and the riotous crew had all flown off to Aphrasöe, the Swinging City. He had grown considerably in judgment and wisdom since then, although, naturally, he was still your wild reckless warrior kind of fellow, to be sure.

He found himself wondering how Thelda would handle the odd circumstances that she did not appear to age as her husband, Lol Polisto, aged. For Thelda, as far as he knew, was not aware that she would live for a thousand years. That was cruel. He would have to rectify that, and, if possible, make arrangements for Lol, also, to take that miraculous baptism. Again and again they'd discussed, in all the various places of Kregen they'd adventured together, he and the Bogandur, just how you dealt with this unexpected gift of a thousand years of life—if gift it was.

There had to be a limit; how to apply that cruel limiting judgment? Milsi, now...

He was about to attempt some blundering pack of lies to explain away this surprising lack of knowledge of his children's ages, when Bamba popped out from the bush pushing her bark apron straight, followed at once by Diomb.

"Seg! We must—"

"Now by all the Shattered Targes in Mount Hlabro!" burst out Seg. "What is it now?"

"We must hide. A party of boltim approach, and they may not be friendly."

Seg grunted. "Won't be, more likely."

Keeping low into the bushes, silent, watchful, the little party watched as the newcomers stalked and staggered past.

The Katakis stalked, strutting in heavy boots, flicking their whips and flicking their tails at the coffle of slaves who staggered, struggling on, naked and chained.

Seg counted the Katakis. Twenty of the diffs, twenty fierce, voracious, unpleasant and highly lethal slavers, twenty packets of sudden death. Flared of nostrils, the Katakis, low of frowning forehead, with black hair wild and tangled, with jagged teeth and hungry jaws. They were half-armored and carried spears and swords and bows. They urged on the slaves, who were of many races, without mercy, shouting the ugly word to force on dead-tired muscles and aching limbs.

"Grak, you yetches! Grak!"

Seg thought of Milsi. He thought, also, of Diomb and Bamba. Well, he could shaft half a dozen and then they'd be on him and slay him. That would not help either the poor devils in the coffle or Milsi and the dinkus.

So, then. He must perforce crouch here like any coward and wait until the slavers had passed.

He did not think it necessary to advise Milsi of his decision. For her part, she stared unseeingly upon the slaves, shuddered at the predatory Katakis, kept very silent and fervently prayed that her great jikai, this warrior bowman Seg Segutorio, would not conceive his honor demanded he rush out to fight and die.

That this illogical behavior might be expected from Seg was to her the greatest proof of her irrationality in finding herself in this position. No sensible person would interfere with slavers about their business, and most certainly not Katakis. The bladed steel strapped to their tails whickered like summer lightning, the flats belaboring the slaves in vicious spanking buffetings. If those steel blades turned edge on...

When the miserable coffle had struggled on and was out of sight and sound, Diomb stretched and said: "Now, Seg, tell me what that was all about. I am most anxious to find out about the outside world. But I own I do not understand what I saw."

"Those ugly brutes were Katakis, what we call Whiptails. Steer clear of 'em unless you want trouble. The slaves were—"

"Slaves?"

Seg tried to explain. Diomb interrupted.

"I know that a person may own certain items—my blowpipe and darts, my apron. But nothing much else. The elders have explained much of the outside world to us, for we are not ignorant savages. I thought I understood the principle of possession. But owning people—"

"There's a lot in the world you have to learn about," said Milsi. "And I shall be happy to show you and Bamba."

The trouble with a lot of this wonderful world of Kregen could be summed up in the one word—slavery. Seg had had his run-ins with the diabolical custom and so he could, while deploring Milsi's attitude, understand it. He did not look forward with any pleasure to what the future held when he began the process of correcting her attitude. He was long past the stage when he consulted his conscience on the matter. He was long past the stage when he worried over the problem of whether or not he had the right to change people's minds on the question of slavery. He had seen enough. He had lost a great deal over the slavery business, quite happily, and he was prepared to go to great lengths to do what he could to stamp out the evil.

He did not doubt that his explanation of slavery would be somewhat different from Milsi's.

A few dwaburs farther on they ran into a marshy area.

"We have the Malar Marshes in Erthyrdrin," said Seg. "I am not enamored of them. We had best find another way around."

That being agreed, they cut inland a trifle to circumvent the noxious areas.

Milsi chattered away to Diomb and Bamba. Seg strode on silently, biding his time.

When he had an opportunity at the next halt to tell Milsi a thing or three, he found himself instead attempting to explain the nomenclature customs of Erthyrdrin.

"My children may call themselves Segutorio, or Segutoria, as a kind of surname when out of the country. That is, if it fits in with the country's customs. But the Torio is reserved for the eldest, and the first syllables are always the same. The girl child will take her mother's name as a second name, and when she marries may attach her husband's name if she wishes."

He picked a scrap of meat from between his teeth with a sliver of clean-stripped wood and not his finger. He was finicky with the operation. Milsi noticed this.

He went on, "My lad Valin, Silda's twin, is called Valin Segutorio at home; but that is not really correct and we would not do so in Erthyrdrin. He—"

"But, Seg. I thought your home was Erthyrdrin? Where is it you call home, then?"

No good for Seg to castigate his loose tongue.

He replied easily enough, and with enough truth to ease his conscience.

"Oh, we have a fine home in Valka. But, as I was saying—"

"Valka? I have not heard of it."

"North of here. But, as I was saying—"

"North?"

Seg sighed. Women were the very devil for sticking to a point you didn't want explored, and likewise the very devil for being loose-minded and scatty when it pleased them. Damned clever, women, usually.

"It's a small island in the Sea of Opaz."

"H'm. It must be a very small island, then, for I know most of the more important ones along the north coast of Pandahem in the Sea of Opaz. Although, Seg, we Pandaheem more often call the sea the Ocean of Panda."

"Oh, yes, that shows how cut off we are there."

He did not dare to look at her in case she saw the unease in him. The devil Chanko-taroth take it! He did not wish to lie to Milsi; but he didn't want too much of his past to be revealed until he was ready to do the revealing.

Milsi ran swiftly over the major islands whose names she knew up there off the north coast of the main island. Valka? There was a ring in the name, a faint memory of hearing it, spoken in great passion by her father. But the memory would not coalesce.

Around almost all the coasts of Kregen the islands clustered as thickly as bubbles on the surface of boiling milk. There were far too many for all to be recalled at will.

"You were saying?"

"Oh, yes. Valin will never be Valin Valintorio unless he gains great renown, is recognized, can persuade the elders and the secret ones to grant him the torio. Then he will have a family, and lands, and may call himself Valin Valintorio. I look forward to the day."

"And the name Seg will go on through the main line?"

"Just so."

"With us it is different." Then she stopped and bit her lip. "I mean, well, here the male line is recognized only if the female line is in accord."

"That means, exactly?"

"Well, Seg, to give the example that has exercised the minds of everyone in Croxdrin lately. The king, Crox, lost his wife and entire family in a dreadful accident. It was through his wife that his legal entitlement to the crown was established."

"So he had to look around for the next legal heir?"

"It has been known in the past for fathers to marry their daughters to secure the throne—in name only, I hasten to add. So—"

"Oh, I see. I heard that this poor Queen Mab whom you served was married to the king and he departed in the same hour to this fateful expedition into the Coup Blag. Then Queen Mab followed—she must have loved him, then, although I was told the marriage was political only."

"It was only political! There was no love there, only a dreadful acceptance of fate."

"Well, you should know, you were her lady in waiting."

"Yes."

"Diomb and Bamba have stopped frisking about and are looking expectant. It is time we moved on."

Then she surprised him.

"Time is a terrible thing, Seg the Horkandur! I could almost wish this journey, which now is far more pleasant than when we began, could go on forever."

"But you want to get home to Mewsansmot!"

"I do, I do. And yet..."

"Come on, you two!" called Bamba. "Diomb is quite impatient in this as in other refined things."

"Coming."

Their route to skirt the marshes lay northwest, north, northeast and then, just to make sure, they curved down a little and struck along east-northeast.

"And, my fine young friends," quoth Seg, lustily, striding along. "At the first decent hostelry we run across, I shall treat you to roast vosk, momo-lams, squish pie, and a heaping dish of palines. *And* there will be ale, and wine—believe you me!"

"We had best, perhaps," said Milsi, most anxiously, "be very wary regarding ale and wine for Bamba and Diomb."

"Naturally. But they'll down their jugs with the best in no time, you will see."

"We have strange stories about the dinkus from the forest. We must take care."

"If anyone offers insult to our friends, Milsi—"

"You, Seg Segutorio the Horkandur, had best stay out of stupid arguments until we—"

"Assuredly, my lady," and Seg bowed a deep and most ironical bow.

"Oh, you!" flared Milsi, the color rising.

Seg could well understand what Milsi meant when she said she wished this journey could go on forever. The forest had now become far less hostile, the Snarly Hills dwaburs to the rear. There were few habitations, as most of the villages and towns were located along the river; but there were villages within the forest. The slavers operated here, and that made life terrible. But for the adventurers marching through the forest, eyes and ears alert, the dangers were by now a part of life, accepted by the two apims in the same spirit as the two dinkus.

The air breathed less oppressively. There was food aplenty, and water—boiled to drink. The life made men and women hardy and inured to hardship. And yet, surely, to a lady brought up as a handmaiden to serve a queen, this rude out-of-doors adventuring life could not hold aught of pleasure? Yet Milsi throve.

Seg, wistful, was reminded of ancient days.

He said, once: "Milsi, do you know the difference between fallimy and vilmy flowers?"

She laughed in an off-hand way. "Of course." Then she saw how serious he was beneath the casual attitude. "One is good for poultices, the other to clean disgusting corroded cesspits and cisterns."

"Yes. And you could tell them apart?"

"Well, would I put a cistern-cleaning poultice on your wound—" She saw him. "Seg!"

"It is all right. I am ashamed. I should not have said anything—"

"Can you tell me?"

"Not now." He walked on ahead, very quickly, and even in the state he was in he knew Milsi would be safe with Diomb and Bamba. He should not have spoken! It was cruel, degrading. It was unholy. Poor Thelda! He had loved Thelda, he had. They had had their quarrels, as who hadn't, but they had had a splendid life. And now she was gone, married to another man, and here he was, a wandering adventurer desperately trying to relive a part of his life that was dead.

He was not the same Seg Segutorio who had so happily marched through the Hostile Territories, all those seasons ago, with Thelda, and with his old dom and Delia. No. He was different now. He'd been a great noble, lording it over rich lands, and he'd lost all that because he'd tried to outlaw slavery. He'd told kings and emperors what they could do. He'd commanded armies in battle. And now he had found a woman in his life for whom he could cherish a great and genuine affection, who might turn back the years for him, cause the clepsydra's water to run back up into the upper vessel...

Milsi wouldn't so confidently, meaning the best, have slapped a harsh cistern-cleaning poultice on the wound in his old dom's chest... Poor Thelda! She was gone. He no longer loved the woman who was Thelda and who was married to Lol Polisto. He recalled the love he had felt for the Thelda of long ago, when they'd marched through the Hostile Territories, when they'd struggled for an empire.

No. It was so.

He could find it in his heart to love this Milsi, for all the oddness he sensed about her history. He had not so much found in her a new meaning to life, as a new reason to live a proper life once again.

As to her feelings for him, they remained obscure, despite that he felt she had been shafted with him by the same bolt of lightning. It was entirely possible when they returned to civilization and her home she would give him a cool "thank you" and then turn away and forget him.

Well, so be it, by Vox! He knew what he wanted, now. So, if that was how the adventure turned out, he'd use what skill and cunning he had to alter that outcome...

All that had happened was gone. It was smoke blown with the wind.

"By Beng Dikkane!" he said, calling on the patron saint of all the ale-drinkers of Paz. "I could do with a wet right now!"

Following on, Diomb kept up a stream of questions.

"What is vosk? What are momolams? What is ponsho? What is dopa?"

Half-laughing, Milsi explained carefully. She was mindful of the responsibilities she had taken on with her acceptance of the two dinkus as companions.

Seg could not fail to notice the way in which she handled them, easy and yet with a quiet manipulation she must have learned as a lady in waiting to a queen.

Bamba chattered as much as Diomb.

"What is a spinning wheel? What are carts?"

And Diomb: "What is a ship?"

Seg slowed, ears cocked, listening.

Milsi showed no hesitation in her reply. She spoke with the same sure conviction anyone would use explaining what a cart was.

"Oh, a ship is a very large boat, and I have told you that a boat floats on water and carries people and things. Ships travel far over the seas, driven by the winds of heaven, and bring strange and exotic merchandise back home."

Walking on, Seg reflected that Milsi knew much and spoke warmly of ships. Here, in the midst of a jungle with a river, a great river, to be sure, as her only source of information? She could have learned this from books. But, from the way she spoke, Seg was convinced she had seen what she so vividly described, had seen the armadas of sail ploughing the shining seas, venturing to the corners of the world, sailing home again, argosies of treasure.

If his honorable intentions toward her were ever to be realized there was much, a very great deal, he must learn about her history. Then he laughed to himself in his old reckless raffish way. By the Veiled Froyvil! What did her history matter to him? He would do what he would do, and play his part manfully, and if Erthyr the Bow smiled on him he would win what his heart desired.

Six

Milsi causes more aggravation

They reached the Kazzchun River in good order and turned north along the bank. The brown water slid past and upon its still amiable flow the keels of commerce passed up and down. There were still plenty of sails to be seen, for Milsi said the head of navigation lay far upriver, and beyond that the paddle driven barks penetrated for many more dwaburs yet.

They entered the first township with due caution, although Milsi insisted that strangers would receive the need that was their due.

"A hulking great Bowman warrior, and two dinkus from the forest may attract unwelcome attention," she said, with that tiny dint between her delectable eyebrows. "But a few cheerful words, and perhaps a small offering to the local godling in his temple, should smooth the way."

"I trust so," said Seg. "Although the local godling's temple I am most in need of is to be found in the nearest tavern."

"I shall begin to believe you are a drunkard, Seg Segutorio!"

"Not so, my lady. Just that a fellow needs to wash away the dust from his throat from time to time."

"We shall see."

The place was called Lasindle, small and rundown, with wooden airy houses roofed with the leaves of papishin that were commonly used for this purpose in many parts of Kregen. Neither Seg nor Milsi felt any surprise that places in the world separated by vast distances should grow the same kinds of plants and harbor the same kinds of animals. That was perfectly natural to them. There were plenty of strange and weird plants and animals to be found inhabiting selected portions of the world to make those found universally to pass without comment.

The local godling was a fish-tailed lady called Kazzchun-faril and her temple lifted above the houses, and its walls were of wood lavishly carved and decorated. The papishin-leaved roof covered a goodly area of cells and secret places. Milsi and the others went into the outer court and the sight of two gold croxes made the priestess's eyes light up with avarice.

"May the great and glorious fishiness of Kazzchun-faril light upon you and your hooks never be drawn empty," intoned a lady in a swathing robe of fish-scales, and tawdry bangles. "Go with the goddess's blessing."

So, with that out of the way, they went across the muddy square to The Hook and Net. Here a few copper coins produced the local brew. Without proper corn or vines, the locals produced their liquor from the bounty of the forest. Seg sipped. He made a face.

"I judge Diomb and Bamba will never touch a drop of the good stuff if this ruins their palates," he said.

Diomb sipped, spluttered and looked affronted.

Bamba sipped, sipped again, looked at Milsi, smiled, and finished the jug.

"H'm, young lady. I shall not carry you to bed."

The delights of roast ponsho were available, for meat animals were carried downstream from the enormous pastures farther north. Momolams, those small, yellow tubers of the delicious taste, complemented roast pon-sho. Also, there were local dishes, mostly of fish cooked in an amazing variety of ways. The bread, baked from flour brought down the river, was gritty and coarse and would wear a person's teeth out well within two hundred years.

The two dinkus lapped up everything new with an appetite at once greedy and charming.

From the caverns of the Coup Blag Seg had brought his pouch-full of gold coins. He used these sparingly. He noticed that Milsi, also, had a pouch of coins, and he surmised that these had come from the same source as his own, or, perhaps, were leftovers of those she would habitually carry as handmaid to the queen.

When the reckoning was paid, and the word was mentioned, Diomb said, "What is money?"

"Ah, now," said Seg, wisely, scratching his nose. "Now there you pose a question that has bedeviled men and women for thousands of seasons. Money! If we did not need it, why, then—"

"We have none in the forest," pointed out Bamba.

"I will tell you this. Money is hard to obtain and easy to lose. With it you can buy—that is, get hold of—many things. But if you think only of money, you're done for."

Milsi gave a more reasoned explanation, so that the dinkus, naturally, said: "Then how will we obtain this money if it is necessary to live in the outside world?"

"Work."

"What is work?"

As Milsi explained Seg looked out of the window. He pointed to the three stakes set up side by side against the larger house with mud cladding to its wooden walls. Each stake was crowned with a human head. Two were men, one was female; two were Fristles, one was an Och.

"See those heads out there? They are there because their owners instead of working stole goods or money from other honest folk."

Milsi said: "Oh, Seg—the penalty here for thievery is to have the hand cut off. I don't think—"

Seg looked meaningfully upon the two dinkus.

"And the hands cut off!"

Then, sotto voce to Milsi, "I don't want them up to their usual common-possession habits. If we scare 'em enough they won't get into trouble."

"Yes, well. I suppose you are right."

Bamba and Diomb were suitably impressed.

"The outside world is indeed a strange place. Far more strange than ever the elders told us."

"There is," said Seg, helpfully, "a whole lot more."

A movement in the mud square took his attention. He pointed again. "Look there! See that fellow with the yellow skin and the blue pigtail? His hair hanging down like a rope, like a twisted vine?"

They all looked out. The small coffle of slaves, trudging from the large mud-walled house, were in a poor state. The fellow Seg pointed out with the shaven yellow skull and the blue pigtail had tusks reaching up each side of his jaw. His eyes were bloodshot. His body was robustly strong and fit, endowed with muscle.

"It is uncommon strange to see a Chulik as slave. They are mercenaries, fighting men trained up from birth. They are first-class warriors and they are not cheap to hire. I wonder what he did to get himself in this fix?"

Chained before the Chulik a little Och slumped along, his six limbs giving him some assistance, for Ochs, although only around four feet tall, use their middle limbs as hands or feet as circumstances dictate. His puffy face and lemon-shaped head looked thoroughly hangdog.

Following the Chulik a beaked Rapa, hawklike in appearance, his orange and blue feathers bedraggled, stumped along, careful not to drag the bight of chain tight.

Other diffs and apims trudged along in the miserable slave column, and the Katakis lashed them with thick whips, or buffeted them with the flats of the steel strapped to their tails.

"If they don't cut off your hands and head," said Seg, heavily, "they'll take you up as slaves. So—do not take anything that is not yours. That is stealing."

"We will remember," said Diomb, most chastened.

The pygmies aroused considerable interest in the fisherfolk of Lasindle. A group of them in the opposite window corner kept shooting looks toward Diomb and Bamba. They were mostly apims, not all, and Seg began to feel a stuffiness in the atmosphere. He just hoped that he would not have to become embroiled in some stupid affray because these fishermen did not allow dinkus into their tavern. That kind of barbaric custom was known.

He also did not fail to miss the interest they took in the great long-sword strapped to his back. He'd kept the sword because it belonged to the Bogandur. As for Seg himself, his old dom had shown him, often and often, how to wield the thing, and to hold it properly, and how to cut and thrust and cleave a path through the midst of a confused battle, as well as how to meet an opponent in single combat. Seg could handle the long-sword; but it was not his chosen weapon. If he came to handstrokes he was most comfortable with the drexer scabbarded at his side, or a rapier and left-hand dagger.

All the same, he firmly believed in shafting his enemies before they got within striking range.

Uneasily, he said to Milsi: "I believe we should leave here very soon."

"Oh?"

"I'm not much enamored of the looks of those fishermen."

"But they are ordinary honest fisherfolk—"

"Oh, aye, indisputably. But they're like any honest folk in their tavern. They don't like strangers, particularly strangers they feel may wish them harm."

"That's nonsense! I don't see—"

"All the same, my lady, drink up and we will leave."

Just as they were about to quit The Hook and Net a rumble of coarse voices from the stoop heralded a couple of Katakis. They stamped their feet. They swished their bladed tails.

Seg stood aside.

Milsi sailed on, oblivious of the newcomers, making for the door.

With the two dinkus at his side, Seg watched, and it was all over in a twinkling.

Milsi quite expected to walk out of the doorway unimpeded and if anyone happened to be there, her manner made it perfectly plain, then they'd scuttle out of her way.

The Katakis did not scuttle.

They pushed in, and where in most races of Kregen people entering a tavern would be laughing and chattering, joyous in the delights to come, Katakis just marched in with their usual dour and grim absence of humor.

They pushed into Milsi.

Her surprise was genuine.

"You boors!" she cried, regaining her balance. "Do you not know to stand aside when a lady passes?"

They turned their vicious low-browed faces toward her. Their bladed tails flicked above their heads. Snaggle teeth showed as—in this situation—the Katakis could take their unhealthy dregs of amusement.

"Shishi! You speak over-boldly—"

"Get out of my way, rasts!"

They did not like that. One put out a hand and seized the Lady Milsi by her arm, and the other wrapped his tail about her waist.

"Ho! One for the coffle, this! A fine promising piece of merchandise."

Seg moved as a leaping leem moves. Feral, deadly, merciless.

His fist struck twice.

The two Katakis slumped to the floor, unconscious.

"Now let us get out of here, and right now! Come on you two—and, Diomb, stow that dratted blowpipe!"

Pelting out from the stoop they hit the square and ran like crazy down the first of the mazy alleyways. Seg headed for the river.

"Where are we going?" Milsi panted it out, running with her head up, her hips going from side to side; but running fleetly and well.

"River. Find a boat. The rains—are due soon. Now, woman—run!"

The dinkus kept up with fleet agility. Seg held his pace down. He would not leave them, and he could not leave Milsi, who had caused all this aggravation.

The rains would come pelting down soon, casting a pall of water over everything and turning the mud into a quagmire. He wanted to be well away into the river by then.

The waterside presented an appearance of lazy apathy. Fisherfolk were not working at this time, knowing the rains were due. The busiest activity centered on a long narrow canoe-like craft where the Kataki slavers they had seen crossing the square were herding the coffle aboard.

Diomb settled the whole thing.

He skidded to a halt. His blowpipe twitched up.

"Dratted Katakis!" he said.

His cheeks puffed, the first dart sped.

Seg howled in frustration; but the damage was done.

He slapped up his bow, nocked an arrow, and Diomb had puffed a second dart. Two Katakis clapped hands to their necks above the rim of their harness, startled. They saw the pygmies, they started to jeer at them, and then they fell down.

Another took a clothyard shaft through his throat and a fourth yelped as a dart stung his lowering face. He, too, fell down shortly thereafter.

The fifth and sixth were punched clean through by arrows. The seventh tried to run and, ironically, the dart took him in the fleshy root of his tail. He ran on and could not stop and tumbled headlong into the water.

A furious splashing followed, and the crunch of jaws.

Seg roared up to the canoe-like craft, known as a Schinkitree in these parts, and stared down on the slaves.

"Who is willing to paddle to freedom with me?"

"I!" and "I!"

"All right. You—" pointing at the Och, "find the keys. You—" with a fierce stab at the Chulik, "chuck the dratted Katakis into the river when we have the keys! *Bratch!*"

At that command the slaves bratched. They jumped.

The key was found, the clever fingers of the little Och released the first of the slaves on the chain, the Chulik, after a dour look at Seg, started hurling the Katakis into the river. Jaws crunched.

"Get aboard, all!" called Seg. "Hurry!"

The two dinkus even in this extremity of urgency assisted Milsi aboard, waiting for her. She went into the Schinkitree with a regal step that looked most becoming. Seg pushed off. He stared back across the waterside to the first of the wooden houses.

From the ragged alleyway men were running out, apims, Katakis, Rapas, all yelling and waving weapons. He did not bother to shaft them. There had been no time to cut out his arrows, and he did not wish to waste any more. The boat was off from the riverside, surging out into midstream as the freed slaves took up the paddles and dug deep.

Then the rain slashed down.

A solid curtain of water hid the bank and the forest and the township.

The Chulik roared out: "By Likshu the Treacherous! I am free again! Downstream. Paddle downstream. We will make Mattamlad at the mouth of the river. I have friends there—"

Seg chopped him off brutally.

"I am in command here, Chulik. We paddle upstream. That is without question."

His bow, arrow nocked, aimed at the Chulik's breast.

"Apim yetch! I am Nath Chandarl! Nath the Dorvenhork!"

"That is as it may be. But, by the Veiled Froyvil, dom, we paddle upstream—unless you wish to become flint-fodder."

The Chulik started. He stared from those narrow eyes at Seg, saw the bow, heard what he said. He lowered his fist.

"You are a Bowman of Loh?"

"Yes."

"In that case—"

"Look, dom. They will expect us to paddle downstream. That is where they will search. We have a goodly craft, strong paddlers. We go upstream and they'll never find us. Later, when we have made our fortunes, we may return downstream and you can rejoin your friends."

"That does, by Likshu the Treacherous, make sense, apim."

The current, lazy though it might still be here, was carrying them downstream. Seg, without taking his gaze or the aim of the shaft from the Chulik, Nath the Dorvenhork, said with a harsh emphasis: "Paddle, doms. Paddle upstream and let us lose ourselves in the rain."

"Yes," shrilled the Och, wildly. "As sure as my name is Umtig the Lock, the apim speaks sooth!"

Once more the paddles bit. This time the boat turned and headed upstream. The paddlers, slaves only moments before, drew their blades through the brown water with strong and determined sweeps. They had been slave; now they were free. Not one of them would voluntarily return to slavery. They would paddle and paddle, strive and battle, to avoid that ghastly fate.

Slowly, Seg lowered his bow. This Chulik, by his sobriquet of Dorvenhork, was a bowman also. With Seg's movement from the stern of the Schinkitree the Chulik relaxed. Merciless, ruthless, like all his race, he had recognized another master bowman, and, also, seen the wisdom of the decision to paddle upstream. He took up a paddle and joined in the rhythmic swing and stroke of the other ex-slaves.

In the stern, with Milsi, Diomb and Bamba, Seg surveyed his new command. They were veiled in the gray and silver rain. The brown river gurgled past below.

Whatever the future might hold, they were on their way to it right now...

Seven

Stranded

A sennight later and well up the river the fugitives found it expedient to make a camp for a few days on one of the islands dotting the Kazzchun River hereabouts. The river rolled along, redolent of brown mud and damp growing things, choked with wildfowl, the mudflats always shimmering with the flash of wings. The denizens of the water fought and thrived, and, all in all, there was food aplenty.

The histories of the freed slaves were interesting and shared a common thread. Folk who are born to slavery are born to slavery, as the saying went. Others, caught in petty crimes, found themselves chained and trudging along in the coffle, punished enough and more for their sins.

The little Och, Umtig the Lock, more than once exclaimed when he spoke: "By Diproo the Nimble-Fingered!" By this men knew him to be a thief.

The Chulik had formed an odd kind of respect for Seg. He had asked to inspect the Lohvian longbow, and made a stupid mewling whistle of admiration as he bent it.

"I am used to the dorven bow, the crossbow, or even the weak flat bow; this round longbow is indeed a marvel."

Seg had never had much time for Chuliks. Raised from birth as they were to be mercenaries, and highly paid ones at that, they knew little of humanity. They were ruthless in their exactment of debts. But, in these latter days, he found that human converse was possible with specimens of the race. He simply handled each eventuality as it arose, and felt distinct relief that Nath the Dorvenhork had desisted from that first desire to shaft him.

Diomb brought up an interesting question, that made Seg roar with laughter, and then sober, and then—lamely—try to explain.

"You stole this boat, Seg. You are a thief. They will cut off your hands, and your head—"

"They have to catch me first."

"Yes—but, you said—"

"I know, Diomb, and mark me! What I said was right. But you saw the situation. All honest men abhor Katakis as slavers, even though they condone slavery. Katakis are anti-human in a way that—" Here Seg looked around the campsite on the river island. The Chulik was nowhere in sight. "In a way even that Chuliks are not. But I do not seek to pretend I did not steal the boat or that stealing is a crime. Just, that—"

"Thievery is an honest profession like any other!" protested the Och, Umtig the Lock, most heated.

"There are degrees, dom, and well you know it."

They wrangled amicably for a space, and then Seg said to Umtig: "And mind you do not lead Diomb into bad habits, you rogue. I cherish your outlook in some things, not all."

The traffic on the river thinned past the last town through which they had paddled at dead of night. Local produce traveled up and down, and the massive rafts carried stone and building materials to the south, as the slender schinkitrees carried wood upstream to the great plains.

"Let us paddle out and seize one of these craft laden with treasure, slit all their throats, and take the gold!" counseled a hulking great apim called Ortyg the Undlefar.

"We are not pirates, not renders!" said Seg, shocked at the uncouthness of it all.

"Why not? We have a boat, we have fighting men, we have—"

"And we have no weapons, apart from those of the four who rescued us," said a Fristle, Naghan the Slippy.

"We descend on them unheard and unseen! We will soon have weapons!" Ortyg the Undlefar showed his contempt for those who did not understand the render's trade.

A Sybli, a girl with the delectable body of a mature woman and the face of an innocent child in the way of her race of diffs, spoke up. "I would like to go home."

Others took up this call. A lath-thin apim, known as Hundle the Design, said: "I agree we would like to go home. But I, for one, would prefer to return with a pocket full of gold. But, doms, I would not like to gain the gold through piracy or thievery."

A Khibil whose haughty, fox-featured face showed that, like all Khibils, he considered himself a cut above everyone else—known as Khardun the Franch—said in his lofty way: "I am a hyr-paktun. Let us find a great lord and hire out our services as fighting men. We will soon make our fortunes."

A mild-mannered Relt stylor, Caphlander the Quill, ventured to say that not all present had the skills of mercenary fighting men, paktuns.

Seg felt the twinge hearing that name. There had been just such a mild-mannered Relt when he'd first met his old dom, far and far away from here,

340

and that Relt's name had been Caphlander. Relts were distant cousins of the ferocious Rapas, and usually they were employed as domestics, stylors, clerical help, accountants.

"We stick together," Seg declared. "We are going to reach the town of Mewsansmot. After that, with full bellies, you may go your own separate ways. There may also be gold in it, too." He cocked a cautious eye at Milsi.

She took the point at once.

"I believe there will be gold for all of you if you help to bring us safely to Mewsansmot."

The only serious opposition to this plan came from the hulking apim, Ortyg the Undlefar. Seg told him that he was at perfect liberty to leave the party. He would be put onto the riverbank of his choosing and from thence go where he willed. Ortyg chilled considerably in his own plans and oppositions to others after that.

The plain fact was that these one-time slaves had been taken up for a variety of reasons. Ortyg, now, was a real villain. The beautiful Sybli was a slave because members of her race were usually slaves. She had been there to be sold to a new master. Some were petty criminals, some were debtors, some had been snatched from their homes.

Seg sorted them out in his mind, allotting them places in his table of possible uses.

He took the opportunity to have a word with the Khibil, Khardun the Franch.

"I salute you, Khardun, as a hyrpaktun. How is it, if you care to tell me, that you became slave?"

Seg knew how to handle Khibils. So long as they believed they were the greatest, then things ran smoothly.

"How I became slave, dom? I will tell you. I am a hyrpaktun, I am a mercenary who hires out only for top rates, who commands, who orders. I served King Crox well. I had a detachment to take downriver, and this I did. When I returned, the king had gone to some heathenish place called the Coup Blag. The lady Mab, who was married to him in a ceremony, so I am told, of the utmost shortness, followed. The Kov Llipton—"

"Ah!" said Seg. "Now I have heard of him. He is the regent, is he not, and rules in the king's place?"

"That is so. I do not know how I offended him. But whatever I did, it was wrong, and I was stripped, my pakzhan taken from me, my sword broken, and I was shipped out as slave." Here the Khibil's savage and resentful look did not surprise Seg. The pakzhan, a golden head of a zhantil, perhaps the most splendid of all Kregen's wild animals that he knew of, strung on a silken thread and looped in a top buttonhole or over a shoulder knot, was the highest award conferred by hyrpaktuns upon members of their trade. It was hard to come by. A pakzhan glittering gold at the throat of a hyrpaktun marked him as a soldier of fortune of the highest renown.

Seg did not think it opportune to mention that he, too, had won the pakzhan and was a hyrpaktun. He had been a noble lord long enough for his more reckless days as a mercenary warrior to recede into the past for him.

"Tell me of Kov Llipton."

"He is like any other great lord, I suppose. He runs the country now. I think that he was mightily displeased that Queen Mab followed the king to the Coup Blag."

Ah! said Seg to himself. That did not take a deal of worming out. If this Llipton fellow wanted to be king, and King Crox dead, then he'd have to marry the queen.

"You saw Queen Mab?"

"No. She came from Jholaix—"

"From Jholaix!"

"Aye, Seg. She brought a dowry of wine so splendid that, well, I swear it was enough to make all of the kingdom drunk for three seasons."

"And no hangovers."

"No. Never! Not with the wines of Jholaix!"

They paddled upriver. No one of the passing craft offered to molest them. Milsi judged that pursuit had, indeed, hared off downriver.

Diomb came up to Seg as they paddled past one of the many islands dotting the broad river here, and said: "I am astonished by what that girl, the Sybli Malindi, says. She wants to go home. That is understandable. But, by Clomb of the Ompion Never-Miss! If she does that she will be slave again. That is what home means to her."

"There are different sorts of slaves, Diomb. Oh, some folk who keep slaves treat them well, almost as part of the family. Syblies and Relts aspire to that condition. It is in the fields, the mines, the terrible places where men and women work until they drop, that slavery at its worst may be found."

"And, another thing. There are mercenaries, paktuns, among us. They take—money—from other people to fight for them. That is, indeed, most strange."

Seg laughed.

"If I do not like fighting and do not wish to risk my precious skin in a battle, then I will pay someone else to go out and fight for me. It is simple."

"Well, I suppose so. But all mercenaries are not paktuns—"

"No. A paktun is a mercenary who has gained some fame. A hyrpaktun is a most famous paktun. Yet lots of mercenaries are dubbed paktuns these days. The custom is new. Just about only the young ones, the coys, are not called paktuns in general usage these days."

"Well," said Diomb. "I think that if I have to work to gain this money, then I will be a paktun."

Seg was not surprised.

"You could. You would do well with your dratted blowpipe—your ompion. That would tickle 'em up on a battlefield, by the Veiled Froyvil, yes!"

The Chulik, Nath the Dorvenhork, in the general way of Chuliks, did not laugh or smile when he made his comment. But for a Chulik it was revealing enough.

"I agree. The little fellow would earn his hire!"

There was, Seg could see, a strange kind of brotherhood developing between the exponents of missile weapons.

He'd always been a feckless sort of scamp and so he'd never thought overmuch of the way he ought to treat diffs. Diffs were diffs; that was all there was to it. In these later seasons he had seen a deal of the world and had picked up new ways of handling exceptional members of odd races. But he'd never bothered his head much over Chuliks; they went their cold, mercenary way, and he went his.

Still, if the Dorvenhork wanted to secure allies, that would be no bad thing.

The political map had changed with the coming of age of King Crox, and he now controlled the length of the river from past Mewsansmot in the north to a new shanty town he'd erected ten or so dwaburs from the coast. King Crox did not control the mouth of the river and Mattamlad. But, then, it was highly unlikely that King Crox controlled anything at all in the fabulous world of Kregen, being no doubt stuffed down in the intestines of some horrendous monster in the maze of the Coup Blag.

A little Ift, Twober the So, went past with a long look at Seg's bow. Twober's ears stuck up in two shapely points almost past the crown of his head. His eyebrows slanted up, and his eyes slanted up. Woodsfolk, the Ifts, not jungle folk, and Twober had wandered down here to South Pandahem from his home over the massive central mountains in North Pandahem.

Various plans were discussed by groups of the escaped slaves. All well understood their peril, and the punishments that would be their lot if they were recaptured. Any slave-owning society is hard on runaways.

Ortyg the Undlefar, although chastened, kept on a monotonous series of suggestions. All boiled down to paddling out and capturing a rich merchant raft, boat or Schinkitree, massacring all the occupants, and disappearing with the gold and jewels.

The evening light, all a glorious mingling of jade and ruby, threw mazy shadows upon the sliding water. Waterfowl sprawled on the mudflats or turned in a glinting pinioned array in the last flights before nightfall. The two second Moons of Kregen were due early tonight, the Twins would cast down a pinkish radiance that would light up the world in a strange and ghostly reflection of the twin suns, Zim and Genodras. The warm muddy scents rose.

The fires were set well back from the banks of the island in secure places so as not to be observed by craft passing along the river. Food there was in plenty. Palines grew in lush profusion. A slothfulness could easily overtake these people but for the ever-present fear of discovery and the terrors that would follow.

Guards were set. Diomb and Bamba disappeared farther back into the interior of the island where the vegetation, although it might not rival in any way the riot of the jungle, gave them a sense of home. Seg settled down, with Milsi and the Sybli girl, Malindi, sleeping not too far off and within call. He placed the Bogandur's long sword at his side, with his own Lohvian longbow. The drexer he placed near to his right hand as he slept.

He had the last watch and would be called when Kregen's fourth moon, She of the Veils, rose four glasses before dawn.

With the habits of a lifetime he awoke a few moments before he expected to be called. He yawned and stretched. He'd never wondered overmuch about the oddity of his own body, which must have some kind of blood-filled clepsydra somewhere inside. He and the Bogandur were old campaigners in matters of this nature.

He stood up and went toward the bank with its screen of bushes where the lookout was kept expecting to find Rafikhan, the Rapa with the orange and blue feathers, just setting off to wake him.

Perhaps he was a little early. The Twins were wheeling away to the west and the new roseate-golden tinge flushing the eastern sky was She of the Veils about to pour her glory upon the face of the world. He reached the lookout post without meeting a soul.

Rafikhan was just sitting up holding his head.

About to let fly with a torrent of abuse, Seg paused. Between the Rapa's fingers a dark liquid thread shone greasily, staining down his facial feathers.

"Rafikhan! What's amiss?"

The Rapa hissed his pain, rocking backwards and forwards. Beside him the body of the little Ift, Twober the So, lay in an ungainly and lax posture. Seg bent.

Twober was dead, his skull bashed in. The blow that had killed him had been delivered with the same force as the blow that had knocked Rafikhan unconscious.

Instantly, Seg looked to the bank.

The boat was gone.

So he knew it all.

The camp roused out and Seg silenced their babble.

He counted heads.

Almost half of the ex-slaves were no longer present.

"May Likshu the Treacherous draw forth his entrails to be devoured by worms!" declared Nath the Dorvenhork.

"By Rhapaporgolam the Reiver of Souls!" Rafikhan's voice hissed in the moons' light. "The cramph hit me shrewdly."

No need to ask who had struck the Rapa and slain the Ift.

"Ortyg the Undlefar!" said Milsi. "He has persuaded many poor deluded souls to follow him—"

"And he has taken our boat!"

"We are stranded here, abandoned on this little island..."

Stranded they were, isolated on their mound of mud in a river boiling with hungry bellies and ravenous jaws.

Eight

Of the sharing of clothes

"Now what are we going to do?"

Hundle the Design, skinny as a spear-shaft, stepped forward. Everyone left in the party gathered around as the twin suns rose. Their warmth on this morning, their refulgence, brought no happy welcome.

Hundle had proved knowledgeable about the boat and the way she should be handled. Now he said: "I was a Schinkitree master before my boat hit a half-submerged log and filled and sank. I lost my boat, all the merchandise I carried for the merchant Dorian Merlo, who was a Lamnia and my friend, my living and my freedom."

They all listened, not shouting out about what the hell had this to do with their plight now. The thin ex-boat master was clearly leading up to something important he had to say.

"Go on, Hundle the Design," said Milsi.

"The king, since he took full command of the river, has swept the whole length he controls free of pirates. The renders were trapped, caught, slain. This poor deluded fool, Ortyg the Undlefar, will surely come to grief. As Pandrite is my witness, this will happen."

"Yes," said Milsi. "I judged him by his talk of renders not to understand."

"He and I," said the Chulik Nath Chandarl, stroking one of his tusks with a thumb, "were dragged upriver together. I think my friends in Mattamlad and his were on opposite sides of the law."

By this, Seg gathered that the idiot Ortyg had probably been a pirate out along the coast of Pandahem and among the islands of the Koroles.

He said, "I thank you for your information, horter Hundle. This means, I take it, that that onker Ortyg will be taken up and beheaded. But, also, that we may signal to a passing craft and hope to be taken off?"

"Yes, horter Seg. They will rescue us, for that is the way of the Kazzchun River. They will, of course, charge for their services."

"Oh, of course."

A wailing started up at this news.

They all cried out in various ways, and it summed up as: "But we are all naked and have no money. We are clearly slaves!"

"Shastum! Silence!" yelled Seg.

He quieted them down, and then went on: "I have a little gold. I think it will pay our passage to the nearest town. The vexatious question is, how are we to become honest horters and horteras, and no longer slaves?"

Milsi said: "Good master Hundle. Is it not possible for us to have been in a boat that sank? We would have lost all in the accident."

Quite calmly, Milsi took off her blue tunic. It was badly ripped, and she held it up high. Looking at her, clad only in a tiny blue loincloth, Seg caught his breath.

"This tunic will make loincloths for a number of us, and horter Seg can spare some of his scarlet breechclout. We will look decent enough when we are rescued."

Shyly, Malindi said: "I would love to have a loincloth of that beautiful blue, mistress."

"And you shall be my new handmaiden, Malindi, I promise you."

It was said so naturally, so unaffectedly, that Seg barely noticed. He could not keep on looking at Milsi like this, and had to turn away, and found he could not.

"Well, Seg the Horkandur! And where is your knife? And your breech-clout!"

With the aid of his knife the women of the party fashioned just-respectable loincloths for themselves and almost enough breechclouts for the men—drawn tightly!

Diomb and Bamba wanted to know what all the fuss was about. It fell to Seg to stumble over an explanation that slaves were expected to be naked or wear the gray slave breechclout, but that horters and horteras, ladies and gentlemen, usually covered themselves up.

"Then it is a sign of this rank you have tried to explain?"

"More or less—"

"The outside world becomes stranger and stranger the more one learns," declared Bamba, giving her bark apron a flick. "I will willingly wear nothing at all most of the time, and anyone is welcome to share a piece of my bark."

Somebody listening laughed. Somehow that broke the fearful tension that gripped the less hardy of the ex-slaves and seemed a good augury for the future. Seg was interested to notice the people Ortyg the Undlefar had failed to impress into his schemes: The Khibil was too proud, the Chulik a highly qualified and paid paktun, the Rapa just not interested, even the little Och thief was not into the red-roaring blood-letting of piracy. The Fristle was not happy in a boat at the best of times, and as for the others, for the best of reasons they had refused to join the render's trade.

All in all, decided Seg, he had a likely bunch with him now, apart from the timid ones who would no doubt do as they were told. If bluff could succeed, they stood every chance of success.

Diomb in his perennially inquisitive way brought up an interesting point. He was puzzled. If, he wanted to know, slaves were property, and the slave owners very hard on runaways, then surely they'd chase after the people here and re-take them?

Milsi took it upon herself to explain that these people had not been personally owned slaves. They had been merchandise in the hands of Katakis, slave-traders, and would be regarded as stock. Anyway, many of the Kataki owners had been killed. No authority acting on behalf of an owner whose slave had run off would be involved. Seg listened, and realized that a great deal of the apathy he had noticed before caused by the absence of King Crox was at work here. He felt pretty sure that the Katakis themselves, should they ever run across these people and recognize them, would act with harshness.

Nath the Dorvenhork and Khardun the Franch, when the skimpy loincloths had been handed out and adjusted, approached Seg. With all the circumlocution and formality of warriors requesting the loan of another warrior's weapon—the Kregish rituals extended in labyrinthine protocol for these occasions—they asked to borrow Seg's knife. They intended to cut stout staves from the woods, and sharpen the ends in the fire and thus fashion spears for themselves.

"Just," said the Dorvenhork. "In case."

"Right gladly, doms," said Seg cheerfully, and he tossed his knife into the air. Neither attempted to beat the other to the catch and the knife went splut into the earth. Seg laughed—but to himself. Khibil and Chulik; there'd be a constant game of seizing the advantage between these two—and not in petty ways, either, by Vox...

The stranded party took considerable interest and delight in the antics of the little Och, Umtig the Lock. He fashioned a long rope of twisted vines, with a loop at each end, and with this whistling around his head he trotted off into the island forest.

The land sloped gently up from the coast to the interior mountains, but the slope was enough to create a varied biosphere. The rain forest that Seg usually thought of as jungle, gave place to cloud forest. The dwarf forest farther on extended for only a short distance between the cloud forest and the plains. Umtig the lock trotted confidently on, whirling his plaited rope of vines.

Here he expected to find a particular species of monkey among the denizens of the trees, the humming birds, the fighting wasps, the horned lizards and all the splendid and various forms of life flourishing each in its own niche.

Chulik and Khibil watched the Och depart, and then turned to the grave matter of who should pick up Seg's knife.

Seg settled all that nonsense.

"If you two are going to cut spears, it would be a good idea if you'd go off now and keep an eye on Umtig."

They jerked as though stung. Then the Dorvenhork said, "You may take the knife, horter Khardun."

"I will carry it, Nath Chandarl; you may use it first."

"As you wish. The Och is almost out of sight."

They followed on with the swift stalking gait of the fighting man. Umtig went about his task with perfect confidence. He peered about most carefully up into the trees. Presently he uttered a little Och exclamation of delight, and whirled the vine rope with deft precision.

The loop spun up into the air. Umtig jerked the line. With a swooshing rush a bundle of multicolored fur tumbled down. Umtig caught the little monkey with a cry of delight.

"This is a spinlikl," he said, and at once set to crooning and making baby-mewing sounds to caress the monkey to quietude. The small creature wriggled and struggled, his eight limbs swishing about, and then he quieted down. His body was no larger than a fair-sized melon, and his eight limbs each stretched out farther than a man's full armreach. Each limb had a fully formed hand, lithe-fingered, deft, powerful, with sharp nails. The spinlikl made no sound, but squirmed against Umtig's chest and settled himself comfortably, three or four arms wrapped about the Och's neck, the rest wrapped about his upper body.

Umtig beamed his pleasure.

The Chulik and the Khibil looked on, waiting for the Och to return to the main party, then they set about cutting staves with which to fashion spears.

Umtig, returning in his personal triumph to the camp, ripped a paline branch free from a handy bush and began feeding a steady stream of the berries to the spinlikl. These sweet yellow cherry-like fruits found growing over most parts of Kregen proved a source of constant delight, a sovereign remedy for a hangover, a necessity with which to conclude a meal, a digestive of the first order, a boon to all humankind.

"My supremely clever spinlikl," Umtig said to Seg. "I will soon have him trained into the veritable paradigm of invisible deftness. I shall call him Lord Clinglin."

Milsi smiled. "I had a little mili-milu once who was called Pantor Fotaix. How we silly humans love to give our pets grand titles!"

Such was the good humor of the party now that they had clothes of a sort, the promise of money and every chance of rescue, no one appeared to express any high-minded and respectable abomination of Umtig's new pet. For, of course, he was no ordinary household pet to be loved and adored and played with. He was a most adept adjunct in the trade dedicated to and cared for by Diproo the Nimble-fingered.

When all was declared ready they watched for a suitable craft passing up the river. Still no one wished to chance descending the Kazzchun River, despite the general belief the Katakis would write off the lost merchandise and look for more. By the time they reached Lasindle they should be dressed properly and able to escape instant detection as escaped slaves... But...

"There!" said Milsi with great confidence, pointing. "Set the fire."

The craft to which she pointed paddled along with forty paddles aside going in and out and up and down with perfect rhythm. Her after parts carried a covered-in cabin from which flags flew.

Hundle the Design tossed a brand into the pile of stump and twigs, of leaves and greenery and soon the smoke lifted, thick and coiling, and only slightly blown by the tiny breeze. Everyone jumped up and down and waved.

No one really believed the ornately large Schinkitree would paddle grandly past and leave them. No one really believed that... But... The moments passed with excruciating agony before, at last, the bows turned and the boat became a foreshortened spear aimed at them with her paddles churning either side. The flags flew and the foam spurted and she came churning up to their little mud bank.

Very few people ever leaped into the water to drag a boat up onto the bank in the River of Bloody Jaws. Most boats possessed a small laddered ramp, something like a corvus, which ran out and provided a safe way to shore. The anchors were often merely large stones pierced with a hole for the chains or ropes. This vessel ran her gangway out and the spiked end went thunk into the mud, and men marched down, alert and watchful.

"What?" said Milsi, suddenly. "What does this mean?"

For the men were armed and carried weapons, and they fanned out as they touched the shore and presented a formidable front. There were ten of them, and they looked rough and tough, paktuns with blue and yellow feathers in their helmets. Then a wispy Xaffer walked ashore, his blue robes trailing, his dreamy face giving him the look of a man who lived in a private fantasy world of his own. He carried a scrip, and his right temple was ink-stained.

"Forgive the welcome," he said, holding up his hand in greeting. "I give you the Llahal. But there have been reports of pirates on the river."

"That Pandrite-forsaken Ortyg," someone to the rear of the party said with great venom.

Hundle the Design stepped forward and, as the most experienced traveler among them upon the river, explained their situation. His story sounded convincing. They were travelers whose craft had sunk. Seg felt a vicious anger at the explanation of the absence of paddlers, but he kept a calm face. Now was not the time. The paddlers, being slaves, and being chained to their benches, had, of course, sunk with the boat...

Not all of them had reached this island. This handful were the only survivors. Seg agreed with that. They wanted nothing to do with the depredations of Ortyg the Undlefar and his band of cutthroats.

"You are fortunate indeed to have survived the jaws of the river. My master will be interested in your story. You are welcome to come aboard."

They all carefully observed the fantamyrrh as they stepped into the boat. Long and narrow, with her paddlers chained to their benches at each side, she offered only adequate accommodation right aft where the master lived in state, and right forrard where the paktun guards were quartered. The rescued folk could, for the journey, sleep upon the central gangway. There were no masts. Along the gangway prowled the Whip-Deldars ensuring that the paddlers kept time and rhythm and dug deeply with all their strength.

The master turned out to be a jolly, perspiring, multi-chinned apim called Obolya Metromin. As a merchant specializing in the buying and selling of saddle animals, he liked to be called Obolya the Zorcanim. This was, to Seg, pitching it a little high; but he was in no case to argue the finer points of nomenclature.

Obolya sat upon a handsome chair, strewn with expensive silks and furs, beaming away upon the new arrivals. At his back his pavilion-like cabin rose, the flags fluttering. His personal guards flanked him, distinct from the boat-guards. Two charming girls saw to his needs, their pale bodies partially concealed by artfully draped gauzes, decorated with strings of pearls in the age-old custom. Obolya himself, in robes of some magnificence, exuded an air of benediction; but Seg was not the only one to see and realize that this fat, happy, charming man was a merchant of consummate shrewdness.

"Payment?" he exclaimed, and held up a fat beringed hand in horror. "Never could I exact payment for performing a good deed. Why, by Pandrite the All-Powerful! Is it not the Law of the River to aid our unfortunate brothers and sisters? You will take wine, of course. I have a middling-fine Markable which clears the throat most effectively."

So they all took wine.

This fine fat animal-trader was on his way upriver to buy what saddle-animals he could from traders out on the plains. Milsi looked at him carefully, and smiled, and intimated that if horter Obolya was going to Mewsansmot—

"Why, yes! I have business contacts there. All this is new to me, this is my first journey so far upriver. I trade normally in North Pandahem; but things political up there are parlous, most parlous. I am confident that if I can secure good cargoes of saddle animals I can sell every last one back in North Pandahem."

Incautiously, Seg said: "Then the journey around the island by sea is less dangerous than crossing the mountains?"

Obolya lowered his wine cup, of polished silver, studded with gems.

"Of course—as everyone knows. My business associate, a fine brave fellow, Naghan Loppelyer, just managed to stagger back home after an attempt to cross the mountains. He lost his caravan, his guards, his girls, his money, his clothes and escaped only with his life."

"You are then from Tomboram?" Milsi looked up.

"Yes. And a pretty pickle we are in up there, I can tell you."

"Yes," said Milsi. Then, quickly, to Obolya: "If you'd kindly take us to Mewsansmot I have friends there. I am sure I could arrange a number of profitable introductions."

"My dear young lady! That is splendid! It is a bargain, as Pandrite is my witness!"

When he had the chance of a private word, Seg said to Milsi: "Look, my lady. You are the lady in waiting to the queen. Why don't we go straight to the capital? Surely your—"

"The king and queen are dead. We know that. The whole country is not sure, but suspects. I want to see my friends first, Seg. You'll just have to trust me in this."

"Oh, I trust you all right. Perhaps you do not trust this Kov Llipton who is the regent?"

"I have no reason not to trust him. Anyway, he will do what he wants to do. I am only a handmaiden."

There was something else troubling Milsi, Seg could sense that with a sympathy that aroused his own guilt that he had not fully confided in her. Yes, they might have been shafted by the same bolt of lightning; but he felt sure that when Milsi did at last confide the more important parts of her history he would discover facts that, just perhaps, might better be left undiscovered.

He considered the interesting notion that she might be Queen Mab herself. He dismissed the idea because he and his old dom had seen the queen dead in the next cell to Milsi's. And it was certain the queen would be recognized somewhere along the river. If Queen Mab was Milsi and she trusted Kov Llipton—and, it seemed sure that so far there was no reason to distrust him apart from the cynical natures possessed by wandering paktuns—then there would be no need to continue with the masquerade. She could just sail grandly up to her palace in the capital city of Nalvinlad and take over from the regent.

Maybe, just maybe, if the handmaiden Milsi was really Queen Mab, she might not wish to marry Kov Llipton if that was his intention. She might have another in mind. If that was the case, Seg couldn't see that other fortunate man being a wandering warrior Bowman of Loh.

He brushed all this nonsense aside.

The facts were that the lady Milsi had asked him to be her jikai and to escort her safely to her friends in Mewsansmot.

This he intended to do to the best of his ability or die trying.

Milsi joined him as he sat on the central gangway trying to keep his stupid thoughts well away from the continuous hypnotic rhythm of the paddlers to either side, and, equally, away from the fantasy scenarios thronging his stupid old vosk skull of a head.

She wore a yellow blouse fastened with bone rosettes through loops of crimson thread. The blouse was almost a bolero jacket, its hem reaching to a point just above her navel. She still wore the scrap of blue loincloth. Her hair had been wound up and fastened with an overlarge stickpin whose head was fashioned into the likeness of a spinyfish, one of the delicacies of the river.

"Well, my Horkandur! You look mighty pensive!"

"Just wondering how all this will end."

"Do not fret. We are well on our way. Look at my new clothes. Obolya is most kind. Why don't you go aft and ransack his wardrobe?"

"Yes, yes, in a mur or two."

"You are grumpy, Seg!"

"I crave your pardon, my lady. It is just—just that—oh! I do not know! I know so little of you, and I was just puzzling if I wanted to know more. There. I'm honest with you."

She looked clearly at him, a long and level gaze to which he responded with his own fey blue gaze just as level and straight.

"Yes, Seg. I also have a family. A single child, not yet full-grown. And I hunger to see her again!"

Nine

In which Seg hires on paktuns

The boat drew into the wooden piers of the wharfside in Nalvinlad. Many craft dotted the brown water, paddles flashed and the shouts of stentors as they guided their vessels joined in the clamor of birds above the fish quays. The slaves from Obolya's Schinkitree were herded out, chained two and two, and taken off to the slave barracks for the night.

The city was not overlarge, girded with a stout wooden palisade strengthened with mudbrick. Here and there, particularly at the river gates and the few gates facing inland, the defenses were strengthened with blocks of masonry. Crowds surged about the business of a city, yet as he went ashore Seg noticed that same apathy that afflicted all the folk of the river since the disappearance of their king.

The palace, built of wood and mud brick, was encircled by its own separate stone wall. The cost of that must have been enormous. King Crox, since he came of age, had bustled about and transformed his kingdom, extending its boundaries up and down the river. He had done nothing about any lateral extension. Kingdoms in this part of South Pandahem stretched along rivers. They were, as Seg put it, as wide as you could reach with your outspread arms, and as long as you could fight your way and win and take territory.

King Crox, already given the name of the gold piece in customary use around here, had changed the name of his new kingdom. When he'd ascended the throne the realm had been called Nalvindrin. His conquests enlarged his domains enough for him to call the whole lot Croxdrin.

When the bandits from the Snarly Hills had caused interruption in the regular flow of commerce along his river, King Crox had taken his expedition in to quell them for good.

Already he had put down piracy on the river, now he wasn't going to stand still for a miserable bunch of drikingers. Well, he'd run into far more than he could handle in the Coup Blag. Still, the regent carried on the good work of keeping the river free from pirates.

Seg and the folk rescued with him stood by the Peral Gate and looked up. A row of stakes lifted into the brilliance of the suns' radiance.

Each stake was crowned with a head.

"There's Ortyg the Undlefar," said Khardun, scornfully.

"And there and there!" exclaimed others, staring up and recognizing the heads of the people who had escaped with them and who had gone off on the render's trail with Ortyg.

"Kov Llipton moves fast," said Obolya, comfortably. "The moment these rasts were taken, swift boats flew up and down the river, warning us. That is why I hired on extra guards."

"The danger is over, I would think," said Milsi.

"Probably, my lady Milsi. But I will check with the authorities first, before I discharge my brave paktuns."

Khardun turned with his supercilious Khibil nose high.

"That is bad news for me, then, horter Obolya."

"Do not rush upon a leem's nest, horter Khardun! You are a hyrpaktun. Keep close. I may have great use for a kampeon such as yourself, and Nath the Dorvenhork."

Seg had not offered to hire out as a mercenary.

By rescuing them and landing them safely in civilization, Obolya the Zorcanim had discharged the duty laid on him by the Laws of the River. He had contracted to take Milsi on to Mewsansmot; nobody else. If Seg accompanied Milsi, he'd have to pay his passage, always assuming Obolya cared to find room for him.

As for the rest of them, they would have to fend for themselves. They were penniless, with the scraps of clothing found for them from Obolya's wardrobe chests, without occupations. They could easily be taken up again as slaves—vagrants, no-goods, people without visible means of support. This Kov Llipton sounded like your stiff and upright guardian of the laws, such as many Kovs when assuming the regency became in a twinkling.

Cautiously, Seg inspected the condition of his purse. The gold he'd taken from the Coup Blag had been in his estimate enough to last him a long time, given that copper and silver were the more common metals of currency. He could hand out three gold pieces per person, and leave himself with ten. H'm... Once you'd been a noble yourself you tended to forget about a lot of the more unpleasant aspects of money, as he'd explained to the two dinkus.

He still would not think too hard of what Milsi had told him of her child. Well, of course she had a child! Didn't that make sense? She was a married woman. Of course she was. She had said that her husband was dead; she did not specify how or the circumstances.

Seg didn't want to know. Nothing had changed in his estimation. He still determined to carry on with what he had sworn.

The mercenaries hired by Obolya congregated in a group under the staring eyeless heads on their stakes. They wrangled with one another, and their talk was hard and bitter. Most were local lads, trying to get into the mercenary trade; there was just the one paktun with the silver mortil-head at his throat. He had assumed command.

The burden of their complaints could be summed up by: "Since King Crox cleaned up the river there is little employment for us. It is hard to find work for an honest mercenary."

The paktun, Norolger the Arm, said: "Since the great wars finished all paktuns have seen lean times. There must be work for us up in the plains. I heard from my twin recently who is in North Pandahem. He said there was plenty of work there, although he did not or could not say whose army was recruiting."

"Then let us go there! You will lead us, Norolger the Arm, and be our Deldar!"

"And who will pay our passage?"

The Chulik Nath the Dorvenhork interrupted to say: "If you wish to sail around Pandahem to the north, you will sail render-infested seas. You will find ready hire among the masters of the merchant ships, or even in the swordships if you are very skilled."

Two of the mercenaries, little more than coys, said they were going home, and although they gave the reason as a longing to taste once more the delights of their mothers' cooking, Seg, for one, suspected other motives. Being a paktun on Kregen, an honest profession, was not an easy life to lead.

The other mercenaries wandered off still wrangling about what best to do.

Seg looked hard at Khardun. The Khibil would be the toughest. Once he had accepted, the others would follow. Khardun the Franch, as his cognomen suggested, was a very bright spark indeed who thought a great deal of himself.

"Khardun! What is your hire fee these days?"

Khardun had no need to explain that while Chuliks might be trained up from birth to be exemplary fighting men, any Khibil was worth at least as much, if not more. By reason of his smartness, of course... This was not a generally held opinion. Chuliks and Pachaks looked to be paid at least a third more than a Khibil. This general opinion was stated, with a firmness that held severe protocol in the address, by the Dorvenhork.

Seg kept the exasperation out of his face and voice. He'd thought he'd handled this giving of gold to the dratted Khibil cleverly, and instead had raised a howling argument.

"When mercenaries are hiring on in times of short supply," Khardun snapped out, intemperately, "many cherished opinions are shattered."

"Here there is an oversupply of mercenaries."

Seg butted in. "Dratted good pay for a mercenary is a silver piece a day. You'd get a lot less here. A Chulik can look, as Nath well knows, for twelve a week. A Khibil will take nine."

"And an apim will take seven!" flared Khardun.

"Oh," said Seg. "I'd stand out for eight."

The Rapa, Rafikhan, fluffed up his feathers and said morosely: "We Rapas are paid the standard one silver piece a day, six a week. I have been paid nine, once, when I went for a varterman and—well, never mind that."

During this conversation Diomb stood, first on one leg, then on the other, listening avidly. He had slung his blowpipe over his back, broken down into four pieces.

"Listen to me," said Seg, and at his tone they all swiveled to regard him, silently. "I intend to give three gold pieces to each of the party with us. That will help them on their way home." He glared at the fighting men in the party, well-knowing that the rest would accept his offer gladly and with thanks. "As for you paktuns, I need to hire on a bodyguard. I shall pay you each three gold pieces. I leave it a paktun's honor for each of you to decide just how long you will serve for that amount. Is that understood? Then *Queyd-arn-tung!*"*

They goggled at him for a bit, surprised—yet the Chulik, remembering their first meeting and the ominous steadiness of Seg's bow on him in the boat, gave a salute with due punctilio.

"So be it, by Likshu the Treacherous."

"By Horato the Potent! So be it!"

"By Rhapaporgolam the Reiver of Souls! So be it!"

Seg nodded, brusquely.

The others in the party crowded round, jabbering away, excited, filling the air with clamor, all thanking horter Seg for his munificence. Seg felt around for his belt pouch and the purse within. The latch was already undone and he hauled out the purse, heavy with gold.

Umtig stepped a little forward, the eight-armed spinlikl, Lord Clinglin, draped around his neck and shoulders. The Och smirked pridefully.

"I thank you most sincerely for your most generous gesture in presenting me with three gold pieces, horter Seg. I shall, of course, repay you." He laughed that high, almost giggling Och laugh. "Oh, and horter Seg, you have already paid me." In his supple fingers three gold croxes glowed.

"What!" Seg looked into his purse, looked at the Och, saw the gold—and he laughed. He laughed with his head thrown back and his huge chest expanded, his shock of black hair dancing.

"You hulu!"

"Aye!"

Khardun looked down his foxy nose at the Och.

"And if you were a mercenary, Umtig, you would receive a mere three or four silver pieces a week."

"Four or five!" spluttered Umtig, cackling with his own ingenuity at his trade. Seg hadn't felt a thing.

Now Diomb stepped forward, bright and expectant.

Seg sighed.

---

* Queyd-arn-tung! No more need be said.

"I do not know, good Diomb. I really do not know."

"But, Seg, I wish to earn my hire. If I need money so that Bamba and I may eat, well, then—"

"You will not go short while I still have gold."

"That is not the same thing, as I now understand."

The Khibil laughed. "A copper ob a day, doms?"

The Chulik polished up his tusk with his thumb.

"Mayhap. It is no concern of mine."

"Now," said Seg, lifting his voice, "as we all have gold in our pockets let us go out and put some wine and meat into our bellies."

"Aye!"

He felt disappointment when Milsi indicated that she and Malindi would be staying within the accommodation offered in the wharf area for paying guests. She offered no explanation apart from a disinclination to venture into the city away from Obolya's boat. He caught the impression that she imagined the rapscallion section of the party with Seg would riot all their money away in a low-class tavern and be thrown out, arrested for drunken and disorderly, or in some way offend the laws. The shadow of Kov Llipton hovered unseen over them.

Many of the main streets possessed wooden sidewalks raised on stilts, and some had decorative arcades and papishin-leaved roofs. When the rains came, it appeared, the good folk of Nalvinlad took care of themselves.

As his comrades started off out of the wharf area, some of them danced little jigs upon the boardwalk. Seg stared after them and turned back to Milsi. "Truly is it said by San Blarnoi, my lady, that a human person is like an onion, layer of secrets wrapped within layer. I shall, of course, not accompany those rogues—"

"Oh, do not be silly, Seg! Go if you want to."

Diomb looked back, waving farewell to Bamba, for the first time since they had left their homes in the forest. Bamba stood with Malindi. Milsi looked cross.

"I do not want you saying that I kept you from all your enjoyments."

"It will not be much of an enjoyment if you are not there to share it."

"A noisy tavern, no doubt a foul dopa den, dancing girls, caff, all manner of spectacles put on called entertainment?"

"I am not in the habit of frequenting dopa dens. Dopa is a liquor so fiery as to make anyone a fighting fool, and, I think you imagine I am enough of that already—my lady."

The movement of her chin would have, in a less composed woman, been a toss of the head. She bit her lip and looked away.

"Go, Seg. Your friends will leave without you."

"They are all our friends, surely?"

"After you have paid them gold—most surely!"

"I only did—"

"Quite! Now Malindi and I are off to the little clothing arcade just over there, where we will outfit ourselves, and Bamba, too. Remberee, Seg."

And she turned with Malindi and Bamba following and walked off with that superb lithe swing of her hips.

Seg did not swear aloud. But, to himself, using one of the Bogandur's favorites, he said: "By the disgusting diseased liver and lights of Makki Grodno!—What a woman!"

Ten

Concerning an ob and a toc

The Rokveil's Ank was not quite as bad as Milsi had predicted the tavern would be; not quite.

It was situated on a side turning from the Street of Anchor Stones, where the sidewalks were fallen away here and there. When the rains came the roadway became a quagmire so tenacious that even a Quoffa, hauling with might and main, would never shift his cart harnessed to him by chains. The papishin leaf roof resounded to the uproar. Inside the tavern the wooden walls seeped water. No one appeared to care.

No dopa was served here.

Seg would not have entered had dopa been served, not because he was too prudish ever to enter a dopa den but because the almost inevitable fights tended to a sad and messy conclusion. Dopa dens, as he had come to know, could yield secrets and offer fine plucked rascals to be used as unwitting tools in intrigues.

The tables were scrubbed clean, the pots and jugs of a similar cleanly style, and the various brews far superior to anything so far encountered along the Kazzchun River. This was only a small unpretentious tavern a stone's throw from the waterfront; but this was the capital city.

A Sylvie came in swirling gauzes and clanging bangles and danced erotically, and a performing animal with heavy chains was prodded by red-hot irons into dancing, and a troupe of jugglers threw balls and hoops and firebrands about and... Seg sat slumped into the corner of a settle and moped about the words he'd had with Milsi.

In all the uproar among the fumes of wine and ale and the blue smells of cooking from the kitchen, the hot fat sizzling in pans as food was hurried by serving wenches to the tables, Seg gradually found himself listening to the different conversations going on.

Naturally, one of the main topics was the capture and summary execution of the renders. Kov Llipton had acted very smartly there, the news flying up and down the river in no time. But, it was clear, even amid all this bustle and the titillation of fresh gossip, everyone's mind dwelt upon the absence of the king and queen. The river was not the same without the guiding hand of King Crox, no matter how smartly the regent, Kov Llipton, acted.

No one knew much about conditions in the Snarly Hills, and a variety of opinions were expressed. That the place was infested with bandits was certain sure, and the king had stopped that, may the good Pandrite be praised. But how drikingers within their forest fastnesses could interfere with river traffic remained a puzzle, and the few land routes were hazardous enough at the best of times. Seg sat, drinking carefully, and he noticed that for all their big talk, Khardun, Rafikhan and the Dorvenhork also drank sparingly. They did, however, eat hugely.

Seg felt it would be less than politic—at the very least!—to mention that a Witch of Loh sat like an evil spider at the center of the Snarly Hills in the Coup Blag.

Nath the Dorvenhork caught the attention of a serving wench and asked if The Rokveil's Ank served huliper pie.

"No, master. Squish pie, celene flan, jooshas—" She would have rattled out the menu, but the Dorvenhork nodded in his dour Chulik way and said, "Squish."

"Huliper Pie," said Rafikhan, leaning forward. "You have been in the army, horter Nath."

"It is no secret. A Chulik follows the guiding hand of Shum of the Four Tusks into whatever fortune brings."

Diomb was agog to taste all the varied delights of civilized cooking.

"Squish pie," said Seg. "I have a comrade, a very great comrade, who dotes on squish pie. Yet his taboos deny him the pleasure without penance, so that he spends bur after bur standing on his head."

Diomb laughed delightedly. He had proved an object of interest to the denizens of the tavern for only a short time. Most of them had seen dinkus before, captured and brought in as curiosities. Times changed, and no doubt the little people of the forest would soon be setting up in business in Nalvinlad. If good King Crox were here, now...

When Seg's roast ponsho and momolams arrived at the table he looked at the platter, frowning.

"What is it, Seg?" demanded Diomb.

"A strange fashion this, to be sure."

Diomb summoned the serving wench by the simple expedient of

showing her a copper ob between his nimble fingers. He was learning the ways of civilization. The girl, she was apim with smudgy cheeks, ample bosom, stringy hair, dressed in a simple gray tunic, and she could carry a tray with ten jugs of ale one-handed, came over at once.

"What is this food?" demanded Diomb.

"It is Weeping Ponsho, master."

Seg said: "How is the dish cooked?"

"Why, master, I know that, although I am but a serving girl. You slash the ponsho and stuff the cuts with herbs. You cut the momolams into slices and then you roast the meat above the vegetables on a rack so that all the fats and goodness drip down." She looked proud in her own knowledge.

"No doubt, one day, you will be the cook here." Seg stirred the mess with his knife. "I will eat this. But I prefer ponsho roast whole, or quartered respectably, with the momolams halved lengthways and arranged around the meat."

"I have heard of that, master. We think it—" Then she stopped, clearly frightened at her willfulness in what she was about to say. You did not contradict a patron. The landlord had a hard and heavy switch hanging at the back of the kitchen door.

All this time she had not taken her eyes off the ob in Diomb's fingers, going flickety-flick up and down in the way he'd copied, the coin a dazzle.

He flicked it to her and, with the unerring aim of a forest marksman he shied it into the cleavage of her gray tunic. She wiggled, laughed in an affected way, and said, "Thank you, master, may the good Pandrite reward you."

Khardun the Franch looked at Diomb, and Seg, watching, saw that the Khibil smiled a genuine smile, albeit a foxy one.

"You want to be more careful with your money, young Diomb. Not all gold comes as easily as that from horter Seg."

"Oh?"

"Why, yes. Didn't you see the look on that girl's face? She never gets more than a toc as a tip, and you get six tocs for one copper ob."

Diomb shoved his blowpipe up his shoulder out of the way, and leaned back against the settle. "I thank you, horter Khardun, for your information. A toc is one of these, then?" And he held up the tiny coin to inspect it more closely.

Somewhat morosely, Seg struck into his meal. A Fristle fifi came in to sing a song and the taproom more or less quieted down to listen. In her melodious meowling way she sang through: "The Lay of Faerly the Ponsho Farmer's Daughter." Then she warbled, "Black is White and White is Black," concerning the doings of the miller's and the sweep's wives. She finished up with a little ditty about a girl who so loved a boy on the opposite bank of the Kazzchun River that she essayed to swim and risk the perils of the jaws in the water. Her courage and love so impressed the goddess Pavish-keemi that she came down from her house in Panachreem, the home of the deities of Pandahem, and spread her shush-chiff across the waters. This elegant flowing garment provided a safe way for the love-sick girl, whose name, in the fashion of Kregen, changed from region to region.

This song was known as "The Shush-chiff of Pavishkeemi the Beloved."

The Fristle fifi sang well and the applause that followed was genuine. Coins showered about her feet. The Fristle with the party, Naghan the Slippy, was so carried away he joyfully threw the fifi a whole shining silver Dhem. Diomb did not notice this. Mindful of Khardun's words, he threw over the little copper toc.

The girl saw. She bent down with a single graceful motion, picked the toc from the floor, and with a scornful gesture, flung it back at Diomb.

"What—?" exclaimed the dinko, bemused.

Khardun blew out his reddish whiskers. "There are degrees of recompense within the world, young Diomb, and you have just demonstrated two of them—in the wrong order."

"I suppose I will understand this silly world, one day?"

The young mercenaries who had served as boat guards for the short trip upriver now came in. They looked disgusted. Deeming the rest of his river journey safe, Obolya had paid them off. They had money which they proceeded to squander.

"Onkers," said Khardun. "They will learn."

The paktun, Norolger the Arm, whom they had elected as their Deldar to command them, made a half-hearted attempt to restrain the lavish spending. But his heart was not in it.

"By the Blade of Kurin!" he said, wiping the froth from his mouth. "Life is hard, doms, exceeding hard."

A man wearing a coat of sewn skins sitting just along the wall hitched his cudgel forward and lifted his jug.

"If you seek work, paktuns, the wolves are out along the plains up past Mewsansmot."

The paktuns swiveled to stare at this unwelcome intrusion upon their conspicuous misery.

"Wolves?" said Norolger. "We are paktuns, not animal catchers."

The wolves they were talking about, Seg decided, must really be werst-ings, and they were ferocious and vicious and yet could be tamed by man into hunting packs. Runaway criminals and fugitives of all kinds trembled when they heard the yeowling of the wersting pack upon their heels.

He scraped the platter clean and pushed it aside. Before he reached for the looshas pudding he took a swingeing draught of ale. It was probably correct for Milsi not to have accompanied him. But, then, had she done so he would have walked farther on and sought out a more respectable inn.

He thought of Milsi, and found he was looking forward to meeting her daughter. For quite clearly her daughter was the real reason Milsi was so determined to go up to Mewsansmot where the werstings prowled.

Milsi, with her new handmaid Malindi and the charming dinka Bamba, found satisfaction at the warm welcome accorded them in the clothing arcade. The proprietor, a Lamnia called Orlan Felminyer, brushed up his pale yellow fur and smiled and spread his wares. His wife, Alenci, took the three into a back room where they could strip off their old clothes, thankfully, and then with many wriggles and sighs, and exclamations of delight, try on brand new clothes.

Bamba was determined not to wear her bark apron again. She declared that if she was to be a woman of the world then she must dress accordingly.

Milsi's gold procured first-class service and sumptuous apparel. In the end, they bought a chestful.

"Have it taken down to horter Obolya's boat, please, horter Felminyer."

"It shall be done, my lady."

The twin suns threw their twin shadows across the boardwalk as they emerged. The rains had broomed away and the sky was clearing. Out in the alley between arcade and wharfside a file of soldiers marched up, halted at a sharp word of command, grounded their spears.

Milsi realized that Kov Llipton did, indeed, run the kingdom tightly. An officer—he was a Hikdar—walked up the few steps onto the boardwalk. He was apim, ruddy-featured, thrusting, wearing half-armor and carrying an arsenal of weapons in the Kregan way. He touched a forefinger to the peak of his helmet and spoke to Milsi.

"My lady. You are from Obolya Metromin's boat?"

"That is correct, Hikdar."

His ruddy features darkened. "My apologies, my lady. Llahal. I am Hikdar Northag ti Hovensmot. I seek information from you concerning your traveling companions."

"Llahal Hikdar Northag. How may I assist you?"

She looked at him quite calmly. He wore an ornate plume of brown and white feathers in his helmet, and although they were not arbora feathers, they looked splendid. Even the swods in the ranks, the ordinary foot soldiers, wore a piling bunch of brown and white feathers in their bronze helmets.

"I have just asked you. Where are the people from Obolya's boat?"

"Gone drinking in some tavern or other."

His gaze bore down on her. At that moment Milsi felt cold. He did not look quite the same fine upright soldierly person her first impression had conveyed.

"Very well."

He swung away, bellowed unpleasantly at the Deldar at the head of the file—it was an audo of ten men—and jumped off the boardwalk. Milsi watched them until the last clump of brown and white feathers vanished past the end of a warehouse with a broken crane over the upper doors.

"What could that have been all about, my lady?" ventured Malindi in her simple way.

"I do not know," snapped Milsi, crossly.

Bamba smoothed down her new green dress with the orange bows and the yellow lace. Milsi had been quite unable to part the dinka from the abomination.

"I did not like them at all," said Bamba, with a spurt of fierceness. "Men like that have chased us in the forest."

"Yes, and I daresay men like your Diomb have shot poisoned darts at them!"

"Milsi!"

"Oh, yes, very well. I didn't mean to be so sharp. But I am worried. What, in the name of the foul Armipand, did they really want?"

The three women began slowly to walk back to the wharfside where Obolya's boat was tied up. The smells of the river grew stronger, mingling with the brisk smells of the wharf, of which fish was the most prominent.

Milsi stopped so suddenly Malindi crashed into her.

"I am sorry, my lady—"

"Enough of that, Malindi! Of course! What a fool I am!"

"What is it?" cried Bamba.

"It has to be so. That rast of a villain Ortyg the Undlefar. They must have questioned him. He told them—oh, I can see it all!"

Bamba looked nervously unhappy; Malindi started to cry.

"We must warn Seg and the others!" said Milsi, and she straight away started to run swiftly along the alley. Gripping her skirts high, head up, she ran panting with passionate fury toward the city.

Eleven

Knives

"We are a bedraggled-looking bunch," observed Seg, feeling the food inside him and the ale cheerful in his blood. "Let us go along to the souks and buy ourselves some decent clothes."

"Aye," rumbled the Dorvenhork. "Clothes are all very well. But there is a greater need we lack."

He had no need to place his broad yellow hand upon the fire-sharpened wooden stake at his side. In almost any location on Kregen a man needed a weapon, preferably a small arsenal of weapons. Kregans habitually carry enough weapons for the task ahead, not less, not more. If a blade breaks in your hands, and you have no other weapons to draw... Equally, no Kregan will willingly burden himself with junk he does not need.

"Agreed," said Khardun.

They rose from the table, pushing the heavy wooden thing away with no difficulty. They stood up, stretching their legs. Only the Chulik belched.

"Weapons first," he said, and there was no argument, not even from Seg.

"All the same," pointed out Khardun. "We will be able to afford precious little."

"A knife, maybe that is all we will need for a beginning. These wooden spears will serve, I judge. As for an axe—"

"Well," observed Rafikhan, blowing out his feathers. "We will never afford a single sword between us."

"You will pardon me, doms," said Umtig. He stroked the spinlikl upon his breast. "I will return to the boat. I had an eye to Master Orlan Felminyer's arcade."

They watched him trot off without comment, merely calling the polite remberees.

Among the many different folk from all up and down the Kazzchun River they excited no particular interest. There were half-naked men and women seeking to earn their daily food, folk who slept under the piles of the sidewalks, folk who were as adept at stealing the copper ob as at carrying the burden from the wharfside.

Very very few men walked about without a weapon of some kind, even though very many of the poorer folk carried merely a heavy bludgeon.

The roadways steamed. The radiance of the suns beat down and very soon the gluey mud would return to its hard-baked consistency. Up ahead the walkways led into that part of the city where the souks and covered alleys ran in a confusing tangle. These areas of cities, known as the aracloins, harbored commerce, money and villainy.

These particular aracloins in Nalvinlad were not extensive and it was abundantly clear that Kov Llipton kept a close eye on them. Parties of soldiers wearing blue and white feathers in their helmets could be seen here and there ready to squelch the first incipient riot.

The party with Seg walked along very meekly when they passed the soldiers. Old-hand paktuns knew when to make themselves small. Particularly when they carried no weapons in their fists.

The odd thing was that while most of the party of ordinary folk whom

Seg had rescued did not go first to the souks of weaponry, instead trotting off to find new clothes, the Relt, mild and gentle, Caphlander the Quill, went with the paktuns.

As he said, "While I am with you, whom I venture to call comrades, I feel safe. And I must buy a penknife."

They guffawed, and jollied him along. But they all sensed the innate wholesomeness of Caphlander, with his innocent beaked face and the yellow feathers rounding his eyes into bright intelligence.

"This looks likely," said Khardun, halting precipitately. They all looked at the entrance to the store, one of many lining the sides of the souk. The sign said that one Jezbellandur the Iarvin provided the best weapons in all Croxdrin. Seg noticed that the word Croxdrin in the ornately embellished hyr-Kregish, was recently painted and already some of the base paint was flaking away to reveal dimmer lettering beneath. That would be the word Nalvindrin, without a doubt.

An audo—only eight of them—of soldiers marched past with careful looks at Seg and his people. These soldiers wore green and yellow feathers. Farther on, chasing a couple of idiots caught thieving, a group of soldiers wearing green and white feathers rushed on, hullabalooing.

Everyone stood back as the rout passed.

"How is it, horter Hundle," Seg said to the boat-master, "that there are differently colored feathers?"

"Oh, each great lord of the land recruits his own forces and allocates a certain number under Kov Llipton to the proper policing of the city. The blue and whites, they are Kov Llipton's men."

"I see."

They all trooped into Master Jezbellandur's bazaar, and gawped around at the splendid display of weaponry upon the walls and in open-fronted cases about the wooden floor.

Master Jezbellandur himself, nick-named the Iarvin, came forward rubbing his hands together. He clearly was a man of substance, a man who knew himself to be smart, clever, supreme master of his trade, and, at the same time, he managed to express a devoted attention to the wants of his clients.

He summed up this sorry band in no time at all. "Not a pair of copper obs to rub together between them," he said to himself. But he bowed. If they did have a pair of copper obs, he'd have them off them, that he promised.

Khardun, like the other paktuns, had patronized places like this many times before. He was brisk.

"We need first quality knives, horter. And we would like to test them in your salle."

"Knives. Well, I have the finest selection—"

"Good. That is settled. Lead on."

So it was that they were ushered into the salle, a large, square, bare room at the rear of the premises. The floor, although gleamingly clean, was not polished. Sand stood ready in buckets to be strewn. No one else at the moment was in the place. Khardun nodded at the targets, stuffed with grasses.

"Knives that cut, stab, and throw."

"At once, horters."

The cases were produced by a bent-backed Och who contrived to balance two cases at a time. The knives were duly inspected and then test-hurled at the targets.

Seg wandered across to a corner and sat on a chair. Business must be poor for the weapons-trader to concede so much time to men merely buying knives. The racks of swords and axes and spears, of armor and helmets, remained unopened.

The door crashed open and a madwoman rushed in, shrieking.

"The guards are coming! We must run, hide—quick, oh, quick!"

Seg leaped up. He stared. The woman wore a brand new dress hiked up to her knees, mud-splashed and stained. He choked.

"Milsi!"

"They think we are pirates! The guards are coming!"

Umtig the Lock, clasping his spinlikl, sidled in after Milsi. That, then, explained how she had found them. The little Och thief would follow their trail with no trouble. Malindi and Bamba ran in, crying, and Diomb rushed across to them.

"Hurry!" Milsi called, agonized, and whirled, her eyes enormous, her hands leaving the hem of her dress and going in horror to her mouth.

The guards clumped in, hard, spears leveled, the brown and white feathers in their helmets lowering as they bent ready to thrust. Milsi exclaimed in despair that her attempt to warn Seg had proved futile. Seg put a brown hand up to his bow.

"Do not attempt to resist, rast!" The Hikdar, brave in his armor, stepped forward. Milsi could see that he had reinforced his original audo, and now a rank of bowmen bent their bows upon Seg and his comrades. "You are charged with being renders. Your heads will adorn the stakes at the city walls!"

Seg took his hand away. He stepped forward.

"There is a mistake, Hikdar. We are peaceable men, stranded in the river. We are not pirates—"

"Shastum! Silence, you yetch."

"But we can explain it all!"

The bowmen were commanded by a second Hikdar, corpulent, sweating in his armor, his brown and white feathers far grander than the first Hikdar's. He stepped up to the side of the first Hikdar and whispered in his ear.

Seg just stood, poised, alert, watching. He and the comrades with him were at a clear disadvantage. They had no real weapons. These soldiers, despite the finery, were well-armed. He noticed that the bowmen had spurs fixed to their tall brown boots. This puzzled him. How would cavalry be employed along the river to make the expense of the arm worthwhile? Rafikhan had mentioned that there were swarths available for riders far-ther north. These were the so-called two-legged swarths of Pandahem. The true swarth had four legs, a powerful, humped reptilian saddle animal with a heavy wedge-shaped head. The Pandahem two-legged variety pos-sessed four limbs, of course; the forelimbs were nowhere as well developed as the afterlimbs, giving the swarths a faint resemblance to sleeths.

These silly fragile thoughts flowed through his head as he watched what went on.

The porcine Hikdar laughed. Seg did not care for that laugh.

"Well, Northag? What do you say?"

"I—you're confident nothing would come out, Pafnut?"

"Of course not. A bit of fun. Then, afterwards, well—who's going to ask questions? Trylon Muryan?"

"The Trylon? He wouldn't care—no, you're right." This unpleasant Hik-dar Northag licked his lips. Then: "My swods. I'm not sure about them—"

"It's my lads who'll be into it, never fear. Send yours out into the bazaar." Sweat showed in the wrinkles on Hikdar Pafnut's fat cheeks.

Seg braced himself. He detested the so-called soldiers who harassed the weak folk of the world. Vicious cowards like that gave soldiers a bad name. The kind of soldier Seg understood was devoted to protecting others from those who would kill or enslave or rob. It was quite clear this unhealthy bunch were going to have some fun with their victims in the salle. Leem-ing, they called it, a rough, nasty knock-about that could turn ugly.

Khardun knew. He said, "I judge this Northag offal to be lily-livered, and easily led by this thing called Pafnut." He spoke so that the soldiers could not hear him. "Brace yourselves, fanshos, brassud!"

"Aye," growled the Dorvenhork. "I mark me this Pafnut and will deliver his tripes to Likshu the Treacherous, personally."'

Hikdar Northag rapped out a command and his Deldar, poker-faced, marched out the spearmen. The leveled bows of Pafnut's command remained spanned on the party at the other side of the salle. Seg put an arm around Milsi. The gesture was completely unaffected.

"The men over here!" shouted Pafnut. He looked bloated. "Bratch!"

Obediently, the men bratched. They walked smartly across the unpol-ished floor, covered all the way by the bent bows and the steel-tipped arrows, expecting to feel fists, or boots, or the flats of swords beating on them as the swods had their fun.

"Outside!" Pafnut's thick lips glistened, foam flew.

Instantly, Seg and the others saw what was afoot.

Only Diomb failed to grasp what was intended.

Now the Dorvenhork was an archer. He was as well aware as Seg of the menace of those drawn bows.

"Outside!" shrieked Pafnut. His Deldar lowered his bow, let the arrow slide down the shaft to grip it left-handed, and drew his sword with his right hand. He moved up to take command of the party.

He picked on Seg. Over the noise of heavy breathing, the chink of metal, the sudden uproar, Seg heard Milsi's voice from the far side of the salle. "Oh, Seg!"

Seg yelled. "Knives!"

He kicked the Deldar in the guts, swiveled, smashed the nearest bowman across the bridge of his nose, feeling the string smart. His own knife whipped up in a blur of speed and flew to stand out full in Pafnut's porcine face.

Other knives flew. In the instant between Seg's call and the hurling of the knives, the soldiers had failed to respond. When they did loose, they were dead men loosing at shadows.

Milsi and Bamba ran across instantly, and Malindi followed. The men were already hard at work snatching up bows, swords, quivers of arrows.

"We came here to buy weapons," exulted Khardun. "And these onkers gave us theirs free!"

Milsi said, a hard note in her voice: "Does anyone claim this dead Pafnut's rapier and main gauche?"

No one appeared to know much of the outlandish weapons. Seg said: "They are yours, my lady. But I would that you do not go too froward when we blatter those outside."

"Our best plan, Seg the Horkandur, will be to leave this evil place by the back door."

Seg looked around. He saw the lads of his party plundering what each required of armor and weapons. He saw the dead men. He saw the way Diomb and Bamba still had not understood what was intended. "Evil place? No, my lady. Not the place, the kleeshes who came in for sport."

"You are right, quibble though you must at a time like this! Come on! Let us escape."

"The lady Milsi is right," said Khardun. "They will think, those with the squeamish stomachs outside in the bazaar, that we are being beaten in a little leeming. Let us go now, and take our revenge later."

And Seg laughed.

"Revenge, good Khardun! Look around you!"

"Oh, aye, well, by Horato the Potent! I shall not forget these rasts who wear brown and white."

"Nor I!" said the Chulik with great menace.

"Are we all ready, then, fanshos?"

"Aye, ready."

Seg cast a gloomy eye on the bows still lying upon the floor. They were dorven bows, compound reflex, good enough for a first class archer. Their arrows were too short for his own Lohvian longbow. Still, he was running short of shafts. Philosophically, he retrieved a bow that looked as though it had been cared for, and with it two quivers of arrows. These he slung on his back, then turned and faced his comrades.

"Wenda! Let's go!"

When they had all vanished out of the rear door, along that clean and unpolished floor lay a scattering trail of ripped off brown and white feathers.

Twelve

The Law of the River

It is said overmuch of Kregen, and is widely believed, that Chuliks have no sense of humanity. Trained from birth as they are to the military art, they possess a strict sense of order, of the need for rules and regulations, for the necessity of ladders of command to avoid confusion. Their codes of conduct are different from those of many other races. They have nothing of the fanatical dedication to honor, to their nikobi, of the Pachaks. They have nothing to do with the races who change colors upon the battlefield as the swing and sway of conflict brings victory or defeat.

Over the seasons Seg had been nurturing a growing conviction that the Chuliks were misjudged. Their own harsh upbringing and sense of values denied them the outgoing frankness that might have changed general opinion. They could not readily accept a proffered hand of friendship.

When Nath Chandarl the Dorvenhork said, "I would not have witnessed the outrage to the little dinko, Bamba," Seg could see what the Chulik meant. He was not, in these later seasons of greater wisdom, surprised, as he would have been even a few short seasons ago.

For the Rapa, Rafikhan, a different set of mores had to be applied. Given the license, it was common knowledge what would happen to a woman of another race if she was thrown into the Rapa court. But Rafikhan had joined in the fight with relish, his flung knife extinguishing a brown and white feathered soldier, his ferocious hands and beak destroying another.

As for the Khibil, Khardun the Franch, his innate sense of superiority had motivated him to protect his friends. Amnesty for wrongdoers was very foreign to a Khibil's philosophy.

The Fristle, Naghan the Slippy, although not a mercenary, had played his part. He said he was a metalworker, and detested the river, and Seg believed him, willy-nilly.

Now they sailed up the Kazzchun River in Obolya's boat, paying their way in solid silver Dhems, and kept a watchful lookout for pursuit. The brown and white feathered soldiery of Trylon Muryan would be after them if no other lord felt inclined to send his paktuns in pursuit.

Obolya the Zorcanim, of course, remained in total ignorance of the malefactions of the ne'er-do-wells who took passage in his boat. He labored under the impression that he had hired on the Chulik and the Khibil. No one disabused him of the notion.

As Seg said, "I give you thanks, friends, for your courage and help. You earned your hire, to speak in base commercial paktunish terms, exceedingly well. But, for now, why not take a holiday from my service and serve Obolya?"

This could be done in honor and so was done.

That it might have unforeseen consequences did not escape Seg, but he felt it to be the best way of making sure of Obolya's friendship.

A mercenary does not leave a dead body lying around abandoned when time and circumstance give him the opportunity to make sure the poor dead fellow has no more assistance to offer.

Seg insisted that the money taken from the dead soldiers should be shared equally.

Khardun laughed. "That is as it should be. Then we are all equally implicated."

The Relt, Caphlander, quivered at this. But he said: "I cannot strike a blow. But, doms, I stand implicated and although I want none of the cash, I am your comrade still."

They made him take his share.

This little band were fugitives from the law as administered by Kov Llipton. Seg expressed himself as mightily dissatisfied with the famous Law of the River.

Milsi corrected him.

"The Law of the River is unwritten. It is a common bond between all who sail the brown waters. We help one another. But the law of the land, as given by King Crox and now administered by Kov Llipton, is another matter. In that, I think you err also, my Horkandur."

"Oh? How so?"

"Those evil men were from the retinue of Trylon Muryan. He hates the Kov, as the Kov hates the Trylon." Then she passed a hand across her forehead. "I wish I knew if Llipton could be trusted."

"You said you had no reason to distrust him. And, anyway, Milsi—by the Veiled Froyvil!—you are the queen's lady in waiting. Surely you should tell this Kov what has happened to the king and queen?"

"And then?"

"H'm. I see."

In this part of Paz on this side of Kregen the highest noble rank was a High Kov. Then came a Kov followed by a Vad. After that rank came a Trylon and then a Strom. There were three more ranks in the higher nobility, Rango, Elten and Amak. As for the lesser nobility, that varied widely, names and positions changing, it seemed, with every individual country.

Seg had had his fill of nobility. He'd willingly forsaken his overlordship on the question of slavery, and his good comrade, Turko the Shield, had taken over and was no doubt bringing a harsher hand to bear on forcing the dissidents into line with imperial policy.

There was no doubt about it. Even though he joyed in the company of Milsi and made the most of every moment of this journey, he sorely missed the companionship of his comrades. Inch, whose taboos made him do extraordinary things, Turko the Shield, Korero the Shield, Oby, Balass the Hawk, Naghan the Gnat, young tearaway Vomanus of Vindelka, all his blade comrades, and, of course, most of all his old dom, the Bogandur himself.

Well, he'd see Milsi safely home, and then find out what the fates held for him. He noticed that the nearer they sailed to Mewsansmot the more edgy and nervous she became.

He was well aware that he had been indulging himself in this knight-errantry. Unsure though he might be about what would happen, he was sufficiently aware of himself and his wants to know that he needed Milsi. There was no use disguising that. Since he had lost Thelda, grieving for her on her long last journey to the Ice Floes of Sicce, he had grown emotionally callous. He'd taken a sneaking amusement from the speculations of acquaintances that he might marry Jilian Sweet-Tooth. That had never been in his plan of life.

No. No, he could find happiness with Milsi. Yet the secret she clearly harbored troubled him. Was it merely the existence of her daughter? That had no possible influence on him; he would love to meet Milsi's daughter, be a new father to her, bring her into the family of Drayseg, and Valin and Silda. And, by the same token, no doubt he and they would be engulfed in the relations Milsi must have somewhere in Kregen.

Just as they reached the last stretch before Mewsansmot, Milsi found Seg right forrard in the bows where the gangplank lay stowed. He watched the brown water and the ripples, spotting the swift slither of great bodies below the surface, the gape of fangs. The capital of Croxdrin, Nalvinlad, was built where the forest ended and the plains began. The Schinkitree paddled now between the banks, low and bushy, and beyond them extended the plains out to the distant horizons.

"Seg. We shall soon be home."

"Home? Your home, Milsi, not mine."

"And not mine, really, either. You must have guessed I wish to see my daughter, Mishti. You are a parent; you understand how our heart trembles for our children."

"I do."

"I left her with friends—Clawsangs—and yet I worry and worry—"

"Do not fret so, Milsi. Clawsangs are bonny fighters. We had a group with us in the Coup Blag. Skort the Clawsang and his people. They were trapped behind a falling stone. I trust they escaped as did we, for the Bogandur mentioned them as being in the jungle."

"So do I!"

The brown water slid by and the twin suns, Zim and Genodras, poured down their mingled streaming lights. Seg drew a breath.

"When you have assured yourself that your daughter, the lady Mishti, is safe, then what will you do?"

"I do not know!"

"Ah! Then—" Seg swallowed. He started again, and again trailed off. He wet his lips. Then, remembering he was supposed to be a bold brave paktun wandering Bowman warrior, he said: "My lady Milsi. I think you know of my affection for you. Well, that affection is grown—"

"No, Seg! No! Stop."

"But—"

"Do not say anything. I cannot answer. I cannot!"

He felt the granite falling onto his heart.

"Perhaps you love another?"

"Oh, you fool, Seg Segutorio! Cheap words from a cheap farce out of the theater souk!"

"Maybe. I thought you could—"

"I could, I could... But it is—no, Seg, no. Say no more on this, I beg you."

What might have happened then Seg never knew.

A hail from aft brought their attention to Obolya scuttling out from his magnificent cabin, screaming, and his guards yelling, and Khardun and the Dorvenhork stringing their bows. An air of grim tension fell upon the boat.

Up from aft, paddling at high speed, foamed a long lean craft, a Schinkitree with many paddlers, and flags, and a group of prijikers in the bows with their ramp ready to drop, ready to roar charging over in a welter of steel and bronze.

Those stem-fighters clustered in the bows looked hardy, tough men, clad in armor, their blue and white feathers waving. When the ramp went down and clawed into the stern of Obolya's boat, those prijikers would leap across like leems. They knew their business. Not one would fall into the brown, jaw-ravening water, not unless he was shafted through.

Obolya jumped onto the curved stern waving his arms and shrieking. The pursuing boat surged nearer.

Seg took up his Lohvian longbow and bent it with the practiced ease he had known since early childhood.

Milsi put a hand to her breast, staring wide-eyed aft. The paddlers along each side of the boat dug deeply, frantic with the lashes of the Whip-Deldar upon their naked backs.

From the boat aft of them a giant voice roared.

A Stentor, using a curly horn from one of the cattle animals of the plain, bellowed commands.

"Steer for the bank! Do not resist! Resistance is useless."

Seg, about to spit out in his bluff way: "We'll see about that, by Krun!" stopped, the words unformed.

The cluster of fighting men in the bows parted. The prijikers moved aside. Clearly to be seen the snout of a varter showed, aimed at Obolya's boat, and in the trough of the ballista there would be a large and heavy rock. Once the ballista clanged and the arms sprang forward and the varter disgorged that rock...

"We shall be holed! We will sink!" gasped Milsi.

Obolya shrieked again, and his personal guards lowered their bows. Once the boat was holed and sank, the jaws lurking in the muddy waters would feast...

"There is no chance, my lady," said Seg. He looked at his bow. He looked at the pursuing craft. He saw the varter and pictured the cruelly sharp and heavy rock positioned in the trough. Carefully, he unstrung his bow. He took the string right off. He coiled it neatly and laid it away in his belt pouch. Then he took up one of the compound reflex bows, and put that dorven bow close by his hand.

Milsi said, "The guards of Kov Llipton will not be deceived, Seg."

"Nevertheless, I can but try." And he put the great Lohvian longbow down, pushing it half under the landing ramp, so that it looked a mere lump of wood.

Without orders, for there was need of none, the helmsman headed for the near bank.

Zim and Genodras threw down their glorious mingled lights, streaming in long swaths of ruby and jade. The breeze brought the scents of the plains, sweet grasses, dust, and the sky washed a pearly blue high above. The prow of the boat touched the bank, and she slewed and so came to rest in a ferny brake. The pursuing boat ranged up alongside, and the Stentor's voice roared forth again.

"Hold fast all! You are renders and will surely die!"

Willy-nilly, Seg and his comrades, menaced by drawn-back bows, watched as the guards poured into their boat.

Thirteen

Trylon Muryan

"If," said Seg, "we cannot cheat, contrive or fight a way out of this stinking dungeon, we are not fit to be called paktuns."

The dungeon itself, sunk into the ground, iron-barred, stank. Outside, at a higher level, the guards prowled. Some guards wore brown and white feathers, and for every guard with the brown and white, another guard wearing the blue and white paced him and kept him company.

Hundle the Design explained this.

"We are in the dungeons of Mewsansmot. This is Trylon Muryan's domain. But Kov Llipton, also, has jurisdiction, seeing that the town was the benefice of King Crox to Queen Mab when they were married."

"Fat lot of good that does us," said Khardun. "It means we have double the damned guards to deal with."

"Mayhap," said Seg, "we can start them fighting one another."

"Would that the good Pandrite willed it!"

"I agree with Seg," growled the Dorvenhork in his grim Chulik way. He strained against the iron chains that bound him cruelly. "We are paktuns. You, Khardun the Khibil, are a hyrpaktun."

"That is so. We are not true to ourselves if we cannot burst a way out of here."

Seg refused to let the scarlet flames of horror into his brain—Milsi! What had happened to her? Where was she? What were these rasts doing to her now?

Of all the men, only Diomb had been sent along with the women. He and Bamba, Milsi and Malindi had been taken off. Seg could feel the passionate terror in him; and the ferocious coldness to push that away, and await what came, and to escape and shaft as many villains as needed shafting, and rescue Milsi and the others...

"Seg! Brassud, dom, brassud!"

"Yes." At Khardun's comradely words, Seg did as he was bid and braced up. He could not go to pieces now, could not betray these men. The odd thing was, he thought, how they looked to him for guidance. Oh, yes, he had paid three of them good red gold to serve as hired paktuns. And the others took their lead from him. But, all the same, used as he was to command, and the giving of orders, he found this situation intriguing.

The little Och cleared his throat.

"Doms," said Umtig the Lock. "There is a way."

They all looked at him, chained in their misery in the dungeon. Umtig still wore the remnants of his finery, and the green-laced blue tunic was ripped only here and there. Seg could not see Lord Clinglin, the tiny spinlikl, in his accustomed place about Umtig's breast.

The tunic moved of itself.

"Ah!" said Seg. And, then: "Can the little fellow do it?"

"Do it?" Umtig sounded mightily offended. "Have I not trained him assiduously ever since he was fortunate enough to come under my protection? Do it! You steer close to offending me, horter Seg."

"Then I crave your pardon, horter Umtig. And," Seg added, "by Diproo the Nimble-Fingered! Let him get on with it sharpish!"

Umtig jumped as though goosed. He bent instantly and started whispering fervently into the opening of his tunic. Presently a long prehensile arm emerged, the tiny but powerful hand grasped Umtig's ear, and with that as a purchase, Lord Clinglin climbed to Umtig's shoulder.

His large round eyes surveyed the dungeon. His small round head with the widow's peak of darker hair giving him a religious look, a sweet and ooh-aahing look to soft-hearted ladies of the court, looked to the chained men in the dungeon oddly fragile to be the cunning object on which their hopes rested.

"Beautifully, now, my lord," whispered Umtig. "Sweetly now, as I have taught you. Away you go!"

Without hesitation, the tiny monkey jumped from Umtig's shoulder, clung to the iron bars of the dungeon, and then vanished up away out of sight.

Trylon Muryan Mandifenar na Mewsansmot held his title and lands at the hands of the king. King Crox had made him, made his family, and took half of the goodness, produce and profit of the Mewsansmot estates.

Encamped a few miles outside the town on the fringes of the great plains where the ruffled rumps of uncountable head of grazing animals flooded the land with color and movement, Trylon Muryan lolled at ease. He was feeling pleased with himself. That morning he had ridden out on his mewsany, a strong and hard-mouthed beast called Black Thunder, and had successfully shot and slain two chavonths creeping among the herds. His crossbow had been placed among the trophies of the hunt. He had called Master Pumphilio, an artist of repute, to capture the moment and the glory in vivid paint.

So, there sat the trylon on his striped cushions of brown and white silk, sipping sazz, nibbling at miscils, awaiting the moment when he could repair to the dinner tent. These tents were more of the style of pavilions, peaked, striped with multi-colors, embroidered. Delicious aromas from the cooking fires where his slave chefs labored filled his mouth with saliva. He drooled at the coming repast.

Around him his chiefs, his major domo, his slaves, his Chail Sheom—pearl-hung, gauzy of garments, painted of face, and chained—waited on his every word, his every gesture. He was a man pampered in this life.

He ate gluttonously. He ate hugely. Yet he remained trim and dapper, with a figure that could still be spanned by a woman's outspread hands. And there were women aplenty who sighed to perform that divine function.

As he said, soulfully, it was a great pity and a wonder under the heavens of Zim and Genodras, that the great and glorious Pandrite had seen fit to take away his wife and his twins, and to cast them beneath the iron-rimmed wheels of a common Rapa's garbage cart.

So it was that when the zorca-rider appeared, dust-stained, bearing the marks of hard-riding, the trylon was prepared to treat him with great solicitude.

"Wine for the messenger." And: "Take your time, tikshim." And: "I am for the dinner table, so do not delay me at your peril."

The messenger gasped out his news, fragile, pallid, in mortal fear of this elegant man in the lounging robes trimmed with silver lace.

"The devil you say!"

Trylon Muryan sat up straight on his cushions.

He snapped his fingers, and his grand chamberlain scurried to do what was unspoken but necessary. Muryan sat deep in thought and then snapped pettishly at the messenger.

"You say they will be here in two burs?"

"Assuredly so, pantor."

"Very well. Get out."

The trylon sat again in thought. On his sallow face graced with a thin strip of chin beard of a dark color that was not a genuine black until it was dyed, a look of growing wonder curved his thin and painted lips. He began to throb with the wonder and the glory of what had happened. He knew, as Lem was his master and guide, he knew he had been appointed, anointed, chosen and selected.

"It must be!" he said, gobbling over his words, to San Frorwald. "The gods shine on me, and Lem is to be praised above all others!"

"You are undeniably in the right," said San Frorwald in his grating voice. He was a Sorcerer of the Cult of Almuensis, a glittering and imposing figure, such a sorcerer of flash and presence as would be employed at the table of Trylon Muryan. San Frorwald glistened in a robe of green and gold and blue, tall of spiral-bound hat, imposing of look, a thaumaturgist of considerable powers. His beringed hands stroked the book chained to his waist. That hyr lif was gem-encrusted, and bound in the skin flayed from a newly slain maiden.

This sorcerer was the only confidant admitted to the secret thoughts of Trylon Muryan Mandifenar na Mewsansmot.

"Prepare everything," he told his major-domo. "Nothing must go amiss, or your head is forfeit."

The major-domo, a butter-pated Gon, bowed, and acknowledged the command, and went to oversee the preparations. The Gon, one Nath the Keys, knew the trylon's threat was no idle one.

"Now the great and glorious Lem smiles upon me!" declared Trylon Muryan. "Now shall the brown and silvers see such a day as this kingdom has never before witnessed!"

The approaching cavalcade of whose advent the messenger had warned was observed, and escorted into the trylon's camp with great pomp. A full regiment of lancers preceded the column, their mewsany mounts hardy animals of the plains tamed to men's use. The carriage was covered with a yellow and green awning against the midday glare of the suns. Slaves with water jugs threw handfuls of water against the carriage to cool it and the occupants within. Feathers waved. There was a full regiment of mewsany cavalry to bring up the rear. In the midst of the glittering host rode the principals, gorgeously clad, riding zorcas, those supreme saddle animals whose hooves splintered the light from burnished silver, whose spiral horns were wound with gold wire. Stentors blew their brazen trumpets in fanfare after fanfare.

Trylon Muryan, resplendent, walked out of his pavilion to greet the arrivals.

The cavalry opened out to left and right. The mewsanys of these two regiments were blacks and grays, hard of hoof, pawing the ground as their riders gentled them into the required positions to take up their guard stations. Pennons fluttered. The carriage rolled to a standstill before Trylon Muryan's pavilion. He felt conscious of himself, of the suns beating down, of the sound of the cavalrymen, of the jingle of bit and bridle. He could smell the dust off the plains, and scent the savory dishes cooking in the kitchen area. He swelled with the importance of the moment.

Being the man he was, he swelled with his own importance.

Being the man he was, down he went, plump, into the full incline before the carriage. His nose dug into the dust of the plains, his rump stuck in the air, he abased himself to all outward seeming, and joyed in it, knowing the inner secrets of his own heart and the fecundity and glory of the schemes hatching there.

"Do rise, Trylon Muryan. Lahal."

He lifted his head, staring up.

The queen looked glorious, clothed in light, glittering with gems, seen from this humble position like a goddess rising supernal into the air.

"Lahal, majestrix. Lahal. You are more welcome than—"

"Very probably. I have ridden out particularly to see you, trylon. Let us go into your tent where we may talk privately."

A frantic scrabbling followed as men and women jostled out of the way, making attempts to maintain protocol, pushing lesser wights clear, shoving to make a passage for the queen and the trylon.

Within the coolness of the tent Muryan swept a beringed hand about the displayed wealth and luxury.

"All I have is yours, majestrix."

Slowly she removed her dust-veil, the shamil of fine blue gauze hemmed with diamonds and seed pearls. Her brown eyes regarded the trylon meaningfully.

"That is so, Muryan. You hold your life at the hands of the king my husband. And he has given Mewsansmot to benefit me. I am glad you do not forget."

Muryan put a hand to his lips. He knew nothing of this woman. She had appeared suddenly, brought at the king's orders from Jholaix. She was the last representative, as far as the wise men knew, of the royal line in the vital female descent. She had been married to the king in a hasty, candle-lit ceremony in the palace of Nalvinlad. The moment the final words had been spoken the king had departed, paddling down the river to go on his fatal expedition into the Snarly Hills. The queen had waited no time at all before setting off after King Crox.

And, now, here she was, back and alive, and of a sudden promising to be an unexpectedly formidable opponent.

"How may I serve, you, majestrix?"

"In two things, which must be done immediately."

"Of course."

"One. You will send for my daughter, the lady Mishti, from wherever she has been banished. You will do this thing now. Your head will answer for her safety."

Muryan bowed that head that, on a sudden, seemed to him to be not so securely affixed to his neck. He rang a golden bell and his Relt stylor sidled in, pale feathers dusty and ink-stained.

"Send for the queen's daughter, the lady Mishti. Send Jiktar Parndan and his regiment. Bratch!"

The Relt bratched, quiveringly.

"And, majestrix?"

Before she could answer, Muryan rattled on: "Please, majestrix. A chair. Sit down. May I offer you wine, parclear, sazz?"

She waved a hand bare of any rings.

"Later. I am not well-pleased that you took it upon yourself to send my daughter away from Mewsansmot. One might think you sought to imprison her. I am well aware of her importance."

"Majestrix! I sought to protect her. Kov Llipton has designs—"

"I will come to that later."

"As you command."

"You and Kov Llipton do not see eye to eye. For every soldier he has wearing the blue and white, you employ one wearing the brown and white. If your mutual hatred flared into open conflict..." Again she made that small dismissive gesture. The shapeliness of her hands fascinated Muryan. She was a shapely woman altogether, the formal heavily embroidered and gold-laced garments barely concealing the proudness, the lissomness, of her body. Yes, decided Trylon Muryan, his schemes would involve pleasure as well as profit.

"The other matter of importance, majestrix?"

"I came upriver in a boat belonging to a certain animal-trader, Obolya Metromin the Zorcanim, under the protection of paktuns."

"I am overjoyed you were able to hire loyal men."

"Ah, yes. It was not exactly a question of hiring the paktuns. My desire to see my daughter caused me to leave them under the protection of one of your officers, a Jiktar called Harmo ti Pallseray."

Muryan nodded.

"A good man. Loyal. He will do his duty."

"So I trust. First, I wish that Obolya be afforded every facility in the trading he carries out here. Second, I wonder if you recall two others of your officers—Hikdars Northag and Pafnut?"

He frowned and then he smiled. "I know all the Jiktars who command my regiments, majestrix, of course. But, as for the Hikdars who command the pastangs within the regiments, well—" He spread his hands, and the massed rings glittered. "Well, majestrix, no, I do not know all of them. But Hikdar Pafnut, I recall, yes, him I remember."

"Well," she said, and she made it brutal. "Both of the rasts are dead, and may they rot on their way down to the Ice Floes of Sicce."

"Majestrix?"

She told him what had occurred in Master Jezbellandur the Iarvin's weapons bazaar. "These men, your officers, Muryan, attempted the queen. They were slain by my protectors. Therefore, no charges can possibly be leveled."

Muryan screwed up his face. "I agree, majestrix. But, Kov Llipton will not see the matter in that light."

"And you have nothing to say on the conduct of your officers and men?"

He saw his mistake.

"It is an outrage, majestrix! Of course—I shall have the matter thoroughly examined. Rest your mind. As for your paktuns, I feel sure Kov Llipton will pardon them."

She stared at him for a moment, not much caring for what she saw, yet knowing she had to use this man, for her own resources in this strange land where she had been made a queen in the game of power politics were parlous slender.

"You are frightened of the kov, Trylon Muryan?"

He blustered. "Frightened? Assuredly not, majestrix. Yet he is the man your husband gave the overlordship of the country to when he went away. His death grieves us all; also, it leaves Kov Llipton in a position of great power."

"That I see."

For the moment there was no more that could be accomplished. Muryan issued the necessary instructions.

She sat down. She put a hand to her forehead, and then, firmly, said, "Now I will take a glass of parclear, if you please, trylon."

Fourteen

Concerning Seg the Horkandur's discovery

Executions carried out in the provinces along the Kazzchun River were matters of elegant if bloody simplicity.

There was, quite obviously, no need to keep an executioner with an axe on the payroll. Prisoners due for the chop were merely invited to take a little swim in the river.

Reflecting on this, Nath the Keys shoved his bent back more comfortably against the straw-filled sack against the guardhouse wall, scratched under an armpit, flicked away a couple of pesky flies, and then took a chunky bite out of his cheese pie. As he was an apim with only two hands, these actions had to be performed in sequence, unlike those diffs with usefully more than two hands who'd do the whole lot in one go, and wipe their noses into the bargain.

The new prisoners stuffed down into the sinkhole under iron bars were very quiet. They, too, must be reflecting on the manner of executions along the river. Down the passageway with its barred cells at either side where less important prisoners were confined, a dolorous series of wails and cries, pleas—and singing—broke the stillness of the night.

"Shaddap!" yelled Nath the Keys, spraying bits of cheese and pastry. The noises did not diminish. He had a party of drunks in there, a couple of fellows who'd robbed a Lamnia of his purse and been taken up by the trylon's guards, a fellow who had commented unfavorably on the trylon's personal habits in a too-public place, and an idiot boy and girl who'd stupefied themselves on caff and staggered doped and dazed into the temple.

Much as Nath regarded Trylon Muryan as an out-and-out bastard, there was still no call for Kov Llipton to come raging up here with his own men to take charge of the prisoners. The queen had said, quite distinctly, that the paktuns were not to be imprisoned, that the deaths of the two Hikdars and the men could be explained. Jiktar Harmo ti Pallseray was a bit of a ninny; but he could obey orders. And then Kov Llipton had arrived like a monster from the brown river itself, and changed everything.

On a board fastened to the wall the keys to all the cells and dungeons hung on rings. Nath the Keys, sitting against his sack, did not notice the tiny spidery hand reaching out from the shadows. Not a single key chingled. He took another bite from his cheese pie, beginning to worry if his ladylove, Nardia the Yellow, really was, or if she was just trying to play him along for more cash. If she was and she wanted to, she could go along to Kov Llipton and... A drop of sweat rolled down Nath's nose and dropped onto his cheese pie.

A tiny grating noise came from the bars of the dungeons. Nath half-smiled. Poor devils. They were going for a swim. Once Kov Llipton got his teeth into you, you were as good as dead.

As this thought flitted through his head, one of the kov's soldiers walked in, a hairy Brokelsh with his blue and white feathers flaunting about him. Nath looked up.

"We're off for a wet, Nath. Nothing more doing tonight, and, by the Resplendent Bridzilkelsh, this place would make a fish thirsty."

Nath eyed him a trifle warily.

"If that's all right with Deldar Stroikan. All I have to do is lock 'em up and feed and water 'em—if they're here long enough."

The Brokelsh did not take this too well. He put a hairy hand to the silver mortil head at his throat. Among the string of trophy rings in his pakai gleamed no less than two gold rings. A man of some repute, then, this Bandlar the Spear. He had slain two hyrpaktuns in personal combat, and taken from them their golden pakzhan rings to add to his pakai collection. Still, slaying a hyrpaktun did not automatically make you a hyrpaktun. That high honor was far more hardly won. Bandlar the Spear was an ord-Deldar.

"I've given Deldar Stroikan his instructions. If he and his audo cannot do the job for a bur or two while we clear our throats, then what is the world coming to?"

Nath was far too canny—and, if the truth be told, more than a little frightened—to make any scathing remarks about the white and blues coming up here and lording it over the brown and whites who were the inhabitants.

A clatter of iron on stone heralded the entrance of Deldar Stroikan. He showed in his flushed face the anger Nath had contained. His left fist gripped onto the hilt of his sword. As a so-Deldar, he was five steps below Bandlar the Spear in the grade structure within the Deldar rank. His pakai showed all silver; it was lacking gold, and it was shorter, a lot shorter, than the pakai dangling so insolently from Bandlar's shoulder.

"Yes, Deldar?" Bandlar's coarse Brokelsh voice conveyed insultingly his position.

As Nath could see, clearly for the sake of explaining his arrival, Stroikan jerked his right thumb at the pile of weapons stacked into a corner.

"The Jiktar will want every one o' those weapons strictly accounted for."

Bandlar simply swept aside the opening gambit in a positional tussle. "Make it so. And, I've looked. Most of the stuff is Krasny work. Those paktuns we've got stuffed down the sinkhole had better crafted kits. But, as for that great bar of iron one of the onkers carried—what paktun in his right mind would lug that about?"

"It's supposed to be a sword."

Nath ventured to chip in.

"I believe it's ceremonial. He probably stole it from the retinue of some noble, maybe even some king in his wanderings."

"Then he's a worse onker than I thought."

Bandlar the Spear stalked off, and after Stroikan so far forgot himself as to make a face at Nath the Keys, he, too, went off to the guard positions to check his men. Nath was left alone to get on with his cheese pie.

So he thought.

A slithering grating sound from the sinkhole again made him give that half-smile through a mouthful of cheese pie. He could feel sorry for those poor devils. He did catch just the one astonishing glimpse of a shadow where the tallow dip could throw no shadow from anything he knew of in the guardroom, then the black cloak of Notor Zan fell on him.

Khardun said: "You needn't have knocked him cold, Dorvenhork. Now we cannot question him."

"Better safe than have him screaming his fool head off."

The others crowded in silently. Umtig felt bloated with pride. He glowed. Lord Clinglin had carried off his part with meticulous and wonderful skill, returning with the keys and making only a single tiny chingle of noise. Now Umtig and the spinlikl wrapped around his neck could let the big hairy fighting men get on with their parts.

Seg found their weaponry piled in the corner.

Each man took up his kit, some with a little grunt of pleasure, some with a feeling of relief. Seg turned the pile of other prisoners' weapons over, picked up the great Krozair longsword, and could not find his Lohvian longbow.

Probably that was still pushed safely under the landing plank in Obolya's boat.

He contented himself with one of the compound reflex bows, and took up two quivers of the shorter arrows. He looked around.

"Right, fanshos. Shaft anybody who tries to stop us. Go more silently than the White Wind that glides across Wistith Waste."

On their way here they had been blindfolded. Now they crept silently along the passageway and heard the drunken discordant songs foaming from the cells. Other voices joined in, yelling for the drunks to shaddap, and so Seg, without a smile, nodded his men on, confident they would not be heard.

The passageway was ill-lit, the barred cells pools of darkness. Seg discarded the idea of releasing the drunks, for although they would create a fine disorder, they would alert the guards far too early. He passed the iron bars of a cell and a voice, hoarse and raspy with wonder, said: "By Zim-Zair! How came you by that sword?"

Instantly, so fast his feet seemed barely to touch the stone floor, Seg leaped at the bars. He peered into the darkness. He said, "Is that you, my old dom?"

A man clad in a tunic that had once been white moved toward the bars of his cell so that a single vagrant gleam from the tallow dip on the opposite side caught and etched his face. He had black hair, very curly, and ferocious black moustaches brushed arrogantly upward. He looked a wild and raffish fellow, and he stared at the sword across Seg's back with a hunger that tautened all the ridges of his face.

He spoke. Some of the words he said were ordinary understandable words, but what he was saying was completely unintelligible to Seg.

At last, the leaden feeling banished from his limbs and the dryness from his throat, the sawdust from his brains—for he'd thought it was, he'd really thought it was!—Seg said, "I am sorry to disappoint you. I am not a Krozair. This sword belongs to a friend of mine and I keep it in trust for him."

"By the disgusting diseased liver and lights of Makki-Grodno! This is, indeed, a marvel. I had not thought to find a single soul in this heathen place who knew of the Eye of the World."

Seg well understood how the people of the Eye of the World, the inner sea in the far continent of Turismond, believed themselves to be the center of the world, and all the enormous oceans and continents about them merely the frame.

"I am well enough acquainted with the Krozairs to believe that if I release you from this cell, I may entrust the safety of this longsword to you, as a Krozair brother."

"You may. I am called Zarado. Llahal—"

"I am called Seg. Llahal. Now let us get you out of it and bash a few skulls and so escape free."

Khardun called back on a whisper: "Someone comes."

The drunks made enough noise to cover what followed.

Ten men, led by their Deldar, marched down the passageway, a full audo of soldiers. Their brown and white feathers frilled above their bronze helmets. These were the men who would hurl Seg and his comrades into the Kazzchun River. Shafts flew. Blades rose and fell, punched past corselet rim and withdrew, darkly stained.

The Deldar went down with all the famous Bells of Beng Kishi ringing in his head. When he recovered he was pinioned, and his men were mostly dead or unconscious. Seg glowered down, hands on hips, his face like a thundercloud.

"You, Deldar. You will answer a few questions."

Deldar Stroikan said: "You're all dead men."

"I think not. Not yet. But you do understand that you will be? Very good. Now, Deldar—where are the ladies who were taken up with us, and the dinkus?"

"This will not do you any good, you rast. You have slain too many of the trylon's men to—"

Seg put his face close into the Deldar's face. He could smell the man's wine-soaked breath, and, no doubt, his own onion-smell was spreading nicely in return.

"The Lady Milsi! If you don't answer, *now*, I'll slit your gizzard up, down and across! Where is the Lady Milsi?"

The man looked nonplussed at this. He licked his lips. "I heard that the king is dead, and all the people with them. The Lady Milsi died, too, in the Coup Blag. Only Queen Mab returned safely, and she has gone to the trylon."

Seg heard this and did not understand it. It was not the same degree of non-understanding he had experienced with the Krozair. He shook his head to stop the ringing and said, "You are mistaken. The queen died in the Maze. We brought the Lady Milsi out safely. Now, you rogue, tell me—"

"I've told you!" The Deldar's eyes widened. It was clear he was dealing with a madman. "The queen was brought ashore with you and your band of cutthroats and rode out immediately in a great cavalcade to see Trylon Muryan."

"Trylon Muryan," growled the Dorvenhork, "is the man who put us down the sinkhole."

"And who threatened to throw us into the river." Khardun wouldn't forget that in a hurry.

Seg would not admit that ice flowed in his veins. He would not admit that a clutching hand gripped his heart with crushing force. He found it damned difficult to catch his breath. And his legs were shaking, he had to admit that, curse his stupid betraying legs though he might.

Lady Milsi—Milsi—was the queen. No doubt of it.

"So they mewed her up in chains and dragged her off to be thrown down before this damned trylon? HEY?"

"No, no. It was not like that. She was received with great honor and joy that she was still alive."

There was no doubt, no doubt at all, that Seg felt as though some gigantic oaf had kicked him in the guts.

"We will have to get moving," said Khardun. Then, in his Khibil way, he added: "I own I am disappointed in the Lady Milsi. But, queens are queens and have their own ways of dealing with us ordinary folk."

The Chulik thumbed up a tusk. "Ordinary folk, Khardun? And you a Khibil?"

"You know that I am not a king, not even a noble, Dorvenhork. But I think our friend Seg has been shrewdly struck."

"Aye. So let us get out of here, by Likshu the Treacherous!"

"What shall be done with this Deldar?" demanded Rafikhan.

"Oh—just thump him gently behind the ear."

This was done. Seg took no notice. Surrounded by the others, who now included the Krozair, Zarado, among their number, he was more conveyed along the passageway than going as an understanding member of the escaping party.

They encountered no more guards, of either blue and white or brown and white allegiance, and so burst forth into the starry night of Kregen, out under the golden roseate light of the moon sailing above the town and the treetops—She of the Veils.

Just for the moment, Seg Segutorio, known as the Horkandur, didn't much care about anything at all.

Fifteen

Kov Llipton

"By Mother Zinzu the Blessed," exclaimed Zarado. "I needed that!"

He wiped the froth from his lips with a scrap of once-yellow linen. Seg's heart warmed to the Krozair. How many times he had heard that heartfelt expression!

Khardun and the Dorvenhork were still on speaking terms, and were sharing a bottle companionably. The others had their bottles and tankards on the sturmwood table, and the slaking of thirsts went on at a prodigious rate.

About them the noise of the taproom of The Aeilssa and the Risslaca flowed on in a muted fashion, for it was late and most of the fisherfolk had already left. The few farmers had gone long ago and only the merchants and the mewsany handlers seemed to have time to spend to sit and drink past the hour of dim.

"This is all very well," said the Fristle, Naghan the Slippy. "But surely we cannot stay here long? The guards will be—"

"Of course they will," Khardun said with his expansive cocksure attitude. "But they have to find out that we are flown. Then they will set up a hue and cry. By then we'll be well out of it."

"If I may venture to ask," said the Relt stylor, Caphlander, in his usual nervous and apologetic manner. "Where we will go to be out of it?"

"Ah," said the Dorvenhork. He did not polish up a tusk, but his small piggy eyes glanced about the taproom. "That is the question."

"If you think," Hundle the Design lowered his tankard, "that we can march over the Mountains and reach North Pandahem—forget it. It'll be down the river for us."

"And you would steer us?"

"If we find a boat, doms, why, yes, of course."

Sitting with his nose in a tankard, Seg took little interest in all this. He was not going to allow himself to become maudlin over a woman. That the woman used to be Milsi, and was now the queen—this famous Queen Mab—merely made his resolve the stronger. These women looked to him. Quite apart from the gold he'd paid out, they sensed in him the qualities necessary for leadership. Well, by the Veiled Froyvil! he'd lead them down the river and out of this hell hole.

And yet—and yet!

He had really believed there was a future with Milsi. They had both been shafted by the same bolt of lightning. He was sure of that. He had known it with all his consciousness, known it unfailingly. Because she was a queen she had betrayed him, left him, consigned him to the dungeons. She had used him, had gained her ends, and then she had abandoned him.

No. He did not feel a happy man at that moment.

"One thing is sure," he said, his voice heavy and leaden. "We are all wanted men. There is a price on our heads, mark me on that."

"Aye. So we defy these rasts, and sail. We go downriver with Hundle the Design as our boat master—"

"That is true, Khardun," interrupted Rafikhan. "But Seg the Horkandur is our Jiktar."

No one argued that.

None of them offered much information about past lives. They did not volunteer information on their homes, what they had done, what seen, where adventured. Only Hundle and the Och thief appeared to own the Kazzchun River as home. What Umtig had done to land up in prison was obvious; the Relt stylor offered no information. The Fristle once mumbled a few words about a broken bronze plate and a death of a ninny; but that passed without comment. Truth to tell, Seg no more worried about the past misdeeds of this happy little band of fugitives than he fretted over the future mayhem they might cause. Nothing much made sense or reason or was of interest to him right now.

The supposed racial enmity between Rapas, Fristles and Chuliks did not seem to affect these representatives of their races, and Seg could feel a tiny twinge of relief that he had no worries of that tiresome nature. He wouldn't have cared had they flown at each other's throats as they might well have done in other circumstances. He felt the most important step he could take now would be to get himself well out of this stupid Kazzchun River business, get back home to Valka and Vallia. He'd find his old dom, and then they could set about putting the country straight for the last and final time. Then there were his Kroveres of Iztar to concern him. They had been abominably neglected of late, what with other priorities like Spikatur Hunting Sword. No, get out of this the quickest way he could and get off back home.

These new comrades of his might be rough paktuns or dubious characters along the river; they were sensible of the blow he had received, and while in no way expressing maudlin comfort, did not—as they would have done to a fellow sufferer—make mock of his affliction.

Seg stood up. "Let us go down to the riverbank and find ourselves a boat."

Hundle stood up, looking troubled.

"I mind me that the Law of the River does not take kindly to folk who steal boats."

Seg looked at him.

"The Law of S.O.N. takes precedence, Hundle."

Kregans love abbreviations and initials. Hundle lifted one eyebrow.

"The Law of Saving Our Necks. Right—wenda!"

Under the light of She of the Veils they crept down to the riverbank, and, by that streaming roseate golden light they witnessed a horrific scene.

A Schinkitree had just pushed off, the long narrow boat laden with bales. The loadmaster had either not known his job or had botched it. The boat was sinking.

The paddlers chained to the benches screamed. They flailed their paddles at what reared at them as the water closed in. Horrible, macabre, disgusting... The monsters roared from the brown water, churning it into suds, and those suds tinged ominously red-black under the light. Huge jaws crunched down. The boat slipped beneath the water, dragging with her the doomed slaves. The free men might just as well have been chained up. They flailed and splashed and tried to swim, and were engulfed. The noise of chomping jaws reached across the water clearly to the bank. Seg half-lifted his new bow, and then lowered it. Any help was impossible. The men tipped into the Kazzchun River were already dead men.

"We do not let that happen to us," he said.

Hundle let out a queasy breath. "The nightmare," he said, and he shook. "The nightmare!"

This distraction, gruesome though it was, gave them the opportunity to find a boat at the downriver end of the wharf, to untie her and climb in unseen. They let her drift gently off downstream for a time before taking up the paddles and driving her fast and true through the treacherous water.

There was no pursuit they could see.

Fishing in the Kazzchun River was an occupation of an entirely different order from fishing in other parts of the globe. You didn't just hang a line and hook, suitably baited, over the side and merrily haul in when you had a bite. Nor did you spread out nets and haul them in, beautifully freighted with the shining catch. If you did the latter, you'd haul in mere shreds and rags. And if the former—idiot!—you'd go headfirst over the side.

One system involved placing two or three, even four or five, boats alongside one another and decking them in. Then, secure behind barriers, the fisher folk hurled long fish-spears. They had to watch for their targets, and select the edible from the predators. A flashing cast, the cruel barbs, fashioned probably from the fangs of the very monsters who lurked in the water, biting in and the quick hauling in of the line. If you hung about during that stage you'd most probably haul in only half of your catch.

A river can support many different species, and the fish and plants sustain each other. A rain forest is a finely balanced biosphere, fragile, and living things learn to live together and contribute their part to the existence of the forest. Nalvinlad, being situated near the end of the forest proper, partook of the jungle and a little of the plains to the north. Hundle expressed grave doubts that they'd escape easily through the capital city without questions being asked.

The Dorvenhork said in his growly way: "Let us go ashore and walk, then. I am famished!"

They were all hungry.

"It would be best, if we are captured, not to be found in possession of a stolen boat," counseled Hundle.

Caphlander expressed the pious hope that all would come well in the end.

In any event, the end appeared immediate and sudden. A number of other boats and fishing craft mingled along a broad reach, and from the tangle of boats a paddler appeared thrusting along with the brown water broken into cream-colored foam at her prow. Seg looked and let rip with an exclamation of so profound a disgust no one else had the heart to comment.

There followed a repetition of what had previously occurred. Their boat was forced to the bank under pain of being instantly sunk. In what seemed no time at all they were chained up and on their way to Kov Llipton's dungeons in the city. The speed of it all impinged only faintly on Seg. His thoughts were not with him at the moment, not fully, not so as to make him the Seg Segutorio who would have put up a fight in his mad feckless way—and probably got himself killed for his foolhardy pains.

The boat that had captured them had been sailing downriver, going along at a foaming pace, her paddlers urged on by Whip-Deldars. She flew the blue and white treshes, and the flags fluttered brilliantly in the streaming radiance of Zim and Genodras.

Kov Llipton looked down on his miserable band of prisoners from his high deck aft. Cloth of gold hangings framed his seat. His feet rested on a balass and ivory stool. Watchful guards stood at his back, waving long yellow feather-fans to cool the Kov's brow.

Seg, chained up, looked at his own feet on the deck.

"You are culprits, miscreants who have slain soldiers in the execution of their duty. You are drikingers. Therefore it is meet you should die with the customs of the river."

Hundle said in an oddly dignified way in these fraught circumstances: "No, pantor, no! We merely protected defenseless women. We have done nothing to bring the Laws of the River upon us." It was clear that Llipton's mention of these famous laws had sparked Hundle the Design.

"Do not banter words with me!" The lion bellow roared about the prisoners. "I have judged. Now you swim."

Seg looked up.

Kov Llipton was a numim, a lion-man, with fierce whiskers and ferocious, lowering lion face. His mane gleamed brilliantly under the light of the suns. Robed in war harness, strong and robust like most members of his race, he glowered down, the lord, the arbiter, the final dispenser of justice along the Kazzchun River.

Seg's tongue crept out and wet his lips. He could deal with lion-men. He lifted his head, and his shock of unruly dark hair bristled.

"Listen to me, kov!" he bellowed out, and with every word his passion grew, his feelings of wrongness, his realization that good men should not have to die for sins they had not committed. "Listen to me, you great fambly, and learn the truth!"

Llipton hunched forward, suddenly. His massive paw-like hand gripped onto his sword hilt. He frowned.

"You speak to me—"

"Aye, you great ninny! I speak the truth!" Rapidly, not wasting a word, he shouted out what had happened in Master Jezbellandur the Iarvin's armory. At each sentence his comrades, with great venom, shouted out: "Aye!" and: "That is the truth!" and: "That was the way of it!"

During this, the Krozair, Pur Zarado, joined in fervently. He knew a chance, slender though it might be, when he saw one.

Kov Llipton listened intently, waving away a guard who would have laid Seg senseless with a blow from his spear butt. Llipton's goldenyellow fur gleamed, his armor shone, his fierce lion-face bent frowningly down. Seg roared on, worked up, determined that he must do all he could to save the lives of his comrades. He forgot about the Lady Milsi as the woman who might have shared his life; she became the object in whose protection they had done what they had done and were now being persecuted.

"And so, Kov Llipton, you have the right of it now. If you condemn men for going to the assistance of ladies, of slaying rasts who attempt a lady and a queen, then your famous Laws of the River, aye! and of King Crox, are a blasphemy and a mockery in the eyes of honest men!"

The kov pointed.

"Bring that man up here to me!"

Seg was dragged forward and dumped down at the foot of the ivory and balass stool. He glared up and the malevolence in his face made the kov's eyelids twitch.

"If what you say is true—"

"If! I thought I spoke to a man of honor, who might recognize another such. Perhaps I was mistaken—"

"You are too proud and insolent, or too mad—"

"I am not proud, I hope I am not mad, and I am insolent only to a few people who deserve it."

Llipton brushed a beringed hand across his whiskers.

"I bear hardly on malefactors, yet I dispense a just justice. If your story can be proved..."

"Ask Master Jezbellandur. Ask the queen."

"Believe me, that I will do." Llipton looked over the side. In a musing tone, he added: "That will not avail you, for by then you will have gone swimming."

"Justice!" screeched Seg. He staggered up, his chains dangling about him. "What kind of justice do they teach you here in this Opaz-forsaken blot called Croxdrin?"

Llipton's hand stilled above his whiskers.

Seg saw that he had to bring this matter to a head by introducing an entirely new aspect to the situation. He drew a breath. He glared; but he got out what he had to say reasonably enough. "Let me speak to you, man to man, kov, or pantor, whatever they call nobles hereabouts. Maybe I can prevent a great misfortune falling upon you and all you love and value."

"What are you babbling about now? Guards!"

Seg tried for the last time.

"You are all doomed, kov, you great fambly, if you do not listen to me!"

Llipton's hand resumed that stroking of his whiskers, and the rings flamed in the jade and ruby radiance. Then: "Drag him up to me. I will hear what he has to say further to condemn himself. Then he swims."

Rough hands grasped Seg and hauled him up closer so that he stood swaying before the noble. Seg's face composed itself, the mad fey glare faded from those piercingly brilliant blue eyes. Even his shock of black hair seemed to settle and grow smooth. He drew himself up. He looked the kov straight in the eye.

"Listen to me, kov. You are a great noble here, and yet your poor barbarian people and your primitive river civilization are laughable. Know this! I am a kov. I am a Kov of Vallia! We in Vallia do not take kindly to anyone who insults one of us. I have an army at my command. Listen, I have already swum in your famous River of Bloody Jaws! I brought a voller down into the water—if you in your benighted ignorance know what a voller, a flier, is—and we swam to the shore and no monsters stopped us. My name is Seg Segutorio. These men with me are innocent of the vile charges brought—rather, you should send for a swim the perpetrators of the crime, if our justice had not already struck. If these men are not released then you must answer for the consequences when the might of Vallia is arrayed against you! Woe, indeed, on that day to all of Croxdrin along the Kazzchun River!"

For a space of time that stretched intolerably, Kov Llipton sat, gripping his sword hilt, brushing his whiskers, saying nothing.

In a voice soft as the kiss of steel, at last he said: "You claim much, Seg Segutorio. A kov? We shall see. Innocent? We shall find out. Insolent—ah, yes, you are that!"

Seg said nothing.

"One thing you claim, that you have already swum the river. That is the most difficult of all to believe—"

"And the least important. I am who I say I am. You may never have heard of Vallia—"

"Oh, yes. I know of Vallia."

Well, that explained the abruptly cautious attitude of the numim, then...

"Take these men to the dungeons of the Langarl Paraido. Do not mistreat them. I will ponder the story, and have inquiries pursued. Until then, you tremble upon the brink of death."

"That," said Seg Segutorio, a Kov of Vallia, "is no new experience."

Suddenly, Llipton leaned forward. "I am prideful of my trust. I keep the Law for the king. You did not say, Seg Segutorio, of what lands you are kov?"

Seg didn't bat an eye or split a second. "Of Falinur. I have given the charge of my kovnate over to my comrade, Turko the Shield, while I visit heathen parts."

"Of Falinur—if it exists—I do not know. But I shall. Have a care, lest you—"

"What do you think can be worse, in your mind, than taking a swim in your river?"

"Ah!" said Kov Llipton, and waved his guards to take Seg back to his comrades. They had not been privy to what went forward upon the high dais; they were agog to know what the hell was going to happen next. All that Seg could do was to assure them that, at least for now, they weren't going for a swim.

With a treacherous feeling of pleasure, Seg realized he was feeling amused. These poor benighted folk in their jungly river! This proud puffed numim—who were a great race of folk, to be sure—and his bewilderment. Vallia! Ah, well, perhaps there had been a grain of truth in the tale Seg had spun. Enough, perhaps, to delay their swim by a few days...

Sixteen

In which Strom Ornol takes cover

The amusement Seg felt increased when the ruling came down from Kov Llipton regarding the due payment required. Whether the story was true or not, they had indubitably taken knives from Master Jezbellandur the Iarvin. Ergo—those knives must be paid for. From each member of the group was, therefore, scrupulously removed the price of one knife. Seg almost laughed.

"This has to mean our story is believed," declared Khardun. He gave his whiskers the first proper tweaking they had received in too long a time. "We shall soon be free."

"Before that we should escape," growled the Dorvenhork in his Chulik way. "By Likshu the Treacherous! Let us break a few skulls and make off."

"I am with you, Dorvenhork," quoth Rafikhan.

"Oh, and I, of course," said Khardun in his offhand Khibil manner. "Naturally."

They were immured in the dungeons of the Langarl Paraido. The iron bars here were measurably thicker than those of the sinkhole in Mewsansmot. Also, they had a nice interesting habit here of sending condemned prisoners for their final swim wrapped in nets so that something could be hauled back and, if the head happened to be among the bits and pieces salvaged, then the heads of prisoners finished off by swimming could be impaled and exhibited along the city walls.

Of them all, Umtig would not be consoled.

He looked shrunken, his little puffed Och face miserable, his whole demeanor eloquent of the Thieves' own description—like a pickpocket with no fingers.

Lord Clinglin, amid much boisterous jocularity, had swung nimbly out through the bars, and Umtig had confidently predicted his speedy return with the keys.

Lord Clinglin had not returned.

Caphlander in his mild Relt way attempted to comfort Umtig. "Nothing harmful can have happened," he said, giving his beak a twitch. "And when we are released we will prosecute inquiries—"

"When? If!"

"So that," rumbled the dangerous Chulik growl, "is why we should break a few skulls and escape!"

"Yet," said Zarado, speaking up forcefully and yet in a smooth even tone, "there are other aspects. They are feeding us. They are not ill-treating us. And we believe they are sending to search out the truth of our story. We can escape now and look foolish—and once again be subject to the Law— if we are found innocent. Or we can bide a few days and see."

"Lull the rasts into a false sense of security," offered Rafikhan. "Aye, that is a good scheme."

The rest of them went at the argument and Zarado moved off to leave them to it. The cell was capacious and reasonably dry, and equipped with a few foliage-stuffed bags on which to sleep. The Krozair plumped down beside Seg, saying: "I owe you a deep apology, Seg—"

"Not so, Pur Zarado. It is I—"

"Listen. You gave into my charge the longsword. I no longer have the brand. So, you see how it is."

"The blade will return to its proper owner, never worry."

Zarado twisted up his ferocious moustaches, one side at a time. "I studied the blade. There were certain things upon it. And there were the letters DPKrzy. I knew a man once—Jak the Drang—who owned sword and letters similar—"

Without thinking through the implications, for the situation had clearly changed, and still embedded in the usual caution, Seg rapped out: "Oh that was old Duruk Pazjik."

"Of Pur Duruk Pazjik I do not know."

Fascinated by the past history suddenly opened out by Zarado's words, Seg had to say: "And this man, Jak the Drang?"

"Oh, he turned out to be the Emperor of Vallia. My comrade Zunder and I hired out for a time, then we drifted off, meaning to sail back to Sanurkazz." Here the Krozair heaved up a sigh. "I miss Zunder. We were parted in some heathen place called Molambo, and I was hired on to serve in swordships and so assisted in guarding boats up this Zair-forsaken river. I wish I'd never seen the place or this Grodno-Gasta of a Kov Llipton."

"The Eye of the World is perhaps not so far as we think. The Chulik asked for huliper pie in a tavern—"

"Did he! The sailors of Magdag love that pie—"

"And he was accused of being in the army for it. Items of food and drink, recipes, fashions, travel widely."

"Humph—that does not bring back our weapons or gain us our freedom, by the disgusting suppurating armpits of Makki Grodno!"

Seg shook his head, devoutly wishing that he could hear another Krozair brother saying these delicious oaths.

Shortly after that the guards came by and removed Seg from the cell. He was pushed along the corridors and into a room where guards wearing green and white waited. He squinted in the lamplight, for dawn was a few burs off yet.

"So it is the Seg the Horkandur I thought! Well met, comrade of the Maze!"

Strom Ornol, for it was he, strode forward with outstretched hand. His handsome, weak, aristocratic face did not look at all as Seg remembered it. Its habitual blot-like pallor was replaced by a crimson flush. A trimmed beard concealed the jaw. In fact, Seg had to look twice to reassure himself that this was the rast Ornol himself. The most astonishing thing was the broad smile on Strom Ornol's face.

Seg grasped the outstretched hand.

"I, Vad Olmengo, am come strictly charged with Kov Llipton's orders to bring you to him straightaway. Now, not a word! Not a word. Hurry!"

The guards with Ornol—or Olmengo as he had newly dubbed himself—closed up around Seg and casually, and yet with purpose, pushing the dungeon guards aside, swiftly escorted him outside. They pattered through the corridors, ascended to the surface, and mounted up on mewsanys waiting ready. In the first pale fingers of apple green and vermeil radiance they rode swiftly for the southern gate. No one spoke. The guards at the gate allowed them through when a Hikdar leaned from the saddle and rattled off orders from Kov Llipton. They cantered through and so entered onto the jungle trackway beside the river. The smells of forest and river mingled. The sound of the mewsanys, the clink of bit and bridle, the feel of leather and the ungainly clip-clop-clip of the six-legged riding animals might in other circumstances have lulled Seg Segutorio.

He remained quiveringly alert.

The weird friendliness of this blot, Strom Ornol, came as distinctly unsettling.

The circumstances of their parting, when the Lady Milsi—who was really this famous Queen Mab!—had told a few home truths and Ornol had reacted in his stupidly vicious way, forcing Seg to stick a knobby fist into his mouth, could hardly cause any friendly feelings. Ornol would in the normal way of the blot have him strung up or sent swimming. So...?

The track reached the riverbank with the massed trees receding to leave a small open space. Here a hut of rotting branches and tattered papishin leaves sagged over a wooden jetty. A boat was tied up, silent and waiting, with the boat master in his typical leaf hat standing shading his eyes. The cavalcade rode up and the guards dismounted.

"Can we talk now, strom?"

"Dismount, Seg the Horkandur. We go aboard the boat."

The guards in their green and white tied their mounts to leaning posts and began to board. Seg dismounted. Ornol—or Olmengo—drew his rapier. Four guards stood by him with bared swords. Ornol's smile changed.

"Step aboard, Seg—"

"What is this about, strom?"

"You call me pantor!"

The vicious haughtiness of the words was more in keeping with the Ornol Seg knew. The noble's expression changed. He was enjoying himself. He put up a beringed hand and ripped the false beard free. He rubbed a kerchief over his cheeks, and it came away reddened, and, lo! his face was the face of Strom Ornol, pallid, like the underbelly of a fish.

"Everyone will believe you escaped with the assistance of Vad Olmengo, who is a stupid adherent of Lliptons." The guards, too, were enjoying the farce. They ripped off their green and white feathers and replaced them. Seg saw the colors of the feathers they placed in their helmets.

Brown and white.

"You are a fool, Segutorio, and an insolent cramph! You are going swimming. Then we shall deal with Jezbellandur. There will be no proof against Trylon Muryan's men—and you will be dead and out of the way. As for your comrades, they are fish food as soon as your escape proves your guilt!"

Seg did not feel in the least horrified. He saw the boatmen had already cast off the rope at the prow of the boat and were holding her steady. Ornol motioned with his rapier.

"Step aboard, you rast."

Obediently, Seg moved forward. They thought they were clever, yet they had not bound him. That wouldn't be necessary when he was threatened by so many swords. They'd just sail out into midstream and push him overboard.

Very well...

"So you work for this fellow Muryan, Ornol?" Seg talked casually, moving toward the guards and their swords, watching the strom.

When he moved he moved like a leem.

He hit the first two guards inside their swords. They toppled backwards, arms flailing. They screamed in mortal terror long before they hit the water...

Ornol skipped backwards, yelling. Seg swiveled, sloshed the next guard so that he dropped, stunned. He ducked without a thought, turning again and sticking out his foot so that the fourth guard, rushing on and yelling in bold fury, tripped. That guard, screeching horribly, staggered on, off balance, and went splash into the murky waters.

"A madman!" screamed Ornol. He jumped for the boat and scrambled over the gunwale anyoldhow, already screeching for his archers to loose.

The bowmen in the boat were not numerous; there were enough to feather Seg before he could reach cover! Seg had a deep respect for the power of bows. He saw the composite bows bending, saw five at least shafts aimed at him. He had the skill to deflect arrows, arduously taught him by the Bogandur, and could weave his way through an arrow storm—but he had no weapon with which to make the deflections.

Very well—he'd run for it, and dodge, and win free.

In that instant one of the bowmen jumped as though stung and clapped a hand to his eye. His bow clattered uselessly to the deck. Another archer whirled around a full circle, dropping his bow. When he faced Seg again there was something odd about his eye.

Seg put his head down and ran for the trees, jinking like a hunted animal, which he was.

A voice ripped from the trees.

"Seg! Over here! Run!"

Seg ran.

Two arrows plunked into the mud of the track before he reached shelter—then he was hurling himself head over heels into the trees and, already, was alert to the dangers of the forest.

He saw a small, lithe form, clad in an astounding rig of scarlet and gold, with green feathers waving, and a long tube at its mouth. Cheeks swelled to enormous balloons, and puffed—and the next dart sped.

"Diomb!"

The dinko did not bother to reply. Seg watched his amazing performance.

As a bowman of some repute, Seg could judge and admire superb shooting.

Diomb's two upper hands held the long blowpipe in a brace. His other two hands withdrew darts from his magazine pouch and fed them in a steady stream into the mouthpiece of the ompion.

He drew, placed, and blew, drew, placed and blew. He sucked in his breath with whooshing open-mouthed gusto. Darts sped.

Seg tumbled down among the muck of the forest and turned, at last, to stare out onto the river-bank and see just what this dustrectium* was accomplishing.

Panic-stricken, the boatmen had cut the stern rope. The boat drifted out and downstream. Sundry splashings and churnings in the water indicated where the river was living up to its name with respect to those unfortunate wights who had fallen in. There was no sign of Strom Ornol. If Seg knew him, he was cowering well out of it, head down.

At last Diomb stopped shooting. The range opened out past the effective reach of the blowpipe.

"Seg!"

"I give you my thanks, Diomb, and the jikai!"

"I enjoyed that. It proves I have learned the ompion and can earn my hire as a paktun."

"You have and you may, may Erthyr be praised!"

Presently, when the boat, still without a paddler in sight, had drifted off, they stood up and walked out onto the wooden jetty. The guard whom Seg had stunned was about to recover his senses, groaning. Diomb put his little foot against the fellow's gut and started to push him into the water.

"Hold on, Diomb. We can't just kill the silly bastard like that—"

"Why not?"

"We-ell—"

"He would have killed you, and laughed doing it."

"All the same, he is just a guard, earning his hire." Here Seg, admitting of no further argument, clouted the guard over the head again with his picked-up sword, and glared straight at Diomb, head down and jutting.

"I shall understand the ways of this preposterous outside world one day, I suppose, by Clomb of the Ompion Never-Miss!"

Seg looked around. "He has this sword and a knife, and that is all. Oh, well, that is better than being empty-handed. Now, Diomb, tell me all about it."

Abruptly the dinko suffused with passion.

"Of course! I was so enjoying this little fight I forgot. Seg! The Lady Milsi—"

"You mean Queen Mab." Seg's voice grated in a surly unfriendly rasp.

---

* dustrectium: firepower

"Why, yes. I do not understand it all. Her name is Milsi. And it is Mab. But, Seg, that great rogue Trylon Muryan has her a prisoner! In a monstrous tower!"

"And I suppose the cramph plans to marry her and make himself king?"

"Seg! You do not sound as though you are Milsi's friend." Diomb stared up, his little face creased into a scowl of incomprehension. "Are you not feeling well? Perhaps you have an ache in the guts...?"

"I've an ache, all right. If Milsi wants to marry this Muryan fellow, then that is her business. I must get back to my comrades, and Jezbellandur. If he is slain then a key witness vanishes. There is no time to waste—"

"There is no time to waste, true, Seg the Horkandur! I do not understand you, after all that you and the Lady Milsi were together! What ails you?"

Seg was already turning away and reaching for the best of the mewsanys. He grasped the reins looped around the standing post. "Look, Diomb. Bamba is well? Good. Then you are all right. As for me, I am alone."

Diomb scuttled across and his upper left hand reached up to fasten on Seg's muscle-corded arm.

"Listen to me, Seg! Milsi is imprisoned, with Bamba and Malindi. She sent me—I escaped, and a pretty piece of trickery that was, too—and she sent me to ask you. I followed this Strom Ornol, who takes his orders from Muryan, and crept through the jungle after you, and—"

"And you saved me, Diomb. I do not forget that."

"But you must go to the Warvol Tower leading our comrades and rescue the ladies!"

"So Milsi turns to me when she is in trouble again, imagining I will come running like a little mili-milu when she rings her golden bell and wheedles and puts out a bowl of milk? Well, Diomb, my comrade, I have finished with that foolishness. When she marries Muryan it is sure that Malindi and Bamba will not be harmed, will be richly rewarded in the wedding party. As for me, time presses, and my comrades fester in a dungeon—"

"There is no time to bring your comrades if they cannot go at once! The wedding is planned—"

"Do not tell me! I do not care!"

Diomb stood there, face a single stricken question mark. He shook his head. He swallowed. He tried again.

"Lady Milsi is Queen Mab, and she holds you in high honor and tender loving care, Seg. This is so—"

"This is feathers from a zorca!"

Diomb let go Seg's arm. He jumped up and down with frustrated rage. He started to yell.

"I don't know what is the matter with you, Seg the Horkandur! You are no jakai! We thought, all of us, only of you when misfortune fell on us!"

"Oh, aye, typical!"

"You are an ingrate! You are not deserving of the Lady Milsi's esteem or affection, still less of her love! After all she has done for you—"

"By the Veiled Froyvil, Diomb! You try me hard!"

Then Seg paused. He took a trencher of a breath. His chest swelled as only an archer's chest can. He was not just an ordinary man, was Seg Segutorio. He could feel the dinko's words like lashes upon his spirit. But, there had to be more to this, there had to be some spark of what he had felt still left to him... He let the enormous breath out and he said: "Diomb, my friend. Maybe I have the wrong of it. Maybe—you spoke of Milsi's love. I have received no sign of it, save for a foolish passing moment soon forgotten. But, mayhap there was a reason for the queen using us warriors to escort her safely home, and then to have us dumped down into a sinkhole and ready to go swimming in the River of Bloody Jaws. Maybe this reason was not the obvious one we believed—"

Diomb looked horrified. Then he jumped up and down and almost fell over himself trying to sputter his words out.

"I see! I see! You blame Milsi for putting you in the dungeon!"

Still wrought up, Seg shook his head, his impatience wanting to brush aside stupid matters of logic. "Well, not exactly. She did not put us in the dungeon. But we were chucked down the sinkhole because we defended her, and she rode off as a great queen and left us to fester!"

The look that crossed Diomb's face would have made Bamba hug him with delight.

"You said, Seg the Horkandur, that mayhap you did not have the right of this sorry business." Diomb spoke in a light, easy way, a tone not nonchalant or casual, but airy and rippling with hidden amusement. He could be a little devil at times, could Diomb the dinko.

"I said this. Go on."

"Then I have to tell you that you are an onker with a head full of the fungus that sprouts on the forest floor. Why do you think Ornol was sent by Muryan to pick *you* out of the dungeons and throw *you* in for a swim? Hey?"

"We-ell—"

"I suppose you imagined it was because you were the leader, the most important, the high and mighty puffed up pantor among us? Confess it, I challenge you!"

"If I had been thought to have escaped, the others would have received short shrift—"

Diomb gave a curt cutting gesture with his upper left hand. "I will tell you. This piece of festering dung called Muryan wishes to marry Milsi and thus hold title to the kingship—I have learned all this. He knows Milsi loves you and he will have you dead!"

"Do what?"

"You heard me, Seg the Horkandur!"

"You mean Muryan wants me dead, not Milsi?"

"Cretin!"

"Then—then what you say is true—there is danger for her—"

"She did not abandon you. She rode to seek her daughter and gave strict instructions you and our comrades were to be well-treated."

Seg glared around on the brown waters of the river, on the bank and the sagging shed, at the mewsanys, around to look unseeingly at the ranked dark green masses of the trees. Again he shook his head. He felt bloated, and yet shrunken. One thing he did know, without a moment's hesitation.

"I shall ride to the Warvol Tower. You must see to Jezbellandur and our comrades. One thing I know, Diomb—if Muryan does wed Milsi against her will, then it will be he who will be the dead man!"

Seventeen

Seg Segutorio builds a bow

A slim paddler skimmed down the Kazzchun River passing without hindrance where any other boat would be forced to halt and declare occupants and contents. The Schinkitree flew the flags of Croxdrin; but the tresh that gained this imperious passage flew from a taller mast than any other banner. This was the personal flag of Kov Llipton allied to the kingdom's messenger service.

Sitting on his comfortable chair in the stern, Tyr Naghan Shor brushed up his fierce whiskers and the streaming radiance of the suns glinted from his golden mane. Kov Llipton trusted folk of his own race to carry secret messages and discover intelligence of the river. The vague form of the Xaffer, squatting to one side, offended no one, for the Xaffers are a race strange and remote, and employed usually as secretaries and domestics. This Xaffer, Ninshurl the Seal, wore a decent blue robe girt with a silver chain, yet he was slave.

"A fool's errand, Ninshurl, I warrant you, by Numi-Hyrjiv the Golden Splendor!"

"Yet the kov was most insistent, master."

"Oh, one does not quarrel with Kov Llipton, not unless they wish to take a little swim. All the same, if the hulus of Mattamlad are mindful to be awkward..."

"We fly the flag of truce, master. They will listen to what we have to say."

"You are right, of course. All the same, I have left a most gorgeous numim maiden for this arduous duty, and I shall not waste too much time, believe you me."

The boat sped on downriver, driven powerfully by the hardened muscles of specially selected paddlers, slaves every one, chained to their benches.

Mattamlad at the mouth of the river slumbered under the suns. Here mud stank into the air, and the heat rotted everything. Tyr Naghan Shor under his flag of truce was allowed passage past the guard boats, for Mattamlad was an independent port town, and owed no allegiance to King Crox or his country to the north.

Reporting in at the bureau for foreigners, Tyr Naghan saw the tall masts of ships lying in the port area. He sniffed. He regarded the folk of Mattamlad with contempt; yet there was no doubt they were in more direct contact with other nations. Still, one day, all in Pandrite's good time, Kov Llipton would sweep down the river and annex all here.

"Your flag of truce and your letters will be honored, Tyr," the port official informed Naghan. "But I think it wise if you concluded your business within the space of a single day."

"I will if I can. But you know foreigners—"

"Oh, aye," said the official, a wizened marcer whose comb and sidebrushes were much bedraggled, and whose curved body showed the effects of a long-ago swim—a quite inadvertent swim—in the river. For that miraculous escape he was known as Nath the Flounder. "Oh, aye, Tyr Naghan Shor. By the Bloody Jaws of the Brown River Herself, I think we know foreigners better than you."

Not allowing his natural numim authority to exert itself over a matter so petty, Naghan took himself off. He walked through the muddy street with a swing, judging that he would just get indoors before the rain fell down like a solid blow on everyone and everything. He passed the inns with a cock of his head at the sign of the Mermaid's Ankle, walked with the Xaffer at his side and rear, into a wider thoroughfare where a raised wooden sidewalk indicated the higher status of the neighborhood.

"There it is," he said, and strode on, turning up wooden steps to a bronze gate. A large house walled off stood beyond the bronze gate. At his ring a man answered the bell with a cheery remark and a genial presence. This man wore a buff jerkin over a tunic whose sleeves were banded in red and yellow. He wore two swords.

"Come on, come in, horter. I shall announce you at once."

Tyr Naghan grunted in a noncommittal way. As he entered, another man was just going out, walking fast to reach the nearest inn before the rains came. He wore a buff jerkin and buff breeches, and his hat possessed a wide rolled brim with a jaunty feather curling at the side. He gave the numim a cheerful "Llahal, horter," before trotting off toward the taverns.

Tyr Naghan Shor, followed by his Xaffer slave secretary, went into the building. As the doors closed and the first drops of rain fell splat onto the mud, he said: "A waste of time. Just a waste of time."

The so-called "big" plains of northern Croxdrin were extensive; but in no way could they be compared to the enormous areas of Segesthes where the wild clansmen rode on and on for week after week and still there was no end to the plains. Herds of animals grazed here, and the predators had their fill during feeding time in the age-old way. Seg rode a mewsany at breakneck speed, two more tailing on the leading ropes, and he no longer carried a sword.

Three quarters of the blade lay far back down the trail embedded in the side of a wersting, and the hilt rested a few dwaburs farther on, shoved well and truly down the sharp-fanged gullet of the leader of the wersting pack.

Diomb's directions had been precise. Seg knew how much farther he had to go when he saw the brown and yellow tents clustered about a stand of trees breaking the level of the plain. He slowed. The werstings were vicious hunting dogs, black and white striped killers; but he had outrun them now for the loss of his sword and two mewsanys. What lay up ahead in those tents could be far worse trouble.

He felt damned naked without a bow, by Vox!

He was tired, hungry and thirsty. None of that mattered until he had taken Milsi and the others safely out of the clutches of Trylon Muryan. He'd eaten all the provisions in the mewsany's saddlebags. He kept religiously intact the last bottle of wine, a mediocre red stuff. The girls might need a refresher when he found them.

When the Maiden with the Many Smiles shone down refulgently in a pink wash of moonlight Seg scouted the camp and the Warvol Tower beyond. As for the tents, they housed simple herdsmen of the plains, who could ride their mewsanys with consummate skill, hurl a rope, cut and slash with their heavy halberd-like strangchis to drive off the werstings. Of bows they appeared to have only tiny self bows that wouldn't stick a woflo's hide.

As for the tower...

The thing brought back vivid memories to Seg Segutorio of Erthyrdrin. Like a Peel Tower, it soared up, stark and brutal against the stars. There were no outworks. Set here to guard a long-forgotten frontier, it was now kept in use by Trylon Muryan to immure his prisoners. Similar towers, stark, simple, separate, had dominated the skylines of Seg's youth. Erthyrdrin might be vastly different from these plains, being a land of valleys and fey folk whose characters were yet shrewdly practical, yet it shared the architecture. The Warvol Tower lofted, tall, unpierced by any window or arrow slot for the first hundred feet. Above that the slits leered down. Near the top there were even trellised arcades supported on slender pillars. Here in Pandahem no thought was given to the defense against aerial attack. These people did not expect a host of saddle flyers to burst upon them from the clouds. They had not witnessed airboats swooping in to disgorge fighting men.

Seg had no saddle flyer. He had no voller.

All he had was a knife.

Diomb had said: "They are kept in the chambers with columns of blue and yellow. The columns of green and yellow are where the quarters for the guards are situated."

Staring up, Seg cautiously circumnavigated the tower. He assured himself that those columns up there *were* blue and yellow. If that blue was really green... Well, that lay in the hands of the all-seeing Erthyr of the Bow.

A ramp curled up from the ground three quarters of the way around the tower before reaching the main door. This was set at a cunning oblique angle in the masonry so that no room was afforded for the swing of a ram.

There was no way, Seg had to face the truth, that he was going to force his way in through that door and then up all the interminable stairs within to the prisoners' quarters at the summit.

He took himself off to the herdsmen's camp like a gray wraith, skulking like a lurfing of the plains.

He kept his saddle animals well away from those of the herders. He did first things first. Instead of stealing some food, he went off to the thickest part of the stand of trees away from the tents, and settled down to work.

Had he not had the fortune to be favored with the knife, he considered gravely, he'd have chewed the damned wood off with his teeth...

To say that he could not remember when he had built his first bow was correct, for he seemed to have been building bows all his life; but he could well recall the very first adult bow. And, of course, there was the stave of the green Yerthyr wood he had cut from Kak Kakutorio's tree. The trees growing here in Pandahem now were not Yerthyr—most certainly not. The Yerthyr, of a green so dark as almost to be black, was lethally poisonous to animals without the special second stomach such as the thyrrixes of Erthyrdrin had. Well, even had these trees been Yerthyr there would be no time to fashion a real longbow in a single night. A longbow took four years or so...

Around him within the trees of this wood lay staves and billets waiting to be released and freed into longbows. All he wanted was one decent stave, for he would not contemplate jointing two billets. Eventually he selected a limb in which the grain appeared to run straight and which had the slightest of curves so that he could compensate for the string-follow. His knife went swish-swish through the wood, smooth and gentle strokes that slivered the heartwood away with full respect to the lay of the grain.

He found places where the grain forced itself up in a curve and so he left that curve there, rightly contemptuous of any stupid attempt to cut the sapwood to conform.

Above him the Maiden with the Many Smiles wheeled through the stars, and the Twins shed down their mingled pinkish light, streaming shadows between the trunks. Seg worked on, head bent, concentrated into a single organism that could do this thing superbly well.

Bowyers there might be in this world of Kregen; there were no finer builders of bows than those of Erthyrdrin. He carefully thinned the limbs of the bow, constantly checking with finger and thumb, with eyes that could judge to a whisker. A lifetime's experience was now coalesced into this one task, to make a bow that would cast aright.

Gradually the rough limb torn from the tree assumed a section something like a thimble. Stout in the handle, cunningly tapering to the tips. He would just have to cut string notches there, no horn or ivory nocks in this bow. Only two pins bothered him, and these he left with plenty of spare wood to be on the safe side. He was working at a pace that, to an observer, would appear cautious and steady and even slow. In reality he prepared and trued the bow with prodigious speed.

Every now and then Seg cocked an eye at the Moons. He checked the time, aware of the passing moments.

When he first tested the bow he used a bowstring from his pouch. At least that was proper, a real silken string from his own longbow. The bow bent sweetly and he held it up, muscles bulging, to see better the way the two limbs curved and to judge the arc. The sapwood on the back and the shaped heartwood on the belly worked together. He made a tiny clicking sound of satisfaction. The fistmele, the clenched fist and upright thumb, that measured the proper distance between string and handle was right. The bow felt right. The handle was a bit of a mess; no time to fix a real handle. Now for the shafts...

In the end he had to settle for the heart of three leaves, cut down to long and narrow flights. He fastened the fletchings with a length of scarlet thread ripped from the edge of his loincloth. There was no need for a head.

He might simply have taken a suitable springy branch and fitted the bowstring and tried that. But he felt that the cast ahead would demand length—or, rather, height—strength and accuracy. For a Bowman of Loh there was really only one way to secure those requirements.

"Now," he said, speaking softly and with great solemnity, "may Erthanfydd the Meticulous approve of this work and bless this newborn bow."

The final flourish remained. Dutifully, he cut his sign neatly into the wood without marring the finish. That sign he felt might help...

The feel of the bow in his hand was odd, of course, for very many reasons. The lack of seasoning would mean that the bow could never, in the opinion of a Bowman of Loh, be a proper longbow. As for the arrow, all his skill and judgment had to serve in getting the spine right, in seeing that the shaft was not too stiff or too weak for the weight of the bowstave.

He'd been forced to tighten everything up in this devil of a rush. And he was famished. Scouting around the herdsmen's tents he came across an abandoned bowl of cheese which, when he dipped his fingers in and sucked, tasted like King Golanfroi's Nosedrops—and every child knew what they tasted like. Still, he sucked down and didn't breathe in too hard through his nose. Then he reconnoitered the piquet lines and discovered the coil of rope he was after. The ropes were used between posts for temporary corralling purposes. With his booty over his shoulder he went back to his clump of trees.

Unraveling a fine strand took time. He'd made the distance judgment with the experienced eye of a shooter. He wouldn't be out more than the length of a man's body. When he had his fine long strand he coiled it with exquisite care and fastened one end to the arrow.

Then he picked up a splinter of wood, whittled the end to a needle point, and set off for the Warvol Tower.

The guards were not foolish or masochistic enough to stand a watch out on the open plain when no one was going to get into the tower but through the one doorway. Seg circled twice, checking, and then stationed himself under the spot where, high above and seeming to reel sickeningly against the stars, the blue and yellow arcade showed.

If that wasn't blue up there...

Now was the time.

Quickly, he pricked the ball of his left thumb with the needle-sharp splinter and a drop of blood, black and shining, oozed out. With the other end of the splinter and in his own blood, he wrote on the leaf fletchings: "Haul in."

Sucking his thumb took no time. He gripped the bow. He held it familiarly, and yet with the tentativeness of fresh acquaintance. The bow felt good. Had he been using one of his own bows he would simply have lifted the stave, drawn and let fly. As it was, he felt his way into the shot, sniffing the faint night-breeze, feeling the waft of air on his cheek. He looked up and the bow followed him.

Seg shot in his bow. He felt the draw, the brace, the loose. The shaft sped upward. The fine twine unraveled at lightning speed.

The arrow soared up and up against the stars. It curved. It hovered. The twine whirled away aft, seeming to vanish where it neared the arrow. With the suddenness of all shafts in flight, the arrow vanished between two of the blue and yellow columns.

No lights showed through the slits above him, and only dimly seen a wash of radiance seeped around the columns. He waited. He held the slender thread in his hand. In only a few moments that stretched like the last day before paynight, the thread jerked in his hand. He jerked it gently three times and then watched as it began to draw away upward.

The check when the heavy rope came on amused him. Then whoever it was hauling in took a fresh purchase and the rope whistled up the sheer side of the tower.

He had judged well. There were perhaps five man-lengths left when the rope quivered and hung still. He waited for them to tie it off above, and pulled. An answering quiver reassured him. He put the bow down, laid both hands on the rope, and hauled hard. He pulled with determination to dislodge any shoddy knots up there. The rope held.

With that, like the little spinlikl Lord Clinglin, up he went. He climbed using his arms alone, hand over hand, only occasionally having to use his feet to fend off. Just below the arcade he paused. He was breathing deeply and evenly. Now was the time for a guard to smash him across the head with his sword, or more simply just to cut the rope...

He struck his head over the edge.

Malindi, Bamba and Milsi stared at him as though he were a magician popping out of an empty chest.

"Seg!"

"Quiet."

He hauled himself in over the edge. There was no time to talk, to do anything but haul in the rope. When he had the end he grabbed Bamba, wrapped a bowline about her and pushed her off with a fierce: "Do not cry out, Bamba!" in her tiny ear.

She lowered down without a squeak.

"If Bamba can make no sound, neither will I," quoth Malindi, bravely. She was scared stiff.

The rope slackened off and then wriggled. Bamba had slipped out of the bowline on a bight and Seg hauled in. Malindi went down with her eyes fast shut, her heart in her mouth, damply—and without a sound.

"She is a brave girl," whispered Milsi. "I prayed you would come to rescue us, Seg, my jikai."

"Quiet."

He hadn't got over his feelings of abandonment just yet, unworthy though they were. He felt awkward in Milsi's presence, almost embarrassed.

Each woman had taken a few clothes and necessaries gathered up from the toiletry table. Milsi glanced about the room beyond the blue and yellow columns, and then, very firmly, slipped the rope about her. Seg payed out and down she went. Presently the signal rattled up and he had the reassuring knowledge that the three women were safely down. He took his sole arrow, stuck through his belt. He went over the side like a lizard sliding over a rock. Down and down and his feet hit the grass with a thump.

"Oh, Seg!"

"Talk when we are away."

Had the rope been dry enough he'd have set it alight to confuse those rasts up there. But it held dampness and so, with a feral look around that boded ill for anyone foolish enough to cross his path, he led off. The women followed silently, holding each other in mutual comfort.

They reached his three mewsanys. Here, immediately, a fresh problem presented itself.

"I could not ride, my lady!" Malindi clutched her thin tunic to her breast. "A saddle animal like the great ladies! Oh, no, my lady!"

Bamba said: "Perch on that great beast!"

Milsi said, with a sigh: "We were brought here in a carriage, Seg."

"I will take Malindi up on my saddle. You take Bamba. And be sharp about it. We must be well clear by dawn."

They jumped at his tone.

They did as they were bid and after a time they changed around and brought the third mewsany in to relieve the extra load. They rode silently, as Seg had enjoined.

The awkwardness persisted, exacerbated by his awareness that Milsi was not aware of it or its cause. He rode abaft her mewsany on purpose, and kept a watchful look out to the rear. The peril sprouted from the front, suddenly, in a long line of riders breasting a hill and racing down with wild war whoops upon them.

Their own mounts were tired and dispirited. With two riders up, they could never outrun this cavalry that pounded down now, glittering in the first light of the suns. Armor winked in ruby and jade fire. Lanceheads glittered. Feathers waved. Dust spurted back in a long line. The riders bore on and opened out into a circle, ringing the fugitives.

Seg slid his bow forward and nocked his single shaft.

They'd done well and come a long way—and now they'd come to the end of their flight.

He looked into the faces of these warriors.

Skull faces... Blunt-featured, with a tightly drawn skin of pebbly gray-green, with the roots of the teeth exposed, with bony brow ridges overhanging smoky crimson eyes, these faces looked the decomposing features of nightmare newly risen from the grave. Bamba let out a shriek of horror. Malindi fainted clean away. The ghastly riders ringed their quarry.

Milsi urged her mount a little forward. She held up her hand.

"Lahal and Lahal! Well met!"

"Lahal, majestrix!" said the leader, his gruesome features writhing with an emotion that might indicate pleasure. "Thank the Good Pandrite we have found you safe at last!"

Eighteen

The queen calls: "Hai, Jikai!"

"I," said Skort the Clawsang, "was told you were dead, majestrix, in that confounded Coup Blag." He used the teeth that appeared to be decomposing to bite firmly into a slice of succulent roast vosk. They were sitting around the camp fire and they were eating and drinking until they burst.

"It was poor Milsi who died. She had the same name as me, as you know, and I grieve for her."

"Aye." Skort wiped his lipless mouth, daintily. "But, majestrix, it is not all good news. That foul cramph Muryan has not released your daughter, the divine Princess Mishti—"

"What!" The regal anger that blazed from Milsi made Seg realize that, by Vox, she was a queen.

"He would not release her into our care, as was ordered. We rode to seek a ruling on this, and our spies told us of the Warvol Tower. But—" and Skort added this very rapidly, "he would not harm her. He dare not."

"That I believe to be true. But I'll—I'll—"

"Do what all queens do, particularly Queens of Pain, and have his head off," said Seg, and buried his face in a tankard of parclear.

"Oh, I shall, I shall! Disabuse yourself of any notion that I will not, Seg the Horkandur!"

Skort, with a mastery of tactics that pleased Seg, chipped in to say: "I own I am surprised to find you here, Seg, and yet pleased. Very pleased. The queen has need of all the champions who will muster to her banner."

"There's going to be a fight, then?"

"Assuredly, a fight, and a battle."

"What of Kov Llipton?"

"If only," said Milsi, "I could trust him!"

Carefully, Skort said: "Your husband, King Crox, suffered the misfortune of having his wife and family killed in an accident. Luckily for us, that brought you here, majestrix, an event for which we are profoundly grateful. This rast Muryan callously slew his wife and family just so that he might marry you, according to the laws. Kov Llipton still has a wife and family. Also, he is a numim."

"I heard Muryan's family fell under a Rapa's garbage cart," said Seg.

"Under a garbage cart, yes. They did not fall. They were pushed."

"And I'll bet that Strom Ornol did the pushing."

"Just so." Skort swiveled that macabre head and his crimson eyes rested balefully upon the queen. "Llipton may be a numim. But there is nothing in the law that says he may not marry an apim. The marriage would be in name only. But then he would be king."

"You think that is his design, Skort?" Milsi looked completely undecided. "You know the River, Skort, you understand local conditions. I am from Jholaix, and..."

"My own personal belief is that Llipton is upright and honest in his own way. He took much upon himself when the king your husband gave him the charge of the kingdom. He may be over strict. But I believe him to be loyal."

"Yeah," said Seg. "But to whom?"

"To King Crox until the king is known to be dead."

"And then to the queen?"

"That is what I believe."

"One thing is certain, Llipton won't have Muryan as a king set above him."

"Ha!"

"If there is to be a battle," and here Milsi spoke with a wistful regret, "Muryan is able to field a formidable force, as he told me with much relish."

"We'll gulp him down with relish!"

"Yes, good Skort, I pray the Almighty Pandrite this will be so. But there was a man in the guard set over us, a man with red hair. A famous archer. He boasted continually of his prowess and of that of his men."

"Oh?" said Seg, at once alert, his professional hackles raised. "His name?"

"He was a Jiktar, commanding a regiment. His name was Nag-So-Spangchin, called Spangchin the Horkandur."

"A whole regiment!"

"Aye, Seg—and his name, like yours—he wore the golden zhantil-head of the pakzhan at his throat and was a zhanpaktun, although he insisted on being addressed as a hyrpaktun, which he said was proper—"

Seg put out his hand and touched Milsi's hand, feeling the tremble. She stilled instantly the moment he touched her.

Following her line, he said: "This is the coming fashion, to call hyrpaktuns zhanpaktuns, to dub paktuns mortpaktuns, and to let the ordinary mercenaries wallow in the name of paktuns. But a whole regiment! This is bad news indeed."

"Aye." Skort nodded his horrific corpselike head. "All men know of the fame of the Bowmen of Loh."

"He wore a flaunting mass of red and yellow feathers in his helmet, and, Seg, his bow was very like yours."

"And his arrows were all fletched blue with the feathers of the king korf from my own mountains of Erthyrdrin!"

"Yes, Seg..."

There was no need to enlarge. Pandahem, like many another island and country, had once been under the heel of the Empire of Walfarg, that was known as the Empire of Loh. The Gold and Red banners had waved in those days, until the empire had fallen and the continent of Loh had turned inward upon itself, mysterious behind its walled gardens, its women wearing veils, soft-slippered and soft-spoken. Now the new countries of Pandahem and the Empire of Vallia were pressing outwards. But men remembered the merciless efficiency of the armies of Walfarg, where every other man had red hair, and of the sleeting death brought to every battlefield by the Bowmen of Loh.

Out of his own jumbled thoughts Seg said fretfully: "I wish we could find Obolya so that I might have my own longbow again."

No one had heard of the whereabouts of Obolya, and it was assumed he was busily trading for saddle animals.

The queen stood up. Everyone else scrambled to their feet. Looking at her, Seg felt the blood in him, the bursting pressure of his heart beating. She lifted her chin.

"We will not be downhearted, my friends! We will go forward, confident in Pandrite. If there is to be a battle then we shall win it. And then we shall make a just administration of all the land. Hai, jikai!"

"Hai, jikai!" they roared, caught up in the abrupt splendor of the moment. Seg yelled, too...

Considering it markedly inadvisable to go anywhere near Mewsansmot where Trylon Muryan hatched his plans, they skirted the town out on the plains before rejoining the river line much farther downstream. Worry over her daughter made Milsi pale and fretful; yet Seg marked the way she contained her irritability and temper with the Clawsangs. Despite continual reassurances that Muryan would not dare to harm the lady Mishti, she took scant comfort, and lived on only by virtue of her own courage and inner resources. Seg watched all this.

No word of love passed between them. His own tangled emotions had still not fully recovered, and Milsi had more than enough problems to contend with. He took every opportunity to reassure her, and she responded in a way that while not listless, saddened him. She spoke bravely, and she encouraged all; but inwardly, Seg sensed, she doubted a happy outcome to this business.

At the capital, Nalvinlad, two items of news greeted them, one good, one evil.

The good news came when Bamba, screaming, flew into the arms of Diomb. The dinkus hugged each other with a frank and open display of affection that made Seg heave up a sigh, and then castigate himself for a dreaming loon. Milsi put a scrap of yellow lace to her eye. In the next instant, there outside her palace of the Langarl Paraido, Khardun, the Dorvenhork, Rafikhan, Naghan the Slippy, Caphlander and Umtig with Lord Clinglin waving his eight arms on his breast, gathered around, shouting the Lahals. Hundle the Design had been pardoned and had gone off home. So the reunion was splendid.

The bad news was that Kov Llipton and six of his chief men had been treacherously attacked. Only Llipton and Trylon Ronglor had survived, badly wounded. It was thought that Llipton might recover, given time and the devoted attentions of the needlemen.

Vad Olmengo brought this news to the queen. This was the real Olmengo, and with his chin beard and full face he did not look much like Strom Ornol; but that disguise had proved perfectly adequate again.

"The rast impersonated me and brought his assassins into the palace, majestrix! The guards slew many of these vile stikitches; but the poor Kov was struck through. I am desolate—"

"It is a sad business, Olmengo, but the kov will survive, as we trust in the good Pandrite."

"I pray so, my queen." Here Olmengo's face drew down mournfully. "But the soldiers! The generals had chosen that night to confer, and the Kapts are slain. We have no one with experience of warfare to lead the army!"

Seg kept very quiet. He did not want to be landed with that job. Oh, no, by Vox, not him!

Milsi said, sharply: "Then the senior Chuktars will decide. Muryan will attack. There is no doubt of that!"

In a very quiet voice as they all trooped up into the palace, Seg said to the Krozair: "Look, Pur Zarado. I know of the fame of the Krozairs. You are great warriors. If these folk have no generals, surely you could—"

"Your pardon, Seg. I am a Krozair of Zamu, as my comrade Zunder was a Krozair of Zimuzz. We are hard fighting men, yes; we do not aspire to the rarefied heights of being a Kapt, not even a Chuktar. I imagine I could swagger well enough as a Jiktar and bully a regiment. But... Oh, no!"

A couple of days later Skort's spies reported that Muryan's army was moving south.

Seg quite expected a huge flotilla of schinkitrees to sail down river. Skort scoffed at this.

"What! No, my friend, no sensible man wages a war on the river. Victor as well as vanquished is likely to fall into the water. Then, well..."

"Yes, I see."

"We will march out and the battle will take place where the forest gives way to a nice battle-worthy terrain."

"Who is to command?"

"The Chuktars argue among themselves. Men are coming in well enough to fill the ranks. Kov Llipton may not be King Crox, may Clansawft of the Perimeters have him in his keeping. But the kov is now recognized as being a man with honor attempting to carry out the duties entrusted to him. He maintained the law."

"Oh, aye, he did that."

"And men see that Muryan is a villain. His own adherents ride in fear of him, believe me. I have high hopes for the outcome of the battle."

"Without a leader on our side."

"The queen will decide."

"Well, she'd best decide damned soon."

Skort swished his sword back, and looked sharply at Seg. Then he said: "The sorest point at issue is this matter of the queen's daughter. We know where she is held. But it would take an army to break through—and that is what our army will do under the queen's direction."

"Oh?" Seg's mouth did not drop open. "You mean Milsi will handle the battle herself?"

"No, no, Seg, you great fambly! That is the aim of the battle, to smash Muryan and to break through to the lady Mishti and rescue her."

Seg rubbed a hand down a raspy jaw. "It's these Bowmen of Loh who worry me." Incautiously he went on: "If I commanded them they'd win the battle on their own."

"But, horter Seg, you command nothing. And you and your comrades live in the palace at the generous hands of the queen."

He felt like saying snappishly: "She owes us that!"

The next time Seg was talking to Zarado, the Krozair caught him up in an excited torrent of words.

"When I was fighting in Vallia for Jak the Drang he often used to say, very many times: 'If only Seg were here!' I wonder, Seg Segutorio the Horkandur—"

"Oh, there are many Segs in the world."

"That may be true; but I have been puzzled where I had heard the name before."

"They still have not chosen a Kapt to lead them. Surely, Pur Zarado—"

"By Zim-Zair! As Zogo the Hyr-Whip is my judge! Not me!"

That evening Seg was just preparing to turn in in the room allotted to him high in the Chungi Tower. Milsi entered without knocking. She looked splendid. Her hair was coiffed and sheened with health, her cheeks glowed, her eyes—well, Seg could lose everything in those eyes of hers. She wore a pale blue gown, loose and flowing, girded by a thin golden chain from which hung a jeweled dagger. Seg swallowed.

"Majestrix—"

"The intelligence is that Muryan will reach the spot chosen for the battle in two days. You, Seg Segutorio the Horkandur, will lead my army in the fight."

"But—"

"Do you truly love me?"

"Yes."

"Then that is settled." And she stepped forward into the clasp of his Bowman's arms.

Nineteen

The Battle of the Kazzchun River

At the queen's express command Kapt Seg wore a bronze harness garnished with golden rosettes. His bronze helmet fitted close, and the blue and white and yellow feathers flew high above on their golden spike. His tunic was of red velvet, lustrous and cunningly changing in hue and tone with the angle of the lights. He strapped on his own drexer, and a plethora of other weapons also. He looked a fitting figure to command an army.

At Kapt Seg's express wish and desire the queen wore a bronze harness, garnished with golden rosettes. Her helmet with its feathers framed her face glowing with passion and conviction in the right and in victory. She wore the Kregan arsenal of weaponry, and Seg's heart joyed in her.

Above them lofted the flag the queen had commanded to be made and embroidered specially for Seg. This was his own tresh. Tall and narrow, it was of red silk. In careful fine stitching in golden thread her handmaidens had represented a bow in the lower portion, bent to shoot upward. Instead of an arrow, a jagged bolt of lightning, lethal and overpowering, skewered skyward.

"Do you then expect me to challenge the heavens themselves?"

"If any man dared—"

Seg looked at her. He could see only Milsi, sitting erect and supple in the saddle, see her gorgeousness. He smiled. He had no need to prattle on about daring anything for her. By the Veiled Froyvil! She knew that!

The army marched out.

Vad Olmengo, quivering, had exuded an enormous sigh of satisfaction and relief when the queen told him that Kapt Seg would take command. Had the chief place been thrust upon him...!

Seg had a plan.

"It is not a great plan, Milsi, not a mind-shattering exhibition of military genius. But a plan we must have."

"I believe in you, Seg, as you know. Therefore your plan is good."

"Ridiculous!"

On the day before the battle Skort had taken Seg out to survey the field of the forthcoming conflict. They fought to protocol here along the Kazz-chun River. He recalled the fracas between the dinkus, and he half-smiled. These armored and mounted warriors with their bronze and leather armor and their steel weapons had not progressed very far along the path of military skills...

He gave the Chulik, Nath Chandarl the Dorvenhork, his instructions. The Chulik nodded, cunning in the ways of battle.

"It shall be as you say, Seg the Horkandur. There may not be many of us, but I will make them fight like demons from the Pits of Gundarlo!"

"And," put in the Khibil, Khardun the Franch, "my lads will hit them with such elan they will all turn tail and run."

"Make it so, and may Likshu the Treacherous and Horato the Potent look down with benediction upon you."

When he spoke to the Rapa, Rafikhan, Seg called down the benediction of Rhapaporgolam the Reiver of Souls.

"I have my task, set to my hands, Seg. It shall be done."

The Jiktars and the three Chuktars of the little army did not demur when Kapt Seg set his own men thus in positions of vital importance. Seg spoke to them. They saw they were dealing with a man who commanded, who had commanded, who knew how to command. They saw his strength, of will and determination as well as of body. He had much of the yrium, that mystical aura of power, charisma, that made men and women follow him willy-nilly. Seg himself made no pretense to the yrium. He was not aware of the charismatic presence he conveyed when he wanted something done...

Two of the Chuktars commanded each his wing of the infantry. This was chiefly composed of half-naked men, many of them fishermen with bundles of their long and cruelly-barbed fishspears. These they would hurl with deadly accuracy. Long before they came within range the Bowmen of Loh would have destroyed them. The infantry carried shields, large, pointed at top and bottom, fashioned of withies or wood, a few with leather, and if there was one in fifty with a bronze rim that was overstating the case.

The remaining Chuktar commanded the cavalry, mewsany-mounted men who were a trifle better armored than the infantry. They carried lances, small shields, and some had javelins. Each regiment was separated out as to type under its Jiktar, and, perforce, owing to training, Seg had to continue with this arrangement.

Skort, well armed and armored, rode close with his Clawsangs. He said: "I now believe this Jiktar Nag-So-Spangchin, known as the Horkandur, commands a regiment of three hundred to three hundred and fifty Bowmen of Loh."

"A formidable force." Seg knew damn well how truly formidable a force that was. "The Dorvenhork will play his part, Skort. Chuliks detest being beaten."

"Who does not?"

"True. But there is something in a soulless Chulik that cannot abide defeat. And I do not believe the Dorvenhork to be soulless, contrary to received opinion."

"There are few who would agree with you."

"There must be Chuliks and Chuliks, as there are apims and apims, and, doubtless, Clawsangs and Clawsangs."

"Aye. But not Katakis and Katakis."

"How many?"

Skort could not pull his lip, but his lipless mouth gleamed blue. "We believe no more than two hundred and fifty."

"Then they must be put down."

"Oh, aye."

Caphlander the Relt rode up on a zorca. Seg gaped at him. He wore a leather jerkin, belted in very tightly, very tightly indeed. His feathered head was covered by a leather cap, in which flourished further feathers—clearly these were not his own. He gave a hesitant salute.

"Well, Caphlander. What does this mean?"

"Why, Seg the Horkandur, merely that I may not fight, but I am a trained stylor. I can carry messages."

The queen smiled graciously. "You are right welcome, master Caphlander. If every man and woman play their parts as well as you, then victory will smile upon our banners this day."

As to that, grumped Seg to himself, there were altogether too many damned banners and flags and standards. If each one prevented its bearer from striking a blow he'd see the lot consigned to Cottmer's Caverns.

He glanced up at the standard Milsi had given him. It really was rather splendid. Its bearer, a horrific-looking Clawsang called Tskarin, would have to be carefully watched, for if that banner fell the warriors and the men who had come to swell the ranks might very well run off.

His trumpeter, another corpselike Clawsang called Ksandic, had proved he knew the calls regulations laid down in the army of Croxdrin—trouble was, did all the people in the ranks know them as well?

Diomb had gone off with the Dorvenhork, beside himself with glee that he was seeing more of the outside world—this time how they got on when they had a real big fight. Seg had had to let him go. Bamba had not cried;

in fact Bamba was not about when Diomb marched off. Clearly—Seg knew about and understood these things—quite clearly Bamba had equipped herself and had skulked off to join Diomb. Oh, well... As for Malindi, she had wailed when Milsi rode off; but a single stern injunction had stilled the pretty infant-like features. A battlefield was no place for a Sybli—well, to be truthful, it was no place at all for anyone with a scrap of sense in their heads.

Military organization must, of course, vary over the wide world of Kregen; in these parts the old methods of the defunct Empire of Walfarg persisted. Usually there were ten men in an audo, eight or ten audos in a pastang, and six pastangs to a regiment. Milsi's army, as Seg watched them marching out to war, were on the low side in regimental strengths. The men raised by King Crox into regular regiments and with whom he had carved out his kingdom, were well enough armed and equipped and trained. Their regiments usually totaled around the four hundred mark. The half-naked fisherfolk and townsmen and riff-raff from the streets, although prettily organized, could muster few regiments above the three hundred and fifty or sixty mark.

This would have to suffice. It was pretty certain that the regiments marching under Trylon Muryan's brown and white banners would muster roughly equal numbers to those with the queen. It was those confounded Bowmen of Loh...

The moment the priests from the various temples had ceased their chantings and incantations and the sacrifices had been made, Seg breathed more freely. The bands started up, blowing and banging lustily. A little breeze got up and blew the banners bravely. The army presented a fine sight, swinging along with the bands playing and the standards flying, and the men singing. Seg humped along on his zorca and tried not to feel too angry at the waste of it all.

The bands played "The Jaws that Bite, the Teeth that Rend." Then they went into "The Forest Stands from Dawn to Dusk." With a fine flush of fury, Seg supposed that cramph Muryan would have his bands playing "The Bowman of Loh."

His mind obsessed with the plan for the battle oddly enough rejected further worry. He found himself thinking of what Milsi had told him of her childhood. Her mother had been born in Jholaix, daughter of one of the wealthy Wine Families. Her grandmother had been born in Nalvindrin, second daughter of the king and queen of the time. Uprisings and revolutions had found, in the end, her grand aunt married and the queen—and her daughter had brought King Crox to the throne—and her grandmother safely hidden in Jholaix. But descent came down through the female line, and Milsi was the one and only legitimate Queen Mab. Thus had all the problems arisen.

All the girls of the family were called Mab as well as their given name.

If Milsi happened to be slain, either in this battle or at the hands of Muryan's hired assassins led by Strom Ornol, then the lady Mishti Mab would inherit the legal descent. No doubt that was what Muryan, having lost Milsi, now planned. The thought that if it came to it Seg would slay the cramph Muryan without mercy gave him no comfort whatsoever.

The idea that he had engineered the deaths of the Bowmen of Loh—or would have done if his primitive plan succeeded—gave him so much less comfort as to make him feel that he bore the sins of the world upon his shoulders. Oh, they weren't his own countrymen. They had red hair, therefore they came from Walfarg. His land of Erthyrdrin, in the northernmost tip of Loh, had been ravaged and attacked by Walfarg over the centuries. Erthyrdrin provided the very cream of the Bowmen of Loh. All the same, it went sore to him to do this thing, and he just wanted this stupid battle over and out of the way so that the future could be entered into sooner rather than later—or at all...

The army reached the area selected for the fight.

To the right flank stretched the river, masked off by a screen of closely growing vegetation. The ground lay open, dotted with a few trees, scattered outposts of the forest, and most of the left flank was open and rolling, ideal country for cavalry maneuver.

As this was what amounted to a north-south confrontation along the Kazzchun River the northern forces must have a marked preponderance of cavalry. They were the people who tended the vast herds of mewsanys and provided them to the southerners, after all. Chuktar Ortyg Lloton na Mismot, who was a trylon, commanding Milsi's cavalry, had a stern task ahead. He had most of the nobility riding in his ranks.

With all the cavalry available to the enemy, Seg calculated that Muryan would attempt to work the old door hinge ploy on him. He'd use some of his cavalry to shoulder the mewsany riders of Milsi's army aside, and then just ride around from his right flank, using his anchored left infantry as the hinge, and roll Seg and all his people up and crush them against the river. If they all went swimming, well, that would put a little extra zest in Trylon Muryan's day.

Inquiries of his infantry commanders elicited the information that soldiers always fought by regiment, and the regiments in their higher groupings always fought together, as was proper.

Chuktar Moldo Nirgra na Chefensmot, who was a strom, wrinkled up his forehead when Seg gave him his orders.

"We need to hold, Chuktar Moldo. This you will do."

"My regulars will stand, Kapt Seg. We are skilled with the strangchi. But—the scum you foist on me—"

"Not scum, Chuktar! Men like you or me. They may be fishermen or laborers but they can fight. You will need the fishspears, believe me." Then

Seg went more deeply into just what these ill-disciplined bands of half-naked men throwing cruelly barbed spears might do when allied with the solid ranks of the regulars.

The strangchi, long-hafted, topped by spear-point, axe-head and hook, was not the strangdja of Chem, that holly-leafed lethality; in these circumstances it ought to prove superior. If it failed, Seg's army would go splashing into the brown waters.

Chuktar Moldo loosed the collar of his tunic under the rim of his corselet, the kax gilded and brave with engravings of stirring battle scenes.

"It is these Bowmen of Loh, Kapt, that—"

Seg lowered a baleful glance on the infantry commander. "I have seen mercenaries refuse their hire and run when they heard they were to face Bowmen of Loh. But you are not mercenaries. You fight for your queen! And our mercenary archers are Undurkers, who have a great contempt for Bowmen of Loh."

With that Seg finished off his instructions, and he thought with his own professional arrogance that he'd always considered these condescending Undurkers a bunch of idiots. Still, they would have to serve this day...

Mixing his light troops, his kreutzin, with his regulars in the right wing, under Chuktar Nath Roynlair na Strainsmot, who also was a strom, he gave similar orders. The difference here was that, Chuktar Nath being a numim, he said: "And on the signal you will charge and let nothing stand in your way. Is that clear?"

"As the streets clear when the rains come, Kapt Seg."

Trust a lion-man for that way of expressing it!

Milsi looked radiant when Seg trotted across to her. The army moved out ahead, deploying to orders. The suns streamed their mingled brilliance upon the field. Away ahead the long serried masses of the enemy came into view, dark and ominous. Seg began checking off numbers, and Milsi watched him, her face expressing as it were in reflection every nuance of Seg's as he counted and calculated.

"Well," he said, and turned to Milsi. "He has more cavalry, as we expected. But he is deficient in infantry. And that is mostly mercenary, and some rascally low-class masichieri among 'em, I'll warrant, no better than brigands."

"He does not really need foot soldiers, does he? He simply puts his Bowmen of Loh to the fore, they shoot and shoot and we are pinned, and his cavalry ride around and—oh, Seg! What have we done!"

"You simply have a slight case of the twitches before battle, nothing to worry about. Everybody has 'em."

"Seg!"

"D'you see, Milsi? We are not deploying out to our left. See? All his gorgeous and famous cavalry are facing empty ground."

"Yes, but—"

"Now watch!"

Trumpets, pealing high and shrill into the clear air, banners, floating and fluttering over the hosts, the dull surf-roar of hundreds of men, the clink and clash of iron and bronze, the excited shrilling of mewsanys and the harsh breath of dust clogging mouths and nostrils...

"They move!"

The Bowmen of Loh trotted out ahead, smart, their bows curves of glitter in the light. By reason of Seg's clumped formations close to his right flank, the archers perforce had to move to their left flank. "They must be licking their lips over there to see such massed targets," said Seg. He looked to the screen of trees following the line of the river.

Out from that concealment ran men, archers, haughty canine faces slanted sideways as they raised their composite bows. Leading them roared on the Dorvenhork. They flanked the Bowmen of Loh. They were well within their shorter range. They began to play on the famed Bowmen of Loh, shooting with flat trajectories that worked down the line like a meat slicer.

Seg smiled. "Very nice. I sent them there in boats before dawn. And, see! There goes Khardun with our paktuns! Oh, he has them by the short and curlies! And Rafikhan!"

Left out on a limb, the cavalry commanded by Muryan started to charge into the left flank of Milsi's army. And, of course, they were met by a hedge of steel and by a multitude of showered fishspears that discomposed them mightily. When Chuktar Ortyg brought Seg's cavalry into action they charged slap bang into the flank of the enemy jutmen and knocked them over, sent them reeling, all jammed up in a tightly wedged mass of frightened and ungovernable animals and men.

Chuktar Nath Roynlair, being a numim, wasn't going to delay when a fight was promised and he simply led his people in a blood-crazed charge dead ahead. This finished Muryan's left wing. His right wing was in process of taking itself off as fast as the mewsanys could gallop. That left the center. Here Chuktar Moldo, having held the charge of hostile jutmen, having seen them repulsed and routed, was feeling mightily puffed up. His trumpeter blew "Charge!" and it was all over.

"Very satisfactory," said Seg Segutorio. "By the Veiled Froyvil, yes!"

"Seg!" said Milsi, staring at him as though she could never bear to tear her gaze away. "My Jikai!"

Twenty

Seg casts a reasonable shaft

"Now let us get after the rast!"

As they spurred ahead, Seg reflected that Milsi was a romantic soul. Well, she had every right to be, seeing what her life had been and what she had been through. Her feelings and expression left him in no doubt. When she dubbed him her Jikai—she meant it with a full heart.

With Skort and his Clawsangs riding in attendance and with Seg's comrades joining with a few of the Undurker archers, they caught up with the fleeing Muryan in not too long a time. He had a small party of adherents still with him, including the red-headed Bowman of Loh, Nag-So-Spangchin.

The configuration of the ground here, a series of shallow depressions and low rounded hills, channeled pursued and pursuers into the valley to the right ahead, which looked broader and easier than the left. The flight hullabalooed along, with the dust kicking and the mewsanys stretching their necks, clumsily thumping on in their six-legged gait.

At the far end of the valley the ground leveled off and stretched off to the next horizon. A clump of trees to the left showed up clearly, with an overturned carriage nearby.

Muryan's party halted.

Seg saw men gesticulating up there and arms raised in anger. Just to the left an uncrossable ravine split the ground. Instantly, Seg saw it all.

So did Milsi!

"Mishti!" she screamed, rising in her stirrups, staring wildly at the small white form trapped beneath one of the shafts of the overturned carriage. A tiny arm waved.

The Dorvenhork in his Chulik way growled to his archers: "Shaft 'em all!"

The canine-faced archers loosed, uselessly. Seg's hand reached around for his apology for a longbow. He had but the one arrow, which he had brought out of comfort, for, as he was the first to say, he felt naked without a good Lohvian longbow and a quiver of clothyard shafts.

Milsi urged her mount toward the ravine; but the beast, sensible in his mewsany way, refused to descend.

Abruptly, the paktuns about Muryan leveled their lances, helmets came down, and they charged pell-mell upon Milsi's party. Skort bellowed and leveled his lance.

Milsi saw what followed. Everyone saw. Nag-so-Spangchin jumped off his mount. He stood proud from the few men still with Muryan. He lifted his bow. The arrow head glittered sharply in the lights of Zim and Genodras. He loosed.

The shaft spat from the bow, soaring up and up. No trained eye was needed to tell where that steel-tipped bird would fall.

"Mishti!" screamed Milsi, frantic, panting, wild-eyed.

Useless to shaft the Bowman of Loh. Too late for that. The charging cavalry with their leveled lances were almost on Seg's people, who rode out to front that wild and desperate last onslaught.

The bow was in Seg's hand. The bow he had knocked up with a knife, working hurriedly, an unseasoned bow, which he had shot in once, a poor apology for a bow, and yet the only bow here that was of any use whatsoever. The silly leaf-fletched shaft was nocked in a twinkling. He could feel the blood, he could feel his heart, he could feel his muscles. He stopped breathing. He laid himself into his bow, holding him just so, every single fiber of his being wrapped up in the shot. Left and right hands drawing together, right hand to the ear and left arm thrusting out with sure power and purpose. The loose, clean, clean! The shaft, speeding away, like a hunting bird, like a gleaming raptor of the skies swooping upon some poor fluttering prey.

High and high against the blue soared the shaft.

It curved. It dipped. Unheard through the thundering oncoming racket of the deadly cavalry charge, arrow struck arrow.

Both shafts tumbled to the ground.

And a damned great mewsany lumbered full into Seg and knocked him all sprawling, and a razor-edged lance point sliced all along his side. The animal fell on him, a bulky sweaty body clad in bronze fell on him and all the lights went out for Seg and he was gathered up into the all-enveloping cloak of Notor Zan.

When he regained his senses the famous Bells of Beng Kishi so rang and clamored in his head that he dare not so much as move that poor abused cranium of his.

They carted him back to Nalvinlad, first in a creaking two-wheeled conveyance drawn by a couple of mytzers and then in a Schinkitree. His head still jumped about loosely upon his shoulders. They put him in a fine expensive bed in a splendid bedroom and the doctors with their needles stuck him and took away the pain, and so he slept.

Milsi kept watch and ward over him. He came to, at last, for Seg had bathed in the Sacred Pool of Baptism in the River Zelph in far Aphrasöe, the Swinging City. He supposed, logically, that he would take Milsi to Aphrasöe very soon. Then she too, besides partaking of this miraculous recovery from injuries, would also live a thousand years.

"Muryan?" he said when Milsi came in, smiling.

"Oh, don't worry your head about him. He never was a good swimmer."

"The lady Mishti?"

Milsi frowned.

"I own I do not understand her. She is still a child yet she is grown into womanhood—and, yet, Seg, she sometimes acts as though she were my mother. It is strange."

"That's children for you."

"You must mend soon. We are being married in six days."

"If you say so, my heart. If you are sure."

"I am certain positive! Do you not wish to be king?"

Seg did not answer but picked a paline from the gold dish at the bedside and chewed comfortably. Truth to tell, he didn't know about this kingship business. He'd been a kov, and kind-heartedness had got him nowhere. Perhaps being a king where they sent people off for a little swim might also prove untenable as a way of life.

"My love!" she cried, and plumped down on the bed and took him in her arms. "I want for you only what is best!"

"I want to marry you, Milsi. You know my past. I own I feel for you so much that—well—"

"We were both shafted by the same bolt of lightning." She laughed, joyful at her own cleverness. "That is the lightning bolt upon your flag, Seg, my dearest heart!"

Holding her close, drawing in the sweet perfume of her hair and shoulders, feeling her firm softness against him, Seg fell into a dizzy state of contentment that overpowered him with its freshness and delight. That this could be! He gave thanks to all the gods and spirits of Kregen that he should be so favored, so fortunate, so blessed.

Preparations for the wedding went ahead and a couple of days later the lady Mishti slipped in to see him.

She surprised Seg. Milsi had been quite right. This slip of a girl, half woman, half child, knew exactly what she wanted, and was unsure only of the best way to gain her ends. She did not look at all like Milsi, and her hair was dark, her nose thin, and her mouth rather too full. Still, she would grow out of imperfections and become a dazzling beauty.

She said: "Kov Llipton mends, pantor Seg. You are to be my new father. Well, mother is old. One day I shall be queen, and very soon, I think. Then, I am almost decided, I shall marry Kov Llipton. He is a numim, of course; but then he will die and I shall marry whomever I choose and have a great deal of money—lots and lots..."

"Go," said Seg, "away. Come back when you can talk respectfully of your mother. Is that clear!"

She jumped into the air, her face blanched, she bit her lip—turned and fled.

Seg started to berate himself, cursing his own folly and pig-headed stupidity. Onker! Vosk-skulled onker!

Now he'd ruptured the whole fabric of his planned life.

Nothing of what had passed was spoken, the days went by, and, suddenly, here he was being dressed in robes so ornate as to need another fellow in here with him to help support the weight. He made sure he had his drexer with him. Obolya had been through on his way downriver, taking Seg's bowstave and quiver with him. Oh, well. He could look forward with pleasure at least to building himself a new bow on his honeymoon... He fretted over Mishti...

The wedding took place in the Temple of Pandrite Risen, and included priests of all the other temples of the city. The occasion was in truth splendid. So much gold, so much glitter, so many lamps, so many robes of wonderful ornateness. The music soared. The scents almost overpowered. The choirs sang. The lady Mishti stood to the side, drenched in silks and gold, and her eyes were downcast and she did not look at her new father at all.

One could feel true sorrow and sympathy for any girl who has to face a new father; that does not mean she may forfeit her respect for her mother. Seg felt his heart move for poor Mishti. He would do all he could, and perhaps that would not be enough.

When the dancing began he said to Milsi: "This is a splendid wedding, my heart. But there must be at least two more, you know."

"Oh, aye, assuredly. One with all my friends in Jholaix. And the other with yours in Vallia."

"The Vallia of today is not like the Vallia you were taught to hate as a child."

"I know. I have spoken to Llipton on this."

He was there, the kov, propped up, joying in the happiness of his queen. His wife, the gorgeous Rahishta, was truly sumptuous and Seg couldn't see Llipton having her killed off.

They were enjoying themselves in the enormous ballroom of the Langarl Paraido. Perfumes scented the air, fans waved, wine circulated, people talked and chattered and danced as the four orchestras played by turn. Seg, looking at Milsi, found he could hardly bear to look away. She so radiated happiness, she looked so perfect, that she dominated everything by her own self and not because she happened to be the queen.

On the second day of the ceremonies, Seg was to be crowned king.

This function took place in the throne room of the Langarl Paraido. More

423

gorgeousness, more gold, more silks and tapestries, more of everything luxurious and sybaritic and heady with the promise of the life to come.

Clad in robes of astounding magnificence, Seg stood forth with Milsi facing him. She was the only person with the power to crown him. She wore a long straight gown of purest white, girded in silver, with the crown upon her head. The chief priest held upon a velvet cushion the crown she would take up and place upon Seg's dark unruly mop.

He stared up into her eyes. So beautiful, so wonderful—a girl who was his wife now. Yet, yet—did he want to be king of this infernal jungly rivery place?

Milsi took up the crown. She held it high and all sound ceased in that immense chamber. The chief priest stood like a dummy. A priest beside him stood on one leg, the other stilled in the act of scratching his calf. The feathered fans ceased their incessant waving to and fro. A little fly upon the velvet cushion stopped and did not move.

Seg knew.

He turned his head and looked at the water clock fixed beneath the east window. No water dropped from the clepsydra's upper chamber. The water in the lower stood as though solid, like a sheet of blued steel.

The blue water in the upper chamber remained where it was, fixed, rigid, solid, unmoving...

Motionless in their ranks all his comrades stood looking blindly on. All the nobles and the chiefs, all the great ones, all the vast assembly—all—stood like stone.

In all that great and glittering company only two lives sparked with energy. Milsi lowered the crown, and almost dropped it, and so placed it back upon the velvet cushion.

"Seg! What is it? What—?"

"It is all right, Milsi, I promise you—"

"But—but—" She looked around, distraught.

He took the two steps up and clasped her in his arms, smoothing the supple curve of her back for he could not smooth her hair for the crown.

"Milsi, hush, hush—"

A golden yellow light blossomed about them. The unearthly scent of surpassing sweetness enfolded them. At the core of the golden radiance the figure of a woman glowed, supernal, divine, shedding benediction. She wore a white gown girdled by a golden chain. Her dark hair flowed in a loose perfumed mass from beneath a helmet of so brilliant a gold it shone as though molten. Crimson plumes bedecked the helmet. Milsi, looking on in awe, saw the woman's face.

A pale face, unlined, with a purity of outline that set her countenance apart from ordinary features, her face half-smiled down upon the two locked in each other's arms. Her eyes of a deep and lustrous brown seemed to melt into them. Her firm, full mouth, a contrast of complexity, curved benignly upon them. Yet in her left hand she held a sword. Upon her breast shone an insignia in the shape of a wheel with nine projections upon its outer circumference.

Seg felt Milsi stir in his arms, stiffen, grow firm.

"Who," demanded Milsi, "are you, lady?"

The answering voice flowed in a golden mellow sound like a million deep and yet happy-toned bells all chiming from the bell towers of a world's temples.

"I speak to the Grand Archbold of the Kroveres of Iztar."

"I am here, my lady Zena Iztar," said Seg. "And I give you Lahal and Lahal, and my devotion, and ask you to share with me my happiness and pride in my lady, the lady Milsi, who is the queen of this land."

"Bravely spoken, Seg Segutorio. But you forget you are my Grand Archbold. To you has been entrusted the furtherance of my Order."

"I own to a parlous state of sin in this, for I have been neglectful of late. Yet there have been reasons—"

"Reasons enough so that I have not called on you beforetime. But, now, you are not fighting the Shanks. You are not battling the adherents of Lem the Silver Leem. You are not putting down the slavers, the aragorn, the slavemasters. You are not opposing the Werefolk. You are not combating the Traxon Ardueres. And you do nothing about the Witch of Loh, Csitra, who commands Spikatur Hunting Sword."

"That is true. I *am* being married."

Milsi could feel the hardness of Seg against her. Her common sense told her that this apparition was real, a visitation from the gods—perhaps a goddess herself. So that her Seg took much upon himself to answer in so proud a fashion.

Zena Iztar's smile curved more. "I joy in your good fortune in the lady Milsi, Seg. But do you wish to stay here as king?"

"I do not know! I wish to stay with Milsi—that is all I do know. And, my lady, I wish to serve you as best I may."

"Do you forget what the Emperor of Vallia drew out for your future possibilities, Seg? Concerning Pandahem?"

"I do not forget. He suggested I should be the Emperor of Pandahem. That is all a foolishness. I would sooner be the Grand Archbold of the Kroveres of Iztar."

"Yet this same Emperor of Vallia created the new emperor in Hamal, did he not?"

"Oh, aye, he did that. I was there."

"I would have you still as my hand in the world, Seg. And your new comrades here will prove fine krovere brothers. Even the Relt Caphlander, for the Order has need of a stylor."

"Agreed, my lady."

Milsi just stood, trembling finely in Seg's arms, listening to this talk of emperors...

"Also, Seg, I may tell you that the Emperor of Vallia has decided on your new kovnate. You are to be a High Kov. He would have you as an emperor like himself out of his comradeship." The mellow voice chimed golden gong notes. "Yet I think you do right to refuse for the moment."

"Look at Pandahem! They'd never accept an emperor. And as for this kingdom of Croxdrin, my lady Zena Iztar, I have decided."

"Excellent. Proceed."

"I shall do whatever my lady Milsi asks me to do."

The smile curved even more in that palely glowing face framed by the brown hair and the golden helmet.

"A very wise and sound decision, I assure you."

"But—!"

"The Kroveres of Iztar need you, Ver Seg. So do others of your blade comrades."

"Yes, and I can tell you why my old dom wants to make me the Emperor of Pandahem! The cunning old leem hunter—he's so fed up with his job as Emperor of Vallia and keeps trying to shovel it off onto his son Drak that he wants to let me have a taste of the same nonsense!"

Zena Iztar laughed. Her smile broadened and it seemed the twin suns of Scorpio flamed and blazed within the throne room there in jungle-fast Croxdrin.

"You are wrong, Ver Seg; but you do have a point. Now you must make your decision with the lady Milsi. There is much to do in the world, for Kregen never sleeps."

And, like that, suddenly the golden radiance vanished and with a last faintly ringing "Remberee!" vibrating on the air, Zena Iztar departed.

Without hesitation Seg turned Milsi in his arms, kissed her lusciously and with immense passion and gusto, grabbed the crown, thrust it into her hands, lifted hands and crown and settled it on his head. Then he hopped down the steps and stood staring up at Milsi as the choirs all broke into song, the priests chanted, the music soared and the blue water dropped down plop after plop in the clepsydra.

When they were alone, the crowds still shouting and carousing in the streets outside and the torches flaring all over Nalvinlad and the wine flowing like the very river itself, she said severely: "I understood a very great deal of what passed between you and the lady Zena Iztar. It seems, King Seg, that you have been keeping secrets from your wife."

After he had kissed her a few times, he said: "True."

After she had kissed him some more times, she said: "And what do you propose?"

"Do you think Mishti would happily go to Vallia?"

"I do not. She has grown apart from me since we arrived here. I do not blame Muryan for that. It is her youthfulness. She wants to be queen. It has gone to her—"

"And you?"

"I go with my husband."

He sat up, looking down on her, glorious in the lamplight. "That's not good enough! I do what you want!"

She moved her hand against his chest.

"I do not like this jungly place, and that's the truth of it."

"You'll like Vallia, and Valka, and—"

"Will they like me?"

Seg laughed, but before he could gather her in his arms, she said: "I told you I understood. How could you be the Emperor of Pandahem? The island is made up of many countries. Yet—wait, wait, my love, let me finish. Yet you spoke of the Emperor of Vallia—and we all know what he did in Hamal. And you said he was your old dom. And he was the Bogandur, and he was—oh, Seg! Was he really?"

"As ever lived and breathed."

"Then I shall be happy in Vallia."

Then she reached up and kissed him on the nose, and said: "And even if the Emperor of Vallia was another Trylon Muryan, still I would be happy with you."

The next day they had to go about the city so that all the people might see them and cheer.

Presents were lavished, and Seg made a great point of acting with exquisite politeness to Kov Llipton who accompanied them. They had reached the royal jetty where the crowds waited, and everything was going splendidly. A slim paddler appeared from a tangle of craft and thrust vigorously for the shore. Kov Llipton saw it, and his great numim face broke into a delighted smile.

The Schinkitree touched the jetty and a numim, waving his wand of office high and shoving a little Relt out of his way, leaped up onto the wooden planking. He went straight into the incline, and bellowed: "Pantor! Kov Llipton, I have urgent information—"

"Stand up, Tyr Naghan Shore!"

Up leaped the numim, fierce, bubbling with his news. Before Llipton could bellow out that the queen and king stood before him, Naghan Shore yelped: "I asked at the Vallian consulate, and they confirm, my lord! This evil-smelling rascal, Seg Segutorio, is indeed a kov of Vallia! I hope and pray you have not sent him swimming—"

Seg near busted a gut laughing. Milsi put a hand to her mouth. Even Kov Llipton in his numim way let out a great guffaw of merriment.

Mind you, said Seg to himself, Llipton might laugh now; but it had been touch and go. He'd have sent Seg swimming, sure as the river rolled to the sea, had events not turned out as they had.

A tremendous roar rose up from the crowds. Everyone swiveled to stare down river and up—up into the bright air.

They soared on, high and fast, swarm after swarm of them. Fleet air-boats, fast compact vollers, enormous skyships, flying up the river in a silent majestic procession. Many banners waved. Seg didn't say a word; but the smile spread his mouth right across his tanned face. Milsi clung to his arm.

Tyr Naghan Shore yelped as though a wersting had bitten his rump. His ferocious lion-man's face crumpled.

"May the Good Pandrite aid us now! Woe, woe! They are from Vallia, and they have come to chastise us for sending their kov Seg Segutorio the Horkandur a-swimming in the river!"

Seg rapped out: "Calm yourself, Tyr. I am Seg Segutorio. I live. They are my friends and we will welcome them in a seemly fashion."

Naghan Shore, the kov's messenger, gaped.

That enormous armada flew down, and hovered over the river, and everyone saw the snouts of the catapults and ballistae, the varters, those special varters of Vallia that could blow the crowds away in a twinkling. Of the many banners the union flag of Vallia dominated all.

A small voller swung out, circled, and landed where it seemed to the pilot the most important personages congregated.

From the flier stepped a lithe lissom man, hard-faced, bronzed, with a wild and reckless look about him. At his side stood a woman of great beauty, poised and regal. He wore war harness, she wore a laypom-colored gown of soft material and easy cut, yet she, too, carried weapons.

Seg smiled. People didn't know whether to stare at the new arrivals or gape at the armada above. The skyships were truly enormous, with decks serried one above the other, each with a long row of varter ports. Over the sides heads showed, staring down, hawk-faces, crowned with helmets, and the glitter of spear and sword, the deadly glint of arrowheads.

From a voller over the center of the river a pot fell. It blazed and spurted and spat fire. The hiss when it hit the water carried a message understood by all.

"Milsi," said Seg. "Here come the King and Queen of Hyrklana, Jaidur and Lildra. I see they brought company."

A hulking great fellow abaft the King of Hyrklana put a trumpet to his lips and blew. That brought instant silence. Into the quiet his stentorian bellow broke.

"We seek Kov Seg Segutorio! I tell you, on behalf of the King and Queen of Hyrklana, and of the Eleventh Fleet of the Vallian Air Service, that if you have harmed one hair of his head this entire miserable little city will be put to the flames!"

Seg stepped out and called: "Lahal Jaidur! Lahal Lildra!"

They ran to him, their hands extended.

"Uncle Seg!"

Then it was all an uproar, of shouting and laughter, of introductions, and of the promise of gargantuan feasts, with much eating and drinking, of dancing and singing. If there is one thing that any Kregan can do—bar a few of the more intractable of the races of diffs—it is have one hell of a good time.

"Yes, it was all good fortune," Jaidur told Seg in a reasonably quiet interlude. Milsi just hung onto Seg and wouldn't let him go. "This fellow came downriver and wanted to know if they should have your head off, or whatever—"

"Send a fellow swimming is the way of it here."

"Yes. Damned primitive. Anyway, a voller was there and old Strom Ornol—you remember him, Seg, whiskers as long as your arm and knows all the gods and goddesses in Hawkwa Country off by heart—spotted how important it was, as it was by Vox! The voller hared it back to the fleet. We're going to help Drak out—seems the idiots out of North Pandahem are trying another stupid invasion. So, here we are. And the quicker we're on our way home—although Hyrklana is my home now—" Here Jaidur in his reckless way gazed fondly on Lildra "—we can set about helping my big brother Drak."

"Ye-es—"

"You're taking this kingship thing here seriously?"

"Well, young Vax Neemusbane, you may have been a king longer than I have, for I've just begun; but I do take it seriously. Also, young man, there is a matter I must discuss with you that may make you sit up a trifle."

"Oh?"

Seg smiled. Give Jaidur a few more years yet before he was asked to join the Brotherhood of the Kroveres of Iztar...

"All in good time."

"This is a splendid party you're having. Your coronation? Well, many congratulations. But Vallia needs us."

"In my own time, Jaidur. Give me but the one day?"

"Very well, Uncle Seg. Oh, and I hear that in this savage country all the queens are called Queen Mab and all the kings mean a great fat wo, a zero, empty of power and authority. I mean you no disrespect, Seg, as you know full well, seeing that you stand to me as my father. But you are King Mabo, majister. King Mabo."

"Aye, my lad, I am King Mabo. Also, the kings meant nothing here beside the queens until King Crox married Milsi's relation. The kings take the name Mab and put it into the masculine gender. Mabo. H'm." Here Seg wrinkled up his eyes and pulled his lip and chuckled a trifle to himself, softly. "Your father is not the only one to gather up names to himself, it seems."

During this day of grace, in which he must make his decision, and in which he and the queen must show themselves to the people of Nalvinlad, Seg debated. In theory during the following weeks they would travel up and down the length of the Kazzchun River so that all their subjects might see them.

He knew one fact for certain. If he went back to Vallia he would take those of his comrades who wished to come. He felt confident Diomb and Bamba would leap at the chance. And as for Malindi—Milsi had outfitted her with a wardrobe that would not fit into a chest large enough to hold six full grown men and demanding another six to carry.

He cornered Kov Llipton when they stopped to take a sup at the villa of Trylon Ortyg Lloton. He gestured for Llipton's wife, the sumptuous Rahishta, to remain. He spoke directly and hard, not softening his words.

"You dealt harshly with me, kov. Now I am king I overlook that, for I perceive you were carrying out the duties entrusted to you as you saw fit. I would have you less sudden and more inclined to look into justice."

"Aye, majister. But I sent to verify your tale."

"You did, and that is why you still live and hold your lands, estates, title and head. Yet I see you delight in thus exercising a king's prerogatives and power."

Rahishta gasped. Llipton merely lowered his head.

"Would you remain loyal to Queen Mab if she left this country? Would you care for the lady Mishti Mab if she remained?"

Kov Llipton lifted that massive lion head, and stared full at Seg. He raised a hand. "I so swear on the life of myself, my wife and my family, in the sight of Numi-Hyrjiv the All-Glorious and of Pandrite the All-Seeing."

"So be it, Kov Llipton, and I give you joy of your task—if the queen agrees."

The hours dropped by, plop after plop in the clepsydras.

"I shall not be sorry," said Milsi as they turned back from a high balcony where the crowds below cheered and shouted and sang. "I shall be downright glad to reach my bed this night."

"'Tiredness is a sin,'" quoted Seg.

When after due ceremony they were at last gloriously alone, Milsi sighed and said: "I know what is in your mind, my heart. I believe that many parts of Vallia are very similar to parts of Jholaix."

"We grow fine grapes and make fine wine, but not as fine as that of Jholaix. It is your decision, and yours alone. You know my feelings—"

"And mine are just the same!"

"The first thing in the morning we shall tell Jaidur."

"Not too early!"

When they told Mishti next morning she tossed her head, declaring: "I am pleased! I am a grown woman, a princess, and I shall do what I do more freely. At least that cramph Muryan knew how to treat me as a queen."

"He told that archer to kill you, Mishti!"

"Yes, mother, he was a vengeful spirit. And where is that man? I will send him swimming, I swear—"

"He was just a Bowman of Loh," said Seg, "earning his hire."

Nag-so-Spangchin had disappeared, escaping clean away. With him went a bare score of his regiment of bowmen. Recalling the cast that struck the arrow from thin air, Seg felt the unease in him. He could be mistaken and, of course, no chance could possibly be taken in such a fraught moment—still and all, the doubt persisted. Everywhere people spoke of this miraculous shot, and marveled.

Everything was ready. Everything was prepared. Seg was not disappointed in his comrades. All would fly with him. He looked forward with pleasure to welcoming them to the ranks of the Kroveres of Iztar. And so the final moments came.

Skort and his Clawsangs held very firmly to stanchions and rails as the skyship lifted away. This flying was a novel and highly unsettling experience to them. Milsi remained cool and regal and altogether adorable, and Seg put his arm about her waist in sight of the crowds beneath and the uproar was prodigious.

"Remberee, majestrix! Remberee, majister!"

"We'll come back from time to time, Kov Llipton, unexpectedly. And we'll bring company." Seg nodded significantly skywards, where the swarms of airboats lifted, soaring up and away under the brilliance of the suns. "Remberee!"

Just before Mishti departed, she half-turned, and then swung back. Tears streamed down her cheeks. Impulsively, she flung herself forward and clasped her arms about Milsi.

"Oh, mother! I do love you, really! I do!"

"Yes, Mishti, of course you do, as I love you."

The little two-place voller took Mishti back to the care and protection of Kov Llipton. Seg felt very sure that that young lady would run a very tight ship down there along the Kazzchun River. Then he turned and looked up and forward.

Presently he and Milsi walked up into the prow of the skyship. Above them the flags flew. He was amused and touched to notice the splendid flag Milsi had made for him among the hosts of Vallian and Hyrklanian treshes.

"Well, my love?"

"And well to you, too."

"Jholaix and Vallia. Life is going to be very good."

"Life is going to be splendid!"

After a small silence, Seg said: "My lady Milsi, I wish to tell you how supremely happy you make me, how much I love and admire you, how deeply—"

She began to smile at his foolishness and then saw how deadly serious he was. She responded instantly.

"The same lightning bolt, Horkandur, my Jikai, Seg the Bowman."

And then King Jaidur of Hyrklana strolled up, cheerful to be on his way to his ancestral home. He saw the way the King and Queen of Croxdrin stood so closely, lost in each other. In his reckless way he called out:

"Done any good shooting lately, Uncle Seg?"

"Oh, a couple of reasonable casts..."

A Glossary to the Pandahem Cycle

Compiled by Els Withers

References to the six books of the cycle are given as:

MOS: *Mazes of Scorpio*
DOV: *Delia of Vallia*
FOS: *Fires of Scorpio*
TOS: *Talons of Scorpio*
MAS: *Masks of Scorpio*
SEG: *Seg the Bowman*

NB: Previous glossaries covering items not included here can be found in Volume 5: *Prince of Scorpio*, Volume 7: *Arena of Antares*, Volume 11: *Armada of Antares*, Volume 14: *Krozair of Kregen*, Volume 18: *Golden Scorpio*, Volume 22: *A Victory for Kregen*, and Volume 26: *Allies of Antares*.

A

absteilung: Kregan term for a certain type of honor deriving from a difficult feat in battle.

The Aeilssa and the Risslaca: a tavern in Mewsansmot. *SEG*

Affliction of the Sores of Combabbry: a type of plague; among the symptoms are suppurating sores running with greenish pus. *DOV*

agio: a custom practiced by mercenaries of putting their wealth into a common pot before a battle, those sharing it out being fewer than those contributing.

Agron the Needle: a physician of Mellinsmot. *DOV*

Almuensis, Cult of: a cult of sorcerers of considerable powers.

Alwim the Eye: a mercenary who signed aboard *Tuscurs Maiden*; the sister of Wilma the Shot. *FOS*

Alyss: an alias used by Delia while enslaved by Nyleen Gillois. *DOV*

angerim: a race of diffs with much hair and large ears; very untidy in their living habits.

annimay: an extremely sugary and creamy type of cake.

aracloin: an area of a city consisting of twisting alleys; a haven for commerce and villainy.

Ashti: a young girl who was rescued from the adherents of Lem in South Pandahem by Prescot and traveled with him to Tuscursmot. *FOS*

Asnar the Grolt: a lookout aboard *Redfang,* killed in combat against the Shanks. *FOS*

autmoil: stranger.

The Awkward Swod: a tavern in Port Marsilus. *TOS*

B

Bamba: a dinka forced to flee her home because of her love for Diomb, a male of an enemy tribe. *SEG*

Beng Sbodine: known as the Mender of Men; appealed to by those suffering from illness.

Benorlad: Murgon Marsilus's fortress in Ribenor. *MAS*

Blackfang: one of Pompino the Iarvin's swordships. *FOS*

Bloody Jaws, River of: see Kazzchun River.

Bogandur: a sobriquet used by Prescot while adventuring in South Pandahem. *MOS, SEG*

boltim: 'big man'; the dinko name for normal-sized *Homo Sapiens.*

"breath of the Ice Floes": said to touch one who experiences a sudden chill or uneasiness.

C

Cabaret Plant: a carnivorous plant of South Pandahem which lures its victims with sounds resembling conversation and the clink of glasses.

cadade: captain of the guard.

The Calsany and Flea: a tavern in Ruathytu. *MOS*

Caphlander the Quill: a slave rescued from Katakis of South Pandahem by Seg Segutorio; a stylor by profession. *SEG*

Carrie: a young girl rescued from the adherents of Lem in Menaham by Prescot. *MAS*

Caterion, Vasni ti Delphor: a much-respected SoR born about five hundred years ago.

celene: rainbow.

Central Mountains: a range of mountains crossing Pandahem from east to west.

Chandarl, Nath the Dovenhork: a slave rescued from Katakis of South Pandahem by Seg Segutorio; an archer by profession. *SEG*

Chandarlie the Gut: the ship-Deldar of *Tuscurs Maiden. FOS*

Chekumte the Fist: a guard in the service of Murgon Marsilus. *FOS*

Chenunga the Ob-eyed: a guard in the employ of Pompino ti Tuscursmot. *FOS*

Chozputz, by: an oath used by Prescot and those close to him.

Chusto, by: an oath used by Prescot and those close to him.

Clansawft of the Perimeters: a Clawsang deity.

Clawsang: a race of diffs with pebbly green-gray skin stretched tight over their bones, the roots of the teeth being exposed, and sunken crimson eyes; in appearance resembling a decomposing corpse.

Clinglin, Lord: the name given by Umtig the Lock to his pet spinlikl. *SEG*

Clomb of the Ompion Never-Miss: a dinko deity.

Clomba of the Fruit Tree Eternal: a dinko deity.

colo: a small creature with large ears, a thin tail, and orange and green fur.

Constanchoin the Rod: Lady Tilda's grand chamberlain. *TOS*

Coup Blag: a maze of horrors in South Pandahem. *MOS*

Crockhaden, Thalmi: the spymistress for the SoR. *DOV*

crox: a gold coin named after King Crox of South Pandahem.

Crox, King: the king of Croxdrin in South Pandahem; the deceased husband of Lady Milsi.

Csitra: a witch of Loh, the widow of Phu-si-Yantong. Lured Prescot to the Coup Blag to destroy him, but became enamored of him, allowing him to escape. *MOS, SEG*

Curstouran: a river in South Pandahem. *FOS*

Cwopanifer, Vanli: the commander of the skyship *Val Defender*. *MAS*

D

Dahemin: twin deities, Dahemo and Dahema, of an ancient religion of Pandahem. *TOS*

Dahram the Bold: a fellow who made Prescot's acquaintance at the Ruby Winespout in Ruathytu. *MOS*

Delphor: a tiny village in Delphond.

Delphor, Ros: an alias used by Prescot's daughter Dayra while in Pandahem.

demon: Prescot describes one type of demon he encountered in the Coup Blag as being hooved of rear feet, clawed of third feet, tentacled of second feet, and bearing human hands on its forearms, with horns that emit deadly sparks of light. *MOS*

dinko: a race of diffs in the jungles of South Pandahem; pigmy-sized, with four arms each; they fight with blowpipes. *SEG*

Diomb: a dinko forced to flee his home because of his love for Bamba, a female of an enemy tribe. *SEG*

Dogan: the strom of the province of Mellin in Vallia. *DOV*

Dopitka the Deft: a servant of Murgon Marsilus. *FOS*

Doxology of San Destinakon: a cult of powerful sorcerers.

Drayseg: the eldest son of Seg Segutorio and Thelda.

Dulshini, Lady: sworn by in some parts of Pandahem.

Duurn the Doomsayer: a masquerade of Prescot's as a soothsayer. *MAS*

E

Elomi the Shining: the former name of the mistress of the SoR.

Elspa: the stromni of the province of Mellin in Vallia. *DOV*

Erivor, Javed: the father of Queen Milsi, known as the Good. *SEG*

Erthanfydd the Meticulous: a deity of Erthyr called upon to bless bows.

Exandu: accompanied Prescot and Seg Segutorio on their first expedition to the Coup Blag; much given to concern over the state of his health. *MOS*

F

Fallager: a prosperous town in Falinur.

Fandarlu the Franch: the landlord of The New Frontier in Peminswopt. *TOS*

Faplon the Chuckle: one of the company of *Tuscurs Maiden*, killed at Korfseyrie. *MAS*

Farfaril: a full-bodied red wine, not too sweet.

Faril Sheon: a greeting used by members of the SoR; the appropriate answer is SheonFaril. *DOV*

The Feathered Risslaca: an inn in Mellinsmot. *DOV*

Febranden: a town in South Pandahem.

Felheim-Foivan, Strom Ortygna: holder of two small estates by the Great River in Vomansoir; the Vallian ambassador to Menaham. *MAS*

Fiacola the Gaze: a witch who assisted Nyleen Gillois in her plot to become Empress of Vallia. *DOV*

Filbarrka: the king of a country in Persinia.

Fischili: the mother of Ashti, who sold her to the adherents of Lem. *FOS*

Flamdelka the Gatherer: one of the older deities worshipped in the part of Vallia near the Ochre Limits.

Floria: one of Delia's handmaids.

Flower Country: a land in Balintol, renowned as gentle and peace-loving.

Framco the Tranzer: the cadade at the Zhantil Palace. *TOS*

Fregeff: a sorcerer, an adept of the Doxology of San Destinakon, who accompanied Prescot and Seg Segutorio on their first expedition to the Coup Blag. *MOS*

Frorwald: a sorcerer of the Cult of Almuensis, employed by Muryan Mandifenar. *SEG*

Frupp: a freymul ridden by Prescot in Port Marsilus. *TOS*

Fynarmic, Vylene: the ship-Hikdar of *Val Defender*. *MAS*

G

Gdoinya: the sister of the Gdoinye, the messenger of the Star Lords.

Gillois, Cranchar na Sagaie: Nyleen Gillois's twin brother; known as the Cranchu. *DOV*

Gillois, Nyleen na Sagaie: the wife of Vomanus of Vindelka; the mistress of the Sisters of the Whip. Plotted to become Empress of Vallia, but was defeated by Delia. *DOV*

GLOG: abbreviation for the Grand Ladies Order of Gratitude.

Golden Zhantil: the name given by Pompino to the airboat stolen by Prescot and Dayra from King Nemo.

Grakvar: the name used by members of the SoR for the whip. *DOV*

Grand Ladies Order of Gratitude: a sorority of Vallia, maintaining a strong force of Jikai Vuvushis; in a position of rivalry with the SoR. *DOV*

Gremivoh: an island off the coast of Vallia.

Gullik, Twayne: the castellan at the Zhantil Palace in Port Marsilus. *TOS*

H

Hanmensmot: a town in South Pandahem.

Hardle, Andoth: a spy serving Prescot in Ruathytu. *MOS*

Harlstam, Vadni Dafni of Tenpanam: in love with Murgon Marsilus, was used by him as bait against his cousin Pando. Killed in battle at the Zhantil Palace. *FOS, TOS, MAS*

The Hersany and Queng: a tavern in Port Marsilus. *TOS*

hiosmim: a race of diffs resembling apim, but with something of a pixie look, with high cheekbones; having creamy white complexions and pale blue hair.

Hirvin: a Vallian soldier posted at the edge of the Ochre Limits; killed by Tandu Jondermair. *DOV*

The Hook and Net: a tavern in Lasindle. *SEG*

"Hope alone does not sickle corn": a saying attributed to San Blarnoi.

Hop the Intemperate: a servant of Lady Ilsa on the first expedition to the Coup Blag. *MOS*

hork: bow.

Horkandur: a sobriquet used by Seg Segutorio while adventuring in South Pandahem. *MOS*

Hukalad: a town in South Pandahem.

Hundle the Design: a slave rescued from Katakis of South Pandahem by Seg Segutorio. *SEG*

Hundral, Ortyg ham: Emperor Nedfar's Pallan of Buildings. *MOS*

Hyrzibar: a talkative shishi of mythology who exclusively serves the minor godlings of various mythologies.

I

Ift: a race of diffs about the height of an apim with tall, pointed ears reaching almost to the tops of their heads and devious, slanted eyes; fond of the forest.

Igbolo: an Ift settlement deep in the forests of Bormark.

Igukwa Valjid: Zankov's swordship. *TOS*

Ilka the Silver Rod: a flunkey of Nyleen Gillois. *DOV*

Ilsa: a member of the first expedition to the Coup Blag. *MOS*

J

Jak Leemsjid: name given to Prescot by his friends after he killed a leem in the castle of Korfseyrie. *MAS*

janul: a fire-lighting device utilizing flint and steel.

Jespar the Scundle: one of Pando's slaves who acted as a guide for Prescot and his friends to Korfseyrie. *MAS*

Jeu O'fremont: a full-bodied red wine.

Jezbellandur the Iarvin: an armorer in Nalvinlad. *SEG*

jikmer: a captain of messengers in the SoR.

Jikvar: a razor-sharp clawlike weapon used by the Sisters of the Rose.

jikvarpam: the sack used by a Sister of the Rose to carry her Jikvar.

jis: short form of address for a male superior.

Jondermair, Dalki: the son of Tandu Khynlin Jondermair; helped succor Delia at the edge of the Ochre Limits; was later captured by Nyleen Gillois and strangled her. *DOV*

Jondermair, Tandu Khynlin: a Djang who immigrated to Vallia; rescued Delia at the edge of the Ochre Limits; was later captured by Nyleen Gillois. *DOV*

Jordio the Hawk: a voller pilot who flew Delia to Vindelka; was later captured by Nyleen Gillois. *DOV*

K

Kazzchun Pass: a pass in the center of the Mountains of the North in Vallia.

Kazzchun River: a river in South Pandahem.

Kazzchun-Faril: a local godling of Lasindle.

Kemchug, Nath: a mercenary hired aboard *Tuscurs Maiden*. *FOS*

Khardun the Franch: a slave rescued from Katakis of South Pandahem by Seg Segutorio; a hyr-paktun. *SEG*

Korfseyrie: the castle stronghold of Murgon Marsilus. *MAS*

KRVI: abbreviation for the Kroveres of Iztar.

Ksandic: Seg Segutorio's trumpeter at the battle for the throne of Croxdrin. *SEG*

"Kurin and the Risslaca of Fire-Cavern": a fine, rousing swordsman's song.

L

Lancival: the secret training site of the Sisters of the Rose. *DOV*

Langarl Paraido: a palace in Nalvinlad. *SEG*

Larghos the Flatch: a mercenary bowman hired aboard *Tuscurs Maiden*. *FOS*

Larghos ti Therminsax, Strazab: the Vallian ambassador to Bormark. *TOS*

Lasindle: a town on the Kazzchun River in South Pandahem.

Lathdo the Eager, Jiktar: a Vallian soldier who flew to Vindelka with Delia; was captured by Nyleen Gillois. *DOV*

likl-likl: a small furry animal kept as a pet.

Linson: the captain of *Tuscurs Maiden*. *FOS*

Lintin the Ancho: a slave-trader in Memguin. *MAS*

Lisa the Empoin: one of Quendur the Ripper's crew of pirates; also his lady love. *FOS*

Little Sisters of Impurity: a sorority of Pandahem devoted to the Dahemin.

Liximus River: in Pandahem.

Llando the Ob-Handed: formerly of the Sixth Kerchuri; after losing an arm at the Battle of Kochwold was posted to the Vallian embassy in Menaham. *MAS*

Llipton, Kov: the regent of Croxdrin in the absence of King Crox and Queen Mab. *SEG*

Lloton, Ortyg na Misniot: the Chuktar of Milsi's cavalry. *SEG*

Lobbi: a little girl rescued from the adherents of Lem in Port Marsilus by Prescot. *TOS*

Logan: the captain of *Tuscurs Castle*. *FOS*

Lower Squish Street: in Tuscursmot.

Lun'elsh: a race of diffs with black body hair.

M

Mab: the name belonging to Milsi as Queen of Croxdrin. *SEG*

Mabo: the name belonging to Seg Segutorio as King of Croxdrin. *SEG*

Magero the Obstreperous: one of Cranchar Gillois's men, who rode Delia in the Shishivakka. *DOV*

mak: black.

Malar Marshes: located in Erthyrdrin.

malko: a race of diffs reminiscent of gorillas; used by Csitra as guards in the Coup Blag.

Malpettar: a kovnate province in Tomboram.

Mandifenar, Trylon Muryan of Mewsansmot: tried to usurp the throne of Croxdrin after the death of King Crox. *SEG*

Mankar the Horn: the caretaker of Pando's estate Plaxing. *MAS*

Mantig the Screw: one of the company of *Tuscurs Maiden*. *MAS*

Mappeltar: another name for Malpettar.

Markan: a clear golden wine.

Marsilus, Strom Murgon of Ribenor: the cousin of Pando Marsilus who tried to usurp Pando's kovnate of Bormark. Killed in battle at the Zhantil Palace. *FOS, TOS, MAS*

Matta: a free port city in Pandahem.

Mattamlad: a town situated at the mouth of the Kazzchun River in Pandahem.

Meek Sisters of Mercy: a sorority of Vallia.

Memdo: the kov of the province of Memis in Tomboram. *TOS*

Memguin: a seaport in Menaham.

Memis: a kovnate province in Tomboram.

Metromin, Obolya: a merchant from Tomboram. *TOS*

Mewsansmot: a town in northern Croxdrin.

Milsi: born in Jholaix; became the Queen of Croxdrin. Ventured into the Coup Blag in search of her husband King Crox, where she was found by Prescot and Seg Segutorio. Afterwards married Seg, making him the King of Croxdrin. *MOS, SEG*

Mimi: one of Delia's handmaids.

Mindi the Mad: a witch who served the Lady Tilda and helped Prescot and his friends battle the cult of Lem in Port Marsilus. *TOS*

mishme: a term of endearment.

Mishti: the daughter of Lady Milsi. *SEG*

Moincy, Lady: a judge in Pettarsmot. *MAS*

Monsi the Bosom: a Vallian agent infiltrating the cult of Lem in Bormark. *TOS*

MSM: abbreviation for the Meek Sisters of Mercy.

Munfoon: a creature all hair and eyes and lolling tongue.

munsha bread: a type of bread with only a small amount of leavening.

Murkizon: the captain of *Blackfang;* washed overboard and picked up by *Tuscurs Maiden.* Helped Prescot combat the cult of Lem in Pandahem. Broke the back of Zankov. *FOS, TOS, MAS*

Mytham, Poldo: a friend of Pando Marsilus; enamored of Dafni Harlstam. *FOS*

Mytham, Pynsi: the twin sister of Poldo and enamored of Pando Marsilus. *FOS*

N

Na-Fre, Kalu: a professional treasure-seeker who accompanied Prescot and Seg Segutorio on their first expedition to the Coup Blag. *MOS*

Naghan the Barrel: see Raerdu, Naghan.

Naghan the Pellendur: the ord-Deldar of the guards at the Zhantil Palace. *MAS*

Naghan the Slippy: a slave rescued from Katakis of South Pandahem by Seg Segutorio. *SEG*

Naghondo the Squint: one of Cranchar Gillois's men.

Nalfi, Lady: found by Cap'n Murkizon and Larghos the Flatch in a school for torturers of the cult of Lem in Peminswopt; though held in great esteem by Larghos, she was discovered to be a spy for the cult of Lem. *FOS, TOS, MAS*

Nalgre the Strings: a master maker of harps, dead now for three hundred seasons.

Nalvinlad: a city on the Kazzchun River in South Pandahem.

Nalvindrin: the former name of the country of Croxdrin.

Nan the Bosom: the soup mistress at the villa of Nyleen Gillois. *DOV*

Nardo, Greasy: a water master at the villa of Nyleen Gillois. *DOV*

Naree-Giver: the name used by the dinkus for the Cabaret Plant.

Nath the Apron: the cabin steward aboard *Tuscurs Maiden.* *TOS*

Nath the Muncible: one among Cranchar Gillois's men who tried to mitigate his cruelty. *DOV*

Nath Ob-eye the Trancular: a slave trader in Memguin. *MAS*

Nath, Silly: one of Delia's fellow slaves at the villas of Nyleen Gillois. *DOV*

The New Frontier: a tavern in Peminswopt. *TOS*

Nogoya: an island off the coast of Pandahem.

Northag ti Hovensmot: a Hikdar in the service of Trylon Muryan; tried to capture Seg Segutorio and Milsi in Nalvinlad. *SEG*

O

oiklt: a beast inhabiting the jungles of Pandahem, with clawed feet, tentacles, and a low-slung maw rimmed with feelers.

ompion: blowpipe.

Oonparl: a river in Pandahem.

Ornol the Rasher: the chief cook for Nyleen Gillois. *DOV*

Ornol, Strom: a member of the first expedition to the Coup Blag; working in the service of Trylon Muryan Mandifenar. *MOS, SEG*

Ortyg the Undlefar: a slave rescued from Katakis of South Pandahem by Seg Segutorio; became a river pirate. *SEG*

Ovin, Pamcur: man who sold Quendur the Ripper into slavery after ruining his family.

Ovvend Opandar: a Vallian galleon commanded by Indur ti Fotor.

P

Pafnut: a Hikdar in the service of Trylon Muryan Mandifenar; killed while attempting to capture Seg and Milsi. *SEG*

Palando the Berry: the landlord of The Swod's Revenge in Tuscursmot. *FOS*

The Paline and Brunestaff: an inn in Port Marsilus. *TOS*

pallixter: a type of sword native to Pandahem.

Palm Kyro: a square in Mellinsmot.

Pamantisho the Beauty: Csitra's boy lover. *SEG*

Panachreem: the legendary home of the deities of Pandahem.

Pancresta: an agent of Spikatur who lured Prescot and Seg Segutorio to Pandahem. *MOS*

Panda, Ocean of: a Pandahem name for the Sea of Opaz.

Pandakor Sea: the name given by some Pandaheem to the waters between the Sea of Chem and the Southern Ocean.

Pandamon Jut Gallop: a dance native to Pandahem.

Pandrite Risen, Temple of: a temple in Nalvinlad where Seg and Milsi were married.

Panigium: a Pandahem name for the green sun of Kregen.

Panronium: a Pandahem name for the red sun of Kregen.

Pantora, Paline: a chatelaine in the retinue of Nyleen Gillois. *DOV*

Papachak the All-Powerful, by: a Pachak oath.

papishin: a kind of leaf commonly used for roofing.

Parlaix, Natema: the mother of Queen Milsi. *SEG*

"Patok Punji the Neemu, the Song of": a ditty of Pandahem.

Pavishkeemi: a Pandahem goddess.

Pelamoin, Naghan: the ship-Hikdar of *Tuscurs Maiden,* later given command of *Redfang. FOS*

Peminswopt: a seaport town in the province of Memis in Tomboram.

Periklain, Nath: the captain of *Schydan Imperial,* who gave Prescot a rapier and dagger. *FOS*

Pettarsmot: a town in the province of Malpettar in Tomboram.

Phunik: the hermaphrodite child of Phu-Si-Yantong and Csitra. Together with Csitra tried to destroy Prescot in the Coup Blag. *MOS*

Plaxing: Kov Pando's country estate in Bormark.

Playhouse of the Singing Lotus: a ruined theater in Port Marsilus used as a temple by the adherents of Lem.

Poll, Tom the Nose: a zan-Deldar in the Pandahem army of mercenaries recruited to aid in the rebellion of Vodun Alloran. *TOS*

Polontia: a stromnate province between Bormark and Memis in Tomboram.

Pompina, Scaura: the wife of Scauro Pompino the Iarvin. *FOS*

Pordon, Boris: the ship-Hikdar of *Tuscurs Maiden* following Naghan Pelamoin. *TOS*

Pumphilio: a painter of Pandahem. *SEG*

Q

Quendur the Ripper: a render captain who joined Prescot and Pompino the Iarvin in their campaign against the cult of Lem. *FOS*

quindil: a Kregan bird similar to a turkey.

R

Raerdu, Naghan: Prescot's personal spymaster.

Rafikhan: a slave rescued from Katakis of South Pandahem by Seg Segutorio. *SEG*

Rahishta: the wife of Kov Llipton. *SEG*

Rasnoli: the stylor aboard *Tuscurs Maiden. FOS*

Ratishling the Sinuous: a schrepim deity.

Redfang: the name given by Pompino the Iarvin to the ship *Flame of Nogoya* after its capture by the crew of *Tuscurs Maiden. FOS*

Renko the Iarvin: a pickpocket who tried to steal Prescot's purse in Peminswopt. *TOS*

Ridzi the Rangora: one of the crew of *Tuscurs Maiden;* killed while carrying Tilda to the Zhantil Palace. *TOS*

Rik Razortooth: name given by Fregeff the sorcerer to his volschrin. *MOS*

Rippasch: vulture.

Rondas the Bold: a mercenary and comrade of Prescot who signed aboard *Tuscurs Maiden;* wounded in the castle of Korfseyrie. *FOS*

Rosala: a woman charged with the care of the mistress of the SOR. *DOV*

The Ruby Winespout: a tavern in Ruathytu. *MOS*

S

Saenci the Locks: the deceased wife of Delia's half-brother Vomanus.

Sagaie: a town in Evir.

Schan: a name for the grouping of continents and islands in the hemisphere opposite Paz.

Schinkitree: a canoe-like boat used in parts of South Pandahem.

Schturgins: another name for the Shanks.

Schydan Imperial: a galleon in the Vallian fleet, which Prescot stopped aboard in Matta. *FOS*

Selsmot: a town in the jungles of South Pandahem; starting point for expeditions to the Coup Blag.

Shamsi: the deceased wife of Pando Marsilus.

Shanli: a servant of Exandu who looked after him on Prescot's first expedition to the Coup Blag. *MOS*

shishivakka: a barbaric race in which men ride on the backs of women.

shiume: lady.

Shiusas the Insatiable: a Sylvie deity.

Shor, Naghan: a messenger in the service of Kov Llipton. *SEG*

Shula the Balm: a physician, an adherent of Lem, who treated Rondas the Bold at Korfseyrie. *MAS*

The Sign of the Jolly Puddler: a tavern in Mahendrasmot. *MOS*

Sisters of the Sword: a sorority of Vallia.

Sisters of the Whip: a sorority of Vallia based on hatred of men.

Skort: a retainer of Queen Mab who entered the Coup Blag in search of her. *MOS, SEG*

Slaptra: a carnivorous species of plant which grows in Chem and South Pandahem; it crushes its prey with flailing stems.

Snarly Hills: hills in South Pandahem among which the Coup Blag is located.

soshiv: eighteen.

Soshiv: a gambling game using six dice per player.

Sosie ti Vendleheim: a Sister of the Rose among the crew of *Val Defender. MAS*

Spangchin, Nag-So-, the Horkandur: the commander of Trylon Muryan's regiment of Bowmen of Loh. *SEG*

The Speckled Gyp: a high-class tavern and hotel in Port Marsilus. *TOS*

Spikatur Hunting Sword: a secret organization; initially devoted to the overthrow of the Empress Thyllis and her corrupt government; it was taken over by the witch Csitra and used against Prescot. *MOS*

spinlikl: an animal living in South Pandahem, with a melon-sized body and eight limbs, each longer than a man's full armreach; intelligent and trainable.

Spiny Ribcrusher: a carnivorous plant resembling a syatra.

splash: sea.

The Spotted Lancrimoil: a tavern in Matta. *FOS*

Standur, Larghos: the ship-Hikdar of *Blackfang*, later her captain.

strangchi: a long-hafted weapon topped by a spear-point, axe-head, and hook.

strangdja: a weapon of Chem similar to a strangchi.

Strazab: an imperially created rank on a par with Strom in the regular nobility.

Stroikan: a Deldar in the service of Kov Llipton; the jailer of Seg Segutorio and his comrades. *SEG*

styrorynth: a carnivorous sea-creature.

Superno, Apgarl: Kov of the province of Malpettar in Tomboram. *MAS*

The Swod's Revenge: a tavern in Tuscursmot. *FOS*

T

Tangle the Ears: the cousin of Jespar the Scundle; used as a guide by the forces of Murgon Marsilus. *MAS*

tenchla: a type of plant native to Chem.

Tenpanam: a vadvarate province bordering on the kovnate province of Bormark.

Theakdrin: a kovnate province of Hamal, tucked in a bend of the River Os.

Thousand Clepsydras, Street of a: located in Port Marsilus.

Thousand Strangers, Street of a: located in Ruathytu.

Tipp the Kaktu: a Vallian agent infiltrating the cult of Lem in Bormark. *TOS*

Tlima: a woman who tended Prescot after he was attacked by a Cabaret Plant. *MOS*

toilca: a six-legged reptile native to South Pandahem; about the length of a man, it has scales patterned in brown and green and is given to hunting in packs. *SEG*

trai: luck.

Trevalmin, Chica the Fangs ti Alvondsmot: one of Nyleen Gillois's Jikai Vuvushis; formerly a Sister of the Rose; defeated in single combat by Delia. *DOV*

Tskarin: Seg Segutorio's standard bearer at the battle for the throne of Croxdrin. *SEG*

tump: a race of diffs short of stature but immensely broad and stoutly built; the men grow beards down past their waists; given to mining and delving into the earth.

Tuscurs Castle: a ship of the fleet of Pompino the Iarvin.

Tuscurs Maiden: a ship of the fleet of Pompino the Iarvin, burned by Prescot.

U

uhu: hermaphrodite.

Uldo: the first water master at the villa of Nyleen Gillois. *DOV*

Umtig the Lock: a slave rescued from Katakis of South Pandahem by Seg Segutorio; a thief by profession. *SEG*

V

Val Defender: a Vallian skyship, captured by the Pandaheem. Later liberated by Prescot and Dayra. *MAS*

Valdwin, Larghos: a sculptor of Vallia. *TOS*

Valin: the second son of Seg Segutorio and Thelda.

Veerling, Naghan: a Hikdar of the Vallian courier service; helped Prescot burn a temple of Lem in Menaham and to rescue Dayra from Murgon Marsilus. *MAS*

Velda the Tempestuous: a long-dead Sister of the Rose whose room at Lancival is presently occupied by Delia.

Velia: the steam mistress at the villa of Nyleen Gillois.

Ventil, Larghos: one of Vomanus's men, who helped rescue him from Nyleen Gillois. *DOV*

Volschrin: a vicious winged reptile with a barbed tail; about the size of a cat.

W

warvol: a black-winged bird resembling a vulture.

Warvol Tower: where Milsi was imprisoned by Trylon Muryan.

Weul'til: a race of diffs, tall and extremely thin, with antennae.

wherezik: a carnivorous river creature.

Whitefang: a swordship in the fleet of Pompino the Iarvin.

Wilma the Shot: a mercenary who signed aboard *Tuscurs Maiden;* the sister of Alwim the Eye. *FOS*

Woodraven, Nadia: the cadade of Nyleen Gillois's Jikai Vuvushis; defeated in single combat by Delia. *DOV*

Y

Yzobel: a Sister of the Rose. *DOV*

Z

Zhantil Palace: Pando's palace in Port Marsilus. *TOS*

About the author

Alan Burt Akers was a pen name of the prolific British author Kenneth Bulmer, who died in December 2005 aged eighty-four.

Bulmer wrote over 160 novels and countless short stories, predominantly science fiction, both under his real name and numerous pseudonyms, including Alan Burt Akers, Frank Brandon, Rupert Clinton, Ernest Corley, Peter Green, Adam Hardy, Philip Kent, Bruno Krauss, Karl Maras, Manning Norvil, Chesman Scot, Nelson Sherwood, Richard Silver, H. Philip Stratford, and Tully Zetford. Kenneth Johns was a collective pseudonym used for a collaboration with author John Newman. Some of Bulmer's works were published along with the works of other authors under "house names" (collective pseudonyms) such as Ken Blake (for a series of tie-ins with the 1970s television programme The Professionals), Arthur Frazier, Neil Langholm, Charles R. Pike, and Andrew Quiller.

Bulmer was also active in science fiction fandom, and in the 1970s he edited nine issues of the New Writings in Science Fiction anthology series in succession to John Carnell, who originated the series.

For more details about the author, see www.mushroom-ebooks.com.

www.ingramcontent.com/pod-product-compliance
Lightning Source LLC
Chambersburg PA
CBHW020249030726
47499CB00001B/118